F
and

"George Mandel's perception is acute, his style by turns poetic, expressive, earthy, his insight into the nature of man profound."

—*New York Herald Tribune*

"Into a language left gray and vapid by many of his contemporaries [Mandel] has injected a soulful fire and color that virtually dart from his page with a special kind of electricity."

—*Chapel Hill Weekly*

"The story has universal human dimensions . . . it is a serious and thoughtful piece of work. Here are people fighting against their doom, especially Diane. . . . The author has endowed her with beauty and a childish grace as well as a stark and believable terror of the world, and the reader cares about her and about some of the staunch characters who try to help her."

—*Harper's*

"Told with terrifying intensity."

—Nat Hentoff, *Downbeat*

". . . A novel that will be talked about."

—*The New York Times*

"In a whirling succession of ghastly episodes, the story chronicles Diane's steady descent into the Inferno. As it stands, the book documents very vividly a sector new to the novel—its jazzy lingo, its weird loyalties, its chaotic habits and surrealistic horrors."

—*The Atlantic Monthly*

". . . An excellent treatise on the physical and moral disintegration of drug addicts . . ."

—*The New York Post*

"Using a bright impressionistic prose as an artist might wield a brush, Mr. Mandel paints a horrifying picture of human rights reduced to the condition of befuddled animals."

—*The Roanoke Times*

"George Mandel is popular in Beat Generation circles for what he says as well as for the way he says it."

—Lawrence Lipton, from *The Holy Barbarians*

Praise for
The Wax Boom

"Mandel has written a novel that is exceptional in every significant way."

—Joseph Heller, author of *Catch 22*

"Mandel climbs the final rung to stand with Norman Mailer, Thomas Pynchon, and Günter Grass, the meditators on our world and our time."

—*Houston Chronicle*

"With desperate and unflinching objectivity [Mandel] chronicles the descent into barbarism and the final disintegration of a troop of American soldiers as they fight, rape, plunder and massacre their way into Germany. It is a considerable achievement . . ."

—*Times Literary Supplement*

FLEE THE ANGRY STRANGERS

GEORGE MANDEL

Thunder's Mouth Press
New York

FLEE THE ANGRY STRANGERS

© 1952 by George Mandel

Published by
Thunder's Mouth Press
An Imprint of Avalon Publishing Group Incorporated
245 West 17th Street, 11th Floor
New York, NY 10011-5300

The author wishes to thank Hoagy Carmichael for permission to quote from the song "Poor Old Joe."

Library of Congress Cataloging-in-Publication Data is available.

ISBN: 1-56025-571-4

9 8 7 6 5 4 3 2 1

Printed in the United States of America
Distributed by Publishers Group West

For Bessie and Sam

Introduction

From the author, after a dream of shame in a great hall lit bright by overweening technology that could make those rich who care little to invest in each other:

Dressed their best, all the sheep were there, hating to think and loving to adulate in their accustomed manner of degenerating to frenzied applause for Tweedledee and Tweedledum as they disputed one another for pay about agreeing as usual that their majestic talent for rapid speech proves how smart they look, though dumb as a rote.

A merriment of dancing girls went stripping down to shy hints of their troubles till a CIA leak got everyone pissed. But joy stayed rife for the door prize of an ingenious device that can squeeze out of its tube the last smear of Preparation Hate.

* * *

Now back we go to chapter one of a story that winds up with this novel, but begins as a kind of occupational therapy hopeful of some recovery from considerable devastation in World War Two.

Blinded (and more) by a sniper's gunshot to the head at the Rhine, one hell of a (third) wound for a prosperous young cartoonist aspiring to fine art, I had to turn it literary. Not for a war book (that took me fifteen years to face), it produced *Flee The Angry Strangers* as mending progressed during a lucky presence in Greenwich Village.

This fourth reprint of the 1952 hardcover verifies its theme's survival beyond the durability of ignorant hostilities toward depicted young souls lost to the terrible bane of narcotics. "They should be spanked," was the smug attitude boasted on TV by one incredibly myopic critic, his hand dangling from a table edge in a blasé pose as rigid as his pretentious brainlessness.

My father (of finer memory) had no such remedy, just the coat off his back that he gave me, for a boy frozen blue. Only the kid sold it for heroin he needed more than wool to warm the elephantiasis he was dying of, in the midst of lesser sufferers who nonetheless felt as bad in their lifelong winter of bitter conditions to escape.

Fortunately, more objective critics were sensitive to the curse of an oncoming drug culture already entrapping a confused generation in the bewildering lunatic asylum. A prototype of defensive ridicule labeled the post-war scene—that long before I learned how really insane an addictive population could become by sheer momentum.

On a less auspicious note, no one in all the reviews and commentaries focused on the book's metaphor of narcosis in society, our national dependence on every venom from lethal nicotine to stupefying television, which prevails to this day with enslavements like elitism and its greed, debt and its gambling compulsion, fashion and its doddering celebrity worship, and so on in a deleterious outgrowth to animosities more systemic than the concept dared anticipate.

Yet that seems but an inkling of the base mentality which has turned recent baseball fans homicidal, and political partisans into blathering adherents equally fixated, having mushroomed to a hysterical epoch wherein nothing—no logic, no facts—can dissuade anyone from anything anymore anywhere in the media, the UN, Washington D.C., or the entire bellicose world.

A better than average psychoanalyst I know feels this rampant discord has seeped a mass dilution of common sense into the body politic. Any touch of agreement occurring so rarely, I could only defer to her ardent counsel against *judgmentalism* and allow the assertion she just as vehemently pronounced that this aggregate dissension is now driving the country to the brink of oligarchy.

Coincidentally, overhearing that very threat in an intense restaurant exchange made it hard to ignore a missing step or two of the question. Yes, government by a few, the game of the name, does look prefigured at this very moment by a White House that condones the FCC-authorized pecuniary confiscation of every local TV and radio station by a modicum of media leviathans.

Even as I write this, the Federal Communications Commission chairman pompously vilifies all who stand for the diversification principle by calling our long-established 35% penetration limit "garbage" and, believe it or not, "bordering on the absurd," a United States Senate disapproval resolution that ethically opposes the idolatry of greed resolve that *anything goes.*

All that although the measure is sponsored, believe it or not, by many senators of the right as well as the left. Yet, the advocates of so arrogant a hijack are declaring the measure "dead on arrival" with pledges to block any vote. Who can but not believe their forewarning of a presidential veto in this rabid election prelude if protection of the public weal does proceed? But that intimidation does persist. Have we not gone crazier than this novel implied when much younger?

Or should its forecast of cruel industrial exploitation render sanity apprehensive of the present ripening into atrocious corporate evil toward an unscrupulous plan of rule already in confident place? Conversely, the optimism that presumed to filigree hope through the book might still rely on our astutely precautious checks and balances to keep us the people in power.

Some such sanguine buoyancy may overcome the categorical determinism of politicians with enriching bread to butter, a copy of

psychoanalysts who feel no permit requirement to legitimize judg-
mental boldness any more than cops do to carry guns prohibited by
law. The best of them, as satisfied with their conjectures as a halfwit,
are as good for a laugh as the worst of critics like that aforementioned
scion of bloated disdain.

Models of comic relief (Tinsel Town's surprising intelligence),
they attest to the saving grace of humor. To an extent the burden-
some responsibility of writing a dedicated book not spare of
philosophastry—and the philosophobia it causes—is influenced to
veer that way, perchance to lighten even the heartbreaking obsession
of fragile temperament to disengage by means of every destructive
evasion from an egregious system of wealth that recklessly fattens
on paralyzing want.

Hoping to make the specter of that tragic life more bearable so,
Flee The Angry Strangers turns from a buffeted brave champion
of women's rights, battered by disciplinary restrictions, to
glimpses of resilient human comedy like the eternal borrower des-
pcrate for a benefactor to keep his modest aid from the jealous
neighborhood loan shark who might replace his exorbitant support with mayhem.

And reputed to have introduced the American novel to a generation
beaten by authoritarian dogma, the story turns up an entrepreneurial
nemesis of racism and heartless profiteering, later kept quaint
through two more tomes for his fabulous impact on the failing old,
initially reluctant publisher that brought him back to live and laugh
again out Indianapolis way where no one ever knew that eccentric
business anxieties could make trembling fingers chronic.

A working title, *The Hook and the Tower*, endeavored to encom-
pass all that. But reasonable editorial aversions to the prevalent triteness of such contiguity forms consigned it to devious contents-page
amphigory, while urging the more comprehensible *Flee The Angry
Strangers* out of me.

At its original publication, a newly celebrated fellow pup found the writing "uncvcn." Shamclcss, thc crafty publishcr dclctcd that from the context of a generous endorsement that called the work vigorously superior to most first novels of the period.

I meant to tell this befriender, but kept forgetting to, that readers who can tolerate grammatical severities like a plethora of past-perfects and pluperfects unto stilted writing, imposed on the vernacular of immature dissent by a well-meaning but domineering old workaholic of an editor (whose grammar proved harmfully defective at that), are not bound to find the misadventures of young rebels dated, or to weary of the Proustian excesses of detail designed to cover the vast human plight of inexpressible emotions forever misconceived by others.

Having two heads in those days, one haunted nightly by dreams of searching after an undamaged substitute, the other that marvel called youth, I slept little and gamboled much in Greenwich Village, where every social advent seems to have commenced fifty years ahead of manifestation in regions less energetic, e.g. adolescent pregnancy out of wedlock, if not promiscuity itself.

Even though seizures common to brain injury regularly harassed every venture, as healing took its sweet time, socializing bestowed friends among the company I could not help keeping, romance too, in those environs of distinctive taverns and cafeterias swarming with bogus artists and drug addicts as amusing for all the misery of their misdirected vulnerability to oppression.

Eventually they filled this book with appealing characters like a son of Eugene O'Neill in amiable disguise, and a girl (as we were still allowed to classify a young woman) who once pointed out an admitted sado-masochist at a table nearby. To an offer of my leather belt for any desire of her own to grant him a lash or two over coffee, she reacted, "Why should I send a creep like that?"

But really, she was the nicest of people, oddly like most susceptible to hard drugs, as if kindness *per se* were a warning symptom. As for *send*, it meant *delight*, couched in *jive*, a language so unknown back then that a lexicon was requested for it in the narrative that follows here with such main protagonists. Her treatment of that perceptive music lent dialogue much flavor, and left me sorry I declined to offer the translations Madison Avenue was already spoiling.

The worst was to undermine *pod*, just a hip slider for marijuana, as *pot*, degrading it from the engorged pronunciations of its consumers to one more ridiculously irrelevant encroachment on the square collegiacs to come.

But life has bonuses for the optimistic. The best for me was my wife, of more than five decades by now since she enjoyed accompanying me to the quirky college classes I attended for GI Bill of Rights largesse, rollicking all night with me meanwhile, slaving to retype my revisions upon acceptance of this manuscript, then allowing my assistance in parenting our kids on her way to serving as researcher for every further text.

Had she not, I would still adore her unassuming beauty and the culinary genius that helps me endure a writer's need of information beleaguered by TV commentators and personalities who exist in a box apart from the rest of us. Apparently they imagine we all reflect their exclusive concentration on sexual, political and media conflict as if not only deadly war but all reality is just a board game on which nothing else matters.

Usurping Bolshevism's "opiate of the people" from religion to disinherit the meek, our latter day shepherds utilize the narcotic of entertainment, which includes what postures as newsworthy observation. Although its lessees represent complex public interests little more than do the inmates of a zoo, it's likely that the outer world mistakes their effete self-absorption as the image of our vaunted way of life, and so we're almost as despised nowadays as those who despise us.

It was thought this book ends an immensity of antagonistic struggle on a prediction that the poisonous flight of America's dregs would inevitably suck also its socially more providential into the voracious morass of drugs. That would be like predicting soy sauce chicken in Chinatown. I leave the practice to simpletons too self-important to forbear potential egg on the face, and to droll individuals of dimension enough to understand a little fun is the better part of their earnest work.

So it's no humorous prediction but a serious evaluation of evidence that justifies the reissue of this novel half a century after a grand distaste for the laws of life positioned my mighty country for an unexpected destiny of fear that we may well be in danger of Fascism.

The basic definition of that scary term is simply "The Corporate State." It does not necessarily dictate a Hitler any more than Communism does a similarly murderous Stalin. No, not in a leadership too diffident to kill us, unless—like the freezing kid who sold my father's coat—driven to for its own desensitizer: elitist self-entitlement.

Elitists, a species opposite to the spirit of jazz, some came to its scene as tourists. One alluded to African-Americans as the opposite race at Nick's Tavern as it jumped with great sidemen like Peewee Russell, the brothers Teagarden, Bob Casey. A bone through the septum, he maintained, compares poorly with landing man on the moon.

Half Native American, but too placid to slam him with his bass fiddle, big Bob rejoindered, "Toss up a clarinet on 125th Street and the first cat that grabs it'll sweeten life better than your whole pale ancestry ever did."

Dangerously divided by able fanatics angrily strange to any concern for the subjugated or the inept, this seems no longer the great land my generation fought to preserve, many like me at the cost of unrecoverable resources of youth.

It looks more like a nation of extortionists too vile to care that, while they gloat in illicit prosperity, kids are starving somewhere and parents are condemned for the crime of desperation, to jails never filled by such new rabble that specialize in a glut of scams and swindles, so remote from human consideration as to mock it as maudlin sentimentality.

We have aged into a nation of values like afflictions, ridden with underhanded manipulation of our markets more insidious than insider trading, and revisionists as egotistical as an obtuse talk show host's delusions of intelligence—a nation to save. For that I pray the young will fight courageously, but not each other. The best weapon for the brave may be compassion—if they can recover an electorate that was the only absolute power in the world.

—George Mandel
October 2003

FLEE THE
ANGRY
STRANGERS

SOUNDS OUT OF GONE DEBRIS

A spill of afternoon rain had frozen on asphalt. From a great window swung out wide, Robert Stoney looked four stories down through twilight, to the street lacquered gray and tinted yellow by a lonely corner light. Where by day a flux of shoppers crowded between the pushcarts and stores, a long row of doorway shadows lay deserted now, but for litter moving lifelike in the wind. Stoney stood scratching his beard and nodding a long time, convinced he was witness to a population moved like litter by any arbitrary wind.

There were few on earth as contemptuous as Stoney. For twenty-five years, since he'd come from Camden beardless but already enchanted with himself, he had watched Greenwich Village draw intensity from every stall of living, watched all attitudes come, magnified, from the outer world to manifest themselves here in some abject way of life. Pickpockets, dope fiends and hoodlums had been arrested in the streets he walked; dilettantes and homosexuals had prattled by his ear; well-dressed tourists from above Fourteenth and tramps from the Bowery down below were numbered alike among the hopeless, reeking drunkards who fell in alleyway dust as he passed. Until, finally, that portion of his brain which handled commiseration turned to ice, and he could feel no more for a wind-beaten sufferer than he felt for the litter in the street.

Nor was there any feeling left in him for his work, but he needed more than a gray-streaked beard for the identity with which to earn his way. His paintings rarely sold, yet his profession often made him a place at some tourist's restaurant table, even attracted arty girls who, once impressed by a colorful pile of pictures, might contribute toward his rent. His rent seemed always to be due, and Tony the Shylock was a landlord with neither sense, soul nor patience. This alone sent the painter nightly into rain or frost, for, though he'd long ago decided that many a long soundless night alone in his Bleecker

11

Street loft was the price of genuine consciousness in an idiot society, he had to keep exposing his soul to irritation, so long as dullards could help him mollify the Shylock.

Covering his bulk with his frayed white camel's-hair coat, he kicked ashes over the embers in the fireplace, then lighted an Italian cigar and passed down the narrow flights, wincing at every creak of the stairs, afraid that Tony might be lurking somewhere in shadows. "'Ey, maestro!" He could almost hear that weird accent abusing him. "'Ey, Bobba Stone-uhmo!" From the street doorway he looked up and down till he knew the way was clear, then hurried west past small stores and the great Dills Hotel front cluttered with tramps, toward MacDougal, two streets away, where barrooms were awakening in night's first even dark.

He felt like a captive bear plodding the path his own step had worn in rock diagonally across the corner toward no real expectation. But suddenly it looked like Stoney's night. A trim girl in green went before him along MacDougal—arty-looking with earrings of gold that dangled•where sleek honey-colored hair was cut off abruptly. He broke into a soft-shoe trot to slip up behind her in the Riviera Tavern's neon-tinted light. "May I warn you—once you pass Bleecker, you're in the Village," and meant to offer himself as guide, but she jumped away like some nervous animal and swung horrified eyes his way. She composed her triangular face once she saw him, and continued to clack down the street. This kind he'd seen before: scared silent by the very encounters they dreamed about in such brooding hunger.

Close behind her, he tried again. "Well, may I speak to you on a purely statistical basis?" His voice's effective ring buoyed him up with old confidence. "Only for a moment—to find out why such beauty walks alone."

The girl swung her draped green coat in a graceful swirl. "Get the hell off, Rembrandt; this is the twentieth century." She swept away so thinly into night that it seemed as though she were careful to take only her share of space—no more, no less.

"Ah, you allude——" But some autohonks shattered the rest. He hustled out before her, blocking the walk where it was narrowed conveniently by a jutting stoop. She leaned on the stoop's iron balustrade, giving him a slanted look which, he reasoned, was some shy sort of invitation. "Do you suppose I'm a tramp?" he demanded, knocking the ash off his black cigar. "These clothes mark my dignity. They distinguish——"

"You're wasting your time, Gran'pa. I'm jailbait." It was a honey-textured sting in his ear; he had to let her by.

But across Minetta Lane she stopped and called his name in that throaty voice. He saw her poised beneath the arc light, black eyes cold as the night.

"You know me?" He danced across while scattered people turned to stare. "What irony! You've heard of this beard and all the while——"

"Yeah, I know you, but you don't have to do it in three acts. You make a big deal out of everything, Stoney." She sighed tremulously, as if she'd said all that her strength would allow. Then she fortified herself with a long breath of air and spoke again. "Let's sit in Garcia's; I don't want to be alone any more." She went through the stucco vestibule arch, head bent back with the weary resignation of a creature who'd been alone for years.

At a table in Garcia's cavelike light, he stole glances at her, but couldn't tell her from a thousand other Village darlings. These wanton kids could change their appearance completely with a haircut or new curve of lipstick—a man could never count his following.

The little green-coated girl saw his perturbation in the wrinkles above his eyes, and reassured him out of her own need for certainty. "I've seen you around, Stoney, that's all. You don't have to be hung up; you don't owe me anything. I've seen you around and heard you spiel, that's all." With another of her deep sighs, she looked across the sawdust floor to the bar, where men were lined up, silent and somber, each turned inward toward his world. She watched them drink in measured, almost habitual cadence, like members of a chorus in some twilight dream. So slow in the dozing light, so much calmer than the day had been, so very much slower and calmer than the blood still lurching mistrustfully in her darknesses. She wanted wine, the sweetness of it on her tongue, and asked Stoney to order it— some of the real sweet kind.

The painter cracked his knuckles, scratched his beard. Somehow this child seemed unimpressed with him; there was something deprecating in that, and it was time he provoked her. "Some people say

I own a coffin in which I sleep, while others maintain I spend my nights on the cement floor of my cellar and have rats run across my body and sleep behind my ears. But all that——"

"Stoney, relax," she said, leaning back in her seat. "Don't put on a show, Stoney. Look at all those guys along the bar drinking out the rocks in their chest—so quiet, right here in the Village."

He called for her wine and fixed her with his philosophical eye, his best unblinking, lidless stare. "If I had my way, young lady, I'd give every one of them a psychological screening. Yessir, then rehabilitate them all."

"Don't you ever drink, Stoney?"

"Never! It's the final abrogation of manhood. Watch them: five or six drinks and they begin to declare that misplaced, that banished manhood in the most compensatory ways." He looked down his cheek as he puffed smoke.

Now her eyes were closed. "What about women, Stoney? When they drink? What's it mean when women drink?"

Stoney chuckled, taking her wine from the waiter while she paid. "They're simply trying to equal men, and in the most ridiculous way. Like emulating a king, who happens to be tubercular, by developing consumption rather than a lordly manner." That had been perfectly put and needed no rumination, but he laughed awhile to give her appreciation time to work. "Aah," he lamented, "it's a pathetic impulse in women today to place themselves out of their position in nature. *Nothing* irritates me more, *nothing*. Why, women can't be men; it's absurd. They aren't creators; they *receive* man's creation and nurture it. It's biologically evident, it's . . ." on and on while the girl leaned back tighteyed, not even touching her wine.

While he spoke of the way he would arrange society, directing each human being along his proper *biological* path, she went spiraling into lost shadows of her mind, recognizing in his rambling—as one knows in dreams—the repetition of half-remembered things. It was the spiraling and pointless Village drift, where no day has a face unlike the next. Ceaseless as the days of hiding that stretched before her, the yammering mouth was unendurable; finally, she made straight for a phone booth in the rear.

Stoney was incredulous—the words dried like clay in his mouth. But, rejecting the fleeting thought that the gleam of her earrings kept him from leaving, he decided that her very indifference attracted

him. Still, the earrings appeared to be real gold; that could hardly
be ignored, either.

Now the calm of the place upset her. It seemed a long time between rings as she waited at the phone for an answer; it seemed as
though everything had slowed down in sudden spite to hold away
from her any moment of relief. Although all day she'd maintained
a determination to bother no one at all, Stoney's voice had shattered
it. The high, tight sounds of domination came from that beard, mechanical and unfeeling, and now she had to speak out her pain to
a man who could know it. She wanted to tell how she had won her
way out of walls and made it, with horror replacing her heart, back
to the city, down to the Village, avoiding the characters, leaning on
no one until her fears had at last become jumbled in her brain and
she could no longer go on alone.

She reached in her purse for a cigarette, but now Carter Webb was
alive in her ear, the clean low note of his voice at once peaceful and
challenging. She tried to say how she had come out of Grand Central fearful of the crowds, hurrying past upturned collars that might
have shielded police planted in wait for her, how she wanted now
only to touch that coal-miner slope of his back, to get away from
Stoney and his rigidity—but her voice shot out of her, tripping over
the rush of her thoughts so that she only babbled.

"What is it? What's wrong?" he said.

"Carter, you know who this is?"

"What is it, Edna? Cool off, take it easy."

"This is Diane, Carter," and it was hard to say more for the
pounding in her chest. She imagined the surprise stretching his face
in a grin, heard it in his voice, and grinned herself.

"Diane! Where are you calling from, Diane?"

"I'm out, Cart, I'm calling from outside. You thought I was
Edna. You never can tell the difference."

"There is no difference," and behind it the whisper of his easy
laugh. "In the voice, anyway. Where are you? How come they let
you out?"

"I busted out. Where's Edna? Isn't she there?"

"Diane, you didn't—you know, hurt anybody?"

His alarm made her laugh; he was such a righteous guy. "No, Cart,
nothing like that. I'm no desperado," and she laughed again at the
thought of it.

"That's *your* story. Where are you, little girl?"

"In the Village. Where's Edna? Can you come out, Carter? I want to see you, Carter."

"She's still in the hospital, baby. Why don't you come on over? I want to look at you, too."

"Still in? It's months. How can she be laid up so long with a broken leg?"

"It's easy. I'll tell you facing you. Come on over, babe."

"Gee, everything happens at once."

"And that's the way the ball bounces. Hurry on over. Take a cab. Do you have money, or should I meet you downstairs?"

"No, Cart, I have some, I'll be right over. Hang up, hang up." She heard the fondness in his chuckle and dropped the receiver into its hook, left the booth and felt the drinkers use her with their eyes as she walked stiffly to the door. She went into a wind that bit at her cheeks and kicked at her hair and pushed the smell of sky like a promise of rebirth into her lungs: this was the season of order just beginning in her life. Till Stoney scurried out behind her, "You haven't touched your wine," those little green eyes and the wrinkled brow a menace representing only what she had to leave behind: faces of the old and all the laws established by them like chains on the newly grown; rigid faces, unbending laws, stiff bricks of detention, discipline.

"Get away from me, Stoney!" over a shoulder and off in a rush to where no law for living would be pounded into her ears.

Rejection was nothing new to Stoney: many a shaky female with an eye on her own inconsequential affairs had failed to understand him at first, to appraise his uniqueness. He turned south toward the Riviera, a reserve soon to fill with surer game, but Tony the Shylock chose that moment to come shuffling along in his labored stride. The Village was full of people you didn't want to see. He waved the old man back, gesturing meanwhile toward Diane, and went after her when he saw Tony's conspiratorial nod. "How can you leave the air fortune has placed between us?" he asked her in his jauntiest tone.

"It's easy," she said, and hailed a cab.

"Look, I need you more than you can imagine," he confided to her as the taxi swung around. "You can't leave me here." He ducked behind her when she stooped to enter, certain in a swelling of intuition that she'd secretly like to have him ride along. But she slugged him across the cheek with her handbag.

Stoney gasped and fell back against the open door. "Aagh! Oh! If I had my way I'd—I'd put you away! I'd teach you to behave, all right!"

That was the worst possible choice of a threat. Diane went at him, savagely swinging the purse from its straps, catching him again and again about the head on her way out of the cab, till he broke and ran. "You son-of-a-bitch!" she screamed one time before she slammed the door, then screamed it again as the cab coughed away, and her voice broke, trailed off to silence on the wind.

Stoney felt anxiously around his shaggy head for blood; with simultaneous relief, he found none and saw Tony the Shylock hurry away, puffing his cigar like an innocent bystander. Landlording was only incidental with Tony; in his daily pursuit as usurer he had developed a formidable air of innocence. Once, booked for assault on a welsher, he gave his name to the police blotter as "Bobba Stone," and only clean English had saved Stoney when the police came to make him stand trial. Even so, Stoney now remembered, one stout, suspicious cop had sensed complicity in the beard and had tugged at it before he was satisfied. It was more than a matter of rent that made Tony's back a better sight than his pink, unshaven face.

The painter ducked into Minetta Lane in case Tony should turn, and sat on an auto fender, rubbing his face where it stung in the wind. "A lunatic," he muttered. "What did she think I was after?" Then he thought of that dark pointed face and muttered again: "Those earrings twinkled like real gold, all right," and gold sent him dreaming off to a golden age, where a department of government would teach grace to female children.

The cab moaned away from her with a squeegee burn in the wet, like a doleful song signing out the strangers and the strangeness that had filled the last two months. Diane went past spare hedges scraping in the wind, hurried up the short flagged walk and was in the quietlit lobby, almost sobbing in the comfort of warmth. In the elevator's upward whisper she ran a comb through her hair, still shaky with anger at the dust-colored beard in her mind, at the yellow teeth biting out a threat, a wish to confine her, to cure her by confinement. A way that stank of age. Even in the Village, when they got old they got stiff. They should all be pickled, and yet the old were in charge of everything.

She found Carter awaiting her at the door, as thin and alert as she'd always pictured him. She went into his embrace and felt a renewal of the warmth which had been out of her for months. There was cleanliness in the smell of him; his shoulder where her head rested and his hand cupping the back of her head seemed more massive than she knew them to be. But she had seen something painful in his face, and drew back to look: a brand-new tiredness was imprinted there, lines not from laughing around those raincolored eyes.

"Christ, you're a lady," he laughed. "Two months ago you were a—— My, my, how you've grown," and together they laughed as she pressed close up on him again.

She wanted him to take her up in his arms and carry her in, but laughed at herself, glad that he released her and went ahead through the foyer to the living room. That sloped back looked burdened now, while before it had always seemed a sign of power.

"I didn't want to bother you, Cart," she said, following him, "but I—I just couldn't get cool." When she kicked off her shoes, the rug felt deep and familiar under her feet.

"Bother me? You can't bother me, little girl." He went past the couch and lowered himself into the red club chair, then beckoned to her.

Diane dropped her coat and handbag on the couch and settled in his lap, gazing around the room to bring herself closer to the reality of it: the two paintings and the abstract drapes, the white stone music of the centaur statue on a corner stand. Then she dug her head into the hollow of his shoulder. She'd live this way herself, she decided. No more Village vacuums and running wild, no more frantic——

"All right, how'd you do it?" he asked. "How'd you get out of Clearwater? Unless you don't feel like talking."

"I feel like *tahking*," she mimicked his precise accents. "Plenty. I'll tell the *whaul starry*. I carved out the frame that held the bars. It was wooden. Old and rotten wood. I did a little every night when I was in the kitchen without any matrons around."

"Was it on the ground floor?"

"It was up one story. There was a telegraph pole about six feet out and I jumped for it. I climbed down and beat it to the train. An hour I waited up on that windy platform. What an hour! I thought everybody was a cop—men, women and children. I had the real horrors. Even back in the city I was frantic. That son-of-a-bitch Stoney bugged me up some more. That phony Stoney with his phony beard. He tried to make me, you know, he got me frantic with——" She halted abruptly, feeling herself begin to babble, to spill it all out on Carter.

"He's harmless. He just likes to hear himself talk. Did you wait at least till after supper before you breezed out?"

"That's just it. I slipped out while everyone was eating and got into the pantry where that window was. Nobody's ever there while they're serving. I cased that pretty good."

"You mean you did it while the cooks and all were in the kitchen?" He'd always told himself he could never really know how this kid functioned. "You chewed out those bars while those people were right outside?"

"Sure. There's so much racket out there while they're feeding, I figured they'd never hear the scratching. All they ever do is argue."

He shook his head and reached out to touch her ear. "You must be starving." He jiggled the dangling golden cross. "Big girl's earrings; you got all togged out for the break."

"No, I had them in my bag. On the train I put them on. And I grabbed a sandwich on the train; I'm not hungry, Cart." It was good, sitting there close to Carter. He seemed always to push those indefinable fears out of her, those frights that came from nowhere to blow empty spaces inside her. She imagined waiting in green evening light for Carter to return from work and wrap her in his arms; but Edna's face suddenly glared at her and she felt a fluttering annoyance with herself. She was glad to answer his questions, just for the chance to keep talking; she made a joke of the way in which a matron's handbag had got itself rolled up in her coat when she hid it, during lunch, under a pantry shelf.

"What'll you do with yourself now?" he wanted to know. "They'll be looking for you."

"They'll have to look hard. I want to get my boy and live cool. No more jackpots." She saw him smile at that, head back, eyes closed as if even the low lighting hurt them. "But Carter—if I go to my mother for the baby she'll call the law. You know that; she put me away in the first place, that goddam old——"

"All right, baby," he said.

"You don't like my choice of words, do you?" She laughed at his uneasiness, yet at the same time felt a part of the fatigue she saw. "It's not that. It's the bitterness; I get sad when you feel pushed around enough to sound bitter."

"You look worn, Carter. That line in your forehead is deeper."

"That's my personality. Leave it alone."

It was a different Carter, marked now by pressures that had once just slipped off him. "How's Edna? Isn't she improving at all? I suppose you visit her every chance."

Now he'd have to say it. He leaned over for the cigarettes on the table, taking a good deal of time. When he had lighted their cigarettes, he said, "Edna may die, Diane. She may, that is."

"Die! Why, what is it? Just a broken leg, wasn't it? I didn't know people can die——"

"Leg's the least of it. It just brought things to a head. Remember how—remember that business about her suddenly getting dizzy, knowing she was going to fall down the stairs, but being unable to stop herself?"

"Yeah, I remember something about it. Vaguely, sort of."

"Well, the dizziness comes and goes. First they suspected it was psychological, but now they're pretty sure—well, just *about* certain it's a serious organic deal."

"I *thought* she was in the hospital too long for a broken leg. What do they think it is?"

"Oh, some special disease. Long name. It's fatal, if that's what she's got." He knew he shouldn't say Edna was still being treated psychiatrically, and wondered why he had felt called upon to tell her anything at all. She had troubles enough of her own right now.

Diane rubbed her head against his neck and smoked silently. "Gee," she finally said, "Edna dying," and in her mind Edna's face took on a new helplessness, a greater pallor. "I suppose I should be sorry," she murmured.

"No, don't be sorry."

"You're supposed to cry when your own sister is dying."

"Not you. You don't cry."

"That's right. That's what's wrong with me."

"I mean you don't carry on. You don't do what's expected, what people want you to."

She stood up and walked over to the window to look through the blinds. That was Carter. Live-your-own-life Carter. He wore a badge in his forehead, one single line of understanding. And Edna . . . blind to his intent, possessive of his flesh, demanding all his thought. She was not sorry for Edna, and Carter removed the edge of guilt from her feelings. "Have you seen my Johnny at all? Have you been over to Mama's?"

"No, I don't much want to see her."

"I don't blame you. You been around much? At the Cosmopole or the diner, or along MacDougal?"

"Not much, Diane. It's got so that I don't like to see the citizens around the tables. Not any more. Lately I feel as if I can see what's happening inside them that makes them act up outside. I don't know, it's crazy—sort of the eyes behind the eyes. Once in a while I guzzle coffee at the diner. Mostly, I lob around the street looking at nothing. Or I sit up here. Listening to music . . . reading." But he stopped to look in at himself, for lately his reading had been made foolish by a mind that would not obey his eyes; sitting before spinning records, he would grow listless, until music he loved went vacant. He would sleep in a chair while chords and jumbled notes slid into his dreams and made them eerie; then he would awaken, always in a jerky trembling, to pace the rug and click the phonograph silent and stand awhile in the hum of soundlessness till hours loomed like walls, urging him undirected from the tired dust of these rooms. "Sometimes I see a show," he said, suddenly thankful she was there.

"Alone?" she asked.

"Yeah, alone." He watched her glide half-dancing around the floor, hands hung behind her, so childlike in her muted plaid uniform, yet so very much like Edna in her eyes . . . in her voice.

"No women, Carter?" She felt foolish for the grin growing in her face, and turned her back so he wouldn't see.

"Nope, no women. I get the same from you as I get from your sister, except that a song and dance go with her beating."

Diane faced him, her mouth undecided about smiling. "She bothers you like that? She always was jealous."

"Well, she's sick. What the hell."

"Are you sad, Cart? Do you love Edna very much?"

"Well, I'm not delighted with things, I'll tell you."

"Do you, Cart? Do you love her? A lot, I mean."

"Don't bother me with trivialities, kid." It was too late in the year to discern between love and duty, for this year had grown old in a month, and with it all his patience had seemed to age and calcify.

Diane was back sitting on the rug before him. "Carter, why wouldn't you sleep with me when I wanted you to? I thought because you loved Edna. Don't you like me, Carter?"

Laughing, he put a hand on her head. "Because you're a baby. Or you were six months ago."

"Baby! I've been a mother for almost a year. Baby, my eye."

"I know, Diane, I know."

"I'll be eighteen in a week."

"Yes," he said.

"Edna was always jealous, wasn't she? She was jealous of me, wasn't she?"

Carter heaved to his feet and his face looked old in its shifting shadows. He crossed the room to the radio, turned it on, spun the dial, listening tentatively to some squawking stations; then he switched it off. Diane was beside him when he turned, reaching her arms around his neck. "Don't be angry with me, Cart."

Laughing with a kind of shame, he danced her around, then pulled her down beside him on the couch. "I'm getting pretty sour," he apologized. "But we shouldn't become vultures. Edna's been withering away for over three months. That's pretty rough on her."

"What's that got to do with us?"

"Us? Oh, you're like steel, little girl."

That square unflinching face was trying to understand her, but sometimes even Carter seemed to go blind to truths she found clear. What harm would they be doing Edna if they—— "It's been damn rough on *you*," she said with finality.

"It's been rough on us all; okay?"

Diane leaned back into the crook of the couch's arm and stared at the clean stretch of ceiling. She imagined him being a father to Johnny, knew he could take her boy as his son with none of the biting hesitation that might compromise a lesser man, dreamed of bearing children who smiled his smile and saw the world through eyes like his. The loves she'd had since her fourteenth year were pale things beside her feeling for this man. Without remorse she told herself they'd been necessary, yet realized with a ghostly touch of guilt that they hadn't been loves, not even real hungers, but simply ways of belonging to life. "It's ugly," she said. "Carter, it's all so terrible and useless."

"What is?" he asked, leaning back on the other arm.

"Everything. Life," and she went forward as if in search of life, of everything, creeping up on him so that her face pointed at his. "We should have each other, Carter. There shouldn't be any Ednas or anything between us."

He felt stiff, but kept his arms up with hands under his head, staring unsmiling at her as she lay against him. That clean little face might have been the clean face of any schoolgirl with a dream and a hundred glittering plans.

"If we can't . . . Carter, there's nothing. There's nowhere. Everything is empty and——"

"Hey, babe, don't talk that way." One hand he put on her waist, and with the other he pulled her head down on his shoulder. "Things are always more promising than they seem. Don't you know that? Always."

Twisting her head around, she kissed him with a quick impact, missing his mouth. "Know why I love you, Cart? Because you're the only one I know who disagrees when I say life isn't worth the job." She laid her head against his jaw, sighing. "Carter?"

"Yeah."

"Can we go for a drive?" She snickered. "Just to keep me out of the Riviera and the Cosmopole rat's nest. I could really use some staying out of there."

"Baby's coming on with such healthy instincts. Except I sold the car. Year old, already; dull and dusty."

She lay quietly, then murmured, "Hospital expenses?"

"Every little bit helps," he said drowsily. "Things aren't moving well with surplus film. The big boys are all—well, what the hell, things are slow." There was Wengel's marshmallow face in his mind's gray space, and he resented more its intrusion on this shadowy quiet than the man's greedy reaching in business. "What?" he had to say to Diane's slurred question.

"Will you go with me to Mama's for the baby?"

"Of course. You can keep him here till you decide what you're going to do. You know?"

The weight of his hands on her hip and neck enclosed her from the strange, forever menacing vastness of the world; good, clean Carter kept cold shadows out. "Carter—" without looking up—"could I clean up and get on some fresh clothes? Some of Edna's things?"

"Sure, babe."

"Something simple, like a sweater and skirt. Gray or black, so Mama won't notice."

"Sure."

Things were so easy now; she felt unshakably protected, and lifted her head to see his face silhouetted against an end-table lamp. For a while she stared in silence at the amber glow that traced his profile and touched the corner of his mouth. Then she laid her head down again. "Carter?"

"Yeah?"

"Just Carter." No words were in her to express the welling up in her chest. She raised her head again and leaned close, kissing him first under the jutting cheekbone, then on the wedge of flesh at the end of his mouth. She pressed her cheek against his, let a leg drop down beside him, pressed her body closer and waited. His breathing grew deep and steady, but he lay still, hands warm upon her. Diane raised her head, looked at his face and saw him smiling in his sleep. "Carter!" she shouted, grabbing his ears and shaking him. "Oh! Another woman—*any* other woman would kill you for going to sleep like that."

"You're no other woman." Only half out of sleep. "You're Diane."

She jumped up and ran to the shadows across the room to keep him from seeing the flush she felt in her face, till anger spun her around to find him sitting up.

"It's not all that important, is it, little girl? That sort of indignation is for Riviera emancipation zealots, with emancipation nowhere but in their poor beery mouths."

She came back working off an earring, still uneasy, searching for something to say. "You won't let Mama do anything? You know, call the police?"

"No, we'll just get Johnny and leave." The lines were deep around his eyes; his light hair looked gray where it was cut close at the temples.

Diane sat on a chair arm across from him. "Maybe you ought to sleep, Carter; your face looks so tired."

"No, I'm not tired; I'm just old. You know I'm an old guy, Diane?"

"You're fifteen years older than me." She laughed to force down the bitterness. "I like it. I wish you had a mustache."

"I'm old enough for a beard," he chuckled, rubbing the side of his face.

"Don't say that. I'd pickle you right away if you were old. They should pickle everyone over forty. I hate them all."

"Don't hate." He went toward her. "It's an irritating feeling. Why bother with it?"

"Bother with it?" She laughed now. "You nuts, Carter? You can't help a feeling like that, like turning it on or off."

"Well, at least don't be so general about it. Some of my best friends are old people." He pulled her wrists so that she stood. "Go take your shower, baby. Then we'll visit Grandma and take back your boy."

"Let's go to the Cosmopole first and eat" came compulsively out of her.

"You really want to eat there?"

"Yeah, I have a rock in my chest; I want to have some fun. I've got two months to make up, two months living like a—like a choirgirl or something."

"Forget the two months," he began, but saw that her eyes had become remote. "Have it your way." He took her by the arm through the foyer, down the long, narrow hallway to the bedroom door. "Get undressed and jump under the shower. Hot and cold, quick varying, back and forth. Then if you still feel like it, we'll eat at *Shanker-la*."

Diane was looking in at the broad bed where Edna had spent some six hundred nights with a man she could never really know. Across the room hung the large framed print of a Degas dancer Carter had once called a chubby Diane. She turned to him. "Carter, you insulted me on that couch. You know that, Carter?"

"Diane—" reaching out for her shoulders—"be a good kid . . . for a while, anyway."

"Okay, but not for long. I've been cooped up two months with old bitches watching me. And I'm young, Mr. Webb, and healthy."

"Healthy?" She could see his eyes strain for a way to tell her what he felt. "They've got a number for you somewhere in their records. And your size and weight and complexion. But they don't care how your eyes look when they're darting around for something to hold to. The records don't show—" awkward words for him, but he couldn't

hold them back—"that your skinny little body is warm . . . and
hungry with all kinds of needs, and scared of shadows. Those——"

"Cut it out." It was embarrassing to hear herself described, and
discomforting that Carter was troubled enough to perform that way.
"Cut it out, Carter. I'm no talent scout."

Huddled in his coat, Stoney went up Minetta Lane with social
engineering solid in his mind, planning his departments of correction
and advice for citizens of a race to come, meanwhile scoring with a
sidelong glance present-day citizens of the Village who passed, avoiding him. He held his head high, puffing smoke, assuring himself he
was proud of the privacy it had taken years of invective to attain, and
sat once more on an auto fender to consider the way in which this abject race could be destroyed.

"Jesus, you bearded wonder! Jesus, you want to freeze right up on
that Chev'alet?"

Stoney looked vaguely at the thin wool-stockinged legs, then a
short way up the shaggy tweed coat to Lizzie Linden's skinny head
and corn-silk length of hair, and the little elf's face, a remnant of real
beauty where, in the ten years since her prime, delicacy had turned to
brittle bone. He slid to his feet, ready to go, but she was upon him
looking up from his chest, and he soured at the old demand in her
eyes. Every jaded Village darling bit with her eyes for attention. Rubbing the cheek that felt abraded, he foresaw a day when that little
black-eyed brat who'd slugged him would see her twilight of effective-
ness and strain like Lizzie for any affectionate gesture.

"You got a fireplace in your trap. Stand here in the cold when you
got a fireplace idle? Jesus, you're crazy, Bob." She smiled, but not
with her eyes—those tawny searchers were braced in occupation with
her thoughts. Thoughts forever the same, he knew. Each man who
failed to show desire for her was an offender, time's accomplice in
the negation of Lizzie Linden's appeal.

He made for Sixth Avenue's larger space, but she caught him by an
arm. "Liz, I have to be at the diner," he said softly to the hard ur-
gency in her look. She asked why, and he replied, "You know why;
you're smart enough for that, Liz."

"Smart?" Her laugh was shrill and toneless in the cold. "Don't be
smart, my mother oweys said; be beautiful, tha-a-at's what she said,"
stretching the words as she often did in her taunting, sidelong smirk,

yet looking up uncertainly, as if he might laugh at the erosion of years in her face. But Stoney didn't laugh: he was gracious with those he feared might detect some nameless, impending failure in his make-up, and anyone with lip was suspect. This Lizzie could sense, and she'd always kept him well-behaved. "It's freezin cold. Let's get over to a fire'n warm our blood. Or maybe you got no blood no more to warm. Je-sus," she whined, flashing pale gums in her grin, "maybe you're like them in the Cosmopole, maybe tha-at's why you got to stand by the diner, so's you can run across to the Ca-a-asmopole'n sit with them, sittin easy with no balls in their way at the tables all night drinkin coffee'n talkin it up. You got to have ba-a-alls to paint right, man."

Some early drunks turned to stare; Stoney shifted his eyes in a burlesque of self-consciousness. "Lizzie, watch your talk. The tourists'll think we're Greenwich Village sex maniacs." He saw her laugh, but *at* him. His humor was always a waste with her, yet he could never remember to keep from exposing himself to her dullness.

"Jee-sus, the tourists! Don't you have *any* balls, Stoney? You a table artist, Bob, like them in the Ca-a-asmopo-ole?"

"You should talk." But he decided not to ridicule her for long nights spent in the Cosmopole with her newsprint pad. He leaned back against the lamppost, lighting a new cigar, holding his temper level. "Don't link me with them, Liz; you know I produce."

"Yeah, miles'n miles of them; I heard it but I never seen it. Take me'n show me. Take me to the fireplace, Bob, I'm freezin," shifting and hopping on those brittle legs.

"I'm too hungry, Lizzie." There was nothing to gain from this shadow of a woman for whom he'd never had an urge.

"Well, you can steer me home, at least. You know that Bleecker Street is evil with all them wild Dago kids after dark. I'm forever scared some degenery to come out of a hallway at me. Ain't you a neighbor? I'm forever scared to get hurt bad'n maybe knocked up to the bargain."

She'd used that wail to lure many an indifferent man, hungering at him out of those busy eyes, forcing compassion with her frail mouth and tiny teeth. He patted her head to shield with camaraderie his uneasiness, then realized, when he heard himself again complain of hunger, that he'd intuitively found a way out of her fragile little clutch—he'd let her play mother! "I can hardly move, I'm so hungry.

I've got to find a patron. I'm actually growing faint, Liz—ah, I'm sinking fast." Stoney looked halfheartedly for the laugh that didn't come.

Even her grin had faded. "Aah, you got to be a man to paint right; it's why you're starvin." She looked blindly to the ground, and he knew she'd quit those longing looks. "Come on, come on, I just bought Lukey the Swede a meal; I might as well buy you. *He* just got out of the workhouse, there's a reason; but you're worse, I swear. Jesus, come on."

"How can you compare us?" he whispered, strained with incredulousness. "He's a dope fiend and I'm——"

"No he ain't. Lukey's no junky. It's oney gauge he's on, a little jive. Marijuana ain't no habit like heroin. Come on, I'll fix you to a veal'n pepper over by the Riviera," going before him, right through the steam from a sewer.

"But how can you—Lizzie, I must say I resent being compared with the dregs. You know me better than that."

"Yeah, I know you."

"I mean, you *know* what my interests are. You *know* how I dream of and plan for the day when——" It was no use; this was the thinker's cross.

"What's the difference?" she said like some tired, hopeless parent. "We're all hooked on something."

Carter didn't want to look inside when they reached the Cosmopole Cafeteria's flat fluorescent pallor. He leaned on a bus-stop sign by the curb, letting Diane run ahead to look through one of the huge windows that flanked the door.

"Bunch of new faces," she called through the drizzle from under one of Edna's kerchiefs.

"Old faces," he called back, then said more quietly, "You have to be up close to see the wax. From outside they look real." Long nights, in the unbroken wail of a thousand sourceless voices, he had looked through that violet-tinted light. Over tables packed with dope fiends and philosophers, prostitutes and poets, artists and hoods, darlings, dreamers, derelicts and every American variety of displaced person, all together in a debris of Babel which some conciliatory side of him had defined as fundamental human affinity. But the affinity never seemed fundamental enough. No golden-haired darling with a newlook bohemian manner could long comprehend some dreamer's old remorse. New ashes fell on Babel's ruin.

Even Edna had piled their disparities high between Carter and herself in those transitory days, presenting each of her remembered sins as a virtue to keep him out of her desperate world. "I *like* to smoke jive. You can keep reality," and "Work is for slaves; I'm free." It had cost a portion of his pride to reach a softness behind those coal-hard eyes, to shatter the protective mask she wore.

"You look like a birthday cake," he would say of her pasty rainbow face.

"Men," she'd complain with a shifting eye, "don't pay you any mind unless you attract them with color."

Words and words.

"Which men? One-nighters or a guy for all the time?"

"I've got to live. I live by men," and charcoal eyes direct in a gesture complacent by intent, pathetic for its failure.

"Wash your face and live by one." *Words, words of brine and waxlike faces packed around tables down the violet-tinted months.* He had gone in one dimension toward her, with no sidelong thought to any of her wayward hours, without a glance at any gunman or junky come to warm himself in the negative sun of her carelessness; he had gone to her, looking straight into those fixed wet eyes as though his looking might purge her of shoddiness.

Now he saw Diane waving to someone through the big plate glass, and recalled glances, thoughts he had spent on waywardness, and all his absolutions. He couldn't let convenient spaces in his memory lay blame on the past, nor could he let his guilt pass itself off on junky or hood or whore. They all stumbled blindly for solace, toward coffee or a heroin needle's gift of stupor, or one night of dreamless sleep.

He went up and watched the little green-coated girl smile in on the chaos with the eagerness of an untroubled child.

"Look, Cart, there's Dincher, over there on the other side."

"Little Caesar." Carter sighed.

"Oh, he's all right, Carter. Gee, I know him all my life, practically. Since I was eight. He's a week older than me, Cart, and——"

"That accounts for the cigar. And his boys are all togged out; they're having a birthday party . . . at the Wax Museum."

"That's right," she laughed. "Let's go in, Carter. I want to wish the Dinch many happy returns and all that. Come on, Cart."

"He'll be dead before he's voting age."

"He'll straighten out. Don't be an old fusspot or I'll pickle you." Carter laughed, following her to the steaming doorway.

When they passed through the revolving door, Dincher plucked the cigar from his tight little mouth and got up, patting the air with a hand to indicate to the pair of boys at his table that all was well. His hair glistened black as he snake-hipped watchfully around tables and came up to meet them in the aisle.

"Many happy returns, Dinch," Diane said affectionately.

"Same to you, dollbaby. Like-nex week I getcha present. Where you been so long?"

"Oh, around."

"Happy birthday, Dinch," Carter said with as little dryness as possible.

"Thanks, pal." The boy smiled, cold-eyed, into Carter's face; his eyebrows arched dramatically, as if that were the tested device for erasing the difference of years between them.

Diane caught Carter's impatience in the weary shifting of his glance, and addressed him just to offer attention. "Get me anything you get, Cart. Maybe they still have those little steaks." Then she moved closer and whispered, "Let's sit with the kids; it'll keep the characters away."

He was looking around at the characters, lonely people of every age, the big city's disinherited in rags or sporty togs, filling the tables like stage props in a tragedy, depersonalized in their vast unanimity.

He nodded and she watched him lumber toward the counter, placing his weight deliberately on each step like a man hauling coal. Four years in the army had never quite brought him out of the Pennsylvania pits. Impressions stayed long with Carter, she had to tell herself, and regretfully she knew he'd be a long time burdened with Edna. She turned to Dincher, who grinned clumsily around the cigar, his heavy-lidded eyes drifting up and down her body as though it were expected of him. Eyes were watching her, she felt, from every side and corner of the place, and an old excitement returned to dance around in her. "You know him, don't you, Dinch? That's Edna's husband."

"Yeah, I know the gen'lemun."

"Don't you like him, Dinch?"

"He don't like me."

"Sure he does. He's a swell guy, Dinch; he likes everybody. He's just quiet, just that kind of guy."

"Yeah?" he said with candid boyishness, as if a disguise had slipped from his voice. "C'mon over'n sit it out; like-we make room for ya. How's Edna's leg? Awright?"

"Still healing," she passed it off, and followed him around tables, squeezing past bodies and the frantic chorus of their sounds.

A hand reached out from one group and caught hers tenderly. "Diane, darling, where've you beeeen?" and Timmy Lawless looked through his sandy matted cowlick; tan coat muddy, the hand gripping hers tipped with flaking nail enamel, the other hidden in a feminine kid glove. "I've missssed you, dear; you look so *lovelay*."

"Hello, Timmyboy, where'd you get the nice blue glove?"

He cocked his sad ballet dancer's head and held the gloved hand up, looking out from that lined-leather face as if he could see down the years to another day's suncolored smoke. "D'you lye-kut? Lizzie gave it to me."

"It's real pretty, Tim." She tried gently to pull away, but his clutch on her hand was tight, begging, pathetic.

"Let 'er go, Tim," Dincher wheedled him. "Like-she gotta go, now."

"Oh, don't take her away, darling." Timmy's droopy, veneered eyes swung with the pale grace of dancers toward Dincher. His glance slipped around the boy's features like a soft caressing feather. "Won't you stay? We're about to open a keg of nails."

Meyer Singler cackled his old man's toothless laugh and two clay-faced women at the table sat staring as before, while Timmy's eyes wandered around the group, half-bowing to any response.

"Com-mon, Timmy," Dincher said. "Like . . . like-let 'er go or I'll never kick the crap outta ya."

Timmy let go, but Dincher had stirred his passion. "Fuh-cue!" he wailed. "Fuh-cue, you ba-ast'rd!" while Diane went through behind the Dinch, and at a table behind, Old Man Moe set up a counter-wail against Timmy, till some talking artists in another group banged their fists for quiet. Timmy sipped some wine he found in the sack of empty bottles he always had on hand, and shrunken Old Man Moe turned eyes back to the table top to cough till his temper cooled.

"Timmy, he likes people should blast 'im," Dincher told Diane. "How you like a bum like that?" He put straight the boys who were shifting close to the wall at his table: "You cats know Diane. This guy comin over, like-he's 'er brother-in-law, so no talkin dirty-like; you hip?"

Their lips curled in greeting, their eyes retaining a conscious frost, as much a law with them as their kind of reticence. Sometimes those affected mannerisms amused her, but now her stomach went empty with fright as she realized how religious they were at their game of hardness. "How you been, Angie, Red?" she intoned as brightly as she could.

Together the boys shrugged. "Red goes up for sentence in a couple days," Dincher proudly offered. "Like-he's good for a sixer-like."

Like-like-like. This was like watching a terrible movie, having it grow out of the screen, take on more dimension and engulf her in its senseless unreality. She was about to say something, anything that might cut through the nightmare film replacing the air, when Carter appeared with a loaded tray. Dincher helped arrange the food, smiling with guarded good nature at Carter. "How'sa wife?" he said, leaning back to puff on the cigar.

"Coming along, thanks."

"That's good; right, Ange?"

Angie nodded with little more than his eyebrows, glanced at his watch, then held it out to Dincher. Dincher arose and flicked his head toward the door, smiled at Diane, then at Carter. "A little business," he whispered out of a smug, toothy grin. "Jus for a li'l while, like-then I be back; awright?"

"Take care, Dinch," Diane said. "Don't do anything dumb, Dinch."

"Leave it to me, doll, I stay cool. Right, Ange?" He strode off, slinging a loose black coat over his pin-stripe suit, his erect little form well guarded by those two replicas of himself.

"Are those punks kidding?" Carter asked, stirring coffee. "They think they really look hard with that Bogart stuff?"

"You think they're not? They *are*, all through and through, till anybody's human with them. Then they get human and generous and not so hard any more." The steak tasted as flat as it looked, but she ate steadily to fill the white, airless space within. "Where's your steak? I thought you were going to eat, too."

"I just want coffee." He undid the buttons of his trench coat in half a hope he'd cool off. But the dust of the place was within him;

a million words were uttered here in a night with no hope for communication. "You ready to go for Johnny when you're through eating?"

But the Cosmopole's electricity was within Diane; the rise and fall of voices were communication enough for her. "Not now, not tonight, Carter. I don't want Mama to know yet that I'm out. Not just yet, Carter." She wanted to see Dincher and scold him for anything he might be up to, then pat his face till that grinning mask of complacency was gone from his boy's bewildered stare.

Carter could see the wild darting of her eyes; he stood when Dincher came swaggering back, even smiled fully at him as the boy scraped a chair up close with a theatrical sweep.

"I'll be home if you need me, babe." Carter buttoned up his coat and knew by her nod that she understood he expected her there to sleep.

He left with the awkward smile of a man getting out of the way, and Diane shook off the beginning of remorse with a smile at Dincher, who was talking rapidly of a trumpet he had bought. "Like-I'm diggin a lot of Armstrong, 'cause he's the man. You wanna hear how I go loose'n take off ridin like Louie. Like-you want to hear me, doll." All the pretense was replaced by an unguarded eagerness in his face. She could affect him that way, she knew. "I got the horn stashed by Paddy Jenks, he likes I should play when he's goofin."

"Paddy Jenks? He's hooked with heroin, Dinch."

The boy chuckled at her display of quiet yet alarmed concern. "Well, don' worry about me, doll. Paddy's on Horse, that don' mean I got to. I jus smoke a li'l jive off'n on, I'm too hip for any Horse. Don' worry about me, doll."

She tried not to worry, but she had to speak up. "Those junkies, they'll bring you down, Dinch, they'll highjive you till you get hooked *with* them. I know them, Dinch. You can smoke all the pod you want, but keep away from the junkies, Dinch. Please, Dinch."

Now he had to assert that professional confidence again: his eyelids drooped heavily as he bobbed with a silent chuckle. "Leave it to me, doll, I stay real cool. You wanna get on? I got some pot stashed by the subway."

"Pod, Dincher; don't say pot."

"What's the diff? You wanna get on?"

"Don't say pot, Dinch. It's the intellectuals from college and all who come on that way. They want to get their hip-cards punched. Say pod, Dincher." And all the while she was speaking she was trying to decide. Those two months in the detention home had been sober ones, drab and oppressive with religious sermons. She wanted the gummy sweetness of marijuana in her throat and the drifting carelessness that went with it. But she knew how easily she could relinquish that sense of responsibility with which she had this time gone to Carter, how simply she could become a Viper again and laugh at the meaning of days. But she'd be laughing at Johnny, that way. If she refused to get high right now and went instead to Mama's for the baby . . . Why had she let Carter go? She'd avoided those tired eyes asking her to come away. "No, Dinch, no, I got to get over to my mother's. I got to get my baby, Dinch," and stood quickly, as if Dincher might hold her down.

"That's good, doll. Like-you gonna get the little kid? I clean forgot . . . " He grew silent in boyish embarrassment.

Diane looked back once to warn Dincher hastily against the junkies, but hurried out, across Sixth Avenue and up into Christopher in a thin drizzle, half-seeing the shimmering reflections of glass, brick and neon glare, crossing streets swiftly toward Carter's, afraid that if she slowed down she might backtrack to the Cosmopole and all its easy, irrelevant noises, the drifting faces that demanded so little of her.

She was sniffling with cold by the time she reached that hedge-lined red-brick building, and hurried through to the elevator. To wait longer, it seemed, than it should take for any elevator to arrive. Then, up in the rattling car, she leaned back to catch in her mind Carter's expression of content because she wanted to get Johnny and begin to live as a woman should.

She rang twice before the elevator left. Then she rang again, and the hallway shrank, lost air and light. Carter wasn't in. She rang and rang, while her heart pounded from anger to despair. "He said he'd be home, he *said* so! If I need him . . ." Wearily, she sat on the cold marble stairs to wait, even if it took all night for him to return. She'd never go alone to Mama's—just to think of her was to hear her preach . . . in that special saintlike voice. She had to have Carter beside her, knowing her every rise and fall of feeling.

Light was pale from the hall window half a flight up, coming down through iron banister rungs so that barlike shadows striped across

her legs. She stood, impelled to hurry back to keep the junkies cool
if they tried to con Dincher onto Horse—*like, like-like*: already they'd
impressed on him the junky-musician's word-sign for stupor. Dinch
was such a baby under his crust. But the junkies would behave with
her around; she could always keep them cool. She went down a step,
then another, tasting in her mind the burnt pungency of marijuana.
Then she sat down abruptly. Her coat looked purple in the orange
hallway light—or blackish, perhaps—no longer green. Carter had to
come back soon. Forever she'd need him by to keep her sensible, and
knowledge of her own compulsiveness was a cold shadow, more
livid than the hallway gloom, growing down from her packed heart
into limbs as heavy as wood. She gripped a banister rung, concentrating on Carter on the chance there might be something between
them that could bring him home before her will went dry of power.
He had to be thinking of her wherever he was; he had to look for
her; he had to point his feet homeward; he just had to sense her
despair.

But Carter's feet were aimless in the streets. Down the wet funnel
of night he lumbered with a heavier man's gait, trying to feel less
wedged in the funnel of his own despair. The drizzle was a relentless
thing, catching light obliquely as he passed half-lit stores. He could
see his pace quicken to escape the pursuit of Edna's tears, the figures
on bills he couldn't pay, the gleaming glasses and bloodless flesh of
Wengel, crazy, pompous Wengel, reaching out a pudgy hand to grab
up the rest of raw-film distribution to add to the half he already controlled, still squeezing cunningly for Webb's color-processing kit. "It's
a secret you're lucky to have," Merwin Fingerhut had said, and Merwin knew. "You got to guard it away from Wengel like you got to
guard he don't pull out your eyes."

It hurt Merwin to process the film Wengel sold, but he contented
himself with the knowledge that his sin was only manual, that he
only worked for Carter, whose moral responsibility it was.

"Well, we give them better developing than Wengel can," Carter
would explain. "If Wengel could get our kit he'd cut us right out.
He needs us and the people need us."

"Vote for Webb. They need us like they need blisters on their
nose. What they need is plain, ordinary decent film, in a country like
this with so much items to sell."

And Merwin was right, Carter always knew when he listened to that chubby young easyfaced man talk about the fat old hard-brained one. Wengel bought up air-force surplus film, originally produced to be shot from ten thousand feet, and cut it into domestic sizes for public sale. He had to commission Carter to develop the exposed rolls, for only Carter's special kit, his own chemical arrangement, could bring out color in developing so that customers were half satisfied. "They use Wengel's film," Merwin often said. "They might as well take the pictures with a shoe box instead of cameras. Unless they got the Mustangs and P-51s." He'd rub his little token mustache while Carter laughed. "If Wengel could make them come out at all, even all purple, he'd process them in his toilet bowl for all he cares about the citizens."

The citizens were the last thing Wengel cared about, all right, for no other man was so single-minded in his concern as that old man: Wengel was conscious of Wengel. The first thing to be seen on entering his offices was a huge portrait of himself, a crude, maladroit work in oils applied sparingly, fearfully, by some amateur who, it would seem, could be paid off with a meal. Beside the thing hung a plaque dedicated by the Welfare Society for the Blind to *August S. Wengel in recognition of his generous contribution to the amelioration of the condition of the blind.* It had startled Carter when he first saw it, and he couldn't hide his incredulousness when he asked Wengel's secretary about it. Marge asked if he'd been through this whole building into which Wengel had recently moved his one-floor plant, and Carter said, "Yes. Only this plaque is new to me," expecting an explanation. But the girl said nothing, keeping her placid face down toward the typewriter, so that he had to ask right out what Wengel had done for the blind.

"He's filled the rolling room with them." Her voice was low with a kind of reluctance. "Seventy-five of them."

Carter, in a leather easy chair, looked over the rail at the girl, enjoying a first happy thought about Wengel. In his old age was he finally turning benign? Then he wondered about the Puerto Ricans who had worked in the rolling room and asked Marge if Wengel had let them go.

"He's got them spread around on the processing machines, on the sixteen-millimeter and the thirty-fives," she said blankly, and sat, stubbornly plump at her typing, sharing none of his enthusiasm over

Wengel's new heart. It was as if she had neither admiration nor contempt for anybody's conduct. But at last she looked up and abruptly blurted out her hidden rancor: "Listen, maybe you'll tell Wengel everything I say, but I swear I don't care any more. I have a little girl, but I don't care, I'll manage somehow. You may think those Spanish people got a raise, but I know different."

She, who made out their pay vouchers, knew different, and let Carter know in a rush from her pursed full lips that, working all day in a pitch-dark room, the Puerto Ricans had been paid a cent and a half for each of the forty packs they rolled in an hour, to earn twenty-nine dollars a week. That the blind, more adept in the dark, turned out fifty-five rolls in an hour, but at *one cent* each, so that Wengel's darkroom now produced much more and cost him something less. Meanwhile, the Puerto Ricans replaced high-salaried men on the movie-film-processing floor, to be paid a wage based on their piece-work earnings in the rolling room. Everybody was being rolled by Wengel, and Carter Webb was next on the list.

"What do you expect from Wengel?" Merwin had asked when Carter had returned to his shop in wild dismay and related what he had learned. "Humanity? The man is a low animal."

A man was a man; Carter couldn't envisage even Wengel on all fours. "Why don't they form a union?" he'd wanted to know.

"They're afraid. Helpless people, they think anyone gives them a rat's chance to live, they got to be grateful."

Carter, in a search for calm, had declared that no normal man could do as Wengel did. But Merwin only laughed and asked Carter how old was he. "You're a big boy, now. Don't start calling people crazy or you'll have to put all the citizens in the funny bin. You got to struggle against nature and you got to struggle against nature's animals."

It was easy to concede that the whole commercial scene was animal against animal. "I don't mind that so much, cutting each other's throats. But when they take helpless people and——"

"Carter, where you gonna draw the line? How helpless does someone have to be before you get riled when they're bounced around?"

That was something to consider in Village society, he told himself now, and circled back to go up the wet highlights of Waverly Place toward the diner. For the solace of coffee cups. To make their steaming centers focal points for rumination.

First, on Sixth Avenue, he swung past the Cosmopole to look with
little expectation for Diane, then crossed over through crossing traffic
to where Robert Stoney stood, erect as the traffic-light stanchion beside him, drawing on the black cigar before the diner's amber glow.
There the painter would often stand for an hour of night, apparently
aware of the picture he made in winds that blew his hair and stark
white coat with dramatic grace, ignoring anyone who smiled at him
in greeting. In two years of crossing paths in every public place
Stoney had never offered a nod, so Carter went right by without a
look at that raggedy beard.

He stepped up into the diner's amber gleam of chrome, into the
hour of quiet between dinner's prolonged clatter and the chatter of
midnight's coffee crowd. Only a muffled song came out of Magoo the
Newsboy, asleep in a booth beside his printed pile of other people's
fortunes. One hand propped up his battered old claw-nosed head
while he sang from a dream, and dreamed of soft little Lizzie as
though music still swelled from their love. Awake, he would stalk to
the Cosmopole and sit, fidgeting, some tables away in the line of
Lizzie's sight, swearing to wall or to audience that she purposely sat in
his view. All this although years, faded with their suns and sounds,
had so long ago set them apart. While Lizzie sat, with no remnant
of ardor, sketching in a newsprint pad the shape of everyone but
Magoo. Only in dreams did anything more than newsprint link them,
and only in dreaming did he find it in his heart to sing.

> "Oney a row . . . of daisies . . .
> Where tulips use to bloom . . . "

"Just in time for the chorus, Mr. Carter." This from the man in
white whose nervous eye and scraggy neck claimed twice the years in
his face. "Magoo got her in a garden now, Mr. Carter, which he's
singin all about flahrs."

"You're mistering my Christian name," Carter muttered, spinning
toward the counter on a stool.

"I know, but that's the respect I give a man, he's reg'lar with
work'n sleep." And the hot coffee, set down with the flourish of a
man proud of his skill. Slinger was more than owner of this sleepless
foodwagon that bathed in pure yellow light all seasons on the
Village Square; he was liaison among the motley cultures crammed

into this core of a motley town, and made himself historian of everyone's affairs. "What's a business guy like you wastin 'is time for in Green-witch Village?" he liked to ask, in a confidential businessman's tone, of this neatest man he knew. Carter was never more than general with Slinger: "Lucky to have an apartment anywhere," rather than to say he wondered himself.

"How's the wife?" Slinger asked this night, and Carter only nodded.

"Any better? Gettin a little stronger?"

"A little worse." He was sorry before the words were out, because Slinger stopped his ferretlike filling of sugar tanks to go blinking into a sorry grin. "Slinger," Carter quickly digressed, "you know what the Greenwich Diner is famous for? The tannest, most unobtrusive coffee in all New York. 'You want to taste some unpretentious coffee?' they say, and bring the tourists to Sixth Avenue and Eighth."

Like a hungry man fed, Slinger laughed with blanched gratitude for the change of subject. "It's the *hottest* untasty coffee in town," he insisted through hissing green-toothed laughter. "It's the damn *hottest* you'll get'n that's important as the taste."

The two night men came on and Slinger filled Carter's cup, then set a typewriter up at the counter's bend, two fingers moving like wild birds to clack out the next day's bill of fare. Magoo, in his corner booth, droned on against the typewriter's rattle, and Carter could almost see the moments doze on the coffee tank's silver, steamy sheen. And almost hear time slip out to leave the diner forever enclosing quiet, a quiet no more than tickled by Slinger and Magoo. By Slinger's able tapping and Magoo's helpless serenade.

> *"Baby if you all alone . . .*
> *Call me on the tellyphone . . .*
> *'Cause Daddy wantsa know . . .*
> *Where baby's gonna go. . . ."*

"Quiet!" Slinger yelled when a drove of trousered girls came boistering in, but they ignored him in the hope that Carter was a tourist whom they could impress to the tune of a meal. One stood by the mirror near the toilet passageway, fixing her bow tie and porkpie hat, pulling her jacket-tail tight over the unfortunate buttock spread that betrayed her masquerade. With a stevedore's scowl on her infant's face she threw a possessive arm around the one dress-high-heel-

and-earring girl of the five, and they jabbered into a booth with the others.

"Quiet!" Slinger ordered solemnly. "Magoo, he's singin'," and they whispered before the baritone whine scraping up from sleep's other world.

"*. . . fuh you, dear girl . . .*
I . . . would gadder up the world . . .
An' lay it at . . . yuh feet . . ."

But when the place filled steadily, overflowing from booths to the long-necked stools along the counter's lip, Slinger's aesthetic sense waned. He shook Magoo awake, cutting him off with a *Last* plaintive *Flower of Love*. "This ain't no hospital," he reminded the newsboy, and helped him out with his newsprint pile. A nightly routine. For Magoo slept only at the late-evening hour of quiet in a diner booth; there were those who said he'd never been in a bed since his month with Lizzie so long ago.

His startled eyes found the Lesbians, and his lingering dream made him spit with contempt at such waste.

"Back to the fist!" one shouted.

"Go twiddle it like you did last night!" another screeched at his back as he shambled out. And they all jeered with their own contempt for men, for fathers and lovers who had failed them.

From wall boxes, coins pushed music that jangled against the hubbub of voices—each note, each voice a thing alone. The city had spilled Friday over into the little yellow wagon, where clerks and stenogs, in their sharpest attire, and Village people, wise enough to escape the rain, translated loudly into laughter the secret tears of their brotherlessness.

Stoney came in out of the rain to have a whispered word with Slinger and took a stool, studying Carter from the counter's other angle. Carter nodded indifferently and looked back to his coffee.

"You know what the Village is?" Stoney wanted to know. "You know what the Village *really* is?"

"A pumpkin," Carter suggested.

Bob Stoney puffed smoke languidly, squinting at the thin, square-faced man with whom he bracketed the counter's turn, half-recalling that deep tired line below the hatbrim. "The Village," he slowly said, "is a magnifying mirror for the whole damn society." Just to get the philosophic gems rolling for this sophisticated mark; a veal-and-pepper sandwich couldn't hold a man Stoney's size. "You know those magnifying mirrors that make your pores look like billiard pockets?" He sat back waiting for the laugh.

But Carter didn't laugh; he only watched his coffee with that wincing stare. "Not my pores, pal, not mine." He saw Slinger watching from the smoke of frying meat and knew how Stoney had decided where to touch for the price of supper. Slinger was not a historian for nothing.

"That's what the Village is," Stoney sighed, pulling his fingers till each knuckle popped. "The world in diminution. It's all the ineptitude and waste and vapidity crammed together for investigation purposes. Man's inadequacy in a nutshell, ready to be examined."

"What a dismal prospect," Carter mumbled listlessly.

"This is the kind of night I *like* speaking with a responsive soul," Stoney declared with sudden vitality, as though his pleasure were indisputably the world's concern. "Yes sir, this is the kind of night I can *really* relate my plan. A golden age is in the offing, and this is the kind of night I can explain how to engineer it. It's something that involves the total species. *That's* what mature minds should concern themselves with. Let me tell you——"

"Why tell me? I *live* in the Village. You've seen me a thousand times; even made occasional passes at my wife."

"I have? I did? Well—well, what's that got to do with what I'm about to say?" But it occurred to him that he might have said it all before in this man's presence, and he snapped his knuckles hard. "You fooled me. You're dressed like—well, neatly, I must say. I mistook——" He straightened out of his crouch, and said in a voice magnanimous with acceptance: "I *really* didn't know you were one of us."

That condescending apology was half insult, half joke for Carter. "What do you mean, one of *us*? Stoney, you don't represent anybody." Some local young hoods were watching from down the counter, and he resented being identified with Stoney; he got to his feet.

But Stoney always felt effective; he suddenly laughed and leaned over, shaking Carter's shoulder fraternally. "Let me show you——"

"I have no time, Stoney." He started by, but caught with a glance at the man some childlike need hidden in his eyes. "Can I lend you a dollar?" he asked as flatly as he could.

Stoney shrugged like a man granting a favor, then held Carter's arm as it reached inside. "One moment, hold it awhile. Here comes Tony the Shylock. He'll get jealous."

Old Tony paused between them and removed the fat cigar from a head forever tilted. "Muh, you got a dough, Maestro, or you no got a dough? 'At's all-uhmo."

"My friend—" Stoney beamed—"it's guaranteed. This time it's in the bag." He held Carter's arm, pulling him to the neighboring stool.

Tony looked with disappointment through his blear eyes. He had wished Stoney would welsh, for he secretly loved a welsher, against whom he could lead his gang of hoodlum kids in mayhem. With a delicate finger, he scratched the sparse gray hairs of his lip. "Wadda you mean? You come across?" and he watched through drooped purple lids while his fingers flicked ashes to the floor. No man enjoyed his role more profoundly than Tony did. To conduct business with him a tryst had to be arranged around some corner—no transaction occurred on the street where a loan was first requested. Fifteen minutes had to elapse; then he'd sidle up to his client in any crowded spot and pass the money in a backhand movement, as though it were a stolen jewel, or at least a heroin cap. And all debtors were potential victims; that was understood whether the debt was legal or contraband. "You got it or no? Muh, no goddam bulshee, Stone."

Stoney's beard stretched with the grin beneath it; his eyes remained cold. "Here, take my seat; you'll delight in this." He knew that Tony could be placated if a confidence were given him over a story concerning women. He had that story and he wanted Carter around as a sounding board for a vocabulary that Tony could never follow. "As usual—" he fixed Tony with his grin—"a lady enters the scene. A *rich* lady."

Tony leaned back on the counter with the bored nonchalance of any man of the world, while Carter caught Slinger's eye for still more coffee, and Stoney laughed. "Yes sir, our troubles'll be over, done with, in one short week. One week—" he chuckled slyly—"of nurturing a potential patroness."

This threw the Shylock into wild laughter. Carter had to laugh at the sight of it, and when Tony found himself joined, he leaned close to whisper, " 'At's a Stone, boy. He's a got a mowd fulla *strunz*," wagging his head, incredibly entertained.

Stoney went unabashed through it all, informing any idle ear in the place that the fiercest fire in a thinker's hell burns in his ignoble stomach. "And—" he laughed almost to choking—"the *worst* part of his position is that all history's creators have shared it. The triteness is an unbearable offense. But—" he shrugged philosophically—"that's the price of talent."

"Hey, you know Lafarge?" Tony pushed his hat back to ask. "He's a best goddam artiss inna Vil-uhmo," leaning in confidentially. "*He's* a Talian."

Stoney gave a condescending grin and spoke on, promising to *make a long story short*, but forgetting to in his love for his own words. Meticulously, he described each step that took him to a print-shop window on Eighth Street to listen, as he often did, for one honest response from tourists ogling the masters. "But only the familiar coo of the dilettante came to me, and a stupid falsetto or two from some idiot who felt called upon to impose his aesthetic impotence on the free air." On he went, while Tony watched his mouth so intently that his own hung open, his cigar all but slipping out. Carter fidgeted, waiting for a break in the painter's yapping through which he might gracefully slip away to that free air. But there was no break; the story unfolded: Stoney was alone at the print-shop window with two females, fur coats, silver cigarette holders, they were fascinated with him, they were stupid, he was brilliant. " 'Oh yes, Gauguin,' " he mimicked in falsetto, " 'the one with leprosy.' Leprosy!" he laughed in his own voice. "That's how she identified Gauguin. And that's a sophisticate, mind you. Leprosy!"

Tony's intentness fascinated Carter, till the Shylock caught his eye and, covering his mouth, whispered sideways, "He's a craze, 'at's okay," meanwhile humoring the painter with a nod.

Stoney needed no spurring; delighted with himself, he told how he had identified Bonnard as *the one with ulcers*, El Greco as *the scrofulous one*, laughing till he strangled, but still talking between coughs into a paper napkin that he tossed over his shoulder into the aisle. Carter had to laugh despite his aversion to the man. He ordered two coffees from Slinger, who had begun to hover, blinking with impatience. And the noise of other voices became only a dim background for Stoney, who swung onto a vacated stool beside the Shylock, pausing for breath only when Tony asked Carter if he knew Bell, inventor of the radio. "He's a Talian," the Shylock declared.

Stoney hurtled on, analyzing each of the girls, while the Shylock looked expectantly past him to the door. The old man got up abruptly and departed without a look or a word, as though he'd been sitting there alone. But Stoney wouldn't be discomfited by anyone as dull as Tony; he blinked just once and slid his cup closer to Carter, taking the nearer stool. A long wave of time had passed, and the painter seemed nowhere near finished. "The kid seemed attached to her friend in that masochistic way modern youngsters have of yielding themselves almost dutifully to the shadow of some less sensitive, more affected, less intelligent, but somehow more colorful spirit . . . and *that* more colorful spirit in the high heels—a tall, blond, sleeky, almost pretty creature—seemed the very thing for my purpose."

Carter now decided finally to buy no meal for this blowhard, but hedged a little, feeling indebted for this chance to blame someone for something. "Well," he said impatiently, "did you or didn't you score? I don't have much more time," and felt like a poseur saying it: there was nowhere he had to go.

Stoney looked over a shoulder and sighed out his relief when he saw no Shylock. "Score? Of course. Louella, that's the sleeky girl, finally got around to asking if I were an artist. 'Yes,' I confessed." He showed little yellow teeth in a grin of unbridled pride. "And I added, 'Occasional toothaches and mild summer colds in the back.' That did it. Before they left I had Louella's enthusiastic promise to visit me at my studio with her poetry. Poetry is the Open Sesame with those imbeciles."

"Imbeciles? Who do you mean, imbeciles?"

The painter gaped with an accused man's affronted features. "Who? Why, those culture perverts from uptown. *Anyone* from uptown. And downtown . . . just about everyone I see about me, for that matter. Everywhere I go. I tell you our society is at the bottom of its spiral. As for me, I *know* we live in a lunatic asylum. I——"

"You're some speaker," Carter cut in, already penitent for the insult he was about to deliver, "but that's one word you use too much—I and all its variations."

But Stoney beamed. "Of course. I, I, I!" He banged the counter hard with each yap of sound. "It's the basic reality," raising his voice till it rang shrill; "it's the source of action and effect. If anything is ever done, it'll be done by—I (bang), I (bang), I!" Bang! Carter laughed. "I knew your grammar would collapse."

"Gents, gents, now lower down the hollerin, please." Slinger was an experienced arbiter: he could smile through his strictest demands. Yet a quick temper was unfettered in him when the Greenwich Diner was really in danger of havoc. His little wirelike frame was under the counterboard and down the aisle before Timmy Lawless, with the rainpasted mat of his hair, could carry that eternal sack of empty wine bottles more than five womanlike steps out of the night. And back into the rain went Timmy, profanity and tears—"I just came in for the sme-ell, you ba-ast'rd"—run by the collar of his grimy gabardine like a sack of so many expended dreams, sniffing a greedy nostrilful of some simmering onion's aroma, into his Village circusland of colored lights and sounds forever new, all roads leading to the Dills Hotel, where even his abused skinful of regret was a target for love.

"I don't want no Dills Hotel whore queerin the joint fer all the respec'bul faces," Slinger told Carter in a half-apologetic rush. His nervous eye stammered over the respectable clay of Izzie the Ghost and Paddy Jenks in a booth trading dreams from their heroin fog, and he came closer to the point. "He'd be tossin them jugs inta evvy mirror in the wagon, half a chance. Let 'im git over to the Dills where them hobos want 'is skin."

Carter shifted agitatedly. "You didn't have to shake him up, Slinger."

"You were *too* indulgent," Stoney complained. "He creamed all over the floor when you pushed him."

Slinger's feeble throat tried to roar out a laugh. "You said it. He loves that, for people to shake 'im up. He prob'ly creamed on the floor is right," rocking his thin-haired head back to work.

"That's a sick guy," Carter said straight to Stoney. "You don't rough sick guys."

"Aagh!" Stoney turned a shoulder to him, then looked his way again. "What are you, a saint? *That's* a disease, that coddling impulse."

"Maybe people should be sicker that way."

"You know what kind of disease that is, sonnyboy?" Stoney leaned over on an elbow like a man about to divulge some secret intelligence, puffing smoke while waiting for Carter to plead for what he had to say.

Carter wanted to be out in the impersonal rain. "Yeah, I know. I just forget the name, it's one of those rare things. It's some exotic disease." And Edna's face careened around the nightcolored bend of nowhere, brooding wetly at him for making a joke of disease. "But I know a good cure . . . Jonathan apples." He started to go, enjoying the warm bubbling of anger, when Tony the Shylock waddled around some milling faces, puffing his important cigar.

"Maestro, wadda you wan' big loft for paint-uhmo? You no wanna worry onna rent, you get lilla trap for scratch a whiska by boardinghouse'n no paint a *no* more."

The painter felt future hungers lurch inside him. "Tony, I'll be *rich* in a week. Why——"

"Listen, I gotta lilla fella, he take a loft, nobody tell a long story *no* more, okay?" He shuffled away with smug finality.

Carter resented it as much as the sputtering painter; he hadn't wanted to sympathize with Stoney, but now he had to. "Here, worry on a full stomach."

"You know something?" Stoney offered to repay Carter double for the buck he handed over. "That habit of kindness for the swine of the earth will kick back in your face. We'll never come into a golden age if they survive. They should be exterminated once and for all."

"What constitutes a swine?" Carter asked, and waited for no reply. Some sourceless fatigue lay like a load of coal on his back, weighed unrelenting as any load he'd ever hauled back home. In the running-days. In the swift unknowing-days. He paid his check, then let the rain feather on his face, and turned into the long, light-scratched shadow of Christopher Street, wanting to be home.

Home—where he could focus his loneliness on some of Edna's things, pretend it was missing her that made him feel so lost among other drifters in the night. He would have to find—somewhere—a photograph. But there might be no photograph at all, and he needed one, for her face in his mind was without depth, like a simple drawing on thin paper. He could feel nothing behind it, here in dark rain's reflections, not even the crazy workings of her suspicions.

When he sat facing her in the gloomy outworld of her hospital room he could feel those machinations, like intricate watch gears grinding against one another, plotting the time he spent away from her, inventing people and situations. His denials died in her ears. She only glared at him with those black eyes glittering, shot with the pain of her fantasies, sunken with the pull of disease.

"*Who have you been shacking with?*"

"*Nobody.*"

"*Don't try to tell me you've been going without. In that frantic Village?*"

"*I have, Edna.*" From a dry and tired chest.

"*Not all this time, Carter. Not you.*"

"*Nobody in all this time.*"

Every visit, always the same. Unaware she might be dying. Still intent upon the healing of the leg, straining her vision toward dubious horizons.

"*Who did you rock over this week?*"

"*Seventeen women named Alice. Four of them were over eighty and one has a brother in Turkey.*"

Then the surge of tears, skittering like panicky prayers for more days on earth, and complaints about tortures out of her nightly dreams, confused with reality by those lost, overlapping boundaries of her days. "*You didn't wave to me on the porch, last time. I waited in the sun.*" When all last times that month the rain had pounded at glass like some willful animal trying to reach inside with a need to cleanse what it saw in grayness there. "*You didn't have to tear up the book jacket just because you don't like Proust.*" While all the time it lay inviolate on a sterile porcelain stool. Well, sick . . . maybe dying. Dying, crying Edna, not any Edna any more, but a dying woman; not even a woman any longer, but a dying. A Dying, now.

"There was nowhere to go. Anywhere I went would start the jackpots all over again." Diane in hallway shadows, like a cat cub huddled in a corner of some dreary cage, was a picture Carter couldn't get out of his mind through the leisure of their week end together. Now from the desk at the office side of his one-room shop he watched Merwin tape over the tacks that pinned blackout paper over the

big window, only half-hearing the chubby man's near-whisper of a
voice. "Enough light bled in before, I could read a newspaper during darkroom work. Now it's taken care."

"You're a genius," Carter mumbled.

"It's a pleasure; now I can't read the papers. Who can stand newspapers these days?"

Carter laughed shortly and gave his mind back to that voice in the
hallway, so weak with waiting that it came high out of its normal
place in her throat. "I waited, Carter, I really *made* myself wait. Like
doing time it was, Cart." He had felt badly enough taking her inside,
but when she said, "You promised you'd be home, you *promised*,"
he had felt dirty with guilt, still felt it and still found himself im-
posing half the blame on Stoney, on his verbosity and the egomania
that was its source. It was evident Diane needed a little securing—
even Edna kept him from lending himself. Sunday had been——

"What's happening, Carter, in your head? You got a terrible look
on your face."

"It's happening in my stomach," Carter muttered and fingered
some papers before him. Childlike on the couch, Diane had slept
huddled beside him and had awakened there in the noon darkness of
Saturday's rain, still a child speaking in Friday's lonely sighs. A hurt
and shaky child all day, so that instead of running her to Mama's for
the baby he'd got her laughing with army stories over lots of wine
in Louie's Cellar, a bar the Village groups had not yet bohemianized.
On Sunday she was more energetic. Afraid she might drift with her
replenished confidence into the Cosmopole and its odd attractions,
he deposited her in a movie till he could return from the hospital.
Out to Queens he'd rushed—calculating time in order to catch Diane
at the show's end—to find Mama Lattimer seated by Edna's bed
when he arrived. For once he was happy to see the pretentious lady,
since he was able to learn she knew nothing as yet about Diane's
escape. In her false bell-like voice—but now the phone bell cut into
that antiseptic pall of domesticity in his dreaming; he gladly let
mother and daughter and hospital white go dusty and fade. He took
up the phone and a man asked for "*Zeeskite*," then corrected it to
"Merwin Fingerflub" after Carter's bewildered pause. He passed
the phone to Merwin and turned to the papers on the desk, seeing
only Diane waiting at home as she had waited in the hallway for
him. He offered himself the comfort that now she was at least warm.

"Yes?" Merwin was saying. "Ah, hello *Meeskite*, wadda you want?"
So free of anxiety she'd been (Carter smiled) that he'd even agreed
to share the bed with her last night, and she'd slept in his arms like
any child bundled in her father's pajamas.

Merwin laughed, paused, laughed a higher whisper, paused and
laughed a long time, then hung up, wiping tears from his face, while
Carter hoped Diane could hold out till evening, stay inside till he
could get there and for another little time keep her from running
wild.

"Cousin Curly." Merwin wiggled into his coat. "I'm gonna meet
him for lunch. Should we see Wengel for you?"

"What for? Curly'll only give the old swine a laugh."

"Who knows? Maybe together we'll bug him up. Maybe we get
something outta him. If not, I'll slip a knife in his liver for everybody's sake."

Carter felt a nervous lack of interest in things around him. "Okay."
He forced a laugh. "See what you can do."

In that effortless, barely audible voice, Merwin inquired, "Anything goes?"

"It's your life."

"It's your business."

"You call this a business?"

"You call this a life?"

Laughing more easily, Carter pushed him out, then went across
the floor to route packages of developed film at the workbench, at-
taching addressed stickers and tossing the rolls into a carton at his
side. He felt mechanical and wasted, felt he really belonged with
the kid, taking her for her baby so that she could have something
solid and demanding to keep her level; she had seemed all set at
breakfast, with something womanly in her live black eyes. An old
sense of his work's uselessness expanded almost to nausea in his
chest. "People have to know what they look like from outside, and
Webb's on the spot to pamper them with film. What a distinction!"
His thoughts loafed along that way in little waves of conscience
that rose to real guilt each time he saw Diane's look of need. Twice
in the hours he worked alone he telephoned home. But there was no
answer; he had to keep assuring himself the girl was afraid it might
be Edna or Mama. That was *all* she needed now.

At about four Merwin returned with a sizable carton and a rare flush of excitement on his round, usually inexpressive face. "Color film. Consignment! Carter, you got to go there and sign for it; you pay Wengel when you collect. Oh, is this sweet! Like falling in love again, Carter. What can I say?"

Carter got up, a little angry. "Merwin, I wouldn't sell this shit to a dog."

"That's just it." He was nearly singing. "You don't sell it; you *give* it away. Is this gorgeous!"

"Lie down awhile, Merwin. A little sleep, a little sleep."

"Never mind . . . just listen." He removed his coat, tossed it to a wall hook almost athletically. "The contract, it's worded so beautiful. You got the goods and you pay only when you collect for it. But you never collect because you never sell it. We advertise *FREE— two-fifty value—FREE.* When they shoot the rolls they got to send it back to us for processing just like always at a buck a roll. The people save half a pound on every bite, we clean up, Wengel's piles hemorrhage. What can be sweeter?" In clumsy excited motions he changed a clip rack of film strips from one processing tank to another. "Curly. You shoulda see Curls with the old man. Like a comedy it looked. Wengel tells his whole life, how he came here a pauper kid and works his way to the top. Every date he mentioned, Curly sings a song from that year, but like an opera star, not show business. He sang "Tea for Two" and "Ramona" and "The Sheik"; it was so crazy. And Wengel, every time Curly gives a scream Wengel leans back, hands on his belly like this, and smiles and nods. Carter, what can I tell you? You hadda be there. That girl Margy standing there laughing, she was holding her knees. Till we show up again she don't stop looking out the window for us."

Carter got his coat on, watched Merwin work as he spoke, then leaned back on the workbench, eying the floor. "Merwin, you'll hate me, but we can't do it. We can't con Wengel like that."

Merwin fell into the desk chair, feeling his mustache as if checking to see that it was still there. "Carter, steal my wife, but don't——"

"*Don't,* your hairy ass. You don't make a Wengel out of me, boy."

"Car-ter Webberoony! Don't be a *child.* Wadda you got for *Wengel* all of a sudden? It's so *sudden* . . . my heart . . ."

Carter shifted uneasily in the fading light. "I'd cut his throat, but not behind his back. It's a cute idea, all right, I appreciate that.

Look, you're hereby promoted to first vice-president; how's that? You may take ten extra minutes for lunch from here on in."

"You may take two giant steps," Merwin croaked miserably.

"What'd he mean by that?" Carter muttered over a shoulder.

"It's a game young kids play before they get working papers. Where you going anyway? It's not Tuesday; there's no hospital today."

"Something else I have to take care of. Mind the store." And he left, pulling on his hat. It was some parental urge hurrying him down the flight of stairs and out into Forty-fifth Street's gray crowded dusk, and he could laugh at himself going with difficulty against the mob headed for the Independent subway entrance near his building. Yet he was satisfied to find a clear way in the gutter, hurrying west with something just short of a prayer that Diane would hold out till he reached home.

The trip downtown was quick on the I.R.T.'s train of clattering old cars, but the four-block walk from Sheridan Square seemed endless from the moment he crossed the huge intersection of streets into Christopher. In the first show of night kids were slowing their ball games to a gesture, leaning giddily upon one another in the flat frost, while parents hurried up old stoops toward food and rest. Carter found himself inanely looking for the spot in his life when he stopped whistling and started feeling a serious depth in every little thing. Then he laughed, deciding the feeling was seasonal, and that he'd whistle again in the spring. Yet fair days to come were already darkened by Edna; he went inside with the weight of her on his lungs.

Diane met him in the foyer. She approached him straight-faced, wearing a towel on her head, a wine-colored pajama top, bedroom slippers and nothing more. Rocking her in his arms, he decided that the child was gone out of her look and the little sharp-eyed woman had again emerged. "Get dressed. We eat and get Johnny once and for all. What kind of getup are you wearing anyhow?"

"I cleaned this dusty trap; then I took a shower." She snuggled against him. "If we bring him here, Cart—Mama—she'll send the police."

"We'll talk nice to Mama, babe. Maybe she'll call the whole thing off. She wasn't too bad yesterday."

"Did you talk about Johnny?" She pulled back to watch his face.

"No, babe, we just talked about God and Mrs. Lattimer."

She laughed and went off down the hallway; her legs were capable shapely things, he realized after she'd gone to dress, and allowed himself finally to sit, to remove his hat. She'd walked right into him in a wine-colored pajama top. But Edna, wet-eyed, met her there, and inside him the sisters fought. "Don't make a scene," he muttered, shifting his weight.

He shifted again in the orange wood booth under photos of poets and beauties, watching her eat Chinese shrimp while her earrings swung at the sharp angle of her jaw. "Don't be nervous," she said, more to reassure herself than to advise him. "We'll handle Mama, don't worry about her."

He wasn't worrying about Mama. He was worrying about Diane— about himself aroused by Diane.

Fourth Street lay windless and bare alongside the park, quiet but for the city's muted noises: the underground rumble of trains, the distant cough of a car, the whining, hydraulic gasp of a bus door. They went into Sullivan Street past an open-air store where the owner chatted in loud musical Italian with neighbors, and carefully around boys moving strenuously through the last moments of their day, shouting lustily in the cold. Through the doorway shadow they went down the long, dreary hall, past the staircase to the door at the end.

Leaning on the bell, Diane could see that Carter still fidgeted just as he always had whenever he waited for Mrs. Lattimer to come to the door. When Edna had brought her new husband home for a visit two years back, Carter had kept an eye on her mother as one might watch a domesticated leopard. Diane knew that her mother's every artifice had been apparent to Carter from his first look at her. The elevated octave she affected had failed to charm him, and despite her pale, angelic beauty he had mistrusted her from the start. "Just no kind of mother," he would often say.

Mrs. Lattimer came to the door and gasped when she saw them. "Diane!" She brushed young black hair nervously back. "How did you——"

"I burned the place down." Diane rushed past her. "Where's my boy? Is he sleeping?"

"Hello, Mother," Carter said.

"Don't Mother me, you fool."

Diane stopped in the living room; it looked smaller, somehow, and cloudier than ever. The musty old portrait of Christ stared out at her, enveloping her in some mysterious fear that prevented her going through to the bedroom. "Where's Johnny? Is he asleep in there?"

Carter sat down in an easy chair without removing his coat. He fingered the hat in his lap and closed his eyes. Mrs. Lattimer looked from one to the other and smirked meaningfully.

Diane had meant to maintain calm, but now rage bubbled out of her. "Well, answer me, dammit. Where's the boy?" She sat down quickly on the arm of Carter's chair. Something was about to happen: the woman's face was loathsome, arranged from within to look concerned and sad.

Stiff-backed on the couch, thin hands folded in her lap, Mrs. Lattimer said, "It's been very difficult," in her special high voice. "You know, it's not easy to——"

"Where's my baby?" Diane shouted.

"Now Diane! I'm trying to tell you that——"

"That *what?* Will you tell me! Where's my boy? That's what I want to know; where's my boy?"

"You needn't—he's got a fine home, where——"

"*Home!*" Diane leaped at her mother, but Carter lurched forward to intercept her.

"Diane, Diane," he said, holding her.

"Home!" Diane screamed. "I'll kill her, that witch, I'll kill her yet."

"It's best for him," Mrs. Lattimer said in the placating tones one might use with children. "He'll have all his needs: a real home with a good family."

Carter eased Diane into the chair, sitting with her in a position that would prevent her rising.

"It's always homes," Diane said in a calmer voice. "Edna and I went from one home to another, all our lives. Now she's got my baby in one."

"You're not thinking of the child." Mrs. Lattimer leaned forward seriously. "After all, I'm a working woman; I couldn't give him a home or provide for him properly——"

"You! He's not yours, he's mine!" Diane turned to Carter. "I'll kill her yet. I tell you, I'll kill that crazy bastard. My own mother puts me in a goddam detention home, then gives *my* baby away. I'll kill her yet."

"Diane, it was for your own good." Carter saw that the woman was really trying to get herself across, was sincere enough so that for once her age drew itself around her eyes in a hundred fragile lines. "Heaven knows it's been difficult all these years. I couldn't stand by and watch you go straight to hell. It's easier for you to do than for me to watch. There may still be a chance for you if—" she looked upward—"if you pray."

"What am I going to do?" Diane wanted to know of Carter. "She's crazy. She thinks she's on God's side. About spooks she worries, about the devil and heaven and hell and spirits and good and bad angels. She's plain crazy—look at her—and they let her run around loose. She ruins everybody that gets near her. What am I going to do?"

"Just cool off for a while," Carter said. "We'll figure something out." Then, "How come—how'd she get the right to——"

"I'm the legal guardian!" Mrs. Lattimer was quickly on her feet, tall and austere by the portrait of Christ. "Diane signed for that, she signed that readily enough. Who are you to butt in anyway, Mr. Nobody?"

Carter wanted to laugh. "Don't blow a blood vessel, Vivienne. It seems——"

"Ever since you came into this family you've been nothing but trouble to me. You came from nowhere, no background. How dare you accuse me? I——"

"Vivienne, that's your own conscience, not me. I didn't say a word."

"I'll have you know I've been a——"

"You've told me that a hundred times," Carter said. "You've been a lady for eight hundred years. It's beginning to show in your figure."

It wasn't so; Mrs. Lattimer's body was trim in her black flawless suit. Yet she sat down abruptly. "What can I hope for?" she said sadly in the direction of Diane. "You lie around with scum like this, a coal miner, nothing more. And your sister's husband, moreover. You don't even know who the child's father is," she added irrelevantly.

Diane was furious again; Carter had to restrain her. "I know damn well who he is. *You* don't, you filthy-minded bitch. You make everything dirty in your mind. Carter and I never——"

"Don't, babe. Let her rave with her goofed-up morality."

"Goofed-up, is it?" The woman nodded ironically. "Any sound concept of living is *goofed-up*. It's easy to ridicule morality, to call it stuffy and all that. Just use the sense the Lord gave you: you'll realize that the moral law is a well-laid plan; centuries of wise experience developed it, not prudes, as you're thinking."

Carter finally laughed outright. "That conscience'll kill you, old mother. Nobody said anything about——"

"Ugh! Scum," she hissed, rushing out to the kitchen. "Scum all around me. Why did I ever marry Clyde? What children he gave me, what children!"

"Ah, you corny bastard with your melodrama," Diane shouted for her to hear. "You're living fifty years ago. I want to know why *he* ever married a narrow bitch like you. Your own mother hated you. All I ever remember her doing till the day she died was cursing you out."

Mrs. Lattimer was back in the room, arms folded tight across her bosom. "Curse me, did she?" The delicate pitch of her voice was forgotten; it was shrill. "She warned me about you! She told me you had no tears in your eyes. And it's true; you never cried like a normal child. And to this day you've never cried." She swept back her hair and fled again to the kitchen.

Diane leaned back and closed her eyes. Dry, cold, they felt detached from the rest of her. It upset her that the image of Johnny was vague in her mind. She strained to see each feature of his face, but she could only almost see him. "Where is Johnny?" she asked quietly, opening her eyes.

Her mother set a tray of teacups on the end table by their chair. "He's in a nice private home on Long Island, where he——"

"Who are the people?" She let her heavy eyelids drop.

"They're a middle-aged couple who were so anxious for a baby that they didn't mind that he . . . They're very well to do and——"

"Come on, Carter." Diane turned to him. "I want to get away."

"Here, drink your tea." He handed her a cup he had filled, undecided whether he was being ironic or deferential to Vivienne.

"Diane," Mrs. Lattimer said with that high tenderness, "you can start again. I'm getting on nicely at the agency. I could have you released from Clearwater; I'll take a nice modern apartment and——"

"Nice! Nice!" she mimicked. "Why couldn't you do it for Johnny?"

"But he's a child. I couldn't attend to him properly."

Diane set her cup down with a clatter. "Oh, come on, Cart. I have to get out. Come on, please!"

Mrs. Lattimer spilled some tea getting up. "Where are you going?" she demanded, following them to the door. "They'll be after you. I'll tell them where to find you, all right." Her voice suddenly tore as they ignored her. "Who are you going to *screw* tonight, eh? Who? Your brother-in-law?"

"Ah, dry up!" Carter said.

"She's been dry!" Diane shouted, pulling open the door. "She wouldn't be a witch if she could——"

"Go on," Mrs. Lattimer screeched into the hallway after them, "*screw* her while you may, while your own wife is away. You probably did before, you may as well go on!"

The hallway was an old ugly mixture of cooking odors and dust. When they reached the street, Diane took several gasps of clean air to cool her lungs. She leaned on Carter's arm down Sullivan and across Fourth into Washington Square Park. Silently they crossed the huge space where Fifth Avenue cleaved the park in halves to end at a circular pool. "The aristocrat!" Diane muttered. "She kept us in those homes after the old man lit out on her, but she never forgot to come around and tell us about our heritage. You've heard that stuff. The counts and countesses, the generals, the ambassadors. Isn't she crazy, Carter? That crap really means something to her."

He only grunted, and they went past naked benches under the new snow clouding the air with its silent gliding mesh.

In the Cosmopole they took coffee to a side table and watched Sixth Avenue go white. "What kind of papers did you sign?" Carter asked.

"All kinds; who can remember? You know the shape I was in—I was half nuts." She felt that way in that moment's rush of fear. What was to happen now? Pictures of fun—smoking jive, choosing men to make it with—drummed in her mind, till she saw Carter's heavy concern in his frown. She thought then of finding Johnny's new home and stealing him away from his front yard, or out of his carriage where he might be left for a moment in front of a store. "I can't figure a way, but I will," she said at last.

"It's a cinch Mama got you to sign adoption papers. She's crafty enough for that." The din of the place was packing spitefully into his ears; he lighted cigarettes for them and drained his cup. "Let's go home; the noise in this place is crowding in on me."

"I can't go to your place any more, Cart. It's a cinch Mama's called the police by now. Your place'll be first on their list."

"Where'll you go?"

"Oh, I'll fall in somewhere. I'll meet one of the characters."

Mama wanted her to go to God, but she'd go to the ungodly. There were not many roads for the trapped: climb a tower to heaven or drown out your brains; you can't long endure reality. "I'd rather you wouldn't go loose again, baby; but you will, so I'll keep quiet. You need some money?"

"No, Carter. I'll meet one of the characters; I'll get some money."

There were a sudden clatter and some quick voices in the center of the place. Timmy Lawless was moving backward toward the door, tossing a trail of empty bottles shattering to the floor from the sack in his arms. "Clean the shithouse!" he yelled. "Light the candles. Old Man Moe is dead!" Then he dashed outside and past the window, his face twisted with his shrieking. A crowd bulged around one of the tables, some women screamed, some men moaned, and a cafeteria policeman shouted his way into the crowd. Diane started to rise, but Carter held her down.

"Old Man Moe, that's the little old guy, Carter, the one always coughing. You remember him?"

That struck him as a description of everyone in the place. "No use running over—he's either dead or unconscious." Like everyone else, he thought.

"Wha'ja say? He's dead, he's dead." Meyer Singler, his aged face lined with fright, stood behind Carter's chair. "Coughing his head off right by my table all night, he suddenly croaks." He shifted a sloppy white bundle in his arms, tearing off loose ends and looking anxiously around the place out of those beadlike eyes. "Well, he was sick, you know. That cough wasn't for nothing. He was sick and dying right along, all these years. It's a shame. He was sick all along." As if to see if he'd convinced anyone, he stood looking from Diane to

Carter and back, tearing paper, sucking his lips. "Right by my table he croaked." Mute then, he stayed a moment before going back to the crowd and trying to see over the clustered heads.

"He was pretty old," Diane said. "Old as Meyer, about seventy. Gee, he used to just sit there, just coughing since I know him. Only time he ever said anything was when he hollered at Timmy for making noise," and she laughed for a reason that she didn't understand.

While Carter watched the arena. An ambulance clanged to a stop outside, and in an instant the crowd parted to let two doctors and the driver through, then closed around them. "Too late, too late," someone laughed out of the mob, and a few men came away grinning. Old Man Moe was carried out on a litter as though there were something special that could still be done for him. At the neighboring table a group of fat old anarchists resumed their venomous, table-pounding agreements. Carter felt with alarming clarity that he and Diane amounted to simply one more microscopic problem among a million others in some vast external noise. Perhaps there was some key riddle to be solved for all of them at once.

He shook his head, afraid he was getting maudlin. "Look, why don't you come on home? If the police come, I won't let them in."

She played with the brim of his hat. "What'll you do, spill hot water on them? You've got to let the police in."

"Not without a warrant."

"What if they have a warrant?" She laughed. He had an eagerness in his face that was almost anger; it thrilled her that he was so concerned.

"We just won't answer the door," he said.

"No, Cart, you'll get in a jackpot."

Shifting back in his seat, he swung a look around the place. "Come on, it's worth the chance. I don't want you messing with the grifters around here."

"Carter! Shame on you."

"You're grinning like Edna now," he said, standing. "Come on home."

Keeping her seat, she put a hand on his. "No. Really, Cart, I don't want to." That was all, she knew, that she had to say.

"Take this." He handed her two dollars. "If things don't work out, come over to the apartment. We'll chance it if it's necessary."

"Okay, Cart. Daddy. Edna used to call you Daddy, didn't she?"

"Yes. I didn't like it." He stooped to kiss her cheek, then walked out very quickly. . . .

Now the blind marathon was on; once more she'd let the easiest winds carry her. Diane dropped ashes on the table, patted them flat with the glowing end of her cigarette, formed designs by spreading the powdery gray specks. Carter knew, she thought; he knew how she was. He knew what the promiscuity had meant before. Edna had been the same way before they were married. One man after another. Looking, looking, waiting for it to mean something. But it was nothing, ever. Not anything physical, nor even very good spiritually. Just motions and the foolish gasps of the man's thrill sensation. Nothing for her and nothing for Edna with her hundred different faceless men. Then Carter. Carter with his serious face and good heart. But Edna couldn't meet him halfway, couldn't really know the depth of him. And she might die soon, never having lived all the way with Carter . . . like Old Man Moe wasting his last hours coughing at a table top.

Her thoughts turned more deeply inward till she became unconscious of the moving world outside her. She dreamed back to her month with Rocky the soldier, father of her Johnny, a man whose face was a cloud for her now, whose voice was a toneless whisper. And the memory of their coupling was bodiless. Then there were other cloudy faces, hissing voices, ghostly leg-lockings, and clearer looks from faces more recent that directed and warned and scolded. She thought of the baby and once more tried to visualize his face but failed. Yet his flesh's texture was closer to the fingers of her mind than any face, place or mood she dreamed: she could almost feel him warm against her.

It was like having a shower curtain yanked open, to find a man smiling toothlessly at her across the table. "Lukey!" she laughed. "Lukey, you bum, what happened to your teeth? When did you make the air? I didn't know——"

"Oh, I been out." Lukey giggled and shifted his long nervous frame. "I been out drinkin air a week. The kind ones gimme air with no restrictions. All the air I want. They swung open the gates and invited me out, because that's when they can look the kindest. But that's all they gimme: air. I thought you was Edna; you look— you know," and he gestured obscurely about his face.

"Older? Like a big girl, huh?" His poor lined face was weakened more by that reduced and awkward chin; she watched her fingers. "You know Old Man Moe just died in here, Swede?"

"Yeah, I know. Timmy Lawless is out in the snow with it. He's under the statue, singin in the park, singin Old Man Moe is dead, singin in the snow."

Diane shook her head. "Gee, that's terrible. It's eerie; you know?"

"Well, Timmy Lawless is all alone now; he's got a right. Moe was the only enemy he had. He's in the park singin it, singin Old Man Moe kicked the bucket and about the log cabin and everything."

"Lukey—" just to stop his rambling—"you been inside a long time. You're pale as a corpse."

He showed his tongue, laughing. "No sunshine. Four months without prayin. Talkin to anyone who listens and it turns out to be me, the only listener."

She could imagine; Lukey never could stand silence and felt always responsible for its displacement. Yet it was with affection she thought of it. He was like any child needing to be soothed. She thought then of taking him somewhere to do it, but the idea died in a chill because there was nothing childlike, lovable in his face. It was lined and drawn, looked even older than the thirty-five years he'd suffered on earth.

" . . . and everybody dominated me," Lukey was gumming along. "They dominated me to work and they dominated me to eat and sleep. They tried to dominate me to pray, but they couldn't push my lips. Wasn't important enough or they'd get in my mouth and dominate my lips to pray. We got to eliminate the dominance in life. When the big kicks the small he's gonna get kicked when the small gets larger. That's the paradox. The paradox is always there and you can't beat it. You try one way and I try another, but you can't beat the paradox. God can't help you and escapology can't help you. God tells you love your brother, but how can you love your brother when he don't love you? God don't know the paradox. Like when your brother loves you it ain't enough because you're too hungry to love him back and he don't love you enough to feed you. And when you try——"

"Oh, Lukey, don't give me a headache." Diane had to interrupt, more to introduce her burst of laughter than to halt him. She'd been imagining convicts climbing the wall to escape that ceaseless lingual flutter. "You don't stop talking."

"Escapology," he hurtled on, "spits in the face of the years. But what do them years do? They spit back and hit you. Escapology stays dry, you get with spit all over you. Escapology knows the paradox, but it don't hip you. It lets the years hip you when it gets too late, when you get too kind to fight back."

Now she was really growing dizzy. "What are you talking about? Man, you're a machine."

Giggling, Lukey took his corduroy hat by the brim and pushed it back. "The other night it comes to me that escapology is a paradox, so I go around knockin on doors, tellin guys escapology is a loser, and I'm like the Salvation Army makin converts till mornin turns everything light-blue and I get weak and a shmecker pulls me in his trap and makes me snort some Horse while I'm hippin him. So I got right back with escapology and I had to quit the mission."

"Lukey the Swede!" she protested, rocking her head. "Slow down a little. What are you smoking? Are you smoking good?"

"Great pod," he whispered, leaning in. "There's great pod all over when I get out. Election is over and the panic is off. Everybody's stickin. Children are smokin in the streets. Babes in arms, even. The cops are yawnin and the boats are comin in, because election day is long dead and the bums is enough to pinch. That's another paradox. The para——"

"Lukey! If you say that word once more . . ." But the momentum of his giggling had bottled up his mouth; she slapped his back while he coughed.

"Okay, baby. Come, we stalk down the street and get you on. If you like we could even jump up to Paddy Jenks in his room, if you like."

"The junky? I don't want any junkies, Luke. I hardly know that one."

"What's to know? He's Mrs. Jenks' boy; what's the hassel?" He tossed a look over his shoulder, then leaned 'way over the table toward her. "Lots of jive and goofballs, maybe a couple caps of Horse. You was never on 'H,' was you? Great, one time; *crazy!* But keep off, better, because if you like junk you keep shmeckin and shootin, then the skin pop goes to the big pipe and you run your head on the wall for sleep when your habit gets so big you can't buy."

They all knew the score on Horse before they ever rode it, yet invariably it rode *them* down the last stretch. They were all *too hip* to be destroyed; still the heap of broken junkies touched heaven. Now she laughed at the second level of her thoughts: there she'd been anticipating marijuana's welling up of sensitivity that sweetens the throat and fills the chest with gummy music, while further forward in her mind she was repelled by heroin, a habit kick unlike the others, frightened of the gray wax faces of its users, their stupid voices, and the excruciating vacancy of their eyes. "Let's just smoke some jive, Lukey. I don't want any junkies, I don't want to go there, to Paddy's trap."

Lukey leaned back, frowning with the injury of a tricked schoolmaster, his close-set eyes drawn closer still. "Why, it's cool at Paddy's. Baby, nobody has a mind to bother you. Just the ball. They got a wire recorder up there, and Paddy, why he's aces, a real saint, like; you know?"

Diane had to laugh, watching the deep concern line his face with a seriousness so rare in him. Lukey was so intensely kind. "Maybe I'll go, Lukey. After we get high, maybe I'll want to go up there." She looked around for nothing she could name. There was really nowhere else to go.

SHRINES TO ZERO

The snow falling slow and sullen, with a kind of quiet
endless as the hidden sky, reminded Joe Letrigo of the snow in Le
Havre the night he returned to France with a patched leg and a thousand patched men puffing with him up a hill the city followed out of
the sea. MacDougal Street was normally level, he knew, yet now, under an alcoholic load he likened to the eighty pounds he had borne
with resignation over those other soggy miles, it was sloped almost as
steeply as that French street four winters back. He told himself that
it was the vast silence and his own stupor, and possibly the fact that
this was a return to New York—that all these things brought back the
white hush of Le Havre rather than other snows which should more
intensely lend themselves to recollection. Other snows had exploded
in his face and shown his blood orange in the sun, but this was a Le
Havre snow: just dumb, floating powder puffs with unending
tedium. Only his aloneness and a restrained hope for some exotic
involvement were unlike that night in 1944.

Joe trudged along, hearing no more than his breathing exaggerated
to a hiss by the stillness, now and then yawning, leaving his tongue
out to be cooled by the snow. The houses standing close, their even
five-story height marked by an occasional snow-veiled fleck of light,
seemed a dimension removed from the neon and doored-in tinkle
of the barrooms lining the way. For an instant he felt detachable and
sailed up from the snowdusted ground, to lurch for balance on landing and to swallow hard against the whisky bobbing in him. Then he
spun about with a remnant of carelessness as a couple passed, leaning
close together as if they could avoid some snow that way. They faded
like ghosts in the blown web of flakes as he watched. "Boy, now
that's for Joe," he mumbled. "Some poontang to cradle my lonesome
frame," and, going on again, "Muh-muh-muh," as a shudder shook
his back.

65

He took to the dark shelter of a store doorway to light a cigarette, then stayed there awhile, recalling this little street without the white which now hid nearly all its identity. In his mind he brought back to the street the summer he had spent here, cleared snow from the stoops and iron grillwork that footed the buildings, and filled the narrow walks with movement, laughter, playful voices. He had known some Village women and now their nameless faces smiled in his brain. He might run into one at the Riviera, he decided. He ducked into the swirling cloud and walked, but a hand clutched at his arm. "Hey, got any money, pal?" A face flat with shadow breathed stale fumes of alcohol into his.

Joe reared back. "Lots of it, lo-ots of it."

Turned to the streetlight, the man's face danced grotesquely, its muscles punched awkward by long, helpless years. "Gimme a dime," he whined, pushing his head close to Joe's. "I'm saving up for Florida."

"Hold off me, boy. Goddam your ass, you smell like an ole cotton-pickin hat," and went quickly past the man while he felt the blood tremble into a knot at the back of his neck. "Refrigeration don't help you none, by God."

"You ain't no lily," the man croaked in boozy singsong. "You give off a lungful of Sneaky Pete yaself; I sniffed you out, brother, Hahahahaha!"

Joe halted and whirled about. The hobo half sat, turned, and ran in a clumsy, high-kneed gallop into the drifting white veil, holding down his hat and chortling till he faded from sight. Snow cooled Joe's eyes, and he yanked his hat tight, rubbed his face and laughed at his own anger, at the snow that was as pointless, at the hiding houses and the sky sleeping far beyond his unimportant bad temper.

At the Riviera he squinted through the long window, its film of moisture blurring his vision still more. It was a hive of movement inside; he gulped wet air and entered, blinking in the loud glare and searching in the crowd of faces for a familiar eye or a smile remembered. Familiarity was only in the atmosphere: in the muddy frameless paintings lost along a recess high in the tooled-oak walls; in the abandon people affected as they hauled their bodies from booth to booth, from toilet to bar, uttering inherited phrases and going through the very gestures he had seen others use thirty months before. He wormed his way to the bar, changed his mind about whisky and got himself some beer for the burning which had begun in his chest.

There was not much he could see in this mass of bodies, but he stretched up on his toes, looking along the bar crowded with heads, and over more heads squirming, as though disembodied, around the three loaded tables that filled the floorspace, and over to the booths lining the walls, packed with faces he had never known. Then, as though his loneliness extended some kind of energy, the crowd parted for an instant to disclose a corner booth near the window, and before people blocked his view again, Joe's eye caught the gray-streaked beard that unmistakably identified the painter with whom he'd had long talks so long ago. He drank down his beer and bought two more, carried them cautiously through the mob and stopped behind Stoney, alone in the big booth where a neon windowsign warmed his table with color. The bitter old Italian cigar, familiar as that beard, gave Joe a first real sense of homecoming, a first memory of fun they'd had together. Feeling prankish, he leaned over to watch the painter absorbedly scribbling little lines of words on a paper napkin and guarding them with his free hand.

"You a writer, mister?" Joe said right in his ear.

Stoney yanked his head away, refusing to turn, just shaking that mass of hair and continuing to write.

"Then what in hell you writin for?"

Slamming down the pencil stub, Stoney turned around. "Just figuring a way to keep stupid tourists—— Joe! Joe Letrigo! Well, kiss my royal . . . You've returned to the Village. Just couldn't stay away from the cesspool."

Joe slid in across from Bob, setting down the beers. "Listen to the man. Here, drink this beer and wrench out your mouth of that turd you're chewin. Same one you had in your moltin ole beard last time I saw you, isn't it?"

"Last saw me." The painter nodded with real sentiment. "How long has it been, Joe?"

"Two years and a half, I guess. Just came away from a ship crawled the Atlantic like a mud turtle with the clap." He gulped his beer twice and felt the burning ease in his chest. "You know, I walked in here drunk—been that way all the trip from Africa killin travel pain —but I'm clear as new rain now. Your face is a soberin influence, show little as it does through the moss."

Stoney's teeth showed yellow and small, clenched on the cigar as he grinned. He leaned back, pulling snaps in his knuckles. "Two and a half years away from the Village; it sounds hardly possible. Where could you keep yourself so long?"

Before Joe could say, a blond girl was there out of noise and movement, pushing in beside Bob Stoney, plucking a cigarette in its silver holder from the drooped corner of her mouth. "Bob, I wrote a poem after I saw you last night, and sent it right off to *Partisan*. It's your duty to hear it because . . . Oh, who's your cute friend?"

Bob's nose wrinkled, and he rubbed it with a thumb. "This is Joe Letrigo, just returned after a long absence. He was about to tell——"

"Well, let's hear my poem first while it's still smoking, shall we?"

Joe closed his eyes, leaning back into the cloud spreading in his head. There'd been thirty long months without this particular kind of nuisance: the two and a half gone years leaving mixed pictures gray with time, of Carolina leisure, of war's tight space—*new* war, against the enemies of strangers, and the warmth of family faces. . . .

"Oh body with its sheen of fiery moisture," the girl was breathing, "oh laden vessel at once bonded and at large, leap! blinded by thy need of living past thy mother's sallow face, into the fire of thy lust, into the doom of thy desire, unto thy completion." She thrust the cigarette holder into the grim line of her mouth. "I masturbated immediately after the writing, it was that emotional." Then to Joe, "Do you believe in virginality?"

Joe gulped beer, let it kick air rumbling out of him, and said, "Lady, I'm an Episcopalian."

The girl was already facing Bob, whose nose twitched like a rabbit's. "If that poem is rejected—" she worked the rows of pearls up and down her throat—"I don't know what I shall do. It would be like having a lover castrated before my eyes. Oh, there's Harry. Harry! Do excuse me, I love Harry; he's so dispassionate. Come get me in a bit, will you, Bob?" and she was scooped up by the mob.

"Christamighty!" Joe fingered his cheek.

"Well, that's what you get for leaving me alone in all this psychic nausea, this—this fringe of reality. For a while after you left I didn't speak more than four words to anybody. And they usually were 'Get away from me!' You know you're the only rational human being on earth beside me, even though you're still wetting your diapers. Where could you have gone, you heartless bastard?"

But Joe was thinking of that girl and her poem, recalling the sense he used to have, in this place, of people living painfully alone behind sad token projections of personal secrets, eluding every challenge of maturity, growing old in adolescence. Even Robert, a man close to fifty——

"Listen, are you drunk? Am I talking to a corpse? I insist on knowing where you've been before you lapse into a coma."

"That Israel rumpus, I got mixed up in it. Last time you saw me was—let's see . . ."

"When you shipped out on an oiler or tanker or whatever they're called."

"Sure enough. Well, one time we unloaded in Marseilles and there was an intrigue hot and quiet while we laid up couple of weeks. Wound up carryin a load of D.P.'s out, had the misery in their eyes could break the devil's heart. Goddam British boarded us and locked our ass on Crete, but I shook loose with a few fine and ready guys turned out to be Sternists, and man, we were big-assed birds for the Promised Land through an underground knit up like twelve-dollar Sunday britches. You want to see something. You want to see a whole land of people know where they bound, know what's in each other's heart. Boy, I'll tell you I got in that like I was born to it."

Robert pushed the beer away and leaned back, cracking his knuckles. He recalled some of Joe's depictions of the war against Germany and now pictured him dodging and blasting again. He could not conceive of a man enduring a constant threat of his own disintegration; the image made him shudder. "You're some boy. Out of one war into another. And willingly. It's a form of masochism; don't deny it."

The girl was suddenly back, with the silver holder empty but still jutting out of the little pouch of flesh which tiredly formed her cheek. "Bob, Harry will look at your work. I'll get my coat and wait for you outside," and she disappeared behind clinking glass and words.

Stoney got up, frowning. "These goddam repression neurotics, they don't hold still a minute."

Joe laughed. "You were saying something about masochism?"

"Look, this is my line—to coin a phrase—of business. A man's got to eat."

"Keep your senile sex habits to yourself, father. Just bring me some beer before you go; I don't want to lose the booth."

"Youth's impunity," Stoney sighed, shouldering a hole in the crowd. "I'd kick your ass up your back like a window shade if you weren't just a kid, six-one, a hundred and ninety. Drink mine; I don't touch that bilge."

"And see if you can locate me a woman," Joe called just before the painter was absorbed by noisy faces. "One who can manipulate her own pillow."

Looking through the trickling beads that bled out of neon, he could see the snow had stopped falling and had left the street padded and mute. Free of passers-by, the view allowed his eye to sail the powdery drifts to a black factory wall on the other side and up the zigzag of its fire escape, brought out of shadows by stark white tracings of snow. There was a beckoning peace in the street that recalled childhood responses to Christmas cards by now yellowed and frayed, and small voices in that time when Roanton was center of a dreamlike universe. The house on State Street was a bulwark of meaning then, sitting solidly white and wooden in the heart of his world, immutable against the shifting skies and changing seasons, forever storing the amber certainty of home: the food, the laughter, knowable faces, the electric visits of relatives, the victrola horn and handle. There was a song back in that time——

"Wake up, you disgusting drunk." Stoney tugged at his shoulder. "If there's anything I hate, it's a drunk. Ugly, useless . . ." He closed up before "unmanly"; he had to make an exception here.

"Come on and sit down. I want to tell you about my home and my parents and little sisters."

"A *sentimental* drunk! Nothing is worse—" he glanced over his shoulder—"unless it's Louella and Harry." Clasping his hands, he rolled his eyes ceilingward. "Oh, give me strength, I'm old and sensitive. Sentimental drunks, idiots, weak pigs from uptown." Blinking as though in tears, he collapsed into the booth and wagged that great, shaggy head. "Look, sonny. These lines that creep into my face with the years, like the lines of age all grownups wear, are not noble badges of wisdom, but the most abject imprints of frustration and defeat."

Joe drank beer, then removed his hat and laid it down beside him. "Your story has touched my heart. It is by far the saddest——"

"Aagh," Stoney grunted, "no feeling. Why don't you come with me? I have to work those two for a little cash or I lose the studio to some underage gangster. Afterwards you can have the girl; how's that?"

"Rather bury my nose in an armpit than do a trip with that nubblehead woman. I'm after a blood-and-flesh one, poppa. Got a dread of a cold, lonely sack tonight. Muh-muh-muh."

"Oh, that can wait." Stoney scratched his beard, rattling the whole booth on his way out, and frowned so painfully that a fierce laugh boomed out of Joe. "Goddammit, why can't you be sensitive like I am?"

"The milk of human kindness is just gushin out both your breasts; but me, I'm flat-chested." The whisky dipped in him, and he swallowed the laugh.

"You're a sadist," Stoney said, pushing toward the door. "They should lock you up." He yanked open the door, faced the crowd and, pointing at Joe, shouted over the heads: "Joe Letrigo rapes children! Boys!"

Swiftly, Joe slipped down in his seat and through the wide glass watched Stoney lead Louella and Harry across into Bleecker Street, white coat and hair whipping around in the wind. When they disappeared, Joe's eyes rode the white path back to the emptiness before the tavern: unsullied, unadorned simplicity. For a while he stared blankly; the pure outside drew him a distance from the rattling hubbub around him that sounded by contrast like Death rubbing its knotted hands. Something he had once read in a Negeb holding position nudged him; it was Rosoff, the Sternist: *Space is a magnificent conception. . . . Space with figures is a tragic conception.* Then he drank beer and shook himself alert. Lord, he'd gone touchy in Israel! The time was not for pondering; he'd have time for that when he went back home. He looked hopefully around for an inviting female smile, but there was only a flat, bloodless look in all the faces; everyone seemed part of the noise and glaring light and beer stink of the place. Joe spun beer around in his glass and looked softly back at the soft outside.

Some people kicked through snow, alert in the cold so that one was like the next, quick shadows in the steam of breathing. Then a girl drifted over, stopped to peek inside as if she were looking for someone she did not know, a person or thing she couldn't conceive of, wouldn't recognize if she found; it was an uncertainty he saw in her eyes, some anxiety that seemed as permanent as their glittering blackness. She wore a kerchief on her head and a draped green coat, yet appeared slight and delicate despite the bulk of clothing that made a mystery of all but her face. It was an angular face with prominent bones and full-lipped, suggesting sensuality and strength, so searchingly beautiful in the vapors of her breathing that Joe's voice escaped in a whisper: "I'd marry her just to hold her little hand."

Those black eyes swung toward the door to meet the approach of a skinny grinning man with a boyish corduroy hat and an old man's stoop. When they came together the man began to talk rapidly and gesture toward the inside. Joe felt an excitement pound in his blood that was like something he had left behind in his cloudy adolescent years, and it throbbed more quickly still as they came in and stood looking around—for a place to sit, he hoped. His empty booth was suddenly a rich, invaluable property in the crowded tavern: when the man's shifting glance chanced to meet his, a hand shot up independent of his thought to wave them over. They came, searching his face for recognition, and Joe, charged now by the whisky suddenly awakening in him, grinned and talked. "You don't know me from a load of coal, but you might's well take up all this room."

"Are you leaving?" the girl asked; her voice was rare, deep into her and rich as honey.

A voice that activated—Joe found himself rising, putting on his hat. "I wasn't fixing to, but if you want . . . *What* am I sayin? Godamighty, I got no place at all to go. I'm a tourist, by God, and this is all of Greenwich Village I know about." He fell back in his seat, removing his hat, pulling apart the buttons of his coat, and when he looked up that man was giggling like a child out of his time-beaten face, poking the shoulder of the little green-coated girl out of whose fixed eyes a woman looked. "This guy's okay, Diane, ain't he? Real cool. We sit in before some hustlers tap him."

The girl smiled but avoided Joe's eye, and slid in opposite him, followed by the man. She pulled the kerchief from her head and patted into place the simple tan silk of her hair. Joe had to pull himself back inside to keep from reaching his finger tips over her face.

"You wait here, Diane," the man said hoarsely, "and I go give Paddy another call. He must be home, but like stoned out; you know?" He slipped backward out of the booth, excusing his way past people.

Diane let her coat drop in a heap behind her. She was riding a violin note, a mellow one that drank in and blended any noise that tried to break through. Now and then a memento of the frantic hours would scream out in her mother's voice somewhere in her neck, but the gummy veil would quiet it, the music would absorb it, and the violin string carried her gently horizontal, sweet where it ran down her throat, stroking through warm insides and slipping out electrically so that she had to tighten her knees, but carrying her, and beaming its music out through her so that she leaned forward to listen.

Joe saw the girl bring thin shoulders forward as if to have new folds in her sweater hide the impudence of virginal breasts. Large earrings trembled at her jaw, black lace-rimmed eyes followed the doodling moves of her hand propelling a cigarette around in the ash tray. He searched through the heavy darkness of his brain for something with which to win her attention, but the few ideas that loitered there seemed dull and trite against the demand her beauty made on him. The seconds began to swell like bloated hours, and the rolling hubbub in the place seemed a mockery directed at him like the hiss of incoming shells personalized when a man is pinned down. He was sweating like any target now, and habit activated him: words slipped out as if thought originated at the roof of his mouth. "Lord, I'm hung up like a smoked turkey. Is there something I can do for you till your feller comes back? I can sing pretty fair," watching the girl turn eyes on him and smile, thick-lidded eyes distant with a wearied sort of awareness.

Her eyes made his face part of the rest of space, but a hard part of her mind isolated it, turned and fingered it: an Indian face, skin tight on its bones, pointed all over. Lighting a cigarette, he did not waste a movement. Like a cat. But a large man and large-boned: something like a tiger was the way he moved, or like a panther, which would have that same strength but more grace. But one horror was branded there in his talk. She asked him abruptly, "You from the South?"

"Carolina. Didn't think it showed through the coat on my tongue. You want a drink? I'm about to get me one."

Still wearing a token smile, she dropped her eyes, then laboriously raised them again not quite into his. "A little wine. Port or any sweet kind." *But black from the South with the black of hate and/or fear of black that makes men black-souled, yet and/or hate/fear* she had to know how it could be, how a smiling man who showed strength in his look could be fearful/hateful. "Lukey?" she was answering Joe. "I don't know what Lukey drinks. Better not get him anything till he asks."

Joe was glad he'd asked, glad he'd referred to the man as "your feller." Her answer meant there was only a thin relationship between them. He saw her realize that her eyes were running over him and avert them swiftly; going through the crowd he carried that image, let it lie incubating in his stomach's hot alcohol, and pointed his chin at the waiter for a shot of rye before he took wine and beer back to Diane. Di-ane.

Lukey sat waving a hand and talking, grinned up at Joe as he set down the drinks. "Nothin for me, friend, I'm just drinkin air like an Eskimo." He looked around and chuckled with Diane. "I'm an Eskimo, I'm tellin her, like with no heat in my blood to bother her."

"Lukey," Diane said, hiding her glance in the ash tray. "Lukey, rest your tongue a minute and maybe I'll go with you after the wine." She tasted it and blinked, then held it out to Lukey. "Here, run some on your tongue; it's like honey, Luke." Joe watched the man taste like an obedient son the wine she held out to him. And her intonations were the mollifying sounds of a mother: she was a blossoming woman in whose face a child would live forever—child and woman, naïve and conscious, helpless and effective. The whisky, having burned his chest clean, now bounced like a fireball to his brain, pushing out the stale, muggy clouds to make space for new cool ones, high clouds splashed vastly over an infinity of sky. Now there was silence in the booth, yet communication seemed to proceed between the girl and him, cutting through the din around them, passing easily between their eyes, oozing warmly into them with the drink; Lukey was candleholder in the act.

Then all at once Joe shook his head and laughed. "Enchantment is a fragile bubble deferential to the material of living."

Diane's smile diminished. "What's that mean?"

"It's proud philosophy. Means how high can you get?"

"You'd be amazed." She laughed, shifting her eyes to Lukey, and together they laughed again.

"How high's the sky?" The Swede giggled. "How wide is time? You know when I learned about time, Diane? I learned about time watchin it, lookin at it out of my eyes, livin in a clock. I was three foot high and senseless, shinin shoes by trade and havin me a ball till late at night, so my old man hated my ways. I didn't love his ways neither . . . he was makin hay while the son shines and payin me no mind except to holler at my habits. So I went down by the docks instead of home one night and I found a little door callin me in just at bedtime and I crawled in and flopped in a shadow. All night long I hear *bam bam bam* like a hammer and I think it's in my head from the ballin around. But in the mornin I see I'm sleepin in a clock, right in the back machinery of the Weehawken Ferry clock, like a door mouse or clock mouse or one of those. I opened the door and looked out acrost the Hudson and what's over on the other side diggin me but another clock facin my way acrost the river with sea gulls and them tugboats comin and goin between us. Two weeks I live there, shinin no more shoes, takin no more parent, just learnin and learnin about time, like."

Diane lowered her head and laughed quietly—in a repressed way, it seemed to Joe. "And there's lots of it, isn't there, Lukey? It goes on and on."

"But it don't wait. You think it's minutes and it turns out to be years laughin in your face. We better cut out or Paddy goofs off again waitin for laughs."

It was strange talk and stranger meaning for Joe, an old remembered kind of strangeness, whenever colloquialisms had isolated him, shut him out, in whatever part of the world. He drank beer, telling himself it was just as well she was about to leave—he wanted a woman anyway, not a shy little girl playing bohemian; his guts were turning sophomore with her around—she might just as well leave and let him off the cloud into a good solid bed full of flesh, sweat and motion. But, looking up, he found her eyes on him, and he could taste her in his chest again, wanting her just so he could hold her hand. Before she dropped them, her eyes stayed with his for a moment, not flirtatiously, but as though her reflexes were slowed by preoccupation. Then she drained her glass and set it down. Lukey stood up, buttoned his black coat and pulled his hat down tight. Joe stopped breathing.

Diane looked at the Swede, then at the Southerner, finally at her fingers around the glass. Her voice rode out easily on the violin note: "Lukey, I don't feel like going up there."

Joe began to breathe.

"But it's cool, baby," Lukey whined. "There ain't no reason why you shouldn't go."

Oh, yes I am, Joe thought.

"I feel like sitting it out here awhile, Luke. You don't want to dominate a buddy; do you?" That was the trigger with Lukey; she was glad she'd told him of their affinity in being dominated, glad in the gummy calm Lukey's smoke had lent her.

"Okay, Diane, you know where it is in case you switch the mind. I'll withhold back some laughs for you." He backed away toward the door, rubbing his toothless mouth as if his pain were focused there.

Several people moved out behind Lukey, exposing the tile floor with the sad dust of decades marking its design. Joe finished his beer and, turning to Diane, saw her eyes pull quickly away, shift uncertainly, and drop to her glass. "You want a refill on that wine, Diane?"

"Okay, but first tell me one thing. Did you ever—could you—did you ever lynch anyone? Did you ever——"

"That may all be so" (the sting, the quick tedium, the old searing shame), "but would you *marry* a Negro?" Now her face would tell the depth of her; her response would determine it for him. Watching eagerly, he saw the bewilderment in her eyes thaw into tentative amusement.

"I don't know what you mean," she said, "but I can tell you're gagging with me."

Good enough. "It's not a gaggin subject, so I thought I'd cut out most of the weary details and bring it up to the punch line. I've endured that thumpin for a good many years."

"What do you mean?"

"People holdin my accent accountable for any horror ever happened under the Mason-Dixon."

Her eyes flickered contritely. "I didn't accuse you of anything. I only asked. I just wanted to know how a Southerner would—you know, justify all that stuff." Now the lift was turning into a drag; she could feel the first twitch in her stomach.

"You mean rationalize it," Joe said.

"Yeah, that's it." She smiled suddenly. "Still—you know, I'm afraid of you; that's why I hung around, I think."

"Of *me?* What on earth about?"

"I don't know," shaking her head, looking downward, fingering her glass. "You don't look—well, I can size up other men, sort of. But you don't—I don't know—you look tough, hard, but not cruel, just tough."

Joe caught his reflection, hazy red in the neon-splashed window. "I need a shave is all. I'm tender as a speckled pup under a red cart."

"That's cute," she chuckled. "Southern talk, it's colorful as . . ." Her lips struggled with a smile. "Would you—would you marry a Negro?"

"Not me. But I might a Negress. Depends on which one; I'd marry *you* if you happened to be one." That embarrassed her, he could see. "I mean, pink, tan or royal-blue, I'd marry who I wanted to, poetry unintentional, but I wouldn't hunt me up a colored lady just to prove I'd beat my used-to-be."

Diane felt the man's rightness, saw it in his long brown eyes, thought she ought to pull away, felt her own confusions an imposition on him. She cocked her head and watched her fingernail scratch without purpose on the table top. "It's hard to believe a guy from the South could see things that way."

"Me? I can hang my hat in any ole land. For I love 'em all where they're lovable at all."

The Tea had turned; she was a victim of it now, lost among the entwining edges of her thoughts, fearful. "Then why am I afraid of you? There must be something wrong in you."

Or in you, he thought with swift alarm. Then he laughed. "Are you high on that little ole wine?"

"Not on the wine. Look, I'd better leave; it's getting late and——"

"No!" His hand shot out and grabbed hers. He felt he'd been a bit forward, but touching her was so good that he followed an impulse and leaned over to plant an exaggerated kiss on her little knuckles. "Now that I've found you I'll never let you go. Never!" Her smile seemed less than she wanted it to be, as though something were choking back her real response. He felt, oddly, that he was failing to give her something he had promised, something she seriously needed. Releasing her hand, he straightened up. "You can't leave yet. Why, you don't even know my name."

"It's not important." She began to rise with the rise of gummy tension in her breathing.

"Wait!" It stopped her. "You're right, it's not important. I hadn't ought to even mention it aloud. It's Joe Letrigo."

There was that fraction of a smile again. "Joe . . . Joe, I'd better leave, because by and by I'll bring you down. I mean I'll make you unhappy, Joe."

"The kind of unhappy you're goin to make me is the kind I been pursuin under my constitutional rights along with life and liberty, long may it wave, amen, pass the plate."

She shook her head. "I can't laugh, Joe, like these people moving and laughing. I can't even move like they do. They have a good time and——"

"You kiddin?" He reached out, covered her hand. "These people act that loud way out of anguish. You know they carry on with big talk and laughin or they'll blow their caps for lookin in mirrors. Lordy, you can laugh where there's call for it. You're just honest with yourself; you're not the one for *inventin* fun."

Her eyes darted around the place, taking in the merged groups that chatted and chortled, lingering where slovenly men and tawdry women made sketches of others, watching unembarrassed youngsters laugh redundantly over spilled beer. Joe hoped she could see the atrophied spirit, the deep, resigned hopelessness that underlay their every move. This was a fearful little girl hunting out her own meaning.

"I . . . used to know what was right," she murmured.

"Well, don't fear me. You're just uneasy because you don't know me well. I don't feature abusin little girls."

She toyed with her glass, made it do a little dance. "You think that's it? Why aren't *all* these people scared of each other?"

"Ask me, I'd say they are." He got up. "Diane, you just stop comparing what you *know* in your little belly with the lies people wear on the face they show about. Don't go way, now."

He took their glasses around two tables to the bar. When he called to the bartender, a woman on a stool turned her freckled elfin face to him. "Joe!" she yelled delightedly. "Holy Jesus, I thought that voice was familiar. How you been, for Christ sake?"

"Hey, Lizzie," he said quietly. "Good to see you again." Then to the bartender, "Please fill these. Port in the little one."

He anticipated Lizzie's next words: "Jesus, where the hell you been so long?"

"Europe and Asia, Liz," reaching over a man's back for the drinks. He looked toward the booth, but could see only the top of its posts. Diane was a disturbed little girl, something like Bob Stoney's Louella, except her repressions showed differently. But Lizzie had been talking to him; he turned back to her impatiently. "What, huh?"

"What the hell 'dyou do over there? Jesus, you can't hear yourself talk in this joint."

"I shipped over," he muttered, taking his change. A girl like Diane, disturbed like Diane, could get up and leave on an impulse.

"I say you have a good time over there, Joe?"

"Yeah, fine time, Lizzie. How you been gettin on?"

"Same as always," she sang. "Boy, you been away a-ges. Nine, ten months, I bet. A year, I bet."

"Sure enough. Look, I'll see you later if you're around, hear?"

"Jesus, I missed you like cra-a-azy, Joe. I didn't forget you not for a minute, not one."

"Hey, I'll see you later, Liz. Okay?"

"Okay," and some more he didn't hear. Lizzie was a sure bedful of submissive round baby-soft flesh, and the memory of long-ago summer nights with her bubbled in his stomach. But she wasn't a woman to be brought home, not simple and pure like Diane. He pictured Diane at his family's table, and she looked born to it, smiling with his mother, joking with his dad. He rolled her name on his tongue and swallowed it.

At the booth she greeted him with a new kind of smile, broad and uncontained, as though a weight had passed out of her mind. "Hello, Joe, glad to see you. I'm not letting myself be scared of you any more."

"Well, that's good music. It's enough to give a man religion."

"Don't you have any as it is?" For she herself felt a divine cleansing now that she had gone over the top of her gauge where the marijuana had clogged in her brain.

"Yeah, I guess I do, sure enough. I flinched when I said that. I'm just not busy with it, but it's around me, sure enough."

They drank and locked eyes over the glasses. Diane sighed with the Viper's postnarcosis weariness, felt a flowing relief at being no longer high, and decided then she never wanted to be high again. She could even control the stabs of apprehension over police seeking her out, blamed the Tea for unnerving her: the cops would never expect her to hang out so close to her own environment. "I'm not afraid any more," she said. "Before I thought I saw something cold in you." "Not me," Joe laughed. "Touch spit to me and I sizzle."

The laughing started there, growing like a curtain across the booth. Diane, overrelaxed, began to ramble and called herself a fatmouth, a word Joe recognized as Dixieland jargon, and they laughed into the music of the South, sang jazz together, with the noise of the place backing them, systematized vaguely like the rocking blare of any jam-session crew. Joe was delighted at the rich old language they shared now, felt at last they were of the same land, wide as it was. "Dixieland is U.S. right enough," he said.

"That's all the music I like. Chicago isn't bad, but I don't like Bop at all."

"Bop? What's Bop? That a kind of music?"

"Sure, Be-bop." Her eyes were wide like those of an amazed child. "Don't they have it down South? It's supposed to be new jazz. Supposed to, but it isn't happy like jazz or sad like jazz can be. It's just— I don't know—it's like the horrors, like sick or something. Except when it goes back and becomes old jazz with a teeny disguise. You mean to say you never heard of Bop?"

"I been away, I been away." He didn't care about Bop; she was leaning back with a grin, and that distant veneer was gone from her eyes.

"Where've you been, Joe? In jail?"

"In jail?" He laughed, then saw that her smile was of the kindly, understanding variety. "Hell, no. I been overseas. Why jail?"

"Oh, I don't know. Lots of people go to jail once in a while. Were you in the occupation army or something?"

"No . . . no, I'll tell you sometime." This time he went on about Dixieland music, about the instrumentalist being more important than the composer so that jazz didn't compete with the classical form, about it being pure American art and how he'd gone blue-gilled arguing it. Till Diane showed her soft, thin throat swallowing laughter. Diane. "You're hidin your laugh, Diane. Come on, now, what——"

The laughter rolled out stomach-deep. "You say idn't for isn't and dudn't for doesn't and it's cute as a little speckled pup on a——"

"Under a red wagon. Lordy, you take the South like Lee took Harrisburg."

They rocked forward, joining their laughter, then sat that way drinking, looking, silently feeling each other. Joe toyed with an idea that the girl's anxieties before had simply been signs of timidity in the face of something that challenged her with permanence; he was sure someone like God had placed them together in this home of empty hours as a sort of heavenly irony to prove all His creation worth while. The idea got a little big for him and began to cloud his eyes; he excused himself, went dizzily through the cloud of faces and down a passageway to the men's room. He let out the beer burning in his bowels and splashed cold water in his face; then he left the little room, stiffly, carefully, not quite believing his head was really clear.

Yet it was clear enough to control the twitch of anger in his stomach when he saw some drunk in the booth with Diane. What the hell, that was the affected informality of the place.

". . . significance down the sewer," he heard as he slipped in beside Diane. The man appeared frightful with the neon skinning the left side of his face and making raw meat of it while the other side remained speckled tallow. Middle age was delicately etched in his forehead, marked in white wiry points at the temples, where great veins protruded, throbbing with a power disproportionate to the rest of his frail structure. He went on, oblivious of Joe, as if he'd been talking that way for years. "Why, you could sit and observe a tiny secondhand following its timeworn path around its pitiably infinitesimal spot on the face of a watch—" the words demanded real effort of his lips, veins quivered in his neck as he strained to speak—"a *miniature* watch."

"It's Ralph Steerman," Diane whispered in his ear, "the big writer."

"Whisper some more, Diane."

"What about?"

"Just anything; it's a little bit of heaven."

He trembled when she laughed in his ear. "Get . . . me . . . some more . . . wine," she whispered close.

Steerman was going strong. ". . . and see once and forever the meaning, the origin, the potential of all existence on earth . . . and in the universe." He looked at Joe and gave him one abrupt, consummating nod.

"So let's all jump on our damn heads," Joe suggested, "and quit making up like there's something to live for. Okay?"

The writer's eyes narrowed and he rearranged his features in preparation for battle, but a sudden gastric spasm intervened, involving his face in unheroic gasps and flexures. Getting to his feet, he rejected Joe with a flap of his uncontrolled hand and staggered off toward the bar.

"Poor man," Diane said. "He's a rich guy, he writes those political books; you know? But he looks like a man who—who was never loved."

"Never had a mother," Joe said, and went off to the bar, putting many people between Lizzie and himself.

Diane thought now about Johnny for the first time since she'd got on with the Swede, yet with no uneasiness, for Joe was an assurance, somehow, that things really could ease into balance. Carter had said it: things are always better than they appear. Joe had Carter's sensitive sort of power to feel out her need so well that he concerned himself with making her laugh. Still, for all the comfort she felt with him, there remained a firmness in the swing of his eyes, in his tight lips, that made her ashamed of her years. And they were *her* years and hers to live as she decided to—as she had to.

Joe returned in time to deflect a man ready to tell Diane why he had dyed his frizzle of a beard lime-green, and they sat, wordless, drinking, stealing an occasional look at each other. For Joe the thing was settled—this was where he stopped being bored with the day-by-day living which had been chasing him into one intense situation after another. He was not a bit drunk, and even his fatigue relaxed him into a kind of clarity.

Diane was smiling without raising those feather-tipped eyelids. "Sometimes I talk up a breeze, Joe, but right now I don't feel like it." She swept her eyes across his face. "We—I have the feeling we don't have to talk. Joe, this sounds corny, but I feel like, I really feel like I know you a long time. It does sound corny."

"Maybe it's corny, but it feels that way to me too." He put a hand hesitantly on the back of her neck; she pulled her eyes away, then pushed her face up against his. He didn't know what he'd expected, but it wasn't anything so smooth with a cool-coated warmth as that. "We're about to put in some good time together, Diane. A long, long time."

She reared back. "Joe, I'm still afraid of you. I don't know what it is, but I can't help it."

"How old are you, Diane? Come on, now, how old?"

"I'm eighteen, but——"

"Lordy—" he shook his head— "you must be scared I'm fixin to—uh—look, time you're nineteen men won't be so mysterious to you. Not this one, leastways."

"Men? Joe, I've been around, and I want to tell you that—" But a deeper look into his eyes stopped her. She blinked and continued with a small alteration in her voice. "—that we're playing a silly game, you and I. Joe, we don't even know each other."

All the night's drinking stirred in his head and bucked; his voice lashed whiplike. "What's there we'd want to know? How many meals we've missed? How many lighthouses we passed? How many goddam walls we've run up on. Christamighty!"

"Hey, don't pull a temper with me. I bet that's what scares me about you. Well, look out, mister, I got one of my own, so look out."

"Come on, let's get out in the air. Guess I'm high as a waitin buzzard. First thing you know, that Steerman be back gettin us busy with one of those Village jawflaps make you feel like you sat through a bad double feature eatin sourballs . . . lemon flavor."

"And when you come outside—" she followed him out of the booth feeling a little that way herself—"it's four in the afternoon and drizzling and you have a headache around your eyes."

They laughed as he helped her with her coat. Small shoulders, precious things; he had never felt so tender and pulled his hands away, afraid it would show. At the door he asked Diane to wait, and the agreeability in the little triangle face lingered with him as he went across to say good-by to Lizzie, who had been watching from the bar. "We goin, Lizzie. I'll be about in the Village for a spell, so we'll be runnin up on each other, hear?"

Lizzie was straining off her stool to look over his shoulder toward the door. She wore the half-smile that bridges disapproval and indifference. "Since when," she said, "did you take up with money trade?"

He looked blankly at her for a hurtling moment. "Money trade! What do you mean, money trade?" There were Christmas trees and cousins in Roanton and sanctimonious aunts humming in his ears against the answer he already knew.

"You-oo know what I mean. That Seventh Avenue hustler you're with. You don't have to get frantic for love, Joe. Je-sus, you know it's like pickin fruit and vegetables. Nobody at my place tonight and *you* are always——"

Diane. Diane with contrite eyes and a halo of vapors around her head stood waiting and smiling for him when he came outside. Now his expended years broke through into the present; he saw again the pious faces that brought back values long forgotten. And here was the girl with layers of colored cloth hiding her indicted body. He imagined her talking to his mother.

Fortunately it was cold. Diane accepted the silence he found so hard to break, and in silence they kicked their way through snow to the diner on Village Square. They ate griddle cakes and bacon, and he remained silent throughout the meal, trying to force his spirit, to restore the buoyancy he had felt before. He looked at her, smiled with her, even chuckled a bit at the things she said, but he couldn't bring his emotions up to the level of his mind, which could rationalize a thousand reasons for prostitution. The fatigue kept growing in him by the pound, and when he tried his own voice it sounded sourceless as a stranger's. They had hot chocolate, and he agreed that it was piping hot. She said she was sleepy and he nodded, tapping his chest with a thumb. They smoked cigarettes and left the place deserted.

Dawn was edging in. Diane held his arm down the pale frost of Waverly Place toward the park. His mind was a whirl of confusion; he was emotionally paralyzed. By the time they reached the untouched whiteness of the park he was cursing himself with morbid severity for his inability to overcome the shock. "*God damn you, Joe. God damn you.*" He said it over and over to himself.

"The hot chocolate was like a blood transfusion," Diane said.

"Yeah."

"Look at the way the snow hangs on those branches, Joe. It looks blue, doesn't it? Look at it. Like frozen air pointing in every direction, all different levels and directions crossing each other all over the whole park. It's gone—it's beautiful, isn't it, Joe?"

"It sure is, Diane." There had been prostitutes in Italy, sweet-looking kids like this, young as Diane, even younger. But that was a matter of acute need; in America a girl could always——

"Look over there, Joe, on that path where the sun is hitting. The snow is sort of pink, almost orange, or gold; it's hard to say which. And on the side, over in the shade it's blue, the snow."

"Yeah, Diane, it's nice."

His collar was up and he had his head drawn down into the warm tweed. It was only when he heard her call his name that he realized he was walking alone. He could tell by the inflection of her voice that she had noticed his withdrawal: it was faint and it broke over the one syllable of his name. Turning, he saw that she had stopped some distance back.

"What is it, Joe?" she wanted to know as he approached.

"I'm dog-tired is all. Dead on my feet, Diane."

"No, it's more than that. You got funny the minute we left the Riviera. What is it, Joe?"

Her eyes cut deep into him. What was he to say? *Can I take you home?* No. *Come to my hotel?* Nah. *Good-by forever?* Christ, no. "Don't you ever look to sleep at all?" knowing that the evasion showed in his look.

Her eyes burned deeper. "Come on, speak up. What is it? What happened to you? What did that blonde—Lizzie—what did she say to you?"

"You know her?" He hadn't wanted her even to know Lizzie, so that it might seem Lizzie had mistaken her, a simple case of mistaken——

"Sure I know her. God, who doesn't? She's an old Village character. What did she say, Joe? She doesn't know *me*; what could she say?"

"Nothin, Diane."

She stared as if she were counting the lines under his eyes. "You're lying, Joe. That woman said something to you."

"No she didn't. Nothin worth a hoot, anyway."

"Joe, I can't make it with lying. I hate it." She made a quick turn and sped stiffly toward the park exit.

Joe watched the hem of her coat whip about her legs, saw the snow fly into powder at her heels, and it blurred his eyes. Each step she took relieved a pressure but destroyed a dream in him. The thing that weighed on him was not so real as those steps that put distance and hostility between them; it was not his problem, it belonged to people connected with him only by memories and religious heritage. "Diane!" he shouted into the frost.

She waited for him to run up to her. Her face was expressionless. Her eyes glittered. The strength he saw that look declare relieved him of the burden of kindness.

"You want the truth; it's all yours. That Lizzie told me you're a—whore."

"She said I'm . . . Well, what if it were true?"

"Is it, Diane?"

"What if it were? Is that why you've been acting that way?"

A million windows looked down at him from the big stone houses surrounding the square. The snow was white as unending space, and cold, cold.

"I knew something was fishy about you," she said flatly. "You want me, but with conditions. You want me pure and a virgin. That's the one thing that sticks to you from the land of cotton. You've come a long way out of the prejudice they brought you up with. You can see a Negro as your equal, Joe, but—not a woman."

"Diane, what in hell you talkin about? What's it all got to do with equality? Goddammit, I only want to know if that woman was just blowin wind or what."

"You can just go and dream about it." She spun around and went.

He took a step, "Diane!" then held, and said in an undertone, "Dry your little feet, honey." Joe Letrigo watched the girl walk swiftly up Waverly Place, saw her size diminish, her colors fade, her motion become imperceptible. Then he sat in the snow fallen soft on a bench and tried to reason through more complex things than simply her dimensions, colors and slender mobility, which all lay so indelibly on his brain.

Spine. Once you were so close to it, the word itself was ominous—*spine, spine*—the word itself tasted like jelly-coated bones with big and little black nerves. The suspended soundless dawn was a time for words to grow personalities, Carter decided, shifting in his pajamas by the bedroom window. Begins to degenerate at some point in *spineola*, if the doctor could be sure. But surely Edna had a spine, inside, under the flesh. A spine for sure and maybe rotten with the Thing, more live words: Amyotrophic Lateral Sclerosis crawling in and out as if all the millions of nerves weren't enough. A microscopic jungle scene: Amyotraffic . . . Edna . . . undone, undone, wrong nerves, broken brain machine . . . dying, perhaps. A Dying, going out, no more, ebbing like night in the sky outside, painted now by the gray and chill of daylight. While crowded houses stared apathetically at time. Time weighed, crept slowly, yawned, stopped, crept a little more. Tuesday, another word that had a face. The day would be a crawling repetition of hollow words, low-level shrewdness; the evening meant the hospital and Edna, the night a looming blackness that offered nothing . . . unless Diane emerged from the snowed-under whirlpool of aimlessness into which she'd plunged again.

Carter clicked off the bedlight and went through deepened shadows to the bathroom, telling himself not to bother speculating about Diane: his concern wasn't nearly enough to stabilize her. Concern reminded him with a laugh of Careless Adams in the army, the most unconcerned man on earth, who was so relaxed that he often took some sleep draped across the barrel of a forty-millimeter gun. Careless had been Normie Goldsmith's discovery. With an arm around Adams' shoulder the lanky man had brought him to Carter and introduced him as the only man in the Army of the United States who earned less than a hundred a week prior to induction. Gladmouth Normie. He could stand a visit with Normie and his family.

The doorbell's ring sliced through the gush from faucets and he went grumbling to answer it. Six o'clock: some drunk, probably. But it was Diane slamming into him, folding her arms cold around his neck.

"I was right; I thought it was a drunk."

"I'm not drunk, Carter; I'm just glad to see you."

"Not drunk? You smell like three blocks of Third Avenue. Climb into bed before you collapse."

"Then I'm drunk and glad to see you. What's the difference?"

"You hungry?" He tried to ease her arms away, but she clung.

"No, I've eaten. Let me hang on you awhile. Did I wake you? You don't look a bit sleepy, not a bit."

"I've been up awhile." He wanted to pull her close, but that was only in his chest; his spine ran into his arms to keep her distant. "Come on, get into the sack."

Diane followed him through to the bedroom, threw her coat and kerchief on a chair, and fell across the bed, digging her face into the rumpled sheets that smelled cleanly of Carter. "Whew! I didn't know how tired I was. Come on over and stay with me a little minute, Cart. Oh, it's good to look at you. Hot dog!" He chuckled, dropping down beside her, and she lay quietly while the light grew in the room, pushing out the shadows and capping the furniture edges with blue highlights. She reached over and played with his ear. "It's like being home, Carter, it's like coming home and feeling safe again."

"Sure it's home. There's your picture on the wall . . . by Degas."

"How come you think it looks like me, Cart?"

"Who said it looks like you? It just feels like you—soft and graceful and surrounded by clean air."

She was silent, looking sleepily across the room, with a penitent look, as if she were trying to dream herself clean of all the errors in her short life. "There's not much clean air around me, Carter. You know that."

"Don't get that kind of conscience, baby. You're not going to blame yourself for all the guys who took you and——"

"Listen," she said with impatience. "Nobody ever took advantage of me. Any time I slept with anyone, it was a guy I picked out."

"Well, don't feel guilty for it; it's your own life," thinking, as he watched the little body stretch comfortably, that he might have been telling it to himself; he put his hands under his head to keep them from reaching.

Diane swung around to the side of the bed and worked off her shoes. She unsheathed her feet and dried them on a blanket end, then stood and began pulling clothes over her head. Carter turned his back to her.

"What's the matter with you?" She laughed. "You're a real puritan. Bodies shouldn't be so secret as all that. You're a real puritan, Carter."

Carter came around to his original position and looked at her standing nude beside the bed. "This make you feel better?" But he couldn't feel as casual as he'd hoped to sound, not with those breasts pointed at him, even firmer than he'd imagined them to be. There was an urge to reach out and pull her toward him by the slender hips cast just slightly forward. But the impulse passed in an instant, displaced in his mind by the weeping eyes of Dying. Carter looked at the ceiling.

"And I'm not trying to seduce you." Diane bounced on the bed. "I know what you're thinking."

"Go to sleep."

"I will, I will. You don't have to be so nasty."

"Nasty?" He turned toward her; there was something tragic in her nakedness, in the way her shoulders were drawn forward. "Baby, I'd sooner cut my throat than be nasty to you." She slipped smoothly into his arms. "You know it, little girl, I'd sooner die."

Diane laughed and pressed closer—Carter whipped back.

"I felt that!" she shouted. "I felt that, Carter. You think I'm trying to seduce you, that's what."

Her voice filled his chest solid, and the sensation burst out of him in laughter. "No, no. I didn't think anything of the sort. It was just a reflex."

"Reflex, my eye. You bastard, you're afraid . . ." and she thought of Joe Letrigo. "Carter . . . I was with some guy tonight and I didn't swear one little time. Does that mean something?"

"It means he didn't get you mad. He didn't pull away when you tried to creep into him."

"I did not try! Oh, you bastard!" She leaped over on him, pounding his chest as he laughed. "And he did get me mad, but I didn't swear."

Carter put his arms on the baby skin of her back, held her lightly to him. "Well, he impressed you, and you wanted to—well, you liked him."

"I didn't like him either. Carter . . . Carter, I like you best."

His hands held her at the waist; her skin was silk. "All right, get off me and go to sleep. Why don't you stay here, Diane? Stay here and get things straight in your mind. Don't run around for a while."

"I'd love to, Cart, but you know I can't; they'll come looking for me. Some people just aren't born to be free."

"Don't talk like that. You sound like a senator."

She giggled and kissed his neck. "Okay, Daddio, but I'll have to keep one leg on the fire escape. Carter . . . I can't keep them crossed, that way," and she lifted herself to see his face.

He wasn't smiling. "Get off me, baby."

"Why won't you love me, Carter?" she said into his cheek. "Other men want me; why don't you?"

"You know why; it's got nothing to do with us. Get off me, Diane."

"I'll get Paddy Jenks to." Then she was sorry she'd used that name. "You know him?"

"The junky? I've seen him around. Why him, of all people?"

"He's a great stickman. I was with him last night." That was a deliberate lie, and right after Joe had enraged her with his lying. But she found in it a kind of truth: it was only a slight inversion of time . . . she could make a whole truth out of it any night she chose. "He's the best stickman in town, Carter."

"All right. Get under the covers and go to sleep. I have to go to work."

"You don't care who I sleep with."

His ears were burning and there was a contraction in his chest that even breathing hard would not relieve. This girl . . . this little wanton child of a woman. . . . "Go to sleep, baby, go to sleep."

"Don't make me move, Carter. This is heaven."

Her body, curled upon him, cradled in his hollows, was a softness without weight. Where her back narrowed into the spread of buttocks the skin was deep to his touch, and warm and dry. Now the street was purring with the noise of trucks, dogs barked somewhere, and all of it was walled out; the naked little girl was his. The rest—the laws and obligations beyond this moment—were a chaos of words, sounds, gestures that had neither body nor reason, words invented for confusion's sake, to dissociate life from the feeling of it. Diane was his child, warmth and peace and responsibility, a saint in his arms.

Carter eased her over, settled her carefully, and pulled the covers up under her chin. With his fingers he traced the contour of her face, childlike in the glow of sleep. It was odd how the region of her eyes sustained the contrite look that hung on all her wakeful glances. Leaning over, he kissed the hollow of her cheek, then came to his feet and looked out the window at the sunlit day.

Winter was packed white in the street, but already several cleared sidewalks peeked through in front of high factory buildings. Down toward Greenwich Street the few little sprigs of trees stood incongruously in the industrial avenue. The apartment house in which he lived was out of place too, yet it stood there not in incongruity but in a kind of boldness. Trees as delicate and house as bold as Diane, Diane bending to strong winds but boldly standing her ground in a society of dependent women, stubborn in her will to live with the same spontaneity in conduct as that of any man. Yet, rootless like no tree or pile of bricks, she flew blindly from normal paths to carry her abused sensibilities wherever they could be free. A daily and unending marathon of horror turned to habit, more ominous than but parallel to the marathon of housewives in this building, sent shuddering to parks with their children by the growl and screech of delivery trucks. Carter turned to look at her, sighed for her, then quickly got into his clothes. He left a five-dollar bill and the extra apartment key in the bathroom, decided to have breakfast outside to keep from clanking around in the kitchen. The phone rang as he passed it, and he caught it up quickly. "Yes," he said with a look into the bedroom: Diane slept undisturbed.

"Carter, this is Mother—now, no wisecracks, you'll want to hear this. I have a letter from the Welfare Board authorities reporting Diane's escape. I'm to answer it, telling what I know of her whereabouts."

He kept silent while she paused, then decided to play no games. "Well, how can I help you?"

"You know very well how you can. I want you to send her back on her own, before the police begin looking for her. It's best that way. She'll have a better feeling in her spirit. She'll be able to rest in God's eyes——"

"Wait a minute. That's not her problem. You want her to feel better in her spirit? Call it off. Call the dogs off. Call off all the hounding if you really want her to feel better. There's a better way——"

"Carter! I'm trying to help her. Why do you persist in standing in my way?"

He didn't know how he might reach the woman, make her realize that Diane had to be led, not pushed. He wished he could call her Mother without feeling hypocritical. "Vivienne, listen for a minute. Diane isn't a machine; she's alive and very young and very confused. Take her out of this mess and I swear I'll do what I can to . . . I'll try to talk to her and get her to stay home and even——"

"Carter, I refuse to go over it all. Don't you think I've thought it out at length? Goodness, I'm her mother; I know nothing will help that girl but confinement. I've tried everything, everything. I'm at——"

"Everything but a real stretch of your imagination. The kid only——"

"Please, please, Carter. Just send her back. My imagination doesn't need to be stretched to tell me where she is."

"Well, then you'd better stretch it. She's not here," and his face burned. "I want to see you, Viv. I want to talk——"

"It's none of your affair!" The woman's voice was slipping out of range with hysteria. "You send her back or I'll have the police up there. I don't want to; I don't want her taken away like a common criminal, but I will. I will, Carter, I will!"

"You'll turn her into a common criminal hounding her that way."

"You send her back, you . . . you sex—you pervert!"

"You've been calling the girls names like that since they were playing potsy. I ought to have you put away. I believe I'll look into that. Diane's not here," and he eased the phone onto its hook at the first bell of the woman's voice. He looked in one time at the child asleep and left; he knew she'd answer no bell that rang, and the very apprehensiveness with which she protected herself made him guilty in his guts for all the mechanical laws in the land.

A wild wind bit into his nostrils, but he walked right on past the Sheridan Square subway to the next street. Somehow he couldn't bear the shadows below. He stood instead at the Tenth Street bus stop.

I've been a lady for eight hundred years. She was a fungus on them all. French nobility. Nobility! Noble! Called them prostitutes before they knew what vaginas were for. Kept them in homes. Froze out their blood till any ability to love was gone, except in their minds where they could still counterfeit it. Edna and Diane. Diane and Edna. Same face, same voice. Only a psychological wedge of years differentiating between them.

The approaching bus wakened him, and he climbed out of the suncold street, dropped his fare and turned to see the boy Dincher seated with his friend Red in the empty car's rear. Staggering, he made the walk to the back and sat in front of the boys. "Where you going, Dincher? Fishing?"

Dincher enjoyed that. "Criminal court." He laughed, pulling on the brim of his gray hat. "Like-we figure we be there early; right, Red?"

Red turned away from the window, his gray hat bobbing as he nodded. "We don' wanna get a bad repetation." He looked at Dincher and they laughed in the same mild voice both affected in their speech, the attempt for impassiveness that sounded like stupefaction. "Where *you* goin?" Dincher wanted to know, flicking a loose hand toward Carter.

"To work, Dinch."

"Doin any good?"

"Holding on. What's happening in court?"

"Red's havin a goin-away party-like." Red continued to watch Seventh Avenue coasting by the window, flashing glass, air and neon.

"He's goin inside," Dincher added casually.

Red seemed younger and as smooth as Diane; he sat unperturbed.

"How long a trip?" Carter asked.

"Six moes." Dincher sighed. "But he'll have somethin like-waitin outside; right, Red?"

Red nodded, looking out the window. A boy named Schoenberg, three days before his destruction, had been insulted when Carter had asked his age. Lying dead before Lingayen, he had looked neither young nor old.

"You know," Dincher said, "I like to send Edna a little gift-like. Like-we know each other from back; it'll cheer her up, like flowers or maybe a little gimmick or somethin. A long time like-we know each other."

"Sure, Dinch, she'd like that all right."

"I could even go visit her, maybe; right?"

"Sure; she's at the Midway Hospital in Queens. Want to know how to get out there?"

"I find out easy. Midway Hospital in Queens. Like-she get a boot out of it."

"Okay. I'll see her tonight and tell her."

"No, lemme surprise her-like; you know?" His eyes remained fixed and wary, but the rest of his face relaxed in an untroubled grin. He looked around suddenly and said, "Come on, Red. Thirty-eighth."

"There a court here?" Carter asked as the boys swung to their feet.

"No, first we got like a little business here, then we go downtown." Dincher bent over close. "If anyone ever asks—you know, like cops —don' say nothin about diggin us. Okay?"

"Okay, Dinch," and marveled at the trust resting in those baby eyes. Kids had a simple formula of trust by association, and so long as he could be identified with the sisters he would be trusted with the very lives of these boys. He had to laugh when he considered the feeling they must then have, on those grounds, for Mrs. Lattimer.

"The name's Webb, right?" Dincher said from the exit as the bus quivered to a stop. And when Carter nodded, "That's like a different kind of name, Webb."

Carter dipped into army banter for something to amuse the boy. "Know where it comes from? The spider's ass."

Dincher threw his head back, laughing as he got off behind Red, and they kicked off across the snow, twinlike in their loose black coats and gray hats.

"Poor little bastards," Carter muttered. Some people boarded and at Fortieth a few more jumped on, choosing seats good distances apart. The faces of Dincher, Red and Schoenberg were with him when he got off at Forty-fifth and crunched diagonally across to the blue-glass luncheonette on his street. He ordered breakfast in a leather booth, thinking then of himself at eighteen; he dreamed of Atherton, the mines, the Hunky catcalls: *Hey, Engelish! Ho, you Johnny-Bull bastar'!* There were the vague, drifting faces of his parents, almost legend to his memory, killed by coal dust and despair so long ago, so long. Jess was a man now with a wife and a dream in Pennsylvania. It had been hard to keep the kid brother in school, and the sun and laughter of those liquid days came more clearly to his mind than the time-blunted stings of hardships, bringing up the boy and crouching in the pits, the need of books, of money to keep himself in night school, the lack of time to breathe; the sounds ringing in that time and his own young face were clearer in his mind. It was all so distant, almost a different incarnation; the war had been the dark transition.

Merwin Fingerhut came waddling in, red-faced with cold. "What happened to me!" he moaned, plopping in across from Carter. "In the movies they couldn't show it. Carter, who can believe about people like this any more?"

Carter called for two coffees and felt the muscles relax all over his body, realizing for the first time that he'd been tightened up like a harp. "Lie down and sleep a little, Merwin."

"Believe me, I could use a couple hours. Maxie Scar got a hold of me last night and it was almost the end."

Maxie Scar was a live citizen in Carter's mind, and he laughed half over Merwin's condition and half over old stories Merwin had told. Maxie had been in the ring, and when a fight was arranged for him with Graziano everybody in Coney Island, including Maxie's mother, had gone to synagogue to pray for it to last many rounds so that Maxie would not get off easily. Merwin had sworn that Coney Island went into a kind of mourning when it turned out that Graziano finished Maxie off in thirty seconds of the first round. Several people departed from God because of that unanswered plea. Old men shaved faces which religion had kept bearded for decades.

"Now he bites ears." Merwin's whisper was strained. "He marched into Weepy's poolroom last night and asked the whole place who knows how to drive a car. Every finger points to Merwin, the whole place turns their heads away and points to me. So I'm driving a hot car, he's got a Great Dane in it. You know how he gets them dogs? A lady walks her dog, Maxie jumps out of a car, belts the dog out with a right to his kisser and before the lady can give scream one he tosses the hound in the car and *zoom!* he's gone. So I'm in a hot car driving two animals, I don't know which is worse. All night we go from one joint to another and when citizens see the dog—like a horse he's built—they get up and go away and Maxie makes me help him finish the drinks all the citizens don't want no more." Merwin sipped coffee, giving Carter time to work down his laughter. "We come to Club Haha on Ocean Parkway, the manager don't know Maxie from a normal human being, he tells him kindly remove the animal from the premises. What can I tell you? Maxie takes the guy's head in one hand and bites off his ear and spits it on the ground. The screaming in the place! This part of the guy's ear, the lobe. The guy is suddenly with half an ear, hollering blue murder, and citizens are fainting, grown men." He pushed his coffee aside and gulped Carter's water. "Wait—" shaking his chubby fingers before Carter could speak —"me, I'm driving with bubbles coming out of my nose, and the dog, he's got his back feet in the back of the car and his front feet beside me, he's licking my face with a tongue two inches thick, every lick is like a slap in the face, but I'm thankful he's between Maxie and me. Maxie has to go home for something, we go back to the Island, he's hollering *Faster!* I should kill people. We turn into Twenny-eighth Street, people are running all over like a panic, Maxie's brother Sam is on the porch blasting with a pistol, he's smiling like an angel and blasting the citizens. Maxie jumps on the porch and knocks his brother dead with one punch and now I'm driving him around he's got a pistol in his pocket."

Carter was sneezing with laughter even though he was horrified. "What was it, his younger brother?" was all he could manage as Merwin followed him to the cashier and out.

"Nobody is younger or older in that family. They were all born thirty years old. All night I drove, every place: Harlem, the Village, in Canarsie he had to see people," breathlessly on past the glass door and up the stone stairway, past Radio Repair and Chiropodist, and inside right to the processing tanks. "In the morning he gets tired of the dog, he stuffs it in a house on his block, a guy runs out screaming *Lion!* a lady whacks Maxie into the street with a broom, he's on the dog like a horse, laughing like crazy he rides away. Hopalong Cassidy. I call the wife, she's hysterical. Go tell her a story like that. Carter, I didn't sleep a blink, but I don't go home now not for money. It's terrible what can happen to a man. Some story I need for the wife."

"Why won't she believe you? I do," he gasped, still wiping his eyes.

"You got no reason not to. A wife can dream up a million ideas. How's Edna getting along? I always forget to ask."

"I'll find out tonight." He watched Merwin mechanically dip a frame of film; the fatigue didn't show on the round face, yet there was a frown of perturbation around the flesh-buried eyes. "Merwin, you know of any union that might be interested in Wengel's setup?"

Merwin grinned around at him. "Yeah, I know one. I'm glad you feel like that, Carter; I been thinking about it on the way uptown." He came around some cartons and sat beside Carter on the desk. "Listen, I figure like this. Where should I begin? Take Maxie Scar and his brother Sam. Why are they crazy like that? Because they never was kids. Why not? Because they never had parents should smile and tell them go out and play in the air. Why not? Because the parents didn't have crackerjack money. Instead of sending them to play in the air they sent them to work. What does a kid know from work? He can't buy nothing for hisself, he's got to give the money into the house for rent and food. So he gets crazy, he gets bad. Take a boy like me, I'm brought up in the same neighborhood, but my father is lucky, he brings home the goods and sends me out I should play in the air. So I grow up good, not exceptionally good, just good enough I obey the laws. But I walk around minding my business, a guy like the Scar collars me and makes life rough. I got two kids, ain't I? What's gonna happen when my boy and girl grow up and meet kids like, say, those Spanish kids they belong to Wengel's working people? You think those kids can be kids on the money Wengel pays the daddies? Certainly not, it's no question. All day they're with the shoeshine boxes and newspapers and carrying packages. Don't worry, I

know some of them can turn out okay, with extra ambition like a
go-getter. But those that don't, what good is it if I bring my kids up
right, they should run into bad kids later on? I'm a father and I got
to think of my kids, I got to pay my kids off. Why should a pig like
Wengel pack money away in drawers and never use it while those
Spanish citizens don't have for their kids? And the blind ones . . .
that's a shame by itself, without kids. They got to have unions, and
guys like Wengel—I spit on them where they breathe."

Carter patted his head. "That's what I mean: up with the unions.
Merwin, what sends you to Coney Island? You live farther up in
Brooklyn, don't you? Where the kids play in the air."

Merwin shrugged, turning his little smile toward the blacked-out
window. "It's my home town, that's all. What can I tell you? I know
all the streets, I know the guys, I know how everybody ticks. Even
guys like Maxie Scar ain't really evil like they sound. They just
breathe that way."

"How does old Wengel breathe? He's breathing too."

"Not like Maxie; Maxie *has* to do those things. Wengel can make
things good but won't. It's guys like that ruin everybody's life in the
whole world. What can you do? There's a million of them like lice."

"You call the union, that's what." Somehow the younger man's
simplicity always served to stultify Carter to such a point that his
thinking lost complexity and came out in short inexpressive sentences.
"Try not to worry, Merwin." He felt false, hearing his own uttered
superficialities, but blamed himself rather than Merwin, since the
man's observations were certainly honest and significant enough.

"If I don't worry, who will? I'm sick of the way things are in this
country, I can die sometimes when I think about it."

"Then don't think about it," Carter suggested in the doorway.

"That's just it." Merwin wagged a finger. "That's just what guys
like Wengel want—people shouldn't think about it. It's easy for you
—I don't mean exactly you, Carter, you're a sensitive guy by nature—
it's easy for guys without families not to think of it, but I got kids
and I owe them something. Did they ask to be born? You bring
kids into this world, you got to give them a decent world. You
know, sometimes I hate my own father for never thinking enough.
It hurts me to say it, but it's true. When I think how the last generation just played with whisky and short dresses I get plenty mad at
them. And then I look at my kids and see someday they'll have a

right to think bad things about me, I get ashamed. Here, take the name of the union before I forget. What's the use of talking? We can talk our heads off and get no place, except some crook'll holler Communist. Or some idiot who don't know better." He scribbled the information, tore the sheet from a pad and handed it over.

"I'm going over to Wengel's." Carter backed through the door, unwilling to hear what he knew Merwin would say. "I'll be back after lunch and you can go home and hit the sack."

"Sign the consignment, Carter. Don't be like a guilty conscience." Merwin's smile didn't involve his eyes. He turned with a weary sigh toward the black-rubber processing tanks as Carter shut the door.

Bouncing uptown in a cab, Carter couldn't help applying what Merwin had been saying to Mrs. Lattimer and her girls. Vivienne swore her daughters were tainted by the *common* people they'd been in contact with. There was something wryly funny about it and he might have laughed if it weren't all so close to him. Inwardly he swung through an attempt to trace his own current problems to some economic source. Ideas tumbled through his mind without order: Edna reduced to prostitution, Clyde Lattimer escaping from Vivienne and duty, Vivienne's family and the degradation they suffered at the collapse of the aristocracy myth—all economically motivated, yet all pervaded with quirks and even basic veins of personality. People just couldn't seem to get on with one another, and passed their failures to their young. And Carter couldn't seem to find a point at which to begin: he felt submerged, and the sea was a murky brine of general incompatibility. There had to be unity, there had to be a point at which people stopped biting at one another and began trying to live together. He left the cab, reading vaguely the information Merwin had written for him, and passed through the concrete portals of Wengel's building.

It was a moment before he realized the crowd in which he lost himself was a parade of the blind, each following another to the elevators as methodically and unquestioningly as any group of workers. Once he recognized them, a double despair grew down on him; the sunken eye sockets and the stoop-shouldered hesitancy preyed only superficially on his feelings, for more frightening was the fact that these unfortunates served as stark illustration of the less obviously oppressed, the millions of men and women blinded to the breadth of their large needs by more immediate ones: the Puerto Ricans, for instance—and now he saw some groups of them around the lobby, jabbering and laughing by the pseudomarble walls. Here was unity all around him, but a unity too circumstantial, undirected, virtually purposeless. And if they were unionized, if a real militance were sparked into their bit of unity, they would possibly slow Wengel down a little, contain him a measure, but the Wengels would keep cropping up. Carter wanted a total unity, he wanted a union of lumberjacks from Washington and ranch hands from Texas and Carolina cotton pickers, Dakota farmers, New York factory workers; but suddenly he felt naïve, like an adolescent coming for the first time into the breathtaking limitlessness of commerce. These things had been dreamed of before, even attempted, but the vast human incompatibility, the tissue-thin cultural disparities always destroyed the dream, and Wengel's counterparts grew unmolested. Sourly he waited in a far corner of the lobby till the shabby Puerto Ricans and the pitiable blind disappeared.

Wengel came through the revolving door, leaning back to balance his paunch, marching to an inaudible drumbeat. His smile, as he approached, seemed set as though he secretly measured its degree, granting just so much to each recipient. Carter found it hard to look at the white, superfluous flesh crammed between hat and coat collar.

"So?" Wengel said. "You're on the doorstep waiting. Come up, come up, there's a nice contract for you. Consignment. Who do I give consignment, my young man? Not even my own brother."

Robert Stoney knelt on the hearth, dropping split boards on the fire. They snapped in the flames that grew wildly—flames hot on his face just short of burning. Spinning on his haunches, he watched the giant of his shadow dance flickering over the sobbing shape on the bed. He straightened up, tightened his belt over the bulge, then leaned lightheaded against the calcimined brick and stared at his bag-kneed, grimy trousers. *I'm being gouged,* he thought; *this melodrama is far too great a price to pay for the borrowed flesh.* He groped among palette knives and tubes of paint on the high wheel-bottomed table, found a cigar and lighted it.

Louella's voice was strained through her gasps: "You . . . you realize what you've done. I didn't invite it. I didn't . . . co-operate. You realize that you've actually . . . gone and——"

"Gagh!" he burst to the ceiling. "No no no no no. Don't do that.

In the name of truth, beauty and female suffrage, don't say I raped you."

"But you did, you did!" Her voice cracked and rode into a high, piteous moan. "You di-id! You held me down and . . . ohohohoh-ahaho." The very whine she used for laughter: the situation altered its meaning.

"Sue me," he said, taking a good pull on the stogie.

"Oh, you're cruel, cruel!"

"And that's specifically why you came here this afternoon. Because you expected I'd be *cruel* enough to free you of that hallucination burning your thighs. Nineteen forty-nine! You're supposed to have grown realistic enough by now to accept the manifest equality of women, and some people are still concerned with hymens, with symbolic virginity, and Christ only knows what other hoodoos. What rot! What ugly retrogression!" Even in the half-dark she seemed awkward for her age, burying her face in the pillows, shaking with sobs. "Well, why *did* you come back? Didn't I say this morning that I'd try to seduce you if you returned?"

"I . . . I thought you said that . . . just to . . . shock Harry."

"To shock Harry!" He threw his hands out and walked across to the bed. "Go home, Louella. Go on back uptown and cry to your mother. She'll comfort you—I certainly can't."

A new kind of wail trembled out of her. "My mother! How can I look at her again?"

"Look at her, look at her. She's got a few secrets herself, I guarantee it." He suddenly became aware of how fully the master he was in this moment. "For all I know you may be my own daughter. My very own. Where did you say you were born?"

Louella sat up abruptly, her clothes twisted, her hair undone. "Don't *dare* say those things! My mother . . . my mother is a Christtian, through and through, and pure all her life, you son-of-a-bitch! And my family always . . . my family . . ." Tears choked her silent and she fell with a bounce to her side.

"Lord, what a tragedy." He sat on the bed's end, leaning back till his shoulders found the wall. "Tradition! Galvanized by religion, tradition remains unaffected by change. It hovers over their heads and renders every one of them an atavism." He could see the shadow of her face pointed his way and knew she was captured by the ring of his words to that point these people reached where they felt themselves participants in posterity's own hours. "You morbid children," he went on in a flat historical voice, "were destroyed at infancy by parents with similar histories: begotten by infinite ghosts of intimidation, as far back as the analytical eye can see."

"I don't know what you're talking about and I don't care. I don't care about anything any more, not anything."

Stoney lurched to his feet and pulled on the light over his easel. The girl let out a shriek and jumped straight up with both hands over her face.

"Put out the light!" she yelled. "Put it out! Oh, I must look hideous." She whipped her back around toward him, snatched her purse from the floor and dashed off to the bathroom.

He laughed and looked at the canvas before him: *Princess Tamar.* Closed pathetic eyes and a hand between the great round breasts. Last night he had told Louella the story of Tamar, David's daughter, tricked, seduced by David's son Amnon. *Whose hand is upon Tamar? Her own? Amnon's? Or . . . the king's?* It had been totally effective with Louella, and now she could defile the deep significance of this story to absolve herself of a lust that needed no absolution, just as she had chosen him as bearer of the blame for an act which was blameless. He squeezed paint on the palette and ran a gold-ocher glaze over the yellow streak on Tamar's right breast.

Perfume and Louella were behind him. "Are you giving Tamar a gold medal now that you've reincarnated her in me?"

He laughed a loud hawk, sucking on the cold, foul cigar. "It's not a medal, it's a little golden flaw in her make-up." *It's something far beyond symbol,* he told himself with a surge of artistic mystery, *it's in the language of paint,* and shook off an idea it was some postorgasmic tremor in him and not intuition at all.

"I suppose I should rub ashes on my forehead like Tamar did. Would you like that, Bob? Should I write your name in ashes on my forehead?"

"That won't be necessary. Times have really changed in spite of your mother. Just tattoo my initials on your abdomen."

"You're a beast."

"And you love it." Turning to the palette, he saw her seated, watching in a small mirror as she applied mascara to an eye spread glaring. He relighted his cigar, then ran a knife of cadmium red lightly over the dark nipples to speck them with fire.

"Can't I have that picture, Bob? Why don't you give it to me? That's the very least you can do under the——"

"The least I can do in payment for your flesh?" He watched her focus her composure on the lighting of a cigarette in its silver holder. "That would make a prostitute of you; I couldn't do that. I'll sell it to you."

She dropped her eyes with an absurd pathos; he turned away. Tamar's eyes were in sad shadow beneath the rich orange arrow formed by the collapse of hair. Indefinably effective, and thus his art lay buried for another age to find: he put a highlight on her lip, a fever, a terminated tear.

"How much shall I make it out for?" She had her checkbook out, sitting stiff with self-righteousness.

"Mm-m-m, two hundred. Or one-fifty, if you feel two hundred is exorbitant." It was a mortgage, a new lease, or whatever those things were; he pictured himself dropping gold pieces in the Shylock's hand.

She handed him the check made out for one hundred fifty. "My address is on it; will you send the thing when it dries?"

"When it's done." He matched her dramatic tones. "I'll send it when it's done, madame."

In her gray curly-haired coat, head high, long neck rigid, she clacked across to the door, whirled, and looked at him, her head cocked. She thrust the silver gleam into a corner of her mouth and whispered with finality, "Good-by, Amnon!"

Stoney raised his cigar ceilingward in his hand, pointed his beard at her and let "Good-by, Tamar" flutter from a whisper. Then when the door closed behind her he muttered, "See you tomorrow," and did a little dance on his toes, circling deftly around the easel. He executed a flourishing bow, then removed Tamar from the easel. "You're done and paid for, you old whore."

A clean, freshly stretched canvas Louella had brought him stood propped against the wall between windows at the studio's end. Stoney secured it on the easel, spat at the challenging expanse of white and pulled the room into darkness. He built up the fire, then tidied the bed and sprawled diagonally, watching the ceiling writhe with shadows of his brushes in their jar, his bottles of petroleum and sunthickened linseed dancing translucently, liquidly. Twenty years ago Louella would have been a cross of guilt on his soul, her pain poignant, her ruination real. But now he told himself he'd liberated her, just as she'd planned the liberation, using him against the miserable dwarfs of her conditioning that were making a dual personality of her. Duality of response was the order of the day for the young: gray old circumspections were directing them against the pull of their own instincts. There was no means by which they could discern between their personal impulses and the imposed perspective, the set of dogmas handed them by their parents, through which they measured meaning and mortified themselves. Taboo and hoodoo!

"Christ!" he shouted, crossing over to the fire. He felt suddenly absurd for the way he spent his days and nights alone, knew by that intuitive burgeoning inside that his proper place was at the head of a throng inspired enough to follow the historical rightness he could feel thumping in his blood.

He killed the fire and ran from the room, pulling on his coat, down into the bite of winter, out of Bleecker marching along MacDougal while his solid plan for government paraded its departments across a brain that almost lifted him soaring through space. Till his name exploded in his ear and he spun around, reaching out a hand for the blazing sword. But it was the yellow flash of a jonquil bouquet he caught.

"I been thinkin of you, love, and I got you these." Joe Letrigo sat cross-legged on a milk-delivery box in front of a store, his hat cocked back so that he looked like some oversize goblin.

Stoney tossed the flowers into Joe's lap and sighed voluminously. The crisp evening did not dispel the muggy whisky mist hung curtainlike around Joe. "Why do you blunt your senses with alcohol?" Stoney asked, sitting down next to him.

"Stoney, you're an opinionated ole gangle-assed joker. It's moot as hell whether the juice blunts or sharpens the senses. What you got against flowers? You never did paint one yet, did you?"

"Why paint them? They're all around you; why immortalize them?"

Joe rocked his head in his hand, laughing into his coat collar. "Christamighty, you never did seem a painter to me. Too damn literal in your thinkin. Why don't you get an honest job?"

"Nothing less than administrating a world government would interest me."

"And yet you paint." Joe laughed his deep chopped-up boom. "Man, you do it like anyone drinks or watches television."

"Agh, you're drunk. Don't deny it—you wouldn't be so prosaic if you were the least bit sober. Come on and have some coffee; I'll reorient you philosophically." And he pulled Joe to his feet, explaining as they walked the subtle differences between escape and diversion, leading with doubling intensity into a discourse on the evils of tradition, every word of which Joe contradicted in a way that made the painter sure Joe was trying to antagonize him.

"You know what I call all that kind of talk?" Joe said before they stepped into the diner's splash of light. "Poetic nonsense, that's what. Poetic nonsense. Something sounds philosophical, you make a damn law of it. Man, you're a juvenile just huntin generalities." Joe was content to get that much across; the whisky was like a little man swinging from his brain, sleeping on his tongue. There were no empty booths, so they took stools at the counter and Joe didn't hear Stoney's voice through the noise till the painter shook him.

"Well, answer me, will you? How'd you come to buy me flowers? You thought it would be funny. It's not very funny and you would have realized it had you been sober."

Joe pondered awhile to find some relevance in that, but gave it up. "I didn't get them for you; I got them for a little girl."

"Well, why the hell didn't you give them to her?"

"Don't know where to find her." Joe turned to the coffee Slinger set down, then looked questioningly at him as he leaned elbows on the counter.

"Better stop lookin," Slinger advised. "If it's the broadie I seen you wit this mornin. She's sick'n if she ain't sick she's married."

"Who, that little girl?" Joe spun on Stoney. "This guy got all his marbles, Robert?"

"You know 'er ole man, artiss. The quiet guy you was snowin the other night, the one beefed you tried the eye on 'er, the one don't like I should bounce Timmy Lawless too hard. Carter Webb'n he's 'er ole man."

"Yes . . . yes," the painter muttered while Joe loosened his collar. "A distinct personality, a man to be dealt with. Scratch her off, Joe."

"She been sick," Slinger reported, "sick in the hospital'n first thing I know he's got 'er in here Saddy night, she's skinnier maybe a little, weaker-lookin like; you know?" and he went off to spread more information.

"It can't be!" Joe protested. "Goddam, it can't. Somebody's goofy sure as your goddam whiskers. She'd've told me. Robert, we just went

for one another like ole cows to a burnin barn. There was a real kind
of enchantment wrapped us up and in a little no time we were just
ready. Man, she can't be married, she's a child, cute as a speckled
. . . She's black-eyed and slender and pours a voice over you like
maple sirup——"
    "And you flatten like a pancake. I know. Spare me the vile details."
    "Along comes ole Lizzie Linden and tells me she's a prostitute."
    "Who is? Lizzie?"
    "No, Diane. She said Diane is. Man, inside I just came to dust."
    "Lizzie said that? I didn't think Lizzie knew what a prostitute is."
    "Don't weary me, Robert." Joe went to his coffee, but the splat of
flesh on flesh brought him around just in time to see Stoney grab at
his neck and look with incredulous horror at a little man ending the
follow-through of a long, loping swing at him.
    "You son-of-a-bitch!" Magoo the Newsboy sputtered. "You ain't
callin Lizzie no whore. He called Lizzie a dirty whore," he complained
to Slinger, who now had him by his arms.
    "The winner and new champeen!" an early drunk called from
down the counter. "Hunnert'n eight pouns soakin wet!"
    Joe was laughing so hard it made a problem of hustling Stoney out,
but only because of a path blocked by patrons: Stoney wanted nothing more than to be out of it. "I'm afraid of those little people," he
told Joe outside. "One punch and you have a broken skull to account
for. It's frustrating. We live in an asylum. A lunacy . . . a lunatic
asylum."
    "Forget it," Joe said, walking him south. "I got a real problem."
    "I had a mastoid operation as a boy. I should be more careful."
    "That Diane said I was backward, that I didn't respect the equality
of women. Now how about that?" Stoney had a ready answer, but
Joe's mind was too busy recapturing Diane's voice in the morning
park really to listen to the painter's abstractions. They had gone down
Waverly and around toward Eighth when he tuned in full on Stoney;
listening, he felt like a minor character in some stranger's dream.
    ". . . and they are equal, but not identical. Trace it from their
physical difference and you build out into their social differences.
The man yields his creation to the woman, who receives and de-
velops——"
    "Hey, you're givin me the d.t.'s. I got a real problem and you're
buggin me up with philosophy . . . or psilosophy."

"All right, what's your problem? Lie down here on this snowbank while I fetch pad and pencil." In pale half-shadow Joe suddenly looked very young to Stoney: his weather-tested skin seemed smooth, his eyes, normally piercing, now wide and gleaming with the uncertainty of a child. "Now, look here, sonny. There's a girl who is married, yet seems to be a prostitute; you want her none the less. Fine! Go get her, take her from her husband if you can, forget everything that happened in her life before you met. Next case."

"She's not married; I don't believe that applehead." He kicked a hump of snow as they rounded the corner into the neon bath of Eighth Street. "It's the rest of it, what Lizzie said and Diane wouldn't deny. And it's my people. Goddam if it doesn't sound like Sunday school, but somehow I by God feel like I'd be doin them a real hurt."

Stoney halted. There it was again: duality of response. Another victim of the parental poison. And in Joe, of all people: a man, a soldier, brave, aware, unaffected. Victimized not by the actual conduct of his parents—that would be horrifying enough—but by the air around them, the vague, disoriented ideas that were their eternal cocoons against a world they dared not attempt to define.

Joe looked around for the painter. "Come on, none of those dramatic pauses. Let's walk some or sit down somewhere—one."

Stoney lighted his cigar and walked, took a great inhalation and felt it scrape challengingly down his esophagus. He cleared his throat. "Your pardon if I seem to be recklessly stomping on toes, but your people are a bunch of gentle bastards who don't count. They've had their time, followed their customs, and now they're dying out of the world, leaving nothing and having derived nothing. They live by words instead of by guts. They recognize superiors. Their only real purpose is to belong. And belong they will at any cost; they'd sell you down the river for a neighbor's good opinion."

"What're you huffin about? You don't know my people from a load of coal."

"Don't I? Listen, sonny," and Joe listened while the painter admitted he'd never been to Roanton, yet insisted he'd seen the gentle bastards elsewhere, standing by while bishops and governors poured garbage over their heads and admiring those superiors for abusing them. He tore at their unquestioning subservience to mores they hadn't made, geographical and temporal moralities they so arbitrarily accepted as universal law. He yapped like a machine in high gear, shouldering through groups of people standing about by cars and restaurant windows. Joe followed along, reluctant to agree, but forced to by conscience, for all his life he'd been aware of a static quality in that world at home. He'd always sensed a fearfulness there, some defensive kind of blindness in his friends, in the chaste little girls with their stylized cuteness. No little girl or her mother cared to know more than the preacher told of the Bible; few men dared to investigate their world from scratch and formulate beliefs on what they found to be true; it had always been easier to accept the dogmas handed them and to formulate ideas *after* their beliefs. "I know them right well, those gentle souls. It's why I got out, enlisted in the army when I was eighteen just to be on my own, just to do something that counted."

"Good!" Stoney bucked through a group of boys who wiggled by, dubbing one another's noses with powder puffs. "So long as you agree they're worthless. I——"

"Worthless? I never agreed to no such. Those are my people; don't you know? I come out of the war with so many holes in me I whistled in the wind and it was them got my feet into walkin position. Maybe they buttered me a mite too careful, too patronizin, but it's the only kind of generosity they know. They're home to me. Goddam, Stoney, you sound off just somewhat too far. You're like a damn machine with no warm blood at all."

Stoney held up at the corner of Sixth Avenue, leaning back on the Nedick's store glass. "But you *realize* that world is dying of its own poison——"

"Aah, you're plain demented. Those are my people, good people, and I'm not the one to hurt them." Suddenly, while the painter yapped a retort, everything seemed unreal in the store's white light; the time itself seemed not in the present but remembered. Joe was ashamed for standing there listening.

". . . begin to block up the roads all over the land with their *goodness*. They'll be destroyed before they learn to grow."

"You! You talk about growin. Only growin you've done in the last twenty years is that brush on your face," and he turned off down Sixth.

Joe was smiling with a steadiness that made more than a joke of what he had said; the painter watched him walk to the Cosmopole window and stare through, eyes searching, face drawn as tight as though man and boy within fought for its possession. Stoney could recall the taste of being twenty-five, a time when, in his own life, illusions clung long after he'd rejected them, tormenting him with wavering doubts. "Joe—" he idled over—"you got angrier then than you meant to. Why?"

"Your goddam momentum. You talk smart a spell and then go shootin on with nothin words and evil talk. Takes a tough man to observe things delicately. You just don't know how to feel things softly."

"Softly!" Stoney mimicked. "Not softly, but coldly, coldly. That's how to judge—coldly, if we're to understand our world and be effective in it. Think coldly and act with equal iciness, and you'll replace God on this earth."

Joe leaned close and whispered, irritating Stoney's nostrils with the alcohol on this breath, "That's the trouble with you. You want to be God . . . frigid, nonhuman. You think from too high up, without stomach. If the road to knowledge is coated with ice, I'll——" But the flash of a body shot from behind the boarded-up newsstand at the curb to land hissing and swinging on the painter's back. Joe plucked Magoo away at the painter's first gawk of alarm and swung him around, setting him down where he couldn't reach Stoney, who, with the identical idea, had retreated to the newsstand and stood snapping his knuckles.

"You gonna keep this up all night?" Joe wanted to know.

"Lemme go! It's slander! He got no right'n I'll mangle 'im! Buster!" he howled toward a group in the Cosmopole doorway. "Buster, c'mere!"

"Look, now, you got it all wrong, feller," Joe told him, then looked up into the face of a giant shining in clothes like some race-track fashion plate. "It's just a mistake, feller, this boy overheard wrong is all."

"Let 'im go," the big man said with soft deliberation. His eyes shifted sneakily under the wide hatbrim; too much white showed under those umber pupils, like eyes inward and alone for too many years in a young life. "Leggo, I says."

Joe looked over to Stoney lighting his cigar, profile to the action, and wondered if the painter would come in on anything fierce. Then he matched the look he gave Buster with words: "I'll by God hold him till he's listenable, feller."

"You heard 'im yaself!" Magoo protested with real pain. "He said Lizzie, she's for anybody got a buck, you was the guy he tole it to yaself. Lemme go!" He looked entreatingly at the big man, who looked at neither of them, continuing to nod with a foolish smirk on his thick shapely lips.

"Stay cool, Magoo, just stay real cool. Maybe it's a mistake. Anyone can make a mistake. Right?" he said to Joe.

Joe let go and went toward Stoney, but the big man held him back. "You got to understand somethin," he said, clicking open a long blade. "I like things should stay cool; you got it? Real cool. It's why I freeze Magoo up like that. Things don't stay cool, I make them red-hot; you got it?" he watched the blade as he carved deftly at a celluloid block in his other hand.

Joe nodded and went up to Stoney; that toy-soldier nonsense could go on for hours if he participated. The painter gave him an exasperated scowl and motioned with his head for them to get away. But Joe looked toward the subway entrance on the corner of Waverly and stiffened. "Diane!" he shouted, and grabbed Stoney by the white lapels. "Where're the flowers? Where'd you leave the flowers?" shaking him, then letting go abruptly, running with Stoney close behind to where she stood waiting in furs and a sweeping black hat, in the pale light of the subway alcove, poised with an austerity that halted him.

It was Diane and yet it wasn't. It was a taller Diane, ghostly with an overlay of years. "Where is she?" the voice was too flatly high for Diane. "Is Diane somewhere near by? Answer me. I'm her mother and I want her."

Joe sighed, leaning heavily on the black guardrail. "Wish I knew where she was, ma'am. Sure wish I knew."

Stoney wished he'd lately trimmed his beard. Though his cigar glowed, he put new fire to it only to draw the lady's eyes away from his stained and wrinkled pants. He was disarmed by her dignity, touched by the delicacy of her face, reduced to muteness by the saintly voice.

"What do you want of her?" she demanded of Joe. "You men . . . why do you . . . Don't you have *any* decency? She's a child, she——"

"Ma'am," Joe cut in quietly, "I just want to hold her little hand is all. I know she's a little child right enough, and mean to let her know it."

"Then leave her alone." But she stopped on her first step down, came out of the staircase again. "If you find her . . . if you happen to see her, please say her mother . . . please say she has to come to her mother quickly, before it's too late." Her half-tone eyes shifted between them and rested on the painter. "If you're at all mature, believe me she's in trouble, she has to come to me quickly. Tell her, if you can find her."

Stoney was knotted up inside; the voice, the straight tragic look: she seemed a girl victimized by time while her back was turned. "Madam, I will find her and pass the information, be assured."

Joe took a chance. "Isn't she with her husband?" and waited breathlessly.

"Her husband! Carter? Is that what they're saying? Well, maybe they're saying that, but it's untrue, untrue! She's delinquent, delinquent, you hear? Oh! Can you find her?" She spun fiercely on Stoney. "Do you know where she might be while he's at work? Do you know all the dives?"

"Madam . . . I am the glans of Greenwich Village," and choked on cigar smoke, cursing himself for indelicacy: this was a lady, who made a junk shop of the bank whose windows backgrounded her in the alcove.

But she smiled and thanked him, then stabbed a gloved finger at Joe. "You leave her alone. I know *your* kind," and down to the subway she swept.

They walked in the silence of their own preoccupations down Waverly and for three blocks of MacDougal, until Joe declared: "That lady's nuts. Damn if she isn't. Least, I found out Diane's not married," but that did little to unburden him of the rest he'd learned.

"That lady," Stoney informed him, "is a sensitive and aware individual. So stately. She's got her troubles with the girl," and he stopped abruptly. "Does she wear a green coat, this Diane? Sleek sienna hair? Big earrings?"

"That's her, that's her."

"I know her, all right." Stoney rubbed his hairy cheek. "Absolutely a problem child, absolutely! Ah, that poor lady," and out of a stark sense of loyalty to the mother he kept himself from steering Joe away from the girl, even suggested that Joe could exercise his vitality on Diane to normalize her. He spoke as rapidly as he reasoned, so that by the time they reached the yellow-stone house on Bleecker

Street he was once again deprecating the background of the boy, calling his people gentle bastards who loved to be enslaved.

Joe turned away toward MacDougal. "Can't talk to you. You get carried away by yourself."

The painter cracked his knuckles. "Come upstairs, I want to start a new picture. Don't shout; where was I carried away?"

"This complete rejection of the unaware as worthless and evil," Joe said on the way up. "Man, I can't figure your mind. Maybe they let themselves be victimized, but when you blame them, when you refer to them as trash . . . well, now. Hell, man, they'll come out of it when they have to, when the bullshit they're bein fed begins to literally make their lives a burden. I can't make out your damn thinkin."

Stoney tore paper, stacked strips of wood, and got a fire started. The tenacity of illusions, he thought. They were a weird confusion in that good mind. The old story: American boy who won't hurt his parents by getting their feet off his neck. And here he was kicking the lad right in his guilt feeling. "You're probably right, Joe." The admission cleansed him, gave him a tenuous sense of magnanimity. He shed his coat and took up a brush, ran some black lines over the canvas, destroying the glaring white threat, blocking in a figure. "You take that girl and straighten her out, marry her." It warmed him to imagine the mother glowing with delight, where her face had been veiled with pale remorse. In bold strokes he'd arranged three heads on the figure whose one hand clawed aloft while the other reached downward toward a fruit bowl.

"Got to shake off this Carter guy," Joe muttered. "Aah, what's the use; that ole Lizzie bust me up worse than gunfire ever did, by God. Even so I ran things through my mind, damn near about decided it didn't matter . . . and then pitched over dead, just kept thinkin about them, my parents."

"Ah, you're a sentimental jerk." Stoney wiped the brush on a rag, dipped it in petroleum, wrung it dry and lighted his cigar. He dipped the brush again in the squid of black paint on the palette, ran two lines in an upper corner to pull the composition together, then cleaned the brush again.

Joe stalked to the window and back, pushing his hat forward, then back, on his head. "Robert, it isn't them, it isn't them at all. It's me, by God. It's in my guts to shy away from her. It's me by my natural

self, but I don't respect that part of me. In goddam deed I don't."
He moved, wagging his head, to the door.

"It's your folks all right," Stoney called. "You sap, they've made
that kind of mark on you. They've imposed that kind of perspective
on you."

"Yeah, I see what you mean." With his shoulders hunched, he
pulled open the door. "You—man, I don't reason you nohow. Sometimes you're incisive as a needle, other times you're just a discon-
tented old maid. I'll be along MacDougal huntin that little girl,"
and he was out, quietly shutting the door.

Stoney yanked the room dark and sat on the bed. What illusions,
he thought, use one's entrails for a battleground! He lay back in the
contorting firelit shadows, suddenly very cold, and pulled the bed
covers around himself. Who was Joe Letrigo and who was the girl
Diane? Not permanent things, not knowable as personalities, but
subject to each erratic tomorrow, subject to the mysterious resulting
force of their blending. And who was Louella Nordvahl? Who was
she without the silver cigarette holder, without her pitiable sophisti-
cation, without the great howling wind of her uncertainty, the fearful space in her emotions which she sought to fill even with artifice?
What was she, blended with Robert Stoney? It jarred against the
face of that mother, stately in furs between the subway and the
bank. To hell with Louella Nordvahl and everything about her! He
wrapped himself tighter.

"*Stoney!*" from outside. "*Stoney!*"

He crossed to the window and swung it open.

"Stoney!" Joe Letrigo looked up from the street, connected to his
shadow like a wild V on the snow. "I got you figured, Stoney. You're
just pro-anti!" and he hurried laughing down the street toward
MacDougal.

The figures that passed were as inanimate for Carter as the
trampled snow. Sounds made no mark on his consciousness, but
reached only a secondary level of his mind, like the glaring fluorescence that bleached the street. His thoughts were of Edna, who was
less than flesh in his imagining. She was a vague conception. It was
difficult to trace the development of their life together. He went
down into the subway, followed the mob through a turnstile, and
got a newspaper while he waited for the E train. The flat taste of

the hasty veal dinner he'd eaten lingered, and he worked a machine for chewing gum. The station stank of flesh, breath and dampness; nobody in the hundreds on the platform was smiling. The human race seemed cold and loveless—that was his thought. With it came a despairing pity for Edna—as he boarded the packed train—for that low temperature she'd always betrayed by affecting great heat, for the lovelessness that had made of their loving a mechanical thing measured by the clock. Through clenched teeth she'd inveighed against *control* that could be exhausted by repugnance.

Carter, closed in by people at the car's far end, stared at his newspaper, at words that wouldn't hold still for the rattling quiver of the train. The people wore one grim face—"*all of us the same be one with me and kiss . . .*" but he wouldn't, and he had to laugh now at himself made small by memory's inverted eye, lying there in stupid sweat, arguing about inhibition, and finally turning to his wife, but really out of it himself, and "*Daddy!*" *fabricated passion*, and then the great, gratuitous confession: *two three hundred men but only kisses only digit sometime dream*, but not she alone, *Diane that way too, through teeth* to form a cult out of a condition, to identify herself, in bursts of religious fervor, with the irritable Eighty Per Cent.

And yet a woman to whom he was responsible. He choked back a wish that she would die quickly, made himself wish well for her, yet his mind created stubborn images of her grave, of his air without her in it. He forced his thoughts to conjectures of the future, filling that afterlife with Diane, her faces and varying smiles and the voice that was like a bath in oil. It was a vague and fleshless relationship he dreamed about, free of the bewildered and anxious Diane he knew, had more the character of that moment at dawn, with Diane asleep in his embrace like a child secure in her father's arms. At peace, and insight had grown with the light in the room, making a mockery of all the moral stains upon her.

He read of a kidnaping that turned out to be an elopement, happy faces, toothy grins; then about a robbery at a Thirty-eighth Street check-cashing service, eight o'clock, two men dressed alike, white mufflers over face, black coats, fifteen hundred dollars, disappeared from neighborhood by time police arrived. Thirty-eighth Street . . . eight o'clock A.M. . . . *somethin waitin outside; right, Red?* and Carter could only laugh. They did the job and made for the subway; straight for the criminal-court sanctuary, better than a church. Probably got rid of the white mufflers in a subway trash can. Possibly Dincher let Red go alone to court, inviolable in his prior guilt. Picturing the holdup scene, Carter imagined Wengel in the role of victim, greasy-jowled, bug-eyed and shaking like anyone here in the subway as he stared down the barrel of the gun. Carter thought he might direct Dincher to the real Wengel and have him steal the old man's teeth.

Just to put him on the other end of the gun for once, for Wengel was of that strange department of the human tribe which lacked the faculty to imagine themselves in the position of others, lacked it just as some of the fat man's victims lacked eyes. And just to crack for a moment the frustrating self-importance in his nasal voice: "It's a big difference from last year, no? This place it ain't like the one floor on Forty-first; ain't it? *Yahahakh!*" The same smug tones he'd use talking of something as impersonal as a shoelace.

Carter still trembled with irritation at the way Wengel had motioned him into a chair with his pudgy white hand. Like a command. Seated pompously at that oversize desk, backed by a wall of shutter-type windows. It was a kind of pleasure now to see the gnarled hands of workers in the crowded car, and he strained his attention on the paper in his own hands, but Wengel remained, his voice wheezing louder than the rattle of cars.

"It was a plenty tough fight, don't fool yourself. Twelve years old I was when I came from the olcountry. In a furrier's shop I worked, no windows, four-teen hours a day, don't fool yourself." He lighted a cigar too long even for his wide face, leaned back too comfortably for any man at work. "Now I got it. You know I'm worth in seven figures? *Yahagh!* Seven figures, yes sir, my young man. You realize what this means? This means I can do anything I want. This is freedom you could never have in the olcountry. Freedom, you got to work for it. You got to suffer hard a good many years, you got to fight."

Carter had seen him then as one of Merwin's never-sent-in-the-air kids, one of those with *extra ambition like a go-getter,* not the embittered, disinherited kind Merwin had illustrated with Maxie Scar, not one of the criminals. Going a little farther in his simplification of things, Merwin could easily have created an economic-sociological picture based on his out-to-play-in-the-air theory with a clean half of the underprivileged children growing up to be lawbreaking terrorists while the remainder developed into law-abiding economic swine incapable of understanding the hardships of their victims. Of course that left those with a childhood playing-in-the-air as victims caught between both categories. "You're a fortunate man," Carter had said. Wengel leaned forward too quickly for so bulky a man. "Don't fool yourself. It ain't luck, it's work. You think you get anything in this world waiting for good fortune? Not on your life, my young man. Nothing comes from heaven but rain. *Yahaghee!* That's pretty good, nothing but rain comes from heaven." His eyes rolled up out of focus and he bared his teeth, sucking air into himself as he leaned back with sudden seriousness. "You know all the churchgoing and praying?" he asked softly. "Take it or leave it, I give you a tip. If you want to make good, if you want freedom—but the real McCoy freedom—forget all that business about heaven and hell, forget about it, leave it for the chain gang. You know the chain gang, they got no gray matter, just muscles, that's how they're born that way, to work, to work with the muscles all their lives. Leave it to them and don't never take it away from them; you hear? You know why? I'll tell you why. They need it. It gives them peace. It gives them—what you call it?—it's their conscience. Can you ee-magine what they could do if not for God? Look, I'm worth in seven figures; you get it? But it's all on paper. You understand that, it's ink on paper. That chain gang, there's millions and millions and millions of them. If not for God, what keeps them from tearing up the paper?" He sat up straight, tucked the cigar into a patient smile and spread his hands, inviting comment.

Carter had to say, "Thank heaven for God," eying the floor.

"Right. You can thank heaven. But don't fool yourself, don't wait for good luck. You got to go out and take, because—you got to re-member—there . . . ain't . . . no . . . God." His voice tapered away to a whisper. "But keep it to yourself, do like the big shots and remind them all the time about God and never, never take it away from the chain gang or they'll take away your freedom before you get it—*yahahahakh-kagh-kagh*—before you even *kagh* get it, they'll take it away. Oh boy."

Carter's eyelids grew heavy and that old swift weariness kept air out of his chest. He could manage no adequate hatred of the man. Wengel's personality represented for him a kind of tragedy rather than an affront: just as Merwin had dispelled blame of Maxie Scar with an understanding of his origin, he couldn't help seeing that Wengel, dissolute and stupid, had been forged by circumstances. Now, watching the train lose passengers at Queens Plaza, he asked himself whom he could blame. Whom on earth could he ever despise? There was something distantly frightening about it, and it rolled up into nausea; he got rid of the chewing gum gone sour.

After discharging passengers at the Queens stations the train gained air, and in it Carter could laugh a bit over the way Wengel's face went dead when the consignment contract was rejected. He'd rapidly recovered, however, to give Carter fifty cans of uncut bulk film at a fair price, along with the name of an exporter who needed part of it. The rest would be wanted by other jobbers, and Carter couldn't understand the act of kindness till he spoke to Marge in the outer office. Wengel had said, "Don't let the jobbers cut price on you; fix the price and make them respect it. Don't let them break your heart, don't pay anything out of your pocket you don't have to pay. Not a lousy dime."

Carter, still dazed by the gesture, had murmured, "You're like a father to me, Mr. Wengel."

The man whispered, holding him in the doorway. "That's it, that's just it, like a father, don't fool yourself. Nobody looks at it that way. Nobody understands me like I'm a father to them. You know who? Merwin, he knows. He's like you, not an extra word out of him. He listens when I tell him. He knows."

"He sure does; he really understands you, Mr. Wengel. Don't fool yourself."

When the complacent nod came and the door closed, he hurried over to Marge to assure her he'd said nothing to the old man about what she'd told the other day. She smiled securely, said she hadn't worried at all, and let him know at last why he'd been given the uncut bulk. "You know what he's after? He wants your kit. Don't let him fool you with his big heart. He's been storming around ever since he took this whole building, he's been screaming that he's losing a fortune letting you process the film he sells. Watch out, Mr. Webb, he'll trick you."

Wengel came out before Carter could thank her for information he already had but seldom related to single events. They went out together, and by the elevators Wengel grinned enigmatically and scrutinized him slowly from head to foot. "While the cat's away, eh? She likes you, I can see that."

"She's a nice girl," Carter said, leaning on the elevator button.

With his hands Wengel traced his conception of the woman's figure. "Me, I don't bother with her like that. I don't crap where I eat," and he stretched the fat of his neck in laughter, shaking Carter's arm a little. "But I'll take mine," he wheezed, "don't fool yourself. You got something extra, bring it around, it'll pay off. My wife ain't dead twenny years for nothing."

Down in the elevator Carter hated himself for extending a smile at that, yet pitied the old man for the dirt of which his life was made. It was nothing as contemptuous as pity that he felt for the man's workers, it was a deep and lurching pain. He took a cab downtown and had a talk in a bare old hall with a union secretary, who promised to put a delegate on the case. There had been a sharp relief in that, and now it showed again in his chest when he left the subway at Parsons Boulevard and caught the blast of cold air.

Boarding the orange bus, he thought about Wengel and Mrs. Lattimer and Stoney the painter and older people in general. There seemed an age in an individual's development when his view of things became fixed and exclusive, when his own peculiar taste became his judging device for all good and bad; "The age of mental petrifaction," he muttered. Perhaps it was the point at which they began to crumble spiritually toward physical death, decaying each after his own manner, but all withering by curse of the same odious subjectivity. And, considering his own occasional uncertainties, it occurred to him that the mind matured at a slower rate than the body. Mentally, people were too young or too old.

The bus turned through gray streets quiet under snow, and eventually pulled up before the clean new hospital, which lay as though flung out across its space, eight stories of porches neatly circling the building in modern line, like the decks of some foundered ocean liner. He was repelled by the muted lights in the hedge-lined hospital driveway, the snowpainted grounds. He could easily have turned and run forever, in any direction at all.

Inside, the lighting was a brilliant antitoxic symbol, like the starched white uniforms that crisscrossed impersonally all over the vast lobby. Carter went in line to the elevator with his visitor's pass ready for the operator's inspection. Up in the packed, silent car, which was filled more strongly with the insolent odors of ether and medication with each floor they passed. On the sixth he stepped out onto scrubbed, disinfected linoleum, into the mute and endless corridor he had followed fifty times, through an atmosphere esoteric and horrifying with its meaning and smells and stiff-backed nurses. Visitors—self-conscious, gift-laden, bereaved, excited, frightened— dropped off into the heavy-doored rooms on either side of the corridor. Carter felt empty-handed; he stopped a moment outside Edna's room, wishing he'd brought some little thing. He heard a voice, absurdly delicate—Mrs. Lattimer! What was she doing here on Tuesday? He heard her say "Diane" and winced. He took a step away, stopped and turned to face the finger of light from the door, while Diane's voice moaned through his sudden nausea and fatigue, telling him of people just not born to freedom, and the faces of the blind and helpless blurred his eyes as he entered the room.

There was no awareness of place or moment. Only a spaceless awakening in endless, black, rolling gloom. Not even a certainty of self. Values, in the darkness, had no conditions out of which to grow, and only fear cavorted, fantasy prevailed. Yet self, with neither name nor features, suspended its search for identity—for the time it took muscle and tissue to reach a point of comfort. In stretching, Diane rolled over, buried her face deep in cool pillows, and through her nostrils an image of Carter blossomed. Orientation began: she wanted light.

She groped, found the night lamp and turned it on. Slowly the fear lingering in her stomach quit bobbing; she felt at home among Carter's things: some clothes abandoned on a tan-leather chair under the Degas dancer, the long gray-wood dresser near the door and his squat chiffonier leaning ponderously toward her in the distorted perspective of her position on the bed. Safety and ease were with Carter, home was where his things were.

But where was the man? Seven o'clock, she saw by the night-table clock. She sat up, wondering why he couldn't come in right then, wanting her as she was, supple with the warmth of sleep. "Carter!" she called. "Carter!" hoping he might be in another room. But nothing stirred outside. There were only the rolling shadows in the long hallway. Why did he stay away, wasting moments that could burn red? Then she remembered: the hospital . . . Edna. Edna had always been first. And now, though she had no way of really using him, she kept him bound with crazy laws. Carter—Carter, he was blinded by it all; the laws, the narrow, sticky paths people had to follow: walk down the straight cold road, forget yourself and walk, forget your heart and walk straight so that you don't upset the other straight walkers who like to walk straight, who can easily afford to walk straight because they were led by the hand down clean straight paths. . . . Carter, Carter, what waste!

She knew he'd arrive home ready to collapse in bed. Up before dawn, unable to sleep, he'd probably tripped over the tangled undergrowths all over the straight road of his day. She got to her feet and pulled the sheets tight on the bed, tidied the covers, turning down the corner on Carter's side. The other side, the part she'd been using, belonged to Edna, who might die and never breathe again, never talk, make no more sounds, not feel anything . . . and never again care. Her face would wrinkle up like poor Lukey's, and Lukey too might die suddenly, not knowing he lay rotting to dust as he laughed, no more aware than Edna. And Diane and Carter and even Johnny . . . she had a creeping fear that all of them were dying away while moments hurtled out of the sun, changed from gold to ashes.

She ran across the rug to the dresser and searched in her purse for the reefers Lukey had given her, lighted one, watched in the mirror the evil face she made puffing on the narrow shaft. It tasted just bad enough to give a tingling sense of vice, just a little vice, enough to run a ripple through the muddy flatness of life. She wondered how Joe Letrigo would react to marijuana, to her smoking it. His corny ideals would pull him even a little farther away. Joe Letrigo the choir boy . . . gone to pieces, pouted when he was told the lie. Whatever could have made Lizzie give that song and dance? Whore! But she had not denied it because whoredom and freedom in love were the same in women as far as those virginmotherlovers cared to reason. Now it scratched in her stomach while the Tea scratched her throat: was it the same? Did Carter, the Carter who had rejected her as a woman, think her dirty as Joe did? The idea, fat with Tea, electrified her, then looped over the gauge to rest in marijuana's solid reasoning: Carter was more than just a mouth full of words like everybody's mouth going with words like priests and kings and congressmen with words and no understanding, like Joe Letrigo and equality short of all the way: Carter understood everybody right down to why one life differed from the next. It was Edna working on his guts because Carter was sensitive and honest at the same time, so his were easy guts to work on. That was it and only that why Edna had really hustled still Carter went and smiling married her yet Edna working on his guts . . . and now she could feel his guts in her own quivering insides.

Insides alarmed now that Joe could back away. And Carter wanted none of her. She looked quickly at the glass to see the body neither one needed, the smooth soft skin others had fought over—then with sudden fright she turned sideways to see if something mysterious might have happened in some crazy unwatched instant to make her breasts sag or wrinkle her skin. The relief was as piercing as the shock of fear: everything was in order, tight and smooth.

She finished the marijuana roach and fell to her back on the bed, letting her feet dangle over the side from legs stretched rubberlike by the jive, laughing at the feel of rubber limbs, then wondering what it would be like to be homely, to be really wanted not a bit, not at all, nohow. In this insanely stupid world where a woman's only power was in her body. It would be pleading and whining as it was with Carter, and trembling empty pride as it had been with Joe, and stone-cold spaces in the stomach as it had been with both. A horror spun with the jive in her head, and she lurched erect, fingered the sure velvet of her nakedness: homely, it would be emptier, even more a vacuum.

She moved catlike to the bathroom, like a Letrigo panther, panther unblack from the South without the hate/fear of black that blacks the soul yet spotted black like a leopard not panther with another fear/hate of no maidenhead women stained out of sunlight and air. "Oh Christ," she laughed, sitting there, "the big rough man from Dixie. His mama never got laid . . . only his papa," and laughed hard till the Tea welled thick in her head and the mind freed itself of the fusing patterns of recent events; throat thick and sweet: she swallowed sensually and leaned back that way letting her eyes absorb the yellow peace of tile and porcelain while her mind detached itself from her gravitated flesh to hover somewhere above her head, free of obligation to that flesh, free of the demands and wants of womanhood, just rolling with the moment through the space that sang in her ears; with her heart buoyed up to join her mind: she hummed a deep-throated blues, felt it churn through her veins with the blood, "Oh mammy's so evil. . . ." A laugh escaped her as she stood up, and, still laughing, she found a key and a five-dollar bill on the basin. "Good Carter," she said, "good Daddyman."

These words she took into the song she'd been humming, into the shower stall past glass and chrome, the nice things in life, and under the tepid flow, still humming, occasionally singing "Daddy, daddy, daddy," she trembled to the exaggerated tingle of water striking stimulated nerves. Leaned back against the tile, strange hands pressed soap around her breasts, down her belly to the sharp hips and her thighs her own, and she tried to imagine how Carter could refuse giving himself to her. Water stung into her; soaping rhythmically, she closed her eyes and lost herself in a song which had always somehow quieted those icicles of fear that came into her stomach from nowhere:

> "I'm an easy-rider woman, never
> Do no one man no good.
> Ah'm an easy-rider woman,
> Ne-e-ver do no one man no good.
> But don't you backbite me Daddy,
> You'd be the same way if you could."

And soaped and rinsed like in a pretty dream, and lost to strange hands till she trembled clean of all the yesterdays, and light and sort of newborn. Dressing and making up were rhythmic with distant, removed and automatic motions, hands danced by eyes like delicate ballerinas. Smoked more Tea to keep alive in her head the musical cloud that kept troubles from being pointed, and let them drift out of her mind like exhaled air to make room for easier thoughts, soaring and turning into one another like oboe music. Inside she was a solid smile, smiling through the snapping air, onto the bus the Calvert poster said someone had switched to Calvert Lukey the Swede has switched to hashish, laughing, bouncing, a man was King Solomon on the bus, telling everybody *I'm King Solomon,* everybody tight-lipped avoiding him with personal eyes, *I'm King Solomon, you think all I have to do is settle your arguments? I have a whole land to govern and take care of,* nobody looked, tight-lipped, he might not even have been there, *To me money is no object . . . I'm a Mason,* popped her out with laughter, she laughed alone, the man raved alone, people tight-lipped alone inside, *I got a hospital here it's my hospital,* King Solomon on his feet proclaimed, *three operations I got here tonight, I got no time for arguments, three I got in my hosp*—King Solomon was out talking to the Seventh Avenue air, unaffected by the change of audience, and Diane smiled and thought and told herself the man was chief of surgery at Travelers' Hospital, for all the world was run by madmen.

By the Cosmopole's bloodless light Magoo the Newsboy, beside the boarded-up old newsstand, shouted over the pile of newsprint at his feet, shouted like an outraged man for help: "*Mizhendy* GUILTY! W*oil*' SHOCKED!" and dug in his pocket for something he handed to the Swede, "CAPIDDLE ALARMED! Read aBODdit!" and Lukey, with his grinning wrinkled face, found Diane.

"Baby, you want to come? Bound for Paddy's trap and you right on time to fall in with me for the ball."

She was about to take his arm when Dincher came out of the cafeteria, straight for the Swede with no look at Diane. "You got it, Lukey'n they waitin for it. Don' take her nowhere," and took her wrist without a shift of his eye. And all the lights ran round in her head, all the faces were white as snow.

"That was dynamite you gave me the other night, Luke," she murmured, and the Swede did a happy little shuffle, patted Dincher on the head and mixed with the passing people. Magoo screamed hoarsely for attention into a night hoarse with traffic sounds and irrelevant voices, distant squeaks.

"You wanna get on—" Dincher eyed her now—"you get on wit me."

She kissed her laugh into his cheek and said, "Let's go."

"You popped outta your noodle awready," the boy lamented. "Like-why doncha wait for me, doll? Like-it's the way to smoke jive —wit your own-like."

She could only say, "Come on, Dinch;" all else was a gummy knot of song in her; she pulled him by the arm.

Now he grinned. "I gotta get over somewhere-like, dollbaby. Maybe I get back soon, but maybe like-I get detained. Go inside'n stick wit Buster till I'm back; awright? Till I get back, doll," with both her hands in his.

"I don't like him, Dinch; he looks to——"

"Buster? Nah, not you. Like-you, to him you're like a kid; you know?"

Diane had to laugh at that, but she kept it inside. The street was suddenly too alive for her: gauge got you busy like that. With some kind of word or gesture they parted, and she was through the revolving door, in among the droning groups, with no solid recollection of any good-by.

Over on the side, directly under a mural in which healthy men and women poured fruit from their horn of plenty, Buster Wallinger sat carving a celluloid ring with his long sharp blade. That knife had entered flesh a number of frantic times, she'd heard; it was as much a part of the man as his thick fingers or the brooding eyes deep and dead in the mass of his face. Buster had always wanted Edna, had made half-passes at Diane herself, but both sisters had withheld themselves, sometimes out of revulsion, usually out of fear of his tremendous size, and not infrequently out of a sadistic thrill they derived in frustrating so powerful a man. Yet in sharpened moments of futility, when purposeless days piled up before her like bricks of an enclosing, suffocating wall, Diane had thought about this man and wanted him to tear the breath out of her with his animality. Now she sat across from him, feeling the hunger in his eyes ride down her spine on an emotion magnified by the marijuana.

"Hello, beautiful," he said with a flicker of a grin. "Glad to see you. Where you been keepin yaself so long?" His teeth had a menacing power behind the heavy lips; a shudder pushed words out as they were thought.

"My mother had me in the slammer." His laughter rattled around the place. "Don't laugh so loud, Buster. I'm hot—I busted out."

"Well, what the hell you doin in this joint? Jeez, this is no place for you. Come on," and he stood up, snapping the knife shut, reaching for his heavy black coat. He was uncommonly well dressed, she saw through the shimmying veil of Tea, and it seemed that he moved more confidently than he ever had before.

"But I'm hungry," she said. "Hold up a minute."

"Well, come on; this is no place. I take you down the street."

Marijuana was a sensitive wire from her to everything outside, and she decided it was urgent not to wait around, not for Dincher or anything else. It was a rubber-leg dance around tables to the air, fixing her kerchief, dodging walkers in the street. Magoo screamed that someone was at war with religion, and she waited while Buster said something in the newsboy's ear. The big man's clothes were more than clean and neat; they were well made, soft with an expensive look. "What did you do?" she said, going with him into the whiter light of Eighth. "Buster, what did you do, knock over a bank or something?"

"Whatta you mean, bank?" He kept his eyes straight ahead, like an official in some parade.

"Your clothes. You're wearing real money."

He grinned, leading her by the arm around a Salvation Army band grouping for action on the corner of MacDougal, across out of the clashing neon toward the Limelight Inn, where uptowners and out-of-towners came to go native in the Village and where Villagers who found themselves with a five-dollar bill and a gracious mood went to be cosmopolitan. "Yeah, I got some new connections, beautiful." He brought the dead sorrow of those eyes down on her. "You beautiful now like a lady, and I got connections. Evvybody's growin up. I could set you up like gangbusters any time you're ready."

Carter leaned on the bathroom door while dizziness faded and the burning went out of his eyes on tears. Christ! Her own mother. Mrs. Lattimer had come here to bring Edna something more to suffer over—"Diane is sleeping with him! She is!" with her neck stretched arrogantly in light that bled her of color, showing fine, barely visible lines in the gray translucence of her skin, like signs of irrevocable waste. And he'd allowed himself to be sucked into a trade of futile words, denying that Diane was living with him, accusing Vivienne of destroying her daughters, wanting to stop but hurtling on as though he were only an instrument for old feelings grown uncontrollable; gagging up the rancid flavor of his dinner, swallowing it back burning in his throat. Edna, with a tremor in her voice and madness in her eyes, had joined her mother in accusing him, and the pitiable sight of her had made him feel wretchedly insensitive. So he'd finally gone silent, letting Vivienne go on with her distortions of morality— "Beasts! Nothing matters but your bodies! Lustful, indelicate animals!"—until her superficial austerity shielded too little from him, and he could see the grease and smell the odors that her imagination made of human relations. He had dashed to the bathroom, where all his sleepless dawns and business agonies and insipid overcooked dinners had finally joined in the nausea that bubbled out of him.

Now he splashed cold water on his face, then dried himself and listened at the door, with Vivienne's grimacing image covering his brain like a film. He heard no voices, but granted himself a little time more to hide away just in case the woman was still outside. Finally he went out—she was still there, stooped over her daughter's wheel chair, kissing her, muttering maudlin comforts in her special churchy voice. She gave him an ugly look and folded her arms to say, "I'll find Diane," with a snide grin. "I have the—some official of the Village after her. Husband and wife!" she added irrelevantly in the doorway, and departed with a sweep.

Carter was alone with his wife, the stranger, the burden. Her nostrils quivered; she looked old wearing the formless hospital shirt and huddled with blankets in the chrome chair. He'd brought her several pairs of pajamas, colorful ones to cheer her, but on visiting days she wore only the hospital blues.

Her beadlike eyes were fast upon him—he couldn't stand the silence. "I threw up," he said.

"You threw up your guilt."

"You believe her? You think it's Diane?"

Edna jerked her head toward him. "You bastard, you just gave yourself away. Do I think it's Diane! It. The one. Do I think the woman you're keeping is Diane! Don't try to crawl out of it, you pig. You disgusting liar!"

He could see those gears spinning and grinding. Her eyes flickered, her nostrils dilated, there was a twitch in her lip he'd never seen before. "Edna," he began. "Edna," he said again. But nothing he might say would ease those sour suspicions: she saw his behavior through the dirty glass of her own experience, saw his compulsions as mirrors of her own.

"Go on, say it. I can take it. I've been preparing myself for it. I've known the words you would use if you ever became honest enough." She laughed, but it was only a sound—her face remained unaltered. "I know the words better than you do. 'Edna, there's something,' then the pause. Not right after 'Edna.' Then, 'Edna, I don't want to hurt you, but,' and another pause. Go on, I've said that much for you. Go ahead, I can take it." A smile was frozen on her lips; tears trickled out of black eyes that were unsmiling.

"Listen, Edna." She looked insane; she seemed to be looking forward with some perverted kind of delight to being stung by him. "There's nobody. I swear it. Why do you insist on thinking that all there is in life is sex?"

She stared out into the black night. "What else is there?"

"Don't you realize I work late, I'm always tired? The farthest thing from my mind these days . . ." It was useless. Her eyes were like a sheet of black glass that stood between them.

"Carter—" looking through him—"you needn't go to all this trouble convincing me. I don't expect you to go without. Just don't lie. Tell them . . . tell them when you sleep with them that I know, that I told you it's all right. But stop lying, I can't stand it any more."

Carter paced around, shaking his head. The girl was mad, a withered creature he'd never been related to.

"There's a doctor here," she said in a distant and unfamiliar tone, "whom you ought to meet. He's very—well, civilized, I guess. You'd like him; he's soft-spoken . . . like you were once."

Carter drew up the white-porcelain stool and sat before her, sighed some of the weight out of his chest. "Now this is getting more like a visit. What sort of doctor is he?"

"Young." She grinned. "And understanding, so gentle and concerned. He brings me things to read; he brought me that Proust on the bed table," as if it were a new book Carter had never seen before. "Carter—" she looked up at him with her mother's fixed complacency—"I intend to have an affair with him." It was the kind of gratuitous candor so frequently assumed as disguise by the inherently dishonest, a threadbare deception for him after such long wear.

"Oh, is that it?" just to offer comment. Let her have what was left to be had. This formless creature who was a neuter sorrow to him, whom he must still address as wife—let her have whatever she could find.

"Who knows how long I'll be an invalid, Carter? Would it be wrong, wouldn't it be dishonest not to?"

"If I said it's okay with me . . ." *you'd wail that I don't care enough* ". . . it wouldn't be true. I don't want you sleeping with other men." *So go do what you want.*

"Oh, goddam you, you're stuffy. You're a smug bastard like the rest of them. It's all right for you, for men to screw around, but not for women."

"Aah, people do what they want, men or women. I never fooled around because I didn't want to, that's all, and that's the way the ball bounces."

"Well, I want to do it." She leaned close to him.

Shifting, he said, "Then go ahead, but don't be asking me to okay it."

She bit at her thumbnail to hide a smile growing through the anger in her face. "You and your phony purity. Just remember, Carter, you're not fooling me. I know you too well to believe you're being a monk for me," and a chime sounded in the hallway like some omen she'd provoked. "Carter . . . kiss me before you go." She clung to him when he stooped over. He made contact with clay. "And Carter . . . tell them I wanted you to, allowed it."

One more weary time. "There isn't anyone, Edna."

She kissed him again with exaggerated passion. "I wish I could believe you." The flesh of her cheek under his eye was a growing expanse of putty that made a horror of their intimacy; he kept himself from recoiling. "How can I believe you, Carter? How, how?" reluctantly letting him up.

"Just leave yourself alone."

"But Diane. I *always* knew about you and Diane. How can I believe——"

"Diane and me! She's a little girl to sit on my knee. If you must worry, wait'll she grows up," and felt dirty for advising her to wait, to wait.

Edna smiled, blinking toward the night outside while Carter slipped into his coat. "I wish the weather were warm again. Then I could be out on the porch to wave good-by till you're out of sight. Like we did last month." He didn't remind her it had been four months. "We were closer then, Daddy."

And cornier. "Spring's about due; we'll do it again."

She turned to him. "Come early on Sunday, Carter. I'll have something to tell you . . . about Dr. Morris and me."

"Have fun," he muttered, walking out.

Like a blind buddha behind the white gleam of glasses, Dr. Scarborough stood waiting outside the door. "I didn't want to miss you, Mr. Webb." His small set line of a mouth closed for an instant in punctuation, parted in a hasty smile, then formed a line again before he spoke. "Will you come to the office, please? There is something

—uh—there are some things." The flash of a smile, and he turned, a compact little figure steady down the hallway.

It would be certain now; it was going to be stated conclusively, and Carter felt a constriction pulling inward on the walls of his chest. Edna was doomed; this was her doom in focus, brought to a point, stated, signed. He clenched his pocketed fists; the word would be uttered and it would ring like a signal to a hangman, crack the air and hover with a clarity sharpened by its utter finality. *Your mother is dead*, a voice faint for its journey through years reminded him of mourning, and mourning was the only tragedy in this new death. A parenthetic flash hissed in his brain: *there is freedom too in this death!* He swallowed hard, as though swallowing could repress that guilty glimmer of hopefulness.

Dr. Scarborough offered Carter a hard seat in front of his desk, flashed his blind smile, and relaxed into his chair with the burden of what he had to say—and the burden of all such moments—heavy on his face. Carter felt a bloom of sympathy for the man, decided to make it as easy for him as possible.

Dr. Scarborough closed his smile and said in a peculiarly level tone, "I want to confirm the tentative diagnosis of——"

"Sclerosis." Carter nodded. "It's Amyotrophic Lateral Sclerosis. Yes. Okay, Doctor, that's that."

"Yes, Mr. Webb." The man kept his eyes on Carter.

"Will it be—will it become painful? Will she . . . ?"

"Not really painful in the sense we understand pain." The smile, the regrouping of features. "The debility will develop over a period of several months, you see. Toward the end, when she—when it is necessary for her to remain in bed—" he offered his kindly gesture of a smile and a cryptic sort of shrug—"there is no reason to believe she will suffer sharp pain," and again the smile, the turning up of lip ends.

Carter felt sorry for the doctor's mouth; all the rest of the man was conditioned to tragedy, but his mouth remained obligated to console. Carter kept his eyes on the green desk blotter, wished he could convince the man it was unnecessary to smile. "Will she remain here till it's all over?"

"It would be the sensible thing. Your hospital insurance will continue to cover the attention she'll need; having her at home would prove too great a burden on you."

"Yes, that's reasonable," and for reasonableness alone he felt deeply indebted to the compact little man, kept himself tight to keep from uttering any sentiment bloated in him by the situation.

"Of course, Mr. Webb, you'll have to carry the same expenses you've been carrying: the psychiatric work and everything hospitalization doesn't cover. She'll need psychotherapy more and more, I'm afraid."

"I should imagine so." He looked up: the smile shot into being to meet his glance, then passed away. "Doctor, how is she? You know, mentally."

A slow, thoughtful shake of the head. "Not very well, Mr. Webb. I'm afraid she's not very well at all. Quite disturbed. According to Dr. Morris, there are marked paranoic symptoms. That doesn't mean she's insane, you understand, but there are marked symptoms. Quite capable of reasoning, of course, and very normal behavior, as you can see yourself, but seriously disturbed by more than this disease. Dr. Morris stays close by her, gives her greater comfort than she imagines. Yes, that must continue. Yes."

Carter realized then he was draped half across the desk, and pulled himself erect. "Doesn't she know he's a psychiatrist?"

The smile and the tiny headshake. "No, Mr. Webb. I imagine it might seem somewhat insidious, but it's quite necessary in her case. There isn't much point in any real analysis, is there? Dr. Morris' relationship to her is that of a trusted friend, much more therapeutic than that of a professional. Quite ethical, of course," he hastened to assure.

"Okay, Doctor—" getting up—"unless there's anything more . . ."

"No, that about covers things, Mr. Webb." He stood and reached for Carter's hand. "Just one thing more, yes. You may find it difficult to sleep the next few nights. These things have a curious way of setting in slowly, you know," and he softened it with that localized dart of a grin. "Take one of these before bed the next few nights, Mr. Webb."

Carter pocketed a vial of pills, shook the man's hand once more, and took himself out into the horrible ether-ridden quiet of the hall. The lighting had been subdued, the play was over, the audience was filing out, deeply moved. In the elevator he found himself shaken with a multiplying sense of dread; new doorways to horror kept opening in his mind. His stomach vibrated hollowly; there was an acrid heat running from his throat up through his nostrils, pushing his thoughts into the gray impossible air of graves. And Edna rode through every organ of his being, a thing of clay and tears.

Then winter knifed into his lungs; with difficulty he kept himself from rubbing his face with the snow billowing on the hedges, and walked quickly to the outer gate, where he found a last remaining taxicab. He gave the driver an address in Great Plains, then pushed himself into a corner and shut his eyes as the cab groaned away.

And that was the way the ball bounced. Normie and his wife would scold him for having stayed away so long; then they'd wrap him in warmth, in their solid kind of benevolence, and the night would pass. He hoped Diane would move with care through the jungle of faces and sounds . . . and words, anxious laughter . . . and words and awkward movements. He felt sleep lower its fog, and in that twilight of consciousness he thought of days overlapping days, stitched together by vague hopes and faceless wants that discounted the hours suffered through: it was only the unknowability of tomorrow, its unseen shape, that gave blood to patience, and fortitude was a greater human truth than any arbitrary faith. Edna, poor lacerated soul, have faith, have it in your mother, in her God—faith is for the doomed.

Food had worn the lift of marijuana out of Diane by the time they were drifting through the smoke-and-beer atmosphere of the MacDougal Street haunts. Buster's swaggering dullness assailed her head and neck along with the postnarcotic letdown, and she had him take a table under the wall of caricatures at the Ninevah Tavern while she went to the ladies' room to smoke her tension to a zero. Zero was the word for Buster, she decided in a stall, lighting a cigarette as well as the jive in her other hand, just to cut the powerful burned-gauge odor . . . as she'd cut the big man's bluster all through the meal. "Don't put on a show for these squares," she'd insisted when he protested, squall-voiced, over her choice of meat loaf rather than steak. "I'm paying my own, Buster. I'm not selling any shares."

His face began to tighten up, but he softened it with a grin. "You'll eat them words someday, beautiful."

When she said, "Stop acting like Humphrey Bogart, you're too big," he pouted, bobbing his bear's head till a strand of hair fell across his face from the shiny pompadour. He crawled out of childish embarrassment by bragging about his hotel suite, his car, his secret business on Long Island in the morning. That had struck a quick familiar note: the baby was somewhere on the Island. "The Marietta Hotel?" she wheedled. "Boy, you're riding, Buster." He blinked with clumsy modesty. "What's on Long Island? Could I go there with you?"

Buster grinned, then suddenly went grim in the face, as if someone were whispering reminders in his ear. "Nah, this is on ice; no visitors allowed," and determinedly snapped open his blade.

She laughed now, coughing up a sip of jive: Buster, in his way, was a man of strict conscience, so much so that he'd gone scornful at the first bad word about her mother. Half high, she laughed, thinking of it. "Couldn't you take me there?" she had pleaded. "I might be able to see my kid if you take me."

"Whatta you mean? What's your kid doin on the Island?"

"It's my goddam mother. The witch adopted him out."

"Heyyyy, don't say that about your mother."

"I don't even know where he is out there, but maybe I could find out and get to see him. Couldn't you take me there, Buster?"

"Maybe I could. I just can't take you where I'm goin. It ain't too far out, neither, so I could take you if the kid ain't too far out. How can you find out where?"

"I'll have to get it out of the old lady. It's like visiting in a lion's cage, but I might figure something out. It won't be easy to con *that* old bitch."

He frowned fiercely. "Hey, that's no way to talk about your mother!"

"Are you kidding? She's a monster, that woman."

"Well, she's your own mother anyway!"

Now, smoking hemp, she let out the laughter she'd choked back with food. She had asked about his mother, and he'd lamented her early passing so dramatically that she could imagine that seven-foot hulk in velvet knee pants. "Maybe I'd of turned out different if I had a mother. Maybe I'd of kept out of all the jackpots I been in. You should never talk bad about mothers," sadly folding his knife and pocketing it.

She'd made a mistake asking about his father, because color turned to grayness in his flat face and his fingers stretched, quivered, and closed around an imaginary throat, their hairs spreading like independent little insects. He'd told a story, chaotic with his sputtering, about a drunken shoemaker, wifebeater, rapist, murderer, till he lost control of his eyes. It was soap-opera stuff alive before her, and the man was mobile danger, a threat of destruction that was subject to his dubious moods and any outside circumstance that happened to cross them. The shock of alarm that had sliced through her before reared again now as she took the last sip of marijuana, and she told herself never, in all the time she might know the man, to refer his brutally simple thoughts to anything in his background. Some girls in the long tiled room eyed her suspiciously, but, fortified with gauge, she knew they were awe-struck, if they'd really smelled it, rather than contemptuous. She returned to the wordy, jangling room of drinkers, squeezed past tables toward Buster.

Dincher was seated across from Buster, and they were whispering, leaning close toward each other. "Dincher!" she interrupted, taking a seat beside him. "What are you plotting with this—" she remembered Long Island—"with Buster?"

Dincher slipped a hand under her hair and held her neck; his eyes searched a moment before finding hers. "Doll," he chuckled, "doll-baby, like-what'll you drink on the Dinch? Want to eat? Like-you wanna go someplace and get on?"

"Dinch, you're popped out." It had begun as reproof, but she tied a smile to it, remembering that she was just as high as the boy. "You're real fluked out, Dinch; take it easy, be cool."

"Come on, doll, what'll you drink, like-I'm the man tonight."

Buster sat back stiffly. "I'm buyin, Dincher."

"Not tonight, man." The boy's eyes were half closed. "Dinch is the man tonight."

"I says I'm buyin, Dincher; got it?" Buster's eyes were fixed on the boy, and Diane knew his side-sight kept watch on her reactions. She whipped her hands up and pointed them like pistols at the dramatic brute. "Okay, Wallinger, keep your hands on the table. Port wine, and make it snappy." He enjoyed it just as she had known he would, and when he slipped out of his seat and disappeared in the crowd she sat back, laughing with Dincher. "The corny—— Don't get mixed up with that ape, Dincher."

"Why, doll? I can do big business with him."

"What business? What's he up to? What's his big connection?"

"Ask him, doll."

"Dinch, look. He's a big moron. You can't trust a moron; he'll get you in a hassel. All he thinks is to look important . . . like an actor, he is."

The boy laughed the Viper's lazy whine. "Yeah, like-I call him the General. Like-he squints'n talks phony like that. You know, I paid off for my horn today, *and* I paid off the school like-for six months'n all I got to do now is play music good. A real hard trumpet, doll, real *hard*-like."

"Solid, Dinch. Could I hear you play? Take me up there and let me listen and we'll smoke pod and everything."

He glanced above the crowd. "Not now, doll. I don't want you should like-be around them up in Paddy's. I get my own place soon, the Shylock got a big trap for me soon'n we really make it-like up there; right?"

Buster put wine before her. Sitting down, he shook Dincher's arm. "You be there tomorrow, Dincher. You be there on time."

Dincher nodded. He stood, grinning shyly at Diane, and found his hat on a wall hook. Dincher was a small yet rangy infant walking out, and it seemed he was backing away from her as carefully as Carter always did, as abruptly as Joe Letrigo. And before the fluttering could mount in her stomach Joe Letrigo stood smiling down at her, shifting from foot to foot in front of the squirming mass of noise and flesh.

Buster ran his eye up Joe and down. "Who you suppose to be, Prince Charmin?"

"Oh, how gauche!" Joe snapped. Then to Diane, "How's my vernac'lar? I'm learnin lots in the Village, pro and con."

She sat there, trying to learn from her insides how she felt toward Joe.

Buster flinched to indicate he was ready to rise and get rid of the intruder. "Go on'n take off; you got it? You think you can talk to anyone you like?"

"But I know the girl . . . and by God I know you too. You must think you really sent me off yipin this evenin."

Buster evaded that. "Well, she don't seem to know you; so beat it."

"I want to talk to Diane." Joe spaced his words, looking fixedly at Buster. "And 'less she asks me to leave I'll consider myself right welcome." The men glared at each other; then Buster turned to Diane, grumbled at her silence, and snapped out his blade. He hid himself at work on the celluloid ring while Joe sat down beside him, across from Diane. It frightened her that he sat so close to the sharp knife, but she comforted herself with the conviction that even a madman like Buster would never use the weapon in such a crowd.

"Diane," Joe said, "could I see you sometime? Like to see you and get some things to hold still in my head . . . and maybe in yours too." Like a freshly scrubbed schoolboy asking her to a prom.

"You see me now, don't you, Joe?"

He leaned away, looked at the back of Buster's head. "You know what I mean, Diane."

"Listen—" Buster found a reason to talk—"you got any idea how to find out where the kid is?"

It upset her: Joe shouldn't know. . . . Then there was swift anger at herself: who was he for her to be concerned over? "I'm thinking about it right now." An idea played feebly in her mind: Buster might visit Mama, posing as a Welfare Board authority hunting Diane. That way he might, with subtlety, work the name and address of the foster parents out of her. But the thought of subtlety on Buster's part deflated the plan. "I'll just have to go to my mother. She'll probably blow her wig when she sees me, but——"

"No she won't," Joe put in. "She'd be right pleased to see you. Told me so herself. Says you're in a heap of trouble and for you to hurry home."

"Why don't you get lost?" Buster growled.

"Just not ready to." Joe watched the brute, felt small beside him, yet knew in his whisky-hot chest that he'd handle him easily. Buster spun the knife around in his hand and curled his lip. "Hey, what is this crummy——" Joe's words stumbled over his anger. "Say, just what you tryin to do, intimidate me? Put away that toy; I by God mangled bigger boys than you just to *get* to a fight!"

Diane gasped aloud; for the first time it came through her own stupor that Joe Letrigo was drunk. "Now, stop it," she insisted. "Buster, you put that thing away before we all wind up in the slammer. Come on, now, don't be dumb."

Buster grinned, made a pathetic failure of bravado, and concealed the knife. "See you on the street one of these dark nights——"

"Joe, is it true?" Diane broke in. "Is it true that Mama—that you—that my mother . . ."

"Yes indeed. Thought it was you and stopped her. She said all that about wantin hard to see you." But he turned slowly on Buster, getting meanwhile to his feet. "No night darker than right now." He waited, and looked shakily at Diane. "This the kind of joker you pleased to be with?" He rubbed at the hot flush at the back of his neck. "Goddam if I couldn't waste him away in two minutes off chowtime. Goddam if I couldn't."

Buster sat grinning at the table top.

Diane said, "Be cool, Joe. You're just getting frantic over nothing." Her stomach was a hive of bees and everybody in the place was a noisy drunk, everyone on earth was on something goofy.

"Nothin! Diane, you just . . . I don't know, I don't know, I don't give a damn. I was fixin to apologize for things and stuff, but damn if two and two isn't four," pushing through the buzzing mob toward the door.

Diane fell spinning into a well of self-disdain. They would all leave, all back away from her, all but the bloated Busters and wrinkled Lukeys. Only the unwanted would want her. Where *was* Lukey the Swede and his kind, rambling, senseless kindness?

"If you gave me the word, beautiful, I would of parked him. I didn't wanta embarrass you; you dig?"

"Thanks, Lukey—Buster, I mean, thanks. Lukey, I have to find him, Buster, he's like a little kid, the Swede; you know that? I left him alone last night and I'm real worried about him; you hip?" Tea was helping her with swift words, yet pulling at her brain so that she needed air and ignored him when he insisted she finish her wine. Her head spun as though it might zoom away and she made it to the frost just in time to restore strength to her legs.

Buster came out, folding a wallet, and followed her south toward the Riviera. "If you find the Swede you gonna spend much time with him?"

"I have to go somewhere with him." It would be a relief to be rid of Buster. And Lukey would be entertaining; she would let him talk her ears off, she would go to Paddy's, anywhere.

"In that case, I leave you at the Riviera."

A nervous shock almost pulled the legs from under her, then at once she realized Buster had not read her mind at all, but had said that simply to spare himself the humility of being deserted by her; his infantile kind of pride was poorly shielded by his childish bluster.

Her head still trembled from the shock: marijuana, the great sensitizer, had backfired on her, given her the wrong end of its kick. Diane
had the "horrors." She and Buster crunched along on hard snow to
the Riviera, and Buster's careful eyes searched over faces through the
window. Then he turned. "Okay, beautiful, see you around."

"Is Lukey in there? Did you see him?"

"No, it's hard to see anybody in that mob," and he started to walk
off.

"Buster—" she ran up to him—"what about tomorrow? . . . Long
Island? You'll take me, won't you?"

He smiled down over a shoulder at her, nauseated her with his
expression. "If you meet me on time. I don't wait." He glanced im-
portantly at his watch. "Ten o'clock at the Cosmopole. You got lotsa
time." He grinned cunningly. "Don't go'n forget your kid."

"Creep," she muttered as he walked away. "Fatmouth sack of lard."
She hesitated at the Riviera door; her brain was a fist whipping the
nerves around within her. She entered finally, on the thin hope she
might find the Swede or anybody else who might shower her with ir-
relevance. Shuddered, moving through the crowd of men, whirled
against each motion of a hand, withdrew from every insipid remark.
She huddled near the radiator in a corner at the end of the bar. Noise
became a sticky fog in her brain and Joe Letrigo's profile mixed with
the smoke until she realized he was not part of her dreaming, but
sat drinking at the bar, listening to the ranting of an animated and
carefully attired girl, a thin, fair and very nervous girl who smoked
jerkily through a silver cigarette holder. Diane had to laugh now at
the way Buster had taken one look inside and left. Then Joe's eyes
swung around, found her, widened, and turned away. Slowly he
looked again and, ignoring the quick lip at his ear, said, "Don't deny
you been followin me."

Diane said, "You go to hell, cracker."

"Later, later, I'm waitin on Robert Stoney right now. Told him
I'd be here, and good manners is the first degree of honor." He
bowed, almost falling from the high stool.

"Who's your charming friend?" the blond girl wanted to know.

"Diane, Louella; Louella, Diane. Anybody want a drink?"

"Very beautiful," Louella mumbled dutifully. "In an obtuse
sort of way. Do you model, Diane? No, I think not, your face is too
pointed."

"Up yours," Diane said at her, repeated it with emphasis to Joe when he whirled. The girl disgusted her and Joe was filthy with Stoney's name on his lips. She sat on the radiator, felt old and wasted, cold even in her bulky coat.

"Well, we're victims of the oddest kind of snobbery," Louella intoned. "Joe, is it true? Really, I mean. Did Bob *really* say nothing about this evening? Honestly? Cross your heart?"

"Honestly," he sighed. "He did nothin but comb out his beard all the time I was there," and hated himself for keeping Diane in the corner of his eye. He thought he ought to shack this chatterer up just to hear what she'd have to say in the sack.

Diane found herself walking, pushing through the crowd, grinning dry-lipped as her spirit lifted, not knowing why till she stood leaning on Lukey the Swede, holding tight to his coat, feeling a measure of safety. Then safety screamed for more of itself in her stomach and she wished it were Carter holding her shoulders and laughing. Laughing "Baby of mine." Chuckling "Diane, baby, it warms me that you're glad and it gladdens me that you're warm and everything."

"Let's get out of here, Lukey, it's a creep joint; I've got the *horrors* something awful."

By the arm he led her out and up MacDougal. Crunch crunch the crunch was good in her ears, Lukey in her ears, "No Law in there, baby, I can smell Fuzz from fifty yards. But the Riviera is screamin if you got the horrors. You got to go where it's cool, you got to get off the street. You ever feel that? Like you got to get off the street?"

She laughed with the settling of her nerves; she began to warm up. "Swede, I love you because you're so kind."

"Hey, don't love me for that. Don't love me for kindness, because that's my hassel. I'm too kind, and human nature bites the kind. I went inside for kindness. You know that? For kindness I went inside where they dominated me. Here is the story . . . of a Swedish boy . . . who got locked in for bein kind."

It was all right. Everything he said was a balm for its pointlessness. He was as high as she, and they were a clever secret against the wind and the world. "Why kindness, Luke? I thought you went up for rifling an auto," and burst rocking into laughter when she remembered *Lukey the Swede has switched to hashish.*

"That's oney official, baby. Official is a step away from the real. *I got a story to tell you,*" he sang, spluttering through toothless laughter, "*about a Swedish boy with no front teeth* haHA! *He got ninety days for kindness and a month for likin laughs and not a day for makin the hyste,*" and they reeled laughing through the park, into Fifth Avenue's white-stone houses and barren, incongruous trees. "I reached in that car because it was gettin gray in October and the coat was the oney coat I ever gonna be alone with and I had to act quick so I reached in. But when I haul that coat out it starts to holler *Help* and holler *Murder* and I said *No, don't worry, it ain't murder* but he keeps up squallin and I keep tellin him *don't worry, pal, I just make a mistake, I oney you know wanted the coat, like* and he——"

"Whoa!" Diane had almost fallen to one knee trying to follow him. "Who were you fighting with?"

"Me? I wasn't fightin. When was I fightin?"

"In October. When you went fishing for a coat."

"That's what I'm tellin you, baby."

"Well, who was the guy you were arguing with, the one kept yelling?"

"Him? He was the guy in the coat when I pull it out of the car. We wasn't arguin, he was squallin, and I was tellin him not to be scared, that's all. Then the cops came and took me away and that's how I went inside. For larceny, I went inside. Four months for a lousy coat."

"Oh," Diane said. On Tenth Street a Railway Express truck crawled like the night, inching its way along, and the vehicles retarded behind it held their pace, calmed by the snowy pavement to restrain their customary haste; even a trailer truck named The Great Continental Express tiptoed like the rest. And the quiet old brownstone was warm, lit dark brown in the hallway up a plain staircase into Paddy's room where laughing Lukey said *Paddy* said *Izzie*, laughed and took her coat, took a pill, then, moving like an exposed nerve, settled on a wooden chair near a table of glasses, spoons and dials.

Paddy Jenks was a tall boy, but a boy in his face despite the ominous lines which ran like thin steel wires around his eyes, and a boy in the whisper of his voice. To Diane the room was smaller than its size and vaguer than its smoky atmosphere. Sunken in a soft chair at the center of the room, Izzie the Ghost stared like a blind, atrophied corpse at Lukey giggling at his own sounds returning from the wire recorder. Diane smoked, sipping her throat full of sweetness and

sleep. She rolled over on the wide bed and looked across at Paddy
as he heated the contents of a bent spoon over a candle flame. His
hair fell darkly over the paleness of his face, and from time to time
he brushed back the cowlick with a mechanical hand. A smile supported his expression as though it were some external force that
motivated his otherwise languid being. Like a boy he moved, pouring
the treasure of the spoon into a hypodermic syringe, and boylike he
smiled into the room, shaking back his hair.

"Setup's on," he managed to say, barely parting his lips.

The Ghost raised hueless eyes toward Paddy and moved his lips,
but no sound came. Paddy went past him, adjusting the setup, walking so slowly he seemed to be gliding. Cocking his head, he tapped
the Swede gently on a shoulder.

"Man," Lukey said, pointing to the wire recorder, "you hear me?
I got no teeth in my voice. Even in my voice. The choppers show up
missin and I sound like a chicken's ass."

It threw Paddy's head back, but no sound of laughter escaped him.
He held out the needle to Lukey, who laughed and bobbed in his
seat. "No, don't scratch me. Leave me stay on the pod." He fished
a marijuana butt out of an ash tray and held it up before Paddy,
waiting for his smile of acknowledgment. Diane's laughter popped
out of her. Paddy drifted his head around, gazed a moment, smiled,
and glided over.

"Get on?" slowly, faintly, forcing out the words.

"Thanks, Paddy, I'd rather stay with the Tea. It's great pod. I
don't want to stone out."

Paddy sat down near her. She wanted to touch his face, to feel his
boyishness. He readied his mouth to speak, eyes focused beyond
her as if they could see through her head. "Won't get hooked on the
first." He whispered spaced words that seemed to roll out without
touching his tongue. "Just take a skin pop. Pod's great after Horse,
Diaaaane."

"No, Paddy, I don't want to." Easily she could pull him into her
lap, cradle his boniness in her arms. She fell to her back, Tea in her
head, horror in her heart, helpless in the smoke around her to stop
him from raising his arm, unable to keep the little boy's shirtsleeve
from falling back to expose the cruel scars of his arm. Lukey, in his
corner, said he needed a continuation. He told the wire recorder *I
need a continuation so I can remember the ball when it's over and*

all the bad shows up I need a way to remember how to feel good it's the secret. Diane remembered the gauge and let it flow into all her feeling till thought was gone and she felt like a quivering skinful of goodness. Yet when Paddy's needle pecked for a soft spot in his arm, she turned her head to the wall.

Carter found himself standing in the sweet half-dark of Grapevine Lane, paying the cabdriver, smelling a winter freshness that dropped from the pure heights, a green cleanliness almost lost to him in the city's poisoned fumes. Then he was up the short brick staircase, talking through the lingering tail of sleep, saying, "Feed me, Rusty" to Normie's wife, who hugged him with all the power of her plumpness. The cab made its turn in the cul-de-sac and moaned away to the highway. Normie, slim and animated, got up from the couch, his unlabored smile furrowing his cheeks, a quick finger self-consciously flicking his nose. "Where you been, moss rat? Two months we haven't seen you. Neither has Rusty."

"That was an editorial *we*." Rusty laughed, bringing Carter by the arm down into the living room.

Normie came over to Carter. "You ought to be ashamed. What's new with you?" He took Carter's head in his hands and kissed him hard on the cheek, clung as Carter tried to pull away.

"Get away from him," Rusty protested, taking Carter's coat. "Wrestle with him after he eats; he's blanched with hunger."

Carter went through and up the two steps to the dinette while Normie hung up his coat. He sat in one of the green-leather chairs and grinned at Rusty when she came through toward the kitchen.

"I'll feed you in a minute, Cart. How's Edna coming along?"

"Coming along," and he didn't know what to do with his face.

"Will she be well soon?" from the kitchen doorway, and Normie was there to wrinkle his nose at her; she turned like an admonished child and slipped out of sight. Rusty had strained to make Edna comfortable the few times they'd been thrown together, but Edna had always leaned away out of reach, mistrustful as she invariably was in the face of extended warmth. Yet Rusty, certainly keen enough to feel Edna's remoteness, had never resented her, and now her concern over his wife was clearly more than condescension—Rusty seemed always to invest an oversize share of herself in the small positive side of everyone else.

"These preoccupied businessmen!" Normie said, seated beside him. "I'm whispering to you, Carter. Why don't you answer me?"

"What are you whispering about? Talk up, talk up."

"Sh, it's only for boys. What've you been doing with your spare time? Tramping around?"

Carter leaned close and, weighting the consonants, said, "Masturbating!"

"Ah, yes, yes." Normie reared back. "I took a course in that at Columbia several years ago. They called it Philosophy," and he did a little dance into the kitchen when Carter laughed: Normie never knew what to do when his wit was well received. In the kitchen he put his arms around Rusty's middle, and kissed her on the neck. He returned to the dinette doing the same little jog. "Someday I'll get out of the publishing business and become a dancer. I'm——"

"Publishing business!" Rusty set a platter of hot cheese pancakes before Carter. "Imagine him publishing a newspaper for members of the cloth. Normie Goldsmith. I married an infiltrator."

Normie continued dancing, watching his long rubbery legs. "Every morning I make it into that office with my eyes closed. I can't look at the door: 'Pulpit Chronicle, Norman Goldsmith, Publisher.' I imagine people grumbling about me. What was once a simple Jew complex is now paranoia with hair on its chest."

Carter ate while Rusty poured three cups of coffee. "It's a real problem to show this boy the difference between anti-Semitism and his own hallucinations. But I don't let up, and I don't pamper him. I nail him on every shot. Sit down, Pop."

"And I teach her Jewish cooking. That's the give-and-take of a good marriage." He did a quick, graceful whirl, and Rusty warned him to sit down before he kicked something over. He danced more rapidly. "Me kick something over? I'm in absolute control. I'm a top-grade dancer; that's the art in me crying for expression. I'm better than Astaire. Look, this is Astaire . . . all hands, nothing but hands. Take away his hands and what've you got?"

"An amputee," Carter said, and their laughter came quickly and mounted, then diminished to appreciative, near-embarrassed chuckles. He had a billowing sense of freshness, saw a sudden depth in the cleanliness and lived-in look of the house.

Normie sat down, his thin face shining. But in a moment he dashed out and down the steps in a hop. "Whatcha doing down here?" He

returned carrying his daughter, white and soft in her sleepsuit, rubbing little fists in her eyes, blinking in the light.

Rusty stood up. "Penny, what's the idea? You get on upstairs;
what kind of five years is that, anyway? You know she's five next
week, Carter?"

"How about that?" Carter ran a finger along her cheek. "You'll
be old as Mommy soon." A tremendous laugh for the child, and she
turned green eyes on Carter; her mother's red-lit auburn glinted in
her hair. "Hello, Carterweb, I'm going to wear a button on me says
five years old like a badge, kind of."

Normie hugged her and carried her through a gentle whirl to the
stairs. "My lucky Penny," he whispered, jogging up to the bedroom.

It was all here, Carter thought, a small dream secreted out here
away from the rest of things, from all the friction. Yet the dream had
color, light and sound, so that its reality rather made a nightmare of
everything outside, where the tortured were screaming away from
the sight of duty to one another. Whether praying step by step up
tottering towers toward some illusion of heaven, or playing notch
by notch down any available avenue of escape, from a stupid movie
to a charge of heroin—the world was hooked. He saw Rusty watching
him, her head on her hand. "How's the baby? Must be big since I
saw her last."

"She's fine. A little angel. You'll have them, Carter, when Edna's
well. You'll see, lots of them. I always said you'd make a swell father."

Normie came in on that. "What do you mean, *would* make? He
was. A consummate father. Didn't I tell you how he fathered me in
the army?"

"No, not the army. Nothing about the army, one time, boys."

Carter, beginning to get restless, tried hard to hide it. "How old is
Toby now?" He was filling a vast silence, killing the time it took to
reach his coffee.

Normie took a quick gulp from his cup. "Eight months, a nice fat
kid. And good—she never cries. Tell the truth, sometimes I think—
you know, maybe the kid's a dope."

Rusty laughed as she spoke. "He expects her to be like Penny was,
a real yowler. Besides, he has a grudge against her for not being a boy.
His father calls him a buttonhole maker, and he does a slow burn."

"Because it's a corny gag." Normie grinned sheepishly. "No difference to me, boys or girls. Pop can't insult me; I've known him for years."

"He wanted to name the baby Nickel." Rusty's laughter came from way down, and it rolled through all she said, words Carter scarcely heard, for there was a trembling uneasiness within him; parallels between Normie's girls and the daughters of Mrs. Lattimer were scratching at the borders of his thoughts. He was tempted to warn them to teach tears to Toby, but he recognized the absurdity of it before the words were formed. The whole parallel was ridiculous, neurotic, rooted in his own anxieties. He sighed with relief, listening to Rusty's banter, followed her down into the living room. " . . . call her Nickel to follow Penny. How about that?" and Normie protested that Nicky Goldsmith was a cute and unpretentious name, while Carter fell back on the low, circular couch, meaning to laugh with Rusty beside him, but only able to manage a smile.

"Then Dime, then Quarter," she went on, laughing, holding out a light for Carter. He leaned back, smoking, in the purple hush blended with the low lighting of the room, a warmth traceable beyond the dark drapes and candy-stripe walls, farther than the deep rug. His own apartment was cold white by contrast, white, cold, impeccable with the absence of living.

"Listen, why don't you show us the Village?" Rusty was saying. "We've never seen—*really* seen it."

"There's nothing to see." His voice came out low.

"Don't go blasé on me," while Normie ran to answer the phone. "It's nothing to you, maybe, but we've never seen it from inside, Carter."

"What do you think it is? Just a neighborhood with different kinds of people, just like any other congested New York area. More noisy bars, maybe."

Rusty looked down her shiny cheek at him. "And intense people who speak out their moods and live their impulses. Just you take us; you just show us some out-of-the-way spots. Can you? I mean will you be free to some night?"

"Sure, but I don't know any characters left over from bohemian times. All I can show you is sick people; they're the only characters I know."

Muttering, Normie came down to sit in the heavy chair facing them. "How do you like that Frankfurter? That was Tom Rutledge who called. You remember him, Carter, the guy with two different-colored eyes. He told me Frankfurter bought a dog and named him Penny. How do you like a miserable bum like that? Out of spite, just to get me mad. Penny!" He danced over to a broad black liquor cabinet in shadows and ferreted around inside. "But I'll fix him. Know what I'll do?" He looked up at Rusty, who paused on her way to the dinette. "I'll burn him up right back."

"Don't be playing pranks with Frankfurter," she warned and went out.

Normie set a tray of glasses on the cocktail table near Carter, whipped a bottle from under his arm and deftly uncapped it and poured. "Good bourbon," looking up for Carter's nod.

Rusty returned with a tray of cashew nuts. "Frankfurter hates kids; he louses up the whole neighborhood."

Normie nodded obliquely. "Especially if their name is Goldsmith."

Carter's bourbon hurried down his throat. Warm inside, he reached over and filled his glass again. "What's he got against you, of all people?"

Before Normie could answer, Rusty said, "It's hard to be sure. He's mastered innuendo on a schoolboy level; it's hard to say whether he's just a crank or resents our kind of marriage."

"What do you mean hard? He's both!" Normie poured his drink and brought one to his wife. "But I'll fix him. I'm going to get *us* a dog, one of those Sealyhams or Afghans or whatever they are. The ones with hind legs that make them look like they're up on tiptoe with bent knees and falling pants. All that fur he'll always look hot; I'll call him, therefore, Frankfurter."

Rusty's laugh was quickly done. "He'll raise hell, hon. You know him; you know the kind of remarks he'll make."

"He won't make them to us." Normie glowered.

"Nor to me, but he'll make them."

"Let him. You can't back away from that crap. Someday he'll say something to me, and I'll blast him. But you can't back away," while Rusty sat on the arm of his chair and put a hand on his neck. "I know he's an idiot, but you can't back away. I'm going to have a dog named Frankfurter, and he can lump it."

Carter saw by Normie's face that all this was a serious pursuit of something deep in him, something his every thought and day-by-day move were geared to. He envied Normie the problem, wished his own troubles were of this particular order, things which could make him angry rather than despondent.

Angrily Normie looked around toward the staircase, running a hand through his thin blond wisps of hair. "You know something? Penny's a nice kid. And so is the baby." He looked across at Carter. "And Rusty, she's—she loves the world. And I'm a puddle of piss if anyone is going to make things rough for them while I'm still breathing."

"All right." Rusty shifted on the chair arm. "Put away the bottle or you can't have the next dance."

But the bottle remained, tipping frequently, and Normie went on with his complaint. "And that goes for the crumbs on both sides. Carter, you know the so-called spiritual leaders who are all spirit and no brains, all sky and no earth? The jerks with the electric word of officialdom who do nothing but separate people from people?"

"Oh, Normie, leave Carter alone."

Normie glanced at her and hurried over to the couch beside Carter, telling, rapidly and with an edge of bitterness, about the rabbi at the local Jewish temple who delivered a sermon against intermarriage. "That son-of-a-bitch bastard white-fingered scumhead of a parasite! With Rusty sitting beside me, I had to hear our marriage treated like a social disease. Imagine how we felt."

Carter could imagine, and he washed it down with some bourbon. "Aah, it's savagery, medicine-man stuff. Why do you bother with those medieval creeps? Whatever they preach—at best, when they're not being treacherous, they're only a big meaningless zero."

"Well Rusty—we like to have God around the house, especially when we look at the kids. But I told that rabbi. I told him a man and a woman are like people from different planets, they're almost different species, I said. Now and then one female and one male get together and it works in spite of all the crazy emotional differences, and you, I told him, want them to keep apart over a lousy superficial cultural difference, a little bunch of fables that disappear in a month."

To Carter that sounded a lot like what had been going through his mind that morning in Wengel's marble halls, and he had a glimpse of the basic direction he and Normie shared, probably had shared long before they met. He got to his feet; the bourbon, warming him at first, had begun to sensitize his fatigue. "Norm, what's believing in God got to do with this temple business? Can't you believe without making an apology of it?"

Normie poured more drinks. "You know, wherever you are you have to belong. You just have to."

Somehow Diane's face was staring at Carter in his mind, eyes pleading, forever contrite. "Give me a drive to the station, Norm," and before anyone could ask, "I sold my car."

Normie looked, blinked, and nodded, then walked without dancing to the closet. Rusty yawned and spoke through it. "Don't forget the Village, Cart."

"Yeah. Normie, Rusty wants me to tout you around the Village some night soon." His neck ached with stiffness. Normie was dancing excitedly again now, assuring everyone, while he got their coats, that they'd have a million laughs in the Village; Rusty was kissing Carter firmly on the cheek, telling him to take care; Carter wished he were hours in bed when the frost hit him.

They sat quietly, driving through the winding darkness of trees out to the highway. Carter watched his friend's thin, clean profile still twitching with the religious problem. "*La guerra continua*, soldier."

Glancing around, Normie grinned. "*Continua* everywhere you put a foot. That's life," he sighed, "a bunch of problems looking down your rain barrel. You have the choice of meeting them standing up or lying down."

"Or waiting for the light in the sky to take care of you?"

"No, that's just an easy way of lying down."

"Then what's your old God for, Normie?"

"To keep your spine stiff till you work out a solution for every little problem. I think He'll have to hang around till we get to where we can gain confidence in one another, till we all put our energies in one basket."

"Now *that* would make a good God." Carter laughed. "The playgrounds and hospitals He could build in a minute! The diseases He could wipe off the earth! What a church He'd have."

"Upon a rock He'd build it. Get out, you're plagiarizing a guy the fat officials nailed to wood several years ago for ideas like that. Go on, or you'll miss the eleven-thirty-six; the machines are in charge these days, tomorrow the birds take over. I'll call you and let you know when we'll be in town. Listen, if you—" he leaned out as Carter came around by his lights—"if you were in trouble, you wouldn't hesitate to—you know, let me in on it?"

"How you fixed for crocodile tears?"

Normie said, "Call you tomorrow," and drove off around the circular lawn to the highway's amber lights. Up the station steps Carter ducked into the wind howling on the open platform. From that stone height he could see a distance into the old section of town, over the cluttered rooftops into a blackness where pinlights glittered and blinked. He was alone with a strict row of lampposts shining like hopeful spinsters in wait for the chance visit of some nephew or stranger. Everything seemed to be waiting, waiting. Everything seemed alone, as he was alone. Waiting for one another. Little children, too young to recognize their brothers. Words: *foreigners, Jews, nationalities and religions*. Myths: *faith, fun, faithful, thrilled*. Games: *success, money, new buildings, bigger towers of stone*. Stone words, stone games, and all of them alone, waiting, needing one another. Each with his own arbitrary God, praying to air when God was the power dormant in the unborn unity of men; building great shrines to the great stone God of industry, while the knowable and effective God lay hidden in the dungeon of human distrust. And all around, the unaffected sky rolled with centuries scored in pinlights upon it, rolled with the fortitude of eternity over man's tragic wastes. For an instant Carter felt Mrs. Lattimer's fear of the sky, and the world's horror of all it didn't know. Then the platform creaked wildly under the impact of wheels as the train roared in like a crazy monster with a thousand eyes, and Carter was cold and alone. He let himself dream awhile that Diane would be there to meet him in warmthcolored light when he reached home, but even the dream perished in the cold night. Diane could stand no loneliness for long. Edna lay in many darknesses. Invalids and the robust, Vipers and the religious, junkies and dreamers and millionaires, all in the dark and rolling unfamiliarity of living stood secretly alone. . . .

DESIGNS COLORED WITH REMORSE

Robert Stoney lighted a fresh Italian cigar, fondly felt the cropped trimness of his beard, glanced across the table at Joe Letrigo staring moodily through the window out onto MacDougal, and rested his elbows before him, careful for the soft new flannel of his suit. The crowd was light in the Riviera, not noisy yet and keeping to their booths. In another hour or so, he thought, the anxious bastards would cram into the place, magnifying and projecting the abominable dullness of their personalities, shouting things that went better unsaid. "The horrible part of it," he announced, "is that everything is magnified and accelerated."

Joe rolled his eyes around, tightening the team of wrinkles above his eyebrows. "What's that got to do with poetry? Last thing you said was that poetry's like tearin bits of paper in the wind. And now this. Stoney, you're just losin your damn marbles."

With a strong extension of patience, Stoney could endure the boy's preoccupation. There was a delightful irony in the situation, in the way they both were attracted to the same mold of woman; he'd always suspected that Joe shared his tastes. Of course he couldn't expect the lad to control his emotions as securely as he himself did; it took a goodly mellowing period for that. Inwardly he glowed over the way he'd impressed the Stately Lady of Sullivan Street. Someday she'd even have him in for tea.

There was nowhere a dignity to match that in her walk, and her presence threw Sullivan Street into starker desolation, as though the very tenements and dirty iron fences were ashamed under her eyes. For many a windbitten night he'd followed her, tearing at his brain for an excuse to speak with her. Then finally Joe, in idle conversation, mentioned that he'd passed the lady's message on to her daughter. Idle conversation indeed!

"Madam—" with half a bow to show breeding and yet avoid bur-

151

lesque—"an agent of mine has contacted your daughter. She will visit you shortly."

Though tapered to memory alone, there still remained the electric charge that ran down his spine when her eyes took in the fine clothes selected so carefully for her (with Louella's money). And the voice of her gratefulness was more than memory in his ears. She'd even confided in him that the man Carter's house was under official surveillance, though she'd not elaborated and he certainly had better taste than to pry. At any rate she had touched his hand at her door. Such composure! "It's comforting to know there are gracious people in this mad world," she had said. "Gracious!" She and he alone in all the lunacy. Now he had to laugh over her demure use of the plural in reference to him—what taste!

Yet there the boy sat in near collapse over the delinquent daughter who, Stoney suddenly realized, represented nothing definite for the boy; she was only a ghost of romantic illusion hovering about to plague him, an image left over from boyhood dreams, and a part of Joe still refused to have that image incarnated by the girl's true personality. All nonsense, and Stoney's own force within, his own live sense of rightness swelled and demanded room, demanded that less consequential matters stand aside. Pulling fingers till his knuckles snapped, he said, "The society stinks, and it takes guts to face it. Anyone can look at the few positive fragments of this world, dwell with them, blind himself to all the decay. In fact, most Americans do just that, thinking they're being real patriotic. They think it's real Uncle Sam to eat horseshit out of the hands that rule them. They——"

"You been tellin me that a week. Why don't you turn yourself in? You're so bitter and miserable you'll hang yourself one day."

"Me? Hang myself? Ha! I'm not miserable; I'm simply misanthropic. Suicide is for cockroaches; I'm too egoistic to feel it's my fault that these social effluvia nauseate me." He laughed with quiet arrogance. "Before I'd hurt one hair on this beard I'd willingly liquidate ninety per cent of these unconscious slaves."

Joe groaned impatiently. "That's right courageous of you. You'd kill them all. That the way you'd bring on the golden age?" He shuttled his glance between window and door, drinking his beer with evident lack of pleasure.

Stoney wagged his head impatiently. He felt the creeping sense of waste that always came when people succeeded in dragging his universal outlook down to personalities. He put a new light to his cigar. "Decay has set in, and before social engineering can be rationally administered the civilization must be destroyed. The values that exist are——"

"Bullshit, Stoney! By God, you gangle-assed fatmouth, you're just a negativist! You never do mention anything with any substance. You just negate everything you can, you ole fool."

Stoney leaned back, laughing. The boy was under pressure, no longer capable of objectivity. "Can't you think in abstractions, stupid?"

"Why," Joe went on, "you never took a positive look at anythin. You're opinionated, and you never think to feel out anybody else's view," thinking of Diane, swearing to himself that he'd try to understand her view if he ever found her.

"You're worse sober than when you're drunk." Stoney was somewhat perturbed. The scene with Louella drifted through his mind. What could have been more positive, more an attempt to understand alien values? He had received her well, and considerately avoided embarrassing her with any complaint out of the millions he stored in his heart against her. He'd taken her romantically through the white and sunny park, even allowed himself by way of experiment to grow soft with affection for her, so much so that when they returned to the studio she was completely charming and acceptable. Love by the fire at dusk—

"Jesus, why'd you cut out so fast last week?" Lizzie Linden complained to Joe. "Right while I was talkin."

Stoney said, "Because he has no more manners than a Saint Bernard."

The little woman looked fiercely at him. "Look who's talkin about Saint Bernards. With a face like that I wouldn' mention a poodle. Don't pay no attention to Stoney, Joe. He'd insult Je-e-sus if he had a chance."

Stoney leaned back, settling himself comfortably. Puffing on the cigar, he told himself he was alone; this would not be a conversation but a trapeze act. The girl would catch Joe where she could and, so long as he remained playful, would follow him in any flip or somer-

sault. She was dressed for it, a full blouse shielding her plumpness,
silk stockings on the skinny legs, hair turned under in a brand-new
way that made her face look fuller.

"Just pay him no mind, honey. You know him; he thinks he's
Oscar Wolfe."

They spoke, but Stoney let their voices merge with the growing
noise in the place. Love by the fire had been without anxiety on
Louella's part, totally successful, and it had seemed then that the
effulgence of his youth was returning, dawning out of their partner-
ship. But then reality intervened. Louella, in his arms on the rug
before the fire, soft and young against him, spoke from her soft and
youthful brain: "Isn't it wonderful, Bob?"

"Heavenly."

Sigh. "Did you ever feel this way before?"

"Two . . . three . . . maybe four hundred times before."

And her exasperation mounted with each maudlin question that
demanded he either lie or torture her. Of course she departed with
the silver cigarette holder unearthed and reinstated as keeper of the
Nordvahl security. And there had been more days and nights, uptown and down, of quite sacrificial efforts on his part to test his
awareness of Louella and her whole ridiculous, crumbling culture: it
could not be saved.

"For Jesus' sake," Lizzie was saying, "she's at least twenny-three,
twenny-four; whadda you think? She been kickin around the Village
for years."

"How come you don't know each other? Says you don't, sure
enough."

"Well, I don't know her personally, but we seen each other, awright. Just a kid! She's married, even, and laid low a couple years.
Now she's back—they oweys come back. Musta left him, or vice
versa."

Joe's face was pale and troubled as he stared into the beer. "Her
mother told me she never married that guy. How's it her mother
doesn't know?"

Lizzie didn't find the question significant. "She's the one, awright.
I can show you guys who traded with her. Jesus. What do you need
huh-stlers for? This ain't the middle ages. Christ, you'd think love
was a *preeee*mium or somethin."

Joe grinned at his beer. Stoney watched the woman's lidded eyes betray with a flicker or a shift the progression of her personal involvement in it all.

"You want a drink, Lizzie?"

There was Joe's invitation to stay. Her eyes dealt with it, tasted the moments one beer offered, planned ahead, then shifted toward Joe with decision. "I don't know, there's work tomorrow . . . all week end. I gotta get to sleep by twelve or them telegrams'll bug holes in my head all day," and, staring toward the bar, she kept Joe in a corner of her eye.

"It's only ten o'clock," he said.

"Well, I thought . . ." and she thought through her purse, found cigarettes. "Awright, jus one beer." She stood to let Joe out. The Riviera was filling steadily. "Don't be lookin at me like a wise apple, Stoney."

"It's just that you look lovely tonight, Lizzie."

She used two matches on her cigarette. "Don't get frisky with me, Bob."

"I'm not being sarcastic. You look very appealing. I mean that."

"I can never tell when you're not fakin. Because I can't see your mouth, that's the trouble, you oweys look like you're laughin." She was inward and wary with Joe on her hook; her eyes popped through the old swaggering mask, uncertain, searching things.

"You know you're attractive, Liz. You always knew it."

"Come on, Stoney, don't irritate me," eagerly making space for Joe. "Got to drink this fast, Joe, because I better get home right away."

"Suit yourself, Lizzie." He watched her drink the beer quickly. "Don't gulp it, though; load of time before twelve."

She stopped drinking and looked at him through the watering of her eyes. "Sooner the better. No good walkin through Bleecker late at night."

"Oh, I see."

"It's a bad street."

"Yeah."

"Deserted; you know?"

"And full of strange characters in doorways," Stoney said. "It's dangerous after dark." Lizzie looked at him with cautious gratitude.

"Tell you . . ." Joe leaned forward. "Just relax and I'll walk you home."

"Bingo," and Stoney lighted his cigar.

Joe said he'd return shortly, but Lizzie corrected him, insisting she felt conversational, smiling heavy-liddedly at Stoney as though she now accepted him as an accomplice. Then Stoney was alone with the Stately Lady in his pulse, smoking, appreciating the first breath of solitude, ignoring the cacophonous giggling and clatter that grew with each slam of the door. Several people he knew were scattered about the place, and he was proud they avoided him, blissful in his unpopularity and fine new clothes.

Until Louella thrust herself into the booth across from him, glaring with her prepared kind of indignation, this night's choice out of the few emotional openings she affected—for she somehow found it impossible simply to say hello. "Give me a light," she ordered him, filling the silver holder in jerky, meaningful motions. Giving her a light, he wished for a way to tell her quite simply to be herself, but, like her whole level of existence, she was almost wholly given over to artifice. He sighed and moved over when she invited two hovering lackeys into the booth. When he examined them, he saw the prematurely bald Harry beside Louella and an angry-looking youth at his own side. "This is he, Philon," Louella said accusingly, and Stoney expected the worst: a brother, an avenging blood buddy.

"Why do you paint?" the boy demanded. His small eyes quivered with the strain of premature wrinkles in his brow.

A *crusader*, Stoney thought, and decided to spend eight or ten seconds in discovering what this particular religion was. Louella could certainly find them. "Why do you breathe?" he asked.

"Precisely!" The boy smiled from friend to friend, his brow retaining anger. "Sublimation! Stop painting and you will be driven mad by an overdevelopment of your inhibitory factors. Morality has deflected——" and coughed back from the cigar smoke. Stoney blew full in his face.

"Please carry your dim-witted mediocrity over to that corner where the other sorority sisters are praying to Freud."

"I'm a Reichian!" Philon protested.

"Go terrify the timid and sicken the sensitive," Stoney whispered close to the boy's venomous glare. "I'm bored with you. Louella must you agonize me with cultists? I've given up my turtle-neck sweater and baggy pants because of the Communist you presented who loved me for them, then hated me for tapping my friend Tomlin with a newspaper because *another* Negro might think it a racial act and intercede violently." He loaded his lungs, for many words were arranging themselves eagerly in him. "You burdened me with some little actress who insisted I was the Antichrist when I let it slip I don't use Christmas trees; you took me to a cocktail party uptown —will I ever forget it?—where I was called a Philistine for never having read the *Divine Comedy,* an anachronism for being a bearded painter, a male chauvinist for supposing women were in a better position circumstantially than men to impart ideas to the young; and Harry here . . . you brought me Harry, who called me a hedonist for saying all things spiritual were rooted in physical organs." He paused for a breath before going on, but Louella slapped the table with a palm.

"Stop it!" she hissed. "Why don't you just *say* you're antisocial? You don't have to sit here with us."

"But it's my booth. You people came and——"

"Possessive psychosis," Philon declared. "The introvert——" and hacked again in a new fog of smoke, while Stoney made his way past with a gentle nudge, turned and patted the tight curls on the boy's head, and went through the crowd to the far end of the bar.

Carter Webb had a shoulder guarding his drink from Steerman while the writer leaned in convincingly. "What's the use? You can't write about acutely interesting people any more, like ineffable women or vituperative men . . . because they're all accounted for by science, the romance is gone out of 'em, displaced by the anemic cobweb of psych'logical significance." His head dropped in punctuation, swinging loosely from side to side.

"Steerman," Carter let him know over a shoulder, "I don't mind if you never write stories. I think I might even learn to bear it if you lay off politics for several years." He began to rise when he saw Stoney watching; one motor-driven tongue was enough in his condition.

But Stoney held him down. "How are you, Webb?" lifting an arm like a fashion model while Carter looked over his clothes. "I've come to rescue you from the middle-class maledictorian here."

"Looga the beaver." Steerman hiccuped. "Clothestore dummy," he said and hobbled away in a fit of belching.

"What's on your mind, Stoney? No song and dance, please. I'm just drunk enough to be hard to get along with," and pulled his hat tight to keep it on in case Stoney was offended enough to fight, then laughed at the thought of it when he remembered what Slinger had told him about the painter and Magoo.

Stoney didn't know where to start. "Your wife—how is your wife?" he blurted, then smiled. "I hear she's been ill."

"And that's what you came over to ask? Well, she's dying. My wife is dying of a rare disease. Thanks for asking."

"Good Lord! Where is she? Her mother should know."

Carter slid backward off his stool and began to back away: the man looked too alarmed for a stranger, and stranger still was his remark. "She knows where her daughter is," he heard himself say. "Stoney, what's wrong with you? What are you up to?"

The painter held his arm, and the crowd kept the two of them at the bar. "Diane?" Stoney said. "Is Diane your wife?"

"No, she's my wife's kid sister. Why? Dammit, Stoney, what's your goddam concern? What do you want to know so much for?"

When Stoney took his stool with an offensive relief, Carter pulled his hat tight down again.

"Where is Diane?" Stoney asked. "Her mother is very anxious about her."

"I'd like to know where she is myself, Stoney. How do you know her mother is . . . ?" and he might have laughed at the connection of Vivienne and Stoncy, but thc Lattimcr faccs in his mind had become smoky images slithering around one another like reptiles in a pit.

"The lady and I are friendly, and she's asked me to find Diane."

"Asked *you?* She's got enough police snooping around town."

Suddenly Stoney was standing, hiding behind him, staring like a caught truant past his shoulder.

"'At's okay, boy." Tony the Shylock nodded, letting his eyes ride up and down the painter. "You no got a dough for yesterday by pay the rent-uhmo, descratziadomereecon-uhmo! 'At's okay, boy."

Carter caught Dincher's shoulder, pulled the boy away from where he stood beside the Shylock. "Dinch, you know where Diane is? The Law's after her and we'd better find her before they do."

"What Law? I jus get back from—I been away, Carter. What's the Law want wit her?"

"The Welfare Board. Her mother has them on her. There's a guy parked in my lobby all day. Where could she be, Dinch?"

The boy went with him to the door, pulling on an ear. Outside he said, "I got an idea like-maybe where she is, the kid. But I can't take you, like-the people, they don't like strangers, but I get in touch. Okay?"

"Will you, Dinch? Here's my number," and he scribbled it on the back of Wengel's business card, hoping that it would be found among criminals so that Wengel—he shook his head to clear it, and went into a spell of sneezing, handed the card to Dincher, and walked off down MacDougal's sullied snow, wiping at his watery, burning eyes.

It bothered him more than he'd imagined it could that Diane had stayed away so long. When he'd awakened that first morning, his first fear had been that the police had arrested her. But the persistence of Welfare Board agents at his door had proved to him that she was still free—at least from the Law. But not from her own compulsions—he imagined her laughing and writhing among dope fiends, locked in a gray-cloaked embrace with some Hindu sailor, holding up gas stations in the company of Dincher's hoodlum kids . . . walking in despondency along a bleak, creaking dock, considering the sea. But the sunlight of many mornings splashed through those dusty pictures, reminding him of the infinite crossings of circumstance which make eternal mystery of other people's moments and make a fool's obsession of any conjecture about them.

Yet now, in the free white darkness of the park, dejection lingered, focusing his loneliness on Diane. General loneliness was a remembered fog, a dryness unnamed in one's mouth, with lazy lungs and heavy-lidded looking into space. But, inspired by someone, loneliness ran like a live wire through perception, throwing a sting of current through every response. Knowing it, those chill first mornings, had only intensified the arid vacancy with which the ringing blue distance of sky had filled him; if Diane had been home, the sky might not have seemed too endless, too cold blue. And now the snow crunching under his stride might not have sounded so obtrusive, the frost in the air might have seemed less an enemy.

Passing stoops high and aloof on Waverly Place he pictured the sisters as children, Edna's full nine-year-old face lighted with alert black eyes always a moment removed from tears, Diane in anxious shift back and forth between a sister to emulate and a mother to dread; Vivienne made dreadful by her suffering, spending uncon-

trollable venom on those two images of herself: "Whore! Pervert!"
And over the years that illusion of aristocracy had so worn down
what elasticity she'd ever known that today she was a boulder of obstinacy. Neither logic nor entreaty had touched her any of the
times he'd phoned that week to persuade her to sign Diane out of
Clearwater. When he had warned her that Diane could be *pushed*
only downward, she wanted to know what he thought detention
homes were for. When, in exasperation, he had accused her of
responsibility for everything destructive in her daughters, she'd
abruptly hung up.

There was nothing he could think of to do. Depression hounded
him. Months and months would suck at his conscience before Edna
would pass into the black finality of earth; months piled on barren
months lay before him, calling for devotion to the breath-wasting
ghost, compassion for the rotting flesh, so cold and unfamiliar.

Edna Webb suspected God. Lying still in light that bled through
glass from the hall, she looked through the glass door (locked,
locked!) over the balustrade, out to the white field blue with night,
past its shrubs to the limitless black, where an October carnival had
once spun lights for her to watch and ride with her higher self. The
sky was only a faint shade darker than the field, the sky was near;
without moving her head she could see it from the farthest corners
of her eyes—she could see God's sky. God . . . everything pointed
to Him. Now she could piece things together, teach herself His deceit
as she had pieced together evidence of Carter's destruction of her.

The glass room was the key! God had known her need and sent
Dr. Morris to hear her deepest understanding, to listen with his
amazing patience as no man but Carter had ever listened before. But
God had promised that Dr. Morris would learn to understand the
outpourings of her eyes and do more than listen to her words, and do
more than speak softly. Yet he'd held her arms away from his neck
and his smile had turned from power to foolishness. And she'd been
moved to this room in the east wing—*walled on four sides with glass!*
She needed no glass to see through walls. At the height of her com-
munions with her higher self, when all sense of body was tran-
scended, she passed easily around rooms and through any wall to
mix with all that IS and all the IS NOT hidden behind it; behind
any wall she could sense the approach of a nurse in time to rearrange

her face so that her divinity would not show. Because she could tell by their eyes, as she'd always been able to see in the waver of anybody's eyes, the very nuances of their thoughts. The nurses and doctors translated into madness a divinity generations of pure blood had developed in her. That was the reason for the glass room: they wanted to watch her, to see what she did with her hands, as though she were subject to the compulsions of this woman or that, weaklings giving in to their flesh—not as she had used flesh with sacrifice, as an invitation to spiritual unity, but for the unrewarding animalism of flesh itself. Like Carter, pressing jagged stones into her heart. It was static air, the way Carter made her feel: opaque, thorny air scratching her heart raw. While people slept in glass rooms all down the hall with only bodily pain, she had to lie bodiless, bearing the ache of alienation in her soul. Carter had destroyed her and Lou Morris had destroyed her, and God stood by, allowing her pain to mount in gelatinous whirlpools in her head. Perhaps He was testing her faith! Perhaps He was taking her to the end of earthly forbearance, waiting to see if she would blaspheme and thus lose the favored place He held for her. But the glass room! Not even God could be forgiven for exposing her to common judges, to be judged in the values of limited judges, condemned only for their sins.

Edna let her jaw sag, putting a hollow in her cheek, changing her eyes from black to pale with a droop of her lids, believing her hair into whiteness. She had given her life to Carter. She'd worn black stockings and a white blouse when he seduced her, and a ribbon in her braided hair. For she'd been a virgin angel then, on earth drawing into herself the sins of men, and they'd all scored nothing against her flesh, which she gave to Carter alone. And he used her out in their first year, then stole hours where he could, to seek an earlier Edna in lingerie clerks and schoolgirls in rainy evenings between work and home. He had denied it, denied all his destructions of her as he denied them now. As if stone and steel of built things could ever shield his conduct from eyes empowered to read his guilty face and add meaning to cautious words by judging their intonations and tying them to words intoned weeks and weeks before.

Trembling, she sat up and slid off the bed into slippers, shifting her weight to the good leg and pulling the wheel chair around under her. Wheeling to the window, she looked out over the field of snow, tawny now like a dark old river, changing to purple as she watched. Nothing ever held still; things were always changing. Why did God let things change? Because the world is in motion, Carter had said, because God has nothing to do with it. Carter had always said to ride the changes like good horsemen, not to try and stop them, not to try and keep the earth from turning. Carter had said change will kick your head in if you try to stop it, and the voice of his advice pulled her suddenly erect in the cold chrome chair. She fingered the spokes of a wheel. Change . . . his sporadic utterances about change had a continuity of their own; she could remember faces he wore as he said those things, certain lines dancing around his eyes. "Bodies change," he'd cajoled her when she wept over sagging breasts, and even then she'd seen in his eyes that his weak flesh dreamed of younger girls.

She closed her eyes and stared down dark tunnels, stared harder and harder through time till the light of other days appeared and she could see shapes grow bolder, hear voices burn the air in her soul. "The season's changed," he says in summer to repel her limbs thrown with affection around him; he says, "Change the gaudy way you dress"; he says, "Now rest, less drinking now," before the miscarriage, "less staying up all night, your life has changed." Oh, how he prepared her! All toward this day when she must accept his change toward her. Oh, God! Who was she, who was the woman he used? Who was in bed with him this very moment? A Negress—he'd never allowed her to speak freely of the black, burned savages, always maintained that hateful objective attitude, accused her with a guilty look (she saw it clearly right now) of being as abusive as a poor-white Southerner out of her own sense of abjectness, just to have something toward which she could feel superior. Always so damned objective, but it was stored in her soul, and now his guilty glance lived again to betray his lust for black flesh. Edna pressed a hand on her eyes, burned them staring steeper into the red light of her soul. A Negress took her place in bed, or—the janitor's wife, allowing him to pursue a perversion for old flesh . . . or (it was hard to see) Diane!

Of course! Diane stealing him, hiding in his bed at night to keep Mama from sending her away! Because Mama went there to look, and . . . Mama . . . Perhaps it was . . . Mama! Mama with her warnings against eggs: "Aphrodisiac when sedentary, oh, be careful, dear"; with her disarming smile, her eyes liquid with compassion, "No eggs or you'll abuse yourself in bed": all an act to throw Edna off her guard. Of course, of course, without a man for years and Carter vulnerable! And the argument they staged here last week—a ruse, prearranged in some noisy, neoned tavern before separating, each to come along with dialogue prepared, to meet afterward and laugh over using Diane as distraction. That was why Mama had left early and Carter had affected revulsion: to embellish the lie. Oh, God!

But God stood by laughing too. God and all the worldly flesh and action were directed like frozen spears against Edna Webb! Blood pounded in her throat, and she clenched her teeth to keep from screaming. They would call it madness if she let her terror turn to sound, and she must control them all for her purposes. She looked skyward and saw stars shift like guilty eyes. God was shifty for his failures. That was her mistake, believing in Him all these years. Believing in Mama, in Carter, in men needing her for cleansing. She would show them all—the unfeeling, inconsiderate animals, she would show them the result of their destructive blindness. Without God as source for her insight, she would show them all.

Edna rolled the chair over to the bed and laid her hands on the crisp white sheet. Carter had loved the long thin fingers. She'd make him remember them with bitter tears. But she must smile. When the nurse came, she must smile and say good morning with a cheerfulness that would make them *unlock* the *door* to the *porch*. No more silences. And she must remember to speak the language of every hour, so that they'd all say, "Mrs. Webb is getting well. Mrs. Webb can go to the porch and wave to her husband." She must see to it that Carter too thought her happy and trusting, so that he'd come smiling and waving up the walk to visit her. She would disarm them all! Alone she would—— A sudden claxon of alarm scraped through her veins and she spun toward the windows black with sky, feeling weak in her bones, cold at ankles and wrists. What if it were true that she had not purged the sins of men but indulged them? Memory and intent descended wildly upon her like enemies in ambush; between past deeds and present needs, she decided to put off rejecting God for another day or two. Her burdened eyes rested on His heaven.

No spoken word could urge Diane to leave the room. Neither Lukey's giggled promises of fun outside nor Paddy's boyish smiles could convince her that anything but horror lay outside. One after-

noon when sunlight found a space between curtains drawn tight,
Izzie the Ghost, with paternal alarm magnifying the normal alarm
in his eyes, insisted she'd perish of rickets too long without sun, and
Diane had almost passed away in jive-charged laughter at such advice from a man whose only sign of life was the occasional squeak of
his voice. So the three men would leave to hustle alone, charging
her only with cleaning the room. With Nembutal goofballs and pod
she stayed free of thought but for remorseful instants the size of a
hair when a hornhonk or outcry told her of the world outside
where Johnny was. Instants that flashed to nothing like the zero of
Buster's face and the bubble of regret over having failed to meet him
one morning long gone by. For hours she would sing to the wire
recorder with Louis Armstrong from a record spinning and sizzling
beside her. She'd break up laughing each time Louis sang ". . . *down
among the ri-vuh*" and fall back on the bed with a gauge heart full
of love for the grand old man of sunshine. To grow engrossed with
creeping shadows that marked the hours. To watch dust specks chase,
lifelike, across the floor and feel as free and unwatched as any speck of
lifelessness. Sometimes the men were about and sometimes there were
only vague faces that turned out, once she inquired, to be recollected
moments—moments of voice and flesh like Carter for whom she cried
out at night from a thick Nembutal sleep, one time . . . or maybe
twice. She couldn't go to him again, for the Swede passed on to her
what all the Village knew: that Fuzz were in town for Diane alone,
alone; and alone he'd have to be, poor Carter.

Straight on gauge and goofballs and dreams that lost substance at
awakening. And the men were straight as they had to be: Paddy
hooked, Lukey forever unquieted, and the Ghost mostly dead in his
chair. They'd hustle by day and ball by night, or hustle through darkness and sleep past the hours of sun, but they never brought the outside in, neither newspaper nor magazine nor tale of anybody's woe.
And days went on uncounted with everyone to his own private habit.

Till out of a goofball veil she reached a hand for the matchbook
a friend held out from his smile, and did as another friend directed.
She held cardboard to her nose and sent each nostril taking powder, a questionless snort, and powder had fingernails that tore
through inside. The kick was nothing she'd known in hemp, wine
or Nembutal, it was Nothing itself in a uniform of gold, and Nothing loomed bigger than Anything ever could hope to be. Her gray

sweater went white, the green room was bleached and she'd never seen people so free of color, nor sounds so pale.

The sounds were Lukey sounds about Tony. "I hysted the king," he giggled, bobbing lankily on a wooden cracked-wood chair, white as snow. "The king hisself and when that Shylock sees no more worldly goods—oh, mama!"

It was a slow dance to the sink where she retched, and the men were consoling over somebody else's vomiting, for though it came from her there was neither pain nor importance to it. She vomited for some paralyzed junky powerless to vomit, and felt saintly for the gesture. But Dincher screamed through a wall or window and floated screaming in through the ceiling as she retched for the Crippled Junkies Benevolent Association. "Make the boy sing," she said, meaning to say something like it but different, and the Dinch threw bigger people around, off chairs, pounded them to beds, one bed. Then somehow there was peace and music and the Dinch blew a trumpet like Louis, like Sunshine himself at last over all the world, and it was on his arm she lowered herself past old wood balustrades white as peace to snow dark as hallway lights in some palsied junky's trap. There was Nothing wrong with the air or winter sitting on it. No light held still, but she kept an arm on Dincher's voice to keep earth solid beneath her. He had Armstrong tucked in the other arm and an angry silence with Christ and his cross on his face. In a cellar Timmy Lawless carried a gold-leaf book to her and knelt where she lay on a floor of blankets. "A pret-ty Bible for Diaaaane," like Paddy's *Diaaaane.* Timmy gave a Bible to her hand, while Dincher made little sunshine on his horn. "Cleanimup good," the Shylock said, "muhfookagoombah!" and lighted a fat cigar in dust-gray, low-ceiling light. "They hysta Tone, how you like-uhmo. Cleanup all a junk."

She found her head on Dincher's lap when she awoke, and knew she'd slept through the night, some night, by the pale green sun-paths of dust rolling from the window overhead. Dincher, back propped on the wall, played half-dead fingers in her hair.

"Didn't you sleep, Dinch?"

"Nah," and no more.

With difficulty she swung around to sit beside him, grabbed at her temple where it seemed a flung stone rapped her, but it was inside and passed immediately. "Why didn't you sleep, Dinch?" and scraped at the roof of her mouth with her tongue to moisten the powder-puff taste.

Dincher indicated with his head a pile of rubble near a huge wooden crate, where Timmy Lawless slept curled in a knot, his sandy mat of hair lighted with sun and dust. Diane laughed hoarsely, cleared her throat. "I thought it was a dream about Timmy," and found the leather-bound Bible buried in a swirl of blankets. "You mean Timmy—— Oh, Dincher, Timmy wouldn't bother me. Are you kidding?"

"Who knows?" The boy shrugged; then, still stiff against the wall, eyes on the concrete ceiling, said, "I don't want you should hang around by Paddy's. No more, you hear? 'N I don't want you snortin no more Horse; you hear?"

"Dincher, don't tell me anything like that. Don't tell me what *you* want for *me* to do." Yet she felt the heat of pleasure over it, over the boy's tight lips. She leaned over and kissed him near his jaw, on twitching flesh.

"I telephoned Carter. Like-he's all worried'n I telephoned him I got a hold of you. You're hot like stoves; he told me Fuzz is hangin by his house. You gotta stay off the street."

"I know, Dinch. . . ." Numbly she sat, trying vaguely to reconstruct the days wasted behind her, caught back only fragments of sound and mood, and gave it up. "Where are we, Dinch? What is this place?"

"The Shylock's cellar. Like-he leaves us lob here till he pushes the genius out. Then we get like-a whole floor, a cool pad for you'n me, doll."

"Dinch, I can't . . ." She didn't know what it was she felt unable to do—knew only that it involved other people. Johnny, Carter, maybe Dincher himself; her brain felt small enough to ride in circles around her skull's inside.

"You jus relax, doll. Later I show you the pad. Like-you be cool in there long as you want." He struggled up and stretched, then lumbered out, his fine soft pin-stripe stiff with wrinkles.

Timmy stirred, let out an eerie infant's wail, and swung that furrowed face, puffed now with sleep, around in the dozing dust of the room. The colorless eyes blinked for focus, stared unseeing into shadows, then halted, pointing up to the window, mirroring its frozen light. Diane could feel him growing conscious as he stared at the light, trembled as he began to whimper, lurched with a staggering shock when he shot to his feet and ran screaming into walls, falling, creeping, bucking headfirst into crates, sobbing like any child lost in a nightmare.

"Timmy, Timmy!" she shouted, and the words tore at her throat. "Timmy, come here, baby, come on over to Diane. Come here, Timmyboy."

He straightened up and grinned from the shadows, glass eyes in the dark, then came shyly like an orphan in his gabardine sack of a coat and knelt before her as in worship. "I gave you a pret-ty Bible; d'you lye-kut?" and saw it by her side, ran sensitive fingers over the heavy embossing, lifted it to place it in her lap. While she fingered the gold-edged pages to humor him, he stared up at daylight again, sighed hugely from his very bowels, and whimpered, "Another fuckin day."

He lowered himself willingly when she took his head to her lap, groaned in a faraway voice as she stroked the leather of his neck. One leg stiffened while the other curled, and both feet were at home on grimy concrete the color of his shoes. Grime and ancient dampness were mixed in the dead smell of putrescence, and another world leaked in on muted cries from pushcart hawkers in the sun outside. Little voices played somewhere, child voices the color of bells, while Diane stroked a leather neck deep in the chill and static colors of remorse.

Tony the Shylock waddled in rich with the smell of cigar smoke. He grunted to his seat beside her, wrinkled his overblooded face in a grin, and patted her head. "Lilla Spaniol, you like a stay by Tone for his a cell-uhmo? We cleanimup a shit make nice a houze," and leaned smugly back on an arm to smoke, panting as if he'd done a mile in record time.

"Stay here?" She tried hard to recall what Dincher had told her. "A whole floor. How about Dincher's floor he's supposed to get?"

"Well, 'at's a Stone, he's a sick-uhmo," tapping his temple with a finger. " 'At's a maestro for paint a pitch alla time, he's a craze. I pushim oud, it's a die in a street-uhmo by whiska for the snow," and laughed in falsetto till he groaned. " 'At's a Bobba Stone, oh boy."

"*Stoney?* Stoney lives up there? Push the bastard out and let him die! He stinks, the bastard, let him die!"

Timmy leaped to his feet and danced, whirling in the blown bell of his coat. "Kill the bast'rd! Fuh-kim! Let him die in the storm!" spinning and leaping and laughing with terrible new energy. Tony applauded while Diane sat frozen in a horror she couldn't name, until Dincher came through the blot of a door with an open cardboard box of food and steaming coffee.

"What's goin on? Come on, I got some eats, like-we have breakfiss."

Diane could take only coffee; everything else was lead, even to look at. While she told Dincher what Tony had said, she wondered why she'd burst out so emotionally over Stoney—whether it was simply because he stood in the way of a cool trap in which to stay, or because of the rigid prying he stood for. She watched Dincher approach the Shylock at the old roll-top desk on the side, where he'd retreated and busied himself with dusty papers as she quoted him. "What's this like-about Stoney keepin the pad? I gave you the loot, di'n I? You wanna make me your enemy?"

Tony grinned up from his swivel seat. "Muh-take it ease, Dinch. You know Stone? He's a stay lilla while for get a new trap. You get a loft next, donja worry, keed," and winked exaggerated confidence at Dincher.

"Nex what? Nex year? Like-you gonna hold the loot like-till nex year or somethin? You get him out right away; you hear? Right away, Tony."

"Hey, Dinch, you what's a ma', you no trust a Tone?" and he struggled out of the chair, shuffled after the boy as he came up to where Diane sat on blankets. "You stay by Tony by cell a keep a you lady friend for sleep-uhmo; ketch on?" and winked as though Diane were not right there watching. "Nobody's a botha you for sleep by cell-uhmo; see? Tony's a sleep by boiler room'n Timmy's a go back for Dillsotel," and found something uproarious in it, laughing as he sat down beside Diane. "Lilla Spaniol, it's a big kicks okay by a Tone; donja? Timmy, descratziado, cleanimup a the broom; whadda you think-uhmo?"

Diane got up and took Dincher to the door. "I can't stay here, Dinch. It's filthy. There's no place even to bathe."

The boy pondered, screwing up his face. "You wanna get on? I got some dynamite, it's from India. Real Gunja." He blinked, looking at her in the plastic shadows. "Nothin like Horse, it's oney jive, but it's good charge. You wanna get on, doll?"

"Sure, Dinch, but what about a place? Aah, I'll find a way. Let's get on, Dinch; we'll think about it later."

When they returned to the blankets and lighted up, the Shylock took Timmy out, and outside in other portions of the basement they rattled about for hours while Dincher and Diane smoked into easy laughter and adolescent kissing play. He spoke of the Bronx and his mother and brothers and sisters and a father he hated. "He's like-crazy. For real, I mean it," and told how he'd had to club the old man with his fists to keep him from beating a sister. And told of two elder brothers growing in the father's image, beating the three girls for anything from wearing lipstick to staying out after ten. "I could kill the whole two of 'em, like-sometimes I forget they my brother'n I could like-really murder both of 'em'n my old man together. The old lady, she listens to evvy word he says, the old man." He blasted fiercely on the trumpet, a vein leaping in his temple, then let the music coast, and he was singing out of it, talking now and then about playing for people like Louis. "*Down among the ri-vuh*," Diane sang, and the easy laughter welled up, and they smoked, and Dincher spoke of the big score he'd make so that he might fill his life with music.

The Shylock called them from the doorway, had·them follow him past the wooden staircase leading down from above to an alcove behind it. "You think Tone, he's a slop-uhmo?" and in a grand manner swung open a slatwood door to disclose a spotless, windowless bathroom, with tub, basin and toilet, even the screen of a ventilator near the sloped low ceiling. "You stay by Tone, goddam you clean like a fish," and laughed, pushing Timmy up the stairs with a bushel basket of scrap and dirt.

Diane tried the bath while Dincher went with the key she gave him over to Carter's for a change of clothes. Soaking in the penetrating warmth. Soaked in the languor of marijuana, singing:

> "*Poor ole Joe, he was only forty-two,*
> *He didn't kno-o-ow the things he shouldn't do . . ."*

in the best facsimile of Louis' sunshine voice she could manage, rattling it 'way down low, as satchelmouth as she could. Steeped in penetrating marijuana warmth that let her blood swear she'd been living only as well as she could, that Horse was the tail of Nothing she never wanted again, she dried herself with a kind and loving towel the Shylock had hoarded in cellophane against just such an emergency. Suddenly the Shylock's shouting began outside, and a thumping and hooting that rattled the slatwood door. "Descratziado sonumabitch-uhmo! You wanna see her *bo-o-ody?*" and a thump, a slam, a shriek.

Diane pushed out into wild mayhem, Timmy crashing backward into barrels that toppled upon him, the Shylock finding him in debris with a foot in his middle, then throwing his full weight upon the shriveled, shrieking half-man. "You wanna see sonumabitch a you wanna . . . look on a . . . woomun," finding Timmy with fists anywhere he scrambled.

Diane snapped at him with the towel. "Leave him alone, you crazy old bastard, let him up," whipping at his back with a fierce power she felt in a thousand electrified muscles.

Tony complained as he sat off Timmy to face her. "He's a pook at a door for look-uhmo," then gagged on the cigar still in his mouth when he saw Diane naked above him, and turned, punching at Timmy seated beside him, blaming that sack of sorrow, in a garbled tongue Italy never knew, for Diane's exposure. Timmy was overpowering him with hugs and kisses when Dincher came down, a bundle in his arms, and fell back paralyzed against the banister when he saw Diane.

"Oh, hell, Dincher, give it here. This is a nuthouse," taking the clothes into the steamy little cubicle, shutting the door against the babble of three voices at once. The gauge was dead in her where her stomach quivered, but the laugh hit her when she went out in a dark-green turtle-neck pullover and black shirt, gliding on flat rubber heels.

Tony was leaning close up to Dincher while the boy grinned, wagging his dark round head. "He wanna see her *bo-o-ody*, eh!" tilt-headed, stretching up on toes in indignation, while Timmy Lawless sat on a barrel sucking wine from a pint bottle. In the brooding light from an old dusty bulb.

"Fuh-cue!" Timmy wailed while Dincher placated the Shylock. "Kiss my lily-white arse, you damn furriner," focusing his eyes far off into his secret world, singing soprano asides to the phantoms that peopled it.

When Diane and Dincher broke reeling into laughter, the Shylock threw his hat to the floor in rage, got it back on and hobbled up the stairs, cursing in Italian. His generation had no place here in his own domain; he had to retreat to calmer places until he could invent some kind of adjustment.

Twice more that day Dincher brought in food. Timmy danced brilliantly to trumpet and singing, hours slid under crates and slept by the forty-watt indifference of marijuana smoke. Pipes squeaked along the low ceiling in their white insulation jackets, while outside the minutes shrieked hurtling by on mad gear-grinding, coughing trucks, and voices splashed till dusk, when inside and outside met in general muteness. Dincher was asleep, Timmy gone.

Only the lights, like blisters on veins black with age; only the dust and stone-brick walls; only unlamenting airlessness in cold corners that had never seen light. Gummy darknesses rolled inside her. The quiet lay covered with dust. Diane stretched up from blankets gray-splotched with the ashes of many cigarettes, brushed lint from her skirt, and found the green draped coat on a nailed-up crate. Her steps to the door were dancelike.

She whirled at Dincher's sleep-cracked call of her name, saw him sitting up, rubbing at his eyes, lips loose as a helpless child's. "Where you goin, doll? You goin out? Hey—" and he was up, hurrying to her —"you can't go out, doll. The Fuzz is evvyplace lookin for you-like."

"Dincher, don't be silly. Maybe there's one or two of them around. What do you think I am, a real fugitive? I've got to get out for a while."

Wordless, he looked at her, then marched about in deliberation. Finally, with a Hollywood sacrificial stiffening, he got into hat and coat, fixed her kerchief tight on her head, and began to lead her out.

"You got a couple of joints to take along?" she asked. "I'm coming down a little, Dinch; I know I'll want to get on. Take some pod, Dinch."

"I don't carry none. Like-I got some stashed by the station."

Bleecker Street was a frozen stretch of quiet nighttime snow. He led her east away from MacDougal and downtown along West Broadway's broad desertion, where only traffic in the road showed life. She listened to Dincher's odd complex of tenderness, hate and boasting hardness, sat with it over wine in some Little Italy tavern on Broome Street, growing uneasy with aftergauge fatigue that sat heavier and heavier on her neck. Till, in the creaking booth, in light weaker than that of the Shylock's cellar, she was alarmed at the mention of Buster Wallinger's name. "The General, he's a jumpin cat, like-besides all his bullshit he's like-makin a real score'n I figger for a hunk of it, myself. He's mad you di'n meet 'im the other day to go out there. He di'n score anyway, so if you want, you can con him to take you to the kid again."

"Dinch, what's his deal out there? What's your connection with him, whatever he's up to? He's a walking jackpot, Dinch, keep off him."

"I jus make a li'l trip now'n then, it's nothin. But he's like-leery, like-he's oweys got the horrors, so I do a li'l trip," grinning with heavy-lidded cunning in that Hollywood-gunman way. "I gotta go home now, doll," and it broke through the film of unreality that Dincher was really eighteen years old.

"Hey, my birthday!" She remembered now out of the dull, blanketed Tea. "It was—what's today, Dinch? Gee, I missed my birthday."

"Not me. It was Saturday'n you was by Paddy's'n I was stickin by the Bronx, jus comin in for an hour-like to look for you. But like-I di'n forget, doll. It's why I wanna go home'n get it."

She had to lean over and kiss him out of a girlish tingling. "What is it, what is it, Dinch?" But he wouldn't say; he enjoyed the game too much himself. She ran to phone Carter, but there was no answer after many rings, and back in the booth she realized that another Tuesday lay upon them, keeping Carter away from her reach. She let Dincher take her back to the cellar, let him kiss her with boyish passion, let him tuck her wearing only her slip into blankets that smelled of dust. Watched him leave and fell quickly asleep with a remote fear of rats.

Then days pushed one another by, scrambled up till one blended into the next. The boy Dincher brought food, the old man Tony patted her head and called her Spaniol, the creature Timmy lamented with wine and dancing for the nameless thing which had taken his life from the shell others could see. Dincher stayed boyish in blankets beside Diane, as though her will to love were an abused thing he didn't dare aggravate. Often he brought word from Carter, swearing he'd refused to expose her place of hiding just as she'd insisted he do. Somewhere within the happy robe of unconsciousness she wove about her with hemp a pinlight of pride, like some waning

star, still had to keep Carter from knowing she slept in a cellar. He
was really such a puritan.

And each night in the murky forty-watt stupor she wore the gigantic copper earrings Dincher had brought her, and the heavy me-
dallion swung from her neck. Each night he blew silver from his
trumpet, rich light into the cold, dark lamenting corners of their
souls. And each night, while shadows lumbered with unearthly
patience, the boy wrung a promise from the Shylock. "Soon, soon,
you get a loft, Dinch, donja worry for Tone," with a pat on Diane's
combed head, an ancient look of love watering in his eyes.

By Stoney's angry fire four flights up, while the painter burnished a
gilt frame propped on his easel, Joe Letrigo searched hard around
Carter's face, as if looking could teach him the secret that allowed
so proper a man to separate a woman from the dank slime of prostitution and marry her. After their first talk at the Riviera he'd been impressed with Carter's easy understanding of people, his strict reluctance to blame a single soul on earth for any warped kind of conduct.
So that Joe had told the painter, as Carter departed, that the man
with a coal miner's slouch had come to earth a hundred years too
soon. Yet understanding alone didn't seem adequate equipment for
overlooking something like prostitution, and now, by the heat of
flames, it was unquieting to feel such awe for a man over an involvement so repugnant to him. He knelt and dropped split boards on the
fire, thankful enough to Carter for absolving Diane in his mind by
being married to the sister who had one time been the whore Lizzie
had thrown in his face.

Carter was glad to have found Joe and appreciative toward Stoney
for bringing their meeting about. Three nights they'd met to sit
around with talk and drink, with vitality he'd rarely seen in the Village, with stories only old soldiers could share. He wondered about
Joe's long career at soldiering, about the nature of the impulse which
had pressed him to the aid of Jews; this Southerner who matched
no Southerner he'd ever known, no recollected soldier type, yet
reminded him somehow of all the people one might meet on city
avenues or lonely backland roads.

"Here, how does it look?" the painter wanted to know, standing
back from the frame, now solid with his portrait of himself as some
brooding Christ.

Joe only laughed when he looked, but Carter could see more than a saintly Stoney; he saw Stoney himself framed for Mrs. Lattimer, and he truly hoped for all concerned that the lady would be touched by the gift, allowing himself the edge of a laugh over such a relationship: they deserved each other. He'd said it aloud to Stoney's pleasure when the painter, one beery night, had as much as asked him for his mother-in-law's hand.

Stoney slipped back on the bed till the wall propped him. "My position is quite questionable. I believe—" nodding his well-groomed head—"that a crisis is at hand. My position——"

"Man of destiny," Joe sighed to Carter, "man against fate, every damn breath he takes. You hear him talk up his *historical rightness* over that first beer he let into himself in thirty years? Godamighty!"

Stoney lighted an Italian cigar, muttered, "These Italian people!" and Joe fell laughing into the chair. "Tony the Shylock," Stoney said, "your *paisan*, has given me two weeks to get out. One week is gone, but I continue to feel a profound admiration for his old-world discretion. I can't imagine what came over him. For twenty——"

"Carter, you're right again. Stoney by God is softenin up, sure enough. You hear that: *I can't imagine*, somethin that man never could admit."

"For twenty dollars out of a hundred forty I owe him, he let me stay."

"He has his own devices," Carter suggested, coming over to sit on the bed. "Maybe he doesn't have a new tenant till two weeks are gone."

"Everything has its reason with you," Joe said. "You really feel strong about that; don't you, boy?"

"I think so," Carter said.

"My position," Stoney began again, "seems——"

"The hell with your damn position," Joe shouted. He got up. "Come on, Webb, let's get on uptown and scuff that Louella around. Scrotum-face says he's done with her."

Carter stretched. "I'm for the ball," meaning a measure of it, feeling some small hint of the spirit he'd left long ago in the army, something in which Joe seemed endlessly rich.

"What should I say?" Stoney called after them at the door. "When I present it, what should I say, Carter?"

"Don't be crude." Carter stopped on the stairs. "Don't say anything, just sign it in a corner. *To Vivienne with humble esteem,* and sign it: *Jesus.*"

Joe was still booming with laughter on the ground-floor landing, where Tony the Shylock leaned on the cellar door, grinned tilt-headed, wrinkling his bubble of a nose. "How's a Stone? He's awrigh?"

"He stinks," Joe said, and found himself apologizing to Carter for it in the night outside. "Everyone's okay with you?" he went on, going toward MacDougal. "That can't be real, Carter. Everyone?"

"Don't misinterpret me, soldier. Hardly anyone is okay with me, but I find it hard to blame them. I keep seeing reasons for their distortions. I get mad at people, but I wind up hating myself for it; I'm a kind of cripple that way," and laughed, a little embarrassed.

"That's no kind of cripple, boy. You got a paper asshole is all," watching obliquely for Carter's reaction, although knowing he'd only laugh.

"Maybe, Joe. I'll tell you, that's how I judge the state of my health. If I love people I'm robust, if I dislike them I'm ill, if I hate them I'm about to die. They're great mirrors, great reflections of ourselves."

"Oee," Joe laughed, hailing a cab. "Tell that to Stoney. By God I'll tell him. Let me tell it just so's I can be there to watch him," and gave the driver an address on Central Park West.

They spoke of Stoney clear to the running lights of Broadway, agreed the man was a despot and laughed when Carter gave a quick description of Vivienne, only in terms of her primness, her formidable religionism. "She'll drive Stoney nuttier than he is, if he ever does connect with her," Carter said, but doubted whether anything could ever come about between those two. After the painter's outspoken interest in the Stately Lady, Carter had looked for signs of newly inspired womanliness in her, some sort of thawing, but she'd been as unbending and icy as ever the last Sunday at the hospital, and only Edna's new cheerfulness in her bright new room had lightened at all that two-hour burden. Thinking of Edna now in the rumbling cab, he felt the breath of guilt over brawling about while Edna lay dying as she smiled, and defensively threw himself back to Stoney's yapping harangues; that voice left little room for preoccupation. "But one's consciousness should never be blinded," the painter had complained when Carter, at the tail of a conversation, had warned him against letting Vivienne know of Edna's doom. The painter had been pumping him for some endearment Vivienne might have expressed, and Carter, reluctant to embarrass anyone with a portrayal of Vivienne's true feeling for all men (beardless or not), had simply told him how delicate a woman she was and had wound up with the warning.

"Everyone should be told everything in this age of self-imposed unconsciousness," Stoney'd persisted, and had agreed to keep the secret only when Carter'd pointed out that the mother, helplessly shocked, might blurt it out to Edna, who no longer needed consciousness in whatever kind of age this was. It had pacified Stoney, who—Carter, watching Joe stare out at Broadway crowds and lights, now remembered—had then digressed with a discussion of Joe: "Incapable, yessir, incapable of blinding his own sensibility in this unconscious world. A soldier who chooses his wars, a veritable crusader for truth. Volunteered into ours at eighteen. Good Lord, when I think of myself at eighteen, looking forward to nothing more consuming than the Saturday-night dance . . . Well, at eighteen he was in Africa, then Europe, fighting and getting torn up quite severely. Four times. Four times wounded. Once a grenade wound in the shoulder, then a fragment wound in a leg, then machine-gunned: three slugs in the flesh of his back—" at a time when he personally surrounded a German squad, Joe himself had later said—"and finally a chest wound from a sniper's bullet that touched a nerve and put him out of the mess for good. But that finished him in only one war. He went abroad again with the merchant marine and got mixed up in the Israel affair. A bullet in his calf there too, but he refers to that as a scratch." The painter had been a child in ecstatic reverence of a hero, grimacing incredulously. "Just imagine being ripped into by something fierce and hot and silent, something you don't really understand. Imagine the horror. You're torn open, see yourself inside out, so to speak. And then to go back into the death, the noise, the chaos, after a stay in relatively composed civilization."

That had always been a mystery Carter could never fathom. He'd never been able really to learn even from Normie how a man could go back, once out of it. Normie, when Carter kicked him all over a jungle for letting them send him back, had only kidded that he couldn't stand Carter being left alone with strangers. Joe had been rarely honest about it the other night. "Form of cowardice," he'd said after rumination. "After that ole grenade bit me I wanted *no* more. But I was ashamed to quit, just hadn't the guts for it. Could have bucked for Z.I., but I turned Yankee overseas and had to keep fightin so long as any Yank fought. Man, that's what'll make a man fight in wars he has no stake in at all; it's how all the fascist governments get good men afightin. Just as scared second and third time, but more in control; you know. That last time was back to the Bulge, when the Krauts were shootin prisoners, medics. I was with some doggies in an English pub when the news broke, all of us just braggin how we kept ourselves in Group B at the convalescent hospital. When that Bulge news broke we just fell into a group cryin jag, those replacement kids scuffin about out there not knowin hide nor hair about them squareheads, not knowin shit from good apple butter, just gettin themselves shot to carrion while us ole sojers—well, in three days we were all of us, includin forty-year-ole Eddie Hague, bald head and all, on our way back to—" and he'd laughed into Carter's speculative gaze—"to soft music; would be to you damn jungle bums, I guess."

It had struck Carter then that Joe had a rare quality of honesty, and now he asked right out, "What chases you into war, Joe? Since you were a boy, seems you've done nothing else."

"Wild hair in my ass," Joe whispered. Then he brought his voice up. "Always been that way. I'm a vagabond kind of guy, Carter, just take naturally to sojerin," yet he knew it was something more than that. He watched the crowds ooze slowly by, reflecting the flicker of lights from movie houses. "This stuff—I think deep down I'm fearful of all this machine-made pageantry. You know, there's a little bit of this in most every town in the Union, a little street of neon, and it runs in everybody's blood, the neon. Well, I been sojerin, I been sojerin. In darker places," knowing he expressed nothing of what he felt. Turning straight in his seat, he watched the street lose the last blinking lights of midtown and become a gray stretch of granite, shadow and mystery. It was an abrupt halt of human motion, yet the empty street spoke more of life somehow than had the glimmering, meretricious Broadway full of mirthless laughter and the vast nightmare pilings of incandescence and neon hysteria. Like Louella, he thought, and all her kind—a nation of animated neon signs. Sometimes Stoney was right, and Diane vibrated in his mind, a strange ambiguity of girlish suppleness and city mechanization.

"Your little sister-in-law, Carter; what ails her? How come she's so soft and gentle one time and tight as steel the next?"

"That's a sociological problem; we'll talk about it some night. Meanwhile, what're we up to now with Louella? Let's get a drink before we take her song and dance."

"Oh, she'll have lots of that ole pink and green for us. Where . . . Carter, where is Diane? Where's she hidin herself?" He felt himself blush for asking; he'd never spoken directly to Carter about her before.

"I don't know, Joe. She's hiding out from her mother's dogs." He didn't know how much to tell the man. "You're pretty strong on the kid, aren't you?"

"Interested. She fascinates me. Why the detention home?" Now he'd go right along asking what his guts wanted to know. "What's ole Vivienne houndin her about, Carter?"

"It's a habit. You know how mothers are. Look at Louella and her demure old girl. I never saw a woman before who could send each eye looking in a different direction. She just doesn't have enough eyes to use protecting her little twenty-six-year-old child. Let's not put in too much time up there if Mama hangs around."

"Okay, and if Mama's not about, we share anything there's two of, and where there's only one, may the best man get into it," and they laughed till the cab swung to a halt in the doorlight across from the park.

In green-and-red woolen booties Louella danced for them at the door, swung a flair in her skirt and drew smoke through her silver holder as she let them know Mother had departed for Florida, then took them across the lighted foyer into a dark room pierced by the shaft of a spotlight that bathed a couch. "Joe and Carter," she murmured dutifully, "that's Harry, this is Mike, and those are Lanie, Roger and Cherie," indicating the glow of cigarettes in the darkness surrounding her as she squatted on the lighted couch.

"Let's get out of here," Carter whispered when he saw Louella pick up a sheaf of papers. "It's the poetry, it's the poetry."

Joe, muffling his laughter, pulled him down on a couch near the door. "We can make it to the pantry once she gets under way."

Louella got under way, picked up emotion as she read about the man who understood her most being gone, about solemn candles lit and nobody looking into the bier. At one point, apparently when the lines were closest to her heart, she closed her eyes and recited quietly, head back on pillows behind her.

Joe was quick; in an instant he had Carter through the foyer to the pantry, and out of that wide white room into the huge tiled kitchen with a full bottle of Scotch under his arm. They poured it on ice and drank.

"Would you believe it less you saw it?" Joe asked and laughed. Then he shook Carter's shoulder. "Hey, don't be so damn solemn. You taken up with that lament of hers?"

Carter wagged his head and took his drink fast. "Even seeing it, I don't believe it. How can she make such a buffoon of herself?"

"Beats me." Joe filled their glasses. "Packs some good whisky, though."

They drank the bottle down to its halfway mark before Carter's conscience began to buck in him. "Let's get back before we hurt her feelings," and pulled Joe along when he frowned. "Come on, maybe she hasn't missed us yet."

Joe held him up in the doorway to the foyer, signaled with a finger at his lips for quiet, and pointed to where a man crept on all fours from the darkened sitting room. They fell back quickly to watch him come up sitting in a corner of the foyer, giggling to himself as he worked open a penknife and in deft moves sliced through the insulation of a light cord. He swung around toward the wall, and they could see his shoulders work hastily under the plaid jacket before the sparks hissed and the room fell into darkness.

The man rushed into the pantry and swung the door closed, but his grin vanished when he saw them beside him in the light his sabotage hadn't affected. "I couldn't stand it any more," he whispered apologetically. "You fellows only just came; I've been listening for an hour." He looked quickly from one to the other and back, his big, athletic frame fairly writhing in embarrassment. "I don't make a habit of this sort of conduct. Honestly. Louella is—she's swell, she's a wonderful girl, I've known her family for years. Honestly. But the poetry!" He slapped his forehead, then laughed when they did. "Don't offer to replace the fuse for her. Please. I'm Mike Williams," and he pumped their hands gratefully when they identified themselves.

The three were around the kitchen table drinking Scotch when

Louella shuffled in. "The fuse has blown," she announced sorrowfully, going past them to a cabinet near the floor. "The lights are all out on the other side," and turned, smiling, with a fistful of long red candles. "This'll be more fun," she said in a high, happy, childish voice. "Come on, there are drinks in there, don't be so antisocial, come on," but she didn't wait for them at all.

Mike sat wagging his lean head when she left. "Poor kid, she's really so kind and generous. She just can't seem to—she's just always unhappy." He looked from one to the other as though waiting for some comment, then drank as they drank. "Why can't people be happy?" he lamented. "She's always had everything, everything. Honestly, I've known her and her family for years. We were even sort of engaged when we were at school." He took a moment to look back at other times, then shook his head. "She can't stand anything for long. And—and whenever she's about to break down she writes one of those sorry poems. It's a nervous breakdown, honestly; every poem she writes is a nervous breakdown." He went on that way till the Scotch was gone, then went with them to the room where candlelight made the vast space eerie. Mike introduced them around to the two girls they'd met in darkness, to Harry, whom they'd met the last time they'd been here, and to the squarely built man named Roger, who sat holding Louella's hand on the couch littered with poetry. There was music, good things by Moussorgsky and Franck, somber here in candlelight. All the talk was in whispers. Louella crisscrossed from Roger to Mike, over to Harry for an instant each, then quickly to Joe and Carter, whispering to them about a pigeon on her window sill that morning. Finally she took Roger across to the farthest side of the room for a long time in the shadows.

The girl Lanie went after coats and brought them to Mike, Cherie and Roger; the four of them left after whispered good-bys, and Louella glided around, blowing out several candles. She took Joe by the hand and pulled him to the shadows where she had sat with Roger. "Joe—" she played with his lapels—"don't leave before the others. Please, Joe, my mother is away and I'm afraid of him. He looks mild, I know, but when we're alone——"

"Who, that Harry? Thought he was an ole friend of yours."

"He is, but, Joe, you don't know, he's very strange. His—he gets ill if he can't have his own way. Joe, please don't leave before the others."

"Okay," and he sat there awkwardly with her head on his shoulder, staring into the lighted part of the room where Carter and bald-headed Harry spoke, drank and smoked. After a silence that grew too heavy he brought her to her feet, chuckled foolishly, and went with an arm around her waist to where the others sat whispering. "Hey, what're we hushin about?" he said aloud. "Like a damn morgue in here."

Carter was the only one to laugh. From the gray look of Harry, Joe feared he had abused some kind of religious law, and turned to ask Louella about it, but she was taking Carter out of the room by an arm. He sighed and sat beside Harry.

"Who is it?" Harry wanted to know in his mild voice.

"Who's what, who's what?"

"First it's this fellow Roger, then it's you. Then it turns out to be him," pointing a thumb toward the door Louella and Carter had just gone through. "It was supposed to be me, but now I don't know *who* it is." He looked around when Carter returned alone, watched as he approached, and studied him closely when he sat down smiling. "Who is it?" he asked Carter despairingly. "First it's Roger, then it's him, then it's you. It's supposed to be me, and then——"

"Listen, boy," Joe began, but broke up laughing.

Carter spoke past Harry to Joe. "She wants to go skiing. Let's get out of here. I don't want to go skiing. She took me out to the kitchen to tell me she wants to go skiing. I told her I didn't *want* to go——"

"Who is it? Who is it?" Harry was shouting now.

"Don't get ill, boy." Joe held him down on the couch. "Who is it, Carter? Harry wants to know who the main man is with Louella."

"It's nobody," Carter muttered. "It's everybody or nothing," and sat shaking his head when Harry ran out. "Let's go, Joe. I don't want to go skiing." He got up for a drink and returned with one for Joe. "Don't laugh. She's a sad girl; she's bugged up. She wanted to know if I minded her being alone with you so long. When were you alone? Am I drunk?"

Harry came in with his head hanging, catching coral reflections of light on his shiny scalp. He carried a glass case of carving knives past them and stooped to hide them under one of the many couches. "Don't tell her where they are," he whispered miserably, and went to sit alone in shadows. "She hates her mother" came irrelevantly out of darkness.

"Where are they?" Louella was in the room. "Where are the knives?"

Joe pointed solemnly and she got them, walked out of the room with Harry behind her.

"Good-by." Carter stood. "This is a circus."

"Well, don't go. Isn't it fun? Man, these people're puttin on a show."

"I got a paper asshole," and Carter went with Joe beside him to find his coat in a foyer closet. He had a sickening feeling that he was watching something through a keyhole, that he was some kind of snoop gloating over some cripple's attempt to walk, and he envied Joe for feeling nothing like it.

Joe grinned with him at the door. "You got a paper bottom is right. Man, you could just sit by and watch; all this is none of your damn fault." Yet when Carter left he turned to face the huge apartment with a bitter impatience growing in him. He went to the closet and searched through hanging clothes for a man's coat that was unfamiliar, found it and found a black Homburg. Then he carried them to the kitchen, where Louella leaned, weeping, against Harry.

"Can't we have some privacy?" Harry's voice arched and cracked.

"Jo-oe," a broken wail and she ran to the door, turned and called, as if from a great distance, "I'll telephone tomorrow, Harry," and disappeared.

"Here you go." Joe held out the hat and coat, trying to keep his eyes from Harry's. He stood that way while the man snatched his things and departed. Then he went searching through rooms for Louella, trying light switches that worked, some that didn't, and finally finding her behind a desk in the paneled study furnished with leather pieces. She sat scribbling grimly on a pad, blond hair hanging over her eyes. Joe fell into a chair.

"This room was my father's," she informed him. "They're separated, but he won't give poor Mother her divorce," writing, as she spoke, with grim certainty, with all the weight of living in her face. "Chains, chains," she muttered, then threw the pencil across the room and stood, her eyes wild in the half-light from the desk's lamp. "Oh, let's not be unhappy, Joe. Just for tonight let's be gay, let's laugh—" pulling him by the wrist—"let's dance."

But she forgot it as soon as they were back in the candlelit room. They drank, and she grew more and more morose, told intimate family stories in a doleful undertone. Of a father younger than her mother, a man she identified for herself through the years only by the women he'd kept. Of a mother forever in sorrow, forever concerned with her home, with the development of her daughter. "When I was eight a huge bug hooked onto my arm and I screamed hysterically. But Mother wouldn't pluck it away; she insisted I do it myself, and she must have suffered to see me out of my mind with horror, but she wanted to teach me independence." On she murmured while candles burned low and autohorns turned to squeaks over the distance from the street. On incessantly in a voice like some despairing child, bringing scattered moments of her life into focus, falling over with her head in Joe's lap, murmuring on till she was more than half asleep. She started when he tried to squirm out from under her, and held fast to his trousers, wailing in a voice muffled now with sleep: "I scared, I scared . . . I scared."

The morning infiltrated through dust. On blankets colored with ashes Diane lay waiting for the shaft of blue specks to bleach yellow and blend shadows into outside noises. It was more than Tony's grunts or Timmy's wailing ecstasies that kept her so sleepless, for those sounds from the basement's other parts had many days before paled into the background, like the squeak of habitual water pipes. A war was on within her between the vague face of Johnny and the cries of marijuana's lazy children lolling about in the gumminess of her chest. This morning Buster was bound again for Long Island, and his vacant eyes were with her, as palpable now in the dankness as they'd been in the hissing heat of a Broome Street tavern, where Dincher had brought him to see her. The giant had leered and sneered a wordless accusation that she was a failure as a mother. Failure was nothing new to her, but the accusation was a scathing insult from so useless a man. It had fastened on the festering need of Johnny in her heart. Yet last night's Tea had pulled her down; she was mired in its gummy languor.

And last night's Dincher still upset her. Though she had pulled him down beside her, he'd been lax in his loving, complaining of Tony outside, dreaming of the loft upstairs and a thousand nights alone. He'd slept in her arms, then left, backed away to leave her in old gray airlessness with an old man outside to guard her. To protect her from pipes and barrels.

Diane sat up, pulled her skirt straight at the waist, and reached into a crate for a last night's roach. She secured the quarter-inch butt in a bobbypin, lighted it and sipped its concentrated hemp smoke. It was a signal for Tony, that absurd old man with a tilted, gray-fuzz head and salivant giggle. "Hokay, you rea-dy?" He dropped shakily to a knee beside her.

She kicked at him. "Get the hell away, you son-of-a-bitch!"

"Muh-what's a ma? Dinch, he's a no mind." He'd been aware Dincher stayed half the night on dirty blankets beside her. "'At's okay; Dinch, he's a Talian, he's a no mind for Tone."

"He'll break your Dago back, you old pig!" leaping to her feet. She took a kick at him and started for her shoes, but went back to kick again till he fell to his back by the stone-brick wall.

"He's a no mind. Lilla Spaniol!"

"I'm no Spaniol and Dincher's only half Dago and—" she was as absurd as he—"I'll *kill* you if you get up, you bastard, I'll *kill* you!" She buckled her sandals, found her boots and coat and kerchief and made it to the door, still dressing. Timmy sat up by the staircase; she rubbed the mat of his hair as she passed.

"Diaaaane—" like a baby's weeping—"d'you have the pret-ty Bible?"

"I'll get it later, Timmyboy," and she hurried out onto sun-splashed snow.

Up into MacDougal and along it to the Masters Hotel, where a doorman let her in, through halls on silencing rugs to the ladies' room. Cold water on the frozen heat of her face, trembling down her spine as she washed hard and made up meticulously, unable to keep her thoughts continuous. She felt dirty inside with every static kind of vice. A dirt that shoved her out, into Washington Square Park, now blank white where summers had enchanted it with group-singing at the fountain, soft voices in the night. . . . She had once seen a barefoot man playing his violin to a girl on a bench. All of it was gone, gone; only dirt remained, only pain.

But she was caught up in a river of children on their way to school. They shouted, sang and jumped, garnished the snow with color, the air with laughter, and challenged time with the joy shining out of their faces. Johnny would run some day, she thought, and ply his sounds into the air. She would have him, somehow, somehow, and teach him truth—somehow—that he could carry into his manhood as a barricade against fear. The old laws, darkness and myth, were the horrors her mother had injected into her just as Paddy injected heroin into his blood. Carter had freed her of the myths of aristocracy and religious superiority, had brought light into the darkness of her isolation from the movement of other people on earth—the heritage of her childhood in twenty secluded homes. None of that for Johnny. Somehow, somehow, no fear for Johnny.

She had turned back and down through the park into Sullivan, past the green-painted fence which ran forty feet before her mother's house. She strained to control the hatred bubbling in her for the woman, the strange, hostile creature who was her mother. In the hallway she paused till she could work the beginning of a smile into her eyes, then walked through dimness, watching the small tiles run like pebbles under her feet. She rapped on the door and held her breath.

The door's decay-colored paint was chipped, scratched and cracked. The door opened an eye's breadth, caught on a chain, closed and, after the rattling of a bolt, swung wide. "Diane," Mrs. Lattimer whispered, "they're looking for you. Oh, you must go back. You must, of your own free will. Before they take you away like a common criminal. Come in, darling, come in and sit down." Elegant in her fur coat and sweeping black hat, but a shivering girl in her voice. "Diane, dear, you must," as Diane sat on the couch. "They have police looking for you," as if she were helpless to call them all off. "Don't listen to that Carter. He'll only get you deeper——"

"Carter? What's he got to do with it? Look—" she got to her feet—"if you're building something in that mind of yours——"

"Now, Diane, let's not argue. Let's not waste time; I'm going to be late as it is."

"Well, don't be saying things about Carter. I'm going back. I came to see you first, and now you're starting to change my mind."

"Oh, darling, don't change your mind." Her voice broke and squeaked. She sat on the couch and took Diane's hand, eased her down beside her. "You're young; you don't see him clearly. They have a way, those quiet ones. I know—your father was that way, full of ulterior notions."

Diane trembled, but remembered control was important. "You don't know him, Mama. Carter never did anything but good for me *or* for Edna."

The woman smiled wanly, looking off into distant years. "The young won't be warned. All a mother's experience is nothing to them . . . they won't be warned." Her voice rode high again. "Diane, if you had listened to me before, all the time before——"

"Mama, what's the sense? I'm going back; why bother?"

"Yes. Yes, Diane. And pray, my dear. Pray, and you'll be forgiven."

"Okay, Mama. I just wanted to know—about the boy, about Johnny."

The woman stiffened. "Diane, that's one thing you must forget. After all, you were fortunate enough not to have grown used to him, and——"

"Fortunate! Not used to him!" Diane was on her feet again. "What's the matter with you? I want to know that he's all right. He's my baby; can't you understand that?" *You swine of a thickhead!*

"Of course, of course he is, dear," and pulled her down to the couch again. "Don't worry your little head over him. Oh, my baby," awkwardly taking Diane's head to her bosom. "My baby, I'm so glad you've seen the light. You'll be glad too. You'll see, you can still be pure in God's eyes. Our Lord is a forgiving God; He'll take you back . . . as He takes us all back."

Diane shuddered with contempt; she could tear the woman's flesh from the bone with her teeth, but the promise of success calmed her. "Mama," she said as delicately as she could, "I—I'm afraid to go back where I won't be able to know about the baby. That's the only thing that makes me waver."

"Oh, you'll know, you'll know. I'll keep you informed, you can depend on that."

"But you won't know, Mama." She pulled away and straightened up, smiling. "I know, I could write to the lady who—you know, the foster mother. Just to ask after his health. Then I'd be content, and . . . and I'd pray to God to protect them all. Nothing would bother me if I heard from the lady now and then."

"Yes. Now that's a way. You just write to the lady. Come along, dear, I believe I'm late for work."

Diane stood with her mother, holding the stranger's hand, feeling a need to continue talking. "You bought a new Christ," glancing at the larger, newer painting in the wide gilt frame, then looking again at her mother. "You're doing okay at that advertisement company, I can see that."

"Advertising agency. Yes, I certainly am. I have charge of the copy writers. Didn't you know? Oh, it is recent, it is. Come along, dear, I *must* hurry. Now, you're going back right away. I'm thrilled, I tell you, I'm really thrilled. I prayed for it. The night didn't go by without me praying you'd realize the proper thing to do. You see? Prayer does help. Oh, let me kiss you, my baby."

Diane braced her temper as the woman pressed lips to her cheek. "Ma, you'd better call up the Welfare Board that I'm on my way back. Gee, I feel good already," to banish suspicion from her mother's eye. "It'll be easy as long as I'm not worried about Johnny. Nothing'll bother me."

Her mother dialed quickly a number she knew well, and in a saccharine voice of delight she told someone it was no longer necessary to seek Diane, that she'd seen to it that the girl would return unescorted.

Arm in arm they went into sunlight that fell warmly on them through the edge of frost. "Oh, the address." Diane laughed shortly as if the thought had just struck her. "Don't forget the lady's address, Mama."

"Of course. I have it here, somewhere," and pulled an envelope from the clutter in her bag. Diane felt the blood race through her while the woman in furs tore a corner from the envelope and handed it over. A swift glance caught the neat array of words which formed a name and address, and Diane's hand clutched the scrap tightly as they walked, crushed it, jammed it into her pocket. When Diane turned west at the black guardrails of the park, Mrs. Lattimer stopped. "Good-by, dearest, I'm going toward Fifth. Here, you'll need train fare," and while she dug in her bag for a bill the old sarcasm reared. "Unless you've managed to——" But she caught herself with a hasty smile, handing Diane some crumpled money. "Don't forget to write me. I'm anxious about my baby too, you know," and giggled like a child.

"By-by, Mama." Diane threw a kiss, then watched the woman walk away delicately on the snow, and it was as though all the darkness from which she herself had sprung went fading now into distant, unremembered air. She had won. Quickly she loosened her fist and examined the paper. Yes, she had won, and it was the rarest sort of sensation welling up behind her eyes. There was a name, there was an address, and the town was Lawrence, Long Island. She'd heard of it, so decided it must be near by in the cluster of towns right outside

New York—near enough for Buster to take her there. She took a last
look at the flickering form in furs, the speck that had mothered her,
and turned up Fourth Street. No, the woman was not disappearing;
she was about to write things and to order others to write things for
millions to read, for millions to have thumped into them on subways
and buses, over radios and television sets. It was a sour taste in
Diane's stomach to know that Mrs. Lattimer had an effect on so
very many people.

But she shook herself loose of it: the moment was precious and
one to be indulged. She could recall no other time in her life when
there had been anything she could anticipate with happiness. She
would see Johnny; she would actually touch the pure flesh of her
baby. The park was a white wonderland, and she fairly danced
through it, kicking the crust so that it burst into powder glinting
gold in the sun. She wanted only the boy, the responsibility of giving
to him, the occupation of keeping him free of her own poisons—and
those poisons would vanish out of her, once she was busy with
him: men would become simply other people passing in the sun;
marijuana would be an absurdity in her need for a clear head. Johnny
would be her reason for living, a happy, rewarding reason which
would alter the hue and fortify the meaning of things around her.
Even now Waverly Place grew enriched in her eyes, its buildings no
longer gray lifeless cliffs, but the shelter for hundreds of human
beings, like herself doing what they could to gain a smiling moment.

Sixth was a wide avenue of freedom now, with no police to fear.
She even enjoyed the bustle of people entering the subway station,
the atmosphere about them of things getting done, getting made,
being developed. Where she had always been depressed at the sight
of people leaving air and light to lose themselves in the dark, gaping
subway maw, now she could justify it because of their purposeful
destinations. Even Buster Wallinger, dwarfing his table in the virtually empty Cosmopole, was a welcome sight to her.

"Right on time, beautiful," he observed, lurching to his feet. "Fact,
you're early. Come on, before Fuzz nails you."

"No, it's all right, Buster, I'm cool. I conned the old lady to call
them off. I got it, Buster, I know the address. Lawrence; you know
that town? Is it on your way out, near the road you take? Is it, Buster?"

"Yeah, I pass Lawrence; I can drop you off'n pick you up again, couple of hours. That suit you, beautiful?"

She sat across from him. "Suits me fine. You're swell, Buster," and meant it. In that sunny moment Buster was a fellow human being, clean of any error as she was clean of hers; only the trip to Johnny mattered now. "Shall we start, or do you want to wait a little while?"

"We got time, if you really cool. You want some coffee, maybe somethin to eat?"

"That's a good idea. Gee, I didn't even think of it. I'll get me some eggs," and began to rise.

Buster heaved to his feet, almost losing his hat. "No, I get them."

"You don't have to, Buster," and he winced like a child pushed out of some bigger boys' game. "Okay, Buster, I'll have them fried." Complacency restored, he swaggered off toward the food counter, smacking a fist into his palm in cadence with his stride.

Diane leaned back and looked around the spotless cafeteria. The artificial flowers arranged in both windows seemed real, blossoming and gaining color as she watched. Outside, people walked with grace in the sun and snow. She sighed out the whole dull pattern of her life, felt that it had cracked wide to let in the air of all the universe, and it was a new kind of comfort, infinite and wordless as space, complex and abundant as all the life on earth. She was a graduate now, emerging from a lower world, out of a stagnant opaqueness, into the clear and clean.

Buster set down the food and sat sipping coffee while she ate. Then, with neither bluster nor arrogance, grim in a kind of preoccupation she'd never thought him capable of, he took her across the street by an elbow to the low black sedan in front of the diner and gently helped her in. She relaxed in the new-leather smell. Smoothly the car rolled past Washington Square's mighty arch, down to Second Avenue—already cleared of snow—and there they floated northward for three miles of old faded buildings to the Queensboro Bridge, and on, moaning under its high, gray, antiquated girders, over the flat, broad silver glint of river. And all around, slowly gliding by, huge smokestacks jutted from the packed and dusty buildings, breathing soot lazily against the sky.

Diane said, "It's like a magic carpet, this car."

Buster grinned, turned to look at her. "Because it's heavy. That's

why I got a sedan, a Buick—it should be heavy." They darted past
a huge red truck on the bridge's downward slope. "I got it a couple
of weeks, oney. Since I make my connections, jus like that," and
snapped his fingers, eyes heavy upon her.

"Watch the road, Buster."

"The road better watch me." He tried to roar with laughter, but
laughter was feeble in him. "How'd you like to chase around in a
rubber like this all the time, beautiful?"

"That's what I like about you, Buster. Your delicacy."

"Whatta you mean, delicacy? I ain't delicate. Whatta you think
I am?"

"Never mind, Buster. Just watch the road."

They were swooping under an intricate elevated structure, hooting
past cars that seemed to be crawling. Then they were on a broad
boulevard, going by factories which scratched at the sky with smokestacks and painted the air with heavy fumes. "Wanna get on?" Buster
asked. "I got a couple joints."

"Not me. I want to be straight when I see the kid." The
sky towered blue before them, and it was a new reality to her that all
the life and all the world's involvements occurred within an inch of
horizon crowded with buildings so tightly compressed to earth. There
was so much room. "You go on and smoke, Buster. I'm getting high
on the scenery."

The car filled with the burned-poultry odor of marijuana and with
Buster's sipping hiss, but Diane felt apart from it, recalling the dead,
forty-watt nights behind her as though the girl involved were someone other than herself. It had all been a mistake, everything in her
life up to now, and only now could she see it clearly, drawn away
from the automatic sense of rightness with which impulse had always filled her. It was truly like examining the life of a stranger, an
unwholesome creature totally unlike her new hopeful self. She wondered whether people like Lukey the Swede or Paddy Jenks or wild
little Dincher ever had a circumstance arise which allowed them to
question their impulses as though they were the sourceless urges of
strangers. She wondered whether there were many on earth who
were fortunate enough for that.

They were out of New York, charging through hasty little towns
which yanked houses past the window. People were quaint little
puppets moving in a dream. But Diane felt less dreamlike than ever

before in the slow short years of her life. This was life, this sunshine and motion, this delight with impending moments.

Buster said, "Next town is Lawrence," as they passed beyond wooden homes and shrubbery, over railroad tracks to a wide highway. "I leave you at this lady's house and pick you up in two hours; right?"

"Maybe you'd better wait till I see if she lets me in."

"I don't wait." Buster looked at her. "If she don't, you got to take a train back. You can't come wit me."

"Watch the road, Buster; you make me nervous."

"Don't worry. This load handles like a pair of shoes. Look, we doin seventy. Looka the speedometer."

"Watch the road, Buster. Buster, watch it, a car's coming."

He looked forward and grinned, keeping the car close to the white center line. Diane had to avert her eyes as the two cars yowled by each other. "You take too many chances, Buster."

"It don't mean a thing. Here we come to Lawrence; where's the place?"

"Three-twelve Bluethorne Walk." Her lungs filled with relief when Buster slowed down to find his way around streets. At any other time she might have enjoyed some excitement over the abandoned way he drove, but this was a totally different world: she wanted to insure staying alive. Looking at Buster's head, it struck her that the extent of his consciousness was visible in his face: it went no deeper than the expressionless eyes.

In a wide, tree-lined street the car pulled up before a two-story house, white and gleaming atop a high lawn. A naked tree grew out of the lawn's canted center, spreading gray branches screenlike across the upper windows. Diane alighted into a biting wind, feeling chilled and trembling a little as a swift fear fluttered in her stomach. She had no idea what she would say to Mrs. Burnell, could not imagine what the woman would be like.

"I pick you up in two hours," Buster said. "Okay, beautiful?"

"Okay, Buster. If I'm not here it means I went back by train. Will you remember the address? Three-twelve. Bluethorne Walk," just talking now to keep from going up the teeth of that stone staircase. To turn when he drove off and go up steps, carrying an image in her mind of the dead rubber madness of his face.

The rustic wooden door opened quickly when she rang, and a thickbuilt, matronly woman appeared, smiling, fingering bobbed iron-gray hair, turning once when the child inside yowled playfully.

Diane's heart thumped so wildly that she thought it must be audible. "Hello." She forced a smile. "I'm Diane Lattimer."

There was an appalling moment of silence.

"Oh, of course," the woman finally said. "Come in, Miss Lattimer. Johnny will . . . Do come in."

"I thought it might be all right——"

"Of course," the woman said, leading her to a clean, oak-walled living room. Furniture and pictures ran together with the golden drapes in Diane's eyes. She fell deep into a chair as the woman went through to another room, graceful despite her solid proportions, graceful and confidently arranged as the whole house seemed to be. Diane felt suddenly dusty. A self was perishing now as she waited, yet the dust of it remained: she felt it in her armpits, at her bosom, and in the darkness where her thighs touched. She felt selfish for wanting to take Johnny from this abundance to her own uncertain days.

Mrs. Burnell carried the black-haired boy whose eyes shot a black fire into Diane. She sat mutely until she realized through clouded vision that the woman was holding Johnny out to her. He smiled with Rocky's shyness, but his eyes were hers and the face was thin and pointed like her own. This was the kindest soul on earth, this stranger who held a world out to her; her arms had him, holding his new, soft purity close to control her quaking. She lifted him high, felt the little body stiffen as limbs stretched for balance and, bringing him quickly back to her bosom, heard the music of his squeal. When she looked around, Mrs. Burnell was gone.

Diane sank to the rug with her boy, relieving watery legs, and rolled to her back, watching his eyes widen with delight. From his seat on her stomach he leaned forward to tug at the end of her kerchief; his grip was amazingly strong. Diane set him on his feet, steadied him, then stood and dropped her kerchief and coat on the long, low couch, and sank again beside her child. He had his eyes on her, grinning eagerly, as though anticipating some trick she might play. Resting on elbows, she let her head drop, and he climbed up on her, puffing a gibberish of glee. Diane swung him around and held him close in her arms, her lips tight to his cheek. "Johnny," she said in undertone, "how can I give you what I have inside?" *There's so much I have for*

*you, my Johnny, and no one has what I have for you, no one in all
the crazy world.*

Back in the room, Mrs. Burnell smiled. "Would you care for something, Miss Lattimer? Some coffee?"

"No, thank you, Mrs. Burnell. I just want to . . . Gee, it's nice
of you. I mean——"

"He grows like magic. Those pants are new; the old ones were too
tight. Honestly, too tight."

The boy wrinkled his forehead at their laughter, looked from one
to the other and folded over, his hands clasped between his knees,
his face screwed up, issuing sounds that were fair imitations of theirs.

"Did you ever *see* such an expressive face?" Mrs. Burnell went on
laughing. "You must have some coffee. I've already made it; you can't
leave me with a pot of coffee on my hands." There was a firm alert-
ness about the woman, and the lines running out of her eyes into the
full cheeks seemed to store the years of smiling which had carved
them. The swift warmth with which she filled Diane went into conflict with the frost of resentment deep inside her. She resented the
woman's possession of Johnny, resented her power to give him things
his mother never could. Yet the kindness the woman was displaying
was not really her duty even as a civil human being. She had to be
recognized as a capable, thoughtful woman who would be good for
Johnny; and that was another source of pain for Diane. It would
have been easier to want Johnny if the woman were arrogant or soft
and sloppy in her opulence. Diane followed Mrs. Burnell into the
green-tiled kitchen, watched her arrange cups and fill them from the
steaming glass pot. She felt meager and inept.

As they drank the coffee Diane could see a spark of tension flicker
in the woman's eyes through her smiling. Her own heart felt like a
stretched rubber band, quivering in the face of heavy words which
had to pass between them before this visit was done. Johnny gurgled
and swung around, holding to the chrome leg of her chair.

"He certainly must remember you," Mrs. Burnell said. "He won't
leave you for a minute; will he?"

Diane brought the boy to her lap, where he bounced for a while,
then fell back to rest against her.

Mrs. Burnell gave a spontaneous laugh. "Look at him. He looks
like a politician. Where's your cigar, Johnny? And your derby, eh?

You a ward heeler, Johnny? Hahaha, you're a little politician." She reached out and took the boy as he rocked forward toward her. Rolling him from side to side on her knee, she made up a little song for him about City Hall and the mayor, and lost herself in it like a junky on his twentieth cap.

A tenuous ache tapped in Diane's temples. The capable lady seemed suddenly to have gone mad, using Johnny as a toy, disregarding his obvious lack of interest in that repetitious kind of joking. Besides, politicians were crooks; anybody who thought about it knew that. But here in the hiding middle class they were remote faces with derby hats, cherubic and comical, smoking cigars a great distance away from the unshakable privacy of suburban life. It was the middle-class vacuum from which she had to rescue Johnny. "Mrs. Burnell," she said right out, "I—I'm going to . . . You know how I was when I signed those papers for my mother? I knew nothing about them at all. I——"

The woman's eyes aged before Diane. "You're going to want him back? I was afraid you'd want—but how could it be otherwise? Donald . . . But how could it be avoided? As soon as I saw you . . . Yes, you'll want him."

"Mrs. Burnell, I don't want to—well, hurt anybody. But it's my own baby, Mrs. Burnell."

"Of course, Miss Lattimer. It's your child." The woman had turned her eyes away and sat staring blankly through the window blinds, fingering Johnny's cheek. Like some invisible animal the silence squeezed Diane; she wished she could run from the place with Johnny closed in her arms. "My husband, Donald, is so fond of him." She turned to Diane. "Forgive me, I shouldn't say things like that. I know you feel badly about it as it is."

"I feel terrible, Mrs. Burnell. I know how you must love him," leaning forward as the boy reached for her.

"He certainly knows you." Mrs. Burnell laughed, handing Johnny over. "Have you been married already? Here I've been calling you Miss Lattimer."

"Married? No, I haven't been——"

The woman straightened in her seat. She smiled, but the smile was obviously intended to hide her eagerness. "But you must marry. The Welfare Board will insist on that if you contest the adoption. A decent home and all that."

"Oh, I—well, I will be married soon. I didn't know about the rule; I'm just getting married anyway." To whom? Carter? Dincher? Buster Wallinger? Joe Letrigo?

"Well, that's very nice." Mrs. Burnell smiled in lament. "Yes, that would help things for you," and again stared blindly out the window. She got abruptly to her feet and smiled with a bright cheer which seemed borrowed from the plaid wallpaper and gleaming white fixtures. "Come along. We'll play the television for Johnny and he'll dance. Will you dance for us, Johnnyboy?"

"Will you, Johnny?" Diane had to take that opportunity to shift her eyes from the woman's guarded sadness. As she watched the wide, expectant eyes of her boy, tears scratched at her eyeballs, and she felt a new emergence of responsibility, not alone for Johnny but to her own life. Johnny was the secret of her tears, her interred heart, her womanhood.

Stiff in her legs, she carried the boy into the sunmellowed living room and set him down to watch his fascination as Mrs. Burnell spun the television set gawking and flickering into service. The music of a kiddie show mushroomed its overbearing simplicity into the room, and cartoon figures set the mood for Johnny's hopping dance. Mrs. Burnell applauded when he turned for response, and her gestures, her expressive smiles, were painful and courageous. The whole scene seemed suddenly a counterfeit of life: purple, gold and pale-blue furnishings were shields against life; the television show was a total caricature, its presentation to the thirsty, tractable eyes of Johnny a crime; Mrs. Burnell, offering fruit, extending kindness, screened an animosity which must be rankling within her for this stranger who threatened her family. Yet at the same time Diane was filled with a dreamlike wonder that such a manner of existence, once the lie of it was established, could go on indefinitely precluding the realities of hunger and cold and dirt and horrible bewilderment which made up the world outside. It was a kind of oblivion, it seemed to her now, hardly different from the transient pleasures of a heroin snort or pop. *Escapology*, Lukey had called it, unaware that he referred to more than junk. Still, she accepted an apple from the smiling woman, even enjoyed the exchange of pointless words which dissolved the hovering conflict, banished it to the secret thoughts of each, suspended it nearly as well as two joints of good charge could do.

Then the whole situation was changed: Buster Wallinger rang and was inside, like a polar bear in a greenhouse. There were good-bys and clumsy amenities, embraces with her Johnny-flesh, Johnny small and tender and helpless and expressive, and they were away into the strange winter, floating in the strange red-leather smell through white and nakedwood roads.

"It's a nice kid." Buster had a new kind of authoritarian voice; a cigarette dangled dramatically from the farthest corner of his mouth. "He looked like he was gonna cry when you walked out."

"Did he?" Diane rubbed her forehead. There was the feeling that half the things she'd meant to express to her boy had not come off. And some things she should have got across to the ingratiating, tortured Mrs. Burnell seemed left unsaid. Thought was altogether a wild confusion with no apparent point at which to begin. She had to have Johnny, but should she deprive him of such adequacy? Or should she leave him in that middle-class vacuum to be tutored by televised idiots? Could she manage to take him away? If she married she might be pardoned from Clearwater. Carter? Carter was married to Edna, who might not die at all—and that bit at an edge of her thinking till she promised the part of God she stored within that she would visit Edna soon. Marry anybody? Decent home, not just anybody. Faces. Men. Find Rocky? Where in the world, where? Joe Letrigo? And she was suddenly afraid of Joe Letrigo, as though he were some kind of austere authority—a judge, a priest.

Buster stopped for a light before it actually turned red. Diane noticed it, and she noticed that when he started again he drove slowly, eyes on the road. "You're creeping," she complained. "Before you were driving like a flip, and now you're creeping."

"You got good eyes." He squinted through smoke curling up from his cigarette, his head tilted like the Shylock's.

"What's the idea? You get a ticket or something?"

"No'n I ain't gonna. I don't want no cops a mile near me." The road was a black streak free of traffic, but his eyes kept straight ahead and he drove meticulously, examining each crossing they approached.

"How hot can you be?" she murmured.

"Hundred grand worth. That hot enough for you?"

"What is it? Come on, don't be a goddam actor."

"You think the snow is here to stay?"

"Aah, you're funny like a nightmare."

"I ain't funny. I think the snow is here to stay. I got a pound of it right in the glove compartment. Because I'm a real Sandy Claus; I make all the shmeckers happy, little ones'n big ones, I got a Horsie for 'em all."

Diane laughed: it was all such a rat race. This ape had a clear picture of himself as a big-time racket king, exaggerating the part so much that he stood a good chance of convincing people, since it would seem nobody could be artificial enough to *act* that way. Like Stoney the painter. She laughed harder. . . . That general in the Pacific during the war who said things for publication that sounded like some Grade C movie: he had to be believed. Dincher had noted that quality in Buster, overlooking meanwhile his own theatrical hardness—— She flinched suddenly: Dincher . . . that was his connection to Buster—they were pushing Horse together!

She said nothing to the dead flesh beside her; now the little towns they passed seemed like useless groupings of dollhouses covered over with artificial Christmas-decoration snow, and people seemed slow, forlorn. She felt a frantic rush of helplessness, wished abruptly for Carter's warm house, warm arms. But with her picturing of him came Edna's face and a guilty glimmer of remorse. The idea loomed that she would never have Carter to lean on, or Johnny to protect. "Come on, Buster, light up; let's get on."

"Later, beautiful, later."

"Oh, come on, the cops don't have you on their mind. You just keep driving nice and careful."

He laughed when she did, then passed her a stick of hemp and rubbed her hand erotically till she drew it away. She lighted up and leaned back, drawing in the cutting, heavy fumes, sipping so that air came along with charge, telling herself she might just as well lose all the needles fighting around in her brain, even though it meant a return to the Diane of cellar pipes and dust the color of remorse.

The student grown old fingered his horn-rimmed glasses in the bare old hall and told Carter, "You can't unionize people who are scared," then leaned over the table on big elbows: "That's how a rat grows fat, Webb, believe me."

"You mean to tell me you people can't get a toe hold up there? One worker with guts enough to know what's coming to him? One man or woman, not among the blind, one of the Puerto Ricans, some young guy, say, who can become your organizer? Isn't that how it's done?"

Farrell stood up, pulled at the tail of his serge jacket as if he could yank it far enough to fit. "That's how it's done. So what? Believe me, if we ever did organize them we couldn't pull a strike. We couldn't get them blind people walking around with signs."

Carter got up and followed him around the hall's hundred chairs. "But that's just it. Imagine what that would do—blind people on strike."

"So what? It's not a store. So people in the street will hate a company, but jobbers'll go right on buying. Such is the case. And if and when the strike fails, the union gets a black eye. And—wait a minute—a lot of other people suffer if the union takes a blow; you got to understand that."

Carter could understand it, but it made him feel no less frustrated. And he felt no better when Farrell, at the door, told him he had the proper spirit for union work. "No, it seems I feel it all too strongly," Carter had to say. "I can't stand it; I'd be too ready to fight a losing try just to take a swing for people. I know that's wrong."

"Well, such is always the case at the beginning. Later on you get more smart and less emotional, believe me. Little by little you get realistic. It becomes your job—not just a time-clock business, you know, but still serious work in which you got to use your head and don't expect favors from the idiots."

"What idiots? You call them idiots?"

"The capitalists. Don't you know that's all they are? They can't see what they're doing. Day in and day out, they step harder and harder on working people, like the working people don't have an eye to see with. They got better than an eye; they got a stomach. The stomach tells them, and what them dumb capitalists'll do, they'll get themselves killed off and the damn country'll go Communist. Only thing can save that from happening, believe me, is the union. But the union can't be idiots just because the capitalists are. Such is the case: the union has to be smart and careful."

Carter shook his hand and left, remembering the face tired with lines of resignation, and on the downtown train he felt still a restraint in the man's talk, as if he had been careful not to overburden this new disciple with too intricate an economic theory.

Once more, when he stood before the one lighted building in

his street, he thought about Diane; once again he looked up with idle expectancy for a light in his windows, and saw darkness. Yet there was no Mr. Phelps to greet him in the lobby, and going up in the elevator, he suspected that the Welfare Board had caught up with the little girl.

He took some tomato juice out of the refrigerator which he kept stocked with food in case Diane should slip in, and noticed with surprise that a package of cheese, new and untouched that morning, was open now. He went quickly through to the bedroom, turned on the bed lamp—and there she lay, asleep in tumbled sheets like any winter flower in a snowfield. He knelt and kissed her under an ear.

Awake, tipping his hat over as her arms slipped tight around his neck. "Carter, Carter!" whispering eagerly, smelling babylike and warm.

He hoisted her out of bed and carried her like a naked infant into the bathroom, where he set her down. "What happened to the dogs? How'd you beat the Law?"

"Brrrr, you carried the cold in with you." She rubbed her eyes with tight little fists—just as Normie's Penny had done. Then she leaped upon him, catching his head between her hands. "But I don't care hot or cold, Carter, you're Carter," and kissed him, holding lips soft as rain to his.

"What called off the Law? They always had some guy waiting down——"

"I saw Mama yesterday—no, today I saw her and . . . and I conned her; I told her I was going back to Clearwater. We're free, Cart, for at least a day or two, free, free!" She spun, dancing, to the shower stall. "We can go out later; we can have a date, you and me, Cart," waiting for his nod before closing the glass door. "I saw her phone the Welfare Board myself," she called over the splash of water.

In the kitchen he thawed a frozen steak and grilled it, got frozen French-fries ready, and set up the silverware, the dishes—Christ! she was a child, he thought, and washed up in the wide kitchen sink.

They ate quietly. Carter watched the girl move with her own kind of grace in the black skirt and loose white blouse; he was glad she made no allusions to the fact that the clothes she wore were Edna's.

"How is Edna?" she said suddenly, her eyes on the dessert.

"He said—the doctor said she's going to die. It's certain now." She looked up sharply, and he was sorry he'd been so blunt. "They were pretty sure before, but you know how they are; the doctor told me for sure last week."

"Gee, it all started with a lousy broken leg. What kind of disease is that anyway?"

"What's the difference? The hell with it."

"I'm sorry, Cart. I guess it's not dinner conversation." She could read that mournful look, a mourning, like her own, coated with a thin guilt over what lay between them besides food. "Do you want some more of this pineapple?"

He shook his head, felt stuffy. "It's getting fine outside. Still a little cold, but spring's a cinch."

"We're going out in it, right?"

"Right, little girl. We'll have a date, you and me."

"Okay, finish your coffee and sit in the living room. I'll do the dishes in two minutes; then we'll beat it."

"You're a real flash in the kitchen." He lighted a cigarette. "You look like you belong."

"Where, in a kitchen or in this one?"

"Go wash your dishes," he said, standing. "Want me to dry?"

"No. Go sit outside." She pouted.

"What's the matter, baby? I say something wrong?"

"You're goddam right you did," striding over to where he stood in the kitchen doorway. "You're avoiding a very serious issue. Don't you want me with you? Don't you love me? Why do you keep putting me off?"

Her very diction tickled him; he held her to his chest and laughed. "Sure I love you, little girl. I want to do things to make you feel right. But anything more would be . . ."

"Well, what? What would it be?"

"Incest," he said.

"Incest! Listen, Edna has nothing to do with this. Besides, she's going to die, and there's nothing we can do about it. Now, stop being sentimental. It would be different if we could help her."

There was neither compassion nor bitterness in what she said; it was an ingenuous statement of fact as she saw it. The rare directness of approach shook him. "I wasn't thinking of Edna. I didn't mean incest that way, as if I were your brother, but . . . well, you're too —I'm too old for you. It would be as if your father——"

"Oh, Carter! That's the craziest thing I ever heard. What the hell's the difference how old we are? We've got to do what we want, or else what are we alive for?" She kissed his words back into him. "Don't be a kid, Cart."

The phone intruded on laughter. Carter slapped her seat and hurried through to the hallway. "Yes," he said into the phone.

A man's voice, booming with importance: "Mr. Carter Webb, of Atherton and New York?"

"That's right," searching his mind to identify the man.

"Carter Webb . . . obviously a fictitious name. This is Norman Goldsmith of the Bronx and Great Plains. What did you call me for?"

"I want to borrow your lawn mower," a little ashamed he'd forgotten their appointment.

"Enough of this horticultural chitchat. We'll be over in fifteen minutes." Then he sang in falsetto: "Friday night, Friday night, no more school till Monday," and hung up with a harsh clack; probably still singing, Carter decided, and dancing out in the street while Rusty followed slowly enough to appear unrelated to him. "It's only Normie and Rusty," he told Diane in the living room. "Don't look so scared; they're my best friends, they're beautiful people."

She came close. "Are they coming over?" and made for the bedroom when Carter nodded. "I'd better leave." She whirled with a look of alarm as he grabbed her. "But they'll think—you know, me being here with you."

"Of all the people on earth . . ." He lowered her to the couch, grinned at her in the orange shadows. "Don't you want to have some fun tonight?" and fell back laughing. "You of all people to worry over that."

"I don't care for myself, you dope. I'm thinking about you—and Edna and—and your friends and everything."

"My friends might as well get used to you, because you're going to be around a lot. As long as Mama doesn't send the dogs around again."

She was smiling again. "She won't for a while, and, Carter, later we'll figure something out to keep them——" The smile collapsed into wrinkles of a frown when she remembered the hours in Lawrence. "Carter, I wanted to talk to you, about a lot of things, Cart, and now those people——"

"Baby, there'll be lots of time, lots of it to talk."

"Carter, you really want me to? You really want me to stay?"

"Of course, kid," leading her to the kitchen.

"No, I mean do you really want me with you? For yourself, I mean."

"Baby, I don't know what I want for myself. In all honesty I don't. A million things are on my mind, and I don't know for sure about any one thing."

"But about me? You ought to know about me, Cart."

He watched her tiny hand clean out a glass. "Baby, Diane, all I know is how I feel about you. You know it too. I'd like to take you and get lost somewhere with you."

She spun around toward him. "Let's do that, Carter. Let's get away, you and me. Let's just leave all this bullshit and beat it. It's all crazy anyway."

"It's not that easy, Diane. There's Edna to take care of. We've got to take care of her till—well, till it's all over."

"How long will that be?" She was looking at him directly with no evident attempt to shade word or expression with any affected tenderness for Edna. Her words came out intact as her emotions were born. For all her confusions, this girl was more honestly involved in living than anyone he'd ever known. He wished Louella a measure of Diane's spontaneity, wished some on himself.

"How long, Carter? You can tell me."

"A year and a half. Two years, maybe."

"Two years! Oh, Carter, are we trapped for that long?"

Which meant, *Oh, Carter, will that sister of mine burden us with her life so long?* The girl could say the sort of thing other people buried in their minds, dissociated from words. "I'm the one who's stuck with it, Diane. You're free."

"Not as long as you're hung up. Carter, I want you. I never really wanted anyone before."

"We'll have to wait till things take some kind of shape. You know, you're liable to grow out of it all in less time than that."

Diane came away from the sink. "Is that what you want? Is it? Say it if that's what you're hoping for."

"No." He reached for her. "That's not what I want."

She held him off and gave his face an intense scrutiny. "If it is, I want you to say it out, Carter. I want—I don't want you lying just to make me feel good."

"No, baby, I don't want to lose you."

She came up close, rubbing her hair into his jaw. "Well, don't say things like that. Don't ever say them."

"You're only a little squirt, you know. A beautiful little kid—you're going to meet lots of men, Diane."

"That won't mean anything between us. I feel so safe when I'm with you. Only when I'm with you." It was true: the faces of other men drifted forever strange in her mind, forever an arm's length strange.

"Then what are we mooning about for?" He snapped off the kitchen light. "Paint your face nice for the company."

"Carter." She balked. "Carter, I get scared when I'm about to meet anybody. I'm scared, Cart."

He held her by the waist and looked at the black, glittering life in her eyes. "Don't be scared of Norm and Rusty, babe, that would be—well, a crime against humanity. They're Mr. and Mrs. People." A chuckle came up from his chest. "Watch how Normie leans over backward to make you laugh and feel good in general. He may even get silly, but it's only because he so seriously wants everybody to feel at home. And Rusty—well, you'll see it in her face, just good heart shining out of her."

Diane pressed her lips together in a little uncomfortable smirk and, nodding, broke away toward the bathroom. Carter tuned up the record player alongside the couch and set three sides of Franck's *Trio in F-Sharp Minor* on the changer—Normie liked that, liked the voices of cello and far-searching violin. He clicked on one more light to keep the room from looking somber, then filled the chrome bucket with ice cubes, set it on the radio console, and relaxed on the couch. Diane came into smooth light, smooth in white, grinning and a bit nervous, and with folded hands sat very close to him. He thought she was too beautiful for a kid sister and, flicking one of the quivering copper earrings, was about to mention it when the doorbell buzzed. He snapped on the record player and went out to the door, feeling cozy and hospitable in the unobtrusive lighting and the full, dipping cello notes which followed him through.

Normie went past him with eyes closed, burlesquing aesthetic intoxication with the clean and sensitive violin design. "You killed my entry," he said. "I meant to come in shouting."

"What about?"

"Restaurants," Rusty offered. "He's getting old, Carter, I swear. If you saw him, the way he grumbled in that restaurant . . ."

Normie pulled off his hat and coat. "First time I ever saw a soup plate with a false bottom. We had lamb chops, Carter, from aborted lambs."

"Oh, did he embarrass me!" She hung up her fur-trimmed coat, carried Normie's things into the closet. "A nun came by with a collection can and he tried to force a lamb chop into the slit on top. Sometimes I don't know what——"

Carter laughed. "Come on in. Some drinks, and I want you to meet somebody."

Normie led the way and paused, evidently startled when he saw Diane. With an uncertain grin he hurried over to the couch and took Diane's hand as she smiled. "Edna? No? Yes?" He turned helplessly, found Carter with his eyes, and wailed in a whisper: "He-e-e-elp!"

"It's Edna's sister Diane." Carter chuckled, and Diane had to lower her eyes, unsmiling, suddenly uneasy at the mention of Edna's name.

Rusty fell in beside her. "I'm Rusty and that's my abnorman husband Normal." She grimaced apologetically when she saw Carter wince.

Pouring whisky, Carter watched his friend squeeze between Diane and the couch arm, slipping a long arm around her shoulder. "Carter never told me about you, Diane. Because you know why? Because he's covetous," and he kissed her softly on the cheek. She looked at Rusty, who smiled and reached down to the serving-table shelf for a magazine.

"He's an emotional miser," Normie said, and kissed her cheek again. "He's a moss rat—" another kiss—"he's . . . he's my daughter's godfather."

Carter brought over some glasses. "Normie——"

"Mingle, mingle." Normie waved him away. "Diane, I am a well-to-do man, and in a few short years, if I may speak without guile, I will be ready to take unto me a wife. . . ."

Rusty let out her rolling laugh and held the magazine out. "Look at this, Carter, so perfect, that Arno."

It was Peter Arno's *New Yorker* cover, black and blue with the first signs of frost, of a bear regretfully entering a cave away from incipient snowflakes. Carter laughed, but more because Normie, whom

he could not hear through the *Trio* music, had Diane leaning back
with good throaty laughter. He took drinks to them, then sat down
with his own in the club chair, facing them diagonally.

Rusty said, "The bears have it. What unsophisticated intelligence
that is, getting the hell to sleep for the whole winter. Couldn't we
arrange something like that? Couldn't humans handle winter that
way?"

"You can stop right there," Normie protested past Diane. "Next
thing we know, you'll want to spawn." He got up, laughing. "Can
you imagine Rusty swimming up a river?"

"That's silly." With a hand she traced the sweep of her hair to the
tight knot on her neck. "Who would I get to stay with the kids?"
Then she turned to Diane. "Me and my anticlimactic gags. Those
are the most unique earrings I ever saw. Where do you find things
that go so well with you? In the Village?"

"Yes," Diane whispered, and thought of the cellar where she first
saw them, of Dincher, Tony and Timmy, imagined them here in
this room, tongue-tied as she, with forty-watt dust on the brain.

"My dear," Normie whispered to Carter, "have I shown you my
new snuffbox? So baroque."

Rusty told Diane, "You not only look like Edna; you have her way
of being smart about yourself. It's not anything you can describe in
a word; it's just a sense of style."

Diane fixed her eyes on the drink Carter handed her, then drank,
turned away from Rusty. She wished Rusty wouldn't talk about
Edna, and realized that Carter could see she was upset.

"Diane goes a long way by her sensibility." He was stumbling over
words. "Sometimes people can't quite follow her, but that's because
they habitually intellectualize behavior."

Diane saw that Rusty was as bewildered as she was, and said,
"Every now and then he talks that way. I don't understand him
either, but—but isn't that a peaceful voice he's got?"

"Just like his habits," Rusty replied. "That's why Penny takes to
him. My older girl. I swear I can't wait to see Carter with a gang of
offspring. How about you, Diane? Aren't you just dying to be an
aunt?"

Diane looked squarely at Carter, who was caught between watching her and listening to Normie, then turned to Rusty. "I—I really
haven't thought about it."

"Well, Edna—doesn't she talk about it?"

"No, we're funny that way." Tension pulled her to her feet; forcing a smile, she excused herself and hurried out of the room.

Carter took the records off the player and arranged a Debussy album, not even looking to see what it was, trying to tell himself that it was unlikely she'd been upset about the conversation, but knowing she had been.

Normie filled their glasses. "Where'll you take us, moss rat? Someplace real sordid? Like an opium den, willya huh, willya huh?"

"We can take in a few bars all the corny tourists like to visit by way of resubstantiating their dubious normality. I'll show you the fairies in one bar, the Lesbians in another, and then for excitement I'll take you to a bowling alley."

"Did a Village artist do this?" Rusty stood before the Latour "Icon"—red and pale-blue forms. "It looks crazy enough . . . but interesting as hell."

"Village painter, all right, but there's nothing crazy about him, I'm afraid. He's a fine man and a serious worker. Stand awhile with it, it's a nice guy."

" 'Has it said anything to you yet?' " Rusty quoted a Hokinson cartoon, and Normie grinned, looking deep around the picture.

Carter went to the bedroom, catching a harsh burned odor high in his nostrils, the old smell of jive that grew stronger as he went deeper into darkness. He found the girl sitting on the edge of the bed, smoking near a slightly open window. "Why in the dark, baby?" sitting down beside her.

"You want to get high, Carter?"

"No, thanks. That stuff bores the hell out of me." He felt a scrape of anger, but her child's face in shadows subdued it.

"Carter, I hate to say it, but it—it shakes me up when people talk about Edna. I have no right to——"

"Well, why smoke that stuff? All it does is sensitize you."

"No, it makes everything unimportant. I don't care what anyone says when I'm high. Why should I suffer? Is that what life is for, to suffer? You don't want me to wait for the hereafter, so why shouldn't I get as much pleasure as I can out of life?"

That was it: the rivers of wanting ran skirting around reality. "Pleasure—it's cheap, that sort of pleasure, baby. A quick drunk is never an answer by itself. You only get sick and indecisive with that stuff."

"But there's nothing wrong with Tea," she sighed. "Doctors say it isn't at all harmful. It hurts you even less than cigarettes, to say nothing of whisky. Whisky makes you rotten, not jive."

"Physically, maybe. But jive—it makes you lazy; you get in the habit of running around things instead of looking them in the eye."

She laughed suddenly, coughing on a sip of hemp. "But, Carter, you've got to get *some* kicks out of life. Or what do you want to look things in the eye *for?*"

Watching her sip studiously, he put an arm around her. "You know better than that, you little creep. Kicks aren't negative things like you get in churches and in this kind of sedation. They're in being healthy and watching yourself accomplish things that wouldn't get done if not for you. And they're in rubbing shoulders with other alive people, laughing with them, sharing real things with them. Don't you like Normie and Rusty?"

"I really do." She pulled back to show him her smile in light dubbing in from the street. "I recognized them as soon as I saw them—I knew they'd be just like you said. But Carter—" she lost her smile —"I still . . . they still scare me. I'm afraid they won't like me, they might not——"

"That's the crummy Tea oversensitizing you. Why worry about what people think of you when they're so busy worrying about what you think of them? Come on, put away the jive. Christ, baby, you can't run away from people all your life, you've got to grow up *some-time.*"

His face so stanch in half-light tripped the gauge in her, and she laughed. "Oh, Cart, don't be so serious. I just want to get high, that's all. Because I like to. Everybody escapes in one way or another." She clung to him, kissing him all over the side of his tight-skinned face, then let go and sipped on the thin cigarette.

Carter sat rubbing a handkerchief on his face, watching her, realizing he could never keep Diane from following her impulses, telling himself he had no right to, wondering whether she herself in all her precocious understanding could ever surmount the background of frustration and inadequacy which had robbed her of emotional perspective. Going out, he supposed Diane was on good ground when she suggested that everybody chose his own dream world. Mrs. Lattimer and her cynical godliness, Wengel and his dollar worship, poor Edna and her focus on sex, a whole nation of people suspending consciousness in whatever way they could: in churches and movie houses, before television sets, in barrooms and in books . . . even the friends he was about to join, living well their honest hours till, crowded in by external, uncontrollable threats, they reached farther out to excitement: a freak hunt tonight. The whole world sought hard for its narcosis, each man naming his fear a virtue, demanding that the world share his enthusiasms, rationalizing his arbitrary way of life into a philosophy, but hardly willing to equate his need with all the other needs on earth. He entered the living room in time for Normie to place a highball in his hand, and he had a thirst for it deep in his soul.

Joe Letrigo had to admit that Louella was a bore, and granted without much conviction that Stoney was right: the class she represented was doomed. All the way from the diner through the windless park he had to listen to the painter's harangue, comforting himself only with the fact that Carter, feeling none of Stoney's venom, had found a reason to leave Louella's early the other night.

"They've lost the very point of living," the painter went on. "They've gone barren inside with a magnification of their morality, poverty-stricken by abundance, sterile with power."

"Carried by their momentum," Joe said. "You've got a way of absorbin what I teach you and rollin it up in your own words. You're the most derivative bastard I ever did meet." He laughed when the painter scowled through the heavy fog of his cigar smoke.

Stoney pulled his fingers, snapping them. "To hell with you, you —you young punk. I have problems of my own; go fathom your own confusions."

"Problems? Listen you ole turdhead, you ain't seen problem one, by God. You know you're just a sheltered boy? Huh!" He yanked the painter by his new tweed coat sleeve to keep him from circling away from MacDougal.

Stoney didn't really care where they were bound. "Where will I go? How will I make any money? That filthy old swine wants me out by tomorrow. Just like that, with no warning, and I was supposed to have three more days. Damn him! Damn the whole swinish country! If I had my way——"

"You don't! Damn it, you don't have your way. You still have fourteen dollars, though; so get a room and stop wailin."

Stoney waited for some people to pass on narrow, dark MacDougal. "Fourteen dollars. It's easy for you to talk that way with hundreds to bolster you. You're insensitive, that's all you are."

"Cold. Think coldly and act with equal iciness. Man, I'm omniscient. And you're not gettin a dime of my fightin money, so get the hope out of your shifty damn eyes."

The painter bit on his cigar and paused by an iron stoop. "But Vivienne . . . how can I—— I won't even have an apartment to take her to. She has me in for tea every evening, every evening. She's impressed with my deportment, she's——"

Joe listened to nothing; he saw a child in a beard and thought of other beards, other problems, Jews turning from Torah to rifles with which to fight off Arabs so poverty-stricken and diseased that they joined invading armies for solvency and engaged in a fight to the death the very people who could someday free their world with progressive sanitation and industry. Stoney was the flabby voice of a culture larger than the subdepartment he found symbolized by Louella, a culture of many unrelated links, connected only by enmity. He wanted to tell Stoney of Asia, its millions occupied in search of no greater satisfaction than a daily knot of rice, about black Africans trekking from inland farms, hunting along civilized shores for a way to bring schools to their people.

"I'd burn the old schools." The painter was raving. "I'd teach them to honor the mind, to regard the thinker as noble instead of——"

"Come on, keep walkin. Every time you stop you give me grand opera. It's only when you live too easy—" pulling the painter along —"that's when you bug up with ideas. You're just a damn vegetable, Stoney."

Vegetable! What did this infant know of a thinker's hell? What did he know of the mortifying humiliation of the brain when confronted with the ignoble biological demands of life? "There are too many vulgar problems. . . . I'm enslaved, enslaved. I can't function properly. She refused to kiss me tonight—that's *never* happened to me before, never. But again—she's—not like anybody else."

Joe had to stop now, losing strength in a burst of laughter, sitting back on a trash can. "Oh, Lordy! Listen, Rasputin, you expect—you really expect that mannerly ole girl to kiss that swamp?"

"Aagh, you're obnoxious." He stalked ahead, with Joe following, reeling.

Joe caught up, then quickly went by, speeding up till he reached Diane in front of the Riviera, going dead in his groin when she turned eyes on him in the bleeding tavern light. "Diane—golly!" he said, and felt idiotic with speechlessness.

"Who's this?" Dincher wanted to know, and Diane said swiftly, "A friend of Carter's," then told Joe, "He's inside—Carter. He told me a lot about you that I didn't know," smiling, framed in sleek copper hair and vapors of her breathing, alive and relaxed, till Stoney came up and she frowned.

"Young lady—" the painter was authoritative—"what are you doing here? You were supposed to have gone back. Your mother——"

Before Diane could spill her rage, Dincher had the painter by his lapels, looking up into his beard. "You keep outta her hair, artiss. You don' like-bother her; see?" When Stoney pulled back, the boy fingered his hat and pressed forward. "You gonna be outta there by tomorrow. You don' give no one like-any trouble."

Joe pulled his hand back, decided to let the painter handle his own honor with this little hood, and held Diane by her delicate arms when she started over toward the two by the Riviera's clouded glass. "He and your mother, Diane, they're becomin mighty friendly."

"What! Mama——" She laughed outright, looked at Joe, expecting him to share the joke, but saw only blinding bewilderment in his eyes.

Or preoccupation. "Diane—won't you get in a fix? Bein out here with them dogs huntin you?"

Dogs: he'd picked that up from Carter, just as Carter said people shared real things. "I was born in a fix, Joe. That's the way the ball bounces," and they both laughed. "I'm cool for a couple of days. Didn't fatmouth over there tell you? My mother thinks I went back." They both looked over to where the Dinch and Stoney were smiling and nodding agreeably.

Dincher approached, grinning out of his little tight mouth. "We keep his pitches up there-like. They like-on the walls. Right?" he said to the painter, and Stoney nodded, cracked his knuckles, lighted a fresh cigar. "You go back like-wit Carter, doll. I see you tomorrow-like, right?"

The strict familiarity embarrassed her and passing people confused her jive-ridden eyes. "Okay, Dinch," she had to say, and smiled because she wanted to. When the boy walked off stiffly with the knowledge they were watching him, Diane led the way into glaring light and blown-up voices, swimming heads, teeth and hands and beery air. Voices in conflict. Glass. She slipped in beside Carter, and Joe closed her in; Stoney sat down next to Normie when Rusty, glowing, moved close to the wall. Carter made the introductions, and Rusty immediately asked Stoney if he was an immortal artist.

Even sharp scrutiny of her expression failed to teach the painter her attitude; he admitted his profession but confessed a resignation to eventual death, growing uneasy while Diane eyed him with suspicious hostility, as if she could read through his skull and might, moreover, bite out his eyes for any deceit.

The three young men chattered around Diane—of warfare, of Europe and Asia and Africa and Palestine.

Rusty said past her husband, "Carter told us you know everyone in the Village. Why don't you bring over some characters?"

Leaning on his elbows, Stoney puffed smoke. "Madam, I have nurtured them all with ignoring."

"Not the army, dear God," she said in Normie's face, then ran fingers through the loose wisps of his hair, and smiled brightly up at Joe Ford who, passing, suddenly held up his shuffling walk when he saw Diane out of those prunelike eye sockets. The hairless head gleamed as he leaned in among them. "It's a tough life if you don't week-end," he muttered in his ancient nasal squeak, then wearily carried his ragged little frame away into the agile crowd.

"He tells me something cute every time he sees me." Diane laughed and lowered her eyes to where she could see Joe's fingers drumming on the green table top carved with initials of the long years gone, Carter's blond hand asleep around a cigarette. It was somehow right for them to be friends: she'd seen a resemblance between them, not in appearance but in something at which appearance merely hinted, a kind of resolve she felt in both, as if each, in the silent region of himself, knew a deep secret about tomorrow which gave him endurance. There was a kind of firm forward motion in both, yet in Carter she loved it with a liquid warmth, while in Joe it served to make him a stranger. She pressed closer to Carter while the painter told Normie he didn't believe Joe Ford was really engaged in writing a spoken history of the world, that he was a dirty old man, a total waste. Joe Letrigo laughed, booming over the clinking and the vocal noises, wagging his head.

Rusty said, "In that other place—what's that place down the road?" and Joe realized he was being addressed.

"The Ninevah?"

"Yes, that's it. I asked him what he wanted to become when he grew up. As a child, what did he want to be later? He answered right off. 'Joe Ford,' he said. . . . Well, it was funny when he said it."

Normie yawned. "Carter, what are you going to be when you grow up? A drummer?"

Diane began to laugh, but stopped suddenly, peering through the crowd, alertly waving to somebody.

Stoney shuddered when he saw Lukey the Swede approaching. The man was repulsive to him: smiling like a crone, his decadence written in premature lines across his haggardness, his mouth devoid of teeth, as if those last symbols of strength had deserted a region which had disgusted them.

"Hello, baby." The Swede giggled. "H'ya, Carter, how's Edna? She cookin and cleanin the marriage okay?"

"Edna's been sick, Lukey," watching his friends react straight-faced to this pathetic wanderer on earth . . . a man stanchly rooted in his aimlessness.

"Oh, that's a drag, it's bad to hear. You never told me, Diane. Where you been since that boy flipped his wig by Paddy's?" and she was unnerved for Carter's sake, relieved when the Swede looked at Stoney. "Hey, what's Stoney doin here with you? Wha'ya say, genius, what's the bad word?"

His foolish giggle turned Stoney's stomach. "Why don't you go away, you leper?"

Diane frowned like an injured child. "You leave him alone, Stoney."

"But he's revolting, my dear."

"Not as revolting as you, you fatmouth! Lukey's a friend of mine, and you can just get the hell out of here if you don't like it."

Carter leaned back, looking upward, but Normie grinned as though he enjoyed the spectacle. Stoney felt sour frustration and suddenly hated this girl, hated them all for the tourist halfwits they were. Standing up, he muttered, "Oh, if I were king——"

"That's the trouble with windbags like you," Diane came back. "If you can't be king you won't play." Now she was on her own in a world of selfish noises, careful for nobody's sensibilities: "How are you, Luke; you sticking? You got what you want?"

"No, baby, I ain't connected——"

"I won't argue with you, Diane--" Stoney spoke past the Swede— "because this is your ground. You're more at home in the vortex of unconsciousness than I am." He looked at Normie and Rusty. "I hope you understand. This man is a dope fiend. He's filthy."

"We're strangers here." Normie shrugged. "Diane, you *know* I hate a scene," and laughed with Joe Letrigo.

"Don't worry, Stoney," Lukey the Swede giggled. "You just go right on livin, man."

"And you," the painter said, "go right on dying!"

"Sit down, Stoney," Joe said. "You look like an ole lady."

Diane pushed out past Joe. "Go on, fatmouth, sit down and bore the people; they came a long way to see the characters. I have to talk with Lukey anyway," and pulled the Swede into the mob.

Reluctantly the painter dropped back into his seat, cracking his knuckles while Rusty spoke breathlessly about the different people she'd seen this night. "And now a dope fiend. Wait'll Frances Rutledge hears about all this. Vagrants who know all about everything: planets in the universe, criminals in Congress, and art and music and some things I never even heard about. Carter, how can you say they're like anybody else in the world?"

"I just open my mouth and out it comes." And so, he thought, were the Puerto Ricans like anybody else, and the blind, living in eternal darkness made blacker by unconcerned fellow men.

"Aah, you're a damn ecclesiast, Webb. You'll talk to any nitwit sobbing for a verbal handout." Stoney shifted in irritation, putting an unnecessary light to his cigar.

Joe had felt a little disturbed himself, but Stoney's impudence was too much for him. "Stoney, how can any one man be so—— Listen, don't you think you're ever a nuisance to anybody? Why can't you just let people live?"

Carter leaned in. "Lukey's habits are his own problem. Where do you get off shouting them about? Look, how does this strike you?"

He sat back, looking at Rusty. "This man Stoney lives off women. He lives by contributions from neurotic girls convinced by his arrogance that they owe him their support."

Stoney shifted completely around, grumbling deep in his throat, feeling isolated by a contemptible world.

Joe spoke up to Carter. "Man, doesn't it bother you none that Diane is out there with that snowbird?"

"Sure it does, but who the hell am I to stop it?"

"Carter!" Rusty said. "You're her brother-in-law and she's just a child. Take her away from that man."

"And lock her up? Or let her run around with people who don't go around in a fog but might be worse than any Lukey? How do I know Lukey's a bad guy to begin with? Who am I to decide about people?"

Normie emptied his drink and declared: "Everybody's drunk."

"Your whole generation is," Stoney grumbled.

Joe laughed and sipped Diane's wine, thought he could taste her in it. "Lordy, I'm sittin between Christ and the devil. Stoney wants to exterminate anyone takes a wrong breath and Carter, he just wants to bless every misfit. Normie, let me tell you how they smuggled hand grenades from America into the Holy Land in matso boxes."

"Matzoth," Rusty corrected.

"Matso," Joe tried again. "Flat holy bread——"

But Stoney's hand went before him, pointing ominously at Carter. "You're a disgrace to your own intelligence. It's your kind who are responsible for this world's decay, because you refuse to take a stand."

"A stand? What do you know about a stand?" Carter was burning with whisky. "You call complaining a stand? Come on, Stoney, I don't want to offend you with what I really think. Just look in your own mirror when you're so ready to blame."

"You'll see." The painter gave his slow nod. "You'll sink with the swine you defend." More slowly, "Mark my words, you're doomed with the quagmire you uphold."

And Joe had the feeling that, while heaven and hell disputed the future, earth wasted away by the tick of time. Involuntarily he stood, made hasty good-bys, shook hands with Normie and Rusty, and pressed outward through the crowd to find Diane.

"What are we doing in Greenwich Village?" Normie wanted to know of his wife while Carter and Stoney continued to argue.

"Yes, what are?" She blinked and laid her head on his shoulder. "Something's happened to my syntax, Norm. Don't finish your drink—you have to drive."

Normie listened to Stoney's yapping and chewed an ice cube to cool himself out of an alcoholic haze. "Let's take Stoney home for the kids, Rus."

"And name him Frankfurter. Oh, that wasn't nice. You'd better hurry and put me to bed, old father."

"The sack, the sack. Oh, what I could do with you in a warmy warm bed." He poked Stoney for passage, grinned at Carter, and helped Rusty into her coat.

Carter sat fast with an irritation over Stoney that tracked up his spine and lay like lead on his brain. "I'm going to stick it out here awhile. "I'll call you," he said when Rusty came around to kiss him.

"It was wonderful," she said, "won-derful, Cart."

"She's old like we are," Normie told him, and pulled his wife through the tumult to the street. Joe and Diane were in the rear of Normie's station wagon and he offered to drive them to the Fifty-ninth Street bridge.

"Diane needs a passport to get past Fourteenth." Joe laughed, getting out, and gripped Normie's hand while Diane spoke with Rusty on the other side. Normie called her over and, when she held his hand, pulled her close, kissing her under the earring, muttering, "Gorgeous, gorgeous."

Joe said, "Fine people," when the wagon charged away, and he took Diane by the arm toward the park.

"I can't be with them," she murmured. "Not anyone like them."

"Huh? Why not?" He watched the feathered snow fall softly down out of darkness.

"You know. That's the story I just told you. I like to get high, I've been in a detention home and escaped—my own mother put me there." She held off telling him of the baby, saved it for a final blow. "I'm a fugitive; what do you think of that?"

"I think very highly of it," he mumbled, feeling something of what Carter must have been up against with this willful kid.

She spread an orange kerchief over her head, tied it at her pointed chin. "And all that is besides what Lizzie told you about me. Don't you—aren't you upset by that any more?"

"I don't give a——" His own face came like a specter to his mind, keeping him from saying he cared nothing about it, demanding he speak the truth. "It's just not so," holding her till a car passed, lighting the drift of flakes. "I know Lizzie was wrong," across into the snow-soft, soundless park. "She confused you with someone else."

"Someone else? My sister?"

He nodded, unable to look at her, and led her over to the shelter of triple saplings connected, umbrellalike, with old snow.

"We do look pretty much alike. And she did—she was . . . Oh, that's it! Now that you know it wasn't me it's all right for you to——"

"Goddam! I was afraid you'd jump on it thataway. But that's not——"

"Listen to this! It might just as well have been me, because I— well, I never did anything for money, but I've been in more guy's pants than you could count."

It stung his ears. The remark was more incongruous with her frosted beauty than the habits it exposed, and it struck him silent as she pressed what was now her attack.

"That rocked you, did it? It would have sounded great from some poor broad you wanted to spend the night with, wouldn't it? But not from someone you want to possess. And don't deny it; that's what being in love means with you bastards: possession."

"I never said I was in love——" but felt more absurd. "I am, I am."

"What a crummy bunch of bastards you are! You're white as snow; look at you. It's terrible of me to sleep with whom I damn please. Only men have that privilege. Women must wait for Prince Charming to ride up at his leisure after screwing all the—all the other women who don't count because they're . . . Well, what about the other women? Aren't they supposed to be waiting for some dasher to ride up? You lousy bastards aren't even logical." She laughed to cover anything that she might have exposed unintentionally.

Joe could feel the heat rushing around his ears, hoped the cold neutralized his blushing. "Wait a damn minute. You—Diane, look here." He paused to suck in a vast breath of snow and air. "I don't even know where to take off at. You shouldn't talk dirty; it doesn't fit you. You——"

"Dirty! What's dirty about it? Deadheads like you make it dirty. You're thinking dirty things about me because I think—I *know* I have the right to do anything you have a right to do. When'd you get laid last?"

"Listen, I don't care to——"

"Answer me. Come on, answer me as you would a man. I'm just as human as a man, or don't you think so?"

He leaned on the sapling, looked through twigs to the dark cliff of buildings on MacDougal, where other hundreds lived and fidgeted around one another behind windows lighted with secret histories. It was all old ground he'd been over and over, in the Village, in the army, even in Israel, where new values were being born. He'd always been on the woman's side of any speculation, but, living it now, it wasn't easy to put into words exactly how he felt. And the way he felt seemed abruptly absurd: like a moron in some Hollywood romance, wearing shallow emotion in the wrinkles of his brow.

"Well, are you going to answer me? When were you with a woman last?"

"Recently, recently," and thought it might just as well have been Carter stuck overnight with Louella. Or it might have been no fool at all if she'd only gone to Florida with her mother.

"And you wince when I say such things. Boy, what one-sided bums you are. Except Carter. He's the only man I know big enough to let a woman live her own life as freely as he lives his."

What was this circus? Visions formed in his mind of Carter in bed with two Dianes, her and her sister, vague images, cold and bloodless. "What's Carter to you? Thought he was your sister's old man, that and no more."

She could have avoided going on, but something in his demanding look forced her to sting him some more. "My sister's going to die. Carter and I—you might as well know—Carter and I are in love; we have been for a long time, be——"

"Die of what?" He'd found it an indelicate thing to ask Carter, yet he had to know it of this girl who could speak of it so matter-of-factly.

"She's sick. Some fatal disease—what's the difference?" (Whore, he thought: syphilis, tuberculosis.) "But don't get the idea we're taking advantage of the way things are; we felt that way before." (Seedy crew. It was incredible how he had become obsessed, yet . . . this was Diane, speaking, breathing a cloud of mist that set her apart from gone days.) "In fact Carter—we haven't even—well, we're that way, not just in-laws. You must have noticed it."

"You haven't even what?" He was very conscious of his face, its solemnity, his serious mouth and eyes.

"It's not important."

"It is to me, Diane. Maybe that's why he lets you do as you like. Wait'll you and he are official. Then watch him let you live."

Diane leaned on a bending young tree and closed her eyes. "Why must everything be hung to that? A man doesn't mind if his wife spends half her time with other men, so long as they don't make love. Why is that the important thing?"

"Maybe because he wants at least the inside of her to himself."

"And that leaves the outside of him free to get inside all the women in the world." Now she'd jar him to his knees. "Joe, one more thing, and you won't worry your head over me. I have a baby; the father was a soldier. And it wasn't a great war romance, and the father wasn't killed before we could be married. It was just a few weeks of fun that produced a baby." The tail of narcosis slithered up her spine and around her brain; she rubbed at her eyes, arched her back. "The father is off somewhere in the West, not knowing peanuts about the kid, maybe singing in the Sunday choir, I don't know. Do you know how many you've produced, Joe?"

Babies, detention homes, and the devil knew what else. Whatever else, she stood there a living result of all that his sisters and girl cousins had been sheltered against, and he wanted suddenly to be home among them. This talk had reached its climax; this wasn't an exchange between two people but between two concepts, two worlds. Logically he had no argument to offer, but logic could change nothing that he was feeling. MacDougal Street blinked lights through the trees out of the solid stone coffin; Diane's profile shone green in the frozen, snow-flecked arc light. Now, at this most dramatic moment, an invisible orchestra was to strike up, and the hero . . . Joe spread his hands, arched eyebrows, and sang, *"Some-where gray skies turn blue, some——"* Charging out of him, laughter shattered the song, and when she laughed too a new hope painted out gone days. He took her shoulders, pulling her close. "Diane, Diane, that's it, that's all it is. We can laugh together, girl, and let dust cover all that's gone by."

But she held him off. "Joe, why bother? It was kid stuff, the way we were mooning at each other that night in the Riviera. We don't see the same in what we look at, not really. We're not—well, dammit, what are we talking so much for anyway? I just don't go for you." There, that cut dead all the vacillation in her chest. "I know how men attract me; it's right away or never. You just don't——"

"That first night I did. That was right away."

"That was crazy; I don't know what that was. I didn't want to sleep with you. That's how it is: I want to sleep with a man right away or never, and I didn't want to that night . . . and I don't want to now."

What a horror! "All wrong, all wrong, by God!" A child mouthing adult jargon, throwing stylized words around, making meaning of her neuroses. "You just had a normally inhibited response to me, by God, and you're wearin it down for not bein frantic. You think anyone——"

"Normally inhibited!" she laughed. "That's the craziest . . . Listen, didn't you hear what I said about Carter and me? Isn't that enough?"

"Don't believe a word of it. Didn't see it in him. Why, he's just a papa to you is all."

She started off, with Joe right after her. "I'll show you. Come on, I'll show you. I'll get him and we'll go and you'll see once and for all. You'll see," horrified, as they walked, that he might be right . . . Daddyman Carter, always there to lean on. She took Joe's arm to keep from slipping on new snow, dead-white in a darkness free now of falling snow. Carter—in Carter's arms she was at peace, safe, free of the necessity to reason and wonder. Joe was a—what was Joe? She could understand nothing of why he frightened her so. Good and strong and sensitive: she should have been drawn to him as she was to Carter—or even as she had been to Dincher there in dank shadows. The image of Dincher made a sudden clash with that of Carter, as if Dincher were asking and Carter offering, as if one were soft inside hardness, the other just oppositely made; one pink, the other a lean shiny tan; one a baby——

Stoney met them at the Riviera doorway, lighting yet another Italian cigar. "Carter left ten minutes ago." He grinned sidelong at Joe. "With Louella, who pulled him away with a rejecting look at me." He leaned back, laughing, against the glass, then looked at Diane. "Would you like me to escort you to your mother, young lady? She'd be——"

"Stoney, you son-of-a-bitch, I'll——"

"Hey!" Joe went past them, shouting "A foot!" to the doorway of the neighboring building. They went behind him as he stooped toward a man huddled awkwardly there, looking dead rather than asleep. Joe turned the man face upward and shook him. "It's what's-his-name . . . Steerman. Ralph Steerman. You know him, Robert?"

"Yes. Is he dead?"

"No, but not a great ways from it, seems like. Stiff as an ole steel rail."

"Good. Leave him alone. Maybe he'll die."

"Goddam your ole—give me a hand," grunting, hauling Steerman to his feet. Reluctantly Stoney caught an arm of the man, and together they shook him.

Diane leaned back on a parked car while other revelers gathered around the rescue. Dincher and Johnny were mixing faces in her mind, and Carter—Daddyman was off with a woman. And Joe, calling for a cab over the heads of spectators, was similar to no Dincher, no Carter—not needing, not yielding, just himself, big and able, saying *Here I am, this is me, who are you, lady*—not *mother*, not *child*, but . . . *equal*, and equality was a demand on one, a responsibility too cumbersome for her gauge-heavy head. Yet now, with new light on the meaning of him, a way lay open and bright for her—later, when the last gluey threads of narcosis were gone, she'd stand with him, ready to share any kind of responsibility at all. "Joe!" she called. "Joe!" and thought she saw only distance in the look he threw her. "Joe!" Diane elbowed through the crowd and caught his arm. "Come with me, Joe, because I have to——"

"Beaverrrr!" Steerman yowled, then laughed in weak falsetto.

"Get off me, you disgusting eel!" Stoney tore the man's hand away and left Joe holding him up.

"Joe, you've got to come with me——"

"Stoney!" he called, then spoke down to Diane. "You want me to help you find your daddy? Not me, girl, I'm not all that saintly. Stoney! Wait a damn minute. He's no bum; he's clean as you are."

"Cleaner," Diane said for the crowd to hear, and went off, with her

purse dangling from her hands, with no call from Joe to bring her
back, no home with Carter to go to, and no real wish for either in
her vacant insides. With only a taste for Tea and the promise of
Paddy's pad to uphold her in the windless, friendless night.

Robert Stoney turned the jet with pliers, tried a new match on the
gas radiator, but again there was the violent sneeze of air and the
hoarse rush of inburning. He turned off the gas, then went around
easel and wheel-bottom table to the fireplace and got a fire started,
puffing as he built it up. He hid his face, laughing over the way Joe
had reacted to the suicide decision. "Damn you, you're no better
than Steerman," meanwhile going fiercely at everything the Riviera
would sell him to drink. "Steerman swears he'll kill himself and you
buy the idea; well, you're just his kind of cockroach, that's what."
    Stoney had chided him awhile: "Just the *germ* of Steerman's idea.
He'll probably jump out of the cab we put him in—mine will be a
rational suicide." He'd played with him while Joe drank silently:
"It's all that's left for me—she won't kiss me, she won't see me as
her true liberator."
    Now, back at the radiator, striking new matches to it, he played
some more. "I very rarely bother with this thing, but I intend to be
warm tonight, this last night of my life." The next match caught, and
Stoney unscrewed the water-tank cap with a long metallic squeak.
    Joe shuffled around in his chair, unable to find comfort. "How you
fixin to pull off this rational suicide?" Whisky and fatigue met painfully under his skull; he slid his hat over his eyes against the overhead
light.
    Stoney capped the tank after filling it with water, got out of his
crouch, and belched. "The return from intensity is not without nausea; pardon me."
    "Where you aim to be buried?" Joe asked, lower in the soft chair.
    "You're not estimating things fully enough. The failure of our
times. This departure from life will be rational, and life is an external
phenomenon."
    Joe had to look away when he saw the painter fall crazily back on
the bed. "Listen, you lippy bastard, I don't care a damn about how
you dispose of yourself; you're just another sack of lard to me. A man
dyin is like a sad song to me: sung and done. Man wants to scrag

himself, I'm the last one to stand in his way. 'Specially if it's over some Stately Lady. I just came along to watch. Go on, go on and do it, you crud-eatin cockroach."

Stoney leaped from the bed and ran to the bathroom, returned brandishing a straight-edge razor, moving slowly around walls crowded with unframed paintings. "This is the weapon, and with it I should take my work with me into oblivion," meaning it, yet trembling before the first wild-colored abstraction.

Joe held himself seated. The whisky was churning inside him and his head weighed thickly, though it no longer ached. "Aah, you spit in the face of all you ever say. Go on, go on and slice your damn throat. You're all muddled and crazy anyway. You might as well. Go on, go on."

Stoney hung his head, laughing to himself. "If she'd only turn her eyes inside and really read the face of that prisoner." Then he pointed his beard forward and followed it toward the bathroom, the razor glittering treacherously in the naked light.

"Tearin pieces of paper in the wind!" Joe shouted as the bathroom door closed. He stood and yanked off the light, and in the fire's snapping shadows he clamped his eyes shut. Robert's bearded face stared in his mind, out from shaggy brows and that pathetically wrinkled forehead. What was the miserable old corny isolated tortured fool going to do? And what was Joe Letrigo of Roanton and the whole wide earth doing here? To hell with the old phony! He thought of Lizzie . . . right down the street . . . she'd be delighted to have him wake her.

"Bullshit!" he shouted when he heard Stoney laughing. "Bullshit," he muttered for all the world around him. In Israel there'd been no distance among men, no personalities decimated by physical ease that softened even tramps like Stoney. There the people had a common eye on the land, demanding it free for their children. In Italy, in France, and everywhere else in Europe there'd been that same earth-loving, flesh-rooted drive for real things, a common respect for tangibility—bread, shelter—and for intangible realities like freedom and the expression of the flesh and spirit, all pursued on common ground . . . and from it real poetry could be made: a man could paint a shoe lying on its side and show the mood of the race. While America bled sterile in his absence: here life was written in flagrant neon script, spaced with chromium, punctuated with a fluorescent denial of blood—and every impulse was mechanical. A horror came over him; he felt the contagion of Stoney's attitude in his lungs— Stoney, who petrified the softness of time, painting rigid lines of literal, unbending allegory 'that pointed at nothing: *cold, cold,* he'd said, *think coldly and act with equal iciness.*

Joe rubbed at his eyes, then jumped to his feet when a dizziness pulled at his temples. It was warm down south where people still smiled; he'd be disinfected, once under that Carolina sun. "Stoney!" he called and ran to the bathroom door, pulled vainly on the knob. "Stoney, you miserable infant, open up! Stoney, you fool!" In the kick of silence Joe decided to leave, but found himself held fast by a fright which drained him of warmth despite his heavy coat and the steam hissing out of the radiator beside him. He pressed his ear to the door, then pulled back, ready to throw his weight and temper through wood. Sweating cold, blaming the whisky. But he heard a scratch inside, the lock's hook undone, and Stoney appeared with a face Joe'd never seen before.

Shaved clean, Stoney's face shone thin and white and bony at the jaws. His lips were thick and wedged together with old obstinacy, and when he smiled neither top lip nor nose were involved. "No flowers for my tomb, no commemorating eulogies. For oblivion has no hereafter, and rejected life no charm. Muller, an irrational poet: he destroyed himself rather than his life."

Joe watched Stoney undress, turn off the radiator, and get into bed still wearing his striped shorts, hunching his shoulders and pointing his new white face at the fire as he wrapped blankets like a cocoon around himself. Joe wanted to laugh, but there was none of it in him. He felt Stoney'd been right all along: they lived in a lunatic asylum—but Stoney was cuckoo-in-chief. It seemed talking had been a substitute for living this night, that it was all a carnival of the despairing, all of whom had uttered their formulas for conduct and in talking had succeeded only in sounding lame excuses for the turgid totals of their days—Carter and Stoney and Diane and he himself. Self? Self felt nebulous there in a fire's dying light, by the radiator's last gasps.

It might all have been a joke, but there was no real life about with which to share a laugh, no fellow men anywhere in this night. "Stoney!"

"What is it, young man?" without opening an eye.

"Where you goin to live?"

"After tomorrow—" calm, pale, his eyes still closed—"only fate knows."

"Goo-by forever!" Joe slammed the door and ran down the three flights, two steps at a time, thinking he might fall, yet going on that way till he was out in the quiet cold, walking fast, faster to the door of Lizzie Linden's building. He stood in the old red-painted doorway, no thoughts built in his head, only pictures: Diane, lost forever, her face laughing through wild tears; Carter, quiet and brooding and considerate and helpless; snow, exploding into blood and growing gray with dirt under shrubs in city parks; Lizzie . . . asleep, dreaming of better sunshines than the pale, unloved light of her wakefulness. Joe left the doorway, walking fast, rocking just a bit, into MacDougal past the dead sheets of glass which fronted the Riviera darkness. Roanton would greet him, fair with spring's first feelers when he arrived. Food, spiced and steaming, faces even warmer with familiarity: little Joan fourteen, and Tooney a woman now . . . with men; maybe even Joan—like Diane, willful with puberty's new and curious senses . . . He caught himself speeding his pace to a trot. Slowing, he cursed himself for ever supposing they were sheltered, for there was no such thing outside of wishfulness. He had to see his sisters and warn them—against life itself. He looked down MacDougal's spotted snow and over rows of dented garbage cans toward the park, where he could see dawn hanging high, lowering Saturday slowly onto the world, pushing out a night that had died unmourned.

In three days or four, all the unwanted children of the cliffs and hovels passed through Paddy's eight feet square on earth. All the fugitives came by to sit with her in humble affinity, and Diane sat as queen in a domain to which she belonged. She sang with Lukey the Swede and listened to Harry Sticks curse the "white sons-of-bitches" with an unfettered vehemence which tacitly excluded her and all the room's light-skinned victims of their brothers. She swallowed Nembutal goofballs with Izzie the Ghost, trimmed his hairline mustache while Muffo Smith slept under the covers at her feet, keeping a distance away in deference to Paddy, who shared the bed in infantile languor. Smoked lots of charge with anyone who lighted her up, sat in stupor while Danny Barber, the silent fugitive from

Canada, made weird abstractions of her face on a paper pad. And not even by night when all but Lukey, Paddy and the Ghost were gone into the chaotic and hostile world did she ever undress, for undressing might submit her to the tedium of faceless love in rolling, spaceless darknesses: she aroused none of the animals so long asleep in these men. No animal stirred within her in the solid gum of gauge and goofball; only her eyes were ever, in light or dark, awake.

Till unthought of and involuntary snorts of Horse from matchbooks held out by comrades made gum into animal and eyes into water that bathed all meaning with laughter, all hours with the gold of many suns. Paddy wore the face of a baby she'd lost somewhere in other people's madnesses, and an animal wept in her while her face laughed goldenly, ceaselessly. "No, I don't want to pop, Paddy. . . ."

And fell to singing it over and over, "Pop-paddy-oo-pop," over and over, in her mind, stomach and part of the air, laughing, back on her elbows while Paddy smiled down at her from the edge of the bed, baring an arm full of grown men's scars. He was a boy. She would take him into the bedcloud later and blend with him. Slip out of her clothes as he watched, and she would see his eyes want her, and give the light little matter of herself to the paddyjohninyobop. Laughter was a solid dizziness plugged in her head, UP sitting for equilibrium. And in the pale-green room, that was it: she would take him, laughing that men thought they possessed women when actually it was the other way around, around. From her depths she saw Vague Paddy sitting there before her.

The needle had found a vein, and Paddy, with setup firm at his hip, drew his real red blood into the gleaming syringe, where it lost color in boiled heroin. A mixture with the power of a thousand snorts settled, and he pumped it back into his vein, drew it out again, in, out, in. Diane was repelled, nauseated; dizziness grew in her head and bullied itself into her chest, where it tasted sweet with old gauge, into her stomach, where it stretched a vacancy, and down to her own feet, cold and tingling, and the room was Paddy needing her. She had to feel her face to know it was there, and her fingers could see thin hollow-cheek olive smooth copper newlook hairsilk new, strange, came the days and days and days after days of sameness seeking same new sameness but the steady air stayed firm as she sank away falling back to unseen distances, back, back, smaller into space the air could hold a sameness that remained unchanged but her feet came up before her lifting her unfeeling torso and the steady sameness air watched steadily her backflip as she lost breath couldn't keep the beating going in her heart and feet formed an arc through the steady pressure space and life was giving out she leaped!

Diane stood laughing on the bed, leaning on the wall and filling her lungs between uncontrollable bursts of laughter. Dizziness was gone, leaving in the void within her the engulfing blossom of imminent sleep. But she would not sleep, she would keep its taste without sinking into its darkness. Lukey the Swede told deep secrets to the great wire audience spinning before him, and the Ghost was a mummy centerpiece; Paddy lay stretched lengthwise on the cloud at her feet, watching her through thick unblinking lids. The others in the room were props, local color, things that fitted like cracked-wood chairs and reefers and Nembutal goofballs and paint chipping off the pale-green walls. Things that fitted . . . all that bound her was undone by automatic hands, and automatic motion brought her to the side of Paddy, whose eyes followed nothing, whose lips smiled at things that never were.

Clung to him, wrapped herself around him, felt nothing of the words pouring at her from behind, from the wall, from the unimportant air. Paddy closed his eyes, stretched his grin, but made no move. For all her love he made no move. Words were seeping in, cursing, cajoling, begging, unimportant words from Swede in bed behind her, near the wall, part of the chipping wall. She ministered to the helpless infant in her arms, allowed nothing to bind him, slipped up to him without a halt in movement, kissed his baby-warm skin . . . felt his dead stupor.

"Junk . . . can't . . . won't," the words were forming in her ears, coming out of Lukey, whining out of his pores with their sweat, out of his wrinkles, carrying the pain of wrinkles to her. She kissed Paddy and shook his face and heard him laugh in babylike singsong. Put into a rush of words all she could make of herself. Tried to make him feel all that her pleading meant to convey of the love she had to give.

"Nah . . . nah," Paddy laughed. "Nah, nahaahaaa."

She shouted: "Paddy, Paddy! You're . . . Paddy, Paddy." Radiator hissed in some corner, some Izzie the Ghost was part of a chair. "Paddy, Paddy," she moaned. "Don't you want me? Oh, Paddy, Paddy, Paddyboy."

"Come on, mama," Lukey was calling, his voice cracking and altering in tone. "Turn here, baby; come on, mama girl." Only the Swede, Lukey alone wanting her from his grave. "He's hooked. He's no good for nothin but him no more. Get under here, baby he's gone he's like a rag now no good for nothin but to laugh now baby."

Diane turned through air and floated under covers Lukey held away for her. The sheets were cold wrinkles. She shut her dry eyes tight.

"Come on . . . junkies is like water . . . mama girl . . . the paradox is always . . ." on and on and then it was the same again, the motions old as uselessness, the crazy game of back to nothing, forth to less, numbers of people . . . seeking reason . . . searching faces . . . angry eyes . . . and where oh why oh what's . . . the breathing searching for . . . and why will sun light days again . . . and why the nights and why the air why the driving groping hurting reaching screaming for a time a space a joy a glimpse of hope a taste a speck a *note of* LIFE . . . and trembling Lukey, cold limbs, spent nerveless clay. Dislocated Diane . . . so far from home. Carter, Carter, Carter, Carter. Face with its line could bring her home, could show the way, the warm, the full, the going on tomorrow fearless more tomorrows smile and warm. The grass was warm. And Edna climbed with ease to Daddy's lap and made a smile in his sad, knowing eyes. *Poor Diane can't climb my knee* and father's eyes were sad upon her as she danced and her legs drifted ribbonlike from her hips. But Edna's hair hung browner than her own, then why was Father's blond? *Why is it blond* she sang *how is Daddy blond and sad? Then climb my knee* he whispered *and I'll make a flower for you here* where an egg sat in the coal-black hand he held by his heart. She climbed with music and breeze but his leg was a shaft of light and bars were in the window before her. It was poor Edna who wept and kicked when the bars came away in their frame and higher up were bars made of paper soft and thin but Mama shrieked *It's the police!*

"It's the police! Open this door!"

The naked Swede ran, pulling things from a drawer to the window and heaving them out. The Ghost moved nothing but his mouth, and from it words came clumsily, as if through thick gelatinous bubbles. "Wha'ya wan'? Who ithid?"

"The police! Open this damn door before I kick it in!"

Like an Indian in the faded blanket, Paddy stood smiling before a mirror, combing the cowlick down over an eye, his hand moving slowly, evenly, combing and combing and combing. Diane was pulling on her boots, already fully clothed when thought lost gumminess and associations became continuous. She could feel the quick pounding in her chest, felt the rhythm echoing at her temples. They would take her back! They would bind her again!

"Who ya thay?" The Ghost paralyzed in his chair. "Who ithid? Wha'ya wan'?"

"POLICE I say! Goddam you, open UP!"

"We di'n then' fa p'leece."

Diane stumbled out to the fire escape and climbed to the roof, a new snowfall blinding her, the fallen snow making her slip in her terrible haste.

A long, long time ago Mama had said *you'll end up in there* as they'd passed this bar-windowed edifice, and in the years between then and now Diane had pictured herself screaming through the bars, stringy-haired and gaunt, screaming drunkenly through to free people passing the Women's Detention House. Now, kicking through feather-soft snow as she passed the Tenth Street wall, she looked drearily up its red-brick side of black, mute windows and felt like screaming to the sky for a little of its velvet calm, for freedom from the rushing circle she ran alone, always alone. The sky had shaken off its veil of snow and now calmly let infant sunrays through to warm it free of wetness. But, though four cups of coffee in a west-side diner had burned her out of the junkload fog, traces still bubbled sporadically in corners of her brain—*Horse!* Powder hoofs clattered down her spine—she'd really been snorting Horse! How charged she must have been on goofballs and jive to pull heroin into nostrils. Like any broken shell of a junky who'd always been hip enough to know better. Like all the old Vipers smoking up the stingpoints of moment upon hour of a chest full of rocks, smoking till everything went obscure enough to give the illusion of freedom, till Tea got like Chesterfields and they needed more than smoke. Poor Paddy, pretty and helpless as a child, and Izzie like a dead man, a Ghost all right. She had to lean on the stone-white stoop at the corner, letting the wind bite at her eyes with freshness, trembling over the escape she'd made from police and the more horrible jailer with a Horse's face. Poor Lukey,

not yet on "H" but riding his record alongside the two on the Gold
Mare to prison—they'd all be punished for helplessness. Helpless
Paddy hadn't wanted this cold, aching thing that housed her trembling life. Begging and hysterical it had been with Paddy, and he'd
not moved a finger for her. But it hadn't been her fault, she gave
herself half an assurance. Heroin made men impotent once they were
hooked. And hooked they got as life got painful, more impossible
to endure, and they were willing to give up the good with the bad
just to be oblivious. And how much more stifling would air have to
become before her own speck of remaining endurance cracked and
she allowed the needle, the *final* futility, to cut into her blood? How
helpless she'd been when she let Lukey invade her with his wrinkles
and leave the taste of painful years in her groin. Diane shuddered
and looked at the high-vaulted entranceway, white against pale-red
brick of an ancient building which might have been a fort some hundred years or so ago . . . long before its square block of a neighbor
sprouted there as a House to Detain Women.

H.I.P., the sign declared with mute pride over the door. Real hip,
she said to herself, and walked on along Sixth Avenue, the Avenue of
the Americas, away from the real hip Health Insurance Plan station
housed in an old fort with tall towers to the sky. *Towers to the sky*,
Carter'd been raving to Normie that night they were drunk. People
who were real hip could sign up for insurance against doctor's bills.
Why not a PIP, she thought, crossing the street past a group of men
plodding with shovels against the snow. Why not a Purpose Insurance Plan to insure people against labor they despised and to direct
them to productive fields where they could be content? Then she
asked that same God inside whether people could ever be content,
and looked for a way, down the distant mists of her imagining, in
which she might ever know peace. And she thought about insurance
against the slumbering, self-destructive force right next to God
within, the old laws other generations had left lingering like useless
old crones: a Progress Insurance Plan, another PIP. What about a
Truth Insurance Plan (TIP) to insure everybody against lies, against
the big lie that made people suffer, made them different from each
other: poor rich black white clean vulgar sick and sad healthy and
happy aware confused—what was the big lie? Where was it allowed
to be spoken? She would tell Carter and see what he thought of a
Reality Insurance Plan to RIP out the big lie in churches or govern-

ment or anything else that directed people. Laughing, she stopped
and crossed back toward the west, over into Christopher, playing
Carter's smile in her mind. Without admitting it to herself, she'd
been afraid to go to Daddyman, or ashamed to . . . because of what
Joe had said, because of Carter's involvement with Louella, and, more
than anything else, because of the dirt of days, junk and sex she felt
in the creases of her skin. But she could clean herself at Carter's as
she could nowhere else, and she hurried west, cleaner with every step.

The apartment was gray behind drawn blinds when she let herself
in. No Louella lay in bed beside Carter, and that tiny last fear vanished from her lungs. She stooped to kiss him but stopped out of
fear she might smudge him with vice. Quietly she undressed to her
underthings, then hurried out and dropped them in the bathroom
hamper, took her shower hotter than she enjoyed, soaping over and
over, rinsing and soaping again, till a song whispered out from her
settled, clean insides. Dried herself, singing louder, and when she
went out cool and naked, Carter stood in the long hallway shadows,
phone to his ear, a hand rubbing his short-hewn hair.

"I think I might find her," he told the phone, shifting against the
wall in pajamas, putting a tight arm about her when she slipped up
to kiss him long on the neck. "Well, that's fine, Vivienne. Yes . . .
Yes, I agree. Yes . . . I certainly believe you're right. By-by, Viv,"
and thought as he hung up that it might be too late for that. "Your
mother has come up with a great idea. Rather than get the Welfare
Board on you again, she wants me to find you and send you to her.
She wants to get a new apartment outside the Village, where you'll
be happy living with her."

Diane laughed, and he swung her up, carried her into the sleeping
air of the room, plopped her on the bed. "Ho! Live with her!" Diane
laughed again. "She'd dress me in gingham. She'd take me to church.
Carter, you know that H.I.P. station with the towers on Tenth
Street?"

"Look, baby, it wouldn't be a bad idea. You could stay with her in
some nice uptown apartment and rest till you straighten——"

"Nice apartment. Now she wants to bring me up. We could have
used a nice place once, but I'm too big for that now. I don't want to
have her on my back mothering me. Carter, I can't make it with her."

He sat beside her, rubbing sleep out of his face. "I know you can't,
baby. But you've got to exert yourself. Just to keep her from sending

you away. You know, we have to lean over a bit sometimes in order
—well, just for balance. You know, baby, that's the way the ball
bounces."

"Carter—" she jumped toward him, hung to his neck—"Carter,
I want to stay with you," and began kissing him, held him tighter
till he eased her away and stood up, found his bedroom slippers.

"You can't stay with me . . . baby."

"Someone else? Carter, is there—?"

"Another *woman?*" he said in travesty, standing stiffly dramatic.
"No, baby, that's not it. That's not it, baby," and went out to the
kitchen.

Diane slung into Edna's chenille robe and ran through to the big
tile room. "I'll make your breakfast, Carter. You go on and dress."

It was hard for him to keep away from her, and at last he decided it
was nonsense. At the stove he took her about the waist from behind
and pressed lips to her cheek till she pulled around to clinch with
him, shivering, climbing, biting his lips. "Carter, Carter, let's go away,
away from here."

"No, no, Diane, we can't do that."

"Carter, we can. Carter, we must, Carter," while agile spirits hurtled through her blood, kicking her breath out in gasps.

Gasps and breathing he couldn't tell from his own. He held her
away. "Baby, listen. Diane, let's keep it . . ." backing out of kitchen
light into the living room's shaded silence.

Diane followed him. "Is it Louella? Is it that phony fatmouth
chick? Carter, you can tell me. Dammit, what do you think I am, a
schoolgirl? You can tell me, go on and say it."

It was Edna's voice and Edna's glinting eyes in half-light. And
Edna's hysterical insecurity shattering his guts. Yet *Diane* took his
face and held it before her with a strained directness she had to assert,
an ingenuousness Edna never knew. "Not Louella, little girl, not
anyone at all," and brought her to his chest, sat back on the couch's
arm with Diane weightless on his lap. "Baby, we'll see. We'll see,
Diane. Stay here and think about it. Cool off. Christ, if there's anything we have, it's time. Hold on awhile, baby."

"Okay, Cart," she whispered at his neck. "Carter, Cart, I'd do
anything at all if you told me to. Because . . . it's right if you say
it."

"Anything? How about a little cooking?"

She danced laughing to the kitchen, and he stood shakily on legs spent as though loins had been used as they might have been. As they'd been with Louella, he told himself in the shower, spent on her embarrassing antics. *"Take me, darling!"* The affected helplessness of her voice rattled yet in his ears through the steamed rush of water. It could have been fun for a week end, but some archaic guilt watered the richness, diluted the sun of loving in her. Responses were so exaggerated that she appeared grim rather than impassioned. She had to explain the absence of her hymen as though it were something over which he was concerned—he'd even resented having to hold up lighting his cigarette till she took her light; the poor benighted girl wouldn't look up into dawn's breath of blue till the confession was out: she'd fallen on a western saddle at the age of ten—in tears she'd told it, and then taken her light. "Can you imagine?" he said in the stall's hollow splatter. Yet he had to admit that it had all done well by him, discharged his own wasteful guilt along with the tension which had been its very spine.

He laughed, recalling Stoney's picture of a fallen *Princess Tamar* weeping from the wall over Saturday's poetry-reading monotony, and the expressionless glances Louella gave him through the day, dead looks meant to convey feeling; then he laughed less for sorrow over the shadow of distorted romance under which she writhed through her days. Frantic days now spent in hunting a durable lover. She'd left him Sunday morning for Slinger's counterman John, but not without one more explanation of something he'd never questioned. She had to learn, from that weary nightman, about the *spirit* that kept workingmen so plentiful on earth. For her poetry—she knew he'd understand. Carter understood, and only wondered how many men would hear about a western saddle in a canopied bed overlooking Central Park, and how much poetry would be made with grim tears before the Florida season was done. Now, drying himself, he searched vainly in his mind for some girl he might know who really loved her mother in a deeper region than her brain.

He was dressed by the time Diane called him for breakfast; bacon and eggs fortified them both, and sunlight lay in through the high window over coffee and cigarettes and Diane's considered decision to comply as far as she could with Mama's directives. "I'll go there tonight, Carter. But if she starts nagging, if she doesn't let me——"

"Leave yourself alone, babe. Wait and see, maybe she'll behave. She's got a boy friend now." He had to laugh at his mind's view of those two.

"Stoney?" and she laughed too.

"She's taking him over the rocks. Real hard to get; you know?"

"Oh, God!" That throaty laugh ran like honey through Carter. "I'd like to watch them wrestle. Hey, you know, I think I could make it living with her just to watch Stoney suffer."

Carter got up. "Okay, baby, I'm on my way. Shall I go over to Mama's when I get back tonight?"

"No, Carter." She hurried over to him in the doorway. "Come home. I'll be waiting here for you. Really waiting, Cart," and kissed him softly all along his mouth.

Lips soft as rain and as precious, yet he had to hold her off. "This is Tuesday, Diane. Hospital tonight, I'll be home late."

"Oh . . . But not all that late, Cart. I'll wait for you."

"Gee, babe, I promised Rusty I'd be over for dinner after the hospital. Tell you, I'll call it off; okay?"

"No. No, I don't want you to do that, Carter. I'll see you. Don't go to Mama's. I'll see you here whenever you get back," and followed him to the closet, waited while he got into hat and coat, then kissed him again at the door. She'd sleep, she decided, till he got back, yet knew somewhere beyond decision that she'd not stay long if she wakened before he returned.

Carter found himself whistling down Greenwich and looked up to spring solid-blue in the sky; the sun burned like a warning to the snow still lying around. A check was due from the French exporter, so he treated himself to a cab. He leaned back, rolling luxuriously into better seasons. And it occurred to him that going to work, just getting early into the days toward some purpose, was the greatest therapy. He leaned out the window, pulling into his lungs long, steady breaths of air, and before him Seventh Avenue poked its tan, red and yellow buildings through the misty veneer of sunshine, stretched up into the Fifties in stone, glass and neon-red: molded silicate, tons of brick, massive, impassive towers real only because of life inside them, pointing like scarecrows to the sky, toward the invention high up in blue nothingness. Joe Letrigo had resented his deprecation of God, and now, leaning back again, he told himself

Joe saw Letrigo in the sky as Normie saw Goldsmith, and it was a kind of concession to the part of himself that loved them both, for both of them seemed good examples set for any God.

Yet something had to be conceded to other parts of his thinking, and stubbornly he admitted that both his friends saw only their faceless fears in heaven, that every man had his blind spot. Like the blind spot Joe named in him at Penn Station in last Sunday's snow-hushed noon. "Stoney's right each now and then, boy, and he was right as wine Friday. You gonna get drowned in other people's tears. You gonna get hurt defendin just anybody." It had been a supplement to a long complaint about Diane's affiliations, but once Joe got on it he couldn't let go. "You watch out, Carter, that kid'll get you hurt. She's just got tragedy tied to her like a tail."

"Joe, don't forget to write," for nothing better to say.

"Okay, and when you take a real rap for some junky or hoodlum or other kind of swine Stoney mentioned, you just let Joe hear about it. I'll send cigarettes and magazines."

"Pray for me." Carter passed his bags to him in the train's dark maw, and Joe reached out for his hand.

"Maybe I should pray *to* you, by God. Maybe that's who you are. The truth—what'd you do with Louella, mess her or bless her?" and they pulled apart, laughing.

Carter took the steps in twos, and when he pushed open his door Merwin jumped out of a sleep in the swivel chair: "Merwin Fingerhut, three-two-one-nine-nine-eight-five-two!" saluted clumsily, and fell into the chair again. "I dreamed I was on the carpet," he groaned when Carter's laughter subsided. "Always I dream that, always. In the army they never believe I was dumb, only a wise guy they thought I was. Old Man gets me on the carpet once for staying out after bed check; you hear? He says, 'Fingerhut, you was out after bed check last night?' As if I can deny it even if it wasn't true. 'Yes,' I tell him, I'm standing at attention stiff without breathing. Like a king he looks at me, he says, 'Yes, what?' So I'm an idiot, I say, 'Yes, I was out after bed check.' Can you imagine? He figures me like a wise guy, throws the whole book at me." He got up, rubbing his eyes, and helped Carter out of his coat. "The check is here from Bouchet right on time. But wait. I got better news. Wen-gel," he sang in that strained whisper, "is on a big hook. Simpsons called up, Wengel is in a jackpot with all the mail-order outfits, the big babies which they can nail him down good. Sears Roebuck, outfits like them, he's going in-*si*-ide. He phoned the *ad*-vertising. So why don't you laugh, Carter?"

"What good'll it do anybody if he goes up?"

"Me. At least it'll do me good. Don't you want to see a happy Merwin around the office?"

"What about the people who work for him, Merwin?"

"Carter, *death* is a picnic for people that got to work for him. Any change they make is an improvement."

Carter pulled the seat close to the desk. "Okay, you want to have a party or what?"

"No rush. Wait till the news gets around, the industry'll make block parties, we'll dance in the street."

If Merwin hadn't thought about it, Carter did now; Wengel kept them standing. When he fell, they fell. "You got any idea where Mrs. Fingerhut's old man and I can find a couple of jobs?"

"Yah! I never thought about that. In my delirium I never . . ." and he sat back on a crate of bulk film. "This has got to happen. With Merwin Fingerhut every silver lining has a cloud. The last block party I saw was when Murray Banana gets hit by the Norton's Point trolley car. He's a bookie, a shylock, a pimp, everything sweet in human nature, and for once God comes through with the right trolley at the right time. He's laying there in his errand guy's arms, bleeding from every pore in his body, they're stringing up the lights from the synagogue to Steeplechase, kids are getting out early from P.S. 188, and P.S. 80 down further where mostly the Italian people live, every store is closing they should go home and put on the new suit, people they owe him thousands, you hear? He's laying there in blood, he got one more breath left, he looks up into his guy's face and says, 'Merwin owes me fifty,' and drops dead. Coney Island, it's lit up like in the summer; Merwin, he's lit out like inside a frigidaire. Go be happy. It's got to happen."

Carter had doubled over laughing, but stopped when he saw three white strips on dark concrete under the desk, recognizable at once, three sticks of hemp strewn in line like a cripple's hand in darkness. He held them out to Merwin. "Your joints?"

"My joints," taking them. "Forgive me, I didn't know you cared."

"Since when, Merwin? I had no idea——" but held up when he realized he might have had more than an idea if he'd ever thought about the tired voice, the languorous movements of the man.

Merwin stood shifting on his feet, grinning as he pocketed his treasure. "You want to get on? Don't be polite, but you can have it if you want."

"How long have you——"

"Eleven, twelve years. So what? Since I'm a kid in Coney Island. It's the vogue. Except now all the kids are on junk, with Be-bop, with all kinds of degeneratecy."

"That's all you use?" Carter had to laugh now at Merwin fidgeting before him, only a superficial smile, for inside on the map in his mind he saw corrosion eating the city from down in Coney Island up through the Village to Harlem and question marks everywhere else. "Nothing else, Merwin?"

"How do I know you're not a Fed?" The round man laughed. "Once I hit some Yompok, but never again. Opium. It's when Hymie Putzlemoyal calls me up—you remember that hurricane last year in the summer? He calls me up I should come over and scratch him. In the storm I had to drive over to his house on Neptune Avenue and scratch him. Can you imagine? All night he's laying on his belly naked and Merwin is scratching him. What can make a guy like that? He's smiling and I'm scratching. So after a couple hours, he's falling asleep, he gives me a lump of Yompok and I chew. I drive away, it's itching like I'm gonna die maybe. So I stop the car and start scratching. An hour I'm scratching, along come three Vipers and some balling chick with them, they get in and scratch me, of course they want to know so I give them the rest of the Yompok, by morning we're all naked in the car . . . scratching. What can I tell you? Never again for Merwin, only charge, no more."

Carter didn't know what to say. He went to the window, pushed it open on Sixth Avenue's honking, yowling sunshine.

"Don't feel bad, Carter, it's nothing. You ever smoke jive in the Village, Carter? I got a connection there on Charles Street."

"Yeah, I tried it couple of times. It stinks. Makes me sleepy and hateful sometimes."

"You're nervous, that's why. It's better than you should be a drunken bum, a wife beater like. Only bad thing is the kids nowadays they ain't got enough from jiveroony. They get hooked on the real hook, it's bad. Marijuana could only make you wish for more, never need for it; you see?"

Carter sat on the window sill, looked out on the river of commerce grinding and hooting below. Spring sneaked in wherever it could crack the frost. "What the hell, Merwin, we have bigger problems to worry over," yet felt that every little thing was connected, problem to problem, street to street, person to person, like any season to its parent.

The freak warmth brought people out of houses, but the remaining frost of the wind sent many of them into the Cosmopole's buzzing fluorescence, and they brought in the night on noisy faces. At the food counter Diane stood smiling for Izzie the Ghost as that stooped, lined and mustached little man shuffled toward her at his crippled junky's pace. But before they could speak, Lizzie Linden had Diane by the wrist, shouted at the Ghost in her whining, nasal insults. "Get off, you lousy bindlestiff! Go on'n lay off the kid 'fore I kick in a rib on you."

Diane turned angrily to look at Lizzie's freckled little face, but before she could speak Lizzie showed her gums in the friendliest kind of smile, meanwhile tightening the grip on her wrist, and through her tiny teeth whispered, "Fuzz!" while the Ghost hovered timidly by. "Smile, you jerky little bitch!" Lizzie grinned, and Diane obeyed. The corn-silk hair swung again. "Get off, snake!" Louder than any whisper to Izzie: "Go on'n leave kids alone!"

Pain was stark in the Ghost's white eyes as he backed away. Through her painful perfunctory smile Diane asked Lizzie, "What's a bitch like you taking care of me for?"

Lizzie outsmiled her. "I don't care rotten apples about you, sister, but I hate Fuzz worse'n poison," taking her by the chin, inspecting her profile. "You'n me, we're talkin about drawin, see? We go to a table'n I draw you on the pad," gesturing with the sheaf of newsprint in her other hand, grinning like a lover of all humanity. "Fuzz is watchin the Ghost for connections; they give him'n Lukey a fin apiece'n turn them loose. The Swede hipped me holdin my lungs like a lover by the Riviera."

Diane, half smiling still in that mechanical way, chose her pastry, ordered coffee for them both. "Paddy? Did——"

"He jus keeps smilin while Fuzz is questionin them. He's gone'n

where he's gone makes no more difference, 'cause he can oney smile
any more. You come behind me'n sit where I can draw you'n I hip
you where the Fuzz is sittin while I'm drawin." Her smile had waned
into tired tawny eyes. She eased the shaggy tweed coat back on her
shoulders to expose great breasts, her last proof against the years.

Diane carried the tray behind Lizzie all the way front, and sat in
the seat the little woman faced. "Now right across the aisle—" Lizzie
smiled, tilting Diane's head with fingers of ice at her chin—"two
tables in from the door, like move your eyes like you're lookin down
your cheek, like sophisticated; see?" and began to sketch. "It's a guy
looks like he sells insurance for his uncle's company'n a guy like pale
from too much hours in church," sketching away as she spoke, shifting her heavy-lidded eyes between Diane and her pad.

Down her cheek Diane smiled toward two men in college tweeds,
one thick-set and bemustached, the other hatless, thin, with blond
crew-cut hair. She had to have coffee for her frozen insides and took
it, stretching her smile at Lizzie to let it include contempt. "You
think this squares with me, you're crazy. You go around telling people
I'm a hustler and I'll break your skinny head."

Lizzie drank coffee with no change in expression. Then, smiling
thinly, she fixed Diane's head in position again. "That was a mistake,
kid. I got you mixed up with your big sister," as if that excused her.

"So even if I was my sister? You fatmouth bitch, you shoot your
mouth off about everything you know?"

Lizzie sketched on, no apologetic look in her eyes. "It's other
things, kid. It's other things made me say it. It's things you don't dig
yet. If you forget to be pretty, you got to get smart. You're pretty'n
I'm smart, so listen to me. The Swede's stickin in Brooklyn'n the
Ghost got no Brooklyn for what he needs. Them Fuzz got four
more around which the Swede ain't showed me, so keep outta Izzie's
way like poison, 'cause where he goes them Fuzz goes till he busts
out sweatin for Horse'n fingers the connections. That's what they
give him a fin for, to buy with'n Lukey. . . ." She had to stop drawing for her sudden burst of laughter. "Lukey, he took all the pod I
had'n cut out where he ain't fingerin nobody'n I got the fin they
gave him right here between my tits where no son-of-a-bitchin Fuzz'll
ever get near," and bent snickering back to her work.

Diane had to laugh a little, yet an ember of her anger remained.

"You're not so smart as you think, Lizzie. I know why you did it, why you said that about me to Joe. Did he rock it for you? I'm hip why you did it."

Lizzie met her with cold steady eyes. "He rocked it good, kid'n good like you ain't gonna know till you got no more looks to use it right."

Obscure as it was, it rattled into Diane's head with Joe Letrigo's booming laugh and the thousand aimless voices in the Cosmopole's pale violet light. While she smiled for Lizzie's crayon and kept an eye on the Law.

While the Ghost came shuffling forward with pain in his white eyes, neglect in the hollows of his cheeks, futility heavy where his back bent forward. Diane forced herself to betray no anxiety as the Ghost came nearer, then uttered a small gasp when he had passed by and through the revolving door. The creaking old door that might have been sounding his need. With a tweedy stump of a man in a sporty hat rubbing a thumb on his mustache through the revolving, creaking door.

"Je-sus, *Magoo!*" Lizzie stiffened, looking past the artificial flowers in the big plate-glass window while the crew-cut boy went through and hovered near the action around the boarded-up old newsstand. Where Magoo, voiceless for them through glass, laid on the Ghost all the years of horror stored in his eyes, pushed at him, shouted. The Ghost clutched Magoo's lapels, opened his mouth in a soundless scream, kicked the pile of newsprint fluttering like freed birds in the wind. And through the glass they saw the mustached man confront Magoo while an audience formed out of the oozing river of strangers.

"Jesus, old Magoo," and little Lizzie led Diane through to the night full of spectators titillated by the rumor of vice before them. "I hardly know the bum!" Magoo bellowed as Izzie the Ghost staggered away with one of the police at his heels. "He's a bum hangs around fuh free coffee!" Magoo squalled at the Law, the kind mustached man who helped him gather the newspapers. "Jesus, Magoo," Lizzie was whispering and staring out of wet tawny eyes: Diane could see that the quiet hint of hate always present in Lizzie Linden's eyes had disappeared as they watched the newsboy being led away. "Oney dumb old Magoo," Lizzie muttered, hurrying on wool-sheathed legs too skinny for a child down Sixth Avenue with Diane close behind her. "The Ghost, he's like a plague, he's plain poison now'n I oney hope they all hip. I hipped who I could'n I oney hope the word got around. Magoo they got, dumb old Magoo."

Down Waverly to MacDougal, along it in fierce trembling silence to Fourth Street, and Lizzie whirled in her shaggy tweed coat, leaned puffing on the massive carved cornerstone of the Masters Hotel. "Magoo they hadda tear down, Magoo. Why'nt they bust a big one, why'nt they like bust the guys which they too big like for anybody? Like Wall Street, I dunno. Like why don't they bust this fat fuckin hotel for lookin at the park?" Lizzie was in tears, and it suddenly seemed to Diane that this small, freckled, tiny-featured face was something out of her own generation masquerading in an older season's jaded look. "Why don't they bust the fuckin skyline?" pointing over the Washington Square Arch toward the high neon dome, unobtrusive with distance. "Why'nt they tear down that Empire State like a big roundo at night it hides the spike, but in the daytime when it ain't able to hide it's like a needle right into you'n through your lousy gut. Go on, go on!" she shouted at staring passers-by. "You never see a human bein before? Go on'n look at the freaks, you lousy bastards. Go on home'n show your aunt all the lousy honky-tonk matchbooks you got," until Diane led her away, compliant as a guided child. "They come from the Bronx'n they come from Brooklyn'n they look at each other—" sobbing, gasping—"'n they go home'n tell their old lady about the characters in the Village. Jesus!" pulling away into Minetta Lane to stand in narrow shadows wiping at her eyes. Diane held a Kleenex to the brittle red nose and Lizzie honked. Minetta was a winding, unpeopled sanctuary from indifferent strangers in the night. Diane patted powder over those freckles while the little woman blinked her heavy purple lids. "He's oney a dope never knew what to do," Lizzie said with a faint smile to end the whole matter, and back into the neon of MacDougal they walked.

Into Harry Sticks, black face tight with guarded uneasiness, rushing out of the Ninevah with Jasper the Painter behind him. "The Ghost!" A hoarse whimper close into their faces. "Don't go in there," and up into Minetta's narrow dark, two dark figures afraid to run.

Two hasty women down MacDougal, up an iron stoop, ringing three letter-box bells. "The Ghost is comin by!" Lizzie shouted to drugged, inquiring voices, and Jacquie Swan was the first one out in her crazy sequin evening gown, her only outdoor dress, glittering out of her trench coat, with her only property wailing for want of sleep in her arms. Canada Dan clattered out next with a brand-new huge black portfolio and an ancient paleness in his face, mucus running down a lip like some last viscid tear.

To the Riviera with night growing cold behind them. "The Ghost's comin by!" Lizzie's shout was an alarming whine that sliced through the hubbub and the glare, and chairs were turned over by a junky or two and several hippies with a lust for being pursued. Then a hand lay heavy on each delicate shoulder, and a man in a stevedore's leather jacket and cap had Lizzie and Diane in tow.

"You come along, ladies," in the pleasantest voice, and one more word pushed back by the comet of a fist. Another crunching blow drove him to his knees, backward under the turbulent legs of the crowd. Dincher had them running toward Bleecker, where frantic Buster lumbered into their path, great hams of hands fluttering out of control. "The Ghost! The Ghost!" He even sobbed one time. "The Ghost is down the street!"

"No, he's up MacDougal!" Lizzie whined. "He's comin toward the Riviera."

"Kippie Marsh told me Bleecker!" Buster tried to get by.

Diane felt a horrible flutter behind her eyes. "He can't be everywhere."

Only Dincher was laughing. "He's like-a real ghost. He's here like-he's there!" stretching up on his toes, flushed with cold and conquest. "Come on, he don' know about my pad, come on. Angie! Angie!" and little dead-faced Angie trotted up breathlessly from a cellar, and the five of them went in stumbling speed into Tony the Shylock's four-story tenement, out of the cold night full of Ghost.

Up the narrow flights full of brown light to the tin-coated door and through with Dincher's proud key. Dincher was the man tonight. Till the door was latched and Buster took seniority. "I should rub him out like a fly!" kicking a stool into Stoney's fireplace. "Little fink, I could bust him in two junky pieces."

"Aw, shut your big hole!" Lizzie protested, standing belt-high beside him. "Whatta you want off Izzie? You want he should say lay down to the Horse? You want he should drink milk or somethin?

You big shithead, you just push junk into them'n then don't know how it pulls in their guts."

Buster pouted and whipped out his knife, caught up a slat of Stoney's wood to whittle, then turned to Angie when the boy's dead face livened with laughter. "Whatta you laughin? You ain't no chick, I'll bust your goddam back."

Dincher hoisted a pile of clothing from the bed to let Diane fall across it. "Pipe down, alla you cats. Pipe down or the rescue squad'll get us 'fore the Fuzz." Diane lurched up to follow Dincher through to the inside rooms; she had to stay near Dincher, she had to be away from the anxiety crowded into the studio walled with paintings.

Dincher pulled on a light and grinned with rare excitement in the naked calcimined room. "The artiss, like-he never uses this part," and hung the clothes in a closet. "We make like-we make this the bedroom, doll. In there like-we make it like-a sittin room. How you like how I blast that Fuzz, doll?"

"Dincher, can't you get them out? Can't you make them go, Dinch?"

His response was an appreciative smile over her wanting to be alone with him, but it slipped from his long look at her. "Business, like-I got business wit Buster, doll. I can't jus——"

"Dincher, get rid of him. Get rid of the lousy business shit and everything. Just push him out, Dincher. You're pushing junk, it's murder, baby. Don't be dumb, Dincher."

The boy sat her down next to him on a dusty window sill, with more years in his eyes than belonged there. "You see Angie out there, doll? A kazoo he plays. You remember Angie when we was little kids, when I live on Thompson Street'n come get you to the circle'n sing the two of us for you. Angie wants to play real music too, doll, oney he ain't got the eyes ahead like me. Like-he pulls a little hyste'n lives off it, but he plays a kazoo oney. Like-when I got a band'n I'm doin the arrangin, Angie he still plays the kazoo, right? He riffs out on a kazoo'n I blow a gold horn'n make real music. 'N I study hard by Juilliard, doll'n that takes real loot'n I still got to give money home'n evvythin. You think like-I can blow a kazoo when people they can wear sharp clothes'n go to night clubs'n live off the fatta the land? Not me, doll," and he passed her a stick of Tea, lighted hers and his. "That leary General, he got the connection or I push him down the toilet. Don' talk, doll, jus lemme do like I gotta. Like-we

get the laughs; you dig?" and led her by the hand into the outer
room now grown quiet in the light of the snapping fire alone. They
flopped across the bed, where Angie shifted over to make room.
Buster sat whittling in the soft chair near the easel, and Lizzie lay
smoking jive on the rug by the flames.

"We got a little cappin to do," Buster told the Dinch. "Angie,
maybe he starts a little trade in Brooklyn; right, Ange?"

"I dunno yet," the curly-haired kid murmured, and sipped on his
stick of hemp. "I don' like with the kids-like."

"Shut up, Ange," Dincher mumbled. "You talk about it later.
Like-we ain't cappin nothin tonight. The panic is on. We stay real
quiet."

Buster reared. "We cappin right now, Dinch; got it? When I says
it, that's when we cap; you got it?" and stood, tossing a paper sack
onto the wheel-bottom table, pulling on the light.

"Put the goddam light out!" Lizzie demanded. "Man, can't you stay
cool a lousy minute?"

"You know what you can do, lady," Buster grumbled. "You got a
trap of your own, ain't you? Come on, Dincher," and he poured
hollow capsules tumbling over the table.

"The panic's on, General. Put it away."

"There ain't no panic up here. We can hear anybody comin up
this way. We got the whole floor; ain't we?"

Lizzie slipped into her coat. "You wanna cut outta here, baby?"
she asked Diane. "You wanna, Angie? Don't stay around'n push junk
on kids for this big potatohead."

"What's this *kids*?" Diane wanted to know. "Dinch, what's that?"

Dincher heaved up and joined the giant at the table, silent, back
toward everyone else.

Lizzie had the door open. "Come on, baby, I'll hip you."

"No. Dincher, what is it? I'm staying, Lizzie; Dinch'll tell me."

"I'm goin," Angie mumbled, and passed through with Lizzie's
hand on his back. They heard her descending laugh as Dincher went
to the door. "I'll hip you-oo, Aaaange," and the door slammed tight.

"She's oney a bohawk anyway," Dincher complained. "Like-one
of them screwy artiss."

"What's with kids, Dincher?" Diane asked, keeping to her back
on the bed, smoking her Tea, not wanting to get near enough to see
Buster packing "H."

"Tell her!" Buster bellowed without turning. "Go on'n tell her. Kids want it; it's business. Go on'n tell her."

Dinch sat down and took her hand. "We don' sell it to no kids. We jus give out a couple free samples to one junky kid, he's a junky from back. Like-he wants loot for his junk he needs-like," and he tried a smile that failed. "He lays some on his buddies'n they get to like it; right, Buster? They like it'n he can get it, 'cause he got the connection, see?" and failed again with his face.

The nightful of faces still fought in her stomach, and the turmoil shook through her blood—hot, then cold. "You mean you school a bunch of kids on junk? Dincher?" He was watching the fire past Buster's legs. "Dinch, you get them hooked?" and the word itself began to draw on her stomach, a gentle push at first that suddenly pulled like a hundred angry fingers. "Dinch, you get kids on the hook for Buster?"

"It's their business!" he shouted, standing up. He hurried over to Buster's side, and his elbows bobbed as he worked, ripples running down the flannel of his back. "Somebody wantsa get hooked, whatta I care?"

A fist yanked her forward, actually pulled her to her feet. It was more than emotion, she felt abruptly; it was something in her entrails, something hostile and strange. "Dincher, Dincher, you don't care? Dincher, how'd you like to see me hooked?" and saw revulsion when he faced her. "Dincher, up at Paddy's I took a few snorts. I don't know how many, Dinch, but it's yanking at me," letting him ease her down on the bed.

"Baby . . . doll, baby, you . . . you jivin me. You playin aroun; right, doll?" He had to be reassured, but she couldn't do it. "Come on, doll, like-you, like-you too hip, you don' get hooked on any——" But he saw differently in her face. "You crazy *broad!*" he screamed.

"You dear sweet crazy broad," she whispered, "you mad lovely creature," and laughed at her own anxiety inside, the padded fist punching now her spine, now her stomach, her liver and kidneys and the gland-that-keeps-you-going under her heart.

"You gonna cold-turkey it!" Dincher yelled on his feet. "See?"

Buster was there, looking down at her, frowning like a boy. "You . . . what about your kid?" He fell backward at Dincher's push, widened those forever-injured eyes and came forward as the boy snarled at him. "I bust you in pieces, Dincher," he said. Then he stopped and whipped open the long crazy blade, stood crouched and shifting his eyes between them.

"Buster," Diane whimpered, "don't . . . it's crazy . . . you——There's somebody coming up!"

Buster straightened up, hid the knife and dashed to the wheel-bottom table, gathered up the capsules and packages of Horse, poured them swiftly into the paper bag while Dincher pressed an ear to the door. Diane stood beside him, suddenly quieted inside by fear. Scrape, scrape, the slow scrape of feet on old naked wood, and Diane struggled to undo the lock.

"Whatta you doin?" Dincher glared in amazement.

"We can look down and see——"

"If it's the Ghost!"

She was out on the landing, straining her eyes down the dusty well, where a hand pulled at the banister two flights down, scrape, scrape. "Don't call out," she cautioned the boy. "Don't show we're here. If it's Izzie, we make it out the fire escape. Is there a fire——"

"Yeah, yeah. How's the Ghost know where?" he whispered.

It was a tired scraping, upward and louder, till Diane heard the clack of heels on the landing below. "It's a chick." She grinned at Dincher.

"Robert?" a high, girlish voice drawled, and Diane went past Buster in the doorway, crossed the room and flung herself back on the bed.

"Robert? Hello, Robert?"

"There ain't no Robert here, lady," Dincher informed the visitor.

"Robert Stoney?" The voice was level with Dincher's. "What is it, some sort of absurd gag?"

"Come on in'n look around." Buster was composed again. "Maybe we hidin him. Huh, maybe we hidin him in the fireplace."

Diane lay back, wondering about that weird pulling sensation which had come and gone like a dream. She could only call it tension, for she felt well enough now to resent the woman breezing in. Then she recognized Louella in a gray Persian-lamb coat, her light hair done up in a bun—recognized her and sat up.

"Stoney, he moved." Dincher strolled in, hands in his pockets.

"Diane!" Louella found her and rushed over as though they were old friends whom circumstance had torn apart. "Is Robert really gone? Can he really have left his *studio*?"

"He can have pitched over dead," Diane said as the girl sat beside her. "For all I give a damn he can have been eaten by rats."

"Really, Diane." The girl was intent on having it turn out to be a little joke of Stoney's. "Where is Robert, Diane? His pictures are still here," and she laughed in a deep, conspiratorial *hohoho*. "Really, Diane."

"We jus boardin his pitches." Dincher grinned by the fire.

Buster kept a fascinated eye on her coat. "Why doncha stay awhile? Maybe he come around to visit the paintins."

Louella looked from man to boy and back, clacked over to Buster and looked up into his polished thick face as though she were measuring him for some future experiment. Then she turned toward Diane and smiled craftily. "What do I smell in here? Is it——"

"Stoney's body," Diane said, and fell to her side. "We just burned him in the fire."

"I know what it is—it's marijuana." And before anyone could protest, "Could I have some?" with a naughty rise in the request. "Couldn't I try it? I really want to try it. I want to write about its effect while it's happening," with a look from face to face that might have invited applause for her daring.

Buster was just a boy in velvet knee pants, grinning wrinkle-nosed at Louella as he approached her with several joints in his fleshy mitt. Louella danced out of her coat and slung it with the gayest kind of abandon over the easel, then rushed with many extra steps shortened to excited clacking back to the bed, where she sat down with a bounce. From her purse she took pad and pencil, dropped them into the pocket her wool dress formed between her body and crossed ankles. She gestured nervously before taking the lighted stick from Buster. Everyone lighted up and smoked.

But only the men got high.

While disappointed Buster lighted Louella up for another try, Dincher whispered to Diane, "You feelin any better, doll? You hurtin too much to get on?"

"I'm feeling okay, Dinch. Maybe I'm too nervous yet to get high."

"You want another joint?"

"Not right now. Listen, you know the Fuzz took Magoo away? I don't know if you——"

"Magoo!" Dincher was back at Buster's chair. "Magoo, they busted Magoo. Diane says——"

"What!" Buster had to leave off nursing Louella along to her first gauge high. "They'll—they might squeeze him. Jesus Christ almighty, he could start moanin names like a tobacco man," while Louella took her little wary sips, asking, "Well?" from time to time.

When the men went, jabbering, into the secrecy of the other room, Diane rolled her eyes up toward Louella. "Take harder hits on it; don't sip it like you're scared." But nothing helped Louella—neither that stick nor two more that Diane lighted. Louella sipped delicately, and the fire across the room snapped and whined; Tea painted gumminess somewhere in Diane's chest, more and more with each hit, yet nothing thickened in her head, nothing shimmied for her eyes.

The men returned and smoked in silence, Buster's attention fastened on Louella. Finally the Dinch bent close to Diane's ear and whispered, "Doll, maybe you better cut out. Magoo could finger us. He's the pusher which the junkies get their charge from him. Me, I oney take the money; but Magoo talks, they come'n get us."

"Does Magoo know this place?"

Dincher suddenly brightened. "Boy, like-I'm real popped out," and laughed at himself as any good Viper knows how. "Hey, General, Magoo don' know about this trap. You hip? He got no way to finger nobody," and laughed, falling backward to the wall. While Buster laughed at Dincher's stupidity and really went hard at schooling the uptown chick.

Dincher was less patient. "Here, I got some hash," showing a flat black two-inch square of the pressed and baked concentration of marijuana, taking from under the bed a water pipe, homemade from a medicine bottle, oiling-can spout and small glass tube. "If hashish don' put you on, lady, like-you better stick to lusho."

Diane sat up for that. "Give me a couple of hits, Dinch," while the boy scraped little chunks with a key onto the kitchen-sink screen fitted into the mouth of the spout that reached through rubber to water. While Louella watched in girlish delight. While Buster, puffing as in passion, yanked out the overhead light and hustled to build up the fire.

Bub-bub-bub, water gurgled at each pull on the tube, and the medicine bottle went around and around. Diane warned Louella, "Don't hit it too hard or you'll gag; just take little puffs," but Louella couldn't measure right and doubled into a wheezing, embarrassed cough till Buster tapped her back with amazing gentility. And the fire crackled and snapped as the bottle went around and around. "I'm on," Diane announced after four gentle hits; "that's dynamite, Dincher," and shuffled back to the wall.

While the medicine went around and around.

"Pass me," Diane whispered from spiraling drones in her head. "You better hold it off, Louella," wondering why she should bother about this fool from the easy world. The dandy-clothes chick from uptown. The woman who had shacked Carter up. She remembered Carter sharply now out of the gum fog. "What time is it, somebody?"

"Ten-thirty," Louella reported, and Diane sat back into the pillow of time on her back, time before Carter'd return, time to watch that smooth uptown profile and Buster adoring it with hoarse and hesitant sounds from his throat. Uptown slob who never had a care. "Listen," she whispered to Louella, "you lay off my—sister's husband," but Louella heard nothing in her stiffening lurch.

"Oh! Put on the light!" and Buster swiftly obeyed. In naked cutting incandescent daggers Louella ferreted desperately through her bag till she found the silver holder, plugged it with a king-size cigarette and jammed it into her mouth. Buster held out his lighter, and she took a vast puff, exhaled elaborately and began to scribble in the pad, swiftly for two lines, then faltered and looked crazily around. "Better . . . oh . . . put out . . . the light . . . please." She sat up straight. "It . . . oh . . . oh . . . it's a snake!" She dropped the pencil and grabbed the back of her neck, rubbing it and yanking the silver shaft from her mouth. "It's crawling around in my head! And—" she giggled with fright in her eyes—"and it—really!" Her dead eyes found Diane, and she leaned over to confide in her ear, "There's a definite glow at the . . . crotch," giggling, sitting erect in the mad shadows while everybody laughed.

"Hit her all at once." Diane had to snicker.

Buster sang:

> "She's the queen of small and large,
> Ridin the sky on a ton of charge . . ."

And Dincher's horn was in golden action, honeynotes up in crescendo to silver that brought light into the room of angry shadows, that made of remembered agonies caressing promises of better, better sunshines. Great complexities that passed like old friends half-recognized through Diane's mind. Till Louella let out a pathetic wail on her way down the long room to the toilet.

"Ooh baby!" Buster shuddered. "That's for Buster tonight."

"If she lives through it." Diane dropped a threat, while Dincher rubbed at his lips. "It all hit her at once; she smoked enough for ten way-back Vipers. Maybe she'll die."

Buster wanted to be incredulous and his face tightened and twisted with the attempt. "That couldn't happen, could it? You better look in on her, Diane."

"Dinch, you play like heaven," she told the boy. "You play real, Dinch, and all your own. There's not even any Louie in it any more," taking his head over to kiss him.

"You better look in there, Diane. Go on." Buster stood nervously, hitching up his pants. "Go on, Diane; you got it?"

"Look in, doll," Dincher said in a Viper's whisper. "Maybe like the chick's flippin her wig."

Diane idled over; inside, she found Louella, her chin on her knees, perched on the closed toilet seat. Eyes rolled stupidly around till they located Diane. "I found my home." She smiled. "Beautiful, beautiful. Never go out any more. Only here, right here I want any more. No nothing ever again."

"Would you like some coffee? Coffee'll straighten you out. It'll bring you right down and you can go home to sleep."

"Nonononono. Don't *want* to go home. Don't *want* to sleep," like any intractable child. "Don't *want* to go in there with men. Don't *want*——"

"Come on, come on." Diane took the girl's arm. "You can't stay here all night. You think you can have everything the way you like it? You have to lean over sometimes. Because that's the way the ball bounces, see?"

"Heyyyyy. Hey, that's . . . that's awfully poetic. Hey, that's very, very, *very* profound. Stay here with me and we'll show them all, all over," laying her head on a knee, reaching up to finger the knot of her hair.

"Come on, Louella, let's go out and you can lie down."

"Oh, *yes!*" She looked up at that. "That's wonderful. I'd *love* to lie down and, ooh, ooh, I'd love to just sleep and sleep and sleep."

Helping the girl out, Diane told herself this was the first Tea-drunk she'd ever seen in her life, a nice package for Buster.

Buster made the bed neat for Louella, hovering over the girl as she dropped down and curled up. Diane went back to where she'd seen Dincher in shadows across from the bathroom. He heaved a pile of rolled canvas from a mohair couch to the heap of rags and dusty picture frames he'd already cleared from that somber old seat. "Come on, doll," he said, smacking dust from the surface with both hands. "Come on, we make it here'n leave the General alone." Took up his trumpet and muted its mouth, then sat back as she joined him, and "Especially for You" went softly about the room for three bars that led into Dincher's own brilliant explanations, rich and running nuances that covered dust with silver. "I'm pullin out, doll. You see, jus wait, dollbaby, like-I tell the General I tell him he can take his shit'n push it hisself 'cause I'm a musician'n I don' need no . . . no . . ."

RARAruRAru. He articulated better on the horn; muted terror scratched through that blast, and he stopped only because Diane pulled his head over to hers.

"That's it, Dinch, you're better than any horn in the world, and that means you play good as Louie."

" 'Cause he's outta the world." The boy laughed, then said, "Diane . . . doll, you gonna, you not gonna snort no Horse? You gonna cold-turkey any squallin you get inside for it-like?"

"Yeah, Dinch," and felt the squalling. "I'm hungry. You got anything up here, Dinch?"

"Yeah, we got some——"

A plaintive shriek from the other end of the room, and in speckled light from the low fire Buster pulled back from the crumpled blur on the bed, then went crouching nearer, covered girl and bed with the hulk of himself, only to dance back when she wailed again.

"That slob bastard!" Dincher hissed, and went quickly forward, past them to the kitchen.

In new light bleeding out on him, Buster sat at the edge of the bed looking at the girl. "Why doncha take a walk?" he begged as the boy came out with food.

"Whatta you wanna do? When she's conked out?"

"Go on, Dinch, cop a walk," puffing asthmatically.

Diane came forward, snapped off the kitchen light. "Go on, it's dark. No one can see you," and pulled Dincher away to their couch.

"You wanna like-you wanna let him?"

"Yeah, let him. It'll do them both good," telling herself she meant
it, that it had nothing to do with her hatred of the girl, nothing to
do with Carter, nothing to do with her fear of a maddened Buster.

They ate Italian bread and American cheese, and it was a quiet
room till the fire went altogether dead and the only light was the
alien smear of the skylight. Then there were muffled whines from
the darkness around the bed, and an animal grunt, an arrested shriek,
and irregular creaking that halted abruptly. Sobbing and hoarse placating.

Diane was too tired to move. Too tight in her stomach to ask
about the time, too gummy with hash to care. "Dincher, you want
to . . . you want to see Edna tomorrow?" She was already halfway
to sleep.

"You wanna go there? Like-I thought you . . . I wanna go. Sure,
we get her a little gift; right, doll?"

And she let herself ooze into the well, back into sweet darknesses
where the only whiteness was a window of bars in the sky.

Edna kept silent about the green-coated girl in the gateway. If
she screamed *Diane* they'd take her in and away from the sun.
Away from the high blue sky and the fields spotted below with snow.
She'd almost destroyed her best-laid plans with last night's outburst
at Carter; it would mean a locked terrace door and grayness forever
if she insisted that that girl was Diane. Yet she should know her own
sister. Still, it was eight stories down.

It had rushed involuntarily out on Carter—all the gangly tentacles
of uncertainty, of whom to believe, had rushed out of her to Carter.
Was it really Diane, as Mama insisted—Diane had never gone back
to Clearwater, where she belonged—or was it Mama herself with a
best-laid plan of her own? He'd actually turned his back on her when
she accused him; like some culprit confronted with evidence, he'd
spun around and gone reticent. For that little moment it took to
form a lie. "Diane? I never did any such thing. How . . . how
should I know where she is?" Oh, that tiny hesitation! It would all
come back on his head; it would soon be balanced forever.

Edna lighted a cigarette with Carter's army lighter. It was a part of
him, and it had been like taking an ear from his head to insist that
he give it up. Only guilt had made him do it, and now she could
laugh at his helplessness. She rolled back from the balustrade and

faced the sun. . . . It would all *fall* into balance soon. And *crash* reality into his very eyes.

"Mrs. Webb, some special visitors from out of town." It was the chief nurse herself, smiling back into the room at . . . Diane! And Dincher, little Dincher. "Diane! Dincher! Oh, my two babies," reaching out for them, pulling both of them close, kissing one, then the other.

Dincher looked up to see whether the nurse had gone, then grinned into the sun. "Diane tells them we like-from outta town. You dig? No visitin today, so she tells them. Here, we bring you a bracelet," and he fixed the trinket on her wrist.

"Gee, Edna, how do you feel?" and Diane poked forward to kiss her again, to keep hidden any show of the tears she felt at the sight of those sunken cheeks, of eyes rimmed with shadow.

"Oh, baby, Diane baby." Edna fingered her cheek, then touched Diane's. Yet she knew through the real love she felt that it was all a best-laid plan to divert her suspicions. Even the decoy Dincher, who had always been around to help her before, was now a tool for Carter. "Are you . . . are you two—?" Shifting a finger between the two on the bench.

"Well, we jus, you know, like-we jus startin. . . ." Around and around went the hat in his hand. Poor Dincher probably didn't know at all what they were using him for. Diane said nothing, looked down at her lap in shame.

And the talk sped on, running like water over old scenes of childhood, isolated days in homes among strangers, to agreements about ridiculous Mama, her primness, her unshakable obstinacy. Till Edna told of times she now remembered when Mama was different, when Daddy, handsome and talented, carried the girls in his arms to carnivals and picnics, with Mama adoring them all. "I remember, Diane. For a long time I never spent even a little thought on it, but here I have time to remember. Mama was so sweet back then. It must have crushed her when Daddy . . ." and she had to stop for the choking tears. "If you were married, you'd understand, baby," she managed to say while Diane held her in her arms.

"Don't think about it, Edna. You don't have to bother yourself."

Dincher had gone to the balustrade, and Diane wished he'd sit back with them. Memory wasn't quite enough to make Edna once more her sister: too many crowded years lay like a barricade between her and the withered woman she patted. "Dincher, come on over and have a smoke."

"Oh!" Edna looked up, feigning as much excitement as she could. "Do you have any charge? Do you, Diane? Dincher?" as he sat at her sister's elbow. "Do you have any hemp you could leave me?"

"I don' carry none," Dincher apologized.

Diane was hesitant, then abruptly dug into her bag. Why not? What harm could anything do Edna? "Here, honey," and fumbled five joints to her lap. "It's nearly all I have, but I'll come back with more, Edna."

Edna giggled in delight. "Oh, I can't wait. Tonight, as soon as— here, baby, here's a light," as Diane put a cigarette in her mouth. A little mouth Carter had to love, and Edna clicked the lighter, vengeance ice-cold and powerful trembling up her arm. She did it! She let Diane have her light, then swept the flame by Diane's hair, and it crackled, flared! An invalid's awkward mistake!

But Dincher was never an invalid. With a sweep of his hand he extinguished the crackling fire before Diane realized what had almost happened.

Edna burst wildly into weeping, burning tears of frustration over the inviolate baby-skin face framed in copper hair hardly singed. "It's nothing, Edna," Diane consoled her, near tears herself. "Anyone can make a slip like that, Edna, anyone can. Don't worry, it's okay now."

"Nothin happened." Dincher laughed. "Like-make believe it di'n happen."

"Nothing happened," Edna wailed. "Nothing, nothing happened."

"That's it, honey, nothing at all." Yet Diane couldn't free her mind of the eyes she had seen when it happened, a quick flicker of passion like that she'd seen in clumsy lovers' eyes. And now, like clumsy lovers with nothing to communicate but too embarrassed to part, their eyes locked uselessly.

"Diane," Edna ventured, "Dincher, you'd better . . . I don't feel well. You'd better call the nurse." The blood was going numb in her arms; she trembled, pulling the blanket closer about cold shoulders.

Dincher went out and brought back a nurse who could smile even through alarm. "You had better go, children. I'll have to take her in," and they kissed Edna's cheeks from both sides, heard her mutter something, and went out to the hallway odors of medication.

They waited for the apple-cheeked, smiling nurse.

"Is it anything bad?" Diane had to know.

"Well, she's very weak." The woman whispered a secret. "Nothing more, just that she's extremely weak," and she left them to ponder on it.

Diane pondered on more than Edna's physical condition. Silently —down in the elevator and out to the sunny, ether-free walk, through the gateway and across the street to the bus stop. "Dincher, you know . . . she . . . Edna, when she did that? Don't think I'm crazy, Dinch, but Edna did that on purpose. I saw it, Dincher, I saw it in her eyes right then when it happened."

"Nah, whatta you talkin about? Your own sister?"

Diane didn't pursue it. She stood loving the sun till the bus rumbled up, and aboard it she sat close to the boy, felt his pride as she clutched his arm in both of hers. That smooth roundish face seemed unrelated to the tight face of the man who had slugged the Law in the Riviera; the man who had snarled at the giant last night sat nowhere near her on this rattling old bus. Here was only a smooth-faced boy who would keep away from Buster and junk. Only a boy full of silver sunshine music. "Where do you think Buster took that chick, baby?"

"Who cares? Like-maybe to his trap, maybe home. Who cares for them?"

There was nothing to care about that day. When the bus deposited them at the station, they walked around the block of shrub-lined lawns, little white houses; holding hands that swung in the breezes, smoking a stick of jive between them. Diane found a corner of her brain for Carter and another wider space for Johnny, the boy grown faceless again in her wanting. She could store them there with love and promises, and use the day for not caring.

Caring nothing about the darkness and shrieking of the subway, caring nothing about the Village downtown. Getting off early to walk into Central Park, coats on their arms, avoiding the puddles of vanishing snow. Smoking pod among other little pods smiling into the sun, under great trees that sang in stately whispers. There was a dry patch of grass on a hill overlooking the granite towers around them, and they sat on their coats, marveled at buildings gone pink

in the sun. Dincher riffed his own ideas of songs they loved, and
Diane fell in with the singing, and took his head in her lap, stroked
the full smooth cheeks of her baby. Listened to his dreams, his talk
of home that glowered to drastic complaint. Assured him that he'd
win, that his talent would win it for him. "The rest of them are all
playing Be-bop," she said. "You're going on from Louie. You're great,
Dincher, you're great."

"Know what Louie says about Be-bop? Like-anybody can play
mistakes; it's what Louie says, so it must be like-true; right, doll?"

Right as wine, like the day they danced through, eating at the
open-air restaurant by the zoo, watching people watch the polar
bears, laughing the daytime Viper's stomach-deep rollicker at people
mesmerized by the bear's repetitious lumbering over old worn paths,
clumps of people bobbing their heads in time with each bob of a
bear. Till the sun fell back to promise night, and little breezes grew
into wind. The Fifth Avenue double-decker took them downtown,
and they were alone up on top where they could smoke Tea while
watching the busy city tremble by. Millions of faces, no two alike,
brothers and enemies busily crossing back and forth in the ceaseless,
purposeless marathon of living. Less busy past Fourteenth, more
pastoral toward Washington Square, with little trees trying to be
green, and churchyards green with shrubs for seasons past. Then
under Washington Arch into the park, a sweep alongside the circular
pool to the last stop at the opposite side of the square.

"Dinch, it was like a song, the whole day, Dinch."

He helped her down the stairs and out. "It ain't over yet, doll,"
and around a turning path he said, "It ain't ever gotta be over-like;
right, doll?" taking a deep breath of dusk.

She couldn't talk about *ever*. She wanted to but knew her *ever*
could only injure the boy. Truth had two faces: one her own and
the other a nebulous mask without eyes. She wanted the Dinch always near, and had to have Carter behind her, forever where he could
be found. And Joe Letrigo . . . but that was only a challenge that
reared in her blood now and then. Secretly she was glad he'd kept
out of her way so long—the priest, the judge.

Tony the Shylock met them in the hall. "Muh-you see the Ghost?
He's a look all ove. He's a wan you from evvybo-o-ody," wagging his
tilted head.

"He come here?" Dincher showed his alarm.

"Oh, no, he's a no come by Tone. Cheez a wadda you think-uhmo? You think Tony's a craze? I donja tell a noplace to Ghosts. Ghost, he's a tell me whose a hyste a Tone, he's a tell anybody evvything for catch a connecsh. I ketch a Swede, make lilla pieces Swedish stew," and rocked back in hysterical laughter, then shuffled away to the cellar.

The jive backed up in Diane. "Christ, I forgot all about the Ghost. Dincher, what'll you do? The Ghost'll finger you as soon as they swing a setup in front of his eyes. He must be going nuts. No Horse, he must be half out of his head."

"He can't finger this place." The boy shuffled tiredly up the narrow flights with Diane behind him, looking around to catch a view of his face.

"But Buster, Dinch. If they grab Buster he'll sing like a choir."

Dincher stopped. "That's right. We be caught like rats up here. Come on, we gotta like-make it outside, like-we gotta keep a jump ahead of evvybody." She led the way down and they found Timmy Lawless staring at the moon from his seat on the stoop.

"Timmy," Diane said, "have you seen Buster anywhere?"

He shook his head slowly; tears were running like gentle rivers down the creases in his face.

"What's the matter, Timmy?" She sat down beside him quickly.

"Come on, doll." Dincher shifted uneasily.

"What is it, Tim? Come on, you can tell Diane."

He sniffled and smiled. "It's the moo-oon," and sobbed. "It's the poor moo-oon," staring at the disk in the pale-gray sky.

"Listen, Timboy," Dincher said, "if you see Buster—Timmy, you hear? Like-if you see Buster, tell him we——"

But Diane pulled him away. "Don't tell Buster a thing. What's the matter with you?" and pulled the boy down the street, quickly across MacDougal, with the old thumping with which she'd first returned to the city going again in her chest.

"Dinch! Dinch!" and Angie caught up with them on Bleecker, boyish in a navy jacket. "Don' go up there. I see the Ghost stalkin on Sixth! Like-he's plain frantic, he's screamin your name like-at evvyone inna street!"

"You see Buster?"

"Oney las night I seen him. Wit you."

"Aah, you dummy! You think I wanna know your goddam memory? I mean *now* I gotta see Buster! Y'undastan that?"

"Dincher, listen . . ." Diane could feel his trepidation. "Dinch, go on home to the Bronx, Dinch. You'll be cool up there."

"Sure I go home. But first I get a hold of Buster for my loot," and walked for anyone who cared to follow him into MacDougal—but at the corner he stopped! "Jesus, he's there!" and pulled swiftly back. "Jesus, it's Izzie!" and led them away to Sixth.

"How can he be on MacDougal?" Angie wanted to know.

"How can he be on his feet's what I wanna know. Jeez, Fuzz mus be givin him halfies. They pop him half'n send him off for more."

"Dincher—" Diane had to run to keep up—"go on home."

"No! I get my loot firss! That Ghost, he's screamin by the Riviera. He's layin onna goddam groun."

Angie still protested, "I see Izzie here, you see 'im there," puffing to keep up.

"Listen, Ange, you see Buster, tell 'im I want four hundred beans. If he don' wanna give, I come'n kill the bastard'n you say it, see? You say I tell you'n I come get 'im if he don' come on wit it. Go on, go on'n look."

They waited for no traffic, but dodged across Sixth Avenue into the thick part of Bleecker where dark had not yet dispersed the pushcarts. Angie held up. "Okay, Dinch, I go look."

"Angie!" Dincher called, and the boy came back. "Anythin happens, you lay the loot on Diane; right, Ange?"

Angie nodded and left; the two hustled around people and carts and out of Bleecker, up to Sheridan Square, into the little park in the triangle. Dincher removed his coat and put it beside him on a bench; Diane had a chill.

"He could never do time, like-he hangs hisself in stir, Buster." Dincher jerkily lighted a cigarette. "Me, I take it hoppin on one toe," as though he were trying to prove something doubtful to himself.

"Go home, Dinch. Later you can get the loot. When the panic is off."

"Nah, nah. I get it now'n then I don' worry about panics."

She took his cigarette and smoked, watched him remove his hat; they watched night settle solidly about them. For an hour or more they sat, silent, hidden in other people's noises: children chasing one another, grown men arguing for amusement. Diane couldn't tell whether the night was warm or cold. There was little that Diane could tell.

"Come on, we grab some hamburgers at Pacco's," the boy suggested with a small note of desperation rearing in his weariness. "Nobody goes in there oney like-the college guys; you dig?"

Nobody was in Pacco's but some nondescript men at the bar and some young couples at the wooden tables under the hung wagon wheels of dust. They had hot sandwiches at the little counter, and Dincher took her to the rear, where the tables were neat under checked tablecloths. The muted light was relaxing, and they settled back in a corner, ordered wine and beer from the stubby old German waiter. Dincher hooked a foot on an idle chair and looked around at the dusty ledges, laughing to himself. "Dust. They got this dust for years'n people come from all over like-jus to see it. Once some college guys don' feel right in this here dust, so they start dustin. Ha! you oughta see the house guy blow his top," and Diane was glad to see him laughing.

"Hey, who's gun pay for de suit?" the waiter wanted to know.

"What suit?" Dincher asked, taking his beer.

"De suit somebody got to clean fon you doity feet on here de chair."

Dincher laughed and removed his foot, and the laughing began and grew steadier while the place began to fill with louder-laughing people.

"Vatch you vatch!" It was the waiter's way of excusing himself past groups. "Vatch you vatch!" every now and then above the rumbling of voices.

And suddenly, "The Ghost is coming!" Both of them thought they heard it, but neither was sure till they saw each other's eyes. The laughter that followed it was strange. "Here comes the Ghostahahahee!" and Ralph Steerman was through the crowd before Dincher was half out of his seat.

"Steerman!" Diane called. "Steerman, where is he?"

"Who?" Steerman staggered over. "Where's who?"

"The Ghost," Dincher muttered, looking past the man.

"The Ghost is coming!" Steerman announced to the house. "It's the newest tidbit of meaninglessness. Everybody's saying it," and he fell into a chair, giggling and wagging his head. "Meaningless'ess, it's the new religion. It's all that's lef' innis crazy hazy."

"Let's go, Dinch, come on."

"No, doll, let 'im sit wit us, it's okay." He took Diane's hand and leaned back on the leather bench with her, studying her face while Steerman drank her wine. "If anythin happens, doll, like-you know where you got a trap for yourself. You get that loot from Buster'n use it, see?"

"The Ghost is coming!" Steerman found in it rare and tremendous humor, but he stopped laughing to watch them look at each other.

"Go home, Dinch. Please, Dinch."

"No," he whispered. "You stay here'n I go out'n find the General. You stick it out wit this lush'n I come back, see? But if I ain't back in an hour, you go to the trap'n get the loot——"

"The Ghost is coming!" Steerman shouted. The waiter stopped at his elbow. "Hey mister, you got heebie jeebies, go in toilet. Vatch you vatch!" and he was off again.

"Churl," Steerman complained, then looked at them again, shaking his fragile head at the boy and girl holding hands. "Oh, the aspirations of the young," he moaned, half laughing. "The plans and dreams of the young that they lay out before them like landscapes painted on thicknesses of concrete," shutting his eyes, shaking his head and feigning a laugh. Then, forgetting the querulous waiter, "Here comes the Ghost!" and for once in his life Steerman was right.

The Ghost, held up by an arm, came groaning through the crowd, glass-eyed, brittle-looking as any china doll. His white eyes found Dincher, but before the mustached man holding him looked that way, Dincher was out of his seat. "Don' say a *word!*" he told Diane.

"*Dinsh!* Gimme a *fix!*" The Ghost had a voice agonized to soprano; he was clutching money, holding it out before him.

"Vatch you vatch!"

Dincher pulled Steerman out of his seat and dropped him back. "You own my eyes? I can look at *any* woman I want; see? You keep her like-who wants——"

"*Fix* me, Dinsh! Gimme a fi-fix!" Ghostly hands on his coat collar.

The waiter had to be helpful. "Dot's *hiss* girl," he began, but Dincher shoved him by the face into another couple's table, spun

and caught the Law with a splatting hook on the side of the face
and ran out the side exit while the mustached man in tweeds was
still reaching for him. "He won't get far," the man told anyone who
cared, while Diane pulled Steerman away, Steerman shouting, "The
Ghost is comingahahehee!" Izzie screaming for a fix, and the indom-
itable waiter clearing his own way, "Vatchoovatch, vatchoovatch!"

From the corner Diane could see a commotion up Tenth Street
by Pacco's side exit, scuffling and bending over and kicking in the
street while strangers watched. She started forward, but stopped,
holding tight to Steerman's arm, trying to control her quaking
that way. It was Dincher they were beating, and she knew it through
the nightmare film which had covered the night, and as in a dream she
knew a horrible helplessness, a horrible pain in her entrails. "He had
to swing at that Fuzz," she muttered to the stupefied Steerman,
then left him abruptly to run across into Waverly's northward arm
and around into Greenwich Avenue toward Sixth. Down past the
diner's yellow spill of light, crossing the avenue wide to avoid the
Cosmopole's thousand mouths. Muttering, "Little baby, little baby,"
hurrying south past the park, pulled by a fist in her stomach down
MacDougal's skinny sidewalks cracked and tilted by careless decades.
To Bleecker and Tony's cellar with noisy laughter in her ears from
the Riviera, banging at the cellar door and wondering why she was
there.

"If he gets away," she told Timmy's abraded face when he let her
in. "Timmy," puffing cracks into the words, "if he gets away make
him stay downstairs," knowing the Dinch could get away from
nothing any more, not Fuzz nor Horse nor any frustrating day of his
years in strange parents' houses. "Timmy, Timmy," among barrels
and crates, "what happened to your face?"

"Buster's upstairs, Diaaaane. He hit me with a pret-ty gun,"
grinning abstractedly like some debutante freshly debauched.

"A pret-ty gun," Timmy whispered while she bathed his cheek
with water on toilet tissue in the old bathroom lately polished new.
When she asked, he told her the Shylock was out hunting Lukey,
that Buster had got in upstairs by the key for which he'd gun-
whipped Timmy.

Up the creaking, narrow flights. Diane felt the brown-lit world
in her guts, forty-watt guts in a forty-watt world pitched forever in
defense against a high-voltage universe around it. She banged on

the skimpy metal door and stood aside in case the giant maniac should fire through it in a cornered-rat frenzy. "Buster! Buster, it's me—Diane, Buster!"

"You 'lone?" through the door.

"All alone, Buster. Open up, quick."

Open, and she passed him, rushing into darkness; not even the fire was going. "Why in the dark, Buster? The place is cool."

"How you know it's cool?"

She yanked on the light. "They got Dincher," and her own statement seemed blown up out of reality. Buster blinked; his big lips writhed like fresh-cut quivering beef. "I was there." She fell into the soft chair. "I saw them take him; they took him . . . they took him, Buster."

He quickly pulled the room into darkness. "He'll sing, he'll sing."

She could have killed him for saying it and cut pieces from him for the repetition. She lurched from the seat and pulled on the light again. "If you're so goddam leery, what're you doing here? You big slob, if you think the Dinch is a squaller, why don't you cut out and hide—hide with that uptown chick?"

Buster hit the bed with his seat. "He keep quiet. Yeah, he knows I get 'im if he don't." She wanted to jump him for that, but knew it was useless. "This place stay the coolest for Buster," and he grinned up at her. "They pin it on him when he don't talk'n I got the whole road."

"Buster—" she sat beside him—"lay Dincher's four hundred on me. He said so; so you better do it, or you'll see who gets who."

"What'd he say?" Buster stood up swiftly. "He say he . . . Whatta you mean? Dincher tryin to hunch me? That little——"

"He'll blast you for looking cockeyed, you big dope. After he sits inside he'll come out ready to blast anybody."

Buster ran out to the kitchen, somehow reminding Diane of her mother. She had to laugh at the thought of *Mother. Mother:* the word had a weird taste. Buster came back, wiping his lips, smiling; he sat down beside her. "Listen, beautiful, I give you the loot, see? 'Cause I wan you should have it better'n him. I oweys wanted you should have. You know it, beautiful. 'N I got more, oney it ain't in yet. You can stick it out here wit me, see? You can——"

"I can! This is Dincher's trap. What do you mean, I can! You're lucky if I don't run your big ass out. I can!"

"Beautiful—" he was wincing and sweating and smelling like old abandoned clothes—"beautiful, listen. Don't argue wit me. Jus relax," and he touched her shoulder with a hand.

She yanked away and stood. "Buster, you can stay here till the panic's off and then you get the hell out. And I want four hundred beans for the Dinch and I want it soon."

He lumbered over to her. "Look, beautiful, I got all the jive you want'n I got Horse . . . you know it. You can have——"

"What do you want?" She laughed up at him. "You want to conk me out and diddle with me while I'm helpless, you big degenerate?"

"Don't say that, Diane!"

"What'd you do with that uptown dope? Cut her up or what?"

"No. No, I take her home, that's all. I take her home like a lady."

"Like a lady! You big jerk fiend, you want to school me like you school kids and idiots?"

His eyes were rolling out of focus; his pupils were nearly up out of sight. "You . . . someday you eat them words, beautiful."

"Go on, go on and get some sleep." She knew where she had to go to get clean. "You make me a key and fix up the other room for yourself," wondering why he didn't just drive out of town in that big car, but wanting to keep him around—four hundred dollars' worth —so she said nothing at all about it.

Now the loose lips flinched in half a smile. "Okay, okay, Diane. I make you a key. Sit down . . . stay wit me, beautiful."

She whipped open the door and ran. Down narrow flights, with Buster squalling above her. "Diane! Diane!" She even thought she heard a sob spiral down after her, its aftertone ringing in her head when she got outside.

Into the long, dead shadows of Bleecker, where clumps of dirty snow lay corpselike by the curb. Treading over the great stone corpse called the Village, past its lighted and beery pores festering with forgetful laughter, through the Sheridan Square park where the ghost of Dincher still brooded, with his could-have-been music silver in her head up Christopher, and only strangers about her, only indifference in the streets. Past Greenwich Street she went, faster in the lightless gloom, yanked by the drawing freeze growing stronger inside.

They had taken Johnny, removed Paddy, and now Dincher had been drawn violently away just as strength was being sucked from her stomach by something hungry and hostile. But there'd be Carter at the end of the rattling elevator ride, and she used her own key on his door. There was darkness inside, but the night lamp popped on when she entered the bedroom, and Carter on an elbow squinted from the bed. She hustled out of her coat and fell upon him. "Carter, Carter, they took Dincher away, he's only a kid, he never did anything—he never *knew* how wrong—well they're all coked up, the whole screwy world, Carter, they——"

"Take it easy, baby." He pulled her head down to him. "Just take it easy, little girl. What happened? Just say it slow."

Diane sat up, watched him reach for a cigarette and light it. "Dincher, Cart. The police took him away. Little Dinch, he's only a kid."

"Yeah? What'd they take him for?" He could have suggested several possibilities, but sarcasm wouldn't ease his little girl's tension.

"Junk. For pushing junk."

"Well?" He saw her eyes shift with perplexity. "I'm sorry, baby. But, babe, that's what police are for," while she stood and pulled off clothes, abandoning them where they fell, moving with a slow and abstracted grace that he watched through the glowing end of his cigarette as he puffed on it. Fatigue robbed his lungs of air, and he let his eyes close. He awakened, realizing he'd been nearly asleep again, when he felt her bounce on the bed, slip under the covers and press close to him, touch his side with hers and tremble just a little. He warmed with a heavy want of her . . . but if he took her it would bear out Edna's suspicions; Edna would have described the thing before it had ever happened. And Mrs. Lattimer—she wore the old distortion of her face in his mind, hissing: "See? See?" Diane took the cigarette from his fingers and talked as he floated back into the smooth weight in his chest till he was half-conscious, half-mystified, so that her words stayed a long time in his ears before he understood them. And as he fell more heavily away she spoke out a fear of *everything at once: all the people and all the different things they do and all the things they build and all the things they want and all the different things people know about . . . too much at once . . . and really scared . . . and animals and some secret light withheld in a faraway, a puff,* a puff, a plan and arrest, and a duet of small disembodied female voices sang *wo-o-o-o-o,* diminished and faded, shocking him with worldlessness, frightening him upright. "What? What?" He looked around for voices.

"What's eating you?" Diane had to laugh.

"Oh—" rubbing his cheek—"I was asleep. What was it you said?"

"They don't really try—hey, you better get some sleep. You never get enough, and I always——"

"No, go ahead. It's still early." He wanted urgently not to sleep, afraid of elusive voices which had sung of mystery . . . like tears magically audible, or long-suppressed memories demanding rebirth. "What were you saying, babe?" with sleep pulling at him again like some cloudy phantom.

There was really nothing to say, now that she was home. "Dincher, he plays *some* horn . . . when he can play," and he wouldn't play now for a time. She huddled close to Carter, and he held her, but when she reached over to crush the cigarette out he swung around and sat up. She went up on an elbow, rubbing at the burning in her eyes. "Something just came to me, Carter. Like a sheet, a white sheet with black thread sewed through it, going in and out; first you see it, then you don't, then you see it again, then you don't."

"What's that supposed to mean?" His head felt heavy and the way she looked past his face troubled him.

"Life. That's what life is. That's all."

When he got up and found his bedroom slippers, she whispered, "Don't go out. Carter, stay here."

"But I got to go," smiling at her, sliding his hand around on her cheek until the frozen hopelessness on her face dissolved into a smile. Carter went out to the bathroom. The *blue flame*, he thought, those nutty flashes of insight that seem to illuminate the darknesses of futility. A white sheet with a black thread, one frantic image to disclose the secret of all her angry days. One meaning where nothing added up. What could he say without pulling her tension tighter? He washed his face and neck, then rubbed hard with the towel. What could he say? Perhaps if he spoke of more objective things, perhaps if he joked with her . . .

But when he returned, Diane lay sobbing, face pressed into the pillows, her naked shoulders quivering. It was something he'd never seen or expected to see, something that unnerved him as if he were watching himself cry. Her small hands were pressed to her hiding face.

"Diane, Diane." He pulled her around to face him. For an instant

he saw the wet eyes and her quivering baby lip; then she pulled him
down to hide her face by his ear.

Sobs shattered her words. "Carter, it's . . . Carter . . . my baby,
my . . . baby. I want my Johnny, I want . . . him, I need my
baby. . . ."

"We'll get him, Diane." He slipped under the covers, pulling her
close. "We'll see to it, honey, we'll get him." He wanted to rock her
in his arms, to sing her to sleep or whatever had to be done for a
child sobbing for promises.

But it wasn't a child crying for her toy. "Car-ter . . ." Sobs
rocked her."How . . . can I . . . take him? Where will I . . . take
him? What've I done? My . . . own baby . . . my own, my . . .
own little boy. . . ." It was not even a young girl needing his sympathy, but a mother crying for her child, a woman wailing for what was
her responsibility. He held her tighter than he meant to. He rubbed
her spine, the tense muscles of her shoulder. Diane's sobs quieted to a
whimper, and her arms snaked around his neck, more a demand than
a plea. A truck gunned its engine outside, again and again with
mounting power, and he felt a shameful kinship to machines when he
responded like one to Diane; he felt like some insensitive savage. But
then it hit him that Diane needed him now more than at any other
time. But did she know it? And if she did, was she aware he knew she
knew? He laughed inside, cursed his old insensitivity that had kept
him from the girl so long. Edna! Vivienne! Their accusations were
well-aimed, burning bullets. But it was buckshot they fired, a thousand pellets covering his space, his time; their broad charges had
finally to find a target. He whispered, "Diane," and grew dizzy in her
perfume. "No more dilly-dallying; make up your mind," and kissed
back her laugh. Now in the darkness his awareness of her was like
sight. A gasp, a tiny whisper of air, and she took his earlobe into soft
lips. He was conscious of her hair fluffed out at her ears and of closed,
expectant eyes, and, without seeing it, he was conscious of her legs,
smooth and graceful and somehow very long. And resting somewhere
beyond his thumping veins and automatic muscles there was an em-
bryonic happiness in Carter Webb, a new cleanliness already pushing
away the stupid soot of his debt to Dyingthings.

Engines purred outside, quietly as in deference to realer things,
and now Diane was home, now she felt muscles that loved her, now

power and tenderness blended, and now rhythmic throbs hinted through blood to tap faintly and die too soon in her head. And they were laughing at their nakedness and the foolish curtains of the world. Worms of the day were returning to her brain, but she hushed them for words casual and lazy between them while they smoked. He returned from the bathroom only half awake and went all the way to sleep as soon as he lay down. So she turned off the light and pulled his arms around her, listening to his deep exhausted sigh, feeling solid in the togetherness now grown between them, fitting herself back into the curve he formed.

But sleep stayed distant. While sounds out of citynight whispered in darkness, a whisper of dryness pulled in her groin. With Carter she'd come nearer than ever before, but she'd been left finally unspent in the dark. Yet the pull in her gut couldn't be answered by that, for it grew steadier, drawing, sucking cold inside, first in her stomach alone, then like a clumsy fist at her spine, pulling, and the absence of real pain was weird. Drumming on muscles in her back, then dipping inside when her hands sought the surface pull. She felt cold somewhere under the heat of Carter's arms, eased out of those arms to sit up, and the first pain came, welcome no more, a knot of chalk at her navel. Then farther back when she pressed on her navel, higher, lower, a pain that ran from the stroke of her hand. Diane was sweating. Diane had to get up on cold legs.

She sat in the gray-leather chair, gray with her uneasiness in the dark. Squeezing wooden chair arms held nothing still inside her, held no galloping still, quieted no Horse in her guts. Dincher was gone beyond helping her. Only cold sweat was real, not Carter, not Johnny, not anything but— "Gimme a fix!" the Ghost had cried.

"The Ghost is comingahahahee!" and "Vatchoovatch!" were real. Vatchoovatchoovatchoovatch!" Diane crept on the floor in search of clothes, while her insides pulsed to vatchoovatchoovatch. There was only Buster on Bleecker Street with a hungry, frightened leer and an ounce or two of Horse to make her human again.

WHILE RIVERS OF ANGRY STRANGERS ROAR

Springtime was upon her, a season faintly familiar, yet new to her new arrangement of nerves. Diane was a shell drifting over unrecalled surfaces, sometimes through an old enchanted park where all the known but unimportant faces gathered to chatter and stare, often through side-street crowds of careless unanimity in which she could be lost, now and then up some beckoning staircase to duty obscure as the face of a baby boy she'd used tọ want.

Now, at the end of some duty's winding stairwell, she finally had to say, "But, Mama, I hardly know you." The woman seemed transfixed on her new maroon couch, in her new bright living room, with her old obstinate control keeping her rigid against the rigid skyline outside. "I can't just live here, Mama. I can't just do everything you say."

"Diane, I only want you to rest. You can buy more clothes, take walks in the park. Don't you like it here?" with a look through the wide wall of windows to the sky, thick blue and heavy with spring.

"I'm staying here; I don't bother Mrs. Burnell; what more do you want?"

"I want you in every night. Is that too much?" A long wail near tears.

"Yes, it's too much," with the tug growing colder inside. "It's— you're not supposed to tell me anything. You're trying to bring me up, and it's too late, it's too late." It was too late for anything at all any more—she choked back the thought when Carter loomed up in her mind. Carter couldn't tell. She'd gauged the shots for daytime hours, and he hadn't yet found out.

"Diane, you're getting ill. I can tell. I want you to—you should . . . Diane, don't you think it would be right for you to spend at least one solid week here? Resting, Diane?" She came across the rug to sit on the sweeping arm of the chair, to stroke hair back from Diane's eyes. "Your eyes—there are circles beneath them," uncon-

269

sciously rubbing under her own. "I know you're unhappy, dear, and
I only want to make you well. Don't you see, Diane?"

Stoney's clumsy face stared out from thorns in the gilded frame,
a nasty-hearted Christ, and she had to laugh, thinking of that face
so lewdly naked now in Village streets. But the laughter knotted in
her guts; she doubled over and held herself. "It's too late, Mama,"
getting up, pulling the black trench coat tight by its belt to tether
the Horse inside.

"Diane!" Her mother followed her through to the dark vestibule.
"Must I start all over again with the Welfare Board? You're still
legally an infant, you know."

"Why don't you adopt me out, Mama?" She sighed. "To someone
who'll let me live."

"To Carter? It was his stupid idea to have you taken out of Clearwater's charge. I kept *telling* him. I kept——"

"You kept, you kept! Somebody's *charge*, it always has to be."
She pulled open the door. "You're not responsible for me, Mama.
Leave your conscience alone."

"That's some *more* of his smart-alecky nonsense. Diane, if you're
not in by ten-thirty tonight——"

"What! What if I'm not?" She closed the door again and switched
on the vestibule light because she wanted her hate to show. "What
if I'm not?" she said more quietly, with some perverse will to hear
out her mother's threats.

"I tell you, I'll call in the——"

"Listen, lady—" through teeth clenched to keep her steady—"if
anybody bothers me—you hear me? If anyone *ever* bothers me, you'll
die! You got it?" hating the face that came to her mind with those
words, hating the only man keeping her alive. "I mean it. Don't ask
me anything," and yanked open the door, went down the carpeted
hallway with her mother's agonized look following her to the street.
An uptown street with little trees. A street still damp with late noon
rain, yet lazy with early season heat and strangers in bright-colored
clothes. Heat that was chilly and strangers familiar as days and long
faceless days. Fallen buds lay like red caterpillars in puddles colored
with waste, crunchy little bugs that squeaked under her step and sent
up a perfume that turned sour in her belly. Belly that ordered her to
Bleecker. Back that might crack before she got there.

She couldn't make it to the top of the Fifth Avenue bus, and had to sit at the street level as the monster lumbered downtown, irritating the animal that twisted her spine, lumbered slowly, hesitantly, like a lethargic and frightened Buster hovering over the hooked shell of herself on Stoney's bed. Scared of her open eyes, even in dark afraid of her unseen eyes. Whimpering. Slobbering till she kicked at him with useless limbs and fell back to dream of snails. Snails creeping on gluey paws, till one blew up life-size, pawing at her with hoofs and she had to kick Buster to the floor, whimpering, promising to remain there all night. And before dawn could break through the skylight she'd hurdled the penitent hulk to the setup on Stoney's wheel-bottom table and slowed her stomach to butter with a cap boiled over the painter's stove. And back to Carter in time to beat his awakening, like some Cinderella or like a vampire or like both— she was a mixture of so many things . . . a little bit of the Shakespeare she'd read in Edna's bed that day: *Once more unto the breach, dear friends, once more.* Once more onto the hook, dear shnooks, once more while Mama prays in her tower, while old Carter travels the dismal road between with only strangers around him, with not even a choirboy Letrigo to hold up his head.

Once more with a stomach of lead to turn to softer stuff up the narrow flights where brown light showed the way through dust to a gray tin door. Once again with a bent spoon, boiling it over a stove someone long dead had bought. And then the long laugh while pouring. What a rat race outside!

Diane could stand the painless hurting while she contemplated the charge. Alone in a cobwebby studio with Buster's promise to stay away by day, and a three-cap hypo ready to go, and a system of Nothing worked out. Carter would find her home, freshly set up for the night, just as he'd found her smiling and dreamy for weeks now; Buster, cool now on the strength of Dincher's incarcerated silence, went about his big business and left her ten caps each day, docile and obedient like a son in velvet knee pants.

Lukey the Swede roamed the Village freely, attesting to its temperature: low with an absence of Fuzz. Junkies roamed, drifted like springtime clouds, creatures apart from the machinery of life. Only the *score* called for effort; money was the devil which haunted them as it did the marchers on the dismal road between hook and tower, but junkies had recourse to games sane conscience never could allow: Danny Barber had his string of bookstores to dip into with those long, white, artistic fingers; Sticks sold pod to squares with hip-cards they wanted punched; Jacquie Swan could take twelve men in a night while her baby played with her toes; even Lukey, skin-popping now, had his route of apartment-house drying rooms where women left clothes fresh from washing machines. Only Diane coasted free even of that single junky's cross—Diane had Buster and his fear of her to keep the caps securely by. She swung the setup around, sat forward on the bed, and pulled up her skirt to show the needle her thigh. Punched into muscle and squeezed. No vein for her (she'd kick it one day), just flesh for the little Horse.

Crawling little felt-fingered Horse that searched for more places to stroke. Little stroker let her look up at the skylight canted north away from the sun's angry fingers, perfect spacing between bars that held the glass in place. Perfect spacing in her breathing, perfect senses in her golden skin. Riffing out what Dincher used to play, little tricks of expression that somehow took their own initiative and made only an instrument of her—*ooriooRAru-liOOrara-RA-raliaruRAruRAAA-mammy's soEEvulbaBABE* . . . while day slipped by on butter. Stoney's fireplace yawned in concrete boredom and she had to drape a blanket over that stone face that mocked all flesh and softness and any kind of motion; with fitful envy she obscured that stony face. And met the first shades of twilight that quieted diamond-colored voice notes from the street. Sounds that didn't matter into silence that counted not a bit. Scratches on tin were Timmy.

"A let-ter, Diaaaane," the vague spirit reported, and she had him read it while she lay back, breathing vast round bubbles. Dincher's report with comprehensible edges shaved so that the message was round and her only name was doll addressed to Tony telling doll not to care (as if doll could care with all going well) and thinking always of doll in music that he scribbledooriaa. Timmy loved music and danced it for Diaaaane, whirling leaping like a finger to skies past the well-spaced perfect glass. Danced to sweating off the raggedy shirt to yellow skin and army pants while Canada Dan laughed like any dying child would moan, and Nao Braun was there, watching, with feeble hands playing with those of her emaciated husband, and everybody was there while Timmy danced in darkness, and Buster exploded the room with naked light and scowled under his broad brown hat, Buster huge in a pin-stripe suit, scowling.

"Put out the light, Busser," Diane sang in Mama's twinkle voice.

"Clear out. Evvybody clear out; you got it?"

And everybody ghosted out before she could move a hand to stop shadows from turning real. "Busser, you big shit. Put out the lie." He held her down on the bed, sat hulking there beside her. "Listen, you listen to me for a change." Buster had reasoned out some new mastery of things. "You keep it cool up here; you got it? No lousy junkies here, see? You want your fix, you keep it cool," and grinned with devilish creases in that butterface before he added, "beautiful. You do it my way from now on."

"You got a damn Ma'iet' Hotel, Busser . . . Dinch's place here," in a squeal that had no power. "Go on, Busser."

"I get too lonely there, beautiful." His grin swam into the naked light. "It's why I never left town when I was suppose to. For you, beautiful, I stick it out when the town's on fire, oney for you, Diane," with no more grin, yet with a much grosser smugness in his begging leer. "Make it wit me, Diane, make it wit me."

Laughing was a failure. "Make it! Soff-belly slob . . . pitiful . . . How you gonna make it? How, Busser kneepanss?"

He had half her body in the hand on her shoulder. "I get use to you, Diane. I swear. It'll be okay. I swear, Diane."

"Cook up a fix, Busser. Cook it up, boy."

He hastened to comply. Took caps to the kitchen while she sank back tighteyed into naked white darkness. Bodiless, a skin of inviolable gold shining in darkness till Buster got back. "Here, beautiful." Such love he had for her that he wanted her unconscious.

"Roll up your sleeve, Busser." She blew out a bubble of glue, and still her mouth went dry as chalk.

"Whatta you mean, roll up my sleeve?"

"Hey, you wanna make it with me, Busserboy? Roll up your lousy sleeve."

"Not me, not me."

"Then lemme oud." *Oorioobop.*

"No, don't go away, Diane. Stay here, stay here."

"Go to . . ." but Carter was an unpronounceable name, a misty face.

Buster held her shoulder, and she hit at his face with Dincher's golden horn, hidden until now between bed and wall. He grinned, taking the trumpet from her hand. "Go to my Daddio," she murmured. "Lemme away, Busserboy."

No more grin in naked light. "You want your fix, Diane? Here's your fix, beautiful. I got it ready for you."

"Dowanno fix. Dowanna make it with no square." *Ooriubopoo-bopjebam.*

"You make it wit me, Diane? If I take a pop, you make it?"

"Roll up your lousy sleeve." She was a white-faced vampire, a mixture of many, many white-face things.

Buster couldn't do more by himself than remove his pin-stripe jacket; he looked away while she punctured his arm and popped the gold into mush. He winced and sniffled and looked agonized, yet sat back and smoked a cigarette like some old-timer immune to a couple of little caps of Horse cut to Pony. A Pony pop couldn't hook so much beef: he wore that on his grin. Then the smirk perished abruptly; she laughed as he was kicked. She swelled with golden conquest as he rushed to the bed. First he moaned, with panic in his eyes. Then his eyes fought for focus; he was a Louella far from home. He screamed when she wrapped him in darkness with a yank of the light cord, and new power put sinews back into her legs; she left the loft while Buster vomited in a heavy darkness broken only by the pale smear of skylight in a ceiling that he couldn't reach.

Join hands,
    "   "   ,
We're building a happier world-toot-toot!
and song changed to *were blazing away at-ebop-and fellow travelers-yawk-gathering storm around the world ----.-. ... . -. -. . - obtain or retain respect of other nations loyalty file of one unidentified State Department FBI undercover-byaweek-about shady morals in the Senate-oo-truck blast and two men blown-ooaw-second straight victory——* "Hey, why'd you change that?" Carter groaned, half out of sleep. "I wanted to hear whether those guys were blown up or down." He sat up on the couch while Diane spun the dial. *Flying saucers in Sheridan Square turned out to be searchlight beams from Jersey City fifty-five degrees fair and warmer tomorrow-CLACK!*

"Not a bit of music anywhere," she said lazily, and idled over to sit with him in the silent twilight, laying her head on his shoulder. "It's Saturday night coming on, Carter. Why don't you go out? Have some fun."

"I haven't seen you since you came in goofy on Wednesday and

now you want me to go out. Have you been home since you
threatened Mama?"

"Yeah, till this afternoon. Stoney was up there having tea with
her," but she didn't say that his presence had made her leave long
ago—it was better for Carter to think she'd been at Mama's those
nights she stayed at the loft . . . with stoned-out junkies . . . with
Buster getting harder and harder to tap for some Horse.

"Don't you sleep nights, baby?" knowing it was more than lack of
sleep that made her so lethargic. "Want to read a letter I got from
Joe a few days ago?"

She lifted her head to attempt a smile. "Read it to me, Cart."

He reached over and found Joe's letter in the pocket of his jacket,
opened it, and read aloud:

"Dear Cart . . . Thing that happened—the damn Winter followed me south. Man, I just prayed for Spring to come up and meet
me to warm these homesick bones, but snow rode along all the way
to home. And when I got there at last, what do I see in the station
but some Roanton colored folks, dandy walking sticks their latest af-
fectation, sporting around like any Riviera crowd. You know that kind
of fun-making. Boy I was haunted, I'll tell you. But since then things
have become more to my liking—a lot warmer. One sister (Joanie) is
a happy little girl full of the good weather, and the other (Tooney)
is engaged to a newspaper man and contented, and my parents are
trying their damnedest to grow accustomed to me. I want to tell you
that I'm drinking alone in my room of a Saturday night and bearing
a bad guilt for it—the drink burns too strongly, tastes like crime itself.
It's always that way at home—first week back I can drink a tank dry,
but once adjusted to familiar faces around town and placid moments
creeping about the State Street house, any kind of roistering falls flat.
As if some cottontail conscience had hold of me. So this bottle will
doubtless perish in the truck like the last few have, while old lumber-
loaders glow at their work. (I haul timber in a trailer to the mill where
my daddy Tom is foreman of the sawyers.) Yet, guilty as it makes me,
I manage to stay fried. For I'm a stranger here—people go into strange
silences when I'm about and I feel like some invalid till an audacious
soul like Hensley Clayburne (my sister's beau) asks me right off about
Israel—"I mean, why there? Why way out there?" I never know what
to say. I look about me and see strangers on the porch under Japanese
lamps, mother telling out her tales of the Averills, family tales often so
pointless, while Tooney picks at her nails, while Joanie tugs at Dad to
awaken him, and insects scrape in the poplar trees—I have to drink
and bear the guilt. For even when I hug my mother and laugh, her
laughing is nervous and she pulls away as if I'm some family friend

grown too forward, and I feel myself an intruder in her eyes. They're furtive and fretful eyes, always searching for some little kid lost long ago and replaced by someone she really scarcely knows. Forgive me for being so damn drunk that——"

"Oh, *stop!* For Christ sake, what crap!" Diane pitched over, whimpering.

He pulled her over to him. "Baby, what——"

"Carter, let me get into bed. Let me sleep, Carter; I don't really sleep at—when I'm at Mama's."

That slow voice had been getting more and more frail, as though she were thinking of other things than those she spoke of, letting words slip out with only a token of purpose. "Baby, you been smoking?" He folded Joe's letter, tucked it away, then turned to her. "A lot? I mean, a lot of marijuana?"

"Marijuana?" She looked up at him now, caught his hand when he reached to turn on a brighter light. "Tea? Jive, pod, hempadoodio?" laughing without mirth. "No, I haven't been smoking, Cart. Not me."

"Diane, what is it, baby?" The phone began a clanging demand for attention, but he only looked once toward the hall and let it ring. "Diane, maybe we ought to take you to a doctor."

"No. No, Cart, no doctor. I just want to sleep," and waited only for the phone to stop tearing at her ears before she struggled up and away to the bedroom. Carter didn't follow. That high, distant voice was deathly, slow as her graceless movement. Doubled forward in her walk as though her head were too great a load to carry, oozing about like someone mesmerized, never wanting any more to plan a way to get Johnny. Only in junkies had he ever seen—— Diane? Diane! He lumbered, heavy-legged, down the long hallway to the bedroom, asking himself how he could suppose that Diane would ever allow herself to fall into a disease under which she'd seen people crumble.

Naked, she stood in near-dark beside the bed, leaning motionless against the wall.

"Baby, what are you doing? Why——"

"My legs. I thought they were cramping up. . . . They weren't cramping up, Carter, they just wanted to stand. Legs have a right to stand, Carter," most earnestly in that babylike voice.

Gently, by the hand, he drew her down to sit beside him. Her body, leaning on him, felt only smooth to his hand, totally sexless, just as she'd been an inert mound beside him nights now and then in recent weeks. "Diane . . . little girl . . . There was—you used to tell me things, Diane, you used to come right out and say what you wanted. Why don't——"

"I don't want anything, Carter."

"What is it, baby?" He had to come right out, just as he was suggesting she do. "Is it junk? Are you hooked, Diane?"

Once Diane had thought she'd die if he ever found out; now his question fell easily, and the answer came easily out. "I'm not hooked on anything at all in this world, Carter. Not me."

"Well, then, is it Mama? Is it living with her? Is it anything I can——"

"Mama. It's Mama; she picks on me, Cart," and the tears that exploded out of her seemed to have been praying for just this chance. "She nags me. Carter, she won't . . . leave me alone for a . . . second, Cart."

It was a long unbroken wail that followed, and he hoisted her to his lap and rocked her, even said, "There, there, there," for she'd finally returned to infancy, letting long-inhibited anguish flow. In a few minutes she was asleep.

Settling her in bed, he was horrified by the lax lean flesh of her buttocks—it was a starveling child he covered well. He closed the door in order to give himself light in the hallway. He dialed Information and got Mrs. Lattimer's uptown number, got Mrs. Lattimer herself on the phone.

"I've been trying to reach you," she said. "Carter, where is that girl? Where is she, Carter?"

"I . . . I just saw her awhile ago, Vivienne, and——"

"Why didn't you send her here? Carter, you promised——"

"She told me she'd been there just this afternoon."

"This afternoon! I haven't seen or heard from her in a week. She said she'd have me killed if I——"

"Yeah. Yes, Vivienne, she told me all about it." His ears burned. Diane had lied to him—how much he couldn't quickly decide. "If I find her again, I'll bring her to you. I have to talk with you about her; she's ill, I believe, and——"

"Oh, do you have any more bright ideas like letting her run around free? Maybe now you'll let me decide——"

"We'll talk about it when I bring her over." He swallowed hard to keep from saying more.

"Not tonight. Tonight I'm going . . . I won't be in tonight, Carter."

"I'll keep her here, then, if I see her tonight. I'll bring her there in the morning."

"But I intend to see Edna tomorrow." Her voice lilted in a high octave, like a child reciting words with no idea of their meaning.

"Are you *crazy*, woman?" It burst out; he could hold it in no longer. "Are you *insane*? Should I bring the kid over or shouldn't I? You're younger in your mind than she is!"

"All right, all right, bring her. Bring her tomorrow. I'll forego my visit to Edna. All right, you needn't shout like some——"

"And you can visit Edna too. You don't have to be a watchdog." He replaced the phone quickly. He was back in the bedroom before he realized that he was trembling; he ran a palm across his forehead, but that only made it wetter. Diane lay squarely in the path of light leaning in from the hallway. Her mouth was open; she was breathing in short, urgent gasps, her arm out and awkwardly propped stiff by the elbow so that her hand was a small begging thing in shaddows. He knelt and kissed her cheek as she slept, more out of guilt than love, though not without affection. He'd felt nearly helpless before—it had forced him to call Vivienne—but now he felt only swinish for trying to pass her off: that was what it had been, and there was no use rationalizing it away. He pulled a chair to the window, opened it and leaned out. It was really spring; he could smell it in the bite of the air.

Spring, then summer, then other seasons of chaos. How many more could he endure? He had to think of it, with only a mild reproof for his self-pity, and he had to think of other things he'd feel much better free of. Edna and Diane and Vivienne—he'd married quite a family —and Vivienne had to go out tonight: Saturday was an inconvenient night for motherhood. He was pushed to his feet by his own venom and left the room with his feeling slowly softening to sorrow. Poor Vivienne and poor her daughters and poor Merwin Fingerhut with his juvenile marijuana kick and poor Wengel with his small eyes. Poor world.

Still, Merwin had to be well regarded, he decided, back on the couch, for keeping the processing kit secret from Wengel. Wengel, with every jobber in the trade contributing money and pressure to clear him of the mail-order fraud, had turned on the steam rather than become an angel. The jobbers needed him alive for their own survival, and, knowing it too well, he accepted their help and with it paid back the monumental amount he'd as much as stolen, then swung around to gnaw at the hands which had pulled him out of the mire: he intercepted a job lot of reflex cameras one jobber needed to carry him through the month, withheld bulk film from another, then bought the two of them out with a particle of his still virtually intact *seven figures*. It was Wengel's "freedom," and by it Carter himself was doomed. For when the first shock had come, when Wengel had had to quit mail-ordering rotten surplus film, he saw to it that Webb was left with no camera lots to sell, no bulk film to export, no legitimate film to process. For Wengel could still sell his rotten surplus anywhere outside the mails, but such slow sales meant little profit unless he absorbed the processing yield. He squeezed Webb and courted Merwin for his knowledge of the formula, but Merwin turned him down flat.

Carter clicked on the light beside him and thumbed through the book that had put him to sleep before Diane arrived. But his mind drifted through the prim lines of words to other, closer things. Farrell. If he took Farrell up on his offer, Merwin could go along with Wengel, do his surplus-film developing and still keep the processing formula secret. Carter stood up again in sheer sudden excitement, only to sit back in despair. Diane would be left to her mother's ministrations if he left town for Farrell's labor school. He slammed the book down, and it bounced off the couch. He opened both windows and leaned through one to stare out over the Hudson's drifting orange lights to the black bar of Jersey twinkling distantly. Feeling feverish, he grabbed his tweed jacket from the chair and left, sure that Diane was asleep for the night.

He went as fast as he could down dark Christopher, alone but for cats that yowled erotically. Crossing the lighted and peopled Sheridan Square, he realized he'd called Vivienne to give her hell about Diane and not to unburden himself at all. He went over to Tenth, feeling better, until in the long side-street shadows he remembered that Diane had lied outright. "Only junk," he said aloud, "only junk, only junk could get her like that," shaking his head in perspiring fury. Only narcosis could blind her to help, to the direction in which it lay, even to any idea that she needed help. *I don't want anything, Carter:* a slow needle of sound that lingered still.

In Pacco's he stood on sawdust and drank by the bar, seeking his own narcosis, with chirpy girlish laughter all around him, and faces he'd seen in other Village meeting places, faces fixed in grins permanent with an expectancy never fulfilled. "People," he wanted to shout, "it isn't here!" And loved the whisky burning his throat. "People," he wished he could cry, "Diane is sick, she's sick, she's hooked like you are and I am and everyone's children will be in the time we're preparing them for. People," he could have said without knowing why, "we're murderers for not caring." While some authoritarian voice warned them all to beware for their watches, cautioned them against loss.

Then, feeling maudlin, he stood in the silent privacy of his thoughts for many, many slow drinks, wanting hard to work with Farrell, the schoolboy grown old and very, very wise. The scholar of solidity, the quiet-looking man in horn-rimmed glasses who thought little of words and a lot of work. The simple man who wanted all the people together sharing the load and the rewards. Feeling more maudlin than ever, he stumbled out and staggered up Tenth toward home. Reckless in his head, weary in his legs, hands in his pockets all the way home. Home. Drunk. Narcotized like Diane and the whole wide world.

She was there as he'd left her, but somehow consecrated now in eyes too fogged to really see. He kissed her more with love than remorse, and hurried through his washing to bed—quickly went unconscious.

Dreamed, and knew it as dreaming.

Yet had to function with the seriousness of reality. In gray air he stumbled heavily over land barren and peopled with rocks. Death-colored stones close to the rotted earth slung in an arc toward a distant horizon, with an arid, gutted tree jutting here and there into the hanging smoke of dim recollection. And when recollection ebbed, it trembled unseen back of the horizon glow and set up an ominous rumbling that put a chill of apprehension through him. He leaned against the thick air and pumped his arms, elbows pointed upward, pumped from the shoulders frantically while the rumbling grew louder, came closer. Straining fiercely, he rose up a foot or two, pumped harder still and lifted himself higher, feeling some tenuous pride over a power rare even in dreaming as he flew higher, straining, working, dizzy for lack of breath, while the rumbling, louder, was built into a strict cadence, a march of troops that he avoided with his power to fly, up, up, till strength was gone and he settled on the flat brick roof of the house standing alone in the wilderness. While a platoon of disciplined and resigned faces marched by in strict garrison formation, a block of men over the jagged arc of earth. With Webb perched out of reach on a flat rock roof. No head looked up to find him. But his dreamchest narrowed with guilt and he had to come down, down, and take his place in the formation. Grim-faced as the rest, he had to march till the rock was trampled flat. On to the horizon, past gutted leafless trees.

Till rolling light relieved him of duty and dream, and he put out a hand for Diane in Sunday's hung sunshine. There were only rumpled sheets.

Carter sat up and hitched his pajamas around. He ran the heels of his hands over his eyes and went barefoot through the rooms. Diane looked at him through the silence of the kitchen, over a burner aflame on the stove, with a waiting look in her eyes.

"What are you doing, baby?" But he knew; he could see the sputtering eyedropper in the fist at her arm, almost see through her naked skin to veins bubbling with poison.

"Diane, why didn't you tell me when I asked?" He sat down slowly, feeling for the chair.

Diane pulled another chair up close, but kept her hands from touching him, afraid he might think her dirty. She had to talk before the Horse reared, before she went dry-mouthed. "Carter, I didn't want to aggravate you. You know, Cart?" turning her head to look for his eyes. "It's nothing, Cart. I can kick it; I never popped in a vein, Carter."

His face felt heavy, and it was a job to loosen it, to keep his rigidity from frightening her. But the smile felt foolish on his face, and he reached over to bring her to his lap. "Baby, you don't ever have to keep anything from me. Can you really kick it? Can you, babe?"

"I swear, Carter. I can, Cart," while a cloud grew steadily out of her stomach, and limbs went rubbery. "It's easy, Cart." Everything was easy; anything was easy as Nothing. "I'll just get the shakes for a day or two; that's all, Carter."

It was a different girl now, and he had to look for something in her face to make him believe what she said. He couldn't forget last night's facile lying; he could no longer let himself think of her as the ingenuous kid she'd been: something was added to Diane that subtracted the better parts from her. But he felt easier when she responded with a shrug and a smile to the announcement that he was leaving her with Mama.

Diane remembered to hold up her head through dressing, to keep up with his step in the sun, to keep from goofing in the cab ride uptown. And although Carter felt black with futility inside, she was convinced by the sun on his face that his smile showed hope and confidence. Smooth surges in her promised that she could control all the approaching days, and she went contentedly from the cab to join the Fifth Avenue crowd, high-heel tall, composed, walking beside Carter.

Even Mother smiled, letting them in. Mother with her hair done up for springtime in her smart uptown apartment, served tea in a single moment and fluttered about voicing high hopes for Diane . . . *dear, sweet, crazy; dear, mad, lovely me.* Diane sat back in a brocaded chair with Carter near by and Mama on the couch across from them and Edna in everybody's speech, Edna superseding her once more with Carter, while everybody drank tea in domestic tranquillity.

"You can sit on the terrace, dear, and read all day and look right down into the museum yard and see the lovely statues"; it was like Timmy describing a Bible or a gun. Diane was already quivering, already terrified of days alone with ideas and ways so alien to her. Still, she could kick Horse and control anything at all; her golden stomach told her that.

"No, we had breakfast in the Village, Mama," though she'd hardly eaten half a strip of toast. Followed her mother to the terrace and let herself be settled in a deck chair overlooking the museum yard. Closed her eyes while Carter said he'd be back after visiting Edna. Edna. Edna.

Carter felt half-drugged himself. Worms ferreted about in his brain, and he knew he'd carry his hat, juggling it in his hand all day. Yet he had to laugh when Vivienne looked frigidly at him from the couch, stiff with her cup of stupid tea, voicing the question she'd stored behind her smiling: "Well, did you sleep together? Don't try to tell me that you slept on the couch."

He sank down in his chair and watched her until he realized she meant to stare him down. "Why didn't you let me bring her over last night, Vivienne?"

"Never mind that. I couldn't avoid . . . don't answer a question with another. Did you or didn't you?"

"Vivienne, you're a very lewd woman." He got up. "I'm coming back to see how Diane's getting on."

She came right up to him. "How she's getting on! I'm sure no one *here* will abuse her."

"You're a very lewd woman, Mother dear."

"That's a cowardly way of avoiding my question."

"To *hell* with you, Vivienne," on his way through the door. Down in the cool shadows of the entranceway he shook his head to clear it. Too much lay on his brain, too much, too much. Only sunlight and brisk women in flowered dresses relaxed him. He idled by the huge opulent stores on Fifth, looking at artistic arrangements of things nobody really needed, clothes few people could ever buy. Then on to the gray reality of the Fifty-third Street subway, toward the bitter reality of Edna Lattimer Webb.

A muggy, rattling ride that roared like an enemy in his ears, in a Sunday car scarcely peopled; long, long, station after station, with a lazy metallic whine at each stop. Then sun again in leafy Queens, and before he stood in line for a bus he had to have a drink to clean out his chest. One drink in a huge, quiet tavern, pleasantly dark, then one more, and out to climb an orange bus with other sorrowers, to stand hanging from a strap, looking at faces resigned to disease.

His watch showed him to be early and he was glad—Edna wouldn't be on the terrace yet, waving for him to wave back like a fool clean up the walk to the high white hospital façade, pretty and white as Vivienne's face, just as ridden inside with disease. The bus rumble traveled from his heels to his head, *my rumble-prone head*, he thought. An elbow was in his back, then a shoulder and a grunt and a meaty body muttered behind him, shoving against his obstinate, angry stiffening. Carter went into a swift rage; he didn't move an inch, while the man behind him swore in an undertone and shoved harder and harder. The bus stopped and Carter held tight, the color burning up out of his neck. The bus started again and the man swore aloud, and Carter saw the hospital loom into view, grow larger and stop as the bus lurched. He looked at a red, hostile face as he passed to the door.

"Cantcha move?" the stout man wanted to know.

"Come on, get off," Carter said. "Come on, I'll tell you about it." He climbed down and waited; the man pulled back to ride another block, and the bus rumbled away.

People were staring at him, and Carter felt foolish when his mouth formed the words, "Wouldn't say excuse me, just had to shove." He felt childish, absurd, idiotic.

Still, he told himself, he didn't have to give way to anybody's aggressions, anybody's damn nudging and crowding. He went muttering toward the walk. But springtime was no time for rancor, he decided, with the booming blue of the sky, the finest tingle of air. Beyond the first hedge bordering the walk a dogwood tree spread twelve feet of white starkly against the horizon, which lay like blue smoke on a distant field he'd never noticed before. He looked up and down the unpeopled walk, then took a running leap over the hedge and caught his balance with three quick steps into the field. He smiled once over a shoulder toward the hospital terraces swimming in his eyes—just in case Edna might have been watching—and plucked a sprig of dogwood, carried it out across the field, over springy crab grass, toward nowhere he could name, but wanting very much to lie down alone and stare awhile at dogwood.

Stoney felt a debt to his face. It hung heavily exposed, and he felt the eyes in the room sharply upon it, so that he had to keep it going while Diane shifted restively and Vivienne nodded from her couch. "My dear," he told Diane, "it's not emancipation at all; it's simply hysteria," and smiled quickly to keep her from bursting out in anger. "You're a conditioned thing, no more than a product of your experience, and as such . . ."

Vivienne nodded as he spoke, hearing the very force of his mind in the straight certain flow of his voice, a power undiluted by anything animal in him. Their round of the museum, while Diane had stayed safely asleep in her room, had been two elevating hours of Robert's vital comment. For years she'd sought so clean a spirit, just one soul free and able to communicate dignity. Fleshless, free of the dirt that flesh called forth through pores from the original sin stored in darkness within, Robert sat there now, advising Diane, really an answer to her own unfaltering prayers. The door buzzer was a rude intrusion; she hurried over and opened it for Carter Webb. "How is Edna?" she whispered and took him by the arm off to one side.

"She had a fine afternoon," he said quietly. "Sang. Hasn't done that in a long while. Why are we whispering?" as Diane smiled at him across the room.

"Robert is giving Diane some sound advice."

"You can't realistically circumvent the imprints of your background," Stoney told the girl ,while Vivienne, on the couch with Carter, nodded in cautious agreement. While Carter glanced at Diane to see if she could bear it. While Diane considered the tail of her Horse, hearing only the yap of Stoney and never his words, wondering whether her stomach would soon be tightening up. "If your background has imposed 'Thou shalt nots' on you, your natural impulses will be thus directed. Any contact with reality that calls on you to transcend those fears can be answered only intellectually. Emotionally you will respond to an awareness forged by your conditioning," and got a cigarette lighted, giving them all time to absorb his meaning.

Vivienne was delighted with it. So clear and beyond contradiction —two weeks of this and Diane might well begin to see the light, realistically, in sensible, everyday terms. She reached over and clicked on another lamp to cut the deepening shadows.

"Young lady, you may teach your own daughters to be emancipated—" Stoney uttered a tender chuckle—"but don't feel obligated to mortify your natural tendencies with intellectual hypotheses." He carefully ignored the fact that Diane was on her way to the terrace.

Mrs. Lattimer stood up to prevent her leaving, looking alarmed at her impudence. But Carter barred any interference. "Let her go, Viv," he said quietly. "She's a little tense; let's leave her alone for a while."

Vivienne saw his concern and matched it with her own. "Yes," she murmured, "yes," yet had to add, out of a quivering frustration in her, "Oh, why did I ever bring my children to the Village?" Rhetorically, but it was enough to set Stoney off as they sat down across from him.

He prattled on about the meaning of the Village, cracking his knuckles while Carter watched his mouth: only the bottom lip moved. "Now here's the summing up of them all. I'm going to give you three basic aspects of the nature of *all* the people who settle there. *All*, not a portion, not a majority, but *all*. The degrees of intensity vary . . ." Blinking with the inward rush of his thoughts. ". . . three requisites that make up the so-called bohemian. One! A critical faculty. Two! A creative compulsion. Three! A poetic attitude. Do you see? Let me expound just a bit," leaning forward with that obsequious smile. "I'm aware of your faculty for reception and recognition of implications," an awareness he'd often declared since he'd shaved his beard, Carter told himself as he stood and went with *yap-yap-yap* in his ear to the terrace. Diane sat doubled over in the deck chair, but she lifted her head and smiled.

He squatted beside her. "Is it hurting, Diane?"

"No," and in this light she looked as she'd used to, eyes glittering black, smiling almost gaily. "It doesn't hurt, but it's supposed to about now, Carter, and I don't want to give it a chance to. I started to get sick while fatmouth was talking. That's how it is with Horse, Cart, every little thing——"

"I got sick myself, babe; Stoney's enough without Horse."

She laughed her old laugh and threw her arms around him, burying her lips in his cheek. "Carter, take me home with you. It's where I belong."

"What . . . Watch it, baby. They'll tar and feather us." He helped her to stand up. "Try to make it here a little while more, Diane," he went on as they leaned over the wrought-iron balustrade. "It'll keep everyone under control."

"With fatmouth hanging around? I doubt if I can; if I stay, I don't think I can kick Horse. 'Contact, valid, challenge . . .' I even hate the words he uses. And—and—" before he could suggest that she simply avoid Stoney—"everything else, Carter, everything. I play the radio, and baseball guys argue about what the players did that day, or the U.N. people talk, and it's like Stoney, with words like they're machines or something. I don't know, like they can't even be trusted, because they don't talk about people. . . . I don't know. Then I sit here and see mothers in the street with their kids. They look so matter-of-fact about everything, about people at work and drunks squabbling around them, and the whole world mixes up in my head, Carter, I don't know what to do with myself, I . . ." holding her head, suddenly looking irretrievably lost, frightening him.

"Diane," he said, "baby, don't trouble your mind that way," knowing that advice at this point was meaningless. "Leave yourself alone. Read books or something. Funny books. Give your mind a rest," and stopped at the sound of her empty laughter as she struggled back into the deck chair.

"It's coming on now, Carter, it's pulling on me. I can't read, Daddy; I can't leave myself alone; I can't do anything till I'm on Horse, and then the only thing I can do is Nothing," trying to pronounce the capital initial.

"Can you stand it?" He was whispering by her side. "Do you think you could hold out, babe? If you can awhile——"

"No no no no." Swinging her head from side to side. "It's terrible. I'm sick as a dog, Carter; my legs are going dead. Let me—I'll take a fix, I'll spread them, I only have enough for two or three more. There must be a way, a special . . ."

He wished he had her somewhere alone, not knowing what he'd be able to do, yet wishing it till he hated the people inside. Her face was pinched; her agony tore at his own chest. "Go on, babe, go on in and do something for yourself. Go on. I'll make sure they stay in the living room and talk."

Her face relaxed at once. "You really love me, don't you, Carter, don't you? It doesn't hurt as bad as it looks. It's here—" touching her head—"it's here like a stranger telling me I'm hurting in my body. You know what I mean, Cart?" not quite knowing herself. "I can hold out; after this I can kick it," and went, guided by his hand, to her feet. "You know which room I have? The maid's room, that's my room. Mama would rather have me than a maid."

It didn't mean anything, and he didn't comment. Inside it was no problem to keep those two busy while Diane went right through to her little closet of a room; Stoney took care of it: ". . . infinitely valid basis that this compulsion toward criticism is a fundamentally emotional phenomenon and only becomes intellectual at verbalization. Fine! You see? Fine! Now! The creative drive . . . ah, here we must be coldly scientific, almost cruel, completely unsentimental," while Vivienne, with remarkable endurance, sat stiff-backed on her couch, nodding, following every word. Carter went past her to the kitchen, letting the door swing closed, putting on no light but only standing against the sink trembling, trying not to think of Diane puncturing her skin with poison. There was a pot of vines silhouetted against the faint streetlight high over the sink in a window, and Carter rested his eyes on it as through mesmerized. Diane needed treatment, the kind for which he was throwing out money on Edna. But Diane would never go through with anything like that—her very problem made psychiatric treatment impossible. Both sisters seemed beyond help now, and their poisoner sat in a black dinner dress listening to sophisms from a pompous idler. He took a drink of water and went back, blinking in light, to sit in a brocaded chair while Stoney prattled on.

"... dynamic, unshakable, importunately surging forward, ignoring ostensibly broader opportunities. Now! See what we've arrived at: a distinction between the artist and the *numero*, the *Village Character*. In short, with the creative drive it's fundamentally a matter of degree, and the variation in degree is a very real and very significant factor to be considered in our examination. In other words some of them just . . . don't . . . have the *drive*. Finish! Period! Now the final——"

"What's this?" Carter wanted to know. "A confessional, Robert?"

"What?" Stoney blinked around at him like a man abruptly awakened from an afternoon nap. "Carter—" cracking his knuckles— "please, please don't destroy the conversation. We were doing nicely. Don't make it a personality issue. Please."

"Yes," Vivienne said mildly, "do behave, Carter," as though he were a ten-year-old boy; Carter half expected some kind of bribe to be offered, a candy bar, a promise of circus tickets. While Stoney went on, Carter watched the woman's deep-set heavy-lidded pale eyes, her uptilted chin, and felt an urge to inform her that her daughters lay dying—but even as the urge swelled, some other part of him was admonishing, accusing him of being blindly vindictive: the woman suffered pain enough, even staying on the surface of things.

"Bless you, my children." Carter was on his feet. "Bless you," going past them to Diane's room, tapping on the door till he heard her voice like a thing out of some dimly remembered dream. He glanced over the wrought-iron fence between foyer and living room, saw Vivienne looking his way without expression while Stoney sat back talking. Carter went in and snapped on the light.

Diane, propped up in bed, stared at him from eyes untroubled by the light, followed his face as he approached and sat down. "Old man," she said unfamiliarly, "old man, I know thee not." Then she began a slow whining laugh and ran her hand over his face. "I know nothing, Carter, nothing. Can you imagine?"

"You sound like Merwin Fingerhut," and she laughed like some gleeful child. "In fact you look a little like him," and she laughed even harder.

"Tell me a story about him, Cart." A toneless sigh. "Go on, Cart; he's a funny man."

He clicked on the night-table light and switched off the overhead glare. Sitting on the side of her bed, he told her of Merwin and Moscow the Fourth, a horse on which the round man had bet his last tenspot at the track—the horse that walked down the track while all the rest ran, and turned his head to the grandstand as Merwin screamed. " 'He looks up at me,' " Carter quoted Merwin, " 'I'm screaming *run*, he walks and looks up at me . . . smiling.' "

While the Horse inside her walked, smiling, on felt hoofs and Moscow the Fifth looked around at round old Merwin and said, "Old man, I know thee not," in her own voice at Carter. And Carter smiled like a kind king and helped her to snuggle into bed and covered her so that she could close her eyes into Nothing all about her, Nothing at all anywhere any more.

Carter left the small light on in case she should awaken, afraid to have her awaken into darkness. He was in the living room in time for tea, took it from Vivienne and sat back in the brocaded chair. "I was about to go and get you," she murmured, then looked rigidly into his face. "What on earth were you doing in there?"

"Telling her a bedtime story, Vivienne."

Vivienne looked at him disdainfully before turning back to Stoney.

"The artist's first endeavor is investigation, the primary requisite for validity in that direction being thoroughness, yes, thoroughness! Now, the operating vehicle for accuracy is integrity, the power lies in the sum total of his experience, perceptibility and mathematical acumen." Carter suddenly burst into laughter, and Stoney winced. "What's the matter with you, Carter?"

"Oh, he's upset." Vivienne apologized for him. "He's had a trying day with both girls," looking at Carter with what seemed real compassion.

It was enough to quiet his laughing: it seemed nothing could hold to its own character any more. Now all that had to happen would be for Stoney to stand and admit himself to be a megalomaniac.

But of course he didn't. "Carter, I'm surprised at you. Literally surprised." Stoney nodded with the gleam of all worldly wisdom in his eyes. "I always considered you equipped for reasoning, able to consider reality on the highest level, in the abstract, where mere temporal and material matters are handled by simple implication. I suppose I was wrong about you. It's disturbing, but I suppose I'll have to face it," nodding deliberately, decisively, like a man with the courage to face any horrifying reality.

Carter took his hat and made for the door. "I'll call you, Vivienne."

"Oh, Carter, don't feel badly. Robert, can't you be more patient? Don't let him go away offended. Carter, you should——"

"It's all right, my dear." Stoney heaved himself to his feet with a tired magnanimity in his smile. "Carter and I always come to an understanding, once we have a private word," and took Carter by the elbow to the door.

Out in the hall Stoney grinned placatingly.

"Stoney, no song and dance, please; I assure you, you haven't offended me."

"Of course not," and he slapped Carter's back, "but women will always be sensitive to that sort of nonsense. Carter—" and his yap crumpled into a whisper—"could you lend me fifty cents?"

Carter pulled out some change and selected a quarter, two dimes and a nickel, handed them over. "Stoney, if you can get off the cloud for a minute, try to convince Vivienne that it's urgent to—that she has to leave Diane alone. She has to let the girl go and come as she pleases."

"What are you saying? You know very well what that'll mean. She'll be back in the Village with those hoodlum kids in a minute if we don't teach her to be more rational, more imaginative, more——"

"Stoney! For Christ's sake, I'm not any audience for that crap. That girl feels tyrannized; can't you see that? Let her feel free and then you can start—— Hey, what's this 'we' business? Stoney, you trying to father her?"

"Suppose you try utilizing your imagination and realize that I have a certain responsibility in that direction. Her mother and I have quite an understanding, and I don't intend to fail the lady in any way."

"Stoney. Listen, Stoney, don't fail anyone, be a hero. But don't hound the girl. Teach her to be imaginative, okay, but let her *feel* free."

Stoney nodded shortly, like a general in the field, slapped Carter's back, and went inside. He smiled for Vivienne as she came up to meet him. "Peace in the family guaranteed. Everything is fine." He led her lightly by the elbow back into the quiet evening light of the room.

"I do really hope so."

He followed her out to the terrace and watched her eyes glide over the street soft below in lamplight. "Dear Lord—" she raised closed eyes to the sky—"help my poor children. Help them." For Carter's last despairing glance had reached her, and with it an ancient uncertainty. There had been those times, in spurts through the evaporated years, when a balance seemed to be arranging itself, as it seemed now with Robert's dignity and sound advice to Diane, but it had always shattered like glass under devilish forces that one could never foresee. "Oh Father, Father!" She stared wide-eyed into the night. "Show us the way," while memories turned into faces she could see too well. She pulled away from Stoney's hands on her shoulders, yet fell into the deck chair with hands out of time heavy against her flesh. "Oh, Lord forgive me," she whispered.

There was silence.

"Robert," and he was kneeling beside her chair, taking her hand, "Robert," and looking at his face, solid and solicitous beside her, she smiled and took a long breath and told herself that she didn't have to think of old things gone to dust, remembered to remember that those things had never really happened at all. "It was altogether someone else." She smiled at him. "It wasn't me at all."

"Who was?" He seemed alarmed.

"Nobody," she said, and laughed.

"Vivienne, look. To begin with, I'll take that position at the agency. I will . . . for you, Vivienne. Reluctantly, but I will take it." And he'd take everything over with it: her family, her will, and even the love she had never really released. Slowly, patiently, logically he'd win it all.

"I'm glad, Robert. You'll be brilliant; you'll dynamize their whole concept of layout. I know you will." She raised her chin to stare into futures, with more of a look of confidence than she could feel.

Stoney's eyes were on the fine muscles of her neck. He felt his chest swell, but he pulled away and stood, never again to blunder as he once had. *Oh, Robert, how* could *you destroy it?* Words a week old, but shame forever new. He walked stiffly away, shuddering ever so slightly. From the balustrade he could see over green saplings to Fifth Avenue's mortals drifting aimlessly about. Gentle, tractable bastards with no fixed attitude at all. Vivienne was a distinct personality, one to be dealt with indeed, and the challenge was a noble one. He turned to face her and said in his most temperate tone, "Shall we take the child to a concert tomorrow?"

"I'm afraid she'd balk at that, Robert."

"Oh, we'll convince her it's best for her. You know, I think she's beginning to like me. I'll have a talk with her," but he was planning the talk he'd have with Louella in which he'd borrow another ten dollars. He'd never met a woman he couldn't control, except the Stately Lady making a throne out of the deck chair before his very eyes.

Another Sunday, another. A heavy climb up the mountain of stairs and Carter was out of the inferno, onto Sixth Avenue—scarcely cooler but not unbearably noisy as the subway had been. At the old abandoned newsstand he bought a paper from Magoo, a silent vender now, penitent in his new freedom. Carter went to Slinger for information, sat at the counter under a fan that only went through motions, did nothing to the heat.

"He gets outside lass night," the ferretlike historian reported. "He prob'ly breaks down'n sings a couple names'n they spring 'im," polishing silver while Carter fiddled with iced coffee.

"I guess all the junkies are avoiding him. Like the Ghost."

"Nah," and Slinger found humor in his reflections on the Ghost. "Nothin like that hassel, man. It was wild wit the Ghost, wild! Magoo, he's cool'n he's back to work, sleepin in the lass boot, singin about flahrs'n Lizzie'n evvythin like before, keepin wide of the junkies."

Everything like before—that seemed to be Carter's own limbo. A gift for Edna, her small pathetic squeal to convey delight, her cheek to kiss, her mother sitting there to be consoled over Diane . . . to lie and say he'd not seen the girl since Thursday (though he'd left her in bed to go there), to lie again and say he had to see Dr. Scarborough (when it was Dr. Morris who'd been waiting for him in the solarium).

"She's bearing up well," the redheaded young psychiatrist had whispered. "Have you noticed it, Mr. Webb?" A voice too careful, and Carter hadn't known whether simple compassion or a guilt over his relationship with Edna had been responsible for the doctor's tone. And in that same tone he'd explained meticulously how nature kept approaching death an alien thing to the doomed, how Edna stayed busy with religious fantasies that left little room for any concern with death.

Carter, then, had asked about the possible use of narcotics, should Edna suffer pain, and he learned that it was common practice to addict patients in pain as death approached. That had been the opening he'd wanted, and, disgusted with his own deviousness, he'd taken it. "Doctor, how soon does one become an addict? After the use of narcotics, how soon, after how many——" and he felt like a caught schoolboy when Morris folded his arms. "It's someone I know; I think someone I know is taking . . . something."

"A friend of yours? It's very serious, Mr. Webb. I'd suggest he be treated immediately. Psychiatric treatment as soon as possible."

"Well, you . . . I haven't told you how long this person has——"

"Not much difference," and Carter saw a tension around the man's baggy eyes, as if his training had abruptly slipped away and some deep sorrow glanced through eyes long inured. "I'd say one is an addict as soon as he narcotizes himself. First shot. I don't mean a sick person in physical pain, but people who—you know, the pleasure seeker who wants to give it a try. We can assume he's an addict to all intents and purposes right on his first shot. Anyone else would be repelled by the idea, but someone with a deep psychological need—don't you see? Immediate treatment—that's what I'd prescribe for your friend."

Carter found himself resenting the man's allusion to "your friend" —he'd referred to "someone I know" and wished it would be kept that way. People around them were watching. The doctor spoke too loudly. Carter thanked him abruptly and left.

Now Slinger spoke too loudly, and Carter stood abruptly, reaching for some change. "Stoney don' show aroun here no more wit that nekkid face. He sticks by the park when he ain' uptown. He even works a week'n quits on account of bad conditions. Tomlin the artiss tells me, so it muss be for real. Bad conditions!" He laughed, showing his neglected teeth. "It means nobody wants to do exac'ly like he screams they got to do. Nobody wants to tear down the system."

Carter took his turn to report and let Slinger know that it was hot outside, too hot for May, and departed for higher ground up Christopher, where Diane might still be, perhaps with no death on her eyelids, no stupor in her voice. . . .

A rumor of this dream glinted in the eyes she turned on him from the bedroom chair near a mirror. Fresh from the shower, she sat naked in light filtered through a drifting window curtain, wet and gleaming hair combed flat, freshly clipped to show her ear lobes. "Carter," and no more, waiting, only looking up till he sat on an edge beside her.

"Let me hear you talk," he said after kissing her neck, damp and cool and young. "Tell me something, little girl. Go on and say something."

She pulled him by the wrist and flopped with him to the bed. "I'm fine, Carter. I didn't touch a thing, and I've been awake over two hours." With her voice a level, honey-rich corroboration, but with a hollowness in her guts as Carter leaned over her, kissing her.

She had a cigarette lighted for him when he finished his shower, listened with a show of interest to what he had to tell her, back in the bedroom.

"Magoo is out," he said. "I saw him selling papers by the Cosmopole."

She lay close to him, trying to quiet her whining chest. "Gee, did you ask him about the Dinch? Maybe he saw Dincher inside."

"No, I didn't feel like talking to him. You know. Figured I'd leave him alone. Slinger says he probably did a little singing. You can't get in trouble, can you? I mean if anybody——"

"No, I don't have anything to do with——" And Buster crashed through a window in her mind, tore down a drifting curtain. Where would she get—if she needed any, if she really had to get a fix, after really turkeying through all the nausea, if she really, really had to get a fix, what would she do if Buster were busted? She clung closer to Carter and kissed him, trying to absorb his strength.

He could feel her anxiety at his back where her nails dug. There was no love in her demand, not even play, but only hysterical reaching for faceless solace, a transient anodyne for her dark, despairing terror of a need. And though his blood called the greater part of him to give her any kind of peace at all, some small monitor kept blood halfway, and Carter Webb was repelled by cloudy reasoning when reasoning had no place. He pulled his towel tight around him, while Diane lay weeping. It was an impotence he knew she'd blame herself for, and he pulled her up to sit beside him: "Diane," he said, "it's nothing, nothing at all. It's just—you know, the hospital, the talking. We'll have time, baby, we'll have all the balling we can hold. Straighten out, babe. Later, later on . . . you'll see."

But a fist punched the future out of her stomach, tugged at her spine for the treachery of *now*. Now loomed like forever and she only wept against him while her insides *bub-bub-bubbed* like the vacuum inside of a hash bottle. "I have to go, Carter, I have to. I have to go to . . . Mama." Anywhere at all was where she had to go. Any point toward which she could move to keep her stomach behind her thoughts.

That would have been fine with him, but he knew no promise had meaning to her any more. "Don't goof off, baby. Hold on. We'll have it shining for us when . . . when . . . you know, when we're free."

And Edna rode a golden horse in her imagining. "I'll kick Horse," she sobbed, "and you . . . you can't kick . . . Edna. You can't . . . do it, Cart," feeling that somehow he was glad to be tied away from a permanent Diane. "You . . . have to wait and after . . . you wait maybe you won't——" And she doubled over on the bed as the fist sprouted iron mail and punched anywhere it could inside her. "Oh, Carter, oh, oh, I'm sick."

He was off the bed. "Let me call a doctor; he'll fix——"

"No! No doctor, no doctor, Cart. He can't fix me. Only . . ." Only Buster could fix her . . . and nag her, and threaten, and wail like a lost elephant because she wouldn't let him touch her in crazy places. "Just let me be. . . . It's going away, Carter, it's . . . letting up now." But she stayed doubled up, afraid the quieted fist would rear again if she moved.

He sat down and wiped tiny beads of sweat from the curve of her forehead while a tugboat hooted somewhere and the city creaked below. He could have cried over the wasted sight of her on crumpled sheets, and felt shame at his own helplessness.

"I'll kick it, Carter. Don't sit there hating me."

"Baby, I'm not—where do you get ideas like that? It wasn't your fault; it was mine. I'm neurotic, that's all." But she failed to laugh.

Still, she couldn't bring herself to touch him; she felt every kind of vice on her skin, smelled snorted Horse in the room and knew it to be in the nostrils of her mind. Dirty with an ineffable odor that clung about her like old memories. "Just don't hate me, Carter. Love me a little while more and you'll see. I'll kick it, Cart, I will," and she straightened up with new confidence, began to pull on her clothes. "You saw me beat that blast. That's all I have to do. Just cold-turkey it. Just let it punch till it's done."

"Diane, I'll never hate you for anything, baby." It sounded as silly to him as he'd expected. "Where are you going, little girl?"

"To Mama—I really am. I'll show her too. You'll see, Cart. I'll show you how to kick a big fat habit. I'll show you. Nothing can hold me down. 'Cause I'm like gangbusters. Watch me come on."

He watched her come on with clean clothes and clean promises, rust-colored ruffled skirt and promises she'd put on clean before and dirtied in a day. He got rid of the towel and found clean underwear for himself, dressed as she dressed, and sat smoking in the living room while she put on her make-up. Still tired with shame, and swearing to himself that all he needed was a holiday from Lattimers . . .

Diane had a way of tying purple silk in a snood behind her neck so that it hung from her hair as background for great copper earrings. If he were fresh from Pennsylvania, a man who'd never seen her before, he might easily have fallen to his knees at the sight of her. But he was long out of the pits, and embellishment hid little of the despair she was made of; he could only say, "You look exquisite, Diane," as she smiled before him in a white blouse and rust-colored ruffled skirt.

"You'll see, Dad—Carter, you'll see Diane. Mama, if she leaves me alone, she'll see. I'll kick it before she ever finds out I was hooked. And she'll still be up in her tower while I'm on earth with you, Cart," laughing as he laughed, sitting on his lap. "Carter, could I have a dollar? I want to get her some candy cherries. She likes them; you know that? She's like a little kid, Mama." He gave her the money and sat there as she stood. "Aren't you going down? You don't have to stay here, Cart. You can go where you like, Carter. I don't mind if you have a date or something."

"I'm going to read awhile, Diane." He could lie to anyone at all by now. He could even keep it from showing on his face.

"Wait for me, Carter. I'm going to wait for you. Will we wait for each other, Daddio?" knowing she'd not be back till the habit was kicked and gone. One dead Horse in the cemetery of broken junkies.

"We'll wait, baby." He returned Diane's blown kiss and stared awhile at the door she closed behind her, then stalked to the phone in the long silent hallway. To phone a girl trying hard to be a woman. To see if she'd leave her silver cigarette holder home with her careful mother. To lose himself, Diane, Edna . . . everything.

Once before she'd waited in a hallway for someone to come and keep her from Charge. A more beloved keeper, and from a charge that was never excruciating, that never made water of her legs. Diane watched twilight bleed the hallway of sun, saw night curtain the world, through the window at the carpet's end; sweated cold needles, but nobody's mother showed up. Candy-coated cherries were all right for a while, but they turned disgusting, once the pain started. Even so, she ate them to mark time, promising herself she'd not leave till she had eaten six. But the sixth was a horror of sweetness lying there in the box, and she heaved herself up from the steps with chocolate from the fifth still thick on her palate.

On the corner of Fifth she hopped from foot to foot till the great monster bobbled up. She boarded it and fought her way to the top deck and back where nobody could disturb her if she decided to die. While scattered citizens chattered about things their voices deemed important enough to share with others.

"It's back to Ireland for her. Imagine!" Cracked soprano laughter. "She disapproves of the country. And after that boy brought her here where she got three square meals a day for no doubt the first time in . . ."

While Diane began to retch dry chocolate fumes.

"It's the *only* way you should wear it. Be realistic, sweetie, you have no forehead at all."

". . . four hits right off. You think those spring games . . ."

"They got slaves there just like the Germans. One false word and . . ."

"Reg'lar fifty-four short. He got his troubles, don't worry."

Everybody had a fist in her throat, a thumb in her eye; there was no
more room on earth, and she had to get up high, *had to!* But she'd
kick, she'd kick! *Had to kick! had to kick! had to kick!*

One step at a time down the steps and out behind everybody into
Washington Square Park, into the enchanted park where slow trees
wagged like contented old men and kids played muzzle tag around
the fountain circle and somewhere under a tree someone barefoot
could be playing a violin for children. Past concrete checker and chess
tables crowded with enthusiasts, their dream fulfilled by a benevolent
city statute. With a kick at some drunk who came out of MacDougal
shadows.

First he laughed and then he sang in his rags: "Nobody cares, nobody cares fa you-oo," and gave up the game to pluck some other
stranger's sleeve to see if anyone cared a cup of coffee's worth for
him.

Past early drunks she hurried down MacDougal with nobody caring
a damn. Stumbling into the gutter and stumbling back up onto
the curb each time some reveler reached for her arm. No one
remained to reach into darkness where she writhed alone; nobody
lighted the way. Not Dincher any more, never Joe Letrigo, and even
Carter was snared by his own directions. Each had his will, his need,
and his penance to pay alone. And each in his own life was a stranger
angry at others for their preoccupations. Fools roaring for the right
of way over dust while all the room of heaven lay about the Hook.
Diane was running down the long, suspended quiet of Bleecker, angry at herself for ever wanting to kick, turning her ankle when her
heels slipped, crossing a crazy pathway full of lights that moved and
honked for the right of way, dashing up a stoop to hide in the Shylock's doorway from the river of angry dust. Panting. With fire and
ice inside her, and water in her legs.

Up, wiping dust with a hand on the railing, hating Carter suddenly
for reading books, for speaking softly, and for being kind enough to
make her want to kick. Key through the tin door and music and Buster hiding back on the distant couch listening to Bop on the player
Lukey had taken from Paddy's. Everybody's own life. "Give me a
fix, Buster, I'm croaking. Give me a fix, fixer," and fell across the bed
under Stoney's vicious light.

Buster shuffled over, passion stretching his rubber nostrils, passion
growing stronger as she weakened. He sat grinning beside her and

stroked her. "Rest a minute, beautiful, I cook it up for you. How much caps, beautiful?" and his hand touched the hem of her skirt.

"Get away, you freak!" Her heel caught him across the face.

"You want a *fix?* You flip broad, you want a *fix?*" He wiped frantically at the abrasion. "You wanna kill somebody, you flip broad? You behave; you hear? You want a fix, you——"

"Sell it to me, you bastard, sell it! Take it out of Dincher's four hundred. Pay off, you filthy bastard!" Even her tears hurt, scratching at her eyes. "Ohhhh, fix me, fix me, Buster."

Buster ran to the kitchen, and she heard the spurt of water, the hiss of a gas burner; the pain became bearable, the light grew whiter beyond her eyelids.

Buster had the needle by her arm.

"No, no," she managed to say. "Not there, Buster, too big, leaves a mark. On my thigh," and he pulled her skirt over her head. "No vein, no vein," as if there were any visible in her thigh. "Go on, Buster, gih!" and it was done. She straightened her skirt and sat up. Buster's teeth were visible, two rows of huge tusks that gleamed in the naked light; he wore a hungry smile, puffing with pleasure and staring at the needle.

Then at once he looked up. "You try to make me on Horse, you lousy broad! You think you make a junky outta me?" She knew he had no need for a kick greater than seeing others suffer. She watched him, not caring what he said or did; she just sat propped against the wall while pain fell off to Nothing. It didn't matter about Buster or anyone else.

"You got a kid'n you don't care!"

It didn't matter what he said. *Oobop,* she thought while a record spun at the room's far end.

"*Oorioobop-yarooee,*" she sang, and it quieted him. The pain was gone; Diane was free of anything she didn't care to think about, and that included Everything; she sang only of Nothing, in flat, careless notes, "*riaZHAoo,*" while Buster stalked about, rubbing the scraped skin of his face, waiting for her to go unconscious. She closed her eyes and waited. She oozed to her side and waited, keeping her lips firm against laughter. Nothing was alive in her, and alive with a felt-hoofed pulse. Her eyelids were thin curtains through which light was white, and her ears could see Buster clomping about on wood, one way, then another, back and forth. Then came the scrape of the light cord, and blackness fell like a sudden silence; she let herself grin, even laughed shortly when he stumbled against the creaking wheel-bottom table. Then she controlled her face and lay there in the excitement of a sheer absence of bodily sensation, in the joy of a game her head was playing.

Buster's breath was on her face; a finger touched her eyelid, poked her cheek. She waited, pushing her breath out evenly, heavily, for him to hear. Bodiless, she felt her face taken into a hand and shaken gently. Then his breathing drifted back, and she lurched into sentience at the heat of a stealthy hand upon her. Fingers sprouted to tens and twenties, ran like vines, and stealthy vines were everywhere, touching, inquiring. Stopping when she twitched. Waiting. Then tapping, searching again in darkness. Torpor was easy for Diane: she lay claylike, measured her breathing to the rhythm of sleep, and kept from laughing. She heard a distant rustle of clothing, and hoarse breath was jerky against her face, a leg was against hers, a hand held her at the hip; she opened her eyes and saw the hulk above her against the smear of skylight. Her arms were adroit serpents entwining his neck. "Come on, Daddio," she whispered in travesty of slow passion. "Rock it for me, snag me good," and came up to her elbows when he fell back whimpering. "Come on, gashman, don't go 'way," with all the stored laughter bursting forth in Horse-stifled little rattles. While the whimpering hulk slid off to the floor, sobbing unintelligible words, pleading in its very intonations.

Diane was one long, lean muscle arching up toward the light cord. She yanked the room into naked whiteness and looked around at Buster out of the clearest eyes she'd ever owned. "Get the hell up! You're supposed to be a *man*," and laughed out in swift derision at the very word. "Come on, *man*, be a *man*; stand up and stop crying like a baby," and ran on legs unchecked by Horse or pain to the other end of the room. She snapped the phonograph into action, stacked music on the changer, straightened her rust-colored skirt and fixed her snood while the music warmed the room.

Still at the foot of the bed, Buster was crying when she returned, his mountain of a head tucked in huge arms as his back heaved under sobs. Diane stood there watching, while a rivulet of remorse flowed through her to her head full of street noises and old eyeless faces and the debris of ancient attempts to make days workable: everything came together in the soft clod that filled her skull—the absence of any charge in her blood, the wormlike demands crawling ceaselessly toward her, the angry faces in the streets unending, the heap of helpless men rolled into one at the foot of a bed—and it was all *oorioori-OObop-RAra* . . . *REEEEruiriOOjeba-amRebop* flat sounds and dead notes and scales leveled to the simplicity of Nothing in a helpless world of purpose hopelessly abandoned*OObop*. No charge, no pain, no sun to nourish or burn; she had only to sing *ooriooriOObop-eemaoomaoobopjeBAM!*

Buster strained and stumbled to his enormous height; his face was puffed. He was a giant nurtured by plunder, fattened on the helpless blood of children; sadistic out of self-hatred, despising her for being witness to the impotence he'd shielded from the world with his powerful façade. And all it meant was OObop! EEbop!

He was suddenly all morality filled with contempt for her failure as a mother. OObop! Glaring at her from the foot of the bed were all the threats to little people, all the self-avenging need of the murderer exposed. BamREEah! Blind as his obsessed eyes, unseeing as his dead-rubber brain, his feet clumped forward to stamp out anyone who knew his guilt. His approach was doom itself, yet all it meant to Diane was the Be-bop frenzied understanding of Nothing from the record player behind her in shadows. "*OoriOOraOObop*," she sang to the giant approaching with a long knife in his hand and rubber death on his face. "*OoliaraREEEE-BAMmammy's gone so reeah*," while Buster stood like all hopeless man above her. "*Go-on-and-REE-bop, no-one-gives-a-oomah, RAruRAROOra, onna sunny EEraRAP-riajevooriAWP*," tilting back her head to show how clean and careless was her throat.

For, though he could kill her for seeing his evil, that brain focused only on itself could feel the penetration of a million watchful eyes; he flinched, writhed, stretched his neck in an agony of helplessness, and snapped the knife shut. "Listen, beautiful, look——"

"You could burn me in the fireplace, Buster. Come on, you don't have to worry about my body," for she'd ceased worrying about it herself.

He took a look at the yawning stone mouth, pondered the suggestion, then let his eyes quiver over her again. "Look, Diane, I never mean anythin bad for you. I give you your fix all the time, don't I, beautiful? Don't say nothin." And now with steps sounding outside, he rushed the words. "*Don't say nothin to nobody, Diane; you hear?*" Panic turned entreaty to threat. "Don't say *nothin;* you got it? Nothin or I . . ." He took her shoulder in a hand. "I mean it, Diane, I don't care for nothin, I get you in the street, Diane," while steps grew louder up the stairs.

"I want to see the four hundred beans. Buster, you bring me the four hundred, and I forget anything at all."

There was a light tap on the door while Buster's eyes rolled crazily —a hesitant tap, a tap like an admission of guilt. "Listen, you—" his eyes hung high into his skull—"I got no cash; I can't jus get cash like that."

"You fat pig, you got a million, you got six pushers in the Village alone; you think you jiving me? Come on, Buster, I'm going to the door," and she slipped easily from his hand.

"Okay, okay." A creaking whisper. "Don't talk; I lay it on you. Okay, beautiful, okay, okay."

"Who's there?" She swung open the door for Lukey, stooped over, rushing in now with a pile of clothes in his arms, giggling toothlessly as he piled them on the wheel-bottom table.

"Ss-ss-ss," he giggled, moving like a wire spring. "Here, Buster, here's for three caps' worth, like you can lay them on me with here's the security, it's good for a fin by any fence."

"I ain't no fence," the giant growled, "'n I ain't no connection for you; you got it? You go lay the loot on Muffo Smith'n Angie giz you caps. Go on, you toothless jerk, go on'n do like you suppose," relaxing back into the soft chair.

"I don't lay any loot on Muffo. I don't get that close to his face." He giggled for Diane. "I don't get over to no guy who you can smell his lousy habit. Like a good shmecker keeps the smell in his own private nose, see? Like if a junky got holes in him, he keeps sleeves on his arm and nobody has to bother for his habit. But him—I don't get close to a guy with a habit everybody can tell," while Diane lay back, laughing, on the bed. Little smiling bald-headed Muffo had his troubles.

"Go on," Buster grumbled. "Go on'n get some loot to lay on *some-body.* Go on'n lay it on Kippie Marshmeller; you got it?"

"Diane—" the Swede came to sit beside her with the furrows of laughter in his white, sagging cheeks—"you hear this—ss-ss-ss! The Shylock he's lookin for me by the Cosmopole, up by the north shore he's lookin, he's tellin squares and bohawks he got to cut off my stones for hystin him—ss-ss-ssss. So while he's there I'm here hystin him all over again, I give Timmy a good goose he should swear on his Bible never to squall about it. I catch him in a clutch and he screams with love. So I got loot for a good pop. BUSter! Gimme four caps."

"I give you four busts on your lousy skull, I give you," with a hasty glance at Diane to see if she felt his power. She felt only a flat, dead, leveled tone of understanding to replace any grief she might in old darknesses have felt for Timmy. Now in frenzied recorded music she granted Timmy Lawless the right to love pain, for it was recorded for all time that the world had gone quite ooriubop.

While Lukey the Swede, with scars under his sleeve and a mainliner standing among junkies, laughed with his old knowledge of Nothing. "I go by the north shore lookin for a score and there's old Magoo, he's sellin news like nothin ever gets busted in his life. He got no Horse to lend me, but he hips me about Tony and I'm headin for a score. He——"

"Magoo!" Diane looked over to Buster, who sat whittling a celluloid ring with his old complacency. "Magoo—you hip he's outside, Buster?"

"So what he's out? I can't use that one no more. Let him sell news for buttons now, he gets hisself busted."

"You know Magoo?" she said. "You know he sings in his sleep? You know that, big head? He sings in his sleep, Buster."

Buster was up, looking wildly about. He ran through to the far rooms while Diane and Lukey laughed. "Like he's born with the horrors," the Swede giggled, lying back on the bed.

Diane leaped up and ran to join Buster. He was flipping paper bags into a larger one, trembling visibly as he moved. "I gotta get the junk someplace, I gotta make it cool."

"You lay some on me," she ordered. "You don't run out and keep running, with the Horse and Dincher's four hundred and everything."

His face was agleam with sweat, and he had to wipe his eyes to see her. "Look, you know the Marietta? I clear outta there. I get a new trap'n I let you know. I let you know, Diane." He fumbled through the paper sack. "Here, here's a few caps," and dropped six pegs of Horse cut with sugar into her hand.

"Come on, I need more than that. This just makes me soft any more; I want a little charge, I want to fly. More, Buster, more," with a power she'd never known in her voice.

He emptied his hand into hers, a pile of gleaming capsules. "Go on. Now leave me alone; you got it? I let you know where."

"I want the setup, Buster. I don't want any needles and eyedroppers; I want the setup. Come on, Buster."

He was quick to fish the hypodermic out of the bag. "Here, go on, go on," but he stopped to look around at her. "You forget evvythin, beautiful?" with an abrupt mildness in his voice and quivering eyes.

"I forget nothing. You behave, I behave."

He pondered it, slowly rolling up the sack. "We square it, beautiful," rapping his palm with the bundle. Grinning, thick-lipped and dead-eyed. "We square things, we behave like we got to. 'Cause you gotta hustle your little frame for charge if you cross me. Like this, I got the good."

There pulsed in her too much power to argue; she clacked out, carrying hypo and Horse and the feeling that she was in charge of all holy Nothing. "Here, Swede, knock yourself dead," and the Swede's blear eyes were grateful while his mouth clamored on for fun.

"It's the ball. We got it, baby, mama girl, and we go Eskimo with no kind of gettin busy but for laughs—ss-ss. I make a big stew with ten caps and we fly away forever—ss-ss-ss." Lukey's face had collapsed over the last month—now it was birdlike and wrinkled.

"None for me, Luke. . . . I'm kicking." For she had that power, and she had the power to make Carter her own again, one Something in the wilderness, and out of it she'd grow a tree of power with Johnny up on top.

"Okay." He laughed on his way to the stove. "I hear you. I hear them all say it. It's why I never say a word like that—ss-ss-ss. We got it anyway if you want."

Buster, in the doorway, said nothing, but his eyes laid a charred threat on her for one instant; then he was gone, clumping downstairs and away. Diane laughed and loosened her snood.

She stood laughing at the window that looked out on the Riviera, two streets away, and watched Lukey shag a vein. Watched him pull a small round-bellied lamp from the bundle of clothes and hook it into a baseboard socket. "For good measure I take it—ss-ss. . . ." He set it, lighted, on the wheel-bottom table, turned the room half dark, and sat back on the bed, waiting to be kicked.

They played Be bop on spinning disks and let Timmy take a snort from a matchbook when he came up with his sack of empty wine bottles and his Bible full of Something. He'd come up to dance, wearing bag-kneed leotards that showed his knot of a puffed belly through the black silk, and he was a whirling sack of weird unexpended energy all about the room.

Well-kicked to gigantic hissing laughter, the Swede went hunting friends and returned after an hour of Timmy's whirling with every wanting junky in town. Quiet people with gifts of food and candy they'd pilfered from unguarded shelves. Diane was queen, clean in the head through night's rolling silences, powerful in her painless insides. Even Timmy hardly ever screamed, and when he did somebody like Harry Sticks, with old grudges stored in his fists, would punch him on a cheekbone to make him purr again. A singer who'd never found her night club sang through the gelatin of her charge; Lukey the Swede taught the house a new hushed philosophy on the tail of every drifting hour; Danny Barber made dragons of them all on a paper pad by the round-bellied light, while his fifteen-year-old brother, freshly come from Canada wearing Danny's face to prove Danny had once been a boy, had his first needle pops of "H" to prove all boyhood nonsense; even Muffo Smith had been invited by that limitless kindness of the Swede—and Muffo had a satisfying friend in Nao Braun, who led him to the couch back in the darkness while her snake-shaped husband Clifford ate things he preferred, like a purple flower he'd found in the park and the leaves of a radish bunch given him by a friend. Some people were vegetarians, he reminded them all. And everyone followed his kick, like angels in a tower as free as God's.

While down on earth the river of angry strangers skittered frantically about in hunt for some release. Sitting on the sill where windows were swung wide out, Diane could see them like bugs before the Riviera's pale neon glow, squalling there till dawn painted them out, sent them to Monday's earth-rooted wheel, each strange to his brother, each plodding his single way over angry earth, toward a promise in spring skies, a reward they'd never name.

With junkies behind her and earth pale down below and Something coming alive in her guts. Something she'd never again obey. She gave each friend a share of remaining caps, paid them all at the door with caps and her blessings, and left herself alone with Timmy Lawless, his wine bottles and the memories no word he'd ever uttered could restore. Glazed eyes on wine bottles run dry, dead hands on legs which could only simulate a hint of gone rejoicing.

While somewhere Magoo the Newsboy sang in his sleep of Lizzie. While Carter spent himself on books. While Joe Letrigo said *Yes ma'am* to the watchful mothers of virgins, and the world spun around and around on some machine-driven, coal-burning axis to the roar of mechanical voices directing its path. Yet no power was greater than hers; she took Timmy's head to her lap and stroked the mat of his hair, her pain subsiding with each stroke on another's head. Each finger of the mailed fist loosened from her spine, each ray of light fell resting near Timmy's tear-drenched face, and sleep lowered with holy gentleness to take away the world.

Another evening whispered in Timmy's voice, and she saw him pink and flowing in a nightgown she'd taken from her mother. "Here's your cereal, pret-ty Diaaaane. Eat it all up and I'll give you a surprise."

She ate a part of it, but didn't press him for the surprise. Her guts were an enemy, twisting spitefully while Timmy sang from the kitchen. He came drifting back with a bowl of steaming soup and a weird understanding in his corrugated face. "Soup, Diaaaane. Make you warm again in your tummy, and you must always stay warm in your tum-my, Diaaaane."

She took it hotter than her throat could stand, and it anesthetized her insides. Yet pains shot through her legs, and her arms went quaking out of control. "Timmy . . . Timmy, hold my hands. Hold them, Tim, hold them tight."

He sat beside her with a tight grip on each wrist, kissing her finger tips. Smiling and weeping, "Poor hands, poor hands," as she made him squeeze tighter and tighter. As she stiffened back against his grip, trembling with a strain that pulled stronger through her than the cry for Horse. She felt cold about the face with needles of sweat, hot inside with a new flame in angry organs.

"Ohoho," she had to wail, "ohoho-Timmy, Timmy," feeling her eyes bug out, seeing her own crucifixion mirrored in his face.

Timmy let go and ran scurrying about, screaming in unworldly terror; then he pushed about in Lukey's pile of Tony's clothes, came out with a stout leather belt. He locked her hands on the buckle and fell to his face on the bed. No need of words; she stood above him and whipped with a fierceness her pain invented, and pain drained upward from limbs and torso to her head, and out into the night with her tears.

"Timmy, Timmy." She fell, exhausted, to the floor, spent of power, pain, and any feeling of her own. "Timmy, Timmy." She wept, her head bobbing with the sobs, up and down on her arm. Afraid to look up at blood. Waiting for the enemy to grow again inside.

But her body stayed dead till she pulled it into motion, yanked the string and spilled light over the blue-and-purple welts on his back, broken at points where blood trickled in rivulets that ran down the curve of his side. She bathed him, found peroxide and iodine in Stoney's cabinet for the welts, tore strips from her mother's night-gown for all the suffering on earth. Then she had to be gone—had to rush with her painfree body from the loft. She left Timmy weeping in his crazy joy.

Down the steps with a head creaking: "I'm a body, I'm a body; it's all I am, a body," for soul was a luxury for easier lives to swill in complacently, up in their towers to heaven. A body in the street at night. Hiding in a doorway to fix her snood, to powder tears and anguish from her face, to touch color to her lips. Adrift up unawakened MacDougal, past trash cans and cats and citizens, forcing Timmy from her mind so that she could be nothing more than a body, with no Horse on hand to make her just an idea.

Diane sat alone in the shadows of the park. Voices played in the springtime, children only, for the grownups never more than whispered.

The body went through the green of Washington Square to Fifth Avenue's austere privacy, walked north faster and faster as the muscles began to shriek. Autos picked this night for squalling, blaring on powerful horns; more lights than New York ever owned pointed piercing fingers into her eyes. Snatches of conversation were aimed barbs thrown by strangers who knew she didn't belong on earth. The street was hostile. Buildings of concrete rising to the sky watched her with their million eyes as she ran, then walked, then trotted, sweating ice from her temples. On and on she went, through the Twenties, the Thirties, afraid to stop.

She stood at last before one huge show window of a department store, looking at crippled mannequins togged in summer splendor. Mannequins were the tops of a junky's dream: things fixed in motionless smiles, unfeeling, thoughtless, free of past grief and future demands; junkies were emblems of a race born to the tragedy of brotherlessness, impaled high on the Hook. Carter had whispered her to sleep with this one night, and now she had to run away from the words of it scraping at the back of her head.

Her legs went dead all at once, and some last grain of good fortune placed her near the Public Library, where she could sit on the concrete ledge which fronted its hedges. Trembling, she sat with no kind of pain but the frozen uneasiness that had sapped her of power. The great institution loomed pale-gray against the night; great toy lions guarded steps that ran up like a vast sheet of corrugated paper to columns saddened by shadow; and, beyond, the trees of Bryant Park looked frail and quivering, surrounded by massive towers of commerce. *Carter, Carter.* He'd learned of the wide world and forgotten her quivering guts, her frail endeavors. Stone lions roared above her with all the city's voice: distant trucks and underground trains and faraway machines of every bloodless kind roared out of massive stone into her head. She got up and went on legs stiff with some other season's cold, across Forty-second Street lights and traffic and citizens in wild disarray. Up Fifth again, past more huge windows that touted easy clothes for leisure.

There was a bronze giant in some great entranceway to a tower, stooped over on a pedestal with the steel skeleton of earth on his naked back: Atlas, like some Junky God, kept the shell of gone civilization as an eternal burden while around him walls on the street were bedecked with bronze and colored reliefs like inviolate riches mocking a world which had destroyed itself creating them. On she went, on, with the fist of Death at her spine, touching bones with a sharp cold fingernail, scratching in toward entrails. People gone silent in her ears watched the very beads of ice on her forehead. She had to sit awhile on church steps before she could try to round the corner, focusing now on her knotted core to avoid thinking of the horror another absence of Mama would present.

Though Joe had been sober when writing, his new letter rambled for pages, half-lamenting, however humorously, over little things with

which family life unnerved him: the cute and giggly ways of Tooney's
girl friends, his mother's strict refusal to let Joanie go unchaperoned
to some public lake to swim with her fifteen-year-old friends. For
Carter it was a warming letter, an ingenuous display of friendship
unclouded by the miles between them. He sat well back in his chair,
in an evening silence marked heavily by Diane's absence. But he read
and, reading, felt a glow of diversion grow solid in his chest.

Now Tooney's beau Hensley Clayburne is a man strong and tender
all at once—in many ways he puts me in mind of you. He caught me
by the scruff of my neck and hauled me off one Saturday when I went
at some fool kicking at a Negro man I know right well. He sent that
prehistoric swine off before I cracked him one time on the skull and
I huffed plenty at him in the Ford. He sat patiently smoking till I
was truly spent and then he told me a thing. Roundabout. Said if all
the white folks who disliked their work or pay were to lie down and
quit they'd be replaced by Negroes at less pay. And telling me, he
asked did I expect a white man living under that threat to do better
than hate the Negro. Hensley showed me how the least educated,
humblest white man with no opinion at all of himself and no fighting
chance to gain a fair opinion of himself just uses the Negro to feel
superior to—and then he told me "Don't go busting any skulls, Joey,"
making me feel like a damn child. Then he says our newspapers that
uphold segregation are not truly the ones down here keeping us hateful. Says they only carry on the word. Northern big hats throttling the
South, he tells me, Yankee business, that's who, and it's easy territory
for them, they name an old dead grudge with tradition. Well you
know I laughed up then for finding at last a prejudice in the man. But
he holds me down saying it's Yankee big hats and not Yankee he hates
so well. Says they own our industries and that unionism'll bust them
loose from throttling us. Says a white man down here who talks or
does bad to Negroes is just knifing himself in the back. Hensley means
to start his own newspaper and free the South with information—he
talks that way, big, but it comes not a bit corny from him. Says it's
saddening that American heroes are to be found only in history books,
things like that.

Carter had to close his eyes awhile, yet it was his mind, not his
eyes, that burned with tedium. He admired Hensley and wanted to
enjoy what Joe had conveyed, but felt too pinched with his own
problems. Skimming through more about Hensley, he lingered over
the general rambling in which Joe gagged about his daddy Tom,
strong man of Roanton, and told about easy talk with the redheaded

Selwyn girls in Tooney's room, talk that led up to his sister and her
beau

setting the date. Hensley, Daisy, Marily and I followed Tooney down
where she ran square into Tom and told him a day in July and he told
my mother and it threw the house into a mess of squeals and kisses
for fair. Every woman in the place planted lips on mine and I thought
I heard one redhead snort when she did it. It was all a dream under
the Carolina sky, the home, the town, the sitting around and easy
talk. I thought about a road we once built out from Bab el Wad to
Jerusalem under withering H. E. shellfire and enemy up close behind
great hillside rocks and down in gullies full of woods, and my blood
began to wriggle because it had all been real, good men dead and
blasted shrines at the end of what old men later named the Road of
Valor, all while the world slept in towns and homes like these I'm in
and argued over ideas. I looked at Hensley who can laugh good for all
his strong talk and my blood wriggled on till Tom handed me a drink
that I bolted and the dream in Carolina seemed good enough to me.
I just helped myself to more whisky while everybody carried on and the
wriggling went out of my blood and I shrugged to myself and promised myself a good summer. My friend Cal Honeycutt, fresh out of
medical school, diagnoses that I'm a case of delayed combat fatigue.
Would you say I'm neurotic?

Carter could hear the chuckle that went into that last line and
tried to chuckle away the wriggling in his own blood, then tried to
concentrate on an answer he might get right off to Joe, for Joe deserved a prompt long letter. But all he could think of to say, by way
of rambling as ingenuously as Joe did, was that Diane was a junky
and dying before his eyes. That Louella had grown more rigid still,
sullen enough for him to have left her early last night to wind up in
Lizzie Linden's artful bed. That Lizzie, in private, was a hundred
times the person she appeared in the defensive masks she wore outside. That Stoney, without his hairy mask, was an unendurable
mouth. That Vivienne . . . But he'd write none of it at all, he could
endure nothing this night but whisky.

He got up, laughing at the way Joe always wound up making him
thirsty for a little dreaming, and slipped his jacket on, promising he'd
write a quick answer . . . as soon as he returned from drinking and
wandering and looking for Diane.

The fumes of ignited gasoline and old burned oil drifted about
till they seemed to seep out of mahogany church doors, and Diane

had to go running again. Past grim-faced people enjoying the evening. Down the street to stop under dark windows past the terrace. To pray that Mama was in some other room. Up carpeted stairs with a prayer unworded in her soul.

Mama'd been in another room. Screaming, she opened the door. Tearfully, "Where've you been?" as Diane went through. "Sleeping with someone? *Screwing* some animal? Some beast like *this?*" and Robert Stoney was her target behind the wrought-iron rail in the living room. "Go on and *screw!*" through horrible tears while well-groomed Stoney lighted a cigarette. "There! The two of you— *beasts!* Go on!" with arms guarding her bosom from anyone who might clutch, with a lock of hair from her bun hung dead and lusterless over a red-jersey shoulder.

Diane hurried without a word to her cubicle of a room, flopped on the bed in darkness. But Mama came behind her, snapping light across the space, sitting with an anguished child's tears on the edge of the bed.

"What happened, Mama?" Diane sighed without really caring a bit.

"He . . . he's a *beast!* Like all the rest of them. He tried . . . to ——" A burst of sobs saved her from uttering the unholy word.

Her mother smelled like a snort of Horse, that nameless odor forever lodged back of her nose and brought forth incongruously in old stores and hallways. "Mama, stop sniveling. Throw the bum out and be done with it." Her stomach had turned to chalk; a thirsty knot was dehydrating her insides.

"It's nothing to you." Vivienne wept with hands over her face. "You . . . it doesn't . . . you can't realize——"

"Oh, *Mama*, for Christ sake!" The chalk exploded into fire; Diane doubled into a knot. "Shut up, Mama, shut up!" grabbing where she could about her middle, sneezing the Horse of her mother out of her nostrils. And Timmy lay bleeding in her mind—she leaped to the closet and found a wide fake-leather lacquered belt while terror bit at her blood. Yet she had to laugh at the woman weeping over nothing, at the fool penitently smoking a cigarette outside. "Okay, Mama," she squeezed out through pain, "don't cry, don't cry," and fled to the foyer, into the misty living room to Stoney's face, lewd and naked near an old-fashioned lamp. He screamed like a woman at the first lash, buried his incredulous face in both arms as she came down again and again with leather, cracking through his brown-tweed

coat with all the fury of her pain. "Swine, filthy pig!" she laughed.
"Brute! A helpless Christian girl!" laughing crazily while he screamed.

Her mother's wail was all that held back her frantic arms, and she
fell, laughing, onto the couch as Stoney bolted to the door. Vivienne
stood tall and avenged, with heavy-lidded eyes of pride on the painter
pulling himself erect and composed in the open exit. "Lunacy!" he
declared, still panting through dilated nostrils. "My dear, let me con-
gratulate you on the easiest victory imaginable." He executed a stiff
little bow and departed, shutting the door quietly while a painless,
laughing Diane cried, "Ta-da-da!" for his exit.

Vivienne, her bun secured atop her head, went across to the
kitchen with all the dignity she could muster. On her side and
propped on an elbow, Diane lay thoughtlessly, swinging frozen eyes
over old-fashioned double-bowl lamps and pale-ivory walls hung with
mirrors. The serving table before her was Chinese antique, dragon-
legged and suddenly set with a tray of teacups and a steaming pot.

"This will calm you. . . . Tea," Vivienne murmured with affection.

The tea did calm Diane, burned her insides clean, but Mama beside her on the couch, stupidly pure, absurdly anxious for her body,
made cleanliness into a shaking vacuum in her stomach. "I'm a body,
Mama," she had to say, "and so are you. You're a body too, Mama."

"It's the least of me," her mother declared, sagged now over her
tea as if she'd suddenly forgotten her trick of a rigid spine which
down the years had shielded all her weariness. "Diane, if you only
knew," and she looked around at the night outside the windows,
fingering the cross and chain suspended from her neck. Slowly, as
though some invisible monitor were guiding her, "There's so much
from heaven, so much more than the greed of evil earth."

"Mama, don't give me a headache; please, Mama. I've been to
church."

"Not really." The woman was smiling dreamily for her unseen
friend. "You've never sat there in prayer, in solemn, unhesitant
prayer, and seen a light emerge from windowless shadows high in
the wall, with the cross of Jesus glowing for you alone. To—to remind
you that crosses must be borne until His kingdom is yours. I've seen
the brilliant light of that cross in shadows, sending a ray of divine
light to my eyes. Shining into my heart and soul, my baby, into my
heart and soul."

WHILE RIVERS OF ANGRY STRANGERS ROAR   313

"I've been to church with you, Mama. All I saw was scared people. I never saw any lights except on the altar and the ceiling and maybe, the windows."

Mama's smile was angelic, with the tolerance of heaven in her eyes. "Diane, you've never gone there alone; you've never tried. You've never gone there to really, really give yourself over to the Lord Jesus." Her voice was serenely low and unaltered. "I've seen the light, my dear, I've seen it. And while this world grows more and more evil, I carry the light and I'm unafraid, unafraid. I have it with me always, and in the darkness of my room at night it glows in my heart and promises me light forever in heaven. And sometimes . . . sometimes . . . I flow into that light and lose my very senses, I flow through it and become a part of it, and it takes my breath away. I know, I know, and what I know is not important. I know without knowing, I feel without feeling." She had taken Diane's hand, squeezing it in what seemed to Diane like some kind of junky's ecstasy as she spoke. "We are light, we are only light. Our bodies are cells, my angel, cells, prisons. I've escaped mine at times, knowing I was a light in darkness, growing brighter and knowing, knowing. Brilliant light mortals have never seen, light greater than the sun." She was panting now and showing her teeth. Diane tried to pull her hand away, but Vivienne held on and squeezed. "The light of holiness, Diane, light growing brighter and brighter till it seemed all must explode, and then . . . then . . ." She looked around now, grinning, wild-eyed, close to Diane's face. "Diane, then His face appears . . . for me alone, for me. Diane, His face is beautiful. His face is Love, Diane, and it engulfs me in heavenly fires; it cleanses me of all that is earthly, it courses through my blood, Diane, it rushes to my head, Diane. *Diane*, I've been to heaven, my baby. Yes. Yes."

Some new kind of restive spirit trembled in Diane. She took her mother's arm as the woman leaned back, weeping out of a soft smile. The arm had gone suddenly limber as the woman's eyes closed, and there was a fright upon the room.

"Mama, come on. You better get into bed, Mama."

Vivienne had never been so easily led. The girl undressed her mother while the woman murmured unintelligibly. Diane brought a cloth to wash her mother's face in bed, promising she'd go to church alone, at will, to give herself to Jesus. Meaning it as she spoke, too.

Yet when the woman was asleep Diane felt only foreboding in the shadows asleep under chairs. She undressed and got under the shower, first hot, then cold, varying the flow back and forth.

She sat naked on her mother's couch and stared at an old-fashioned lamp. The music of another world filled her head, and she truly felt bodiless. "O father," she murmured, "O father," the only kind of thanks she knew. The only offering in gratitude for painlessness. And it was familiar, only a mind's finger out of reach, an ease she'd known before. But an autohonk from the street shattered through her head, and body came back to being, tingling with remembered agonies. "I'm a body!" she wailed, and ran to her room for fresh clothes. "I'm a lousy body and that's all I am!" For the absence of body was recognizable now: it was the Nothing she'd known with Horse!

But an easy charge to come off of. No holes in flesh, no scars. She found crumpled bills in her mother's purse, put a five-dollar bill in the pocket of her plaid dress, and made herself up in the bathroom mirror. She fixed the door lock so that it wouldn't catch, and hurried out into the night, into springtime, into air fresh on her clean, fresh body, on her cool, slick head.

A cab took her to the Cosmopole, and Danny Barber was there with his brother, with chubby little pretty Nao Braun, with Harry Sticks at another table full of strangers. In violet light the bohawks argued about the meaning of art, the art of meaning; rubbernecks in uptown clothes picked hassels with Lesbian groups who swore like soprano sailors. And other citizens of no identity at all passed through their lonely hours, watching no argument, no swishing fairy, no junky running mucus at the nose or offending sleep with open unawake eyes. The junkies were still charged on Diane's largesse, and they gathered round to sit in silent homage while Canada Dan sketched everything his brain thought it saw.

The night was easy and passed with no pain to chase her running from herself. Till at dawn Magoo the Newsboy took a table by the wall under the Mural of Plenty and slept himself to singing in a cafeteria emptied of citizens, with none but junkies and tramps for audience.

"Poor old Magoo." Diane had tears for the newsboy four tables away, and tears brought a throb back to her body.

> "There . . . ain't a thing I . . .
> Wouldn' do . . .
> Fuh you, my sweet ba-by . . ."

With no Lizzie at all to hear him, with none but the hooked to watch and laugh the junkies' whine. Diane had to leave, to run in the dawn of a Tuesday away from Magoo's restless sleep. She ran to the park and sat there with none but pigeons to cluck for her pain, with nothing but a rumor of rain in the sky. "Poor Magoo," she tried to sing, "he was only forty-two . . ." but words had a certain ugliness that magnified her pain, and only "ooriubop" was meaningless enough. "Oobop-eema-yopjebam," with no melody to plague her, only flatness and nothing.

As if by signal the pigeons arose in a body, like a great gray papier-mâché sheet in high wind, disappearing in a whir of sound over the high wall of trees behind her. She ran through heavy drops, ran to the shelter of a hotel canopy diagonally across the corner, before the rain came pouring, hissing, raising a silver haze through which surface highlights glittered. The inside of her was hot ice now, and she wanted to double over on the stone steps, but a cloud of vapor in the park caught her eyes, and she stood straight to watch benches leave their moorings in the ground, free themselves and hover in trim formation about the performing trees, which swayed and sang in whispers. Pain lifted in bubbles to her head and out through her eyes as she watched the walks of the enchanted park—walks only vaguely marked off in mist by their volatile wire borders, running like shimmering rivulets in search of the silver horizon, where heaven blended with mist around the vast face of The Son. . . . He smiled with Love, and she went to Him, into the downpour from heaven, through silver butterflies that splashed away from her step, down hazy rivulets toward His face in steaming mists.

But heaven wouldn't linger for a novice. Rain stopped falling, mists quit rising, and she searched around and around in Washington Square Park for the face she'd seen for a moment. Around and around over concrete splashed with mud, with a brain of sawdust in her skull, a skin full of empty on her legs. Legs carried Nothing out of the park, into a new drizzle up Waverly, to the Avenue of the Americas, and the garden of industry was in bloom around her. Gleaming black mushrooms of umbrellas floated by in a weird unanimity that smothered all the life that activated them. Out in the wide road monstrous trucks roared like stone lions, this way and that, grinding in a mechanical indifference to any soul that drove them. Now and then a taxicab darted out of the colorless sea of trucks, a quick splash of orange or yellow to whisper of men and their directions. Diane wailed beside the locked door of a bank. She wailed for a faceless want and sat down in her own dankness on dank, cold stone. Wailing into a half-sleep, freezing in her damp, clinging clothes.

It was Harry Sticks, the pod-pushing junky, who lifted her with strong black arms. "Baby, you goofing in the rain," laughing despite his dismay, holding her up till her legs discovered the ground. "You'll catch your *death* of cold," and laughed louder as he helped her down Waverly, laughed and told her it was something Muffo Smith had once told a college chick when she leaped naked from a parked car. "You'll catch your *death* of cold, he told her." Harry laughed. Like Joe Letrigo, Harry laughed, like a dark Joe Letrigo Harry laughed big and rangy, helping her down MacDougal with his big black jacket around her. Down around Bleecker with only rain in her head. Over to a squall between the Shylock and the Swede on the stoop, Swede laughing, Shylock shaking a fist.

"*Lukey the Swede . . .*" she sang. "*Tony the Shylock has switched to . . .*" and many, many arms helped her up the stairs while a toothless mouth promised Tony he'd find the latest hyste and return it.

"You go down and cook up some soup for the Face. Go on, Tone, me and Sticks, we get her in bed, and I run and hyste back your rags," and two men undressed her, dried her with towels, and pulled the covers tight around her. While Harry felt her forehead the Swede wrapped Tony's clothes in a tidy bundle, hid the round-bellied lamp, and giggled. "It don't mean nothin, baby, nothin at all—ss-ss-ss. It's all for laughs oney count. Oney the laughs. 'Cause if you try any more than the laughs old paradox spits in your face. Oney them that got it made tell you different. I go downtown on Broadway where them Broad Streets and Chamber Streets got the big old buildins with old studs in the chambers like and they rulin the senators, you know, and I want work, 'cause they got it made; see?"

"What's he saying?" Diane asked Sticks out of a burning face. "I feel slow in the head; what's he saying over there?"

"I *been* slow in the head to hear the Swede," Harry laughed. "You got to have a cipher device for the Swede."

"So I figger I better go to the Commonists, 'cause like this—if the Commonists hate them old studs who want it all, they must be okay after all, even if they foreigners from Europe. It must be them old studs squallin lies about them Europeen guys 'cause they afraid, so I figger the Commonists is best. But I connect with some guy takes me up a house which they suppose to be like Polacks, but it's a plain-English guy and he tells me cop a walk. He don't like me neither. It's the paradox; see? Oney for laughs, you can't get bugged with no more. Ss-ss-ssss."

Diane was too numb even to get bugged, too hot about the face to feel more than lazy pulling in her blood. Lukey never stopped talking and Sticks never stopped stroking her head. And they awoke her for soup the Shylock had to serve her himself, chewing his cigar, telling Lukey he'd give no more than three dollars as a reward for the uncovering of his merchandise. "Muh-you take a cut for hysta Tone before a no shit. You take a three doll-uhmo," and tilted his frizzy head back to feed the *lilla Spaniol*. And he sent the others away, to stand there himself while she slept through the day. By night he fed her a chicken section he'd cooked, and brought Timmy to dance for her. He'd never forgotten that she told nothing to the Dinch about a morning in the dust of his cellar, and for days that bled into each other he fed her, medicated her, brought her entertainment in Timmy and Canada Dan, kept Lukey from talking too much, had Jacquie Swan read a letter from Dincher in the heat of some feverish noon.

One day she walked about the loft for an hour to regain her legs, and she was convinced that fever had burned Horse forever from her blood, till a fist came out of the evening's first gray to shake loose her spine, then quickly pass. On the arm of Lukey the Swede she went out into weather that smelled of perfume, laughing a little at the Swede's rambling nonsense while children shrieked through the park's blue darknesses. They sat on a bench in shadows while Lukey told her his favorite stories about priests.

Diane wanted to laugh, but the face out of rain mists admonished her. "You shouldn't lie like that about priests, Swede; it isn't right."

"I ain't lyin and I ain't squallin about religion. This is still a guy even with the starched collar, and he had it saved for forty years. You think that's nothin?"

"I know someone who has it saved and she's no champ except in her dreams at night. Don't talk like that about priests, Luke."

His eyes looked like Izzie the Ghost's in speckled beams from the arc light through trees. If she didn't know the Ghost was with Paddy Jenks and French Therry in Lexington, Kentucky, she'd have taken a punch at him for busting Dincher. "Dincher's coming out soon; you know that, Luke? They're springing him because it's a halfie rap. They found nothing on him but somebody's words."

"That's good to hear, it's good. Come on, we go for beer by the Riviera, 'cause you be makin it with the boy if he makes the air and the Swedish boy don't see you much no more, no more."

She really held his arm on the way over, so that he could look proudly at the tourist squares one time. But the Riviera was beery and hot and full of new-look darlings from the college on University Place, and all their squeals found root in her. The fist swelled, tapping painlessly till it went ironclad once more, then rusty, and she ran out to vomit in the street. Lukey stood faithfully by, brought her water, eased rubbernecks out of the way.

"I want to go to church, Swede, I really do. Take me to a good church, Swede."

"Come on, I take you to a real respectable place through the park. I use to roll my pod in there when I was a young Viper," and he stooped to hold her elbow through to Fifth Avenue, his ruined face more a rubble now in flat gray compassion.

Through the high iron gate feathered with hedges, up a step into amber shadows, old mahogany benches and walls, ancient silence, a space apart from all worldly motion. "It smells like Horse," she murmured as they sat in a pew. "It smells like a snort, Lukey."

"Horse don't smell," he protested in a whisper. "It's all in your head," and they whispered their argument though no one else was there.

Diane looked high about the ceiling gloom for a light, gave herself willingly with her shrieking muscles into the fierce quiet, concentrating on the rain-mist face that still veiled her brain. *"Heavenly father,"* she even sang without shame, *"father, father,"* while her belly burned. The smell of old snorts lingered in the core of her head, trickled nausea down to throat and chest, till she lurched over to her side and vomited on the floor. Retched and heaved while Lukey patted her ribs.

"It's okay, baby," he whispered, "millions they leave their troubles in church," and couldn't resist a "ss-ss-ss."

They changed their pew to one across the aisle, and Diane prayed some more, agonized some more in muscles and entrails. While shadows hung solemnly with no divine light out of any darkness. "Nothing's happening, Luke; oh, I'm dying, I'm dying."

"Come on, I need a fix myself. Come on, no use bein stubborn, we get us a fix and everything is normal again. Come on, baby."

"No, no," while her head bled ice, while she quaked all over and ran at the nose. "Why doesn't God fix me? Why? Why?"

"Whatta you expect—miracles? This outfit hardly knows us."

An autohorn exploded outside, and Diane began a horrible dry retching; each vain heave tore at a part of her abdomen, her chest, her lungs. "Oh," she had to call for air, "ooh," after each heave. While salt ice burned at her eyes, and shadows came close and black around her in separate sheets, like bad old days returning to enclose her in suffocation. "Lukey, Swede, get me out, get me air, Swede, I can't breathe . . . *uh* . . . *uh.* . . ."

But air did little for her lungs: great gray sheets of shadow whirred out of trees to entrap her. "Lukey! I'm not . . . getting any air." She hung on the iron bars of the church gate. The Swede's hands clutched and squeezed on her ribs, pressing and letting up while she sucked through a wide-open mouth for little dry dribbles of dustlike air that kept her barely alive. Streetlights came together in her head, danced down like so many sparks to burn her stomach and die into heavy ashes.

Lukey helped her along to the park, where Angie found them near a railed-in sand pit. "I need a fix, and it's almost bad," the Swede whispered with agitation.

"I got nothin," Angie complained while he pulled Diane's arms from the bench against which she'd collapsed. "I don' see Buster for days, like-he don' even come to see if I got anythin to push for him."

They spoke in powdered sparks, words that were only moans for her frozen, sweaty ears. Everything happening outside her had an elusive familiarity that terrified her; old things appeared out of memory, mixed with trees and words and faces, then vanished before they could be named. While she prayed silently and saw the rain-mist face that wouldn't or couldn't help her. All that had ever occurred by her will lay down upon her; days turned to shadow sheets trapped her

within suffocating walls. Tears cleared her eyes and she saw herself
alone with Angie's curly-haired, freckled face. "Little Ange," she
managed, "Dincher, he's outside soon," and tried to smile for the
boy.

"I look all over for that General'n he ain' nowhere, nowhere." He
sat down beside her with a long-lasting sigh.

Old days were back with their single, endless hours, trying to have
her see their faces, demanding she name all her guilts. Pain let up,
but she was feverish, burning and sweating cold. "I'm kicking, Ange,
I really am."

"What for? Whatta you go through all the pain for anyway? You
oney be back on again; whatta you think? You hooked, baby."

"Not me. I'm kicking. I got it nearly beat," while a face still damp
with rain, still vague in mists, told her a whispered *no*, and fever ate
at her skin.

"Don' worry you hooked. We all hooked on somethin-like; you
dig?"

She didn't know when she'd left Angie, but her legs had found a
route down Thompson Street toward Bleecker. Italian voices were
music to her fever. Words that didn't trouble her with their meanings
rolled from under mustaches on old musical faces. It was a dreamwalk
to some unrecollected melody, some ancient promise that had never
come true, and an easy kind of happiness played in the lighted street
around her, up and down old stoops, out of peopled windows, till
the thorns sprouted and she doubled over on a doorstep, knowing
she was a vessel forever apart from happiness, loaded with fault, error
and helplessness: she prayed to die there on a foot-high stone.

A hand helped her up, forced her easily up, and she wished it
would dash her head on some iron fence and kill her. "What's a matter, beautiful? You need some help? You come right to my doorstep
for help, beautiful."

There was nothing strange about it. "Buster, Buster, I'm dying.
Get me a fix. I can't make it. I'm dying, Buster."

"I got nothin to fix you wit, beautiful. I'm clearin out 'cause it's
bad climate for big boys like me; see?" with a grin she could see
through the mists.

"Take me upstairs, Buster, put me in a bed and sit on me or—oh!
Oh, Buster!" Flames and knives and all the mailed and thorny fingers,
with no power at all in her limbs. No strength in legs punched with

needles of old gone Horse, legs of all her enmities. And up the road
of legs bustled all the voices in a street of musical Italian, all the
eyes that knew nothing of her pain. "Upstairs, oh, Buster, oh, oh,
oh!" with evil legs pumping in her brain.

"Come on, I take you home to the loft. I don' want you croakin up
in my trap. I take you to the loft just 'cause I got a good heart. Then
I cut out, I'm hot like stoves. I got to . . ." words she couldn't know
apart from the musical voices around them, and the mushy lurch of
legs in her guts. Buster in a plaid jacket, grinning under his shiny
pompadour, around into gray Bleecker, up brown light in narrow
flights. "I'm just a body," she had to say aloud, "just a lousy body."

"You just a lousy junky—" he laughed—"and you just a lousy
mother to a bastard kid," throwing her down on the bed under
Stoney's naked light, flinging her hard so that her legs kicked up to
hang for a vast instant before her eyes. "You just a lousy tramp
wit——"

"Buster! Tie my legs, tie them up quick!" It was the secret to everything, the way to cut her loose from the needles and errors and faults
of all the days lurching inside her. "Tie them—" she laughed—"tie
up my lousy legs good and tight, tie them away!"

"I got no time! I got to cut out. Evvy junky bastard knows this
place. You told them all kinds—you told them evvythin you know,
you lousy tramp bastard! They find me here, Magoo sings, all the
junkies——"

"Buster! Nobody knows anything! I didn't say . . . Magoo
didn't . . . Buster! Oh, please, please," tearing at the covers with
futile nails, "tie them, Buster, tie them for me; it's the way, Buster,
tie my legs." There was a horrible quiet while she sucked for breath
under new rolling sheets of shadow.

Her ankles were pinned. "Tie my legs!" he mimicked. "Crazy junky
broad. Tie her legs. I tie your legs awright, I tie them," and he pulled
a tasseled bathrobe cord, soft silk, tight around her ankles, around
and around her ankles.

"Higher. Tie them higher, Buster," but he secured a knot under
the bulk of cord by her ankles, then whipped her body around with
one hand and brought the cord to her wrists, puffing hoarsely while
she screamed, "My legs, Buster, my legs! Tie them all the way up,
Buster, tie them so they can't—Buster, not my hands! Buster——"
But the meat of his fleshy mitt snapped ringing against her mouth,

and through sweat of her own she saw his face purple wet, pupils barely visible in those unfocused eyes, thick lips quivering like a freshly inflicted wound. "Buster!" as he folded her like an accordion from ankle to shoulder. "Buster, I'm dying; oh, oh . . ."

A wind howled hoarsely from his nostrils and mouth. "Go on'n die, you lousy junky broad," puffing hysterically, prodding at her with nails and knuckles. "Your lousy nose is runnin'," he gasped.

Diane, a knot of burning barbs and frozen skin, wailed between suffocating walls, while the fevers and shadows of old mistakes tore at her flesh and pulled at her agonized blood, and she shrieked out her last bubble of strength when an animal bit through her wasted, penitent soul.

It was all for laughs. Carter told Merwin Fingerhut's story to Normie in a Riviera booth surrounded by the noise of mirthless laughter. Normie had left Rusty with her bridge-playing visitors because he felt he should stay close to Carter after learning a lot about his friend's responsibilities to a dying wife, her delinquent sister and a mother who couldn't be described. Both men were nearly drunk, and Carter told Merwin's story. *It was all for laughs and everybody was a child coming out of the shock of depression. Big children were drinking the remaining alcohol of the Twenties and their offspring, seeing their parents' poisoned, bloodshot faces, found a less toxic narcosis for laughs. Marijuana had no physiological target to corrode and left no lingering regrets hung over head and stomach. Recovery was official, an act of Congress promised it, and destiny was in the hands of a beloved national father. The children had only to play, and laughs were the noblest attainment: the bigger the laughs, the more fulfilled the life. The old drank out dark memories, the young smoked into fabulous dreams—the Thirties were for laughs. So that when a man named Adolf began to strut like a toy soldier, everybody laughed at his very seriousness: the benign and wise national father would care for his young against all seriousness. They smoked for greater laughs, and called anyone with a serious eye a "square" who hadn't a heart for laughing.*

"That's Merwin's view," Carter reminded Normie from time to time. "He knows and cares nothing about hidden disillusionment turning them to narcosis." *And when Hitler started to march, and when his drumbeat pounded in the streets full of laughs, the laugh-*

ing marijuana cults complained of noisy "squares" who were elbowing into their world. Nobody had a right to do that. There they were, content to watch automobiles ooze around corners, with no complaints about movies that honored the fallen men of industry, named them as heroes who'd someday come back; with no despair over ungratifying jobs, meager pay; uncomplaining as long as they had the price of "gauge," and the "squares" were muscling in, making life serious. Then BAM! it was on, everyone was on a crazy kick, a horrible intrusion on the joyous who'd polished good jazz to good swing —for music was the face of the nation, and it had been smiling, laughing with "jive" till the "squares" interrupted laughs with seriousness.

"Merwin came awake after the depression; he never saw really hungry people." Carter took the last drink he wanted into his bubbling stomach. "You remember them, Norm, but you didn't see them like I did around the mines. You didn't see them herded by soldiers ready to fire at any man, woman or child gone frantic for food. I think Merwin smoked marijuana because of terror he never saw but had to feel. It's the chain, it's the chain."

"What chain, Carter, what chain?" Normie spoke quietly, not even knowing why Carter had to tell Merwin's story, afraid that his friend was in a state of near-collapse.

"We're all connected. Here, look at this letter I got from Joe Letrigo. Only full-length letter he ever wrote, he says; I'm duly proud," burping over it with a dull cynicism Normie'd never seen in that firm, square face, "Joe's getting a new brother-in-law—I wish Diane had one—Joe quotes him," and he read from the scrawled letter: "*Society is a single organism, localized eruptions are felt all over, et cetera, et cetera. Tell you more later. I want to go on with the Viper Story.*" While Vipers and drunks and other depersonalized people cavorted in the glaring light of the place.

War was on in the world: drunks were turned away and Vipers went into uniform along with the "squares." But laughter collapsed for everyone but drunks, who nursed ulcers and spent big war money on things they neither needed nor loved. Vipers forgot their identity when their spilled blood mixed with the blood spilled from "squares," and some people came home, bewildered, uncertain, seeking a place they thought they'd find for themselves. But there was no special place prepared. The home front had been fighting too tough a war for anything so utopian as that. Vipers became Vipers again, for just

*a few laughs. A younger generation joined them. But the kick was
mild to the grandchildren of drunks. Not narcotizing enough for kids
who'd felt the scars of chaos as their brothers and uncles had felt the
scars of war. Each generation must surmount the last: the new es-
capers found "junk." Heroin, and they called it "Horse," and they
went dead all the way, they worked a little more on jazz, killed the
polished version called swing, and emerged with the voice of their
times, out of sheer and native honesty, and called it Be-bop . . . the
dirge of our civilization. For music is the face of a nation, and in Be-
bop there is no lament, no tear, but only a sentimental acknowledgment of Death.*

"It's Merwin's view, and I mostly share it," Carter said as they
rocked around people out to the street. "The night is heavenly," with
half a gesture toward the sky. "Smell springtime, Normie, it's perfume, and only you, I and the animals know about it," sniffing a
lungful as they walked.

In a week springtime was settling and hinting of summer, but
nothing had settled in Carter. The threads of agitation, woven tight
before, were dispersing into ravelings now, like nerves exposed and
vulnerable to any little irritant. It was sharply apparent, and so. Normie drove him once more to town after the hospital, and once more
sat with him till they were drunk in the Riviera's Sunday din while
Carter complained about his inability to find Diane. Now, in the
park, Carter looked almost boyish in his loose blue sport shirt.

"Everybody, everybody," he was saying as they walked away from
Lizzie, who'd been as pretty as a girl in the half-dark lane. "This is
the season for everybody to crawl out from under their rocks and
come to Washington Square. Everybody but Diane, and nobody'll
tell me where she is; nobody thinks I ought to know about the kid."

The years had been shaded even in her voice when Lizzie had
wanted to know why Carter hadn't come to see her as he'd once
promised, but Carter had yanked Normie away, with no more than a
slurred mumble. He felt guilty for it now, as he felt guilty for having
told Normie that Edna was doomed, for having unburdened himself
at his friend's expense. He didn't know what was right and didn't
trust himself to move about among people, but the whisky urged
him along. Christ, how he'd snapped at Normie over his suggestion

that he leave town and the whole Lattimer family once and for all. Thinking about it, he stopped walking and patted that long, thin, apprehensive face. "Don't worry, Norm, I'm not really blowing my top." Normie smiled and tried to say something, but Carter walked off. "Watch. This one knows Diane. Watch me get ignored. Hey, Nao," and Nao Braun looked up from the flower in her hand, turned great brooding eyes upward to search through her cloud till she found him. "Nao, have you seen Diane lately?"

"Loo-ook," she whispered, holding out the flower, "hurt li'l feller," with a long sigh that shuddered almost to tears.

A crippled grasshopper lay on the flower's yellow petals. Carter looked at Normie shifting there as if he didn't know what to do with his smile, then took the grasshopper from its bed just to humor the girl. "Have you seen Diane? All week, have you seen her?"

She watched his face awhile, then whispered, "Dinch's back. He got back Wensey. You know Dincher? You know what's today?"

"Sunday," he said and felt foolish—she was looking off at a man shuffling by with eyes fast on the ground. Carter put the grasshopper in her lap.

"Kippie, whatcha huntin all night, Kippie?" she asked the man, and as the two walked off Carter heard him say that he was looking for good things people were forever losing.

"See?" Carter said. "Nobody wants to talk. Didn't Nao look nice? She's a way-back junky. Look how nice everything looks: the trees are swaying, all the people are chatting. You'd never know we're at the brink."

Normie went along uneasily, across the road blocked from traffic to the wide circle of a fountain, dry till the peak of summer, crowded with kids chasing each other across its area. "What brink?" he finally asked. "You're getting mighty strange, moss rat. You say weird things."

"Civilization, it's collapsing."

"Your head's collapsing. You have the Cold War jitters, and on top of that you're drunk like a sakihead missionary."

Carter sat on the rim of the pool, rubbing the side of his head where all the whisky seemed to be lying about. He saw Stoney across the way near the guardrail under trees, his stomach showing slung under his belt. "Christ, without his jacket he looks like an old woman. Stoney! Robert Stoney!" and Stoney turned toward them. "All right, you asked for it. He'll tell you about the end of the world in gassier terms than mine."

"Where's his beard? He looks ridiculous."

"He's not sure himself," as Stoney approached, hands still slung lazily on his seat. "He shaved it for some Delilah, and now she's cast him out, so he hasn't shaved in a week or two."

"Uhhhhh!" Stoney came sighing forward. The effects of his fifty weary years, hidden somehow in winter winds, showed now in lines across his cheeks right down into the stubble. "Uhhhhh!" He dropped ponderously to the pool rim, settling his weight carefully. "What a life, to coin a phrase. This existence of inquiry I've led has narrowed natural stimuli to such a point that my only remaining pleasure lies in watching pretty young ladies affect composure as their dogs defecate in the park. It's what I was doing when you so vulgarly distracted me."

"You can use the conserved energy," Carter grumbled.

"Not much doubt about that." Stoney passed it off with a slightly overdone smile. "The truth is, I've been persecuted by some ambitious creature who holds a rather vague membership in the female sex," and he went on to describe the evening in a barrage of words that jarred individually in Carter's head. "But in the end there she was, totally oblivious of my agony. In desperation I allowed her to take me to a movie, which turned out to be a worse ordeal——"

Carter shrugged. "Okay, take us to a movie. We're not too dense to recognize so broad a hint."

"You're too dense to breathe the same air as I do," Stoney said irritably. "I thought you liked me, I——"

"I more than like you. I need you. You're the only one I know whom I can actively dislike," and with it came the guilt over his own irascibility; he turned away to keep Stoney from seeing it.

Stoney whirled on Normie, who had been shifting in embarrassment. "How do you stand this—this church squire, this unemployed deacon? He'll speak gently to any blithering idiot, but to me he . . . First he calls me over, then—gah! It takes stature to recognize stature." He turned back to Carter. "Look, I don't object to your stupidity, but must you seek me out to display it?"

Carter fidgeted when Normie threw him an admonishing look; Normie was amused by Stoney and apparently couldn't see that all

Stoney's humor stemmed from contemptuousness. "Robert," Carter said, standing up, "sometimes you act like a little forty-year-old," and before Stoney could come back, he called out to Dincher, who was crossing toward the trees with two other boys.

Dincher came up to meet him, and they shook hands.

"How was it, Dinch? Pretty rough?"

"Nah, on one toe I do it. Phony rap anyways. Like-they hadda spring me; dig?" as Angie and a taller boy came up to flank him. "Disawd'ly, that's all. They lump me up a little, like-nex they can me, jus for bustin a couple lousy Fuzz; right, Ange? You know Carter; it's Edna's husban." The boy had all his old swagger, but the soft round cheeks had tightened into thick, bony contours of flesh.

"Dinch, where's Diane? No one wants to tell me. You don't have to," he added quickly. "Just how is she?"

Dincher pulled some change from his pocket and jingled it while a breeze blew out his shirt. He twitched his head and the other boys walked off. "Not so good, Carter. She got hurt bad by the General, like-Buster Wallinger."

"Hurt?"

"He give 'er the works-like; you dig? Like a rat'n it hurt 'er bad."

"You mean she didn't . . . He forced it?"

"Sure," with sudden indignation. "Whatta you think?"

"Who is he? That big hard guy?" Just to keep talking, just to keep from running up a tree and screeching.

"Hard guy! I make 'im hard if I see 'im. Like-I make 'm stiff."

"Diane, is she being taken care of okay? Does she need anything?"

The boy shrugged. "Not so hot. She got that pansy Timmy nursin 'er. You know, what the hell. Me, I can' stay there-like. I got a parole issue; dig? Gotta be in by twelve'n all. I tole 'er go to you, but she says you don' like 'er no more."

"What? Why'd she say that?"

"I dunno. I din' believe it. She's different now; she use to like my music how I played it; you know? Now, I dunno," and he shrugged again.

"Is she—you know about the junk? Is she——"

"Yeah, I know. She kicks it okay, but it knocked the meat off her. She's different, Carter, I swear. She thinks evvybody don' like 'er."

"Take me over there, Dinch. Come on. If she doesn't want——"

"No, no, I can' do that, man. She blow her stack. She's different,

Carter," and sniffed like a child ashamed he might cry. "Like-maybe
I tell 'er you wanna see 'er; okay? Then you keep 'er by your house;
okay? I don' like she should be wit them freaks alla time; I don' like
it."

"Yeah, you tell her, Dinch. You tell her to go home where she belongs," and it was a form of the deviousness he'd recently learned; he
had to look away from Dincher's wary eyes, and as he did his own
were blocked by cool hands.

They were cool wrists he took down from his eyes, and he turned
with swift excitement to look for Diane's sleek hair, black eyes, but
it was a blond Louella wrinkling her nose in her happiest springtime grin. "Why haven't I seen you, Carter? I can't believe you went
away angry."

He tried not to be angry now, though his head quaked with whisky
and disappointment. "Louella, you know Dincher? Dincher——"

"Yeah, we meet once." The boy grinned. "Maybe she tell you
about Buster. She knows how he is; right, doll?"

"He's very nice. Buster is sweet," fingering a new gold cross that
dangled between her breasts.

"What're you doing with a triple bosom?" Carter asked, and saw
he'd really embarrassed the girl. He shook Dincher's arm to quiet
his laughter. "Dinch, I'll be right over there by the pool. You get her,
Dinch?"

"Okay, man. If you see sweet Buster, you don' fly off no handles;
dig? Leave it to the Dinch; right? I fix 'im smooth; you dig?" He
flicked his head in a nod and walked off, then paused. "I'm suppose
to be home in the Bronx soon, but firss I go tell Diane," and went
toward his friends, waiting under the trees.

Carter started back toward the pool, but Louella held him.

"Carter, you're becoming a real Village loafer with all the cynicism
and . . . Were you angry because I wouldn't get rid of my friends,
just so——"

"Not angry, just impatient." Lighting a long cigarette in slow,
careful movements, she filled him with impatience now, just as she
had with her slow, careful prattling about art that night he'd left
Central Park West for Bleecker Street. "Too much talk about nothing. That shmoe Philon analyzing all the little girls and never knowing he's reading a damn mirror he can't see in front of his face. Art

—what the hell do you people know about it? It comes out of life, and that's something you've been sheltered away from since——"

"Oh, Carter, now stop. . . ." She followed him to the sidewalk near the pool where Normie was listening to Stoney and stopped him again. "Carter——"

"And all the stupid talk about avoiding the 'static hordes.' You bastards have a philosophy made of toilet paper, and what kills me is you're *militant* about it." He saw her wince and held himself from going on.

Louella stared at him out of her pain. "Diane, she's your idea of life; narcotics and decay of every kind . . ."

"Narcotics," he muttered. Something hotter than whisky and duller than fatigue was trickling about in his skull. "She's a junky and you're a dilettante, and the reason's the same for both of you. It's your special groove; you can be away from the world with your special language and special pleasures, and you can look down your nose at the 'static hordes' who don't realize what they're missing. You both have your ingroups, you poor little bastards. Look, Louella —" while squealing adolescents crisscrossed around them—"we don't owe each other anything. You live your life and I live mine."

She glanced at Stoney and flashed a smile at him in return for his, then turned straight-faced abruptly. "Carter, listen to me." Strained wrinkles appeared around her eyes. "I had to collect myself; I had to think things out. You know I'd been running wild; I had to make sure of everything I did. . . . I had to just stop sleeping with every man who——"

"Oh, hell, it wasn't that," he moaned. "Collect yourself! In all that nausea you surround yourself with? It wasn't the sleeping with that chased me; it was the damn calculation where there should be experience," and grew promptly sick with himself for being drawn into it. "I'm doing it myself—maybe I see a bit of myself in you and can't be patient with it. Maybe——"

"There is . . . there is a bit of you in me, Carter." It was an entreaty, quiet, with a real furtiveness. "Cart, it's because of you I had to stop and think. Don't you see?" She was really whispering now although they were yards away from Stoney's yapping and Normie's choppy laughter.

It was like some springtime ritual dance, words tossed foolishly about and whirling to a clogged core in his brain. "What's the cross for anyway? Supposed to replace the cigarette holder? Silver to gold standard? You can interrupt me any——"

"Carter! What's happening to you? You used to be so relaxed and——"

"I'm having a nervous breakdown. What's with the oversized cross?"

She fingered the trinket again. "I need it, it makes me feel good." She shuffled quickly in her ballet slippers over to sit on Stoney's lap. "Robert, are you glad to see me?" Carter, as he sat beside Normie on the pool rim, heard something pathetic in that.

"Delighted." Stoney smiled out of shifty lidless eyes and told Normie that she was his proudest creation, while Louella pulled his nose in embarrassment. Then she insisted he show her his little room —with a quick glance at Carter—and they both giggled good-bys as they left. Carter watched them and drifted off with his eyes, down springtime lanes full of strangers, while Normie talked, and vaguely Carter heard him tell of Stoney's lament for the absence of a capacity for fun; vaguely he heard of Stoney's stories about the Village in the Twenties. Vaguely he saw his friend's thin, tired face go into a smile.

"Stoney's Twenties and Merwin's Thirties!" Normie was trying hard to cheer him. "Now all we need is someone who remembers the Forties, and we'll know from Onesies to Forties." He looked nervously about, found some kids hovering near by. "Hey, boy, you remember anything about the Forties?"

"You wanna fat lip?" one small boy asked, and six larger ones gathered around, shifting, squirming, looking insulted and hostile.

"Come on." Carter took Normie away to the street and a barroom on Eighth, talking himself up to a frenzy, as they drank, about years and stupor, narcotized ears and shock and evil men ready to sacrifice the world and finally, after many, many drinks, about Diane and what she might look like. "All bones and black circles. 'At'sa least of it. She's kicked, but'll be on a hook again . . . like Louella in her tower . . . or somethin. . . ." A blurred rattle and a belch.

"Carter, you know you're scaring me? You're babbling; I don't know what you're talking about." Normie pulled Carter, unprotesting, from the booth and out into air again, took him along MacDougal back toward the park.

Lights of the tavern still spun in Carter's head, faces, caroming notes of the juke box back on Eighth, all losing their separate edges of identity, all squeezing into one nameless dimension with his thoughts. "Can't last another month without a throw-off deal from pig 'cause Wengel 'buses the blind," while Normie held his arm, teetering himself. "Could work for Farrell's meat to that all right all right." In the park he whipped his arm away from Normie and swayed with trees that swayed in arc light.

"Hold on, kid. You wanna go home or stay here? What's up?" They were in the middle of the forum and Carter was swinging his head around.

"Jus drop me on a bench and you can beat it home." He went quickly to the side and fell back on a bench, looked up and saw Normie bearing down on him, heard the faraway scratch of crickets, and felt all at once resentful, felt he'd been trying to reach Normie and failed. "Go on home," he blurted when Normie sat down. "Go on, go on'n . . . repent, for the time is at hand. Hell with it all," waving a clumsy hand. "Letcha chil'ren clean up after you."

"I'm afraid leave you here. Straighten up."

He straightened up. "Go write your newspaper," speaking carefully now, pulling his chin back against a biliousness in his throat. "Tell 'em God'll save 'em," feeling himself turn all his bitterness on his friend, but unable to stop. "Teacha suckers to pray, before they tear up the paper. . . . Build institutions f'blind'n Wengel's money."

"Hey, Carter, I don't hear you laughing. Liddle smile would at least show me how——"

"Not smiling worth a damn." He said it slowly and deliberately. "Teash Diane to pray, teach 'er about . . . soul . . . what's good of anything?"

He could feel Normie's eyes on his neck as he darted away, and he made himself care nothing for any eyes at all down the eastward walk to aloneness.

He found a bench just short of an arc light and sat there fighting thought, for thinking had become painful and he was too hot with whisky to endure his own consciousness. He whistled something that came out flat, so he stopped and sat there dry-mouthed, goofing at the lights he saw through a wall of trees, sinking back into the humming alcohol fog . . . and it was heavenly all at once. Hiding there

in darkness, free of any debt to relative, acquaintance or friend. He
was anonymous beyond the arc light of living. In warm springtime
and shadowcolored breezes he could watch the lighted arena where
a ring of benches pointed every eye toward a statue of the inventor
of steel. A noble head. But in darkness he owed no esteem to statues
or the flesh they represented, or to anything at all any more. Carter
had finally escaped himself, free of the worst jailer he'd ever known;
he leaned back, reading the sky. While people about whom he
didn't care idled by, caring neither for him nor for one another. Carter really didn't care.

Stars were pale in a sky bleached violet by city lights, pale pin
lights marking the centuries over man's domain of nonsense. All
history lay still under pale, ridiculous dust. Till Diane's fire-black
eyes were searching down at him. "Carter? Carter?" A tiny, fragile
voice in the darkness, and he swung around to where he could know
what was real and what was dreamed. He stood and brought her
about to face the arc light. "Baby," feeling warm shoulders through
the white-rayon sleeves, then wrapping her tight in his arms so that
neither of them could say a word.

When he released her, she said without smiling, "I've been circling around and around. You were hiding from me? Dincher told me
to go by the fountain."

"Not from you, little girl, not from you. I just learned how to hide,
and I couldn't resist it." In shadows her face was still the pretty face
of a girl, and no tension showed in her voice; he scooped her up in
his arms, carried her, weightless as a breeze, perfumed like high winter skies, up the side lane and its shadows, while strangers sighed,
cheered, and complained at the sight of them. Only through shadowed streets to hide from any sight of sunken eyes or wasted cheeks,
while she breathed against his neck.

"You glad to see me, Carter? If you are, you ought to say it."

He didn't have to say anything with her in his arms. For they
were only beginning to hide, with no debts to anyone on earth, and
only careless strangers to remark on their manner of travel.

"I only smoke a little pod," she said against his cheek. "That's all.
I kicked Horse good, Carter, I swear. There's no harm in just a little
pod," rearing back to see his profile bucking with the strain of his
lumbering gait across the Avenue of the Americas. "There's no harm
in a little pod."

"I know, babe, I know. There's no harm in anything at all." He spoke out of the moaning dizziness of his head, waiting for the cars of tourists to pass after rubbernecking them up and down, walking with the voices of strangers demanding that he set her down, into the undemanding shadows of Waverly, to its northward arm, and around into Christopher's straight line to home.

Letters flown over many horizons, over the long arc of earth from Joe, came like an exchange of dreams to Carter. Joe, nudged only gently and occasionally by Hensley, remained otherwise free to bound carelessly about with a fiery redheaded daughter of a planter. Carter, and he had no reason to keep it from Joe, had grown numb to anything deeper than visible motion: he lived with Diane while waiting for his wife to pass beyond visibility; they were content in a relationship of such untroubled affection that each was free to express unsatisfied emotions in other directions. Louella had replaced artifice with a better established religion that somehow absorbed her guilt, leaving her free of grimness in her loves. . . . Lizzie, though her features crumbled more as each day passed, still repaid any attention with an unpossessiveness Carter had rarely seen matched. The Village was in love again, as Stoney claimed it had been before the war. Stoney, Carter reported, was well on his way back to beardhood, and back toward a misanthropy all but vitiated by his ill-fated romance with Vivienne. Now the last pretenses were gone and Stoney was a talker, never more a painter, who lived in a small room, sat at tables everywhere from the Riviera to the Cosmopole, with doom to presage for anyone who'd listen. But youth was no time for calculation, Carter told Joe he'd learned, and Joe laughed in agreement over each note he sent, asking about Diane as politely as one might in soundless ink. Carter told him Diane was in good health and content in the kind of love they shared. He didn't ever say they shared many fogs together over marijuana and wine, nor that some indestructible corner in his brain still marveled at how normal one could feel in an aimlessness that an old self would have called depravity.

"It's geographical," he would tell Diane as they lay naked on the bed while charitable breezes lent them comfort. "In Roanton it would all be immoral; in some Greek civilization it was moral; in the Village it's amoral," pulling his consciousness away from that death-

less corner of his brain that insisted this was a Greek civilization on
the decline.

She'd shrug her little tan shoulders and say, "Leave yourself
alone," then sip on the stick of hemp before passing it back to him.

Each evening when he had no hospital to go to, he'd roam the
park alone while Diane was off with Dincher. Till Lizzie or Louella
or some transient darling with a bohemian urge appealed to some
urgeless leaning in him. Sometimes he'd even sit with Stoney or some
other talker till Dincher delivered the girl before reporting home to
his parole officer. "Take care of 'er," the boy would charge him in a
voice of confidence and trust, and Carter would reassure him with an
ambiguous smile over which he felt no shame.

Even Merwin Fingerhut was aware of a change, though daylight
somehow demanded its measure of propriety and Carter never
smoked Tea with the man. "You're growing up fast," Merwin said
one afternoon in the heat of an inventory. "Two months ago you'd
let Wengel have the kit for peanuts, just to keep him friendly. And
next breath you'd curse him for being cruel to the blind guys and the
Spaniard ones. You used to be crazy with kindness."

Carter nodded. "We're finished in two weeks; you know that? I
need money for the hospital and for the big party at the end," and
saw Merwin turn away. He'd shocked Merwin as he had Normie
with an abrupt statement about Edna's imminent death, yet he felt
neither crude nor indelicate: there was no value at all to death—in
reality there was none—and he couldn't honor sentimentality enough
to lead up to it gently. "What are you planning to do, Merwin? You
won't have crackerjack money when we fold."

"I'll find some little business." Merwin piled cartons in a corner.
"I think about it all the time: maybe a lox-and-cream-cheese route.
I deliver sandwiches Sunday morning; the citizens don't have to get
out of bed."

Carter flopped into the swivel chair at the desk. "Why don't you
work with Farrell? He'll send you to school for a couple of months
and make a real union man out of you, then send you out
organizing."

"Not me. My fingers would fall off if I went to school. I got no
patience. You're the one he wants, Carter. Why don't you?"

"Lost the spirit. Unions are like private little armies all operating alone. That's not what I want. I'd get in probably if there was one big union that had every working guy voting in it."

"Go on and do it for them. Get in and work it out that way."

Carter looked around to see if Merwin were joshing him, but that chubby face wore nothing but the day's heat in its creases. "They tried it before . . . better men than I, and it never came off," yet had to think of a remark of Hensley's Joe had quoted in his first letter: *There are no heroes of the people anywhere but in history books any more,* then relegated it to a coffin in his mind and drove a dooming stake: Carter was no longer a victim submissive to vampire images or guilts. He had finally decided to leave calculation to the old.

Old Farrell had no attraction for him. Carter would listen to the man's devices, feeling embarrassed only that they showed past the sincerity of purpose that used them for articulation. "We need tough people," the man would say flatteringly. "We need young blood in the labor movement," and Carter couldn't help feeling that the schoolboy hadn't grown old enough.

"Labor's dying, Mr. Farrell . . ." *along with everything positive in society.* "You can't get anything done with labor split up the way it is. Of course you need young blood, but they're busy. . . ." *Forgetting, forgetting everything in any way they can,* and wished it were night so that he could smoke some jive and have his brain slip down to his throat and grow gummy.

"We need young blood, believe me," the man repeated with a helplessness distant and old.

And old Wengel too could calculate his head off: once Carter made his terms, he stayed adamant. "It's a crook's price." Wengel, hunched over his oversize cigar, made sure that he sounded hurt. "It's not like you, Carter. I been a father to you three years, maybe four. Where would you be if I dint kick in with bulk lots, to say nothing of all the processing?"

"Same place you'd be if every jobber didn't support you after the advertising fraud. In the gutter. Broke. And I'm broke now; you never needed me enough to see that I flourished." He could laugh at the fat, white, calculating face. "Look, Wengel, by rights you should dump your surplus film in the river, but it's okay with me——"

"In the river! I got ten million feet I ain't allowed to advertise even no more. Lucky I got a jobber here and there to push some rolls."

"Not enough to keep me in business. That's no worry of yours, is it?"

The man grinned and came around his desk to lay a fatherly palm on Carter's shoulder. "We got to take care of ourself, it's true. But not with crook prices, Webb, not with crook prices." He looked insane and sounded more so, but Carter was no longer surprised. It was the sort of thing that had made him reluctantly concede Stoney was right: *We live in a lunatic asylum!*

"Don't fool yourself," Wengel wheezed. "That fraud swindle they pull on me took a big bite on me too, don't fool yourself. You got me on a hook, I'm surprised at you."

"You've *been* on a hook, Wengel." Carter rose. "I'll break up the formula before I give it away at your price. Save your breath and write out a check for five grand out of your petty cash before I boost it." He watched the round man hurry back to his big spot at the desk.

"Listen, Carter, it be a year before I see that kind of money come back on surplus crap. You forcing me to do dirty like you. I don't like it that way, to do dirty, but if you force me . . ."

Carter leaned over, hands on the cool glass, to get a closer look at those steady sanctimonious eyes gleaming behind spectacles. It was remarkable: the man seemed to believe every word he'd said. "There's no formula written down, Wengel. If my place is broken into, I'll have you in the slammer like that," snapping his fingers. "Like that, Wengel, if you take one jug out of the whole processing kit, one jug."

"I don't have to steal. You'll see."

Carter left, wondering about Merwin, but assuring himself that Merwin could be trusted. Back in the shop he said nothing about it while they packaged some near-to-last batch of developed film rolls, and they gagged around till the lowered sun threw shadows of other buildings on them. Carter saw in the man's flesh-buried eyes an old devotion that demanded trust despite the one blind spot marijuana put in his character. A Viper had certain impulses, but Merwin could have sold the processing formula long ago, had he wanted to, and Carter felt secure enough when they parted for the day.

Yet the riddle of trust stayed with him and exploded in his brain when he reached Vivienne's for their Tuesday conference on Diane. He listened to his own easy lying as if some stranger were the culprit; his very power to keep from blushing was painful to that corner of his mind that watched forever. "I saw her Sunday evening," he said over a steaming cup of tea. "She said something about going to work, that you were getting her a job."

Vivienne, girlish in bangs, spoke in a voice still more juvenile. "She was supposed to appear Monday morning, but she never did. Where does she stay, Carter? I'm not prying, not prying, but I think I have the right——"

"Well, I don't ask her." He was ashamed that he was able to meet her pale, heavy-lidded gaze: "Maybe you have the right, but I can't help you."

"Why don't you ask her? She'd tell you anything. You're a father to her, Carter, she'd let you know in a minute. You should ask, you should. Psychologically, she wants you to. They want to feel their parents are concerned. I read it, Carter. I really——"

"I'm not her damn father!" He stood abruptly and walked to the window, then quickly back again to the brocaded gold chair. "Besides, what good would it do to know? We'd only upset her again—she's looking well, isn't she? No more circles under her circles."

Now Vivienne got up to pace. "Carter, it's difficult. I'm trying to exercise the most rational approach." She sounded like a falsetto Stoney as she glided flat-heeled over the rug. "I can't just allow her to sleep with——"

"You can't stop any of that. You have no right. Nobody has." He felt real justice in that: he himself had never kept her even monogamous, never protested when she spoke of Dincher's endurance.

Vivienne took her place on the couch, adjusting the blue-satin sleeve of her blouse. "It's ugly, ugly. I know it's futile to speak of it to you, Carter, with your background. What on earth do you expect to become of her? What do you expect, Carter?"

It was a good question, and he could see the woman's real need of an answer. "I hate to say the same thing over and over, Vivienne, but I'm afraid it's too late for that kind of question. I don't expect; I only hope."

"Well, what do you *hope*? Whatever can come of that kind of life?"

"I hope she gets married and bears children. How's that for an original idea?" But he saw no child of his in the family his imagination had arranged. He couldn't name his true feeling for Diane;

there was little these days he could identify with any real certainty. Not even Merwin's character, he brooded, continuing to watch himself lie. "Next time I see her I'll have a real serious talk, Vivienne. I'll try to have her go to work and everything."

"Good. Make her stay here more than one night or so a week. Make her understand——"

"I'll see, I'll see. Would you care for dinner?" he asked involuntarily on his way to the door, breathing more easily when she complained of no appetite. She obviously had no more desire to spend time with him than he had to spend it with her. "I don't have much appetite either. I'll keep you posted, Vivienne," and he shuffled down the carpet to dark, musty stairs.

Outside, the evening still glinted with lazy sunlight; each store window stabbed silver beams at his eyes, quivering needles that lingered at his temples. The homegoing crowds had thinned, and he went to a Madison Avenue restaurant, more to beat the tail of the rush hour than to eat the salad he ordered.

The subway had taken him well into Queens before he realized that his mind had been occupied with idle speculations on Merwin's honor, stabbing blindly about for evidence that might predict the chubby man's actions. Merwin hated Wengel too much, if nothing else would prevent him from selling the chemical setup. Carter went out into the slow twilight air and boarded the bus, assuring himself that he had Wengel trapped, convincing himself as he rumbled down blue avenues that he had nothing to do but take Edna's beating that night. . . .

When through Edna's glass wall he saw Diane and Dincher in the doorway facing the porch, he knew how to smile with the false delight he'd hated in other faces down the years. "What are you kids doing here?" he asked, taking a cue from Diane: he had to trust that she'd warned Dincher not to let on that she was using Edna's home.

"Can't they visit their own sister?" Edna asked with the small hint of joviality her debility allowed, and they all joined her on the porch.

Carter was careful to watch Diane only in flicking glances, just as he remembered never to touch her in Dincher's presence on Sunday afternoons in his own bedroom when he'd return from Edna to find them bathing after love-making. Though Dincher's mind reasoned a filial relationship between the in-laws, there was evidence of a suspicion now and then. Like the rest of them, he was in a kind of trap that Diane alone didn't seem to mind. Now she was vibrant, chattering with a nervousness that couldn't be suspect in these circumstances

Edna's eyes shot about from face to face. Her suspicion had grown as her body withered and crumbled, until adultery was only a minor part of the hot kaleidoscope of her mind: her Best-laid Plan for vengeance shrieked always for attention. For she had grown weaker and weaker. "Sunday, Carter, Sunday." She smiled with a burlesque of smoldering love. "Don't fail to come on Sunday. Everybody come on Sunday; it's a special day, a special, special one," and she wheeled to the balustrade to check her remaining strength. "Carter, little Diane and little Dincher, they're going to be married soon. Isn't it wonderful, Carter?" She was crying now.

Carter started to look at Diane; it was Dincher's shifty glance that forced him to look away. Still, he'd caught some attempt at reassurance in those black glittering eyes, and with it a tenuous triumph that was totally alien to her. They were four people alone on a terrace with Death hovering by; Carter felt dirty inside.

"We're cutting out, honey," Diane told Edna. "Give you a chance to be alone with Carter," and she squeezed his arm in passing.

Dincher grinned toothily in the doorway, winked with exaggerated swagger at Edna and nodded with a clumsy sort of formality to Carter as he backed away with the little sleek-haired girl in large copper earrings. She said, "I don't know if we can make it Sunday, Edna, but we'll try."

"Oh, please, please." Edna's face worked frantically. "Sunday is special. Bring Mama; make sure Mama comes too. We'll have a party Sunday."

They were alone under a single light. Carter held his wife's bony hand and thought idly of Merwin Fingerhut and money for a funeral. Thought of his own dirty air and focused his mind on Normie Goldsmith and Rusty and Penny and Toby and the red-stone house on Grapevine Lane; he had to call Normie and apologize for that night in Washington Square Park, for not getting in touch with him since.

"Don't miss Sunday, Daddy. Not Sunday," she whispered hoarsely.

"I don't miss, do I, Ed?" He offered the best smile he could manage.

She pulled him close till he could smell the breath of graves. "Daddy, say you love me; say you love me no matter what."

"I love you no matter what," he said meaninglessly, and felt harsh silence follow like a thud.

"Even if . . . I'd like to take Dincher, Carter. You still love me?"

"I still love you, Edna."

"Even if I slept with Dincher?" and he saw the bead of an eye quiver, knew it was time to perform.

"Why must you think of things like that?" *As if you could do it, you crazy corpse.* "You know I don't want you to screw around," pulling her head to his shoulder as he leaned forward from the bench.

Then she was kissing him with lips made of cartilage, up and down his jaw, muttering endearments as he patted her back and searched desperately in his memory for the day promiscuity was initiated in his affair with Diane. Lending his mouth and its practiced answers to his wife meanwhile.

There'd been three nights or so of drifting in Village society after Dincher would leave for home. In Slinger's diner they'd sit over coffee, overlooked by gossips who knew them as in-laws, approached by all sorts of people hungry for a word. To drift along home, hungry for each other. For three nights or so, till Lukey the Swede slipped into their booth and asked many questions about Edna, which Carter answered while Diane looked only at the table top. Now, holding Edna's bones in his arms, he could name that night as the start, for Diane had fingered a poet in a corner booth and in the whorl of amber light and freedom-loving words had taken Carter's consent and the poet's hand away to Dincher's loft. Returning from work, he'd found her at home next night with complaints about a limber poet who took all night, and an abraded eyebrow, a puffed lip Dincher had delivered when he found them together in the morning. Dincher, a hand holder out of pure love before, made himself a lover out of vengeance, and Carter had freed himself for Lizzie, Louella and faceless transient darlings; the game was on. And now he held in his arms a blanketful of bones. "Edna, there's the chime; I have to go."

"Where are you going now, Daddy? Who are you going to?"

"Over to Normie's, Ed. Over to Normie and Rusty."

"Don't fail me on Sunday, Carter; make sure you come."

"I'll be here, Edna. You know I'll be here."

"It's important, so important," as he backed through into her glass-walled room. "It's so terribly important, Daddy," and threw him her last kiss. She wheeled herself to the balustrade and pulled herself standing. She trembled only a little as she looked into the black, rolling world, weeping only gently for black years gone to dust. No one had seen her heart; no one had ever bothered to look at the unending tears inside. But black years would teach them all. Carter would see the avenging God he'd scorned, and on God's Sabbath Mama would see the devil wearing her own face. For they were ignoble mortals, each powerless to feel the other, each greedy in his own intent, using ill the image of Himself God had lent them all.

Lizzie Linden's face collapsed forever the Saturday on which Village suicides began. They'd found Magoo's broken body flattened in the shape of a swastika on sun-splashed, blood-spattered dirt in the back yard of his rooming house on Cornelia Street, beside a young peach tree and some forgotten barrels of cinders. By nightfall Lizzie was a weeper with panicked yellow eyes and a freckled skin sucked into the shards of a skull cracked and shattered like brittle china. "He never sings oney about me," she wailed on a stoop outside the Riviera. "He don't sing about no lousy Horse man; he oney sings about me, about me." For she swore to the world that Magoo had been thrown from his room by a powerful madman frightened by a guilt that told him Magoo had given him away to police. While junkies like Lukey and pale Canada Dan assured her Buster had gone forever. Nobody pushed his wares any more; Horse had to be traveled for, hunted uptown. Yet she swore out of a face twice her age that Magoo never sang about anyone but her, and that Buster would kill them all.

Diane had to comfort Dincher on their way over to Carter in the diner. "You don't go packing rods, Dincher. You got another couple of weeks on parole, and they'll give you life if they catch you with a piece. Buster doesn't have the guts to show his face, let alone kill anybody. You know Lizzie's plain crazy. I don't want you to . . . You just stop trying to be like Bogart," angry more over his hardened face than over his hard-guy impulses.

"Like-he's crazy, he don' need guts to kill somebody when he's crazy like that," keeping his eyes on pavement and cracked stoops, on anything at all but her face, the way he averted those brooding little boy's eyes when he'd finished beating her one morning, the way he kept himself from looking at things he knew to exist, just to let himself love her without reason. "I'm hip you gonna likefall up to the loft now'n then, I'm hip, I'm hip. I keep the piece up there'n you can blast him yourself if he busts in."

"You changed the lock, didn't you? He can't get in, Dinch. We don't need any guns to get us in a hassel."

"I said *bust* in, din' I? You got a key yet, aincha? Gimme the key. Gimme it so I know you wit somebody alla time. Come on'n gimme the key."

She had to laugh as she handed it over. "No guns, Dinch?" and he nodded with humble reluctance. Rounding the corner of the Masters Hotel, she took his bare arm in both her hands as though something had warned her to control him. It was Carter she'd been worried about in her concern over guns. She realized it suddenly and starkly and took Dincher into a hallway, kissed him with a passion she could affect in the dark. Though she told Carter always that Dincher was her most satisfying lover, it was Carter himself who kept the boy clumsy: some suspicion hovering in Dincher's inarticulate brain made him reluctant to bed with her. He'd voiced it only in hesitant questions that she answered easily. "One bed, of course," she'd say, "but would you bother Edna if she had nowhere else to sleep but your bed?" Enough of a salve for a morality which made sex a function initiated by the male. Yet Dincher stayed clothed more often than not, trying to alter jazz in his horn to Be-bop out of a gnawing will to please her nonetheless. Now she squirmed against him in darkness while his arms kept her close and his lips searched hers in boyish hunger.

"Carter, he's okay," Dincher said as they went west on Waverly again. "He's a cool cat," as if in answer to somebody else's worrying.

Carter sat across from Latour the painter in a diner booth, listening to words of ceaseless vitality pouring from under that solid black mustache. The short squat man departed politely when Diane and Dincher appeared, and Carter sent him off with an inept warning to leave himself alone. "He's in a real hassel with Louella; even the noble have their pitfalls," and he told Diane and Dincher about an artist's frailties, because there was nothing to shield any more in the world. He laughed. "Nothing is sacred, and in it all there's a paradox Lukey would enjoy."

"You're popped out, Carter. What would Edna say?" pulling her eyes away from the stung glance he gave her. A thick-lidded glance heavy with jive and fleeting agitation.

"Edna would say!" He laughed halfheartedly. "Latour, who holds love sacred, can't stand the sacred cross of Catholicism. It seems to have given Louella dry loins for him, and it baffles——"

"Oh, I'm hip to that crap," Diane put in. "Anyone can find an excuse to keep guys off," and wondered why she'd implied any woman would want to, then shifted her glance from those rain-colored eyes that seemed to know her reasoning.

"I gotta cut out." Dincher heaved to his feet. "Like-you watch out; you take care of her. Okay, man?"

"I'll take care of her, Dinch," looking at the pointed face backed by gold earrings and a white-silk snood, afraid Dincher knew what he meant.

But if Dincher knew, he showed it to no one. He gave that formal kind of nod and swaggered away toward the Bronx, toward hostile parents and a stranger with authority to check up on him for another couple of weeks.

While Saturday night spilled over into the little yellow wagon and Slinger traded orders in anxious yaps with two anonymous men in white. All boroughs of the great city were represented, all classes, all attitudes and manners in one hum of a meaningless voice.

Carter reached for Diane's hand. "Why so glum, little girl? You still holding that grudge?"

"What grudge?" She remembered and smiled. "No, silly." She'd thrown shoes at him when he arrived late from Normie's that night, angry that he hadn't phoned—with two rings and a pause—to let her know that he was safe. "It isn't anything like that, Cart. I don't know what . . . I think I don't like to see you high. I think that's it, Carter."

"Why not? Can't you stand me relaxed, baby?"

"You're not relaxed. Jive doesn't relax you, Carter; it makes you jumpy. Let's get out and give the squares a booth. We can go to the park."

On the way past Waverly's high stoops Carter confessed that jive did make him jumpy. "But I don't mind being jumpy when I'm high; that's the kick. I don't mind it around here," he hastened to add. "I don't mind it with you, babe," recalling the stark sense of error he'd had when he arrived at Normie's high on half a joint he'd found in his pocket. He'd seen creases of anguish around his friend's eyes, fear in Rusty's glances, and only a strained tolerance in their hospitality. It had been a situation pockmarked with moments of unreality, and he'd hated himself for going there high. "It's a sensitizer," he told Diane. "That's all jive is to anyone, and I'm jumpy on the stuff."

"That's why I don't like you smoking it, Carter. It doesn't go with you," and he had to agree with a dark corner of his brain that told him nothing in the Village went well with him. She said, "What did Joe say in the letter you got this morning?" just to change the subject as they settled back on the first bench they found.

"He's going around with some girl friend of his sister's, and his sister's getting married in a couple of weeks. Her boy is ready to start a small newspaper and wants Joe to work with him."

"Is he going to get married too and stay down there?" She said it more quickly than she had meant to. "He should," she added. "He belongs down there. Carter, let's go home," grabbing his hand. "I'm jumpy myself. Did you hear about Magoo?"

"Yeah, I heard about him. I was with Lizzie this afternoon when Slinger spread the word. I took her home and put her to bed."

"Did you get in it yourself?"

He looked at her clumsy smile. "Know whom you sound like? Vivienne, your mother, keeper of the faith. You're getting a dirty mind."

She made a joke of it, pulling him to his feet and away, laughing past all the chattering faces. But jokes had to be better than that for his gummy chest to brighten out of shadow. "It's Saturday night, Diane; don't you want to ball around a little? It isn't even midnight."

"We'll ball around at home, Carter. That's another thing. What kind of Viper are you, drinking beer and whisky all the time? You might as well not smoke at all. You seem frantic, like you have to be popped out all the time. Like you don't want to know from nothing."

"I'm a citizen." He laughed. "I stay popped out because I don't own a television set and I can't stand movies and I can't read any more and I don't want to think of Edna and Wengel and Merwin Fingerhut."

"You don't have to worry about him. He promised, didn't he? He won't sell out to Wengel if he promised."

Carter ran her across the Avenue of the Americas before the Saturday-night traffic could overwhelm them. "Promised. Yeah, he swore he'd sooner visit Hitler than cross me for Wengel. But he's got a family, and he's like everybody else. . . ." *And people are hostile strangers with affinity only on their faces.* "Wengel still won't come across; that means something. I don't know whom to trust any more, Diane." He gave her an odd kind of look as he pulled her into Waverly's northbound turn.

"How about me?" She held him still in the shadows. "You still trust me, Carter?"

He looked directly at her. "Only with my life, not with yours." He went on before she could question what he had said. "Joe once told me you were tragedy on the hoof. That may or may not be, just like anything else. . . ." He laughed at some secret joke, then pulled her close to kiss her. "I'm jumpy, babe, I really am. I still find myself thinking you're really going to marry Dincher, even though——"

"I told you, Carter. I told you it was to cool Edna off. Dincher's a kid; he's like a baby. You know who I want to marry, Daddio, you know."

He took her arms from his neck as some people strolled by. "It's a long way off, Diane. Don't think about it."

"Carter, you sure you want to?" She choked up at his silence, stumbled along beside him to Pacco's open door. "Carter, answer me," as they went through into the sawdust and the crowds talking in Saturday-night gibberish.

"Sure I want to," and he laughed at a secret joke again. "I want to everything and I want to nothing. Let's have some beer and drink a eulogy to Magoo and my perished brain." He shouldered a hole in the crowd, ordered beers and read the toasts lettered high on the wall. "A votre santé . . . Salud . . . Skoal . . . Lechayim—that's real Yiddish printing; Normie taught me how to read backward. You know, Normie can read backward and forward, and he knows a Chinese guy who can read up and down, and suckers like us——"

"Carter, shut up. You sound like one of these frantic college guys who have to be the life of the party."

"Diane, why do you sleep with Dincher? Why do you sneak in other guys? We're coming on toward each other; you'll soon be having——"

"Carter, what's the matter with you? Gee, it has nothing to do with you. I don't nag you about other women, do I?"

"No, but you come around at it from behind. You know you don't like it; you're just stuck with the convention. Nobody, *nobody* is as conforming as a nonconformist. Did I make that up or did——"

"Carter, I love you for you, not for myself. I love you for your kicks, not for mine. Don't you understand? I want you to love me that——"

"As devious a rationalization—have I introduced you to Manowar? Manowar—" he gestured toward a picture behind the bar and read its inscription, *"four feet off the ground,* meet Dianowar, eight feet off the ground. Larry, give us two shots of the worst fire you're allowed to sell."

Diane caught a look at her face in the mirror, saw Carter take his drink and screw his face up to show wrinkles like Lukey's. Her face was a baby's next to his wide jaws. "Carter, you're a sick man; you know that? You're hooked worse than I was. Take it easy," as he swallowed the other drink and chased it with beer. "You don't want to be a corny lush like these squares, Cart," and pulled on his arm till he followed her into the air.

"I don't know, babe, I don't know. Let's get the hell home."

"Okay, Daddio," she said mildly.

Past Sheridan Square Saturday lay in the dead shadows of any other night. They went on in silence all the way home. She showered while he puttered around with old papers at the desk that held the phone in the long, slumbering hallway. When she was done she found him in bed, eyes closed under the dark-orange light on the night table. "Carter, you asleep, Carter?" She kissed him softly.

"Yeah, I'm gone," he muttered, and she pulled away from the stale odor of whisky about him. "I'll see you in the morning, babe."

"Carter . . . we'll be happy, you'll see. When all the hassels are over, we'll be happy."

"Is that when you'll want to get Johnny again, Diane? When all the hassels are over? Unless some new ones come up?"

"Carter, wake up. Wake up, Cart. Are you saying—Carter, say what you mean. You think I'm avoiding Johnny? What can I do till I'm married? You want me to marry Dincher?"

"I don't know what I want. I told you to see a lawyer; I told you just to grab a lawyer and tell him the whole story. I don't believe anything that woman told you. You don't have to be married or anything at all if you prove you didn't know what you signed."

"Why don't *you* get a lawyer? You know more about those things than I do. Gee, you're older than me, Carter."

He turned toward her to smile at that, but the smile never reached his face. "You know why I don't see a lawyer? For the same reason you don't. I'm not that deeply concerned," and shut his eyes when he saw her wince.

She fell against him. "Carter, you talk so—not like Carter. I don't . . . Carter, I'm just coming out of the Horse, I still am, Cart. I'm like a kid learning how to walk. Be patient, Cart. Like you used to tell me. Be patient and you'll see, you'll see. We'll be happy, Cart."

He was on a revolving circle behind closed eyes, with his ear coming around and around to repeated words that formed old designs with dull old colors. He reached for her and pulled her close so that he could feel nothing but the heat of their nakedness, and let himself sink that way into the draw of sleep. The long, beautiful cloak of cloying darkness.

Diane clicked the light out and let tears she'd recently found fall on both their cheeks. "Don't disappear on me, Carter," she whispered in pale filtered light from the street. "Don't become someone else, Daddio," although she knew she'd had a part in any alteration in him. "Don't fade away from your baby, Carter Webb." He inhabited an alien space; he walked on ice with bleeding feet; yet she prayed that he'd never leave her alone with angry strangers. For she couldn't make it alone; she'd wind up in her mother's tower or back on the dead man's hook. "Don't fade away," she murmured over and over, and dreamed of an Indian with a panther's glistening legs who wouldn't let her ride his back, who let her weep and even wept himself, but wouldn't let her ride.

"I don't want to ride," she told an empty Sunday room, then screamed: "Carter! Carter!" and bounded so fast into the broken squares of sunlight on the rug that she fell dizzily to her knees. There

she wept in a crouched position till Carter stomped over to pull her
up.

"What is it, baby? What's wrong?" he demanded as she pressed
close to him. "What happened, a bad dream?"

"Yeah." She still wept. "Yeah, Carter, that's what it was," and let
him ease her down. After a little she pulled him over on her, kissing
and biting him till he took her, and they were laughing like they
always did, then laughing again over cigarettes.

"I'll take you to a museum when I get back from the hospital," he
told her as he dressed. "Then I'll——" and he stopped when he saw
her look at her hands.

"Dincher," she muttered, lying on her side. "He'll be here when
you get back, Carter."

"Oh . . . yeah. To finish you off. I'll take you both to a museum."

"No, that's not it. Carter—" she came up to stand close—"Dincher
doesn't . . . he can't up here. He feels . . . You know, he feels
strange, he doesn't feel right up here. He never feels right, Carter."

"Okay, babe, it's nothing, it's nothing. Come on, let's eat."

Eating was funereal. They spoke in little bursts that were related
to nothing that mattered to either. She stayed close as he went from
room to room, finishing with his clothes, changing papers from last
night's pockets. They traded thin smiles as she adjusted his black tie
and gray gabardine lapels; they kissed at the door like people married
too long.

The lazy spring Sunday drifted under his feet down to Sheridan
Square, where the heat told him that summer was on hand, and at
once he was repelled by an image of the Cosmopole festering with
people he didn't want to see. He hopped down the iron stairs of the
I.R.T. and took the rattling old train to Times Square, where he
climbed out into deserted streets and walked east to the Independent, pulling his hat low against the sun. Then down again into dank
shadows. The train roared mercilessly, and the few faces that shared
the monotony seemed caricatures of faces that grinned and grimaced
from the advertising posters girdling the ceiling, irritating faces he'd
traveled with so often on this repetitive trip. "Is this trip necesses-
sary?" he muttered in time with clattering wheels, "necessessesses-
sary, nessery, necessessassess," over and over again, the trip, the
waving to a speck on the terrace, the patting of useless bones, meaningless assurances, dead, dust-covered guilt, wasted hours, over and

over and over again and again. His temples throbbed in rhythm with wheels, to the heat of the unseen sun that beat through concrete. He found a joint of hemp in his watch pocket, couldn't recall putting it there, and immediately tore it to little shreds and specks that fluttered around his shoes. He didn't want to be sensitized to Edna's sunken features and bony voice and agonized beady eyes. He didn't dare to magnify the guilt he felt when he looked at her.

"Carter Webberoony," he asked himself aloud, "where are *you* going? What are you doing in this jackpot?"

A portly man across the way promptly left his seat for a section of the train more populated. "Fool!" Carter called, and the portly man pulled open a door, made his way into the next car. "Fool! Shall each wronged and restless spirit dare taint such wine with the salt poison of his own despair? I ask you," while five men and two women testified by unruffled calm that he didn't exist at all. "That's poetry," he informed them all, "and this is the wine I vex with sighs, this is thy simple solitude," spreading an arm to indicate the trembling drab-green car roaring through underground depths. He sat quiet and unembarrassed then until the train stopped at Jamaica, and, though it would go no farther, nobody made a move with leg or eye till he was at the door, saying over his shoulder, "Such a nice-dressed man."

Reflected suns on windshields parked in the hospital yard were treacherous fires in his eyes; he started to wave his hand before he looked up and, looking up, saw Edna in her royal-blue robe waving him on. The little speck that grew taller as he approached, taller and taller as he waved, taller, too much taller as he neared the broad steps of the building. He wasn't moving that fast. She grew higher rather than larger as he approached to where he could see her bony smile. The sun was at his back, fingering his neck. Edna was standing higher still; he could see her tremble as a feeble leg came over the balustrade. His arm was still up and waving and he waved her back, brought his other arm up to help. "*Edna!*" He'd begun to trot. "*Edna, get back!*" Heard his own voice crash and crack "EDNAAaaaa" and go into a slowness

as everything slowed down and she spread her royal-blue arms poor lady smiling.

Slowed—he could count her teeth trace her bony face rope hair and finally into the sun snagged robe on trough a rip and down—"Back,

back!" his voice his hands pushing toward poor floating lady begging her back swearing he never hated her for more than hatred back poor back again. A rush of salt sea water engulfed diluting just in time a knowledge of blood's dread thickness a memory of it and he was submerged and amazed as he sat back legs sapped of strength down in a sun-splashed ocean roaring in his ears. Cool. And amazed to see legs bouncing in his own gabardine, his feet so far away in perfect perforated-leather toes, embarrassed that they were there before him pointing at the pock-marked sun. Underwater sounds a thud a thwack or *splash* the sputter and scrape of feet a searing knowledge of *end* and many memories and many many feet in white. The sea persisted, at least its rushing its cold. They lifted him those cheeks and mouths of teeth he told them things as they directed him in dizzy slow hey cheek hey starch official ficial something in slow oh sun and green stone steps by elbows and indifferent sounds down gray checkerboard halls. There was one instant of ether, one penitent shrieker crowded in by starchy white and anxious arms wanton teeth all backed away at his certain sounds, certain. Disclosed contrite beauty still savable. Whimpering. In sea to stroke. To stroke. Then. Promise more daughters. For salvation. Whimper whisper retrospective sighs. To vex the salt sea tears, the rush departing and the cool ghost of mobile waters, dank sunshine to comfort Vivienne. To tell her nobody was to blame at all. To stand above her in the chief nurse's room and say again and again as she wept that there wasn't any blame. Any use.

"Don't torture yourself, Vivienne," he said with a hand on her smooth satin shoulder, while some last remaining little pool sucked at his brain.

"It's good you're here, Carter; it's good, Carter," words shattered as she stifled her wails. "It's not your fault, no, it's mine, it's mine," with a handkerchief up to her face, while Carter fought the pool in his head to find out how he'd been left alone to care for the mother. Of the deceased. The dead. Really Edna? Really deadedna?

There he was, coming up the walk. She waved, smiling, and climbed. "She was—Vivienne, I should have told you before. Edna was . . . she was dying, Vivienne, she was going anyway. A fatal . . ." Edna? She'd been waving——

"But she'll never get to—oh, Carter!" A shriek that doubled her over on the desk, where her shoulders bucked uncontrollably. "Now

she . . . won't . . . There's no salvation. . . . Oh, what have
I . . . done? What have——"

"Vivienne, don't do that; don't hurt yourself any more." He pulled
her carefully up and took her face in his hand, looked at the deep
creases in wet translucent skin. "We all feel we're part of it. Don't
hurt yourself."

Mrs. Lattimer stood feebly, leaned on him. "Take me away, Carter;
take me home. Don't let them see me. I'm . . . glad you sent them
all out; I'm glad you're strong. Oh . . . forgive me, Carter . . .
what have I done? Oh Lord . . . Lord, forgive me, forgive me . . .
what have I . . . Edna, Edna, my ba-a-a-aby," and he muffled her
wail against his chest.

He settled her back in the black-leather chair, told her to wait until
he got a cab, and went with more a hop than a walk to the hallway,
caught a look at himself in a glass partition, and finally removed his
hat. A clump of faces in starchy white awaited him at the hallway's
checkerboard end, faces he half-recognized as cheeks and teeth floating about in the sea outside, braided-straw hair and breasts, glasses
and mustaches. "Get me a cab, please, I have to take——" then turned
abruptly and went stiff-backed down the hall to the room where
Vivienne wept. Too late for her tears, too late for her beauty, too
late for all the words that poured from tardy remorse.

"She always made me wait inside," the woman wept. "Always made
me wait while she went out to wave. Carter, what have I done?"

They knocked on the door and he didn't have to answer. They led
the way, those cheeks and mouths and heads of hair, to the sun
down stone stairs to a cab drawn up in front. He helped her to the
seat and turned to a mustache he must have known. "I'll return
tomorrow and arrange . . . You tell them, you say it . . . tomorrow," and never heard or saw acknowledgment, only saw the great
white building fall back with its gleaming windows, only heard the
despairing whine of the engine as they rumbled through the gate.

Vivienne whimpered quietly in her corner while Carter sat stiffly
in his, fighting the pool grown to mud in his head. "Fifty-fourth and
Fifth," he leaned forward to say, and sat back swiftly when the cabbie
said he'd been told.

"What have I done?" Vivienne murmured, and Carter didn't
bother to say. "What have I done to us all?" while Carter began to
look for himself down muddy avenues of his brain. "Good Lord, good

Lord," she wailed. "Dear Holy Father—" now without tears—
"what have I done, what have I done?" Level in an unaltered voice,
looking straight ahead like a child come suddenly awake. "Where did
I go? Where did I take my children?" and the tears burst forth again.
"Carter!" She looked at him, wiping, choking back all lament. "Carter, my goodness, my goodness, I loved him so, I loved him so!"

Now Carter reached for her shoulders. "Listen, Vivienne, try to
be——"

"Carter! I loved him, I did, and I . . ." with her face screwed up
to keep tears inside. "Oh, where have I been?" looking wildly through
the window as though some answer lay outside in shrub-fronted lawns
hurtling by. Carter shook her gently till she laid her distant pale eyes
on him again. "Listen to me, let me say it now, Carter, let me say it.
Clyde, I loved him, and I didn't know what it meant. I didn't know,
Carter, I didn't know how to show it. Carter, let me say it. He
was . . . no, he wasn't excellent, I won't say he was, not excellent.
I wanted him to be, I oppressed him, Carter, but I loved him so. I
challenged him, Carter, forever I challenged him. Oh, what have I
done? I plagued him with . . . yes, with other men, Carter—not . . .
not immorally, not in any such way, but he never trusted . . . he
didn't believe . . . He should have known, Carter, I never did, even
with him, I never . . . carnal pleasure never . . ."

"You don't have to talk about those things, Vivienne," wishing
she wouldn't talk at all. "If they embarrass you . . . Vivienne, it's
none of my——"

"Don't you under*stand? I *loved* him, Carter," leaning in to shake
him by the forearm. He did pity her—for an ugliness that lay like a
new skin over that fine, delicate face. "I want to tell you, I want to,
Carter. I see you now, I know you—Carter, let me say it," while her
eyes shifted nervously about. "He worked hard. He loved law and
worked like three men at it. Yes. And I . . . Carter, I was young, so
young, I didn't realize what—— I flirted, Carter. Only that, only that.
I attracted many men, various sorts, it was only a game. Do you believe it, Carter? And I grew confused. I . . . It seemed . . . other
men loved me and I thought . . . sometimes I thought I loved other
men. But not, you understand, not . . . unless . . . until one,"
and she turned away as if his eyes had contradicted her. "One
man . . . I knew him before I married Clyde . . . kind, understanding man who needed me." Now she focused dreamily at a point im-

mediately before her, smiling like an insane child. "He loved me so much that . . . it never hurt Clyde, but . . . still, Clyde always thought, he never knew what . . . Oh, Carter!" and she doubled over in tears that shook her. "My baby, my baby, what have I done?"

Carter let her cry alone. He held to the strap and watched houses grow taller into sleeping factories, and searched for a grain of feeling in himself, for Edna, for Vivienne, for Diane. Diane's black eyes touched something mushy inside and he hated it. He had to be away, he had to be away.

The confessional was on again. Dry-eyed, hoarse, she grew bolder against the veils of time that were trying to color recollection with sanctity. "There were others. They needed me, or . . . that was how I felt. Edna, my poor little girl . . . she . . . that man, it was so easy to love . . . I never knew . . . Oohhh, what I did to Clyde, what I did to poor Clyde, I loved him so, I didn't . . . I never learned how to share. He never learned about me, Carter," almost whispering now. "I never let him see me through and through. He loved the children. You can't know how he loved them, Carter. You can't imagine how maddened he must have been to . . . run away. You can't imagine the pain he must have suffered."

Carter swallowed hard against nauseating pity. "Vivienne, stop beating yourself, will you? Every day is a problem, and you've stumbled over a few. So what? You're just letting your guilt choke you," and it bounced off the mirror in his mind like good advice. "We're a guilty race," he muttered. "You're not alone. Let yourself be."

Her silence brought him around; she wept mutely, huddled in a corner, a pathetic little ruin quivering in voguish embellishment: purple-satin top, black bottom, tight bun of her hair secure in a net that bound pearl earrings. "I'm a misfit on earth," she whispered dryly. "I've always been. A misfit, and I've made misfits of my girls. *Oh, Edna!*" she shrieked while trucks roared by on the Queensboro Bridge and girders flicked forward and back. "She's gone, gone. I've destroyed her. *Ednaaaa!* Diane, Diane! I want my baby, my baby." Her head reached her tidy knees and lay there.

"Listen, Vivienne—" Carter pulled her erect by a shoulder—"stop agitating yourself. We're all misfits for looking backward. It's all done; we've crucified each other; we're all to blame and none of us to blame. Wail for tomorrow, not last year. Be a big girl and live like one; there's so much time for it."

"Not for me, not for me. I don't belong on earth. I don't," skirting around his eyes with hers, quivering with remorse and the rattling of the cab. "There's nothing left for me any more. Diane hates me. I know it, Carter. You hate me yourself, you do."

"That's nonsense. Nobody hates you for just . . . Diane hates your possessiveness, not you. Leave her alone. She's maladjusted; give her a chance to find her own way." His mouth soured at the taste of words that meant nothing. "It's all ahead of you, Vivienne; nothing is behind you, nothing at all; nothing ever happened. You're a free woman. Let yourself live."

The cab had pulled around into Fifth Avenue's sleepy sunlight and stopped where people in pale clothes drifted slowly. He paid and helped the woman out, guided her by her thin young arm past small trees up the street. "Come up," she said at the door. "Come up and have some hot tea, Carter," pressing a hand to her temple.

"Thank you, Vivienne, but there are a lot of things, lots of things I really have to do." He knew she didn't want to be alone, saw it in the unguarded panic in her glances, but couldn't feel any duty at all to her. "I'll find Diane; I'll send her over."

"Yes. Please do, Carter, please do. Send her . . . and if you see Robert . . . please tell him I want him. Will you, Carter?"

He promised and left. Went quickly without a look back, down to the corner of Fifth, where he leaned on a granite wall and watched the people walking by, forever strange to one another. He took off his hat, then replaced it, then removed it again. He walked south a block, slowed down near the corner and stood there, staring down the sunlit funnel toward the Village unseen in the distance, while strangers spoke of strange things going past his ear. Diane would be rolling in his bed with Dincher; Stoney would be teaching nonsense to indifferent ears; Vivienne sat alone with regret and hot China tea. He turned back uptown and lumbered past Fifty-fourth toward the great park where Louella took good Latour to torture him with her bewilderment. He turned and went south again to another stop on Fifty-second, loosened his collar while Edna's face grew bolder in his mind. He went into a fit of coughing, leaning against a Fifth Avenue half-size tree, while people he could see through burning tears neglected him with their eyes. But they owed him no attention, he told himself with fierce impatience, and went off northward again, hating every maudlin pang he'd ever honored with meaning. Edna was dead!

Good for everybody concerned. Fine! Diane was a little girl he'd expected to be a woman for his pompous sake alone, just as her childish mother had demanded she be even more a child than she was. The thought of Central Park full of idlers unsettled him, and at Fifty-fifth he turned back south. Walking swiftly by big store windows, going south to tell Diane he was free, to see what she'd do with Dincher. But he stopped at Fifty-third, weak with indecision in his legs. He climbed the stone church steps and sat to ponder on Diane, like a man who'd been sleeping with his daughter. "Guilt, guilt!" he muttered, and started up again. Guilt. It had kept him pampering Diane no differently than it had kept him at Edna's side for long, wasted months. Nameless guilt that kept him entombed in the Village, bewailing his bewilderment by naming the world with it. Farrell had warned him, "Sure, people can't get along. Such is the case. But you can't just cry. You got to do something to help them work for each other. One guy picks one way; another guy picks another. No wishing, only working, believe me. This is my way and you're welcome to do a better job at it if you can." Carter's real guilt, he suddenly knew, was his stagnation.

He ran down the steps, the rubble of a ruined tower to God, across toward a barroom phone, with a rich distaste of everything on the Village hook: the hemp, the whisky, the idle romance, and all his aimless days. He found papers in a pocket, caught Wengel's number and dialed it, muttering, "Be home, pig, be home one time," and heard the scratch of that voice with a happiness he never thought he'd know over it. "Wengel, this is Webb. Listen, I'll take three grand. How's that? Is that okay? Talk up, because if it's no good——"

"What's the gimmick? Why all of a sudden? Must be a ketch somewhere."

"The gimmick is you take Merwin in to do the processing. That's the gimmick. Fair enough?" throbbing from his throat right up to the skull full of weeping Lattimers, dead, dying, and alive.

"Maybe I got Merwin, hah?" and the old man gave his snide chuckle.

Carter hung up with an angry rap, found another coin, and dialed Merwin's number. "Millie? Carter. Is Merwin around?"

"No, he's still playing ball, Carter. Maybe in an hour he'll be home. How's Edna, Carter? Feeling any——"

"She's dead, Millie. She died today. Tell Merwin to call me when the ball stops bouncing," and hung up before condolences could begin.

Automobile horns sounded around him as he hurried toward a bus stop, grating at him, somehow becoming the derisive voice of Edna yowling in his mind. He burned all over as though in a fever, but he swore as he crossed the street that nothing would keep him mired: not Merwin's sellout, nor any need for him on Diane's part. He was going to Buffalo to learn how to teach people to work for one another, rather than to stick knives in one another's livers.

"I got kids to feed, Carter." Merwin's strained whisper strained harder over the phone. "I never gave Wengel no kit, not for money I wouldn't. He's gotta work it the same way like before. There's less work, Carter; it's enough to hold one man going. You said you was through, Carter; otherwise I never tell Wengel okay. I never gave him no kit."

"Sorry I blew my top, Merwin. I'm upset . . . you know. You want to do one thing, though?"

"Anything you say. But lay down a little, Carter. You don't sound too good. Please, take care of it tomorrow, please, Carter."

"I'm all right. Look, call Wengel up and tell him you're leaving town with me. That's all. Don't let him give you any beef. Just say that. Tell him you just spoke to me and that I'm home packing. Okay, Merwin?"

"Oh, Carter, you're growing up." The mild voice allowed itself a chuckle. "I get it good. You let me know after. Meanwhile, lay down a little, Carter. Please, for Wengel's sake."

"Okay, Merwin, I'll call you. Yeah." His face burned; something hammered at his spine. Back in the living room Diane sat quietly with Dincher. The boy couldn't meet his eye, but Diane came forward and took his arm. "Carter, wouldn't you be better off lying down? I put up some coffee, but lie down till it's finished."

"Why does everybody want me to lie down? Dincher, would you like me to lie down? I have to arrange for the party. Anyone know a good mortician? Got to be a guy with a dust broom. . . . I'm sorry, I'm sorry," when he saw Diane wince.

"I take you where they got Muffo Smith," Dincher began, but stopped when Diane shook her head.

"Who's got Muffo Smith?" Carter asked conversationally. Then,

"Hey, what is this reticence? Don't treat me as though I'm in shock. Who's got Muffo Smith, Diane?"

She didn't say he looked worse than a man in shock; she only forced him into the club chair. "Muffo knocked himself off this morning. This is the season. Remember last spring? Jimmy Cole, Frenchie Davids. Last year it was gas; this year it's real violence. They jump, the first two, and Muffo does it like in the movies. He blows his brains out."

"Maybe he din' do it'n maybe Magoo——"

"Oh, Dincher, come on, leave us alone. Maybe Buster went out and got Edna too," and sat down next to the boy while Carter went to answer the phone. "Don't talk so much, Dinch. He was there; he was right there when she jumped. Gee, it's a wonder he didn't die. Dinch, go home after we have the coffee. I'll see you tomorrow and tell you about the funeral and everything. Carter and I have to go over to Mama's. I can't leave him alone; you see how his face looks? Gee, poor Carter."

"What about your own sister? Poor Carter, poor Carter."

"Stop squalling, for Christ sake. I got dressed, didn't I? Is that all you can think about?"

"Aah!" He shoved her away. "You mus walk aroun like that wit your ass out oweys up here."

"Dincher, baby." She pulled over to him and kissed him. "I just forgot, that's all. Come on, let's look at the coffee."

"You mus oweys wear that pajamas wit no bottom," following her to the kitchen. "Like-you don' care who sees you."

She said nothing as she poured coffee in the dusk-blue kitchen. Dincher had his troubles keeping cool with her. It made honesty impossible. . . . Even Carter had been getting grumpy, as if her relation to one intruded on the other, as if it really mattered at all . . . like Edna now with her hundred men behind her. It didn't mean anything now.

Carter clicked on the light, sat grinning at the table between her and Dincher, red in the face with some deathless excitement, twitching in those shoulders sloped under his shirt. "Where's that mortician, Dincher? Where they have Muffo Smith. Who's paying for it anyway?"

"His aunt," Diane said. "She came just in time to keep them from taking him to the morgue after the medical examiner . . . well, you know." She suddenly felt the air stir, as though something were warning her to be more sorrowful, to lament in some way for Edna.

"Aunt," Dincher mocked. "Some aunt. Muffo never had no aunt, he——"

"So what? She wants to be his aunt, let her. At least she's having him planted decently." Dincher seemed more disturbed than Carter himself with his deep, unchanging red face.

Carter said, "Where is this funeral parlor?" and the word struck for him the first reverberation of finality in all the day's stark meanings. It was really over—really, really done; he finished his coffee in one long pull to burn out the tenacious soot of Edna.

"It's down on Wes Broadway," the boy said. "Diane knows where."

"I know, Carter. I'll take you there. Gee, it's hot; isn't it hot in here?" wishing Carter would think so and throw cold water over that burnt face, over those parched emotions. But he was preoccupied and went out like a sleepwalker. "Dincher, you better cut out, baby. I'll take him down to the place and then over to Mama's. Maybe he wants to like talk himself out, maybe like he's ashamed; you dig? Because you're around; you dig?"

"You gonna like-make him feel okay; hah? You like that, to make guys feel good. Like you make Angie feel good too, hah?"

"What do you mean, Dinch?" First a whisper, then louder when she heard Carter shouting on the phone. "What's that supposed to mean, Dincher?"

"I'm hip what you was doin wit Ange while I was in the slammer, I'm hip. I din' believe it when Lizzie told me, but I dig now. I'm hip you're for all the cats. You just a lousy tramp. I'm hip," turning his eyes away when she frowned, but talking on, spilling out words crusted with long storage. "Lukey the Swede'n Harry Sticks, a lousy blackbelly'n——"

"Shut up! Shut up, Dinch. Don't take it out on Harry. He never even lifted a finger to me. What are you talking about? None of them . . . Maybe Angie . . . once when I was goofy. I didn't want Lizzie bugging him, so I showed him it was easy. He was becoming a pratt boy for her, he——" *Crack* across her face. Reflex carried her out of the chair and over to the sink, where she grabbed a milk bottle. "Dinch, I'll bust your skull." Then she quickly set the bottle down. "No, baby, don't made me mad."

"My own friend. That's what hurts, you lousy bitch," with a face redder than Carter's. "I din' wanna believe it. Inside my head I say no, it never happen, no, no. They all score you, alla them. Even him, your own sister's husban. I'm hip even him. I dug it in your face all since he's home. I keep quiet till he's home'n I can look for it'n I see it, I see it."

"Dincher, baby, it doesn't mean a thing," going toward him to teach him reality, to show him that it didn't reflect on him. But he flashed a small nickel-plated pistol, pointed it at her face. She saw his little mouth curl at an end and ran screaming: "Carter! Carter! He's got a *gun!*" into Carter's arms in the hallway before he could put down the phone.

The impact spun him around, and he knew by the fact that her body was pressed against his while Dincher was about that it was real: everything was real today; everything insane on earth had spun in a whirlpool this day to find a target in his brain. He eased her away and went out to Dincher, but the boy only waved an abrupt gesture of disgust on his way through the outside door. When he got back, the hallway was empty and he found Diane crying on the bed. "What's up now? This is a circus; this is a nightmare."

"I'm sorry, Cart," she sniffled, sitting up. "It's my fault—it's why he's popping Horse already. Dincher, you'd never expect . . . Dincher, he thinks I'm a tramp, Carter. He——"

"Wait a minute, Diane, wait a minute. I got this from Mama, the same damn stuff. Soap opera. Will Gwendolyn's philandering be misunderstood? Tune in tomorrow. Find out if Gwendolyn is a tramp or a trump, a slattern or a pattern of the new——"

"You too, Carter?" Her eyes dried quickly. "You think so, you, Carter?"

"Me? I don't think any more," laughing out of a crazy red face.

"You think I'm a tramp?"

"No, no." He sat down beside her. "There's no such thing. No tramps. Just frantic people, all of us. Just flips. What the hell, it doesn't matter."

"Carter, I thought you understood. I thought you didn't mind like other guys. Carter, you've been getting tense, and now it's all busting loose. You'll get cool again, Cart, you will." She reached her arms around him, but he moved away.

"I'm going away, Diane. To school. I fixed Wengel's ass good. I'm giving him the boots. Come on, I'll tell you about it on the way over to arrange for Edna's party," with a flushed smile as he knotted his necktie. "That's the place I want, a mortician who knows what to do for suicides. It's a special kind of party, you know, a quiet kind, no fireworks for suicides, because they've been dead for years and God isn't allowed to get them even if He wants them. . . ." On and on while she dressed hurriedly, afraid to interrupt for fear his face might explode at any instant. "You hear me tell Wengel? I told him right in his pig belly. Give him the boots, and Merwin is a happy little round man, he's been saying it all along: give it to them like they give it to others; give them the boots. Ten million feet, and he paid three cents a foot himself, three hundred grand right down the sewer without Webb's processing kit; you hear?" Out and down into a soft summer night, walking fast through familiar Christopher Street shadows in a salt mist from the Hudson behind them. "One thousand for me to cover the funeral and to hold me through the summer while I'm at school, and Merwin runs a whole department in the pig's big fat building; takes over the ten million feet, with three and a half cents a foot to Wengel—it's the boots, the boots—to cover distribution and overhead, with blind people rolling for Merwin the foreman, Puerto Ricans packing and shipping and processing. See? The pig makes his money back okay, but that's all, that's all. Leave it to Merwin, he's going to make a block party from the synagogue to Steeplechase and back to——"

"Carter—" she took his arm to lead him south across Sheridan Square toward Bleecker—"Carter, take it easy. You sound like Lukey the Swede," and had to laugh alone while Carter rambled on, red-faced, bug-eyed.

"And that's the way—give them the boots, without getting sentimental, without feeling guilty, without griping about things in the air. I'm going to school and learn unionism and save America for the creatures; I'll learn how to put the boots to pigs. I don't even have to hold out for that thousand when I see Wengel tomorrow. If that blocks it, I won't press for any loot at all. I'll have enough when I sell the furniture, and I can——"

"Carter, Carter, you're not really going away; are you, Cart?"

"I sure am. I sure am. Cutting out to go to school, that's me. Cutting out fast, get my fingers into something solid, and when I'm through in Buffalo . . ." An old vacuum crawled into her stomach like something long asleep. It grew cold as he spoke on and on from his hot, perspiring grin. Down dark Bleecker they were free of tourists, but ran into more on Sixth, lost them on side streets, picked them up on lighted avenues, but neither crowds nor shadows on ancient cracked sidewalks could hold Carter's tongue. He was an instrument of many passions brought into focus, so that little tentacles of feeling either fell into that single direction or were chopped off and abandoned among trash barrels and shadows of gone decades.

The cold vacuum was a terror in her stomach, and she had to bring him around. "Carter, Carter, we're free now. Don't run away from me now. Don't go away, Carter."

"You want to get married? No, you don't want to get married. You know it. Maybe later. I'll be gone only over the summer. It's nothing; it's nothing. Other things to do, baby, real things finally. We're free now and we can do real things instead of goofing and moaning."

"Carter, you're just frantic. After you cool off . . . Carter . . ."

"Yes? You want to settle down? You want to give Dincher up?"

"Oh, Carter. Do you really care for that? I need Dincher, I need him. There are things about him . . . And I need you, Cart, more than——"

"Glad you're not saying how he needs you. That's the line that gripes me. You can have him, and when I get back, maybe me too. You're not for marrying. What do you need it for? It's an institution for tired people, people with no more gut for goofing around any more. Not for you, pretty baby, and I'd be the same way if I could."

"But Johnny. I want Johnny and I have to be——"

"Look, babe." He stopped walking right at the corner of West Broadway. "Let me tell you something," taking her shoulders in hands that trembled. "You hold on to Dincher and you won't be wanting Johnny. And you can replace me with Stoney; he's over at Mama's and he'll make a sweet father once you set him up right. That's all. You haven't looked for a man your size yet," and pulled her along.

"Here, here's the place. Carter, here."

"This? It's dark; nobody's home." He tried the door, and it pulled open. "Come on, maybe they left a ghost in charge," and he disappeared inside, leaving her to follow or wait.

Reluctantly she went after him into a darkness that smelled of dead flowers, over a deep rug toward a crack of light in the rear. She went in behind Carter and saw Muffo Smith sitting on a chair, straight-faced, while a little man hammered a toupee onto his head with a long, thin nail. Her knees buckled and Carter whirled around to catch her, eased her into a soft chair while the little man put up a squall. "Why you sneak in like that? You scare the livin Jesus outta me," while Carter fell back laughing on a table.

"What're you doing to Muffo? Nailing—oh, Christ, it's a lunatic asylum, it really is. It's a nuthouse, a big, big funny bin. You mustn't desecrate the dead, mister. You can go to——"

"Listen, he can put a bullet in his mouth, I can put a little nail in. There's hardly any skull left to paste on a damn toupee. Better take the lady out. C'mere, lady," and he went through to put on a light in the parlor. "Bring her out, mister, come on."

She needed help and wanted to get out. Carter took her to a mohair bench and turned to the little man. "I have a job for you. No nails," and Diane shuddered, tried to blink out the image of Edna's skull full of nails. This was a weird Carter. *Old man, I know thee not. . . .*

"I'm just an embalmer." The little man went back to his shop with Carter behind him. "I take down the figures, that's all. I don't talk price, things like that, I just embalm."

"Okay, just embalm." She heard Carter's high, sharp accents. "Take down the figures and the address and the name and send out the party. The dead are dead; use all the damn nails you want on the dead," half laughing as Diane went through dead flowers again to the air. Walking fast to quiet the frozen crawling in her bowels. Sweating.

Massive towers walled the broad street in, and down the road a river of wild-eyed autos flowed. She escaped into a side street, running over shadows strewn like wasted bodies, away from wild-eyed autos and massive towers and a saint gone wild-eyed in a week. She looked into no doorway she passed, afraid that Edna would screech from any one of them like some stranger of a vindictive ghost ready to touch fire from hell to her hair. She ran all the way to Sullivan while everything in her body went soft and collapsed. Gasping, she ducked into Mama's old hallway, knowing it as Mama's abandoned home, comforting herself in ugly dust and cooking odors as dim as the light. Then out again and around, up to MacDougal, with her eye on the neon-splashed light of the Riviera, with nothing in her brain. The glaring light of the Riviera froze her up.

The faces making noise were strangers, fagues, and familiar rubbernecks in plaids of every gaudy kind. Diane squirmed past bodies, looking in every booth till she found Harry Sticks, big and beautiful black in the side door, just about to leave. "Harry! Harry, you see the Dinch? Has he been here?"

"Yeah, he took off with Angie and Lizzie. They took her home to stop her squalling. You know, she's hollering Muffo was scragged like Magoo. You know her story." One hand was busy with a paper napkin at his nose; with the other he drew her into the street. "I'm bound for a fix . . . before the rocks come on," wagging his head as he spoke, turning it slowly in that junky's uncertain roll. "You see Jasper, tell him——"

"I'm not staying, Sticks. I got the horrors. Like you want to take me along? Just to keep me cool, Sticks."

"Sure, Face. See now, you *will* smoke that evil weed," and pumped his heavy laugh into the night. "Little Face, that'll drive you frantic, that old buzz." He took her along to the middle of the block, up the old stoop on MacDougal where everyone from Jacquie Swan to F.X.J.C. Dorfrum, the poet with five good names, lived behind anonymous doors, everyone from junkies to artists and down the line through dishwashers and department-store clerks, all the representatives of guarded isolation, lived in religious privacy. They went up four flights and rapped on the door of Canada Danny Barber, who understood the knock as Harry's and welcomed them with his pale-faced nod. "I got your lance up here," Harry let Diane know, and he pulled from a drawer the hypo she'd taken from Buster. Brother Barber lay asleep on the single cot, and Danny patted his head on the way to a chair, where he took up his paper pad and sketched by a twenty-watt light from a lamp over his shoulder.

Sticks filled nearly the whole room; he moved with a careful knowledge of his power. "Go on and sit on that cot, Face. You won't wake up little Brother," and emptied a couple of caps into a spoon's bent cup, heated it with some water over the two-burner range. He neither spoke nor looked at anyone till he'd filled the setup and popped in a vein the size of a finger, where little knifelike scars rode white down the surface, nudging one another along.

"You got a little cap for me?" Diane asked, and everyone, including Brother Barber, looked her way.

"We running mighty low," Danny whispered, then went silent

as he watched her. She couldn't decide if he'd simply expended that night's quota of sound or if he'd been stopped by a recollection of ten caps or more in his hand as a farewell one night in the loft.

Harry Sticks remembered it well. "We got for her. I'll run uptown myself later on," blinking from his seat on the floor while the charge limbered him up to a steady purr. He danced erect and went into action at the stove. "For I'm an athlete on Horse. Man, you want to see me play ball today, you want to see. Can't play next Sunday or I don't score for any Horse. My good connection got his heart on the other team and he won't lay nothing on me if I don't promise not to play." Laughing and cooking all the while, pouring a fix into the setup.

She'd kicked it once before, and she could do it again. Like childbirth. Only women were successful at it. Brother was asleep and Danny was sketching dragons in his book while a dragon devoured the world outside where Edna's crazy ghost chased Carter laughing and talking till his face would explode good blood on the dirty streets. Lead lay about inside her now, gray insulation over mush.

"I want a blast, I want it quick," she whispered for no one to hear. "Give me something to work up a vein; I want it main line for one blast," and let Harry tie a necktie about her arm, watched him twist it till a vein showed blue. She applied the needle herself, jabbed quickly and gasped, then pumped the charge and drew it back with her blood, the way a child called Paddy once had. In and out a couple of times while Horse burned gently in her arm. She was scarcely out with the needle when the charge set in. Not Nothingly like a skin pop, not scattered like a snort. It was a quick, sleek, golden Horse, a steed of gold, and gold all about, molten gold oozing into every last organ, erasing lead, enriching mush to cool gold forever. Forever was a long way from shadows.

OVER DUST BETWEEN HOOK AND TOWER

Sky burst with blue and boomed with giant puffs of cloud. Sun bouncing rich deep yellow-gold off the growing puffs. Musical kids at their musical ball games were dwarfed by granite backdrops, supported by horizontal squares, counterpointed by trees and rolling baby carriages. Unclipped blades of grass looked in unison at nowhere.

Washington Square Arch, a monument to some forgotten victory, stood like a great stone terminus to the polished towers of the Avenue. Below it lay Little Italy, in sour colors of ancient, neglected brick and iron fences. On the rim of beveled stone that edged the circular pool in the Square, Diane sat with Harry Sticks, watching school-sized boys play one of the last ball games before the heat suffocating the city reached high into office buildings and reminded the city fathers to fill the pool for perspiring carriage-sized kids. They sat baking in summer's first rancid breath, on blue stone they barely felt, in a drone of small voices and drifting machines that might all have been the dream of a stranger. They sat there, and it might have been the core of the world, and it might have been nowhere at all under the blue dome of sky.

An airplane roared across the sky, louder and louder, but not a soul looked at it and yelled hooray. That was the complaint of Harry Sticks as his head bobbed involuntarily from his bull-size neck. "Not even the kids," he lamented, "and they used to be great at yelling hooray. Kids don't even play ball as def'ly as they used to in my day. Unless the Horse is making fun with my perspec. But modern kids got their hassels . . . mass neurosis . . . all the political hysteria . . . waiting for the Russians to come pebble us to Zero," laughing like an athlete, and Diane laughed too, like water trickling in the sun.

"People are forever getting in and out of cabs," she murmured.

She told Harry how when Carter had soldiered in the South, in heat less offensive than it was up here, he had gone to a carnival or fair and found a man scraping balls of ice and popping pineapple or lemon sirup over it the way they used to when he had been a kid back in Coaltown. Happily he had bought some pineapple kind of ice and carried it behind a tent, where he had garnished it with a shot or two of corn whisky from the pint he was carrying in his rear pocket. When he ate the stuff he vomited, so he had the man sell him some clear ice, with no flavoring at all, and he squirted corn whisky over that and ate it and vomited again. "Later that day," she laughed, "he got himself into a fight."

"Who's that?" Sticks half-wanted to know. "Who's been fighting?"

"Don't be goofing off on me, Stickso. You're a baseball man, not a goof popper. Listen to my story next time," and she watched vaguely as a thin boy in the pool missed a ball. "That's how it bounces," she said, feeling vaguely responsible for the error. There'd been a funeral she'd missed, and a leaden man she hadn't seen since he laughed about nails in a dead man's skull. She'd abandoned leaden duties so that molten gold could light her darknesses while Mama cried on Stoney's wooden lap, cracked-wood limbs and dry loins all over the worldo. "Hey, Sticks, where's a world? Who's the mayor, Harry?"

"You got to tell me the date first." Sticks always knew how to laugh.

"Who's got the next score, Harry Sticks? Nobody has any gold."

"Oobop. Eema ooma, oobop jebam."

As sound an answer as anyone on earth could give. Dincher never showed his face any more, and Angie said he'd lost a friend over Diane. Angie had begun to run to Lizzie.

"Depravity, Sticks." She had to laugh. "Where's Angie getting his Horse? She looks like a mummy—Lizzie. Where's she getting Horse?"

"She's hustling. She never hustled when she was on pod," he lamented in a whimper from his shiny bobbing baseball player's head. "Pod never made a hustler out of no one," still vaguely loyal to the weed of his boyhood, bewailing the fact that hardly anyone was smoking any more.

Any more was a big word in living. "Tony the Shylock is any more too."

"You said it." Harry made a meaning of his own out of anything at all.

Still, Tony the Shylock was a man robbed of his world. Hoodlums gone junky hadn't the patience to punch welshers for an old man. He'd watched his gang dwindle and, abandoned that way, he hoarded his Shylock money. "You can't get a cap's worth out of that old man," she moaned while Harry suffered with kids who couldn't catch a ball. Diane was nowhere at all, yet sat on stone the color of evening, while gold cooled to the middle temperature of the sun, and she was really responsible for fumbled balls and leaden alleyways to a good Daddy's heart. And Brother Barber had to come along then with tears on the sallow cheeks he'd borrowed from blond Canada Dan.

With blue skies under eyebrows running like his nose, and powder words from his mouth. "She's a dead one now. She gassed her and the little baby dead. Jacquie Swan did it like she said," while, before them, kids argued over errors, idlers watched and laughed.

"It's the season" was all that Diane could say, though she meant to make more meaning of her words. No words came from Harry Sticks, nor did the expression of his eyes show he'd even heard the little Canadian boy. And Jacquie Swan was a stick of lead because Diane had never nursed her baby, any baby at all. But the baby wasn't dead because of Diane, and she could prove it in the sun. Sun that put rays like silver threads from her eyes to her hands and the air. So that, although she reached for the little Canadian boy, it was a stranger reaching for a ball she grabbed. And while a bunch of little athletes squealed she clutched a writhing child and kissed him all over the face, kissed him while he squalled, sucked at his lips and bit them to make him understand.

Fists punched at her and women set up a screech and Sticks had her in his arms like a sack of overripe fruit, running her out of the park and up Waverly, cursing the enmity of whites. "God burn them in Hell!" he puffed, setting her down by the bank on the Avenue of the Americas, as though he were finally returning her to the dank stone where he'd found her one morning. She stood up obediently and leaned on the grille cage barring the door, feeling around for cold rain water, looking up for a rain-mist face that promised love to all the world. But there was only black Harry burning white fire out of his eyes. "Animals! White mamasloppin beasts! Come on, Face,

don't let them see you take a fall. Don't let them——" remembering
suddenly that she was white, but helping her up nonetheless. "Come
on, Face, come on now."

"I'm not taking any fall, Harryooba." She could even smile for
him, though Jacquie Swan lay dead in a gray closet of a room and a
little fat baby had died from gas like any guilty grownup. "It's nothing at all," she assured herself. "Know what it is, Harry? It's old
Nothing," and they laughed in a dreamwalk toward the Cosmopole.
They stopped by the subway station to greet Timmy Lawless, to
keep him from nagging the soft old shoeshine with the hairless face.
"Come on, Timmy, that's no one who'll send you," she told him in
the alcove near the five-and-dime door, then had to pull him away
because the store smelled of snorted Horse. "That shoeshine is no
man, Timmy; you can't get a punch out of her."

"You lousy bulldike!" Timmy screamed at the shoeshine. Sticks
laid a hand across his mouth and dragged him away. "Don't mess
with her," Sticks scolded in the dead shade of the Cosmopole. "Leave
her be, Timmy; she don't bother no one at all. Not even little broad-
ies going by."

While Timmy wept, sitting across from Diane, Angie came through
the revolving door with panic in his eyes. "Buster!" he whispered
hoarsely to Diane. "Lizzie says Buster come by. He come by nuts in
his head. Like he got the solid horrors, like-he digs Fuzz evvywhere
he looks'n knocks Lizzie goofy when she says he scragged Magoo'n
Muffo Smith." He took a seat next to Timmy, looking for a word
between Sticks and Diane.

"She's *been* goofy," Diane moaned, laying her weary head on Harry's shoulder. "She had a goofy dream, and I only wish Buster really
showed. I'd score some Horse from him if he showed. Lay a cap or
two on us, Ange. We'll straighten you out for it."

"I need a fix myself. I'm boilin. I ain't got half a cap left'n Lizzie
she needs a fix herself. I gotta hyste a fish market tonight," naming,
with that homely title, anything at all that could be tapped for loot
in the drab alleyways of commerce. "I leff Lizzie wailin in her trap'n
I can't hustle any loot till nighttime."

She grabbed Angie's hand. "Listen, you come with me, you come
with me. Harry, you go on over to Darowitz on Fourteenth and get
some loot. Tell him Angie's on his way with clothes, men's clothes,

good stuff; see? Get a fin at least and everybody gets a pop. Get it
and go on uptown to score."

"Who you gonna hyste?" Sticks wanted to know while Timmy
wailed over a scrap of newspaper in his hands.

She had to search through fogs in her mind to find a proper identity
for her victim. "He's a leadhead cat I used to used to know-biabubari-
bop," and everyone but Timmy grinned and fell in: "Bubadubadu-
baREEbop."

Timmy only wailed of a man shot by a girl with larceny in her
heart, and Sticks told him it happened long ago. "A week at least,
you applehead freak, it's old news and that's the trouble with all
the folks, they think the world is round. It's square, man, square,"
and led the laugh for the table, singing: "*Ubadubadub*," while Angie
tapped on a chair. "This week's news," Sticks announced loudly
enough for all the half-conscious patrons of the Cosmopole to hear,
"is about night riders in masks flogging folks in Alabam! Haha! You
know that? For they care about no law, they just whip folks and we
care about no law and just hyste folks," while Diane and Angie uba-
dubadubbed and Timmy wailed that the Metropolitan Opera House
was all but burned down, just to show that his finger, in an old blue
glove, was right on the pulse of the world. A timorous dish collector
in white, sent by the frightened manager hiding somewhere in the
rear, came up to ask that they be quiet.

The last straw for Timmy: he bolted to the side and caught up a
pile of plastic trays, dropped them clattering to the floor one at a
time as he backed toward the exit, screaming: "Montclair is a punk!
Montclair Boles is my fairy sister!" while Montclair the manager hid
somewhere in the rear, and other agents in white came rushing for
Timmy, who clattered on out. While three junkies at a table on the
side sang *ubadubaREEbop* in the excitement of an imminent pop,
and people sipped iced coffee without turning their heads to look,
for, seeing nothing, they could believe nothing went on.

And nothing went on in the street where Sticks took leave of his
renegade whites, went north toward a hock shop on Fourteenth while
Diane led Angie away. "It's a cinch hyste," she assured the boy,
as if he had the emotion to spare for worrying. "I just need you along
to carry swag, that's all there is to it, just to help me carry swag
away."

For nothing remembered kept her from leading him up Christopher toward the west, nothing wailed in her chest but a thirst for molten gold. Nothing in the heat of the sun reminded her of any gone days, and ballooning puffs of cloud reflecting the yellow-gold told her only that gold was reflectable substance, stuff easily borrowed for any purpose at all.

A heavy silence rode with them through dark Grapevine Lane bordered with darker trees, black against a pale-violet sky, and rubber tires slapped asphalt unevenly—*tedious harangue, tedious harangue,* over and over in Carter's ears. Another tedious harangue had risen out of him. And though Normie had maintained a certain levity through it all, preoccupation showed tight now on his face, touched by the orange light leaking toward them from the highway they were approaching.

Around and around, the harangue still burning in his ears, in Normie's voice and in his own, riding on his blood, nauseating. *Radical neurosis!* a flat, blunt catch-all phrase painful to hear from a friend. "But don't you see I'm trying not to be an *emotional* radical?" Yet he knew he'd never been so emotional. "That's why I'm going to Buffalo—to learn the *science* of economics; don't you see?"

Normie couldn't see. To him Buffalo represented a diversion, a *vacation,* and the harangue went on. While Rusty had stayed in the kitchen doing the dishes immediately after dinner in an uncharacteristic way, he'd shown Normie from his own newspaper how statesmen lied by not stating facts or by speaking in the same sort of double talk they themselves had used to trick Penny upstairs to bed. "Are you a Communist?" Normie had studied his face with that half-burlesqued seriousness of his. "Is that another thing they did to you in the Village?"

"Normie, don't make me vomit. You're too thoughtful to ask questions like that. Leave it to the pinheads, that hysteria."

Normie was no pinhead, and unhysterical enough to see Carter's tensions at a glance. He'd begun to placate him, and that had made Carter all the angrier. "You go on and have fun in Buffalo," and the harangue was on once more, hurtling, spinning through a course Carter couldn't follow now in retrospect. Only sharp edges of it reared in his mind: "Real-estate people call the President's program a socialistic scheme for socialized housing without saying *just what* is wrong with socialism . . . *must* I be partisan . . . *loyalty* bull-shit . . . new catchword with all the false emotion Hollywood ever taught . . . only thing that deserves loyalty is truth . . . men without honor in government should be restrained, dismissed," while Normie fidgeted impatiently; asked what it all had to do with Carter; insisted that he sell his furniture when he left, just to have no remaining ties in the Village; told him, as they drank, to forget Diane, that only some distorted guilt kept him feeling obligated to her. It was all so true that he'd had to get away and had carried his drink to the kitchen for ice. But he had not escaped.

Rusty had stopped him dead. She'd been sitting there, chewing on a thumbnail, and when she saw him she tightened her lips but failed to hold in what she felt. Tears splashed out with her cry: "Carter, Carter, oh, Carter," until he had grabbed her hands. "Carter," she'd wailed again, and he'd asked her what was wrong, and, asking her, looking around for Normie to hurry in, he'd wondered if he shouldn't have expressed some grief for Edna during the afternoon, lie or not. Rusty's eyes had been red with tears, and he'd shouted for Normie, half angry as he pulled a chair near.

When Normie had cautiously entered the kitchen she'd subsided, but was still murmuring Carter's name. She'd looked as awkward, Carter thought, as he'd felt then—and felt now at the recollection. He slunk lower into the seat as they rounded the great lawn near the station.

In all the bustling about at the door Normie had kept the talk down to immediate things, getting Carter to talk about his conquest of Wengel. It took a little winning now and then to stabilize a man, and infrequent winning made a man love to talk about it. He felt foolish for the way he'd spurted out: "The old rat finally gave in. I still own the processing formula; it took only an agreement signed by Merwin and me, but it amounts to a patent. Merwin has an inside consignment deal on Wengel's ten million feet of surplus; we allowed him a nickel a foot and Merwin gets the rest, pays the Puerto Ricans and the blind people decently out of it." He had to add, "I got only three hundred . . . but good contracts," and it grated in him now as wheels ground on gravel in the station driveway.

Normie pulled the brake. "You intend to pay the rent, I suppose, for two months while you're away?"

"Yeah, that'll clean me out and leave me fresh to go to Buffalo.

Let's not labor it: I want the kid to have a place besides her mother's home. Just in case she needs it. Or else she'll be sleeping all over town."

"You going to hunt around for her again tonight?" Normie asked wearily, compassionately.

But the weariness alone was for Diane; Normie couldn't know what it meant that she'd really kicked heroin, that she'd always managed to stick by her guns about her freedom. Carter had to admit he'd been hysterical that night they had run through streets after someone to bury Edna. He wished he could get something of the truth across. "You going to hunt her, moss rat?"

"Sure I am! So what!" Fiercely, though he felt no fierceness toward Normie. "Boy, you publish that godly paper and then insist I let her go to the devil!" He laughed, a sound weird to his own ears.

"You can't . . . Carter, you can't cure the world by yourself, you——"

"What the hell makes you *insist* I mean to do that? You once spoke about it—on this drive to the station—about putting all our energies in one basket. That's all I mean to do: contribute a little energy where I can. It's easy to relax into an apathy just because you're too small to change the world. But that isn't humility; that's cowardice. You publish that damn news sheet for sanctimonious men who wear different clothes from other people. What do you publish? Archaic repetitions that have nothing to do with real life."

"Wait a minute, wait a minute," and they were in it again, with Normie agitatedly defending churchmen, insisting they dealt realistically with problems in society, proving it by quoting some contributors. Normie's thin face was rigid in the station lights, and it seemed as though a delicate balance hung, threatened in the man. It went sharp clean through Carter, and at once he felt that he'd trampled blindly the grass of Normie's world.

"Norm, I'm sorry. You're right. It's just that you can't be patient with mild reformers when you live in the middle of hell. Someday I'll tell you about Edna, how she was when I married her, and Diane won't seem so horrible to you. Normie, this narcotics kick is all over town—all over the country, for all I know. Diane was just caught up in it. School kids are using it. When it all comes out, like boils through the surface, everyone will have a cute idea for controlling it. But every idea will be an evasion: they'll hang buckets under the roof to catch leaks; they'll never dare go to the source because if they do they'll see blood on their hands, all those protectors of mankind who come up with patriotic bluster, those ugly, dead-brained, stupid people in charge of——"

"Hey, you *are* a Communist!" and Carter saw a stranger looking at him in hazy, filtered light. "You're saying a lot of things the propaganda boys——"

"Don't say that, Normie. It's frightful. It's panic. Am I a Quaker for hating war? A fascist for wanting the trains to run on time?"

"Hey, you'd better beat it or you'll miss your damn train," with a swift touch of a smile to keep from offending.

"Normie, are you a Communist for hating officialdom? Or don't you remember once saying it's the officials who tear people apart? A little bit from everybody—this young country has grown old by forgetting it was born on that principle. They'll go along plugging holes in the dike with weak fingers, Normie, and they'll teach frightened little children to call it patriotic to call their own friends names that have no meaning." He opened the door and went around before Normie's lights, came up by the driver's window. "I'm no Communist, Normie, because I'm no partisan. But if those people share some realities with me, by Christ I'm not shutting my eyes to those realities because of that." He was really angry now, angry with the stranger looking at him out of a friend's unchanging eyes. "It all connects, all up and down the line. One thing leads to another; I'm going to Buffalo to get myself some reasonable and scientific roots."

"Carter, take it easy. You're getting red in the face. They'll arrest you for it," laughing with a kind of entreaty for Carter to join him.

Carter laughed harder than it deserved, took Normie's head in his hands and kissed him on the forehead. "I'll write often." He ran up the iron steps with the gunning of Normie's engine in his ears.

On the platform he began to pace along the row of lampposts running along its center. Lights in the old part of town were clusters of blind eyes hung out of darkness and silence. He paced for many, many minutes, wondering whether Normie knew that the train wasn't due for a while, whether his friend had just needed to be rid of him. He couldn't blame Normie; still, he wished he knew if it were so. It was not knowing, he decided, that tore holes in the emotions, and worrying about it that reduced a man to helpless rubble.

Or a woman. Edna had ruined herself with that ceaseless inquiry
into things she could never really know, and now he had to shake
himself loose of blame for it all. She'd been dying all along, he insisted to his guilt; she'd been dying over things she couldn't know
long before the bugs crawled up her spine. Only a thin line divided her intensity from the intensities of the sane, and now a line
divided her cheap side grave from the stone-marked graves of saner
deaths. He was leaning hard on a lamppost with a dread of being
alone on deserted concrete under this pale and brooding light.

He was an eager passenger when the train screeched in, shaking
the whole platform. Faces in the white light were a comfort; he settled back in the smoking car and lighted a cigarette, enjoying the
smoke as if it were some rare luxury for his lungs. Diane knew all
about the poison of secrecy: she'd kept nothing from him but the
fact of her habit . . . just as he'd kept the truth about Edna from
anyone he could, only to spare them the pain of knowing. A clumsy
consideration. Diane had her kind of honor wherever she found that
honor allowed. He decided to spend the night hunting her if he
had to, to let her know the apartment was hers, to live there with
Dincher if she cared to, to do anything she found necessary in her
throttled life.

There were just enough people in the rumbling car to keep him
feeling accompanied, yet not closed in. Little towns slid by in silent
darknesses outside, distant houses lighted modestly in the violet
night, like children tired from a day of playing but reluctant to close
their minds. Little children standing alone in darkness.

Clacking rhythms in wheels and gears made his eyelids heavy. He
let his head rest on the straw back of his seat and composed a letter
he'd send to Joe Letrigo. Something about heroes to tell his brother-
in-law. That the time was too ripe with conscious people to permit
anything like heroes or giants more powerful than the multitude.
That heroism had been reduced to a sentimentality by the awakening of a billion minds, that the only leadership lay in people themselves, united to face their tragedies.

He was awakened once by a conductor collecting fares; then he
sank deeper into a dreamless sleep and got up stiff-necked in the
murky New York station. Crowds on their way out of town for the
week end made his passage difficult, but he finally reached the doors
that opened onto the taxicab stand, and told his driver to drop him

at Sixth Avenue and Eighth. Almost immediately he changed his destination to Christopher off Hudson. He'd take that barely hopeful look at home for Diane.

Seventh Avenue was an oozing shadow in summer heat, with people slowed down for the night, drifting under arc lights as though they had nowhere important to go. In a side street a set of early fireworks crackled; some hasty kid hadn't the patience to wait till the Fourth. He wondered what Buffalo would be like over the Fourth of July, wondered if he'd enjoy the long week end with the same long breath of release holidays had given him when he worked the week long.

Past the gas station and around into long, unmoving shadows, into the dark street and home. He looked up to his dark windows before he even paid the fare, then got his change and ran inside. Up the elevator to his door and—it swung open when he touched it with his key. He clicked on the foyer light and saw that the lock was ripped loose and dangling. He put other lights on in every room: nothing seemed disturbed. Till he looked through closets.

Two raincoats were gone, but his trench coat hung smugly in the wide space left it. An old topcoat he'd rarely cared to wear was missing, while a new tweed he'd not yet got around to wearing hung soft and untouched. Suits were missing from other closets, and shoes, but only old things that he hadn't bothered to discard. Many of Edna's things were gone, things he'd wanted Diane to have. And that sat him down laughing. Diane! Of course, of course. Not a thing he ever used or meant to use—no stranger, however considerate, could know his habits so well. And *habit* clanged like something electric through him, shot him to his feet. Diane . . . the only reason she'd hyste him would be desperation, and only one thing could make her desperate enough for that. Diane was on Horse again, and Carter was in the street, hurrying to find her before she got hooked . . . if she wasn't hooked yet.

Street shadows hurtled by under his feet, and he was puffing when he got to the Cosmopole. He looked from table to table at people who ignored him. He asked people he knew vaguely if they'd seen Diane, though he could anticipate their negative answers: they were long accustomed to denying anything at all.

It was a browned and stalwart Paddy Jenks he met coming through the door. By reflex he caught the man's arm and swung him gently around. "Have you seen Diane, Paddy?" and saw eyes that recognized neither him nor the name of the girl. "Diane Lattimer, you know her. The little thin, black-eyed pretty girl with a voice like honey and a face——" *What the hell, what the hell.* "You look great, Paddy," and saw him break into a grin, saw clean, fine teeth when the man prepared to speak.

But it was a whisper that emerged. "Thank you," and nothing more: almost a squeak, a little whine.

It was Paddy's body they'd cured in Lexington, Kentucky; his frightened mind still lived inside those robust walls, like some enfeebled prisoner in a palace. Carter shook his head as he hurried down Waverly toward the park. People sat around the forum in shadow-shattered light from arc lamps dusted by trees; he went around the complete circle of benches looking for a face he might know. Nothing familiar was in a single look that met him, but Paddy was back there at the entrance to the park, rushing to meet him with a smile.

"Man, I know who you mean." His voice was still thin. "Man, you mean that fine little chick; she's like wine, man. I'm hip who you mean, I'm hip. Diaaaane!" It was a pronouncement, an illustration of infallible memory.

"Where is she, Paddy? Have you seen her at all?"

"No, man. I just . . . wanted to tell you. I just got back, man; I ain't seen a good junky nowhere abouts," and Carter knew how he'd been identified. "But you come along with me, man, I'll dig them out right at the roosts," with a deathless grin that had nothing to do with eyes looking beyond anything anyone else could see. And he'd said all he had to. He took Carter along down MacDougal to the Riviera, where all they found was Louella, minus her cross, minus any cigarette holder or symbol of any kind. Only a brazen smile as she spoke to younger darlings around her at the bar. "Be satisfied," she told them all, "with whatever titillation you get out of it," and they all made hohohos out of their giggling. "Well, here's my titillation for tonight," she announced when she saw Carter. "Oh, who's your cute friend?"

"Have you seen Diane?" Carter asked, and began to move away before she even shook her head, for he felt he might bite a piece out of her cheek if he stayed near her.

"Carter, wait up for a gal!" collecting her purse from the bar as if it were some hard-to-handle sack of squirming animals; jangling bracelets and kicking her legs, a great overdone commotion that became the target for what he couldn't hold in.

"Get the hell away from me!" and he pulled Paddy through the mob to the street. Nao Braun fell into Paddy's arms while her long, bent husband stood inexpressively by. "Nao, where's Diane?" Carter shook her by the arm. "Paddy, ask her where," still trembling, half with shame, over his outburst at Louella.

"Where's Diaaane?" Paddy asked out of his tireless grin.

"Up by Canada," she whispered, playing with buttons on Paddy's shirt. "You don' go." She shook a finger at Carter. "Give the peeble horrors," and slipped up against him from Paddy's limber arms. "Stay here in a sky with Cliffie'n me, man. Laughs."

Carter leaned back on the window, keeping his hands back as the dreamy-faced woman leaned on him. Her husband stood like a drunken soldier trying to bring himself to attention, looking straight ahead through the Riviera to some fanciful world's· quiet designs. Paddy nodded and worked something reassuring out of his smile to Carter, words that never found voice, and then spun on a heel to make it with his head up high down the cracked old shadows of MacDougal. "You're a pretty man," Nao whispered huskily, still leaning hard against Carter, "but you oney love me for my body," and giggled as though with her last breath.

Carter squirmed out from between her and the window, went to a car parked at the curb and found himself laughing as he sat down. Nao drifted directly to him, while her husband stood transfixed in the white bath of light and voices from the open Riviera door. "Tha's Cliffie," Nao whispered. "He loves me for ever'thing, he really does, my Cliffie. He can eat flow-ers'n ever'thing nice," easing herself with a shuddering sigh to silence.

Nobody who passed molested Clifford Braun until Robert Stoney shouldered him out of his way into the tavern. Stoney in a seersucker suit, smoking a black cigar, rubbing a sizable beard.

Carter dashed over to the painter. "Robert. Come on back out," almost glad to see a man intoxicated by nothing but his vanity.

"I came looking for you," Stoney reported. "Where is that girl? She's ruining my life, I tell you. Yes, sir, ruining it!"

Carter looked at the beard. "You seem to be keeping the rubble in fair shape. You look even better than you did before she started victimizing you. How's Vivienne?"

"Impossible! All she thinks about is that girl. Nothing, *nothing* will divert her; she *must* know where the girl is."

"How's your career coming along? Have you taken over the agency yet?"

"Now, Carter——"

"Stoney!" Lizzie Linden, aged almost beyond recognition, slithered through the tavern-front crowd, her small hands wrapping her tweed coat tight about her. "Stoney, I been lookin for you. Carter . . . Carter, I been lookin for you," with tawny eyes shifting as though uncertain of where to look, whom to address. "Take a lady home. He's layin up there waitin to get me; you hear? He's stickin there with his big knife to rip me open, I swear. I'm scared, he's a degenery'n he'll get me. You know it, Carter, you know he'll get me like he gets that kid of yours. You know it, Stoney, like he gets Magoo'n that baldy one."

"Lizzie," all Stoney could think of to say, "it's too warm for that coat. Much too warm, you'll——"

"Come on, Liz." Carter put his arm around the little hunched shoulders, took her past the giggling, arguing faces. Lizzie had crumbled from a woman who'd almost made the grade in her own narrow league. Before panic had invaded her world she'd been up on her own skinny legs, meeting men eye to eye with all the mixed firmness and compassion any human could sustain. Firm and compassionate in direct response to what she saw before her, what she honestly felt. He was still amazed by the store of artistic understanding she displayed only in the privacy of her hospitality in a Bleecker Street flat: she played good recorded music written in this century, showed prints by the best of contemporary painters; it was as though she'd breathed the very life of her culture while hapless Louellas supplicated to the word itself: *Culture!* But now Lizzie'd crumbled under a weight she couldn't support alone. Yet his greater sorrow was for Louella, for her days full of senseless words.

"Take a lady home." Lizzie trembled, searching Carter's face for some special reassurance. "He'll rip me up somethin terrible."

He held up by the curb and motioned to Nao Braun. "Nao, listen . . ." and had to stop, for he suddenly saw the sleek-haired gamin gliding toward them like some emerging memory. Long bead earrings dangled from the clipped line of Diane's hair, tapping on her bony jaws as she drifted along on soft flat heels, her mouth curled in half a smile. Carter stood there, unable to move, while Nao rubbed against him and Lizzie Linden whimpered.

"Get off him!" Diane said viciously to Nao. "Get off!" with a stiff push on the woman's shoulder.

"You don' love nobo-dy," Nao whispered and wrapped her arms around Lizzie, began to stroke her hair and kiss her.

"Take her home, Nao." Carter patted Nao's back. "Go on, Nao, and stay there with her awhile."

"She'll stay there," Diane called after them, "long as the old lady has something she can mooch." She laid the iciest look Carter had ever seen right on his eyes. "Hello, Carter, how you feel?" A slow low voice: heavy-lidded, lusterless eyes. "What did you want to see me about? Don't tell me about any funeral, because I got no ears for it." She had ears for nothing at all, and only some old music struggling around in her head gave her eyes an obligation to look at that clean, square face. "How you feel now, Carter?"

"Come on, let's take a walk. Stoney's around lookin for you. Mama sent him to find you."

"Let him find me." She pulled her arm away. "I'll kill the bastard. He don't rule me. Like you think he——"

"Come on, baby, come on," hauling her along by the smooth silk sleeve. "I want to tell you about a gentleman who committed a murder and disguised himself as a lady in order to escape the police," while she hung to his arm for her footing over the cracked, uneven sidewalks toward the park. "He was doing great till he made a mistake. The cops were always on his tail and he slipped under their noses in that disguise, but one day he helped an old lady off a bus and the cops collected him."

Diane walked along, listening to music that danced in her head around Paddy's new shiny face. All the world was dust and she trod over murky gray only because dust couldn't reach organs warm with molten gold. The voice beside her was a stranger's, similar to any kind of strangeness at all; it had become easy to tread dust past strangers because there was always a golden steed at the end of the road, and now a smiling boy sat waiting for her in the saddle.

"Diane . . . little girl, you gave yourself away; you took my old things because you've not gone far enough to care nothing. Why did you hyste me, Diane? You could have asked me for money."

As if he'd give her money for Horse. "What do you mean, hyste you? I never hysted you, Carter." *That was easy . . . ask me a hard one oobop.*

"How hooked are you, Diane? Can you kick it like you did before?"

"I'm not hooked. And if I was, I could kick it easy. I can do anything, Carter. Just name it; I can do it."

"You can lie better than you were ever able to. You talk like a crippled foghorn. Like Nao Braun, you talk."

Diane spun on him as he sat down on a bench in the west-lane darkness of the park. "I'm nothing like that phony. She . . . her with her damn . . . She gets money from her old lady and never has a cap for a friend."

"*You're* not hooked, are you? You just like a cap now and then from her for friendship's sake. How much did you get for my clothes?"

Diane sat next to him, took his hand. "I didn't hyste you, Carter. Like I wouldn't do anything like that to you. I'm surprised at you saying that. Like you think I would——"

"Never mind. I don't need the stuff anyway. I want to travel light. I'm selling the furniture over the week end and leaving right away." He meant that, but couldn't tell himself why he was pouring it out to the girl. "But let's talk about you, Gwendolyn. What happened to your mother love? You given Johnny up completely?"

"No, not me, Carter. I'm going to get him one of these days."

He'd begun to sweat fiercely; he removed his jacket and hat. Diane was gone. Though she'd dressed in skirt, blouse and sandals like the little girl she once had been, though she'd combed her hair flat right down to huge earrings like the little gamin he'd always adored, she sat there now—a shell, with no compensating concern for truth remaining, her very blood poisoned with forgetfulness.

Yet he had to take her face in his hand and bring her eyes of clouded black to look at his. For one last try before he abandoned a hopeless fight. To see if she could find something in the mirror of his face, some hovering memento of the truth she'd lived on, something to pull her out of the hell she'd allowed to enclose her. "Diane, baby, little girl, say it to me. Tell me about it. Cry, Diane, let it all out because I love you so much."

"Carter—" it was an icebound face with nothing behind it, no hope, no plan, no remorse—"Carter, if you think I did it, there's nothing I can tell you." A face he really didn't know at all, one that admonished him for any sentiment he'd ever felt in his life. "Carter, you'll just never, never know."

She took Paddy along with her to hell. An outside hell with an inner ease no heaven could afford. They lived in a room on Mac-Dougal Street faintly haunted by the ghosts of Jacquie Swan and her baby, and Paddy was a smiling stickman just as Diane had told someone so long ago. The most compliant soul she'd ever found, one who lent himself to anybody's need, smiling always, breathing only the mildest words on the air, as though he'd long ago decided his visible parts were a fair price to pay for the golden privacy inside him. He lent out the great power he'd acquired in Lexington, loved her as long as she needed him, and Diane knew a release she'd never believed herself capable of. Till summer heat and heavy pops of Horse wore love out of their interests, left them to wander like silken ideas over the rough roads of living.

Paddy was much too mild to accompany her on trips for loot in every kind of fish market from a drugstore to an uptown linen emporium. The Swede was handy for that, and sometimes little Angie would join these forays down the straight dusty alleyways of need. Angie—always sullen and querulous, always complaining he'd lost a friend over her, a boy named Dincher she remembered from childhood days in a Village with broader spaces for adventure.

"If Dinch was with us," Angie complained while they hurried down the glistening night of summer's first rain, with Diane shaking Lukey to quiet him, "if Dinch was with us, it's one hyste we never woulda fluke up."

"You bust his head." Lukey said it over and over, as if he couldn't believe it. "He's a goner; you scragged the man; you really bust his skull."

"Forget it," Diane said. "Just forget it, Swede; it never happened at all." But she herself still trembled; her mind couldn't lose sight of the fragile druggist lying where they'd left him, bleeding from the head, or of the bloodied nickel-plated pistol Angie had in his kick. "We got the loot anyway." She kept talking just so that others wouldn't prattle on. "We got for my rent and for enough caps and

even for some ice cream," for ice cream was the staple when more
solid food would stay in nobody's gut. "Like forget it, Ange, just forget it."

"Yeah, just forget it!" he mimicked. "People they seen you, you
hadda stay'n wipe his face, you hadda let evvybody——"

"They don't know. I tagged you like maybe Buster and Tony, like
two different guys, like one big and fat, one a little old stud. Me, they
think I'm a nice kid going by."

"It's no fish market for me." The Swede shuddered on the way
across University Place. "Me, I'm a slinker, I don't go crackin guys,
not me. I don't want it no more, no more, not forever, me."

And before he vanished into some government cell he spent one
week touting the news with Harry Sticks at a Cosmopole table.
"They wanna give away a billion and a half green beans to all them
Atlantic Pacts in Iran and Filipino Island and K'rea to make cannons
for shootin at the Europeens. Me, I do the job for a twenny-dollar
bill and have enough left for five caps a day," while Harry shuffled
through a bundle of discarded newspapers to find something more
pertinent to tout. "You hip what's in a billion and a half? Nah, you
ain't hip, nobody can dig that much loot. Eight hundred grand . . .
you dig that much? It's what they cracked a banker guy for, he run
away to Florida with all that loot. You know how much caps? Man,
it's good for seven years with a twenny-cap-a-day habit; you hip?
Easy for seven years, maybe more."

But Harry wouldn't stay quiet long. He found the news from
Birmingham, and told Lukey and Timmy Lawless and Diane and
Paddy and any square who cared to listen that justice was winning
in Alabama. "They got seventeen cats indicted down there; dig me.
They got the Brookside chief of police on the blotter, and a sheriff
too and they even bust open the jury for having a Ku Klux Klan cat
and an ex-con. . . . They got them all bugged, and justice is gonna
win." He laughed alone in a group not sworn to justice, not sure of
the direction in which it would run next time it veered.

It veered toward Lukey the Swede the night he tried marijuana
for old times' sake, the night summer breezes made him want to return to his childhood, for that thorny time seemed smooth in contrast to the pinch of the days at hand. "It's great after 'H,' it's like
the old buzz," he cackled toothlessly for all his bored acquaintances,

and he sang old Vipers' songs while one by one they drifted away from the cluster under an arc light in Washington Square Park. Only Timmy hovered by for a puff or two on the weed that never made him happier, nor sadder, nor in any way more sensitive to colored lights and sounds he never understood. It was Timmy who told of the frisk, the pinch by two red-necked bulls from an uptown precinct. "He laughed," Timmy told Diane in the Cosmopole while other junkies wandered down their own smoky pastures at the table around her. "The Swede just laughed," Timmy wept, "and laughed because they were tickling him on the frisk. Lands, he laughed, and they never hit him once," a lament that increased his tears.

Paddy smiled out of a face grown thinner, paler, as though some mask had been peeled to show wirelike lines about his eyes. Diane, freshly popped, spoke gelatinous bubbles in place of words, yet everybody listened. She spoke powder puffs into the violet-tinted light while people without identity, squatting all about the place, spoke out their agitations, their mild pleasures, their ancient dreams and regrets. Now and then a squeal rose up to the high ceiling from some bohawk darlings at a table. Now and then a fight broke out and subsided, to show it wasn't Saturday night, when any little scuffle lasted out its hour.

Dincher appeared one time and another out of the fog before her eyes. He'd cast her a glance and a smirk and stalk out, followed by little freckled Angie. All for the laughs, for she'd risen to queen-hood as the days fell away into disappeared heat: every junky and hippie came to sit around her table and listen to powder words bubbling out of her mouth. Words that described a region back of the sky, a space painted with the color of time, full of air that smelled of Nothing. Even Lizzie would spend an hour there, just to be among people who could keep Buster away. They all had their ghosts, and no junky begrudged Lizzie hers. She could sit in the whirling Nothing while Diane spoke bubbles about a bubble of a world, while Paddy told a weird kind of story about a Ghost they all had known many, many golden charges ago. "He lobs in a thicket," Paddy would say of Izzie. "He plays the thicket like a lonesome spray; you dig? He lays in there alone for no cats at all to dig him. Izzie the Ghost don't want a thing in Lex but some waist-belt pop; you dig?" Smiling forever, though he knew nobody dug, no junky understood or cared or bothered to make meaning of anything he dreamed out of his mouth.

But for Diane he began to sound too much like the world in his aimless ranting. "Get out and hustle some loot one time," she said in a sweltering bath of sun from Jacquie Swan's window. "Get out and make yourself good for me," she said, kicking at his limp legs beside her on the bed. For all power had gone with the flesh from his bones, and he was an aimless ranter like any square in Congress. Some squealing defense still alive deep inside her warned that he was a leech living on her blood. There'd been a half-square cat come out of the earth with coal dust around his eyes and a back sloped from working to keep her on the dusty road. There'd been such a stud, and he was gone, and he'd left a shadow in bed behind him. "Get out and hustle for me," she told Paddy as the sun went from yellow to orange, and Paddy was compliant and smiling, so he went out and hustled for Diane.

Two squares in seersucker suits he hustled up to the closet of a room, and she laughed because she'd sent him out to hustle. Paddy entertained in the hall while she took square after square after square and sailors and dark Spanish kids drifting downtown. The easiest score she'd ever known, and Paddy was a smiling hustler, a ready agent for trips uptown to score for golden Horse. She rarely had to leave Jacquie Swan's room, with a hustler like Paddy Jenks to bring her ice cream and Horse and hotstick cats who had to dip into her honey. Street was a drag with once in a while Stoney to bug up her ears, to say words like *unreasonable*, words like *disloyal*, carrying words like little brittle skeletons of worlds on his laundered linen back, and his beard trimmed to a point for Mama Long-ago. Street was a drag with flip Lizzie Linden wrinkled with Buster in her birdy face. With uptown chick talking about coal mines and a post-card from Buffalo, about half-square cats gone to Nowhere, uptown chick with a big gold cross once more rapping her soft little tits, look-ing at the sky like a long-ago Mama. Street was a drag and park was a drag where Mama found her in the sun, stiff on a bench under the gold of sun with gold pressing back from inside.

"Diane, you're so *thin*," Mama moaned while Stoney chewed his cigar.

"Summer, Mama. Makes you so *thin*. Makes you so *thin*, Mama," then got up and took the pretty lady's arm just to keep from having again to use her marshmallow voice. Walked Mama-woman to the church on Fifth Avenue with Stoney dogging it behind. Into a special session where an organ played from heaven and many people moaned, many people sang, while a man in white masquerade taught them how to moan. Diane saw the light come white out of an amber ceiling, but saw no cross inside it. She saw a light and it was enough to kick blood screaming where blood had been asleep before. She hooked her eyes into the light and felt it seep freely into her head, down through her empty frame. Then a face appeared, and she grabbed her mother's wrist. It was an Indian face with the eyes of a watchful panther, and she wasn't afraid at all. "He's there," she whispered. "It's there, it's there," and shook her mother's wrist. Light took her over and cleansed her into some sleep-world. She was outside before she knew she'd been helped. "I saw his face, Mama," but Vivienne only scowled, blind to the Divine beyond her private experience, a skeptic in the broiling public sun. "I really did—" bubble words rolled out of helpless laughter, so that her mother backed away.

"It's nothing to laugh about, Diane. If that's your idea of a joke. . . ."

"No joke . . . I saw the Face you told me about." Yet she couldn't hold the laughter. She laughed, leaning on the black-iron gate, while Stoney led her mother away, left her with something like a warning in the voice of her mother, but she couldn't isolate and name it for the cloud of older warnings that intoned around it down the doorless lane of recollection, the hallway of ceaseless voices.

Laughter shook her all the way through the park, and she fell feebly on a bench. "I saw Him," she told some boys who held up their ball game to watch a skinny lady laugh. She told them His face was Indian, and they were fascinated enough to circle her on the grass behind the cracked-wood bench. They listened till the sun began to lower, till Dincher and Angie broke up the act. "Go on'n beat it," Dincher told them all, and advanced toward the more arrogant loiterers till they all disappeared down a walk. "Go on, you cut out too," he told Angie, and stood hands on hips till his friend disappeared in a shuffle. "You look murdered," he told her with a harshness forced in his voice. "Christ, you gonna die. Like-you finished, you look," and sat near her with fierce anger in his face and old tenderness in the hand with which he felt her shoulder. "Jeez, you crazy broad, you crazy broad. Jeez, you flip broad," and gathered her like loose rags in his arms. "Jeez, baby doll, you don' wanna die, you don' wanna die."

Diane let him lead her through to Bleecker and up the stairs. Into the old loft to the bed she'd once had as throne. Loosened the tight snaps at her wrists and worked off her blouse. "Main-line hitches," he muttered with no surprise, "main-line, main-line up both them little arms." Dincher was older, thinner, she could see through the veil forever with her. Dincher was no longer a round-cheeked baby. When he shuffled out to the kitchen she stripped naked and pulled a bed sheet over sharp jutting bones she didn't care to see. She heard the hiss of a gas burner and closed her eyes, kept them that way till the Dinch returned with a small hypodermic.

"Don't want a fix, Dinch," she murmured. "Not till dark, Dinch."

But it wasn't for her. The boy peeled his shirt and tightened his fist for a vein to show, looked at her once, and drove the setup, searching for first blood in that vein. "For you, doll. Because I lose, I lose. You'n me, we main-line it together, doll," and popped a good kick into that thick and hairy arm.

Immediately he went for his horn behind the easel in the corner to the side of the tall white fireplace. Before the kick could reach him he was on the bed with his back propped against the wall, blowing short notes that grew shorter as he went into charge, short riffs that told how both of them felt in a bare loft walled with angry pictures, designs colored with the smoldering designs of an egocentric. Dincher played short, breathless laments, like a man half asleep, about a world gone dead before he could grow into it. He played unmelodically all the truth he knew of pointlessness, all the reality she recognized of the dusty alleyways they'd both traveled among indifferent grim-faced strangers. *RAru raREE! RA rarurariAA ruliooorabop! BEEdliba RIbop!* Short blasts untroubled with invention, uncreative as the world outside.

"It's the real, Dincher, it's the true reebop picture."

OodloodloodloodlooREE . . . udludludlooBAHree! BAA-Aaaa, he said on his horn, then took it down to sob for breath and bite his tender lips. "My old man—" he grinned, heavy-eyed, around at her —"he don' like Be-bop." He rolled over on his back beside her, one foot on the calcimined wall. *REEaah!* he blasted. "He don' want me

aroun; how you like that? He don' want me wit crazy noises. He don'
know I find them under the chairs-like. Down in the street I find
them, in the faces, on the radio I hear guys talk like this"—*oodlood-
loodloodloodlOOeeee! OOkaw! OOkaw! YAdararaBIdlawBArara!*
"He never hears it, the old man, he thinks I make it up outta my
head." He threw the trumpet over his head, sent it clattering metal-
lically into the shadows behind him. "That horn—" his laughter was
a whine—"it plays by itself like-all alone it plays Bop from the air.
Listen, doll, listen to the Bop-bah." He closed his eyes to look at
regions more colorful than these walls.

Diane felt no need to cradle his head in her arms: he was no
round-cheeked baby, but a hooked man with muscular jaws and an
angry shadow of a beard, a tight little mouth and a small hawknose
with nostrils sucking fiercely for breath. "Dincher," she whispered,
"Dinch, you want to help me get my little baby-kid? Dinch, we could
get him easy."

"How we get 'im, doll? It ain' easy. Like-they ain' no easy way
for nothin; you know it, doll."

Her silence was a prompt concession to that much, yet the first
surge of real feeling she'd known in months pushed up out of her
stomach. "We can do it, Dinch; I want my own kid, and I'll get
him." This was no splash of light in some church, no soaring sense
of gold any charge of Horse had put through her. It appeared the
only sunlight in all the craggy space of reality, and she felt it in
every fleshless bone, through heat dank and quivering riverlike between her and the limp white sheet.

Though faces contorted with sunshine around the concrete checker
table were ludicrous with awe, the idea was to keep their own faces
straight as the weird game progressed. They were equipped for the
look of seriousness: Stoney with his beard, Latour with his solid black
mustache and shock of hair. All speech around them was politely
muffled. Stoney held his laughter tightly back, moved his black
checker from a black square to a white, slid it diagonally through four
more, jumped Latour's red checker and removed it along with one
red from the opposite side of the board. He thumbed some sweat
from his forehead and lighted his cigar, watching Latour and the
faces around them, hoping the painter could carry off the nonsense.
Hunched forward, Latour pondered, then sat up thoughtfully and

began to hop a red checker backward, across and around indiscriminately over black squares and white, skipping over three of Stoney's checkers that were nowhere near one another—a perfect display of idiocy carried off with a serious face. He removed all but one of Stoney's checkers and put them on the side out of play. Stoney scowled, puffed hard on the cigar, then beamed, snapped his fingers for the crowd to see, and picked up two of his blacks from the side, put them back into play, one in each hand, and hopped them crazily around over all the reds on the board while Latour travestied anguish with hands pressed on his face. But Latour rallied—he pulled a red from his pocket, grinned, his silver-capped tooth shining in the sun, and jumped Stoney's three blacks. He stood, reached over to shake Stoney's hand, and walked off while straight-faced spectators watched in silent fascination.

"There you have it." Stoney caught up with him, and they went laughing down the west lane. "People will believe *anything*, so long as you convey it with a straight face. That's the coin of advertising. Why, if I'd wanted to, I could have convinced all those people that you're a crook—*while* picking their pockets. I can go back there and convince them I won the game even though they saw you win. *Anything*, so long as you act serious and say it loudly."

Latour yawned. Flat brick façades, high ones and low ones around the great verdant square, looked vacantly down on trees and ice-cream venders' wagons glinting yellow and white in the sun; children's voices ran their chimelike scales; small breezes faintly, faintly rustled leaves and silk kerchiefs across the shoulders of women here and there in Washington Square. "It's all ephemeral, Robert, a speck on the window of time, and we should address ourselves to eternal things. Come over to the studio and let me——"

"No, no, no." Stoney waved a hand. "You don't get me back to dreaming. Ephemeral, shmemeral. I—today is today, and I——" He looked toward the bench Latour was heading for, to Louella Nordvahl clean and white in the sun, fingering her gold cross, unfolding note papers in her lap. He went along reluctantly, hoping that no old relationships would be brought up to complicate things with embarrassment on Latour's part.

"Hello boys," cheerfully as they flanked her on the bench.

"She called us boys," Stoney muttered, and Latour shrugged philosophically.

"Carter Webb." She held out the note papers. "A letter from Carter. Joe Letrigo is engaged to be married," and felt herself wince, secretly admonished herself for the wayward pang of jealousy she couldn't seem to prevent. "Carter and Joe communicate *furiously*, and Carter tells me so much. He's sorry—" she giggled a bit—"for behaving badly toward me," and automatically fell to reading aloud: "*I want to apologize for outbursts I made against you. I once thought you represented something I hated, but I've learned you don't at all and I suffer great remorse over some things I remember saying. Our tempers seem to settle as we learn more. There's lots of room for lots of people and lots of time to ponder those things that happen to be not painfully urgent.*" She looked at Latour and saw strange new creases working among those defined lines around mustache and eyebrows. Swiftly she turned to Stoney. "Here's something that'll interest you, Robert. Joe's new brother-in-law, Hensley Clayburne— Carter thinks very highly of him and thought I'd be interested in what he tells Joe." She read hastily Hensley's theory on the chemistry of an organism, about cured boils of the neck returning unless they're traced to source, in the liver or kidneys or wherever the chemistry is most off balance. "*Society is an organism like the body; America is the core of society today and down here in the South is where the chemistry is most poorly balanced. Although evidence of inequality is more intense in other parts of the world, America, leader of society, has an innate duty to humanity, and we down here vitiate the power to perform that duty, to set one great and deathless example, by continually destroying the concept of equality. We are not the criminals but the blindly willing victims. The criminals grow fat in their mansions up North, the victims stay lean and angry down South, and the heroes are not yet born.* How is that, Robert? Isn't it——"

"Very well put." Stoney nodded slowly—he hadn't really been listening. "Very well indeed. But it's *such* a waste of energy," and he sighed, looked around at the lazy drift of promenaders.

"Carter quotes Joe a lot," Louella said abstractedly, and pondered on that fact. It showed her the core of her interest in the slope-shouldered man. Knowledge of her relations with other men never seemed to grieve him. That injured only her vanity, she confessed, and for the rest she could be glad that he knew her, that there was nothing to hide from him, nothing to feel guilty for. She read aloud from the part where Carter said he was glad her parents had been reconciled, glad she'd got a job to free herself of any sense of debt to them; where he expressed a real desire to see her as soon as he returned.

"I've had enough," Latour muttered, and it was a sort of whispered shout. "I can't stand this infantilism, Louella. You're reading that— you're just pitting one man against the other out of sheer infantile vanity!" and squirmed restlessly, avoiding Stoney's eye.

"Fred!" Louella began to tremble, held tight to her cross. Sad, patient, vulnerable Latour, whose painful adoration had never transferred more than its pain, had gone angry, impatient, defensive. *Infantile!* and he'd looked collegiate himself in the awkward twisting of his lips. She could have stroked that yearbeaten face as one might a child's.

Stoney walked off. "I'll meet the winner over in the forum," and he waddled around the lawn full of trees to an empty bench in the shade.

Latour stood quickly. "Someday—Louella, someday," as he backed into the sun, "you'll grow up and realize it was me who—" he had to lift his head decisively to finish—"who truly loved you!" and hurried to join Stoney.

As though one could go without loving to where she was loved . . . one so desperately in search of a real relationship to herself. She had to remember not to let Fred Latour's pain compel her, had to remember she owed him only sympathy . . . and admiration for his work, the realest side of him. *Real, real, reality, realistic,* the words formed a tortuous web in her brain; she rubbed her forehead and looked up at the splendor of golden sparks high in treetops. Adolescent shouts cracked the air and sailed off, purring, to the sky; dogs barked, autos honked: real music all in place but for certain edges forever coming apart.

"Let me see," she muttered, and began to sing softly when she thought passers-by had seen her talking. People moved slowly; slowly the sounds and breezes rolled; slowly the sun stroked people and voices and air. "Let me see," she said without moving her lips, but couldn't remember what it was she had to work out. "Me," she whispered through motionless lips, "he wrote to me to say . . ." and became aware of motion, realized she'd been walking south down the lane. Slowly, slowly milling along with people, one hand on her

golden cross, facing the sun's caressing heat, with lots of time to ponder in sunlight on a Saturday afternoon.

When the dust of living grew too thick in her lungs Diane would
enter the amber-colored shadows cool forever without sunlight in
the church on Fifth Avenue, to sit there in a polished mahogany pew
waiting free of thought for the divine light. Sometimes there were
other worshipers around her, and, though at first she resented them
as intruders, she had come to feel some half-familiar unanimity in
their midst, an affinity that made her part of a higher world and allowed her to tarry through the dust a little more, to take on Paddy's
trade in the closet of a room on MacDougal, to withstand Dincher's
demands that she get the boy Johnny to her bosom, away from the
Long Island squares.

Dincher worked hard at tapering her off Horse, just as he worked
hard on himself, and only her insistence on freedom for her will, on
her right to independence, tricked him enough to let her spend
afternoons in her own little room, where she took her clandestine
pops, where she earned the money to buy them. For the money
Edna's clothes brought, piece by piece, from Darowitz on Fourteenth was all the income Dincher knew of, and the fish-market swag
he mustered did little more than buy them food. Now and then he
used her to lure some drunken rubberneck down Bleecker, where he
and Angie would apply a rap behind the tourist's ear and leave him
penniless in an alley. Dincher had his laugh over squares who thought
she'd whore, and Diane had her laugh privately each secret time she
popped Horse bought with whore's gold. It was an easy tightrope
walk over dust between Horse and God, and in His tower no stranger was angry, no voice was loud.

Now she floated out of church in spiritual unanimity with a crowd
purged as she was of gone dusty days. She smiled at any face that
pointed her way, and entered the park by Fifth Avenue's route past
the fountain, lingered awhile to watch the children splash in the
pool, then passed down a winding lane through sun-splashed greens
to MacDougal. Paddy met her at the stoop with a boy in a soldier suit.
She patted the frightened round face and whispered, "Not on Sunday," left Paddy to cool the boy off, and climbed the stairs to the
closet of a room. She took off the flowered print dress and in her slip

boiled four caps, emptied two more into the water in the serving spoon. For there was not much in a four-cap charge any more.

No gold oozed through her from the six-cap blast as she went into Bleecker with Paddy on her tail. "Get lost, Paddy," she told the smiler, "don't let Dincher see you near me or he'll start looking for where you sleep."

"I'm goin up to Lizzie," he bubbled from his glue mouth. "Lizzie don' worry for Sun'ay, not Lizzie."

It was a good laugh, though no sound of laughter traveled higher than her throat. "Where's your soldier boy? You think he wanss a sack of used-to-be like Lizzie? Squallin about Busser in her room?"

"I got him drinkin beer, don' worry 'boud him." Paddy smiled. "See if she's home'n I got a good score, you'll see, Diaaaane."

She took his wrist and dragged him past the red-painted door, with a sudden electric urge in the sun, hot waves of power burning through the white-cotton brunch coat wrapped around her naked skin. "You come with me, Paddy," over to Timmy stacking pictures on a push-cart. "Wha' you doing, Timmy? Tha's Stoney's crap you piling; where you hauling them, Timmyboy?" while Paddy smiled and made no objection to her clutch on his wrist.

"The ar-tist hired me. He did, pret-ty. He's upstairs getting more."

"Stoney? He's up there? Any woman with him, Tim?"

"No, just Dincher," wiping sweat from under his sandy cowlick.

"Come on, Paddy." She pulled him up the stone stairs and into the shade of Tony the Shylock's hallway, pinned him to the wall, kissing him with a will to be caught at it and reprimanded by Robert Stoney himself. "Come on, Paddy," up the stairs, creaking and puffing through old static light to the very door between them and Dincher. She opened the cotton dress and clutched at Paddy, kissing and biting him with a will to be caught at it and killed by Dincher. "Do it wild," she hissed against Paddy's chest, "do it crazy, stickman, snap it one time."

But Paddy only laughed. "Naa, naahaa, Diaaaane," laughed though his eyes went frantic; he wrapped the dress about her, tied the cotton belt at her waist. "Dincher'll cut me open," he laughed, not quite able really to suffer fear. He ran tripping down the stairs as she banged on the tin door, and she was alone when Dincher let her in. "Doll—" he tried to keep her in the doorway—"Stoney, like-he——"

"So what?" She passed him and went down the room to where the painter meddled with his pictures. "Get them all the hell out, Stoney. Go on, all of them. In a hurry, Stoney."

"Diane! Is this where you've been staying?"

"Yeah, you want to come here and teach me the golden age? I know the golden age better than you ever dreamed, Stoney fatmouth," though no gold touched her anywhere at all, no Horse did anything but keep pain a stranger. "You want to learn about the golden age, Stoney?" She turned to Dincher, laughing, but Dincher stalked off, muttering, to the kitchen. ,

Stoney raised his head till the beard pointed at her eyes. "Your mother is ill, Diane. She's in bed and——"

"Go get her, fatmouth. It's set up now; go get her," she laughed, sitting down on the dusty couch. "What do you want me to do about it? Nurse her?"

She smelled greasy to his sensitive nostrils, as though she'd painted out an odor of decay with some unperfumed salve. There was evidence enough in her behavior to convince anyone she needed attention. If Vivienne saw her this way, she'd know her duty was to put her daughter under observation—to free herself of any more anguish. "Diane, your mother has a letter from Carter. Wouldn't you like to hear how he's been?"

"Who cares how *he's* been? What are you trying to do, con me into going home to Mama? Listen, Stoney, I can take care of myself, I can——"

"You must be terrified of me." He turned and lifted two pictures.

"Of you!" She laughed. "You don't scare me and neither does she!"

"Well, then, why don't you come see her?"

"Come on . . . I'll see anybody. Who cares?" She went toward the kitchen, talking over her shoulder. "Go on, carry your stuff down and wait for me." She found Dincher crouched over on a chair; he looked up out of an old man's pinched and worried face. "What's eating you, Dinch? Everyone's frantic today, everyone."

"You took a blast," he whispered. "I can hear it in your talk. Where'd you take a blast, doll, where?"

"Aw, bullshit. So what? What's the difference?"

"How you gonna take care of the kid if you're on horseback? How? Go on'n tell me, maybe you know what I don' know; hah?"

"Sh! Wait'll fatmouth cuts out." She went to the studio and saw

Stoney pass out through the door with a load of pictures. "Listen," she said, back in the kitchen, "you want me off Horse and you want me to get the kid, and don't think I ain't hip why you want it. You got it figured. Like everything nice and we get married and you get a job and me with the kid, I can't do anything you don't know about. You get a job! That'll be the day."

"Doll—" he was out of the chair, putting his hands on her waist —"I get a job is right. We make it like human beins, we——"

"Don't bring me down, Dinch, cut it out. Like we don't dig the same way. You got to know everything I do, but you couldn't stand what I want to do. I mean it, Dinch; you couldn't stand it."

"Whatta you mean?" He began to shake her. "Whatta you do I couldn' stand? If you're off Horse, whatta you wanna do I couldn' stand?"

His twisted face frightened her with more than a threat of violence. There was a passionate hatred there, not of her but of things that made her, things that lay between them, things he couldn't name. "Nothing, Dinch, I'm just running from the mouth, that's all. Dinch, tomorrow we go out to Lawrence and case the road; you dig? We watch and see when they go out and everything; right, Dinch?"

His face relaxed, and he wiped his nose as it began to run. "You wanna snatch the kid?" Pondering, he stalked out to the studio, where she followed him around the wheel-bottom table. "It's your kid," he muttered. "It's your own kid anyway. Like-you got a right. It's yourn."

"Tomorrow, Dinch; we case it tomorrow," while he nodded. "I'm going to my mother and look her in the face. Tomorrow, Dinch."

"Yeah, go on, I'm gonna start bustin out soon. I'm not poppin at all today'n you don' have to stick aroun'n see me squall. But you be here at night; you hear? Don' lemme wake up'n find you ain' here."

"Okay, Dinch." She smiled, kissed him and left, hurried down to find Stoney sending Timmy off with the pushcart. "Come on, Stoney, come on."

He gave her a bow, foolish in his beard and silk shirt. They found a cab on MacDougal, and Stoney helped her in with more absurd graciousness. "That's a very pretty dress," he said as he lighted a cigar. "Unique. I never saw a summer dress with sleeves on it."

"I made it myself," with no fear that he suspected the reason for sleeves. Smug eyes like his, looking for distant meaning, never did see realities under the nose that blocked their view. "You don't have to make conversation with me, Stoney. Like you don't owe me anything; you don't have to be like hung up."

It was a statement with which he concurred heartily. Words were wasted on her; any kind of attention to her was a waste. It only disturbed him that Vivienne was tied by blood to this wanton brat. Tied and bound so with anxiety over an emaciated little nymph that her own womanhood couldn't emerge. One look at her daughter and the Stately Lady would know the proper course to follow.

The cab pulled up at the corner, and Stoney handed over a dollar, waved the change away, and ran around to help Diane out. "Your mother will be happy to see you, my dear, very, very happy."

"What did Carter say in his letter? Did he mention me at all?"

"He asked for you. Yes, he did that," keeping his voice soft. Up the carpet of stairs and down the hallway to the door. He knocked and sucked in his abdomen. "You should have left it open, my dear," he told Vivienne as she pulled her robe tight about her, blinking at Diane.

"Baby, my baby!" She embraced the girl and wept. "Diane, stay here, stay with your mother. . . . I need you."

"What's wrong with you, Mama? Get back into bed and tell me. What is it? What's wrong?" She helped her mother to her room, out of her robe, fixed the sheet over her legs, and sat on the bed. "What are you sick from, Mama? You can tell me."

Her mother lowered her eyes and giggled, turned away with the shyness of a child. "Helplessness," she murmured in her special holy voice. "Just helplessness, Diane," and giggled again.

"What do you mean, helplessness? That's no kind of disease."

Vivienne raised her soft eyes and immediately burst into weeping, with feeble words tripping over the sobs. "You . . . don't you understand, my baby? You . . . it's you . . . I don't know what . . . what to do any more. Tell Robert to come in. Call him . . . for me, please," and moved a sewing basket to the side as if she needed something to do with her bony white hands.

"Hey, Stoney!" Diane shouted without making a move. "Stoney, come on in! . . . You don't have to do anything for me, Mama. I'm okay; you don't have——"

"What is it?" Stoney asked with elaborate anxiety. "What happened? Did anything——"

"Oh, take it easy, the two of you." Diane leaned back on her elbows with the feeling that she was watching two children playing "House." The room was large and immaculate with flimsy curtains over the blinds and coverlets on all the wood furniture; it was spotless, almost as sterile as a hospital room.

"Tell her, Robert. Tell Diane what I've been through over her."

"Well—" he took a small carved chair—"I hardly know where to begin."

"Don't bother," Diane said. "What's Carter got to say? How's he doing at school? Did he tell you what marks he got?" and laughed at it all alone. Her mouth had dried out and she half expected a sucking call for Horse in her legs. "Stoney, get me a drink of water, would you?"

He was quick to go. Vivienne sat up and reached for her hand. "Diane, he's very much concerned over you. Carter is. He told me to write and tell him how you look physically, whether you've lost very much weight."

"What's his damn business? Who's he supposed to be anyway, my father?"

"Diane, he's tried very hard for you. You know that. He——"

"Boy, you're all for him now all of a sudden. As long as he's nagging me you're all for him." She reached for the glass Stoney held out and took huge gulps of water that tasted like sand.

"I wrote and told him. I said you're wasting away to nothing. I told him, Diane, I did," as though she were applying the worst kind of threat imaginable. "You'll see, he'll write and tell me to have you hospitalized. He will, and I'll do it too, I will, Diane."

"Hey, who's he supposed to be? And this big pig Stoney. What are they, my fathers? And you—you're not even my mother. To hell with you all!" She got up, ready to leave.

"Diane! You wait! Remember, remember . . . Oh!" She doubled over, holding a breast. "Oh, my heart, my heart!"

Stoney leaped to place hands on her shoulders. "See! Now see what you've done. Diane, you're a cruel little——"

"Blow it out your ass, Stoney!"

"Wait!" Vivienne was up again. "Diane, I'm going to have you committed. Go on, threaten to kill me. Go on, I'd rather die than see you waste away. I would!" She burst out with new tears. "I don't want to live and——"

"You have me put away," Diane said through her teeth, "and it won't be you I'll kill." She saw her own hands leap to the sewing kit and come toward her with the scissors, straight for her heart—a force just as strange kept the point from plunging. "I can do it like combing my hair. It'll be your fault," looking wildly between two transfixed faces. "It's all your fault—everything. Why am I alive? Who asked you to bring me into this ugly, ugly . . ." She threw the scissors at Stoney, laughed when he screamed, and ran from the place.

Stoney felt his belly, where the scissors had struck, bent to pick them up, feeling absurd for the move. He heard the outside door slam, saw Vivienne with bloodless hands at her face. "Now . . . control yourself," he said, and heard his voice quiver in a false pitch. "Vivienne," slow and low as he sat puffing on the bed's edge, "no emotion. Emotion won't help, won't change matters. Coldly, as coldly as we can. Logic is the proper——"

"Oh, Robert! Robert, did you see her face? Oh, Holy Father . . ." She was quaking visibly before him. "Heaven forgive us; what have we done?"

"Vivienne." He took her hands down and held them, even squeezed them carefully. "There is only one thing, one thing. She must be put—she must be prevented from doing herself any harm. She's irresponsible. She'll—she'll really injure herself if we don't stop it. Call the Welfare Board, warn the police; let the authorities, the proper authorities——"

"No, no, Robert." She was whispering now, with eyes drifting in search of something to fix upon. "No, no, she'll do it. If we confine her, she'll do it, I saw it in her face. Ohhhhh," shaking her head with futility. "She will, she will."

That would be solution enough, but he knew better than to voice the opinion. "She will at any rate, even if we leave her to wander." He kept his tone mild to soothe her. "The only thing we *can* do is place her where she can be watched and rehabilitated. It's our duty, Vivienne; it's all that's left to us, our only recourse."

"They watched Edna." She sat, staring. "Watching doesn't help. I've watched them for years . . . and had others watch them. But watching . . . watching . . . Ohhhh, did you see my little girl's face? Diane. It was Diane's face."

He summoned patience with difficulty. "My dear, we must be decisive." He swung around to sit right beside her, touching her pajamaed shoulder with a hand. "Diane . . . the poor child is irresponsible. We must act for her; we must take the initiative."

But Vivienne had withdrawn from him. Days that lay on her brain in disarray could never be recalled, could never be differently arranged, and upon that yellow mound of errors lay the broken bodies of her daughters. "No! No!" she cried. "She'll do it. I know she'll do it, just as Edna did. I've killed my babies, I've——"

"Don't say that, Vivienne. You didn't; nobody made them do——"

"I didn't, did I?" She was up, wailing, an entreaty in her eyes. "Robert, I didn't know, we're too small to know. Only the Lord, only the Lord knows. We can't know what . . . We're helpless, Robert. Say it, Robert."

"We are, we are, Vivienne," taking her shoulders in a slight, uncertain embrace. "Don't blame yourself; you mustn't do that. We'll save her; we'll put her where she can't harm herself. You'll be free, Vivienne; it won't be your responsibility."

She pulled back. "No! It *is* my responsibility! I won't shun it. I won't confine her." Confinement would be murder. She knew it by the wild face of her daughter still glaring in imagined shadows. "I'll pray, Robert, I'll pray for the Lord to guide her."

"We'll see." Stoney patted her back. "You rest and get well, my dear, and we'll decide later. You can't make decisions when you're upset, you know," telling himself that at any rate they'd be free of the girl. He only wondered how he'd get the rest of his pictures, his easel, his wheel-bottom table—he certainly wasn't eager to expose himself to a madwoman, juvenile or not.

Dincher had been silent on the trip out, and he was silent now, except for the noises he made sucking his hard candy, as they left the Long Island Railroad by the Eighth Avenue subway for home.

"It's the hottest I ever remember it," Diane complained. "Bad enough outside," she went on, "but down here it's like hell itself." She couldn't yet tell whether or not she was glad that the Burnells were away for the summer; it was a confusion in her gummy mind: her eagerness that morning had been a deference to Dincher's watchful eye, yet when they had found the shuttered windows in the house on Bluethorne Walk a pang of regret struck her, then passed; kept returning and drifting away as they traveled back. "It's only another month," she had tried to comfort Dincher. "We'll snatch him when they get back in September," failing to convince herself she'd be alive three more long and tedious weeks. Three weeks. Hundreds of sticky hours between Horse and Dincher. He'd kept her from her morning pop, given her hard candy to suck till her jaws ached, and now she decided she'd not stay a minute in the loft if he refused her again. There were forty shining caps in a box under the dresser at the MacDougal Street trap, and a smiling Paddy who wouldn't have taken more than five. She looked at the Dinch's twitching face, running wet as though each pore wept in pain. "What do we have to kick for now?" she asked in his ear.

He laid an evil look on her, showed his teeth with a curl of his lip. "Jus because! Jus because; awright?" and pulled her by the sleeve when the train stopped. "We be straight when September comes; you hear?" yanking her up the stairs through gray light to the sun pressing cruelly outside.

Sixth Avenue was desolate at the height of the afternoon; figures moved here and there around parked automobiles, slowly like awakened dead in heat waves visibly rising from the gutter. The air stank of a month's perspiration, of garbage long gone from store fronts, of the whole city's breath hanging on stagnated air. "Dincher," she had to say, "you know what? Like he's better off, the kid. Maybe it's not right to take him away from that lady. Now he must be on the grass somewhere; you dig?"

Dincher trudged along beside her down Waverly. Heavily he lumbered along, grinning mirthlessly into the sun, panting, grabbing her arm to keep her from turning into MacDougal, leading her across into the park.

"Come on, I want to go home, Dincher, I need a blast."

He held her arm through the center of the forum circled with people immobile on green benches. "Here, you see kids?" he finally said. "See, in carriages wit their old ladies sittin aroun?" He led her down the lane toward the fountain pool at the middle of Washington Square. "See them jumpin aroun in the water? Laughin? Like they don' have to be in the country if they can't."

She pulled back. "But we'd be running all the time. We couldn't just sit around if we snatched the kid," afraid to go near the pool right now, terrified that someone might be around who had seen her smother a small ballplayer with kisses of remorse. "I can see them splashing; we don't have to jump in with them."

He didn't press her; he only slung his hands into pockets and followed her through to MacDougal. Paddy Jenks sat on the stoop, smiling in the sun as they approached. But when Dincher mumbled a greeting and Diane passed right by with the boy, she took one look over her shoulder to see Paddy's face dead-white with a straight unsmiling mouth. There was a nervous tug at her stomach, as if she'd witnessed a child turning to stone; she hesitated, but Dincher pulled her along.

Down Bleecker they saw Timmy Lawless sitting on the curb beside an empty pushcart, and when they got closer they saw that tears shone out from the gleam of sweat on his face. "Forever he's cryin,'" Dincher complained and passed him to go up the steps, waited in the indoor shade while Diane went over to inquire.

"What's eating you now, Timmy?" while impatience tugged at her spine.

"The ar-tist." He turned that creased face up, glass eyes into the sun. "He's supposed to give me more work. I did the work yes-t'rday and he promised me mo-ore. Five more trips," he wailed, "and I could be free."

"What do you mean, free, Timmy?"

"The ar-tist . . . with the beard," he sniffled. "Gave me three dollars to take the pret-ty pictures over to Sixteenth. Supposed to give me three dollars for every trip . . . lots of pictures . . . and a painting stand and a table."

"Well, he'll show up, Timmy. Don't sit there and cry," hating Stoney in spite of what she promised.

"I need it . . . or I'll never be able to pay Tony. I'll have to . . . stay down there . . . for-ehhh-ver," licking tears from his lips as his shoulders trembled under the torn old shirt.

"What? Pay Tony? You mean you clean up and everything because you owe him—you're like a prisoner?"

Timmy nodded miserably. "I hate to work . . . but in the Bi-ble it——"

"Come on! Get up off your ass. Come on, where's that old Shylock son-of-a-bitch? Come on, we'll find him and cool him off. You don't have to work for Stoney." She tugged at his shirt collar. "You don't have to do anything."

"Sto-op!" he wailed, holding away from her tug. "It says so. . . . I *want* to work, I *want* to pay Tony back. I like it, I like it," weeping louder to prove it. It wasn't for her to decide; she went up behind Dincher.

When she asked for her Horse he poured milk and made her drink it. When she cried he slapped her across the face, threw her on the bed, popped hard candy into his mouth and sat beside her, blowing short scrambles on his horn while longer ones pulled at her stomach. By evening she was nauseated and pushed away the eggs he had scrambled. She screamed when the place was completely dark, and he quit playing the trumpet, heated up a two-cap charge and injected her himself, without pumping it back and forth, just splashing it in and yanking out the setup. "That's no charge for me," she shouted. "I won't even get a buzz. I'll get rocks—I'll get paralyzed in my legs."

"I'll pop you again like-when it's too bad to stand," he said tenderly in the dark. But he slapped her when she began to yell, and yanked on the light the better to watch her, the better to show her a face swollen with pain and intent. His fingers crept about on his lap as he sat watching her with a stranger's agonized eyes. "You think I'm dumb," he panted. "You think I don' know anythin about what you like to do; you think so."

"Dinch—" she watched him labor for breath—"Dinch, better take a pop yourself. You look crazy, Dinch."

"Me, I am crazy awready from you. I wanna go away from you 'cause like-I hate you . . . but I get crazier when I go away. I don' know, I get plain crazier; see? You gonna kick'n I die before I let you out. You stay here till there's no more Horse'n I kill you if you sneak out. You hear me? I kill you if you run away."

Her hand went automatically to his face to feel for a round cheek she'd used to know so well. Sallow skin lay rough on muscles that twitched beyond his knowledge of it. Still it was little Dincher who loved her to hurting, and the fear she felt wasn't for the threat but for the horror in him that made him mean exactly what he said. She pulled him over on her and held tight while Horse failed to soothe her of pain. They lay sweating upon each other till the dull burning began in her groin. "I need more, Dinch; I need it bad, Dinch."

"We both need it," he whispered, "but we're holdin out."

They held out till morning, though neither slept more than minutes at a stretch. Doubled over in a hundred cramps, he moved through the rolling blue of dawn, boiled up a fix that couldn't get either high and used it on them both. Pain subsided to gentle tugs, strength never got to her legs. He played those short agonies on the golden horn through the fever of another day, fed her milk and tomatoes with the junky's knowledge of substitutes for well-rounded meals, ate eggs himself, vomited them up in the kitchen sink. By evening he collapsed in welcome exhaustion and tossed fitfully through nightmares he identified with shrieks of "Cut it off!" and "Kill 'im!" among less coherent outbursts, till she could hold out no longer and fixed a good load into herself with no luxurious power to concern herself with Dincher's probable reaction to five caps gone from his ten remaining.

But as pain vanished and her legs let her feel their muscles she began to tremble with a fear greater than any kind of doom. While he tossed in the stains of his sweat she slipped out and down and past the Riviera. She went short of breath on the way up sighing stairs, let herself into a dark closet of a room, and reached under the dresser to feel nothing but clusters of dust. Like a nightmare. She switched on the light, saw no Paddy, found no cardboard box of Horse caps. Searched through drawers, emptied them of underwear and rubble no one ever used, tore up the bed for some reason she'd never understand, and ran, panting, from the room. Directly to the Riviera. Searched faces. Cursed squares who swore they were born for her. Ran out and froze on the airless corner, not knowing where to go.

From the sweating crowd before the tavern Louella Nordvahl appeared, her fingers worming around a cross the size of her hand, hung from her neck on a chain thick as cable. "Diane—" her voice was borrowed from angels—"are you busy?" with the demurest kind of smile in a face grown thin.

"Busy? Am I busy?" The term seemed weird. "Why? What if I'm busy?"

"I wanted to speak with you," holding up the monumental crucifix.

"Put that thing away. You think I'm a vampire or something?" She might have been one at that, for the paleness she felt in her face, for the drained veins she felt lying dead around her muscles.

"It's about Robert. He's a good man, Diane. He's sorry for all——"

"Robert? Who the hell is Robert? Listen . . ." But she saw Robert, knew who Robert was by the beard pointing out of the crowd. "He sent you over?" and had no need for a reply. She looked frantically over the ground, ran in through the Riviera's door, and snatched a beer bottle from a table, ran out again, saw Stoney hurrying across the street, and threw the bottle with all her meager strength, ran down Bleecker with the crash of glass in her ears, and was panting in Dincher's loft with no memory of stairs. She heard no sound in the darkness, hurried to the room's end and collapsed on the dusty old couch, sucking for breath, till she could feel blood running freely down the walls of her life. She sweated Edna's tears with her sister's face weeping where a skylight used to be. She fixed her mind on the few kinder things it could invoke: the knowing eyes of a long-ago Carter Webb, the husky apologies of Letrigo; Dincher's young round cheeks, Paddy Jenks when he was only a Viper girl's idea; Johnny, her baby, close to her bosom for one ambitious afternoon. Pain ebbed and all afternoons were forever gone dark; only the fear of Dincher's pain bit at her heart. But her eyes were dry with a remembered hopelessness that had kept them dry for years. She even tried to cry, but her eyes were dry forever.

Diane counted minutes in the dark by the tick of her pulse, puffed air hotter than her body, plucked at clothes sticking to her skin. Stood and removed limp clothes, spread them over the couch and fell back, naked yet cloaked in a fabriclike, motionless heat. Felt the couch transmit dirt wherever its old mohair found her skin. Heard a woman cry for help outside, a man curse. There was a tapping on the roof, a scratching . . . or in the ceiling . . . rats, and she imagined too well their bead eyes and twitching noses. But a long whir relieved her; the voice was of rain, not dirty animals but fresh water from the sky. Still the heat oppressed her, closed in, and she had to pant for air in the black corner on a filthy couch. There was no promise on earth outside of sleep, but sleep held off like some new spiteful enemy. She heard Dincher moan, tossed as he tossed, sat up, rocked forward on her face into dusty mohair, rolled over with her head hanging back over the arm, a leg on the couch's back. Under a blanket of black heat. The night laughed at her for trying, and when sleep hid behind minutes that bobbed into hours she decided to trick it into service. Once and for all, with no despair, no regret or anger.

A few quiet steps over wood, and she closed the door before pulling on the bathroom light. She blinked in the knifelike light and found iodine in the cabinet above the old stained basin. The bathtub was cool to her thighs as she sat back on it; uncapped the bottle, and caught the burned smell of iodine deep in her nostrils, saw the fluid gleam black under the near-by light. Rain lashed down the tin ventilator like a shocked beast, the walls sweated in the small room. She brought the bottle to her mouth and laughed back at the night, at sleep trying to foil her. Tasted the iodine and yanked it from her mouth—the taste was of pain, burning, torture. She capped the bottle, set it down on the basin, and got up to search again in the cabinet for something quicker, less painful. Found razor blades, chose one with a clean, unbroken wrapper, heard frantic pounding on the staircase below her, louder and louder, heard, "Dinch! Dincher!" and ran to the couch to get into the wrap-around dress by light borrowed from the bathroom.

"Dincher!" she called, putting on the light.

"Dincher!" She was echoed from outside while fists pounded on the tin door. "Diane! Diane! Dincher!"

The voice was hoarse with panic, but familiar. She opened the door, and Angie ran in, circled back to the bed, and pounded the Dinch frantically on a shoulder. "Get up! Dinch!" He looked up at Diane. "Paddy! He's dyin, he's blue like—like my pants!" nodding to indicate faded dungarees. "Dincher!"

Dinch reared up, greasy with sweat, rubbing his eyes with flat fingers. "What! What! Eeeeah!" sucking for breath. "You crazy? What!"

"Come on! Paddy, he's stiff up in Lizzie's. Come on, quick!"

Diane had her sandals on before Dinch slipped into moccasins; they stomped down into a street cooled by vanished rain, swiftly over to Lizzie's, and up. "He's dead?" Dincher finally said. "He's stiff, you sure?"

"He's like-blue like my pants," Angie puffed. "He popped a gallon of Horse. He's cold-like, I swear!"

Paddy Jenks lay stiff on his back, unmoving, blue as Angie's pants all over the face, blue-white about the throat; Lizzie came out of a closet, whimpering; Diane thought only of Paddy, unsmiling for the first time she'd ever seen his lips arched downward, unsmiling on his stoop in a hot afternoon sun. "Grab him out!" she ordered the immobile boys. "Take him down," and it was her own body she helped them carry out, dead by iodine or razor blades.

A scream from Lizzie that paralyzed them all! Her finger pointed up the stairs where Buster Wallinger stood, crouched and highlighted by a forty-watt light, chewing the air slowly with tusklike teeth, flashing a long silver knife, then turned and disappeared up toward the roof. "You seen him! You seen him?" not sure any more of anything at all.

"The hell with Buster!" Diane shouted. "Get Paddy down, or we'll all go inside forever."

Down on the street level Angie let go of his end and everybody fell. Stiff Paddy rolled over; Angie vomited in a corner, splashing on the tiles.

"Guy can' help it like-he gets sick," Dincher apologized for Angie, and they took their burden up, Lizzie whimpering as she held a token hand to Paddy's leg: "He popped fifty caps at least! On top of evvythin Buster shows up! Ohhh, you seen Buster? You b'lieve it now? He's flip, he walks all night on the roof. Paddy he's stiff, he's——"

"Pipe down, Liz." Diane's voice was steadier and kinder than she'd expected. She ran out ahead, looked up and down Bleecker, and motioned them on into deserted predawn quiet. Puffing, they followed her down to the corner of West Broadway, across after hasty glances all around, and down Bleecker again toward Wooster, to a stoop where Diane had them stretch him out. Away into the start of a drizzle, and she made them return to pull Paddy into the hallway, muttering that he might still be alive, for all they knew. "Like-they never find him in here," Dincher complained, but she pulled them down Thompson to an all-night poolroom and had Angie call the police, told him the very words to say. Angie hung up when he was asked his name, and the four went as casually as they could back to Bleecker and westward again in the first whisper of light.

Diane didn't complain when Dincher invited the panicked Lizzie to stay the rest of the night, even brewed coffee for them all, and they watched dawn tint Stoney's cracked-wall kitchen. Coffee didn't calm the bird-faced little snorter. She prattled a weird mixture of fright over Buster and mourning over Paddy, Magoo and Muffo Smith, and Dincher felt a duty to mention Edna in the requiem. Diane didn't care about anyone at all, couldn't feel any fear over what Dincher might do when he found five caps gone from his poke, his paper bag gummed to the undersurface of a wheel-bottom table.

Dincher played Bop on his trumpet till everyone was asleep across

the narrow bed, and Diane felt a fleeting horror when he shook her
awake by the arm. "You took a pop?" he asked gently, and she nodded. "You took five caps?" She nodded again and he laughed, walked
away in the dank sunless morning, shaking his head, came back smiling, sucking a hard candy. "Well, it's five caps less for kickin. Like-you
gonna cold-turkey it now, doll. Me, I'm omos done," and blew his
small hook nose into a sweaty rag.

"You don't want to help me, Dinch?"

"Sure I wanna. But I ain' bringin in no more Horse." He fell back
into the soft chair, mopped his forehead, and bit down hard on the
candy as his face knotted up in pain.

"Will you get me some goofballs? Maybe I'll sleep through it,"
wondering why she cared at all.

"Sure, I get you some goofballs." He lurched up and away as if he
couldn't stand looking at her.

When pain began to bloom in her, when sweat turned to ice on
her forehead and neck, she tried to walk her insides quiet, but her
legs cramped and she had to sit on the couch in dust and ancient
dirt. She had to watch Dincher spitefully fix a snort for Lizzie on a
matchbook, had to look at the shriveled woman's arms, flabby but
unscarred. Angie promised to return as soon as he scored for some
Nembutal; the little aged woman went, close by the boy, and Diane
sat silently through the afternoon, biting her pain back so that
Dincher wouldn't see her take a fall.

For, reduced by his own tortured guts, he had little room for compassion and milled about as indifferent to her as any stranger. He was
an enemy just as she was an enemy to the world, just as all men were
foes in the narrow space of their suffering.

Diane drank milk, ate tomatoes, and threw it all up. She listened
to music about Nothing and understood it as she understood nothing
outside. By nightfall Angie returned with a jar of Nembutal capsules,
and Dincher let her take two. She was kicked to sleep with the force
of a hammer blow to the head. Woke up to retch in the dead of night.
Found Dincher playing a muted trumpet for Angie and Lizzie in
the chipped kitchen, returned to bed to lie alone and sleepless with
agony as bedmate. She saw Lizzie slip to the rear and fall on the
couch, scream for Angie when the boy tried to slip out the door.

"Shut up!" Diane cried out with all the stifled pain in her guts,
but no tears lubricated her throat.

"I hear him on the roof!" Lizzie wailed. "Je-sus, I hear 'im. He's stalkin arou-ound wit that big kni-i-ife! Angie, don't go way, stay by me, Ange."

"Dincher!" Diane shrieked. "Shut her up, shut her up!"

Angie went to the couch in shadows, Diane stared at the patch of skylight, Dincher clicked off the kitchen light and came over to flop on the bed.

"Keep off me!" Angie squalled. "It's hot; cancha sit quiet?"

Lizzie wailed with cracks in her voice, and Diane fell asleep in madness, ran with cramped legs through a stinking morass hung over with ghostlike trees. Ran, while swamp sucked at her feet, toward a distant neon sign in the shape of a cross. Toward a black panther that ran off when she got near, while she called "Buddy, buddy," meaning something else; till Dincher shook her awake and she heard Lizzie whimpering in some nameless morning's sun.

"You're no good!" the cracked voice whined. "I make a man outta you'n you good for nothin now," from the couch while Angie stalked around the squeaking floor. "You think I'm o-o-old? I ain't so old, you fagot kid!"

"Shut the hell up!" Diane heard her own voice burst like a broken claxon. "Go on, get the hell out of here. It's daytime; Buster won't come around; go on the hell out of here. Dincher, get them out, get them out."

Dincher went silently to the kitchen and returned with a glass of milk. "Don't pay her no mind. Drink it, go on'n drink."

Angie sat whispering to Lizzie on the couch, whispering to a wrinkled head the size of a fist. She fell back to kick at him with both legs; Angie jumped away, then leaped forward to smack her so hard that her head snapped and she fell unconscious.

"Jesus!" Diane bounded over. "You crazy? You must have broken her head, you flip kid," and lifted Lizzie in her arms. Lizzie came to and sobbed against Diane. "Get her some water," Diane ordered the frantic boy. Dincher played Bop while Angie fed his victim water.

Diane went off to retch over the toilet, and the days spiraled that way, with Lizzie weeping by night and milk turning sour in guts and hard candy in the mouth for grinding against pain and for energy in a stomach that couldn't hold food and goofballs to bring on fitful sleep. Hot baths to burn against a fierce burning inside, and sweat and retching and metallic pain and sitting in the Cosmopole with

the living mixing with apparitions of round-faced baby boys and gone
yellow-haired Daddio and women who looked like Edna. Ghosts in
violet light, and Red was out of jail, bitter against Dincher who had
nothing at all saved for a friend who had taken everybody's rap.
"Evvy dime," Dincher whined with guilt and the misery of a weakened body. "Evvy dime, Red, to put in a fix they shouldn't like-set
me up for a junk rap. Four cats I hadda pay off'n Buster he cuts out
wit no pay-off. I get him, Red, 'cause he shows his face, yet. He digs
he's hot, he digs evvybody sung about him to the Fuzz. I get him for
lotsa things; you hip?" and he turned eyes stored with old feeling on
Diane.

Diane sat fixed at her table, sniffling into toilet tissue plucked
from a pink wad in her bag. Sat there and told anyone who cared to
listen that pain was only a feeling, that one might just as easily suffer
as not, once feeling itself was understood. Junkies and derelicts and
poets who needed to learn about life—somehow convinced that life
and pain were synonymous—came to sit around her, and she dressed
in black as often as she could to convince everyone as though she
were a voice from old graves, with nothing to gain for herself, with a
preachment of Nothing to offer them all. Quit painting, she told
artists; throw your books away, she told students from the university
east of the park. "Come sit in the Cosmopole," she invited habitants
and tourists alike. "You don't need anything in this world; only poverty is holy." While Dincher bled the fish markets with Angie and
Red and came each midnight to take her to the loft, dole out Nembutal capsules, and tuck her in bed. She'd sleep each night with a
capsule clutched in her hand, wrapped in paper to keep it from melt-
ing, and she secreted many goofballs in a black-raincoat pocket for a
day surely arriving when she'd trick sleep into staying forever with
her.

Paddy Jenks turned up smiling the afternoon Steerman's funeral
procession wailed by. Though officially the writer was said to have
died accidentally, everyone in the Cosmopole knew better. There
were no accidents for the defeated; they chose their days and their
ways, and only the living who inherited their sorrow made excuses
for the one success in their lives. Paddy Jenks knew that not even an
overdose of Horse was an accident, and he smiled in his quiet knowledge, neither thanking nor blaming efficient doctors in a city ma-

chine for bringing him around. "It don't mean a thing," he said in the airless afternoon Cosmopole as Ralph Steerman's remains rolled by. "Go or come, it's nothin at all, it don't hurt and it don't feel good and it beats me why anyone squalls," for he had surely died one night on a stranger's doorstep, and spoke surely of the void he'd so solidly felt enclosing him.

"At least Steerman, he omos made it right," Lizzie Linden eulogized. "They suppose to wait till autumn to scrag theirself. That's what the psychologiss say. Here evvybody is contrary, they pick springtime. But Steerman, he omos makes it, not like them in the spring," as though, now that others had to admit Buster was somewhere about, she could afford to part-way believe suicides and not murders had occurred in early June. "He was fifty before he caught on that nothin means anythin," Lizzie went on. "He tole me so hisself—evvythin means nothin at all."

Diane knew by Paddy's white face that it didn't mean anything at all. Blue one day, white the next, while Harry Sticks stayed black as her blouse, black as the shrouded ladies in a black car behind Steerman's hearse. Nothing at all in the hot blue sky, but knots of fire unnecessary in her guts. Pain was only pain, yet she left the Cosmopole without a word and drifted through streets deadened by too much sun to sad Bleecker, breathless Bleecker with pushcarts and lazy shoppers. Up into shadows, automatically to the cellar to find out about shouting. Down to the shouting, around to the slat-wood door of a bathroom Tony the Shylock had once polished for her.

There, past the door, Tony in the tub rapped Timmy's thighs as the slave scrubbed the old man's back. Tony almost lost his cigar in surprise when he saw her standing there. "Hey, lilla Spaniol," while Timmy hitched up his shorts, "muh-you stand a look for Tone? Hey, what's a ma?"

Old welt scars on Timmy's back reminded her he loved his slavery; though she could easily drown the old man, she couldn't rob Timmy of his need. She spun and went, softly up through unobtrusive light, into a smoldering loft, to the closet in the rear, to the black-raincoat pocketful of goof. She peeled her clothes in order to lie in state, brought Nembutal and water to the bed, and lay there, propped on an elbow, drinking down a cap at a time, spacing them with minutes, until at last she fell back and was asleep before she hit the pillow. With the black body of a panther lying on her chest, dead as her mother's miles of threats, dead animals, dead dangers, dead warnings on her chest. Nothing at all.

Darkness. No place, no moment, never more an awakening in rolling gloom. No history of self or universe, still a cavorting fear, still a knowledge of sound and quivering shapes that had to be believed in darkness. But darkness could never be complete: other shapes than those of earth, other areas than space, nameless horrors in darkness, by far angrier than any eye of man. *Oh,* but she had no tongue to voice it; *Eeee,* but no throat to scream it. Yet fever found a target where body used to lie, and scorched all area and shape and quivering sense. Tears, fires in darkness . . . till a curtain lowered with the darkest black of all to hide shapes, tears, areas of fever, animals and threats and indifferent eyes, histories, rolling gloom, sounds. A long, long silence.

But hands and breath chose this night out of all nights for love. Anxious grasping, foolish impassioned breath in darkness that had no shape. Stupid rhythms. Husky words demanding, "Come on, come on, you dead or somethin?" Dead for sure, yet thumping where organs used to shiver. "Come on!" Then quiet again, no motion, only panting heat. "You got a blast! Like-you popped outta your noodle!" A slap and Face existed, Face, fever and limbs; and fear cavorting in darkness, shapes, a terrible yearning for light, oh light, oh light.

"Dincher, no Horse. Goofbaw, Dinsh, Nemby, too much. Assiden, Dinsh." *Get me back, get me to the light; one more time, one more, once again in light.*

Light was all about the place, and Dincher hauled her erect, dragged her over a mile of wood to the tub, rolled her over the side, turned ice water hissing over her fevers as she lay on stained porcelain. "Crazy, crazy!" he screamed. "Crazy, crazy broad!"

"Dinsh—" through bubbling ice water—"Dinsh, assiden, Dinsher, ack-siden-tt!" He had her sitting, held her by the hair, pounded her back and forth across the face, stinging, burning across the ice-water face while layers of shadow fell downward inside her. While Death sucked at her heart like a cheated vampire. Veins thumped faster than Dincher could slap.

He hauled her standing, supported her with an arm while his free

hand dabbed and rubbed with a towel. Carried her out, threw her
on the couch . . . wrapped her in white and tied the belt, slipped
sandals on her feet, dragged her downstairs into a hot black vacuum
pierced with drifting white lights. Around to a Sullivan Street lunch
counter. "Coffee, black'n hot," he ordered, and ordered it again on
Broome Street, and again on Sixth Avenue, silent while men he'd
have killed at another time jeered and made remarks about drunks.
Burned her insides with black coffee, let her vomit outside, and
walked her over all the cracked sidewalks and new concrete squares
in the Village. Got Angie and Harry Sticks and Brother Barber to
relieve him for the hours he needed for sleep, walked her without
rest for three nightmare days of black coffee and vomiting, finally
threw her into bed, where she slept a few hours before he wakened
her again. "I'm all right, Dinch," she begged, not believing it, not
thinking it mattered, only wanting to rest. "Dinch—" she caught him
about the neck—"you really love me, Dinch."

"I hate you. Like-I hate even lookin at you. I don' wancha; you
hear? Go on'n get outta here if you awright. Gaw 'head," yet never
pushed her arms away.

"No . . . no, you don't hate me, not you, Dinch. We'll get the
kid, we will. Don't hate me, baby, don't."

"In my trap you wanna knock yaself off. In my place so the
Law——"

"Dinch, it was an accident, I swear."

"Accident! Boy, you think I'm dumb! You get outta here. I mean
it." And now he yanked her arms away, threw her violently back on
the bed.

She wept, but her eyes failed to water. "Dinch, let me sleep awhile.
I'm okay now, let me sleep. Then I'll go, Dinch . . . then I'll go,"
not knowing or caring where, only wanting hard to sleep past the
terror in his wasted face.

"Go on'n sleep. But I wake you up in a couple hours, before it
gets night." It was late afternoon, she noticed now, that expiring
time when even the bright sun goes static, and in long rectangles of
yellow dust he walked up and back in his undershorts, reaching finally
for his horn behind the easel.

While his lead-colored laments did something to equalize the pressure of heat, she lay back into pillows damp with her sweat, pitched

about from side to side as the hungry sucking drew at her heart, and she hoped, as she began to ooze back into darkness, that she'd just never waken again.

Carter Webb dropped the handbill in his lap and looked down on Times Square aglare and pulsing in the night. Surging, crying out, blinking with the force of life, a great faceted diamond lying on the heart of the world . . . while small corners of living writhed in darkness. He ran his eyes over suitcases still packed tight on the bed, over walls painted with time, decorated with prints of pretty, pretty postcard skies, then looked again at the handbill Joe had sent. It all might have depressed him bitterly a season ago, but now he could hold it before him like a target along with old knowledge of such things, and face it with a detachment he'd learned in two months. He took up Joe's accompanying letter and fingered it open like some fine morsel he'd saved for last, glad he'd tucked it away before boarding his train so that he might sleep from Buffalo to home.

Dear Carter—
    Here you have a thing which doubtless has changed my life. What happened over it is something I'll never describe in a letter, but I'll tell you the minute that handbill was passed to me in City Square a chemical change took place in me and all my connections to things around me.
    Hensley, Tooney and Daddy Tom were along with me when we came by folks we know well tossing those sheets out to anyone coming by. Doc Cal's daddy Cuff Honeycutt, who was overseeing the work of passing those sheets, didn't pay Hensley much mind when he said softly that it would be a smart thing for us all to wonder awhile why labor leaders want to mix the colors. But Cuff paid me mind when I asked something about that list of Negroes here and Negroes there. His face fell and I thought he'd cry and maybe it was because I kicked up a real fuss. In all my life I've never been so ashamed of anything as I was of that list. Couple of things came together for me in it and I asked old Cuff how come no women were addressed at all. (You'll notice that if you read it one more time—"you, your wife and daughters," never "you, your husband and sons.") Well, you can't know what that little question gave rise to that night in City Square. Old family friends looking at me as if I'd turned into a buzzard before their eyes, lots of talk about "fools" who want to end segregation, "fools" this and "fools" that, with me never hearing an answer to my question. And Daddy Tom, I saw him go chicken beside me, hand-

WHITE PEOPLE
WAKE UP

BEFORE IT'S TOO LATE

DO YOU WANT?

Negroes working beside you, your wife and daughters in your mills and factories?

Negroes eating beside you in all public eating places?

Negroes riding beside you, your wife and your daughters in buses, cabs and trains?

Negroes sleeping in the same hotels and rooming houses?

Negroes teaching and disciplining your children in school?

Negroes sitting with you and your family at all public meetings?

Negroes going to white schools and white children going to Negro schools?

Negroes to occupy the same hospital rooms with you and your wife and daughters?

Negroes as your foremen and overseers in the mills?

Negroes using your toilet facilities?

Northern political labor leaders have recently ordered that all doors be opened to Negroes on union property. This will lead to whites and Negroes working and living together in the South as they do in the North. Do you want that?

GRAHAM STANDER FAVORS MINGLING OF THE RACES
    He admits that he favors mixing Negroes and whites—he says so in the report he signed. (For proof of this, read page 167, Civil Rights Report.)

DO YOU FAVOR THIS—WANT SOME MORE OF IT?
IF YOU DO, VOTE FOR GRAHAM STANDER

But if you don't

VOTE FOR AND HELP ELECT

JESS WILKINS

HE WILL UPHOLD THE TRADITIONS OF THE SOUTH

See-the-Truth Committee

shaking those maniacs, apologizing for me. Cal Honeycutt told me
again I'm psychoneurotic, delayed combat fatigue and all, and I took
it that he was one of them and I nearly did cry to think of it, for
Calvin is the oldest friend I have. Later that night, when I couldn't
stand to hear Tom fighting himself for a reasonable explanation, for a
way to convince me I had ought to hush, I ran from the house and
headed for town just to run into some of the maniacs who had got
bloodthirsty down there in City Square, and a group of men surrounded me in a doorway, and when I saw Cal Honeycutt scowling
at me I had to laugh, for had I seen his eyes studying me from behind
a white hood I'd have laughed at his whip, old Calvin. I found out
then that they were intent on keeping me hushed just so's I wouldn't
ruin the good work they were doing in their mannerly way, for it
seems Calvin and many more are of a mind with Hensley down here,
and blowtops like me are poison to their aims. And afterwards Hensley showed me how it all fits in a piece—inferior race, inferior sex, and
all of it part of a pattern perpetrated by economic savages who gear
it to tradition. Hensley just begged me to stay here with him and
fight it all with information, but I can't do it. I have only hostility
and violence to offer in a fight, and Hensley needs greater strength
than that. So instead I'll be moving off again, to keep from kicking
over the good work stronger people than I am are doing, maybe to
find me a shooting war someplace, certainly to come by the North
again and look some things in the eye.
    You should be heading back to the big lights soon yourself, so
I'll see you up there and tell you more firsthand.

    Carter looked out again at the big lights hundreds of yards below,
where the small specks of life scurried along, each so gigantically important to himself. He took a vast breath of autumn's first hint and
felt how important he was to Carter Webb. "New York, baby, here
we go," and he got to his feet, took four steps to the bed, and began
unpacking, hanging two suits in a closet, piling shirts, socks and underwear on the dresser, laying bathrobe and raincoat out on the
faded green hotel bedspread—deftly, with real organization, in as
few moves as he could manage. Shoes were in the closet and coats
were hung, and he had begun to fill the dresser drawers when a name
scratched on the mirror caught his eye—*Diane*, scratched in a quivering line and repeated more strongly right below . . . not *Diane*
at all, but *Anne*, just *Anne* scratched twice by some nameless hand
an unknowable time ago, some petty vandalism alive with reflected
light, faint lines just barely there, yet enough for his blood to charge
and shake. Diane . . . And, though the first image that came of her

was that of some woefully decrepit child, his lips still went into smiling over older images of a shiny gamin with great earrings swinging at her jaw.

But he had no more impulse to coddle and advise, this first night back, than to swing into work with Farrell. He reached for the phone to call Louella, a lot of woman to the eye, and hoped she'd really begun to seek herself, just as her letters had implied.

Convinced of Dincher's alienation, Diane left the loft one night while he was blasting from his nickel-plated gun at shadows that might have been Buster on the roof. While Dincher fired at shadows of his animosity, secure in the knowledge that backfires left city ears uninterested, while his steps pounded overhead, Diane went into summer's breathless end wearing black skirt, black blouse with sleeves that reached her wrists. She held court in the Cosmopole's ceaseless rumble, surrounded by disciples who brought their troubles to be ridiculed away. "Well, then starve," she told any lamenting poet. "All you can do is die. That can't be as bad as living," while junkies nodded in agreement and derelicts muttered in mild protest, with no real argument to offer. "If you're here, it's positive," she philosophized for the defeated; "if you're gone, it's negative," and everyone nodded because nobody knew how to contradict so tidy an observation. She spent nights with any soul who needed her, wanted her, or felt a debt to her poverty. Listened to Lizzie Linden's lectures on Rouault and Marin, slept in the frail woman's bed to awaken when Lizzie shrieked "Buster!" from dreams or hallucinations. Spent whole days in Harlem at the home of Harry Sticks's mother, helped the silent old lady tidy up and clean where no dirt was visible at all in the crazy apartment built around a central cagelike room where cousins and strangers lived. Slept between Nao and Clifford Braun, never quite sure who it was who bored her in the black of night. Lived three days with an artist square, watching him design pictures for magazines, overlooking his staid manners till he complained one night when she undressed by a window. Stayed anywhere at all with little change in feeling, returned always for evenings in the Cosmopole to sit and talk while disciples of Nothing gathered around, to go off for a small pop of Horse with friendly junkies who loved her.

When old Meyer Singler went mad on his seventy-fifth birthday, shrieking that he could no longer wait for peace, she sat making de-

signs on a table top with ashes from her cigarette while others
laughed or wept at Meyer's shrieking. When Paddy Jenks placed
twenty ten-dollar bills in her lap she did not return his silent smile,
but passed from table to table placing bills in twenty ragged laps; nor
did she question Paddy about the source of his wealth or his reason
for largesse. For there was no feeling in the girl, nothing she could
name; she gave no thought to life or death or the ladder of days she
descended. Dincher made her laugh from the surface of her face
when he offered to take her back if she'd willingly go with him for
Johnny. "I don't have any baby, man," she told him in his loft after
both of them had popped Horse into veins. "I don't have anything at
all. Like I'm God with nothing at all to plague me." Dincher left her
there to go shooting at shadows on the roof, and she returned to the
Cosmopole alone, with no regret, no kick from Horse, no need for
anything at all.

It was Carter Webb who pronounced her dead when September
was surely there. From the Cosmopole he'd taken her to a hotel uptown and loved her for a week end. A Carter Webb older than the
red-faced Carter who'd once accused her of being a thief. A Carter
newer than the man she'd rescued from her sister. A man strong
about the jaws, steady in his raincolored eyes, even and restrained in
his blunt Pennsylvania accents. A man who knew where he wanted to
go and why, too presumptuous an attitude for her, and he brought
her to Washington Square to sit under trees facing the arch, the
yawning stone mouth of the greatest mound of stone on earth. A
first autumn wind whipped around in circles, carrying discarded news
sheets to an endless sky, carrying along her discarded pasts and
futures while Carter pronounced her dead: "You're done, little girl,
because there's nothing you want any more."

She could have told him that herself, but didn't care to speak. She
could easily have turned a hopeful glance his way, but she didn't
care to strain for his comfort. She might have assured him that it
didn't mean a thing, but she really didn't want to destroy his philosophy with one incisive word.

When he said good-by with permanence ringing in his kindly tones
she had a swift recollection of what he once had meant to a girl who
needed a father, and, though the finality of his good-by lingered after
that recollection passed, there was nothing explosive about it, nothing shocking at all. It seemed as natural and preordained as the fall-

ing, floating, delicate scratching expiration of the leaves around them in the brutal dreariness that had once been an enchanted park.

Diane didn't bother to watch him go, for her mind easily made the scene and in it she saw a slope-shouldered man lumber away with the shell of a world on his back, into an enclosing fog—a scene more dramatic than any eye could show her. She sat there, uncaring, through the night, till at dawn a gentle nudging began at her groin and she went to Paddy's for a snort of Horse. The kick was slowly going back to snorting in this spiral of a world that spun and spun in one directionless path.

It was easy to endure the glaring Riviera light, the stink of beer, the mad voices of people frightened by their own apathy, impassive to their fear. For she'd mastered the highest mathematics, where all motion, hope and application added up to Zero. Through Louella came messages from Stoney saying that Mama was well as long as Diane remained calm. Louella, with rambling sentiment about Carter's patient understanding, accompanied her to church, where they sat in private devotion to their particular kinds of God, and Louella begged for the secret which allowed Diane to detach herself so thoroughly from earth as to care nothing for the passing of time, fear nothing in the demands of biology. "I'll tell only you, Diane. . . . I feel the need now and then to relieve myself as the ancient monks were taught to do," with a faint giggle reminiscent of a long-ago sophisticated girl.

"I let anyone use me who will," Diane deigned to say, more to the sky than to her prayer mate. "I have no worldly destination, and God can bring me who He will. That way I have no need; I have no body at all to sin with." It was an explanation Louella couldn't quite comprehend, but she had still a strict need to protect her soul from sinners.

Neither regret nor elation hovered about the girl without a body as she sat wherever she happened to be. She drank coffee in the Cosmopole with ice cream some junky would provide; ate an occasional sandwich on a dark stoop in Waverly's northward arm with faces she sometimes knew, sometimes never even saw; drank wine in the Riviera with Paddy or Canada Dan or some frantic tourist wanting to hold her hand or Harry Sticks and his smoldering hatred of whites.

The night of the Peekskill riot, when Robeson and his audience

were attacked by Red-hating citizens of a city to the north, and Reds
and blacks and whites and even some folks colorless enough simply
to like Robeson's rich baritone song were stoned and beaten and
struck back while the Law tried its clumsy best to stop the breach
of Peekskill peace by foreigners from New York City—that night
Harry Sticks, the ball-playing junky, blamed violence on the whites,
indiscriminately blaming all Caucasians out of an old frustration
that erupted finally into loud tearful bellows: "Savages! Animals! No
law holds up when white sons-of-bitching savages start screaming
for black men's blood," forgetting in his confusion that it was Red
men's blood no law was made to defend. The Riviera was aglare
with plaid jackets from uptown and men with last remnants of
pride focused on the color of their skins. The booth near a neon
window was surrounded by whites who felt their mothers insulted
and had fists ready to defend their reputations. So that Harry Sticks,
with a swift will to protect Diane and the Barber brothers, stood up
and left the booth before shouting at four men in sporty jackets
that violence was all they knew. "But I ain't backing away from no
damn pink-belly savage, not me," and stood with his bull neck in-
clined, his eyes darting yellow and black over four faces growing
paler with indignation and anxiety, four men of assorted size closing
in. "Come on! Come on!" Harry yelled with his back to the boards
of Diane's creaking booth, and it was the first emotion in months for
the little green-coated girl, the first lurch of nerves in her darknesses.

But a long lean man with a panther's grace sidled up beside Harry.
"Here comes the U.S. Cavalry," Joe Letrigo muttered to Harry,
leaning a shoulder on the black man's. "Come in or back away," he
drawled at the attackers, " 'cause we by God'll take as much as you
got the guts to give."

"Come on, fellers," a little stocky man said, "this place is full of
—full of them, you know what."

"Break it up! Break it up!" A bartender came between with another at his elbow. "Break it up!" while glasses clanked and voices
sang and laughed.

"Come on," a round man said, "the place is full of 'em."

"Bunch of damn Reds," another of the four said right at Joe, and
then shot back from a long swing that Joe hardly felt himself throw.
One man in the City Square turmoil had tortured him with that,
and finally in New York Joe had his revenge. He was in the booth

with Harry on his lap, black hands holding two angry bartenders back. "You heard what they called us, Mario," and Mario had to nod while other barhops pushed the uptowners out.

"Nobody got a right to say that about a guy." Mario shuddered till his big cheeks shook. He plucked the cigar from his mouth. "Nobody should call a man that," pushing through the crowd, wagging his squat head from side to side.

Harry swung around to sit beside pale Danny, and Joe choked when he saw Diane, not promptly sure it really was Diane. He pronounced her name twice before he took her hand, fighting to keep from clutching her to him.

"Joe Letrigo," she whispered, "my man Joe," as he squeezed her hand, not wanting to see the black sockets of her eyes, her drawn cheeks, swearing in his heart that he'd make her well as surely as the sun would rise, living again the moment in City Square when he'd wanted to look into eyes the color of a rainy night and admit he'd failed quite to realize how important was her will to stand as high as any soul on earth.

Harry and the Barber brothers were laughing over some larger victory than that won before the booth. "Man—" Harry touched Joe's arm with a finger—"you a Southern . . ." Hesitantly, yet knowing Joe as a friend past all bewilderment. "How come you to —how you come to——"

"I'll tell you," and wondered if he should, then knew he had to say it and did. "I don't know what it was about, but by God I *like* to see an angry colored man." He waited for nothing more, and pulled Diane through squirming bodies to the street, where a mist halfway between rain and fog made the night pallid. Up Bleecker to the west and into a doorway full of shadows that let him see her face as it once had been, as it could be again: eyes wetter than the night, blacker than all that lay behind in gone days, face smooth over the bony jaws tucked into his hand. "Diane, I never met you halfway, never——"

"Don't be a fatmouth, Joe," and she caught his lips in hers with waves of something she'd never felt before bobbing in her, rising out to wrap them together against the chill of September dankness and any frost that lay ahead.

He held her to his chest, shocked at her tininess; felt the bones of her back through layers of colored cloth, and bent to kiss her again, in the hollows of her cheeks, around the shadows of her eyes. While Diane knew his strength and remembered it as something promised to a woman she'd never been.

Westward through mists, silently past lighted avenues and forgotten side streets to the wide wooden docks leaning over the Hudson. Laughing together in wordless agreement through swirling, salt-smelling incandescence to the Jersey Ferry, arm in arm till the gate swung open and they boarded the old vessel with other silent passengers. They went through the bright, bench-lined hall to stand by the gate facing out across the river, and when the vessel sighed, shuddered, lurched, kicked up a froth below them, it was time to talk.

"Joe," she said, "it's not easy; you know that, Joe."

"Sure . . . I know it's not easy, Diane," holding her close by her shoulders, wanting her near him while the river lashed them with spray.

"Harder even than before, Joe, harder than before."

"I know, Diane."

"No, Joe, you don't know everything. I have a habit, Joe, like a sickness. I take dope. Not just marijuana . . . I take real stuff, Joe," and waited with a fierce anxiety that she'd missed so long, a quaking that she loved.

"I know all about it, Diane. I know even that you cured yourself once before and that you can again."

"I almost *did* again, I—— Joe, how do you know about it? Did Carter——"

"Yeah, he wrote and told me. Not gossipy, Diane, not that way. Forlornly, more like. That's a good man, Diane."

"Too good for me, too good, Joe. Have you seen him since you're back?"

"Just *got* back. I didn't know he was. Where's he at?"

"Uptown. Did he write you about Edna, about my sister?"

"Yeah, that's sad. But he expected it, he knew she was passing away."

"Didn't he tell you she killed herself? Right before his eyes?"

"No, he didn't—he said . . . He wrote that you were doin it, that you were killin yourself before his eyes."

Diane saw the rough skin of his face gleaming with river spray, reached to touch it. "He went nuts when she did it. She jumped off the porch at the hospital as he came up the walk. Landed right next to him. Eight stories." Saw the lines in his forehead tighten.

"Lordy. All he said was—over and over—she was dyin right along."

"I love Carter, Joe. Do you mind me loving Carter? He loves me too, Joe."

He waited, looking down at the lurching opaque waters cut by the vessel's blunt prow. "Sure, sure I mind. But I'll live it out; I'll win you from him, I will."

"No, you don't have to—Joe, you can't win me, I'll never belong to—Joe, don't you see? It has nothing to do with you. Carter . . . he won't have me either. Nobody has anybody in this world. That's where all the trouble comes from: people wanting to own each other. It's crazy, it isn't real, Joe. Don't you see, Joe? Joe, I have a love for you that I can see now. I know why I was afraid of you; it's because I was scared to meet you face to face. That's true. . . . Carter hipped me, Carter showed it to me. Babies and fathers were the only kind of men I dared get near. You're no father and you're no son, Joe, and I know I can make it with you. But don't make me lie, I don't want to lie any more. I'll do what I can, what I have to, Joe, what my body and soul want me to do, and don't, don't say those things are wrong. I've been told so many things are wrong that I did real bad things and thought they were right. Joe, you understand? Do you? If you said you didn't . . . Joe, I'd promise never to do anything you thought was wrong, because I want you now, I want to be a woman, not a baby or a governess. But, Joe, Joe, I'd have to live a lie to please you or lie to please myself. You understand, Joe?"

"Sure, just forget it," and he leaned on the rail to watch the Jersey lights come closer. "Words, they don't answer much. Let's see what happens."

"Joe, are you cold? You should wear a coat, it's getting colder these days." Saw him shake his head without a look at her, pulled a kerchief from her bag and tied it over her head while a chill shook through her. "Joe, come on and hold me. We'll see how it is, Joe."

He grinned and swung around, pulled her close while little cries for Horse began inside her. Unimportant nonsense in her gut . . . only pain, simply pain; she'd kick it in a week, she promised herself, and rubbed her face hard into his jacket.

They stayed aboard when the ferry bucked in between the log

barriers; on the trip back he told her of the last frantic week down
South, of his sister's husband and Hensley's deep similarity to Carter.
Showed her the handbill that would bring a charlatan to the Senate,
told how his leaving home made things safer for Hensley and others
who were showing the true heart of the South.

Diane was aghast at the handbill, said she wished Carter could see
it. "He'll show up in the Village looking for me," she said when Joe
asked where he could be found. "He tries to stay away, but he has to
see me just like I have to . . . I don't really, I don't really have to do
anything," she added, more to herself than to Joe. She could kick
Horse so long as there was reason to kick it, and there was reason at
her side, a man with right in his heart and a promise to see her right
in his brain.

He wanted to take her home, to whatever she called home, but
she insisted on going with him to his room in the Alphonse Hotel
off Irving Place. She told him right off that she was in pain she
wouldn't respect, had him hold her close, knew he was awake each
time she ran to the bathroom to retch. "It's like childbirth," she told
him in the morning. "Women can kick that habit easier than men;
that's the way the ball bounces."

But when he left to look for work she had to run over for a small
pop at Paddy's, telling herself it was allowable to kill the pain, to
taper off as she knew she could. She hurried back to the Alphonse
and slept till Joe returned, kissed him with a powerful surge of love
when she awoke to find him beside her. "You find a job, Joe? Gee,
you've been gone all day."

"No, nothin I wanted. I have enough money to be choosy for a
spell." They had dinner in a Fourteenth Street Hungarian restaurant,
and he took her uptown to see a play called *The Father*, swearing
there was nothing significant in the choice. Had coffee on a side
street afterward and returned to the hotel.

Diane got into his pajamas in the privacy of the bathroom, laughed
at her own modesty, then cursed herself for the truth. "Joe, you want
to see the scars on my arms?" she asked him.

"If you want me to," he said, lighting a cigarette, missing the ash
tray when he dropped the match. He looked at the pink arrow-shaped
marks that ran down the course of veins on each arm, felt a drawing
despair, but smiled past his weariness. "Those things'll go away,

Diane," hoping, telling himself that all the marks on her would pass into gone dust.

"Maybe," she murmured, and bounced on the bed in a way that called him right out of his chair to kiss her and hold her tight enough to choke her.

That was as far as he went in making love for some nights after shows and concerts and movies along Broadway. For he was determined to make no demand at all, to establish for them both a certainty that living together might be relaxed rather than anxious.

Yet to Diane it meant that something in her must still repel him. She took it well, with a strict mustering of patience. Each morning while he was away she ran out and had her pops smaller and smaller from smiling Paddy Jenks, whose voice grew quieter each day till his lips moved uselessly around words nobody ever heard.

On a Friday night she took Joe past trash cans and idlers along MacDougal in search of Carter, but the man whom both of them wanted to see was nowhere, not in any tavern. "He knows what he wants to do," Diane said on their way home. "He's on that union kick, he must be working hard."

"Walk softly; don't wake the clerk," Joe muttered, and they entered the hotel laughing, over the quiet carpet in the lobby, up in the elevator to the little room across the hall.

"Joe, why don't you try to get an apartment?" she called into the bathroom from the bed, pulling off her white-silk snood, kicking off her shoes. "I can cook up a storm; wouldn't you like me to cook for you?"

He looked out at her, grinning through the lather on his face. "I been lookin, Diane. If I ever do find one in this town, I'll take the next job offered me," and turned back to his shaving.

She lay back with her feet on the wall. "You know," she half sang, "you're lucky to have me, Joe. I can cook and sing, and on top of that I'm a glamour girl." When he came in she held him close. "Joe, you have a girl down South? You can tell me, Joe."

"Yeah, I have a pretty redheaded girl down home," and waited for her response. He'd phoned Marily the day after "City Square" and had been told she wouldn't speak to him. But she'd come through a day before he left, slipped out to meet him, just to cry for him to see, and to swear she held nothing against him in her heart, that only an angry father had made her act curtly toward him on the phone. "She's quite a fine little girl, right enough."

"Do you love her, Joe? Tell me the truth."

"Sure I love her. Not like I do you, though." Not to a point where he ached over her—that was what he meant, but he couldn't put it into easy-sounding words; he took Diane's face between his fingers, shook it gently, hoped she knew what he meant.

"You see, Joe? That's how we're made. We're only animals after all."

He shook his head. "No, we're more than animals. We reason, and it gets down into our impulses. Diane, even if you said you didn't care, I'd never have a splash with some other woman I was fond of . . . just for fear it might hurt you somewhere inside."

"But that's wrong, Joe. You've got to do what's natural." She slid into slippers. "If anything bothers me, it's my own hassel."

He followed her to the bathroom, sat on the bathtub ledge while she washed and brushed her teeth. "Diane, it's all how we let ourselves grow. There's some things you give up in order to have others," and promptly left the room.

She turned down the lights and slipped in beside him. "I love you, Joe, I really do, I really do," dug her nails into his neck when he kissed her, heard him tremble in his breath. "What are you so nervous about?" she laughed.

"That's passion, not nerves," he whispered.

"You're nervous, don't kid me. Joe, you're an old choirboy."

He kissed her quiet, kissed her until she trembled as he did. He had more than an urge to take her, he had to make something more of it all, he had to bring it around to their special togetherness, had to clean her skin of unfaded fingermarks, of other lusts, and had to make her know how clean she was for him. "It's just that—" and he had to whisper again to keep from sounding as foolish as he felt— "this . . . it's the first time I ever did have a virgin."

"Me too," she said softly.

Though Diane had brought her clothes from scattered places to Joe's small room, she'd not managed to bring herself altogether there. He felt it vaguely even when she was always on hand, knew it one evening when he came to a room as silent as an abandoned town. He idled for an hour in a hot bath to loosen his muscles after a day on a construction job out on Long Island. "Buildin for other folks where I can't build for myself," he muttered, and knew he'd work there no more after the week was done.

He ate in an Italian place around the corner, then returned for another look; she wasn't there, and he left for the Village, to circle the park, do the taverns and go up along Sixth to look in the Cosmopole. It was too early for anyone but transients in the Cosmopole; he pulled his hat low as it began to drizzle, slung his hands into pockets of his thin coat, and ducked around into the glare of Eighth Street, just walking. Looked in bookstores, windows, saw Robert Stoney with a foolish pointed beard cracking his knuckles beside some women at a print-shop window, didn't want to hear that yapping voice, and went around into MacDougal, past the Christian Science Reading Room, read some literature set up in its lighted window, went on and up Waverly again, across Sixth and over to look through the windows of the diner. Went in and down to where Slinger clacked on his typewriter at the counter's bend. "Hey, Slinger, you see Diane about?"

The little eyes lighted on him. "No, but I seen Carter. He just leaves after a tank of coffee. He hates my coffee, but he drinks it. That guy he muss sure like me," and laughed back to his work.

"Where's he gone? Did he say?" and hated himself for fearing that Carter might be meeting Diane somewhere.

"No, he don't say. You know him, he never says nothin. That's the guy's nature, he can't help that. One time I ask him . . ."

Joe nodded and left, meant to turn up toward Pacco's, but found himself running across Sixth to where Carter stood in his trench coat and hat talking to Lukey the Swede.

"Hey, Titanic *sinks!*" the Swede bellowed beside the boarded-up old newsstand. "*Read aBOD it! Biggest ship sinks! Titanic lost!*" waving a paper from the bundle he held in an arm, pulling a cap low on his head in nervous little flicks.

"Carter!" Joe called, and grabbed the man's hand, pumped it as Carter thumped him on the shoulder. "How're you makin it, boy? You look like an ole general, standin here. But good, good."

Carter patted him on the face. "They always come back to the Village. Goddam, it's good to see you, Joe."

"That's the way the ball——"

"See them?" Lukey giggled, his mouth tight over even little teeth, his chin somehow smaller, though skin had tightened out most of his wrinkles. "See them? They don't care I holler *Titanic* sinks. They walk right by; they think its nineteen-twelve ŏr somethin—ss-ss-ssss. *Read abod it!* Titanic *a goner! Ss-sss-ss.*"

"You really sellin them, Lukey?" Joe asked, still holding Carter by the shoulder.

"Sure, but it ain't the *Titanic,* it's the *Noronic,* and it don't sink, it burns from stem to stern as they say in the nautical. Ss-ss-ssss."

"Everybody looks good." Carter laughed. "Look at Lukey the Swede—he looks good and he feels good. Tell him about it, Luke, go on."

"Ss-ssss-ss. I learn the secret, and it's there ain't no secret. Everybody lookin for the song, and there ain't no song at all. No secret, oney what's gonna happen next. It's wonderful, what's gonna happen which you can't dig but you can be around when it does; you hip? Oney when you're stiff you lost the secret 'cause you ain't gonna be here when the next thing comes. Me—dig this—I get bust; see? They bust me, the Law, and incarcerate me like a sardine, but who do I meet there? A guy he must be from God 'cause he digs me I'm not bad inside. This guy gets me teeth, and, man, when I'm with choppers, well, it's like new eyes to see with; you dig? New eyes like. This cat, even he's a professor-type guy, like he's the examiner doc; you hip? Even so, he's on the track, he hips me I ain't gonna find no song till I'm right in the body. He pulls strings, man, you want to dig. He puts me on a taper, man, he works me outta that slammer and I make the air with no more vices, just with one secret that there ain't no secret, just I got to remember how to feel good it's in the body, it's in eatin and sleepin. *Read aBOD it. Moronic stinks!*" and faced them again, wrinkling his nose in laughter. "They never listen. You can say *Noronic* sinks any way you like. Okay, man, I see you."

"Ooee," Joe laughed as Carter led him away, "what did that man say?"

"Nothing and everything, it's how Lukey talks," stopping with Joe at the corner. "When'd you get back, Joe?"

"Couple of weeks. You don't come around much, I hear tell. What you doin down here tonight?"

"Looking for Diane." He grew abruptly sad and smiled to hide it.

"You haven't seen her in a while?"

"Not for a couple of weeks. But she's around, I'll find her. What's doing down in Dixie, Joe? How's Hensley getting on?"

Joe spoke of home, of Hensley starting up his newspaper, and as he spoke he looked over Carter's face, wondering how much he could say about Diane. He felt it a duty to be open with Carter, yet didn't want to hurt him. "How's ole Lizzie? You makin it with her at all? And Louella. She still——"

"You'd never know Lizzie, Joe. Screams at people and rambles on to herself. Nothing attractive about her any more."

"That's too bad. She was good trimmin, right enough. What about——"

"Louella . . . I'll tell you. She's just about got a grip on herself. She still needs something, though, something to help her. Walks around with a copy of Reich's *Function of the Orgasm* under her arm, but she won't start experimenting yet. She's got poor old Latour crazy. . . ." He saw them both bewailing their own loss, talking of those women as though they were pieces of depreciated property, and it shamed him. "Louella's okay; there's really a woman under all that dilettante crap of hers, and she's working her way out of it. You'd be surprised, Joe. I sit and hold her hand, sometimes."

It had stopped drizzling, and they stood there in the light of Nedick's, talking of the South and of Carter's new work with Farrell. Carter spoke quietly now of his intent to *put the boots to the greedy*, told how, with Merwin's help, he'd organized Wengel's Puerto Ricans—but not the blind. "The blind can't see where to go," he quoted Merwin.

Stoney was suddenly upon them, the belt of his trench coat flying, a twitching anxiety on his face. "Joe Letrigo! I thought it was you." He grabbed Joe's hand and pumped it. "Can't stay away, can you?" He gave Joe a quick, vacant smile and turned seriously to Carter. "Listen, you'd better get over to——"

"Lordy!" Joe laughed. "You've got that beard right back on, and with a snazzy pointed shape. Guess Vivienne never did kiss you even shaved clean."

Stoney lifted his head. "She quite likes my beard. It's never been my *beard* that stood between us. Which brings me back to what I started—Carter, you'd better get over to MacDougal and get Diane. She wouldn't come with me——"

"Where's she at, Stoney?"

"Now, Joe, there's no time for any romantic nonsense. The girl is ill on a doorstep, right between Eighth and Waverly." He turned to Carter. "That wide place with books in the window on——"

Carter and Joe ran together down Eighth, swiftly around people into MacDougal and stopped by the Christian Science doorway. No Diane. "She's sick from . . ." Joe puffed, walking fast with Carter down MacDougal. "It's that stuff; she's tryin to get off it."

"You've seen her? You know about it yourself?"

"Yeah, Carter." He knew he'd have to say it now and let Carter meet it in his own manner. "We're makin it together, Carter," and waited for that flushed face to explode. "We've been doin okay till tonight. That's why she was gone. Runnin out with pain. Carter, we——"

"If I find her, I'll take her to your place . . . if she tells me where."

"It's the way the ball bounces, man." Carter had stopped, and Joe walked backward away from him, not wanting to be held up. "Don't you want to come along and let her choose?"

"No." Carter called it from the corner. "Joe—" walking a few steps forward—"try to make her sleep, Joe. Don't expect too much—well, what the hell." He turned and walked off.

Joe hurried along where MacDougal grew narrow and crowded and noisy. He looked on every stoop, in each bar, turned back and went up Third Street, where more night clubs and taverns rocked with revelry. He found her doubled over on the doorstep of a darkened tailor shop, like a bundle left there to be renovated. "Come on, Diane." He tried to haul her to her feet, but she stayed down and stiff.

"Go away, Joe," through clenched teeth. "I'll come back myself when . . . You go. . . . I'll come back. . . ." High-heeled shoes and purple snood and a knot of pain between. He tried again to pull her up, but she kicked out at him. "Get away; you hear? You don't . . . know what to . . . do for me."

"I'll take you to a hospital where by God they know what."

"No . . . that's the . . . worst. Go on, Joe."

He could as easily have stuffed himself in a sewer as go. People paused for quick glances and went on. He stood off to one side, stepped forward, then back, sweating with fierce helplessness.

Diane couldn't stifle a scream. She let him haul her up and fell against him, whimpering, dry-eyed. "Oh, my head, my head," she wailed. "Joe, my head."

"What has to be done?" he panted. "Tell me, Diane. What can help, what has to . . . Where can I get some of that stuff?"

"Nobody has any," she managed to say while revolving razors chewed at her brain, "nobody anywhere. . . . Dincher, get goofballs, Angie . . . get some . . ."

"Diane, Diane, tell me where to take you. What place."

"Stoney's loft. You know where? Joe . . . I'm dying, Joe."

He lifted her and ran, around into MacDougal and down past laughter and whistles and stupid remarks to Bleecker Street and a wind that blew fruit wrappers and newspapers around their ears. Puffing while she gave little stifled barks, up the squealing stairs to kick at the door.

Dincher had his pistol in a hand when he let them in, looked bug-eyed over Joe's face when he lowered Diane on the bed. "I got nothin for her," he shouted. "She knows it. Gaw 'head, get 'er out."

"Goofballs, Dinch," she cried from the bed, tightening her eyes against the angry white light. "Put me away, Dinch."

"Goofballs! You think I'm crazy? Listen," he told Joe, "she tries to knock herself off. She gets you in hassels, that's all she's good for."

"Two, Dinch. You give me yourself, Dinch."

"Please help her," Joe said. "Please do, feller."

Dincher grunted like some baffled lion, ran to the bathroom, and returned with water and pills. Diane swallowed them from his hands and fell back, whining. "Go on, Joe, go on home," for she didn't want him watching her helplessness. "I'll see you, Joe, go on."

He sat in the soft chair while she shuddered against the wall. He got up and went past the transfixed Dincher to the fireplace, tore sheets of paper and ignited them, snapped strips of wood over the licking flames, then laid larger slats across. "Keep her warm," he told the little man. "Put that gun down, nobody's gonna hurt you."

"Go home, Joe," lethargically from the wall.

"Go on, buddy," Dincher whispered. "She don' want you here."

"She's half asleep." Joe sat down again. "What's the gun for?"

Dincher looked at Diane and pulled the room dark, motioned with his head for Joe to follow him, and they went together to the kitchen. "There's a guy wants to kill her'n I wanna kill him. So like-I let him dig she's here'n when he comes I blast 'im. Now she's here'n maybe he comes in—oweys on the roof, oweys on the roof; you dig?"

Joe had to look hard to remember the boy. It was as though a mask of madness were pinching that face, spreading the eyes in some sourceless terror. "Who wants to kill Diane?" he said hesitantly.

"You know Buster," and Dincher shot his hand up to indicate height, so fast that Joe hopped out of his seat. He sat back again while Dincher went on, "You know the General? Buster? He tells Lizzie'n nobody believes her," whispering as if an enemy were near. "Nex he grabs Angie'n tells him how he got to slice Diane up. Nuts; you dig? Plain nuts, flipped. Me, I got somethin for him, wit'out bein nuts; you dig? I blast 'm out, I got a right in my own trap; see?"

Joe couldn't tell who was mad and who not. He remembered Buster well enough and, if the giant had gone as berserk as this boy, the best thing to do was to get Diane out. He sat and listened while Dincher told of Buster's masquerade as a big-time dope peddler, of his "pratting" for an unseen pusher who paid him just enough for a big front, not enough for any pay-off to assistants. Dincher spoke of things that Joe didn't need to know, like a man speaking for fear of storing words that burned. Passion sought articulation weirdly through this night, and the night seemed mad itself, with Diane screaming in her sleep, Dincher running to the roof, and dawn rushing upon the misty dark with a whirring rain.

The fire was dead and no wood lay about to burn when light was at last full in the place. Diane woke up and looked around, saw Joe and turned to the wall. "Joe, go away, Joe," she said, and pulled her arm away when he touched it.

"You better beat it." Dincher looked at Joe as if he'd never laid eyes on him. "Go on, mister, like-you heard her."

There wasn't anything real in the place. Joe ached all over his body, felt a heavy tug in his lungs. "Diane, you feel all right? Just tell me that and I'll go."

"I feel all right," she said. "Go on, Joe," without turning to look at him.

Joe went to the door but stopped. "Christamighty! I can't leave you here, Diane. Come on, you've *got* to come along with me."

"Beat it." Dincher pointed the gun. "She means it," and Joe saw tears in the boy's agonized eyes. "You no different—" he began to laugh—"you jus another pushover for her. Doncha dig? It's how she operates like that. You ain't the boy like-you dig you the boy but you ain't."

Diane sat up. "Joe, don't listen to him. Just go home. You understand?" She wouldn't have him see anything like this night again. She'd go to him when she kicked and not before. "Please, Joe, I mean it, go on."

"You're all right?" he muttered foolishly and went. Telling himself she had her reasons, hating himself for paying them any mind; down creaking stairs and out. He pulled his hat down tight against the rain and kicked through puddles in the empty lavender of dawn.

They spoke of insanity in Village characters and he'd always thought it nonsense. But now it was all emerging before him and he really had to believe it. Yet a greater insanity lay in the acceptance of it all, in all the lazy shrugging of people who felt too small to do anything about it, and particularly in that lust for power in men who cornered the wealth that could clear slums, provide schools and hospitals, tender aid to the tormented in side streets and alleyways the world over. And Carter wanted to put the boots to the greedy. Carter wasn't mad.

Carter was confused. The night ran like a river before him, lights swimming like tugboats on the Hudson, drops pelting on his hat while Farrell's warnings drummed still in the crevices of his brain. "That's too radical, that's Communist kind of talk. We have to operate individually," Farrell had said. "Such is the case," and stood with an almost hostile finality in eyes and facial lines so long shaped in kindness, patience. The others had turned away, ruffled and coughing, while the secretary hurried into his cagelike office, and Carter had gone from the union hall like an outcast, with no answer to his suggestion, with the words of it still lying on the tongue of his mind. "The greatest task," he'd said, "is to bring all the unions together into a solid labor bloc," an old dream now alive in him as a purpose, with a definite direction, a material end in view. "We'd be in a position to hold a majority in the Democratic party; we'd be able to put sound statesmen in office and——"

"There's solidarity enough in the two big unions," Farrell had said patiently as he gathered up his papers after the meeting. "The independents usually go along anyway."

"Not solidarity enough," Carter had persisted while organizers and business agents shifted in their seats, every little scratch resounding in the great hall. "One solid union could dictate the will of working people and——"

"Wait!" Farrell had stood, fidgeted in his skimpy serge jacket, rubbed an eye under his glasses, and made that pronouncement. It still rattled nightmarishly in the thump of rain on his brain: "Communist kind of talk, too radical . . ." *Mustn't . . . mustn't . . . mustn't care about torture . . . mustn't look too deeply for cures . . . let God take care of salvation . . . let people die each day toward everlasting life in Heaven.* It had been too simple an answer to suppose that personality problems kept unions disunited, that leaders were reluctant to give up particles of power in order to have unity, but now, in desolate October rain, he had to take it as an answer—unity abandoned by the very people who knew so well its power, its purpose, its rightness; avoided for the petty complacence of a few men on top; branded with a *mustn't* word so that even the fighters for equity and reason coughed and stammered in embarrassment, as though any kind of composure, any willingness to ruminate, meant complicity in some unnamed plot against . . . "Against *whom?*" he said aloud, and saw Wengel laughing on a housetop while blind men marched over rubble in grim formation.

At the corner of Eighth and Sixth Carter leaned on the window of Nedick's and laughed himself, wagging his head in the slow perpendicular rain. Slowly, slowly, he assured himself, slowly, and focused on the fact that he'd won an inch from Wengel, that others would win more inches from more Wengels on the revolving table of living. The slow-motion repetitions, he thought on his way past the Cosmopole, and stopped to look inside through wan fluorescence over old faces waxlike in the violet light. The talkers and the goofers were packed around coffee-drenched tables. The whores and unremunerated darlings, the derelicts, the poets, the people with nowhere to go, all there at once in the violet-tinted dust still hovering where Babel crashed. And off to the side, under a mural of khaki-colored abundance Diane sat clothed in black, with Joe Letrigo at her side like a consort, with Lukey the Swede, Dincher, Angie, Red, Paddy Jenks, a dust-colored court listening to her tell Joe: "I *like* to smoke jive, shoot Horse; you can keep reality," or "I live by men, and I've got to live," or "I die by stagnation; I've got to die," or anything at all while Joe sat by with lines cut permanently into his forehead, with eyes looking hard through her wayward hours toward some shapeless and improbable sun that only God could bestow. He left them all to God and waited for traffic to churn by over the drenched coal-black street; he drifted across and entered into the steamy gleam, the amber-colored drone, the diner's chatter of a midnight coffee crowd.

To shed his coat and hat, sit beside Latour while Stoney delivered a harangue about *total* embrace . . . *total* life . . . and . . . contact with . . . valid partner . . . adequacy in nothing less . . . must find the child and woman all in one. . . .

"Okay, Robert, you can marry Vivienne. Slinger!" as the thin man flashed by. "Some coffee, if I may call it that."

Stoney flicked ashes onto the floor, careful not to dust them over his trousers, careful too that he didn't lose his temper with Carter— that, he'd learned, was a kind of defeat—smiled and cracked his knuckles. "It happens—" he chewed his cigar back in place—"that I was giving Latour some advice on Louella. Louella, you see, is a virgin," and he looked for Carter's conspiratorial grin. It never came. "I've been telling him that Louella is one of those rare children of nature who never lose their maidenheads, but merely misplace them," and even Latour had to grin.

Carter swung around to watch faces ooze by under the low steamy ceiling, and behind him the artists wrangled—around and around on the slow carousel, around to where it all began and nothing ended. Then Joe and Diane were there, Joe smiling almost apologetically, Diane with no expression at all, not even her old contrition in her pale olive face.

"Come on, Joe." She was weary. "Come on with us, Carter."

"No, baby, I—" he was standing, looking past them all—"I have to make a phone call," and found himself in the small toilet alcove with a withering need for quiet. He dialed. "Are you alone, Louella?" Yes, her happy parents were vacationing, she'd asked her friends to leave so that she might get to bed; but she didn't want to sleep, she wanted to see him and show how relaxed she was, how easy it was for her to be herself. They were both laughing, reaching through wire for each other with words that didn't matter. He went out and stood beside Latour, watching the man button his yellow corduroy halfcoat, sorry somehow for the deep fleshy creases in his face. Diane and Joe were standing there watching the man, too.

"Stoney," Latour said, and wriggled, waiting for words to form, working his lips till he could taste the proper terms, "the vision of a role based on intuitive power and historical rightness is dependent on a capacity to forget thoroughly one's errors." He reached for his water-stained hat, nodded to each singly, and departed, smiling as he shifted through the crowd.

Joe laughed. "He sure knows how thorough you are, Robert," and followed Diane, who whirled abruptly and left.

Outside, he had her tie the kerchief under her chin, and held her about the shoulders, his hand on the damp black folds of her raincoat. "Simmer down, Diane," he said, with a look through the window to where Carter was putting on his hat while Stoney worked his mouth. "Shouldn't let that fatmouth worry you."

"It's Carter. Why does he have to listen to that voice?"

"Well, Carter's leavin right now, Diane." But she went steadily down Sixth, trembling visibly.

Hollow saxophone notes ballooned out of an upper-story music school, weary notes on the midnight rain. The gleam of lights, their reflections on wet stone, rushing engines, sounds and lights pointed in at her nerves. "Joe, it's coming on again. Go home and . . . No, you don't have to go—go anywhere you want, just don't stay with me, Joe." *Oh, again, again, oh God, again.*

"I'll stay with you, Diane. Don't make me put in another week like last. You won't ever come—you'll go lookin for——"

"No, I haven't had any at all, Joe. I swear, not even a snort. Just—oh, Christ! Listen to me a little bit!" She ran off over whirling reflected lights, as though she could ever escape the great, great calamity. Ran to the corner of Fourth Street and whirled once to see Joe standing a block back, a long figure under a hat, sagged, motionless in the rain. She ran across Sixth, down and around into Third Street neon, leaned on a tenement stoop while her legs quivered and buckled so that she had to grab the iron balustrade. Then she walked, almost limped, around into MacDougal, kept walking while her sweat burned out to meet the rain, kicked through the deserted little street, past the Riviera, past Bleecker with nowhere she wanted to go. Just walking to break the rhythms of pain. Into Little Italy, into the winds that came up as the rain thinned and stopped. Down side streets, trying to follow the wind, turning around to meet its kick on her face. Running when remorse welled up in her, hating herself for making Joe a part of her pain, despising him for loving her, wishing a truck or a madman would kill her. Around streets and avenues while fever rolled globules of blurred recollections through her mind, blew them up to quivering globes that burst in the heat of her insides. "Sick, sick," she muttered, and fell retching behind some trash barrels. Vomited on her knees while distant lights passed through her head. "Sick," she wailed, and went on again as if into her fever, as though heat were some external culmination of all half-remembered things. Dizzily, sweating, "Give myself away," with a sense of deep meaning in it, some weird evidence of hope in the sound of it, "give away, give myself away," over and over, upstairs to wrinkles, to someone farther gone than she. Banged at Lizzie Linden's door. Kicked at the wooden base, banged again at the lighted glass, at the frosted yellow shadows, "Lizzie! Lizzie, you bastard!"

"Get away!" from inside, and scuffling by the door. "Get away; you hear? You lousy *bitch!*" scuffling beyond the door, and it swung open, a huge shadow, the saddest eyes on earth, and Diane was plucked in by the wrist.

"Go on, kill me, Buster!" laughing with all the power of pain.

"Get 'er ouwwwwda here!" Lizzie whined from the corner, from the carpeted floor near a chair. "Get ou-out, you lousy bitch!" weeping over into her lap, wild corn-silk hair over her wool-stocking legs.

"Go on, Buster, I dare you, go and kill me."

"I don't wanna kill you, beautiful," whispering, leaning on the door, blinking the saddest, shiftiest eyes on earth. "I never wanna kill you, Diane." Grinning, walking up to take her hands, easing her down beside him on a bedful of tousled sheets, touching her face with finger tips. "You never say . . . oney what I did it, you said," giggling hoarsely. "I'm hip you don't say bad things about me, I'm hip."

"You're crazy, you bastard. Everybody knows what you did. Everybody knows everything. Don't you know that?" She punched at the last knife in her stomach, fell back to wait for new pains, closed her eyes when no more struck.

"Beautiful, you come with me, come on, Diane. I show you. I make it witcha okay. Right, Lizzie? Lizzie, right?" fingering the little buttons of his shirt, rubbing sweat from under his glossy disturbed pompadour.

Lizzie only whimpered, lifted her face to lay eyes like tawny entreaties upon them. "Don't go 'way, Buster, do-o-o-on't go 'way from me. Don't take 'im, Diane, no-o-o-o," and doubled over again to whine.

"See?" Buster beamed, stared at Lizzie like someone watching a figure squatting between a dream and his awakening, not quite sure to which it belonged. "See?" He grinned around at Diane with rows of tusklike teeth joined, talking through them. "She's gone on me. See that, beautiful? You come on wit me."

Diane lay there, horrified only that this was no dream at all. "Where's Dincher's loot?" just to bring things to reality. "Where's his four hundred?"

"I got no loot!" he cried, spreading those huge hairy fingers. "They beat me for the loot. I told Angie, I told him."

"Sell your car, you big ape."

"No!" He grabbed her by a shoulder and sat her up. "You come wit me, Diane; you got it?" with the indignant flash of self-pity in his look at Lizzie, his features contorted painfully in the innocence of the imposed-upon. "Diane, Diane—" a sudden whisper—"you come wit me . . . I show you how I make it. I . . . I get the loot for Dincher even, I get it."

"Come on and get it." All the slow air was rushing about now, some new intent was building up in her. "Shut up, Lizzie, quit squalling."

"I let you . . . fall in here, Diane, don't I? I . . . I give you the King," and she ran to the Rouault print guarding the door to other rooms, tried to work it from the wall. "Here, take the King. . . . I give it to you, Diane."

"Come on, Buster." Diane sat up and wiped grime from her knees with the bed sheet, ran it down over her splashed ankles. "You fatmouth bitch," she laughed, "go on out and tell Joe Letrigo I'm a whore, go on, tell him. Now you can really say it. Go on, get away from me with that thing!" pushing at the large frame that Lizzie held toward her. "Go tell Joe."

"Joe, he's . . ." Lizzie smiled while she sniffled, looked inward on new ideas floundering about in what was left of her brain. "Where's Joe Letrigo?"

"He's around. If you came out once in a while, you'd see him; he's around," and began to laugh at a picture of Lizzie slinking up on

Joe, laughed at Joe himself, the worried choirboy waiting in the rain for her. "Come on, Buster. You lay the loot on me and we'll ball it up, come on."

Buster lurched into action. Even his smile was avid as he plucked his jacket from a chair and got it on.

"You'll come back." Lizzie giggled now. "You won't stick it out wit dead tail, you-oooooo'll see," while her yellow eyes, still running tears, played over other last hopes.

Diane laughed over the fact that at another time she'd have broken Lizzie's skull for that remark; now she pulled Buster away and down, followed him when he found a way through the dark cellar to the back yard, down an alley to the street back of Bleecker. "You got any Horse?" she asked as he worked a key in his car-door lock.

"I got some stashed," he said nervously, and nervously went on while they got into the car, "but I don't push nothin in the Village'n I don't use none," voice quivering as he drove off. "No one ever make a junky outta me." He laughed craftily. It was an irony: though fear made junkies out of people and Buster was the most frightened animal she'd ever known, his closest, most immediate fear had saved him. . . . Buster was afraid even to scratch his skin. "You cool Dincher; you hear? I give you the loot'n you cool him off; you hip? Then . . . then we . . . you'n me, beautiful—" puffing, hunched over the wheel—"you never say bad things about me, I'm hip, Lizzie she says evvythin she hears'n she never tells me bad things you say. She——"

"She never said you raped me? She sure must have been busy with——"

"She says that, but it's all'n it ain't . . . she's okay, Lizzie, except she goes'n falls for me hard. It's no good because . . . *You the one whose hand I got to hold*," he suddenly sang, "*to get to where I live*," and when Diane burst out laughing Buster laughed maniacally, as if he'd been named master of ceremonies.

He drove east and a bit uptown, parked, and told her to wait as he alighted in a foggy unlighted street.

"Don't you want me to go with you for the ball?" For she really meant to try him, now that Lizzie had tutored him; she meant to try them all and laugh at the waiting choirboy, at the wordy old man so long out of the pits. This was her new intent, a new glorious lust that laughed even at an old will in her to sleep forever. "Don't you want to make it with me, Buster?" she whispered seductively through the window as he shifted, grinning, in the fog.

"Not here." He coughed. "It's oney a stash over here. I take you to my real trap later."

"But I need a fix," she whispered, though pain was nowhere about. Only a new lust moved inside her, for kicks wherever they could be had, for sex she could really respond to as she had only with Paddy Jenks when he returned from Lexington with real endurance loaded in him.

"Come on," he whispered after pondering a moment, and opened the door for her.

She was glad for the fog because it let her laugh while he locked up the shadow of a black automobile. "Crazy, crazy," she muttered, "trying to make it down the straight road with Joe." *Crazy,* she thought, clacking along beside Buster for a block, *letting the kicks go by, as if I had anything better——*

"You can't come," he suddenly decided. "You can't come wit me, Diane." That strict conscience was at work in him, that distorted sense of propriety. "Nobody suppose to know my stash, nobody."

"You think you can leave me here?" She looked around at pale drifting mists, at lights near the river. "You crazy or something?"

"Here, you go back to the car." He handed her a leather pouch of keys. "Go on, don't argue. You go back; you got it?"

"Who wants to see—who cares for your stinking stash? What the hell do I give a damn where your stash is?"

"Go on back, Diane." His eyes shifted, pupils almost out of sight; his big lips worked in the fog. "I bring you a fix, I bring you a cap to snort."

She snatched the keys and began her way back, but turned and saw his jacket tail flap as the hulk plunged forward toward veiled lights along the river. She ducked after him, stayed back, never far enough to lose sight of him in the mists, crossed the avenue, and hid by a pile of planks when he stopped by a riverside shack. Laughing in nervous spasms, Diane waited till she saw a light go on in the window, then ran back across the avenue again, looked up at the street marker, and ran up the street, laughing. "Ninth Street, Ninth, Ninth," laughing in anticipation of a snort, anticipating many charges she'd get even after she walked out on Buster for some new lover in the string she was prepared to develop. "I'll bust that shack

wide open." She giggled as she worked the keys around, found the
one that opened Buster's Buick.

For it was all nonsense. She sat laughing in the smell of leather,
planning a short happy life, a wild one full of sensation. Buster hove
up and plumped in beside her, dropped an envelope on her lap,
held out a capsule of heroin between his thick fingers, looked at her,
and sent an electric tremor through her shoulder blades.

"The four hundred in here?" She felt the bulky envelope.

"Yeah, go on'n take your snort," starting the engine, dead eyes
on her. "We find Dinch'n you lay the loot on him, cool him off; you
got it? Go on, go on'n take the snort awready."

"I don't want it." A nausea was growing in her with the sick oozing
rhythm of the fog outside. "Drive away from here, get out of this
fog, Buster." She had to decide now against the snort, with some
last surge of will—for the habit was almost kicked, and Horse in a
nostril would keep no pain out of her blood, for reasons she couldn't
define in the confusion of nausea and new intent. She began to
sweat as he drove off; she closed her eyes, hoping he wouldn't
begin talking in his hoarse voice. She swallowed spit in gulps to keep
the nausea imprisoned. "Stop," she finally said, "stop the car, Buster," and opened the door as he coasted over to the curb.

"It's where I wanna stop anyhow." He yanked at the brake.

She was outside, retching, stamping her foot in a puddle, trembling where her hand gripped the doorhandle. Parked cars and the
windows of buildings swam in a fog created by her tearful eyes; the
fist was at large inside her, rubbing, burning, punching. "Let's go,
Buster. Walk. Move, Buster."

He led her away by an arm, inside somewhere, over hallway tiles,
up marble steps covered with grime, some other decade's aspiration
faded in the dirt of real life. Real life was a hound at her heels, an
enemy, a terror in her guts. "This your trap, Buster? You got a setup
for popping this cap?" Old, old words, all too familiar. The room
now plunging into light was something known to her, too, though
its dark-green walls, its shiny modern wood-and-leopardskin couch,
little prints hung on green, its rug, striped drapes, were made up into
a gaudy face of a stranger. "Where is this place? You got a setup for
me, Buster?"

"I got no setups here. It's real cool here, real cool." He shifted
angrily, then suddenly leaned over toward her, eased her down on

the couch. "How about a pin, like a diaper pin? You can pop like that; right, Diane?"

"Yeah, get it," and began to pull her clothes off, frantic to get them away from the heat of her sweat.

"In here, Diane," and he pulled her through a door, pulled on the light to show a gaudier bedroom: orange walls, a small room plugged with a bed on one side, a dresser on the other, a yellow-cotton loop rug on the floor, yellow-cotton worms rearing to watch her undress.

"Go on and set me up," she said, and stomped all over the rug to put down the worms. "Go on, Buster, the cap's in my raincoat; boil it, bring me the pin." Watched him hurry out, pulled off all her clothes and got under the covers. Cotton worms were crawling up to get her. . . . She laughed at the idea of cotton worms.

Buster handed her a safety pin stretched straight, ran out again and returned with a bent spoon that he carried with elephantine care; she dug the pin into a space between scars on her arm, dipped a corner of face tissue into the hot Horse in Buster's spoon, squeezed it out against the pin so that the kickjuice ran into the pinhole of blood, did it over and over till the spoon was dry in the big man's wet hand. "Any goofballs?" she whispered. "One cap . . . it couldn't fix a toothache."

"Sure, sure." He stood, delighted, eager, ran out for a minute and came back with a small druggist's jar. "Oney Phenobob." He giggled. "But you take about four of them'n you'll goof awright." He brought her water and she drank down four little white pills, flat little disks of peace. She lay back into all her bobbing fires, felt the Horse stir like some feeble child helpless against her pain, nodded when Buster reached for the light, and watched his bloated shadow writhe in the dark, move here and there as though the room were a cage. "Come on into bed," she said, "come on and show me what Lizzie taught you," laughing in the dark because her body had no want for him, because she knew he wouldn't climb in till she was asleep.

But he did, puffing, grunting at the side of the bed. Got in beside her, patted her shoulder and her back. "Go on'n sleep, Diane, gaw 'head," with an astounding real tenderness, nothing else in his quivering voice.

She slept undisturbed. Even cotton worms lay yellow and dormant in her dreams, fires cooled in the space of her feelings, and she awoke in a pool of sunny breeze, hungry and smiling and alone.

Buster came in with a tray of food: coffee and cinnamon toast made in Lizzie Linden's manner. Buster was shining in checked slacks and a clean white undershirt. "How you like this trap?" His tusk teeth glittered white against the orange walls. "Nice pitches on the walls'n evvythin. It's the finer things for Buster, beautiful. I don't need no Village trade for that," and went on talking about connections he had that didn't even know they worked for him. "The schoolboy route." He laughed. "Nobody like these blowtop hoodlum kids to push charge for me. Come on, don't look bad at me, Diane; if I don't, some other pusher will," and she had to nod, had to say *leave yourself alone* to her sad old soul.

He fixed her bath in the kitchen and, when she had bathed, carried her back to bed, tucked her in. "You rest, beautiful, put in a good day restin." She rested with magazines about movie stars, silly things that made her laugh, stories about the *real-life* tragedies of the beautiful people: divorces, misunderstandings, frustrated ambitions . . . strained attempts by old women to prove that people were human in Hollywood, as though anyone would ever believe it.

Buster fed her again in the evening with a roast chicken he had gone out to buy, and her appetite was enormous. She dressed, put on sheer black stockings he'd bought her, and they went out into a warm night with four hundred dollars in an envelope for Dincher. They went around the block up to the Bleecker Street loft—with Diane swearing she could keep Dincher from running wild against Buster, with the giant loitering behind her up the stairs. There was no answer when she banged on tin. Buster gave a huge sigh on the way down, unbuttoned his jacket and the collar of his shirt.

People sat about on stoops; the world looked almost sane. Even Timmy Lawless was reserved as he came down the street behind his pushcart. "I'm working for the ar-tist again," he said, smiling. "All his pret-ty pictures. Lots of honest work for me, Diaaaane."

"How you going to get in, Timmy? Dincher isn't home."

"I have a key down in the cellar." He laughed and let go of the pushcart to do a little whirl. "Hey!" he called after them as they walked off. "Dincher's in the Riviera with the ar-tist." He ran up to touch Diane's purple kerchief dangling behind her ears. "Diaaaane," he murmured while she smiled. "Pret-ty angel," and tears ran down the crevices in his face.

"Go on." Buster had to assert some of his new authority. "Beat it, Timmy; take your hand off her; you got it?"

Diane didn't bother to make peace; she only patted Timmy's leather face and took Buster up the street.

"I wait here," he said at the corner of MacDougal. "You go see the Dinch and make him cool," and stood in the shadows of a store doorway, rattling change in his pocket.

She ran across to the early Riviera, found no Dincher anywhere in the booths, but Joe Letrigo stood up while Stoney turned away to light his black cigar. "Diane, where you been?" Joe wanted to know. He took her black-wool arm and drew her to the side in the little passageway between the tavern and restaurant. "I waited all night for you, Diane," half-beaten yet deathless in his eyes.

"Where's Dincher?" she said. "Do you know where he went?"

"No, I don't know. Diane, what is it? Is it that habit or do you——"

"What's the difference, Joe? Gee, you're frantic like Carter, you act like the world is coming to an end."

"Maybe it is," and he looked around, over to where Stoney was watching from the booth. He thought he ought to repeat what the beard had spouted, that he was waiting for Diane to show beyond doubt that she belonged inside away from people. "Diane, your mother . . . she and Stoney are gonna——"

"I know about them. He'll *have* to marry her to get in." She laughed and reached up to touch his face. "Don't be so frantic, Joe; take it easy. I'll come around, just let me get some of the hollering quiet inside me."

"What hollering? That habit, girl?"

"No . . . no, it's other things. There are things I have to answer inside me, important things, Joe," knowing she was making more drama than her new intent deserved.

"Diane, Lord, that's not where living is, not inside you. . . . It's outside, Diane. Don't keep looking for a damn song——"

"That's it, Joe, I'm looking for the song, I'm looking for the . . . the different . . . the . . . I don't know. Joe, look at the people eating in there. Swells from uptown, they never come in here, and the people from here never go in there. Two worlds right in the same place. I don't know, I don't know, I have to . . . you know . . . Wait a little while," and ran past him as he grabbed, ran out the corner exit and across to the shadows where Buster waited.

"I don't know how to love," she told Buster. "Never mind," she said, quieting him when he tried to protest. "Dincher isn't there." She pulled him along down MacDougal. They looked in the park, examined faces living through some gone springtime. It was a night in which no one they knew showed up, a night she recognized as something once dreamed, though she knew she'd really lived such nights before, hunting for a friend while loneliness sat like an overgrown child on her back. Buster hung back on side streets while she went through the diner, through the Cosmopole, finding only Lukey the Swede and his new straight kick, his newspapers and the cap that marked his new philosophy. Only Lizzie in her tweed rag of a coat, screaming at men who backed away from her. Only sullen Red, his face still soft though longer, his hands grown knobby and agitated into constant tapping. "Where's the Dinch?" she asked Dincher's old friend. "I got some loot for him, and part of it's yours. You know he'll——"

Red shrugged. "I don't know about the Dinch. I don't want no hassels, I got me a job by the docks," and she became conscious of his shoulders, thick and square, almost vibrating under his shirt. She wanted him and promised him to herself, but now she only smiled and left.

She let Buster take her to the Limelight Inn on MacDougal, drank much wine as he admired pictures brown with age on a distant wall. "Paintins are nice," he laughed, tossing drinks into himself, carving a celluloid ring with that glittering knife. She laughed now, remembering the old rumors of his viciousness with that weapon, then quit laughing when she remembered seeing him in a flash the night they carried Paddy Jenks away from Lizzie's flat. "Did you scrag Magoo?" she said automatically and choked, expecting him to run wild, kick over tables, stab patrons who sat quietly about in the muted lighting.

But Buster only grinned at her. "The Law don't think so. . . . Lizzie don't squall no more. . . ." He shrugged and went back to work on the ring.

It electrified her—she liked it.

They went back to the street behind Bleecker, to Buster's gaudy flat hidden in the squalor of an old neighborhood. Buster watched her as she began to undress, and she laughed with the weight of wine on her lungs when he begged her not to remove her high-heeled shoes. She ignored him just to work up his anger; she sat to work on a shoe buckle and laughed when he struck her across the face with a heavy hairy mitt. Jumped over on him and bit his cheek till he screamed.

When she finally stood in high heels and stockings he threw a pillow onto the floor and pushed her over to stand on it. "Jump," he said from the edge of the bed. "Turn around'n around. Keep . . . jumpin."

She'd heard about it but had never seen it. She jumped and saw his freak passion grow, jumped till her heels cut the pillow, letting out the feathers. Then she grabbed her raincoat and ran.

Down quickly with Buster screaming down the stairwell. Only half into her raincoat when she passed a couple in the doorway. Laughing at their astonished faces, buckling the belt as she skidded around into Sullivan and away.

Up Bleecker to where Timmy piled pictures on the cart. "Where's Dincher?" and saw him sitting on the stoop with Angie. "Dinch, Buster's got your four hundred beans. He wants to pay you off, Dinch," and knew by the boy's dead face that it was another pay-off come too late. "He really wants to lay it on you, Dinch, he does."

"Yeah? How'd you get him to wanna? Like-what you have to do for it?" And got up quickly, went into the hall with Diane behind him. "Go on, get away," he said near the stairs, but took no step upward, kept his back to her.

"I didn't do anything with him, Dinch." She pulled at his shoulder, pulled to see his agonized love for her, for her alone.

Dincher turned, crying, showing his teeth in his attempt to control himself. "Why you do—why you cut a guy up like——" but stopped talking in a swift recognition of futility. "Go on, go tell Buster I blast 'im out if I see his lousy face. Go on'n tell him," and grabbed her, pulled her close and kissed her till his teeth cut her. "Doll, doll," he wept, and she pulled him around to Tony's cellar, down into darkness that smelled of dust, and spread her coat. . . .

She ran again, ran, electrified with a thumping sense of escape though he didn't call after her, didn't even call her name. "Diane." She whispered it herself just to be convinced of self, ran past Angie on the stoop, past Timmy, past leering, cackling drunks before the

Dills Hotel, into Stoney at the corner. "Where's Carter? Where's Joe?" and ran down MacDougal before he could speak. "Stoney!" She whirled and spread her coat, then closed it, ran on again laughing at the incredulous bearded face in her mind, ran crying dry-eyed past chessplayers in the park, through black groves of benches, faces and trees, ran till she made the Alphonse Hotel off Irving Place and stopped in the anteroom before the lobby, straightening her coat and patting down her sweaty hair.

"He's upstairs," the clerk said, and returned to his newspaper at the desk.

She took the elevator whining upward, ran down the hall, and banged on the door. "Joe! Joe! I'm back, I'm back, Joe," and laughed, thinking she cried as she waited, leaning back against the wall. "I'm back," she whispered when he slipped out of the room in a bathrobe and closed the door behind him. "Joe? Let's go in; let's not stand here, Joe."

"We can't go in. . . . Someone's in there."

"Who? Who you got in there, Joe? I thought you—you said you loved me, Joe."

"I do, I sure enough do." His bathrobe was too short. He trembled, trying to tie its cord. It was a stark royal-blue robe. The color of Edna's robe. The color of reality that was forever an enemy to Diane.

"You said you'd never . . . you'd never hurt me with some other . . ."

"Come on, now, Diane. You know you never did give me the damn *privilege* of bein true to you." And now that he'd said what he'd planned to say, he was ashamed of the plan he'd begun tonight in which he'd keep his bed occupied for her to find it so any night she returned.

She went close, hating herself for what she meant to do, but too weak to keep her arms from working. She loosened the raincoat, but he held her wrists off.

"Now, now, girl. Hell, you know that isn't it. You know that stuff hangs from trees for the pickin," and all at once didn't want to go back to the depersonalized Village darling he'd picked from the Riviera's withered bark.

"I need clothes." She backed away, buckling her belt. "I can't walk around like this."

"I'll fetch you all the clothes you want," he said. "Just name them, some of them or all, you're the one who says."

"You . . . want me back, Joe?" not knowing why he should, smiling up at the heavy bones, the tight weatherbeaten skin. "You'll be here for me, Joe?"

"Not for many days," though he really believed he'd wait longer.

"Just get me . . . anything at all; some underwear, a dress; I'll wait near that bathroom down the hall." She went there in a sweat, wondering where the cry for Horse had hidden itself, warning herself that she'd better get back to Joe tomorrow. This was no pampering Carter, no begging Dinch, but a man her own size. She'd better not forget it.

But then there was Red, a boy growing somewhat larger than Dinch but nowhere near as frantic; not so tall as Joe, yet quite as easy in his manner, wanting to *live on the outside* with uptown shows, clean clothes and easy lolling on benches in Central Park. Like Joe he let her rest; he was kind to her. So after two weeks of staying clear of the Village to avoid her pursuers—the men she imagined looking everywhere for her—she grew weary of soft-spoken Red and left his Lower East Side flat for the Village, with a kind of autumn longing for old things in a body free of any longing for Horse. "It's like childbirth," she told Lukey the Swede beside the boarded-up old newsstand. "Women kick it easy."

"Well, maybe I got a wound in my belly nobody knows about." He laughed. "Maybe I get myself knocked up and collect a million green beans from Lloyd's of London, 'cause I'm a kicked junky," and showed his fine teeth like a sign of strength, giggled that way for all the night to see.

So with a memory of a long-ago night in Paddy's Tenth Street trap she took the Swede and a feeling of debt to Paddy's MacDougal Street room and got Paddy to leave. Swede left next day; Brother Barber came, and then his brother Dan, and Diane was surprised at junkies on their uncharged days. And even smiling Paddy showed his old endurance with no apparent thought to self-satisfaction. "You're the stickman joystick daddy," she told him. Then Harry Sticks showed up with everybody's Horse. Harry himself, now sporting a small gold ring in his ear lobe, had a peculiar pride that kept him from touching whites, renegade or not, and Diane left her bed and even went outdoors.

She found schoolboys playing ball in the windy park and went with four of them to a clubhouse they had in a cellar, came out into the November night feeling like an educator—but more like a relic when she found Carter Webb alone in the diner. "Carter, Carter, I think I went nuts." He ate and nodded. "I mean it, Carter; I've been doing terrible things; I've been screwing everybody under the sun," while he nodded and ate his French toast.

"Have some food; you'll feel better."

"I'm hungry, but I feel so . . . in here." She parted her green coat to touch her chest. "It's like hollow; you know?"

"It's fall," he said. "Everybody feels that way. Joe's mad as hell at you. Dincher's mad. Even that big ape Buster grabbed me on Seventh Avenue——"

"What's Joe say?" She found herself grinning. "What's he say, Carter?"

"He's just mad because you took your clothes while he was away at work."

"That's all? That's all he's mad about?"

"It's all he said to me." He handed her a menu and nodded at it. "He's going away next week."

"Where? Where's he going, Cart?" He shrugged. "Carter, don't you love me any more? When'd you stop loving me, Carter?"

He started to smile, but whirled and caught Slinger as he came by. Slinger took Diane's roast-beef order and hurried away.

"Carter, answer me." She reached out to meet the hand seeking hers. "Don't you? Don't you love me, Cart?"

"Of course I do. I've just got it in its place, baby. I'm not mad at you for never being able to get enough."

"Carter! Well, what the hell. What else is there to do?"

It might have been Edna talking to him, for all the futility in that curl of a smile. He felt suddenly the very thing he'd felt with Edna —that he was speaking to someone about to die and unaware of it. "You want an answer, or did you say it to make conversation?"

"What did I say?" She dug into the food a waitress brought her. "What else should I do? Is that what? Tell me—what should I do?"

"Get psychoanalyzed." He waited awhile after she threw him a look of annoyance. "It's worth trying, Diane, where there's no other way. . . . How's it with the junk? You off it?"

"Yes . . . but you've heard that before, haven't you? Carter, aren't you *worried* about me?" for he looked so relaxed in his striped tie and dark suit. "Is that all you can say—get psychoanalyzed? Don't you *care* that I'm going to hell with myself?"

"Well, Diane, that's why . . ." Oh, Christ, her eyes were going through him; she listened to nothing, really, being so busy with things going on in her head. Going on nineteen, nineteen years old, but old . . . The world has—— But Farrell had warned him to focus on closer things than the world. *Don't split yourself up*, the schoolboy grown old had said, *don't make yourself useless; you're doing good work on your own level.* So he'd practiced it, kept himself from blowing off steam, gone hard at his work and soft at his leisure, avoiding Stoney, taking in shows with Louella (good girl who was really learning that her only uniqueness lay in the most natural unaffected depths of her personality), sitting around with Joe over beer and army stories, watching the boy eat away at himself behind a mask of joviality. "Baby, I thought you went for Joe. Why'd you run out on him? He's a good man, as good a——"

"Oh, he's a choirboy; he doesn't think I have a right——"

"You mean you're still not ready for a man, is that it? You're still for the ball. Well, that's your business, all right." She hid with her food, and he decided to irritate her into some sense if he could. "Stoney says you're doomed to tragedy. He's got Vivienne half-convinced; she doesn't even ask about you any more."

"Well, that's good by me. And Stoney, he can go and . . ." She wanted to prove Stoney wrong, but while the heat of coffee worked down her throat the ice of some old fear moved upward, and she pictured Stoney grinning over her bier. "To hell with him," she muttered. "What did Buster say? Did he threaten to——"

"Not in any words, but he had murder in his face. Said you insulted him, said he'd square it with you, that he'd fix you good."

"He better watch out Dincher doesn't fix him." Yet she wasn't sure that Dincher wouldn't fix her along with Buster. She didn't know which of the people who'd expressed concern over her, from her mother through various men to Carter, really had her interests in mind and which their own greedy need for her well-being. She watched Carter smoke, with eyes on her, transparent once but now opaque—unfamiliar, waiting eyes, waiting for her to crack and fall at his feet. She recognized the irrationality of her thoughts even as they occurred. "Carter, Daddy, I'm going nuts; I must be. I don't know who to believe. Mama wants me home, Joe wants me . . . to knit, or something, you want me to go to a damn . . ." She shook her head to clear it. "I mean, I don't know who's out for my good and who just wants me for themselves. I mean——"

"Diane, Diane." She really did look a little unbalanced now. "Just do what's best for yourself. Even if *Stoney* suggests it."

"Go home to your mother." She laughed and stood up. "Young lady, go home to your mothaw."

"I didn't mean that, Diane, but it's a good idea. You're lucky she has money; she could get you a good doctor. Here comes Normie. Why don't you stay awhile, Diane? Where's Joe?" he asked Normie Goldsmith as the man came up and blushed at Diane. "Wasn't he at the hotel?"

"Sure. He's getting a newspaper. Hello, Diane, how are you?" throwing a smile as if he'd just remembered the duty.

"I'm poison," she said. "Ask Carter." Standing there, she formed her lips into a kiss for Carter and smiled quickly at Normie as he took the seat she'd vacated.

As he removed his hat and stroked back his hair he mumbled something faintly amusing, but Carter spoke through it. "Joe's coming in soon, Diane," but made no real move to keep her there. "We're going over to Jimmy Casey's and listen to some jazz. You want to come along, babe?"

"No, thanks, Cart. Cart, Cart," she repeated, trying to feel that old knowledge of him she'd once had, a special trust which had reduced words and even situations to unimportance between them. But she couldn't find it in the sound of his name, in the familiar face. She shifted from foot to foot, smiling at nothing, feeling nothing but the breath of doom sifting through her lungs, spiraling about in her head. "I don't mean to bother you, Cart. I don't want to bother anybody," as she walked off on heels too high, past faces, coats, out of warm lights into the night, with no longing for old things in the November wind. She stood there, watching, as Joe Letrigo came across Sixth Avenue toward her. She held out her arms. "Joe, Joe, take me away."

He kept his hands in the pockets of his coat, puffed on a short cigarette while static and moving lights backed him like stage props in a comedy. "You can't go where I'm goin, ole girl." He spat out the butt, grinned, and tried to go by her toward the diner.

"Joe—" she held his arm—"I'm practically cured; I've just about kicked that stuff, and now——"

"You just about kicked me, you sure have. You know—" he brought his hand out of his pocket to hold her chin—"it embarrasses me when I realize I never did have a basis for thinkin I hold a more important place in your life than other men do; it's right embarrassin."

"Joe, you do." The heavy smell of liquor from his breath nauseated her. "You're drunk if you think you don't."

"If I do, Diane, you sure as hell lack a sense of reciprocation," and he left her standing there in a swirl of wind, pushed through the door and up a step into the light and the steam, with the sound of his voice still ringing in his head. "Some coffee, please, Slinger," in the same voice, and it seemed ironic. "How're we doin?" still in the same voice as he sat down next to Normie. "Anyone seen Stoney?"

"No," Carter said, "but Diane was just here."

"I saw her," he said and turned to his coffee, uneasy in the silence that followed. After a while Carter and Normie began to talk about unionism in a way that made him uneasier still. Carter was trying to make a point about something or other, and Normie was accusing him of hastiness. Joe watched the two old friends talk past each other, saw Normie frown with a half-amused futility, shake his head at everything Carter went on to say. The words of both sounded in his ears like the buzz of motors in the sawmill down home or the timeless cacophony of engines and horns in Times Square traffic. Altogether too much talk. Like that weird night when Daddy Tom had led them all home from City Square and then talked to Joe for an hour, trying to make him realize that he had to knuckle under to the order of things. It had finally sent Joe running toward town with a will to crack skulls too thick for reason.

"Let's bust their heads," he muttered now. "Let's start comin down on anybody makin it rough for folks to live," and decided, when they ignored him in favor of talking past each other, that he'd do it alone, he'd start with Bob Stoney just for his evil mouth. "Where's Stoney?" he shouted to Slinger, and fidgeted when Slinger shrugged. Joe drummed on the table top while Carter and Normie wrangled, and told himself it was time that Stoney got a little

shake-up. "He's a curse," Lukey the Swede had insisted half an hour
before, biting his lip in a face newly fallen, "a sure curse, that man."
Joe could accept that much without detail, just on the basis of emotional evidence inside himself. Still, he had to ask and find out
Stoney's latest mischief. "Like he's got me shakin," and Lukey illustrated with a small quiver on his stool in the drugstore. "I can feel him
inside me like Jersey Hemp. Bad charge, that's what he is, that
Stoney. Like he put me down . . . that I'm trapped, he says. I'm
trapped with my back to the wall. That I should scrag myself, he
says," tearing bits from the pile of newsprint on the stool beside him.
"Oh, he got me right, he didn't say no lie, that man. He just sits there
in the Riviera, smokin the stinker, tellin me. He puts me down like
I'm countin days, he says. I tell him it's when you're seein nothin,
like with closed eyes, that's the time you're done. The rest is okay,
long as there's somethin you don't know comin up and you're
standin up and lookin, it's okay. But he laughs in the whiskers, he
gets like impatient on the lips, he shakes his head smirkin at the
Swedish boy. He tells me good, like I know it, man, inside I feel it
turnin around and around."

"Well, what was it he said?" Joe hadn't really expected any direct
quotations from this agonized chatterer.

"That's what I'm sayin, man. Like I'm trapped; you dig? Like I'm
lyin; you dig? It's no use lyin, he says, and he was sincere, that man.
I'm hip he was, he told me like I'm not sincere, like he hit it right;
dig? He put me down, that man," with eyes alarmed forever, his lips
white above that pinched little chin.

Everything Joe had said had fallen flat. He had tried to convince
Lukey of the sincerity his very conduct revealed: "Even frettin so hard
is sincere, and that's a sight more than Stoney can boast." He'd even
attempted to show the Swede that Stoney had in reality been crying
out over what he'd been hating in himself half his life.

But Lukey had only wagged his head miserably and stood to gather
his papers. "No, man, I got it right here in the guts. He hit me right,
I'm folded up inside; you dig?"

Joe had dug then and he understood now: words were no match
for any gut full of something else; they were things that evaporated
as they fell, like the flimsy crystals of the season's first snow, fluttering in faint swirls outside. "It's snowin," he told the others, "and so
are you."

Carter laughed and took up the checks, slung into his coat and followed Normie down the aisle to where Slinger awaited them at the cash register.

"Let's go start us a war," Joe persisted, and Carter laughed again, at the heavy-lidded cloudiness in Joe's face, at the guarded alarm in Normie's.

"Hey, where's the artist?" The Swede came in, looking from face to face among them. "It's his idea," he told Joe through the gum of a recent charge of Horse that had failed to wrap him in unconsciousness. "He got to gimme the price for rat poison 'cause he told me to scrag myself. He in here?" He went quickly past them to investigate the loaded booths.

"Nex spring's firss suacide." Slinger laughed, ringing up the check. "Watch, Lukey jus moans through the worse part of winter'n busts loose out of a window in June. Evvy season they do it." He laughed while Carter went straight out, with sisters, dead and dying, in his mind.

"You think it'll stop snowin soon?" Joe leaned in to ask.

"How should I know?" Slinger the historian dealt only with events he could prophesy with certainty.

"Service in this place is terrible," and Joe pulled Normie along. "Let's start us a war, sojer, just so's I don't have to leave the country huntin one," and laughed when Normie shook his head and rubbed his sprout of a mustache.

Joe stood awhile to watch the wriggling of the Cosmopole neon sign across the street, saw the countless faces through its window and laughed at himself and his talkative race. "You talk up a storm," he said as he got into the station wagon beside Carter, "about the damn big hats and you'll talk till you're too old to move. Let's just start fightin like men and, Lord bless us, we'll get them big hats off their damn mildewed asses."

With Louella to meet later and Diane on his mind, Carter felt dispersed, as though too many things were going on at once. "Violence never gets anything done, Joe." He was nearly whispering, automatic words he'd put together long ago; his mind was abstracted in lights and faces sliding by. "Hey, what is it with you?" He came awake now. "I thought Hensley taught you something about violence. You never win a war. You've got to build, not tear down, and that's the way. That's why it's cowardly to resort to war."

Normie stopped for a light in a last wan flurry of snow. "You both give me the creeps. Relax! It's Sunday night." Then, incredulously, to Joe: "What do you want to fight for? You really *like* wars?"

"No . . . I guess I hate it, sure enough. The fightin, I hate it, but that's just it. Because it's a tragedy everyone shares and there's room for no small talk or big talk and little greeds; just singin, man, the steady eyes, the good hearts, and every——"

"That's what I mean," Carter said as the car stopped across from Jim Casey's canopied entrance. "It's easy to just shoot it out. It takes guts to talk till you hate your own voice, and come to agreements all around."

"Talk, talk, talk," Joe grumbled, yet he was glad Carter had interrupted him. He'd sounded absurd to himself; he had never been able to express that sense of everybody moving in one direction, the thing he'd looked for but never found anywhere but in armies. And of course armies were nonsense.

They crossed the narrow way and held up for a cab drawing to the curb. Two fat men piled out and stood in their way as they went around the cab. "It's a dog-eat-dog world," one of them said past his cigar. "You can't letum get the jump on you, it's a dog-eat-dog——" Joe was upon him, clutching him by the neck and shaking while the man screamed and his thick companion punched at Joe's shoulder with panicky, ineffective little jabs, yowling incoherently. Carter and Normie plucked Joe off while a crowd gathered, watching in delight.

"Caught him stealin tires," Joe muttered as they hauled him away.

"I ain't gettin any air," the victim wailed hysterically.

Normie drove off quickly. "No jam session for us; we're lucky we got away. Boy, I'm driving around with two Asiatics. Me, I'm a family man. . . . I ought to turn the two of you in before——"

"Hell, you guys just lack spirit." Joe sat hunched up into his coat, rubbing the back of his neck. He saw Carter's bewildered eyes on him and had to laugh. "You think I'm really bugged, Carter?"

"I sure do, I sure do. Boy, you're a wild man. You can't do things like that, Joe. That stuff just——"

"Wow, if they caught my license number! I can see the headlines: *Handsome publisher arrested for strangling innocent bystander.* That innocent-bystander angle, they'll play it up and say I *bit* the guy. I just know it."

"Don't fret, Carter, I'm gonna shove off just as soon as I find me a war someplace." Joe saw Carter turn his head away, exasperated to silence somewhat as Daddy Tom had been in that last week down home. "This country's turnin to crud right before my eyes. I don't have what you call patience, for I call it somethin different."

Carter waved a hand in disgust without looking around.

"Well, I by God got no sittin ass. What would you *have* me do?"

"Go on home and work with Hensley. Stop being a damn kid; go on home and work like you should. Where're we going till eleven, Norm? Only till eleven; I don't want to keep Lou waiting—she's leaving a party early just to meet me."

"Let's go up Tenth Street, Normie; they got some Sunday jam at Nelson's. Let's do listen to some good ole music. Some good Dixie." Joe wanted hard to hear the vitality of men poured forth in sound: the jubilation of freedom expressed first by Southern Negroes at their liberation; and the blues, a remembered lament from their days of drudgery. He wanted to hear it played by white men and black, he wanted to hear the shared jubilation and the inherited lament. "By God, that's America to me," he felt he had to say.

For Carter the music at Nelson's was a reprieve. He hadn't *wanted* all the earlier talk, but he still had a way to go before people who preached apathy the way Normie did, and those with hostile hearts like Joe, would fail to compel his retorts. They sat drinking for two hours while exuberant men played brilliantly, and the army stories began and went on all the way down the street to Pacco's where Louella sat waiting in that rare calm she'd been displaying the last few weeks. No silver cigarette holder, no oversize cross, and no cavorting need in her to have all eyes on her. Still, she took hold of his hand and didn't let go for three rounds of beer and hilarious army stories by Normie and Joe, holding tight in an awkward way that reminded him she had to have something to hold to. And she held it as they walked from the station wagon toward the diner in the still night's renewal of autumn. Carter could be patient over that much in the light of all she'd done for herself—security would be a long time coming. They were laughing as they chided each other about the *tinsel shindigs* Louella kept attending, while Normie locked up the car. "There's no real communication at those things," she admitted. "And besides, you'll do me fine when it comes to talk." Joe, particularly, enjoyed that, and leaned on both their shoulders in laughing.

But Stoney, charging up toward them all, put a chill over the night. "She's done it, she's gone and done it! Diane, she's gone and—oh, God!"

"What!" Joe and Carter said it together, grabbed him simultaneously, with the same horror lurching through their minds. "What's she done?" Carter shook the bearded man while Normie stood off, shaking his head as though it were all something he'd long expected. He took Louella's arm and they moved closer to the others.

"The baby, she's gone and kidnaped the baby!"

"What the hell are you talking about? We saw her this evening."

"This afternoon! She went out there to Lawrence and kidnaped the boy! I kept telling Vivienne she would. If I told her once, I told her——"

"How you know she did?" Joe kept his hands pocketed by way of saving Stoney's life. "We saw her before, a couple of hours ago."

"Who else would do it, you fool? The people—the Burnells are over at Vivienne's right now. Come on over and see them if you can't take my word. Who else on earth would want to kidnap that child?"

They went behind him to the station wagon and waited for Normie to open it. Louella pulled Carter around, brushed a wind-whipped strand of hair back of an ear. "Cart, you said . . . You're getting mixed up with her again. Don't let her . . ." He turned away from her, annoyed at the way her subjective little fears translated themselves into concern over him.

But, alone with Stoney in the back of the charging car, Carter leaned forward with his head just behind Louella's, smelling the subtle mixture of night air and perfume in her hair. He wondered if all this weren't too much to ask of one so lately come out of shadows. Still, there was no way to avoid it, and perhaps this night would help her learn a little more about facing things. He turned to Stoney, watched the man agitatedly bite his lips. "Did they see Diane around there? Did the Burnell people see it happen?"

"They saw a car drive off. Mrs. Burnell recognized it—the car belongs to some man who drove Diane out there before. Now is that evidence enough for you?" His voice was shaking as he fidgeted and pulled on the skirt of his trench coat with frantic fingers. "I've been looking all over——"

"What'll you do if you find her?" Joe swung around to ask. "Have her arrested? You don't even know for sure——"

"You keep out of it, you—you young—you——"

"Look here, Stoney, don't you shake your voice at me!" Joe could laugh now that he knew Diane hadn't done something horrible to herself, knew Carter was laughing with the same kind of relief. Only Normie was agitated nearly as much as Stoney. He couldn't tell how Louella, between him and the driver, felt, staring straight ahead all the way uptown.

She insisted on staying behind with Normie after they parked, saying that she and Normie might only confuse things if they went along. Stoney led the way upstairs, and Vivienne, dry-eyed, spoke with a tearful voice when she let them in. "Carter, where is she? How could she do a thing like that?"

"How do you know she did it?" Carter caught in one quick look the several policemen sitting about in foreign gray uniforms and familiar navy blue, saw the lady in iron-gray hair blinking at tears while her thin, bald husband, beside her on the couch, held a cigarette up near his face, oddly, between thumb and forefinger. Carter went past two plainclothesmen to the couch. "Did you see her, Mrs. . . . Burnell?" he repeated after Vivienne voiced the name. "Did you actually see Diane take the boy?"

"No, I didn't. I told the police I didn't," and a detective looked in a notebook and nodded. "But the car—it belongs to that big man, a very large man who called for her once when she visited Johnny. Quite some time ago. I know that car; I knew it as soon as I saw it driving off. From the window it was just as it looked when I watched them drive off that other time."

"I know who that guy is," Carter told the detective with the note pad. "Buster Wallinger—if the lady is right, if it's really his car. But I tell you, Diane couldn't have been with him. I saw her just a couple of hours ago. She hasn't seen Buster in days; she told me so."

"That's just like her!" Vivienne stood tall, stiff. "Carter, you know her deviousness. You of all people should know her trickery by now."

Carter threw a look at her, didn't know what to say, finally suggested they go downtown and seek the girl. A soft-spoken detective said there were men doing that, said they had her description and photos, and he took Buster's description from Carter, stepped up into the foyer and took hold of the phone. Carter spoke in a near-whisper to Vivienne. "You settle down a little. Don't be such a damn enemy to your girl. You don't know for a fact that she's——"

"Oh, you disgust me, Carter! I'm—I'm just about up to here with you," indicating a level at her throat. "You're so ready to defend her. Always. And like a fool I listened to you; I let her roam around like an animal. What happened? What has she been these months? Hmm? Answer me."

The woman was actually smiling, as though she'd finally effected a victory over him. He took her wrist and pulled her around into the kitchen, with Stoney following indignantly. "You get the hell out of here, Stoney!"

"I'll have you know I——"

"It's quite all right, Robert; there's no need to worry. I can——"

"Get out!" Carter moved forward, and then they were alone in the great white room. They sat by the table, silently staring at each other. "Don't turn on her, Vivienne. Wait'll you're sure before you shoot off your mouth."

"You're not the one to advise me, Carter. I've listened to you for the last time. When we find her, she's going to be put where she can't do anything disgraceful again." Her nostrils were dilated: she'd determined what she meant to do, and any logic she offered now was an apology for that part of herself she'd lost, the human, the sanguine. "I've tried; I've been patient beyond my endurance. I've offered her a beautiful home, I have. Anything, she could have had anything, and what did she do? She became a common prostitute, that's all, just that."

"Just that. That's all there is to it. Just like Edna. You spilled it out when Edna died, but you've swallowed back all that guilt. Just that. She decided to become a prostitute. For laughs." He saw her blink those tentacled lashes, but her nostrils remained obstinately distended, immovable as polished granite. "Just to disgrace you she did it; is that how you feel? Vivienne, you're the worst——"

"Oh!" She stood. "I won't take that from——"

"Sit down!" He pressed her back with quick hands at her shoulder. "You listen to me. In one day of your filthy morality you whore more than any daughter of yours ever did in her life. Because you've given your body and all your imagination away to a bunch of dusty, destructive, sterile mechanisms for living; you sold yourself cheap, and the worst thing about it is that you sold your daughters too. One's dead and the other dying, all for the cheap words that mean so much to you—*honor* and *disgrace!*"

"You're crazy! You're a lunatic! Let me out of here or I'll——"

"Shut up! Listen to me. She never was out there. I know it by the way she spoke to me, not only by what she said. She hasn't seen this Buster. He's mad at her and—and he said he'd fix her good. If he took the boy . . . *If* he did, he did it to hurt Diane. Can you understand that? Can you listen to truth once in your cowardly life?" Now she was folded over, crying on her tidy knees just as she'd cried that afternoon in the cab. "Listen, you know what you're going to do? You're going to stand by her when all this smoke clears. You're going to get her psychiatric attention any way you can manage——"

"I tried that. Didn't I try?"

"She's about ready for it now. And you should be ready, even to keep your mouth shut and Stoney's stupid mouth shut around here. You've got to slave for your girl—slave, slave, like other parents do naturally when they have to. Do you have any idea what that means? You, with all your talk about God?" The woman was nodding, hands over her face. "Go on, go out there and tell the police she isn't the one to look for. Tell them, because . . . Vivienne, police arresting her might give you another suicide for a daughter." He stood up, but she grabbed at his jacket.

"Carter, stay. Till I dry my eyes." She ran, sniffling, to the gleaming white gas range: polished—everything was polished, the woman, the furnishings, the very surface air. He leaned on the polished white sink beside her as she went through automatic preparations for hot tea. "It's been difficult," she whispered. "You don't know. Before I got this position at the agency . . . the Welfare Board . . . I tried to take care of Johnny, I tried. But the Welfare people nagged me; they put me through such red tape, such humiliation; they cut me down and down; they just wouldn't give me enough. Believe me, Carter, it's true."

"But it's done, it's done. Only one thing matters now. You're going to help skinny little Diane. Not by crying that you mean so well by her, not by apathy, but by hard work. Even if you have to quit your phony job just to sit and hold her hand." He felt hatred quivering in him again. "Maybe you'll have to give up a concert or two; maybe you'll have to give up a little *graciousness* in order to sweat; you might even lose an hour or two of church and go through

whole days with no divine light to ease your conscience." He knew
as she rocked her head in her hands that he was trampling on her for
more than what she'd done to her girls—for the crimes "gracious"
people had committed against Louella—and at last he stopped. "All
right. All right, Vivienne. I'm sorry . . . I really am. Don't cry, don't
cry. There, there." It was a child he comforted. "I'm sorry, Vivienne.
I don't . . . really want to hurt you. Come on, let's work together
a little bit. For someone we both love."

She nodded, pulled away and sniffled, dried her eyes, looked in
the small mirror hanging over the sink. "It might not be Diane at
all." She was trying to smile. "I'll tell them, I will, Carter. You'll send
her home? You'll try, I mean?"

"Sure. I think she's ready to be helped. I think she is." He was,
suddenly, terribly aware of how his passion could make him strike
out blindly at anyone for that person's very helplessness. "I'll go and
look for her. You clear these people out and get some sleep. Okay,
Vivienne?"

"Yes. Carter . . . take Robert with you. Make him go along."

"Okay, Viv." He patted her shoulder, exchanged feeble smiles
with her and walked out. Joe sat in the gold-brocade chair shaking
his head while Stoney and two detectives hovered above him.

"Nothin!" Joe said. "I got nothin to teach you about her. You got
your damn nerve, Stoney, and you're mighty lucky a mess of police
are standin about or I'd bust your face wide open."

"Now, take it easy, son," the soft-spoken detective said. "If you
know her habits——"

"I know some of them, but I by God won't tell you peanuts. You
all listen to this ole fool and you'll arrest everyone in the Village
just for havin mannerisms." He nodded shortly as Carter nodded to
him.

"Joe—" Stoney spoke patiently, like a man wisely exercising some
grand authority—"it's for the best. Try to understand that. We're
only interested in——"

"Shut up, dirty Bob." Joe began to rise. "You stand back or I'll
light into you, cops or no cops. Diane didn't do anythin, Carter says
so, you say no, and I know who to go along with. Get him away," he
told the police.

"But her habits," the officer said. "They might lead us to this Wallinger. Don't you see, son?"

Carter said, "Wallinger is out to hurt her. He told me that himself a few days ago. She just learned about it tonight—when I told her. She's not the one you want to follow. If you haunt her, you might frighten her into——"

"Raagh!" Stoney threw his head back impatiently. "This is lunacy! These sentimental fools'll only confuse you . . . while that lady's heart breaks; while that gentleman goes mad with grief." He indicated the Burnells sitting limply on the couch. "Diane probably has that boy in some dive with a bunch——"

"Stoney." Carter went past the police to him. "We're going to look for Diane and bring her here. But not as a prisoner. As Mrs. Lattimer's daughter. You want to come along?"

"Go along with them, Robert." Vivienne was at the serving table with her tray, setting it down as the other lady, automatically compliant in her grief, cleared a space with domestic efficiency. "See if she's in that loft. You know where."

"I've looked there," Stoney protested. "I'd best stay here with you, my dear, and——"

"No, Robert, I want to get some rest. . . . I want to go to bed."

"We *should* be going." Mrs. Burnell stood and straightened her dress.

"Oh, do have some hot tea."

Mrs. Burnell forced a miserable smile and sat back, took her husband's hand.

"Stay for tea before you go," Vivienne told the men.

"We'd better go," Carter said. But the police gathered around Vivienne's tray, and Carter took Stoney's arm. "Come on, Robert, I won't let Joe take you apart."

Stoney lifted his head and grunted. "Do you mind if I have some hot tea?"

"Come on, fatmouth," Joe said, going through the door.

"Vivienne!" Stoney called. "You're letting this sentimental—" he glanced at Carter—"you're letting him compromise you again. That girl——"

"Robert, we'll see." Her composure amazed Carter; her recuperative power was something preternatural. "Let's wait, shall we? Let's find her before we jump to conclusions," and looked toward Mrs. Burnell, who by now was content to agree with anything at all.

Stoney went along reluctantly, stiffly, on Carter's arm. Down the stairs and out Carter began to suffer waves of uncertainty: Diane might have been lying straight-faced just as she'd done over robbing his apartment so long ago. Still, there was time to find out; he told himself he'd acted properly—except for his attack on helpless Vivienne. That guilt still burned in him like a fever, so he sat beside Louella and pulled her close as a kind of assurance to her whole befuddled class that it was capable of turning human. "You behave," he warned Joe when he saw the boy glaring at Stoney in the rear. Then he leaned back, felt his breathing quiver. Emotion was a wild, sightless danger, something he'd known before but not like this. He saw Normie and Louella trade glances, knew they'd done a lot of talking in their time together. "We have to hunt Diane downtown," he muttered, and waited for someone to speak.

It came from Normie. "Carter," he whispered, "what are you mixed up in this for? Go home. What are you doing here?"

He saw Louella lower her eyes. "Diane . . . she's in trouble," he said.

"She was born that way. You can't help her, Carter."

"Louella, was she born that way?"

The girl pouted silently; she looked smug, and so did Normie as he drove off down deserted Fifth. Carter looked from his friend to his girl, feeling the same kind of venom that had taken him over when he'd been in the kitchen with Vivienne; he tightened his jaw and remained silent, just as the rest of them did, all the way downtown.

Once, as they all searched through the park, Stoney began to rebuke Carter for his *sentimental attachment* to Diane, but sensed that his views weren't welcome and kept quiet again until, looking through the Ninevah, they were told by a man named Tomlin that Latour had burned all his pictures. Stoney found great artistic significance in that and held forth at length, though it had been said for Louella to hear.

She caught Carter in the doorway, looked at him with some remnant of histrionic days. "Did you hear that? About Fred Latour? His work, all his work. I have to go to him." She spoke quietly, as though some balance were being struck for his concern over Diane. "I have to go to him. . . . We have lingering duties of our own, Carter." He smiled and nodded and wished she'd go without making much of it, but she went on compulsively about her responsibility to Latour and her affection for him and finally, "I'll come back later and wait for you. I really should go to Fred, shouldn't I?"

Again he smiled and nodded, and watched her sweep away to play mother, just to compete with his role of father to Diane. Small, but he had to be patient; she needed these little rungs until she could finally climb out of her well. He went behind Joe and Normie down MacDougal, keeping well back so that he wouldn't have to talk and give voice to his dejection.

Faces and noises in the Riviera were repeating days that had vanished: time seemed the only reality in all the Village; time devoured the noises and faces and dreams, while defeated hearts begged it to allow for still a little while the consciousless abandon of bohemianism. Carter rubbed his eyes and looked over at Lizzie Linden wrapped in her old tweed coat, sitting capsized on the radiator near the bar. He smiled, thinking she'd seen him, but she was speaking to no one at all.

"Je-sus, nobody got to, you know. I got my big boy, you know; I got him hidin out for meeeee. The bigges boy of all'n he jus got to sleep," as though sleep were her own master, hiding behind the lie of open tawny eyes.

Carter met Joe in the doorway, and outside they found Stoney and Normie. "I'm going up to the loft," Carter announced and crossed the street, letting anyone follow who would.

"I've been up there," Stoney said. "No one was there."

"Maybe they're there now." Joe followed Carter; Normie and Stoney came along. Across silent shadows where litter remained from week-end pushcarts, kicking about in a rising wind. Down two streets to where Dincher sat on the stoop of Tony the Shylock's tenement.

He looked them over with weary eyes, got up when they tried to pass him. "Where you guys goin?" He jumped before them to the doorway.

"We're looking for Diane," Carter said. "Is she up there, Dinch?"

"No, she ain' up anywhere," shifting eyes aged with wariness. "Nobody's up there but Timmy. Like-he got a job for Stoney; right, artiss?"

Stoney nodded, looked around at the empty pushcart before the house. "Well, is it all right if I go speak with Timmy? I want to find out how much I owe him." He laughed.

Dincher considered it, shrugged. "Gaw 'head." But Timmy came lumbering out with two large pictures in heavy frames.

"How much more to go, Timmy?" Stoney put a hand on the man's checked cap, patted him, and smiled like some benevolent guardian.

"She told me," Timmy whined. "You're not her father, you li-ar," and went haughtily down the steps to his cart. "You owe me nine dol-lars," he called. "You pay me before I take the rest of them, because you lied to me."

Stoney ran down to the pushcart, reached into his coat for money. "I didn't lie; I'm sort of a father to her. Here's your nine dollars, Timmy. Have you seen Diane?"

"Shut up, Timmy!" Dincher stood between them. "Mind your own business, artiss. Don' say nothin, Timmy."

Timmy was smiling as he counted the money; he listened to neither of them. He looked up to the sky and did some arithmetic, then shot up and whirled around, down and up in little whirls that filled the bell of his grimy coat with air.

Normie applauded; Carter put a hand on Dincher's shoulder. "Come here, Dinch." He took him off to the side. "Dinch, the kid's in a hassel. They think she went and kidnaped her boy. If we don't find her, the cops'll be looking for her. They all think she has the kid."

"It's her kid," Dincher protested. "She got a right; it's her own little kid, her own."

"Dincher, has she got him?"

"I dunno! I din' see her in a long time," and tried to pull away, but Carter held his shoulder. "Listen, you lookin for a bust lip? Leggo!"

"Dincher, you know where she is. You want the cops to get her?"

"Buster, he snatched the kid. Lemme alone. He snatched the kid."

"How do you know? Come on, Dincher, tell me. I want to help her. Before the cops——"

"Yeah, you wanna help 'er." A young boy was pouting through the tight mask. "You wanna help 'er like you help her the lass time. You think I don' know what you do wit 'er?" He yanked his shoulder away and grabbed Carter's shirt front. "I bust your goddam head, you come aroun tryin to——"

Joe grabbed the boy by his collar and pulled him away. "Don't go gettin rough, sonny; you'll get yourself hurt."

"Leave him alone, Joe."

But Dincher had swung at the tall man, a blow that glanced off Joe's cheek as he turned with it.

"Joe, don't!" Carter shoved Joe away and turned to Dincher. "Listen, you . . . Dincher, goddam you, don't try to be so rough. Nobody wants to——"

"Bullshit! You wanna take 'er away from me, like-it's all you want."

"You think she's an animal? Nobody can take her or give her. What's the matter with you? Hey!" as Stoney went through the doorway. Carter ran up and grabbed him. "Don't you go up till he says it's okay. Dinch! Dinch, is she up there? Come on, before the cops just take over and sit on you."

Dinch walked through and stood facing them all near the staircase. "Listen, leave 'er alone. It's her own kid; see? Cancha understand that? Like-it's her own——"

"There's such a thing as law!" Stoney shouted. "Legally—did you ever hear of the law, Dincher?"

"The Law!" Dincher was in a sweat. "Yeah, I heard of the Law; I heard of it awright. It's her kid! You ever hear that law? God makes that one, God! There ain't no bigger law."

Stoney turned to Carter, grinning, nodding. "Well, are you convinced now? Do you think she took the boy or don't you?"

"Buster," Dincher said, "he snatched the kid. Timmy tells us'n we go get 'im back." He looked wildly from face to face in the dim hallway. "It's her kid; cancha understand that? Diane . . . Carter, you know Diane," holding out a hand. "You know 'er, Carter. It's her kid." He pulled his shirttail out of his belt, opened buttons. "Look, look, Buster giz me a rip." He showed them his bandaged side. "I wanna blast 'im, but she don' let me . . . I swear to God'n His Mother. Down by the river, I coulda blast him dead 'cause he's no good; you hear? Like-I had the piece right in 'is lousy face, but she don' lemme do it. Like-she's a mother; you hip? It's her kid, man; whatta you want from her?"

"Dinch—" Carter went forward—"let me talk to her. Just talk to her, Dinch. We know she's here, you might as well."

"What's the sense of all this?" Stoney turned impatiently. "I'll call the police and get it done with," and really meant to go, but Normie and Joe together grabbed him.

Dincher let Carter go by. "Not upstairs," he said miserably, and pointed back toward the cellar door, then walked out with eyes on the tile floor.

Stoney ran over behind Carter. "Let me see her," and jumped back as Carter swung so hard that he fell to a knee when he missed. Joe and Normie ran up.

"I'm responsible for her!" Stoney shouted.

"Get him away before I kill him," Carter said. "I want to see her alone." He pulled open the slat-wood door and entered, felt his way down.

"I'm practically her guardian!" Stoney went for the door.

Joe grabbed him by the beard, tight up near his chin, and slammed his head close to the wooden cellar wall. "By God, there's only one way to handle kids, sojers and ole men, because they by God got no sense of human responsibility at all."

Carter groped through shadows toward a lighted doorway, looked in on pipes and crates, saw Diane huddled on blankets by a wall on the other side, rocking the sleeping boy in her lap, looking up with eyes that were frightened out of recognition of anything at all before her. "Diane, it's me," he said quietly. "It's me, baby," smiling to reassure her. She followed him with her eyes as he sat on blankets beside her; she kept rocking the sleeping child, touching wet cotton to a bruise on his head.

"It's my Johnny," she said, and caught Carter by the wrist. "Carter, this is my little boy, Carter," looking to see whether he caught the meaning to its deepest extent. Smiling to help him along. "Johnny," she said again, "this is him. Are you going to let them take him away, Carter? Nah, you won't let them do that." She started a hearty laugh, as if she'd suddenly become aware of some deep, unshakable reality. "Not you. You'd kill them all before you let them do a thing like that. Carter . . . you're my Carter Webb. Daddio, it's my baby boy Johnny, and I'm going to take care of him so no squares let him get kidnaped again."

"Where's Buster now, Diane?"

She shrugged. "Who cares? He can't get near my baby any more. I have him now, Cart. Me, Diane. You know me, Cart. He can't touch my baby now."

"Diane, we . . . we have to straighten out with the law. Then you——"

"What do you mean, the Law? Carter—" she hadn't stopped laughing—"you won't let them take him, and you know it." She ran a hand over Carter's face, pulled at his lips to make them smile. "I know you, Cart, you don't lay down on your face for paper laws. You know the real laws; you can smell them, Carter. Carter, where's Joe Letrigo? I want to show him my Johnny."

"He's right upstairs, little girl. Shall I get him?"

"Not yet. First let's talk, you and me. Because I don't care more for any other man. Even Joe. I love Joe, but you and I, Carter, nobody can change that. You tell them about it, tell them all. Tell them they can't have my baby because he's mine. Tell them about that law, Daddio."

He leaned back on the stone wall, rubbed greasy sweat from his head. He saw Diane bathe the U-shaped bruise on the dark little forehead, wondered whether she could do any more for the boy than bathe a small bruise. It seemed a problem for Diane alone to solve, yet it all had to be decided along the pathways of law, or every perplexed and wronged soul on earth had the right to make his own law. "Diane—" rubbing his head again—"you can't stay—this is no place for him."

She studied that, remembering somewhere in the drifting smoke of her mind that she had a reason for being there. It came to her, and she smiled for Carter. "Buster, he swore he'd kill us all. If I stay upstairs, he'll be able to do it. He's nuts, Carter; you ought to see him. But I wouldn't let Dincher kill him, because I remembered. Even when it's right, it's really wrong to kill, because it's the end, like. You know what I mean, Carter?"

"Sure, baby. But, baby, they'll arrest Buster when you tell them what he did. You can tell them, Diane. Come on, we'll tell them."

"No, don't go away, Carter. Don't make me go out there. I don't want to tell the cops anything. They'll slam me around. You don't know, Carter. That's how they are, cops. Ask Dincher, they slam people around."

"Not you," he laughed. "Only criminals."

"Anybody, anybody. Carter, I swear. Before they know who you are. They don't know what a criminal is; they don't care; they don't think. It's how cops are; they like to slam you around, Carter."

"I won't let them do that, baby; I'll stay close to you. Come on, we have to get Johnny into a nice warm bed."

"Buster hurt him," as Carter helped her up. "He threw the little boy at us when we busted in on him. I mean it; he's nuts." It was a new horror for Carter. "Maybe he's hurt inside. We'd better get him to a doctor, Diane."

"No, he's okay. You ought to see him play and laugh before he fell asleep. He likes me, Cart, and he can talk, real words, not baby talk. He even called me Mommy one time, just as if he really knew I am. I really am his mother," she whispered abstractedly as the boy stirred.

Carter kissed her on the cheek, pressed his lips hard as she laughed, then took her by the arm through the dark and up the sighing stairs. "Where's Stoney?" he asked Normie, who ignored it to smile closely at Diane's little boy.

"This is my Johnny." Diane showed him to Joe. "He's my little kid, Joe."

"He took himself down the street," Joe said. "Disgusted with everything; you know?" Joe had his troubles smiling at Diane. He didn't mean to give in to any gnawing in his guts for her; he didn't mean to pamper the girl at all.

She was sitting on the outside stoop, rocking her little boy. "You ought to see him laugh," she told them all. "You'll like him, you bet." She looked up to Joe.

"Well!" Stoney came along, bouncing, agile, puffing on his cigar. "That was a fine thing to do," he began.

But Joe stood around in his way, showed him a face that warned him to say no more.

Dincher and Tony the Shylock stood by an iron rail to the side, the boy kicking at stones that weren't there, the old man puffing a cigar, his head tilted, watching the group on his stoop as though they were of another world, filmed and flashed on some screen for his pleasure. He began to laugh when Timmy came out with pictures in his arms. But when cars rounded the corner, pulled up along the curb, the Shylock turned abruptly; unsmiling, he shambled off, puffs of smoke trailing him down the street.

Police were all over. Strangers were gathering to stare. The Burnells, Mrs. Lattimer. Diane stood up, holding the baby away from them all while Carter ran forward, talking. Joe grabbed Stoney by a shoulder: "You swine, you called them, you no good gangle-ass hog. I ought to crack you wide open."

"Let go!" Stoney pulled away. "I'll have you thrown in jail along with her." He laughed, ran up and in, with Timmy close behind him.

"You have no *reason* to take her away," Carter said hastily to an angry captain. "It's true, she got the kid back from that guy Mrs. Burnell saw."

"Can you prove that?" a detective asked in a hostile whine.

"Yeah," the captain said, "pipe down if you ain't sure. We want facts."

"Vivienne, you'll be responsible for her, won't you?" Vivienne nodded anxiously. The police had become bellicose since leaving Vivienne's. The seriousness of the case had invoked their best professional manners, but now, under a threat of having no one to arrest for all this, they'd begun to sound as brutal as Diane had feared they would be. "Mrs. Burnell," Carter called as the woman stumbled into a police car with the awakened boy. "Mrs. Burnell, you don't want to press charges, do you?"

"No, no." She laughed in a nervous burst dangerously near hysteria. "Leave that poor girl alone. For goodness sake, leave her alone."

The captain ran over to the car, stayed a moment and returned. "Where's this Wallinger? Why ain't he here if he really took that boy?" He looked around at gathered people and bellowed: "Geddada here!" With the detective he went to another car, spoke awhile, and got in. The car drove off, followed by all the rest but one, at which two uniformed cops stood silently.

Joe had Diane by the iron railing beside the house, holding her shoulders, shaking them as she wailed, "It's my own baby, it's my baby!" Tears burned all over her cheeks, burned sharper where she wiped them away with a palm.

"You got to hold still, Diane, you just have to," Joe kept saying as she tried to pull away from him. The wind kicked at her hair, cut into her through the gray sweater. Strangers were watching; Carter and Vivienne came over as police cars rolled away: indifferent oozing lights, unknowing strangers, some stranger's sanctimonious voice: "It'll be all right, you'll see, my baby, it will, it will."

"*My* baby, mine. What about *my* baby? That woman can't have my boy. He's mine. I want my baby!" She crumpled against Carter, crying deep into the warmth of his coat. "You said you wouldn't let them. Car-ter, Car . . . ter," though she knew he'd been helpless against the Law, powerless as in a dream, and all of it was nightmare, a hallucinatory night, the breaking into Buster's flat, the pursuit down to his shack by the river, the fight and flashing knife and Dincher's blood, Dincher and the nickel-plated pistol she wouldn't let him use. All a dream, the months gliding from Horse to church, fleeing the angry strangers, all a nightmare over the dusty rock of living. "Carter . . ." She looked into his pale old face. "Joe . . ." She wept, swinging around toward the dark-faced man by the rail. There was nothing more in her. She looked at the woman who was aging before her. "Mama," and repeated it for the comfort of its sound, "Mama, will you help me? I want my baby. Mama, will you help me get my boy?"

"Diane, dearest, try to understand . . . Yes," when she saw Carter's signal, "yes, we'll see about it, dear, we will."

One of the policemen yelled, "Break it up!" He sent some strangers off, then turned to the group at the rail. "Okay, the show's over," then looked closely at Diane. "What's this kid cryin about?"

"Hey, officer." Dincher stood there, jangling some change in his pocket. "You want this guy Wallinger? I tell you where to find 'im."

"What's *your* name?" the cop wanted to know. "Okay, break it up over here," and he walked to the car with Dincher, stood there writing in a notebook, then helped the boy in, followed him, and the car drove off.

"Where's Stoney?" Carter asked, and it seemed that he'd been saying it all night. Diane was tiny beside him, all huddled up, a little child he felt like carrying away.

"He's upstairs with Timmy," Joe reported, looking Vivienne up and down.

"Carter, will you tell Robert to look in on me tomorrow? At the office?"

"I'll tell him something, all right," Carter muttered, and then Timmy was screaming through to the street, down and around the pushcart, flinging small pictures around as though they were useless old wine bottles, empty and done.

"Through the skylight!" he yelped, racing around and around the pushcart with his coat flying like some stained, shredded wing. "He's got Diane's faaaaather!" while all of them watched, rooted to their spots. "I told him it's her faaaaather, but he's af-ter him with the knife! Buster's through the skylight killing the artist! Light the candles, turn on the snow!" with delirious shrieks around and around the cart, going like a machine.

Carter dashed up the steps with everyone after him.

"Carter!" Normie grabbed him by the collar and yanked back ferociously. "Keep the hell out of it, you crazy son-of-a-bitch! For once——"

"No! No!" He broke loose, charged through to the stairs. Joe caught him about the waist, slammed him against the stair wall. "Let go, he'll be killed! Joe, let go!" with every face a static unseeing mask now with Death at large upstairs.

Joe trembled, holding him to the wall. "You're worth ten of him. Hell with him, man, don't you go——"

"You—Joe, you can't let him be killed! What's the——"

"Good riddance, by God—one more wrong guy gone!"

"Joe, that doesn't solve anything! Dead men don't——" With a lunge he rocked Joe over into Normie and dashed up, Joe bellowing, "Too much, too much, Carter!" and Diane flashing by, screaming, "Carter, he's crazy! He'll kill you, *Carter!*"

A chill portent pressed against Joe's temples, and he went up behind the flash of a girl, with Normie tripping in mad haste up the crazy flights after him, past tenants in forgotten doorways.

Carter plunged into the naked light where Stoney yelped with his back to the fireplace, frantically poking the wheel-bottom table at the giant, who was snorting and crouching and thrusting with his long gleam of a knife. Carter rammed Buster with the full force of his body. "Come on, *Stoney!*" he shouted to the paralyzed bearded man. Buster shook Carter off, showed his rolling sightless eyes, and lunged, head down.

Diane saw Carter grab the flashing blade in both hands low, catch Buster's head in his chest. Saw the painter, transfixed and voiceless as she herself, saw framed with skylight shards the two locked bodies hurtle like overweighted birds, a new unknowing face on Carter as he sailed clean through the yawning shutters of the window, arms outstretched, bloody palms, out the window, and she couldn't scream, couldn't believe, saw Joe crash by and leave his feet as all his limbs struck out at the reeling giant, fists to the face, two knees in succession to the madman's groin, the most awkward attack, the most unrhythmic delivery of a knockout, and over the crumbled hulk a nickel-plated revolver blasted, roared with Dincher's hoarse laughter: "In my trap, in my trap, I got a right!"

While Carter flew incredulously through parted space, knew he was dead, longed to grab the swinging window he had forgotten to grab, never believed it was Carter who crashed—all space and stone structure and single fatal mistakes on earth erupted in the small enclosed area of sense—one diminishing ring in diminishing light, the incredible self splashed over a pushcart of pictures while voices squandered time.

A cargo of art for Timmy Lawless to roll through gathering faces down the wind-blown litter of Bleecker, chanting, "Pret-ty pictures, pret-ty pictures," till Joe Letrigo caught up with him at the corner, plucked him loose from the pushcart and let him run, with tears down the river beds of his face, screaming of horror into a night forever deaf.

Joe eased the cart to the side while Normie sped to phone for an ambulance; he let faces plunge in to inspect the contents of the pushcart, pulled Diane away to the side screaming a dead man's name, thrashing herself about in his arms. While one of the cops who had brought Dincher back from Buster's shack sped away in his green coupé.

"I saw it! I saw it!" Mrs. Lattimer shrieked beside her moaning daughter. "I saw him jump, I did!" she swore to the faces hungry for communication, and the word passed through the gathering mob.

Normie wore a plaster face beside Joe, an expressionless mask. Not till all the police cars whined officially to a halt did Stoney appear again, and the police were swift to pluck Normie from the bearded man who had designated himself informant. The neighborhood had gathered and soon had the facts: it was the machine-gunned body of a giant the police carried out and took off in the same ambulance with the murderer who had finally jumped out of a window when the Law closed in—muffled tones and distant giggling attested to all of it, and no one in the crowd of strangers knew where Dincher fitted in, protesting on his way to a green-and-white coupé: "I got a right, he busted into my own dwellin, I got a right." No one knew, not even friends who had faithfully gathered to watch the boy roll away, smiling and waving from a window.

Stoney gave the names and addresses of all the participants, taking full responsibility for a thoroughgoing detailing of facts, patting Vivienne's limp hand and departing, cigar in mouth, with a captain of police in a gleaming black sedan.

"Take me away, Joe," Diane still wailed against Joe's shoulder. And he could only say, "There's no place at all to take you."

For there was no live person to take away, no spirit ready for living. Only a specter quivering in his arms, and a stain on framed pictures in a pushcart at the curb, the blood of a purpose carried too far. A stain, beside him, where friendship had to die for no one to receive it, muttering, "He should've danced more, he should've danced more," out of a plaster face. A street stained with strangers who laughed in that sad longing that marks the close of carnivals, who sighed and grew sober as they took last half-hopeful looks for any players who might be lurking still in some littered, wind-bitten shadows.

While the shell of Diane obeyed her mother's arm, hid herself away in a gleaming orange taxi, the crowd dispersed, brooders to their Bleecker Street houses, smilers to the Riviera glare.

Normie and Joe remained, their eyes sparring like careful boxers, silently, as though each were choking back some secret with which he didn't dare burden the other. Immobile in slumbering shadows, neither caring to move. Till a bell-shaped shadow clacked toward them, Louella slowing down as she approached, stopping dead and saying, "Dead?" when she was near enough to know them.

"Dead," Joe said, and went up to hold her. "That man is truly dead," and caught her, though she only rocked.

Dead leaves were covered over with snow that whispered down over the city like some long-awaited peace, but there was little peace in Joe. Older friends had died in moments of exploded snow as he'd watched and expended one sigh for their passing, yet sorrow like that of these last chill days he'd never known before. It had been more than mourning over one single life; it had been the sense of waste born that night on Bleecker and spiraled to its full height on Central Park West, where he'd watched a shattered Louella fade through a revolving door.

After the funeral he'd stood with Normie in winds grown angry, winds kicking old news sheets to the sky, and Normie'd promised to ship a small press south along with format designs and articles he thought Hensley could use. But still, though Hensley expected him any day, Joe kicked snow each night toward the Village, with that lingering breathlessness of waste, nearly helpless to leave for home. Now, through eddying flakes, he went forward in one more compulsive search for Diane, the little girl no mother could control, reluctant to believe that even a good man's love was wasted on a girl running away from life.

Before the Cosmopole he found Louella with Harry Sticks, both bleached by fluorescence and snow. She smiled distantly and worked her lips around words that didn't come to sound, then went through the revolving door, faded into it as she'd done before, into the revolving waste of days. "She on junk, Harry?" watching her drift past tables.

"No, man, she's on Paddy Jenks, who doesn't say, though he talks. She thinks she's the sole one to dig the boy. They do that way through the night—just move their lips and smile, no sound at all to worry them." Sticks shifted the wool hat about on his head, rolling his head in that unconscious junky manner. "I'll be seeing her in a bit. Diane," as though he'd been asked. The good flesh was gone from Harry; he'd reached that point of crumbling that any junky will, athlete or not. Only his voice had power. "Come on, I'll show you Diane," in a way that frightened Joe, made him hurry along beside the man, around into illuminated snowflakes on Eighth, rapidly down to MacDougal. "She's okay," Harry assured him, instinctively aware of his concern. "She's okay, old Diane."

Past chess tables piled with rounded mounds of snow, Joe saw the mobile green-coated figure, went closer and saw her tossing snowballs at a lamppost, called her name and ran when she turned. "Where you been hidin?" He tried to pull her close, but she held him off.

"Joe . . . How are you, Joe?" A small voice creating hardly any mist. "I got to go someplace, Joe," waiting for no answer to her question, drifting over to take Harry's arm. "Come on. Man, I had to throw snow like a kid just to keep from busting out. Come on, like I'm frantic for some."

Joe saw her face in the arc light, pinched and shadowed, eyes quivering as they blinked against snow. "You still runnin away, Diane? Thought you'd get on with that doctor your mother——"

"Joe, don't talk." She saw him through a greater veil than snow—

through a dense pall enshrouding her mind. "It's not me, Joe, don't talk . . . don't bother. Later, Joe. Wait for me. We'll talk, we'll talk." For she was a stranger in the torment of sobriety; nothing she'd ever felt to be real came true. She wiped at her wet nose. "You got the key, Sticks?"

"Sure," rolling his head, glistening where a gold ring pierced his ear.

Joe waited by an iron balustrade on MacDougal while Diane went inside with Harry Sticks. He thought little of himself for standing there, for waiting in a ceaseless mist of snow for only a ghost, for a small futility. To carry her off? His bones were too chilled for any such fiery nonsense. Still he was rooted there in unrelenting eddies of powder, waiting, on a narrow and deserted walk where the stains of passion and sorrow were covered over with a purity from the skies: white, white, blank softness over the rude cracks of decades.

Diane came out alone, slow in her walk, yet swift to take his arm, agile in her eyelit smiling. "Harry got to find the Swede." Slow and low in her voice. "Can't look at the Luke, wansa cut his ear off like Van Gogh and send it to Stoney. Kills me to look at him, can't look at anyone." Rapidly, words falling away like bubbles. "They all, you dig, they bug me. Mama, she wants me to this and she wants me to that, bullshit smiling at me, bullshit voice, Carter's out and fatmouth Stoney ubadubadubadub, and you don't want me, you, like why you walking with me, Joe, why you talking with me, Joe?"

"You put me in mind of a shell of someone I loved right well."

"I can kick. You think I can't? Like childbirth. I can do it, you think I can't?" Half through her nose, half falsetto, shattered with puffing.

"Yeah, I think you can't." He took her alongside the park, trying to remember her the way she had looked one dawn ten long months before.

"Take me down South where it's warm, and I'll show you," easily convincing her impressionable bubble of a charged brain that only the cold winter kept her on Horse.

"Ole winter just follows you no matter where. Mighty cold down there."

"You're going? When you going, Joe?" and inside her his departure had its redemptive side. Somehow it was good: a judge would be gone with the man.

"Tomorrow . . . first thing."

It hit her harder than any of the pains she'd known, clouded her brain foggier than Horse. "Not tomorrow . . . You can't do that, Joe," crying now as he took her into the lights of Eighth. "Don't— not so fast. Why'd you bother me? Why didn't you just go without looking for me? Like you have to be a cowboy like, to make me hung up or something?"

"I wanted a look at you, Diane. I wanted to see how you're gettin on."

"Then take me along. Take a chance, come on."

"No, you don't want to kick. If you wanted to, you'd have kept with that doctor you saw one little time."

"Him? He never told me anything, he just wanted me to do all the talking. What kind of doctor is that? Why should I talk to *him?*"

"That's how they do. It takes a while. If you had any guts you'd stick it out . . . on guts or hope, one. They're one and the same thing anyway."

"I can do it, Joe. I'll *show* you," dancing around in front of him with a delicious anger sparking her. "I'll show you guts; I'll show you."

He took her across the street. "Come on, we'll get us a cab and I'll take you to your mother. When'd you eat last?"

"My mother! My mother! Sure, let her spend the loot. Who cares?" There was something indecent, yet something realistic, in the feel of it for her.

They left from the hackstand on the corner, sitting silently for many blocks of slow driving. And they might have gone quietly on, but Diane pitched over with abrupt crying and let out a weird, stored-up lament that confused Carter, Dincher and Buster, with most of her sorrow being spent for Buster, who *didn't know how* . . . *didn't know what* . . . *couldn't do right.*

"Dincher," she was wailing as he helped her upstairs, "they'll taper him. . . . They'll sit him oud on Riker's Islan'. And even Carter . . . he did 'imself oud. But poor Busser, poor din' know what." Joe half-carried her, wondering what he'd say to her mother, wondering what he'd do if they got hysterical together.

But Diane herself took care of their entrance. "Sleep!" she shouted when Vivienne opened the door. "I need sleep," pulling Joe by the wrist to her room, and he saw Stoney stand quickly from a living-room chair.

"Mr. Letrigo," Vivienne began embarrassedly, holding up a hand of caution, and Joe gave her a reassuring nod over his shoulder, following Diane into the compact little room.

"Your Mama's worried," he said as she began pulling off clothes. "I'll wait outside and be back again in ten minutes."

"Five," she muttered drowsily. "Come righ' back in."

He found Mrs. Lattimer right outside the door, a foolish child of a woman standing there to guard her daughter's virtue. She giggled and went off to the living room. "Will you have some tea, Mr. Letrigo?" she asked, pausing at the kitchen door.

"No, thank you. I won't be stayin that long." He sat across from Stoney, silent there beside Vivienne as if muted by the placid lighting, but really that way because he had no further need of argument. This scene of grace and comfort was laid desolate and wasted by Joe's knowledge of those before him—greed and ignorance sitting side by side. He lighted a cigarette. "You . . . what you fixin to do with Diane? Not you, Stoney," as the beard finally parted for speech.

The woman was pale and flustered. "Well . . ." Her voice rang high and she paused, then spoke in an easier tone, modulated to the lighting. "The psychiatrist is ready for her any time——"

"She needs more than psychiatry right now," he interrupted, and got up to get away from where he'd have to go on being rude. He didn't know whether the woman was aware of the scars on her daughter's arms. He went quickly to Diane's room, found her nearly asleep by the yellow light of the bed lamp. "Diane?"

She opened her eyes, stared without recognition as he sat down near her. "Joe? Joe?" As if he'd been missing for years. Her arms went for his neck; she pulled him down, kissed him delicately, small lips cool on his. "Don't leave me here, Joe."

"Diane, don't be askin me to baby you; you're not the one. Take a cure, like a grown woman."

"Oooh, Joe, don't leave me with them. Take me away, Joe."

It wouldn't take much for him to give in to her and to himself. But he had to let her be as capable as her own need demanded she be. He saw her hand wipe brusquely at tears she really hated, and knew he had no right to oppress her with indulgence. He found a pencil inside his coat and scribbled his address on an envelope, tore off the scrap, and felt her fist close over it. "Come down and find me when you feel equal to it," and saw her smile in recollection of old words on equality.

"You'll wait for me, Joe? I'll do it right; I'll have them send me to a sanitorium. Stoney'll get her to agree."

"I'll bct hc will."

"You'll wait for me, Joe?" She was already almost asleep.

"Yeah, I'll wait . . . " *but not for many, many, many months.* For he'd heard of mounds of broken junkies who'd spent their days swearing they'd kick, only to have cured bodies attacked again and again by minds forever plagued. A guided taper, years of psychiatric help . . . and a rational world to live in, to keep that sensitized mind from being plagued and plagued. A big fat chance for the little girl lying here so sweet in sleep, so rhythmic in her sighs, so hopelessly, hopelessly hooked. He held his lips a long time on her neck, then turned off the light and eased his way out.

The couple, in coats, stood up from the couch when they saw him. Joe took his hat. "She wants to stay in a sanitorium." Just a string of token words that took a lot of strength for utterance. "Will she be able to, Mrs. Lattimer?" Just to make it all sound natural, part of life, the way folks talk.

"Decidedly," Stoney said; "decidedly," he said. "Now, Vivienne, it's the *only* sane course to follow. I know how you feel, my dear, but in the long run . . ." trailing off when the woman stopped wincing. *Dream now, Robert,* as they followed him out, *and make a blueprint for society, a golden age with its hierarchy of the gracious, the sensitive, the born aristocrats of soul,* golden halls and splendor drifting abstractly through his mind down the dim stairway to the street.

Stoney laughed aloud. "The snow has stopped; we didn't need the umbrella after all." But he swung it like a walking stick as he started off down the snow-packed walk.

"It's only around the corner." Vivienne sighed. "Would you care to join us for evening services, Mr. Letrigo?" Joe shook his head and walked along, a step behind them. At the corner Vivienne sighed again. "It's peaceful," she said in her highest tones. "Christmas will be here very, very soon." It was some sort of signal that set her and Stoney grinning at each other, locking hands, smiling like adolescents as Joe Letrigo watched.

Arms awkwardly entwined, they started down Fifth. "Aren't you going downtown?" Stoney called over a shoulder.

"The way is up." Joe was rooted there against the somber wall of some swank gentlemen's club, while the bearded man and his Stately

Lady in furs kicked small swirls of snow, heads high, like two people for whom the earth was made, proud parents of all the concrete towers. Stoney worked loose his umbrella arm, pecked at snow, pointed his beard around in inspection of lights and towers.

Joe watched them mount the church steps and disappear, even from his mind, where other parents smiled. Old Daddy Tom, hung halfway between fear and conscience, would put his shoulders with his sons or against them—the choice was his. For this wounded generation was not yet on its knees like the last. Joe thought of it as a generation with wider eyes with which to judge. He shuddered when he pictured his bespectacled mother hearing how he had spent his time in the North. "Disgusting!" she said in his mind as he, in imagination, related details of all his hours here; and in his mind he kissed her as she sat on his knee, and never told her that he'd brought home new scars again, yet somehow pointing out that a threat sat gray and deadly in the coral glow of her home, because Louella'd gone back among the helpless and Lizzie had loved a maniac and Normie had been tricked away from suburban comfort by a friendship; and all were linked invisibly to a hooked little girl by an unending chain of . . . something.

Now Joe Letrigo walked south, huddled in his coat, past varicolored windows done up early for Christmas, down the pure-white boulevard where scatterings of people stopped by windows like hungry little sparrows. Separate little agents whom Carter had wanted shoulder to shoulder against old men who hated the young. Joe was anxious now to be with Hensley. He'd take a train as soon as he could pack, aware before he'd start that winter would follow him south.

Under snow the city lay mute, Lukeys and Lizzies in its dirty pores, all painted over with white like a whore's face; hovels hidden with all their endless anguishes, their steady pulsing pain that promised to erupt every now and then and scar even children of the solvent—all silent now, narcotized under a neat white surface peace.